THE COLIN MACINNES OMNIBUS

THE COLIN MACINNES OMNIBUS

His three London Novels

City of Spades

Absolute Beginners

Mr Love and Justice

ALLISON & BUSBY · LONDON

Allison & Busby Limited
13 Charlotte Mews
London W1T 3EJ
www.allisonandbusby.com

A CIP catalogue record for this book is available from the British Library.

First published by Allison & Busby in 1985.
Reprinted in 2005 and 2007.

10 9 8 7 6 5 4 3

ISBN 978-0-7490-8368-7

Printed and bound in Wales by
Creative Print & Design

City of Spades

COLIN MACINNES

ALLISON & BUSBY

FOR RICKY

CONTENTS

PART I

Johnny Fortune hits town

1

Pew tentatively takes the helm

'IT'S ALL YOURS, Pew, from now,' he said, adding softly, 'thank God,' and waving round the office a mildly revolted hand.

'Yes, but what do I *do* with it all, dear boy?' I asked him. 'Why am I here?'

'Ah, as to that . . .' He heaved an indifferent sigh. 'You'll have to find out for yourself as you go along.'

He picked up his furled umbrella, but I clung to him just a bit longer.

'Couldn't you explain, please, my duties to me in more detail? After all, I'm new, I'm taking over from you, and I'd be very glad to know exactly *what* . . .'

Trim, chill, compact, he eyed me with aloof imperial calm. Clearly he was of the stuff of which proconsuls can even now be made.

'Oh, very well,' he said, grounding his umbrella. 'Not, I'm afraid, that anything I can tell you is likely to be of the slightest use. . . .'

I thanked him and we sat. His eye a bored inquisitor's, he said: 'You know, at any rate, what you're *supposed* to be?'

Simply, I answered: 'I am the newly appointed Assistant Welfare Officer of the Colonial Department.'

He closed his eyes. 'I don't know—forgive me—how you got the job. But may I enquire if you know anything about our colonial peoples?'

'I once spent a most agreeable holiday in Malta. . . .

'Quite so. A heroic spot. But I mean Negroes. Do you happen to know anything about them?'

'Nothing.'

'Nothing whatever?'

'No.'

He emitted a thin smile. 'In that case, may I say I think you're going to have quite a lot of fun?'

'I sincerely hope so. . . . I have certain vague impressions about

Negroes, of course. I rather admire their sleek, loose-limbed appearance. . . .'

'Yes, yes. So very engaging.'

'And their elegant flamboyant style of dress is not without its charm. . . .'

'Ah, that far, personally, I cannot follow you.'

'On the other hand, for their dismal spirituals and their idiotic calypso, I have the most marked distaste.'

'I'm with you there, Pew, I'd glad to say. The European passion for these sad and silly songs has always baffled me. Though their jazz, in so far as it is theirs, is perhaps another matter.'

He had risen once again. I saw he had made up his mind I was beyond hope.

'And what do I do with our coloured cousins?' I asked him, rising too.

'Yours is a wide assignment, limitless almost as the sea. You must be their unpaid lawyer, estate agent, wet-nurse and, in a word, their bloody guardian angel.'

The note of disdain, even though coming from a professional civil servant to an amateur, had become increasingly displeasing to me. I said with dignity: 'Nothing, I suppose, could be more delightful and meritorious.'

He had now closed his eyes; and stood, at the door, a Whitehall Machiavelli.

'Some might say,' he told me softly, that your duty is to help them to corrupt our country.'

Up went my brows.

'So some might say . . . their irruption among us has not been an unmixed blessing. Thousands, you see, have come here in the last few years from Africa and the Caribbean, and given us what we never had before—a colour problem.'

His eyes opened slowly in a slit. 'Could it not be,' I said, 'that we have given them just that in their own countries?'

'My dear Pew! Could it be that I positively find myself in the presence of a *liberal*?'

'My dear boy, of course you do! What else can one comfortably be in these monolithic days?'

He smiled with every tooth.

'A liberal, Pew, in relation to the colour question, is a person who feels an irresponsible sympathy for what he calls oppressed peoples on whom, along with the staunchest Tory, he's quite willing to go on being a parasite.'

Though I sensed it was a phrase he'd used before, I bowed my bleeding head.

'I own,' I told him mildly, 'that I *am* one of those futile, persistent, middle-class Englishmen whom it takes a whole empire, albeit a declining one, to sustain. . . . Remove the imperial shreds, and I'd be destitute as a coolie, I confess. . . .'

This pleased him. 'To use the vulgar phrase,' he said, 'you must learn to know which side your bread is buttered on.'

But this excursion from the concrete into the abstract seemed to me unhelpful in so far as learning my new job was concerned. I made my last desperate appeal. 'You haven't told me, though . . .'

'Please study your dossiers Pew: the instructions are pasted inside each of their covers. Look:

Government Hostels;
Landlords taking non-Europeans;
Facilities for Recreation and Study;
Bad Company and Places to Avoid;
Relations with Commonwealth Co-citizens of the Mother Country.

And so on and so forth, dear man. And may I advise you' (he looked at his watch) 'to hurry up and read them? Because your clients will be turning up for interviews within the hour. Meanwhile I shall say goodbye to you and wish you the good fortune that I fear you'll so much need.'

'Might I enquire,' I said, reluctant even now to see him go, 'to what fresh colonial pastures you yourself are now proceeding?'

A look of mild triumph overspread his face.

'Before the month is out,' he answered, 'I shall be at my new post in one of our Protectorates within the Union of South Africa.'

'South Africa? Good heavens! Won't you find, as a British colonial official, that the atmosphere there's just a little difficult?'

In statesmanlike tones he answered: 'South Africa, Pew, is a country much maligned. Perhaps they have found a logical solution for race relations there. That is the conclusion to which I've rather reluctantly come. Because if my year in the Department has taught me anything, it's that the Negro's still, deep down inside, a savage. Not his fault, no doubt, but just his nature.' (He stood there erect, eyes imperiously agleam.) 'Remember that, Pew, at your Welfare Officer's desk. Under his gaberdine suit and his mission school-veneer, there still lurk the impulses of the primitive man.'

He waved—as if an assegai—his umbrella, I waved more wanly, and lo! he was gone out of my life for ever.

Alone, I picked up the dossiers, crossed out his name, and wrote in its place my own: Montgomery Pew. Then, like a lion (or monkey, possibly?) new to its cage, I walked round my unsumptuous office examining the numerous framed photographs of *worthy* Africans and West Indians, staring out at me with enigmatic faces, whose white grins belied, it seemed to me, the inner silences of the dark pools of their eyes.

2

Johnny Macdonald Fortune takes up the tale

MY FIRST ACTION on reaching the English capital was to perform what I've always promised my sister Peach I would. Namely, leaving my luggages at the Government hostel, to go straight out by taxi (oh, so slow, compared with our sleek Lagos limousines!) to the famous central Piccadilly tube station where I took a one-stop ticket, went down on the escalator, and then *ran up the same steps in the wrong direction*. It was quite easy to reach the top, and our elder brother Christmas was wrong to warn it would be impossible to me. Naturally, the ticket official had his word to say, but I explained it was my promise to my brother Christmas and my sister Peach ever since in our childhood, and he yielded up.

'You boys are all the same,' he said.

'What does that mean, mister?'

'Mad as March hares, if you ask me.'

He looked so sad when he said it, that how could I take offence? 'Maybe you right,' I told him. 'We like living out our lives.'

'And we like peace and quiet. Run along, son,' this official told me.

Not a bad man really, I suppose, so after a smile at him I climbed up towards the free outer air. For I had this morning to keep my appointment at the Colonial Department Welfare Office to hear what plans have been arranged there for the pursuit of my further studies.

In the Circus overhead I looked round more closely at my new city. And I must say at first it was a bad disappointment: so small, poky, dirty, not magnificent! Red buses, like shown to us on the cinema, certainly, and greater scurrying of the population than at home. But people with glum clothes and shut-in faces. Of course, I have not seen yet the Parliament Houses, or many historic palaces, or where Dad lived in Maida Vale when he was here thirty years ago before he met our Mum. . . .

And that also is to be one of my first occupations: to visit this house of his to see if I can recover any news of his former landlady—if dead, or alive, or in what other circumstances. Because my Dad, at the party on the night I sailed right out of Lagos, he took me on one side and said, 'Macdonald,' (he never calls me John or Johnny—always Macdonald) 'Macdonald, you're a man now. You're eighteen.'

'Yes, Dad . . .' I said, wondering what.

'You're a man enough to share a man's secret with your father?'

'If you want to share one with me, Dad.'

'Well, listen, son. You know I went to England as a boy, just like you're doing. . . .'

'Yes, Dad, of course I do. . . .'

'And I had a young landlady there who was very kind and good to me, unusually so for white ladies in those days. So I'd like you to go and get news of her for me if you ever can, because we've never corresponded all these many years.'

'I'll get it for you, Dad, of course.'

Then my Dad lowered his voice and both his eyes.

'But your mother, Macdonald. I don't very much want your mother to know. It was a long while ago that I met this lady out in Maida Vale.'

Here Dad gave me an equal look like he'd never given me in his life before.

'I respect your mother, you understand me, son,' he said.

'I know you do, Dad, and so do Christmas and Peach and me.'

'We all love her, and for that I'd like you to send me the news not here but to my office in a way that she won't know or be disturbed by.'

'I understand, Dad,' I told him. 'I shall be most discreet in my letters about anything I may hear of your past in England when a very young man.'

'Then let's have a drink on that, Macdonald, son,' he said.

So we drank whisky to my year of studying here in England.

'And mind you work hard,' Dad told me. 'We've found two hundred pounds to send you there, and when you return we want you to be thoroughly an expert in meteorology.'

'I will be it, Dad,' I promised.

'Of course, I know you'll drink, have fun with girls, and gamble, like I did myself. . . . But mind you don't do these enjoyments too excessively.'

'No, Dad, no.'

'If your money all gets spent, we can't send out any more for you. You'd have to find your own way home by working on a ship.'

'I'll be reasonable, Dad. I'm not a child. You trust me.'

And afterwards, it was Peach clustering over me with too much kisses and foolish demands for gowns and hats and underclothes from London, to impress her chorus of surrounding giggling girls. I told her all these things were to be bought much cheaper there in Lagos.

And to my brother Christmas, I said, 'Oh, Christmas, why don't you come with me too? I admire your ambition, but surely to see the world and study before fixing your nose to the Lands Office grindstone would be more to your pleasure and advantage?'

'I want to get married quickly, Johnny, as you know,' my serious elder brother said. 'For that I must save, not spend.'

'Well, each man to his own idea of himself,' I told him.

And my mother! Would you believe it, she'd guessed that some secret talk had passed between Dad and me that evening? In her eyes I could see it, but she said nothing special to me except to fondle me like a child in front of all the guests, though not shedding any tears.

And when they all accompanied us to the waterfront, dancing, singing and beating drums, suddenly, as the ship came into view, she stopped and seized me and lifted me up, though quite a grown man now, and carried me as far as the gangway of the boat upon her shoulders.

'Write to me, Johnny,' she said. 'Good news or bad, keep writing.'

Then was more farewell drinking and dancing on the ship until, when visitors had to leave, I saw that my Mum had taken away my jacket (though leaving its valuable contents behind with me, of course). And she stood hugging it to her body on the quay as that big boat pulled out into the Gulf of Guinea sea.

3

The meeting of Jumble and Spade

PRIMED BY MY BRIEF STUDY of the welfare dossiers, I awaited, in my office, the arrival of the first colonials. With some trepidation; because for one who, like myself, has always felt great need of sober counsel, to offer it to others—and to strangers, and to such exotic strangers—seemed intimidating. Perhaps I should add, too, that I'm not quite so old as I think I look: only twenty-six, Heaven be praised; and certainly not so self-assured as my dry, drained, rarely perturbable countenance might suggest.

Picture my mild alarm, then, when there was a first polite knock upon my door. Opening it, I beheld a handsomely ugly face, animal and engaging, with beetling brow, squashed nose and full and generous lips, surmounted by a thatch of thick curly hair cut to a high rising peak in front: a face wearing (it seemed to me) a sly, morose, secretive look, until suddenly its mouth split open into a candid ivory and coral smile.

'I'm Fortune,' said this creature, beaming as though his name was his very nature. 'Johnny Macdonald, Christian names, out of Lagos, checking to see what classes in meteorology you've fixed for me.'

'My name is Pew—Montgomery. Please do come over to these rather less uncomfortable leather chairs.'

I observed that he was attired in a white crocheted sweater with two crimson horizontal stripes, and with gold safety-pins stuck on the tips of each point of the emerging collar of a nylon shirt; in a sky-blue gaberdine jacket zipped down the front; and in even lighter blue linen slacks, full at the hips, tapering to the ankle, and falling delicately one half-inch above a pair of pale brown plaited casual shoes.

'Your curriculum,' I said, handing him a drab buff envelope, 'is outlined here. You begin next week, but it would be well to register within the next few days. Meanwhile I trust you're satisfied with your accommodation at the hostel?'

'Man, you should ask!'

'I beg your pardon?'

He gave me a repeat performance of the grin. 'It's like back in mission school at home. I shall make every haste to leave it as soon as I find myself a room.'

'In that case,' I said, departmentally severe, 'the rent would be appreciably higher.'

'I have loot—I can afford,' he told me. 'Have *you* ever lived inside that hostel, you yourself?'

'No.'

'Well, then!'

The interview was not taking the turn I thought appropriate. Equality between races—yes! But not between officials and the public.

'I should perhaps warn you at this juncture,' I informed him, 'that to secure outside accommodation sometimes presents certain difficulties.'

'You mean for an African to get a room?'

'Yes. . . . We have however here a list of amiable landladies. . . .'

'Why should it be difficult for an African to get a room?'

'There is, unfortunately, in certain cases, prejudice.'

'They fear we dirty the sheets with our dark skins?'

'Not precisely.'

'Then what? In Lagos, anyone will let *you* a room if you have good manners, and the necessary loot. . . .'

'It's kind of them, and I don't doubt your word. Here in England, though, some landladies have had unfortunate experiences.'

'Such as . . ?'

'Well, for one thing—noise.'

'It's true we are not mice.'

'And introducing *friends*. . . .'

'Why not?'

'I mean to sleep—to live. Landladies don't wish three tenants for the price of one.'

'So long as the room is paid, what does it matter?'

'Ah—paid. Failure to pay is another chief complaint.'

'Don't Jumbles never skip their rent as well as Spades?'

'I *beg* your pardon once again?'

'Don't Jumbles . . .'

'Jumbles?'

'You're a Jumble, man.'

'I?'

'Yes. That's what we call you. You don't mind?'

'I hope I don't. . . . It's not, I trust, an impolite expression?'

'You mean like nigger?'

I rose up.

'Now, please! This is the Colonial Department Welfare Office. That word is absolutely forbidden within these walls.'

'It should be outside them, too.'

'No doubt. I too deplore its use.'

'Well, relax, please, Mr Pew. And don't be so scared of Jumble. It's cheeky, perhaps, but not so very insulting.'

'May I enquire how it is spelt?'

'J-o-h-n-b-u-l-l.'

'Ah! But pronounced as you pronounce it?'

'Yes: Jumble.'

It struck me the ancient symbol, thus distorted, was strangely appropriate to the confusion of my mind.

'I see. And . . .' (I hesitated) '. . . Spade?'

'Is us.'

'And that is not an objectionable term?'

'Is cheeky, too, of course, but not offending. In Lagos, on the waterfront, the boys sometimes called me the Ace of Spades.'

'Ah . . .'

He offered me, from an American pack, an extravagantly long fag.

'Let's not us worry, Mr Pew,' he said, 'about bad names. My Dad has taught me that in England some foolish man may call me sambo, darkie, boot or munt or nigger, even. Well, if he does—my fists!' (He clenched them: they were like knees.) 'Or,' he went on, 'as Dad would say, "First try rebuke by tongue, then fists".'

'Well, Mr Fortune,' I said to him, when he had at last unclenched them to rehitch the knife edge of his blue linen tapering slacks, 'I think with one of these good women on our list you'll have no trouble. . . .'

'If I take lodgings, mister,' he replied, 'they must be Liberty Hall.

No questions from the landlady, please. And me, when I give my rent, I'll have the politeness not to ask her what she spends it on.'

'That, my dear fellow, even for an Englishman, is *very* difficult to find in our sad country.'

'I'll find it.' He beetled at me, then, leaning forward, said, 'And do you know why I think your landladies are scared of us?'

'I can but imagine . . .'

'Because of any brown babies that might appear.'

'In the nature of things,' I said, 'that may indeed well be.'

'An arrival of white babies they can somehow explain away. But if their daughter has a brown one, then neighbouring fingers all start pointing.'

I silently shook my head.

'But why,' he cried, 'why not box up together, Jumble and Spade, like we let your folk do back home?'

I rose once more.

'Really, Mr Fortune. You cannot expect me to discuss these complex problems. I am—consider—an official.'

'Oh, yes. . . . You have to earn your money, I suppose.

I found this, of course, offensive. And moving with dignity to my desk, I took up the Warning Folder of People and Places to Avoid.

'Another little duty for which I'm *paid*,' I said to him, 'is to warn our newcomers against . . . well, to be frank, bad elements among their fellow countrymen.'

'Oh, yes, man. Shoot.'

'And,' I continued, looking at my list, 'particularly against visiting the Moorhen public house, the Cosmopolitan dance hall, or the Moonbeam club.'

'Just say those names again.

To my horror, I saw he was jotting them on the back page of his passport.

'To visit these places,' I went on, reading aloud from the mimeographed sheet I held, 'has been, for many, the first step that leads to the shadow of the police courts.'

'Why? What goes in in them?'

I didn't, perhaps fortunately, yet know. 'I'm not at liberty to divulge it,' I replied.

'Ah well . . .'

He pocketed his passport, and took me by the hand.

'Have you any further questions?' I enquired.

'Yes, Mr Pew. Excuse my familiar asking: but where can I get a shirt like that?'

'Like this?'

'Yes. It's hep. Jumble style, but hep.

He reached out a long, long hand and fingered it.

'In Jermyn Street,' I said with some self-satisfaction, but asperity.

'Number?'

I told him.

'Thanks so very much,' said Johnny Macdonald Fortune. 'And now I must be on my way to Maida Vale.'

I watched him go out with an unexpected pang. And moving to the window, soon saw him walk across the courtyard and stop for a moment speaking to some others there. In the sunlight, his nylon shirt shone all the whiter against the smooth brown of his skin. His frame, from this distance, seemed shorter than it was, because of his broad shoulders—flat, though composed of two mounds of muscle arching from his spine. His buttocks sprang optimistically high up from the small of his back, and his long legs—a little bandy and with something of a backward curve—were supported by two very effective splayed-out feet; on which, just now, as he spoke, gesticulating too, he was executing a tracery of tentative dance steps to some soft inaudible music.

4

A pilgrimage to Maida Vale

THIS MAIDA VALE is noteworthy for all the buildings looking similar and making the search for Dad's old lodging-house so more difficult. But by careful enquiry and eliminations, I hit on one house in Nightingale Road all crumbling down and dirty as being the most probable, and as there was no bell or lock and the door open, I walked right in and called up the stairs, 'Is Mrs Hancock there?' but getting no reply, climbed further to the next floor. There was a brown door facing me, so I drummed on it, when immediately it opened and a Jumble lady stood there to confront me: wrung out like a dish-rag, with her body everywhere collapsing, and when she saw me a red flush of fury on her face.

'Get out! I don't want your kind here.'

'I have to speak to Mrs Hancock.'

At these words of mine her colour changed to white like a coconut you bite into.

'Hancock!' she called out. 'My name's Macpherson. Why do you call me Hancock?'

'I don't, lady,' I told her. 'I merely say I wanted to speak to a lady of that name.'

'Why?'

'To bring her my Dad's greetings—Mr David Macdonald Fortune out of Lagos, Nigeria. I'm his son Johnny.'

By the way she eyed me, peering at me, measuring me from top to toes, I was sure now this *was* the lady of Dad's story. And I can't say, at that moment, I quite admired my Dad in his own choice. Though naturally it was years ago when possibly this woman was in better preservation.

Then she said: 'You've brought nothing ever to me but misery and disgrace.'

'But lady, you and I've not met before.'

'Your father, then. Your race.'

'So you *are* Mrs Hancock, please?'

'I used to be.'

'Well, I bring my Dad's greetings to you. He asks you please for news.'

'His *greetings*,' she said, twisting up her mouth into a mess. 'His greetings—is that all?'

I was giving her all this time my biggest smile, and I saw its effect began to melt her just a little. (When I smile at a woman, I relax all my body and seem eager.)

'Your father's a bad man,' she said.

'Oh, no!'

'You look like him, though. He might have spat you out.'

'I should look like him, Mrs Macpherson. I'm legitimate, I hope.'

This didn't please her a bit. She stared white-red at me again till I thought she'd strike me, and I got ready to duck or, if need be, slap back.

'So you've heard!' she shouted out. 'Then why's your father never done anything for Arthur?'

'Arthur, lady?'

'For your brother, if you want to know. Your elder brother.'

Clearly she didn't mean my brother Christmas. Then who? I began to realize.

'I've got a half-brother called Arthur, then?' I said, trying to act as if I felt delighted. 'Well! Can't I meet him?'

'No!'

'Oh, no!'

'No! You certainly can not.'

At this very moment, there glided up beside her a little Jumble girl, quite pretty, seventeen or so I'd say, who I noticed had a glove on one hand only.

'Don't shout, Mother,' she said. 'You'd better ask him in.'

'Oh, very well,' this Mrs Macpherson said, coming over all weary and looking even ten years older.

Their room was quite tidy, with assorted furniture, but poor. I do *hate* poor rooms.

'I suppose I'd better go and make some tea,' the old lady told us both.

(These Jumbles and their tea in every crisis!)

The little girl held out her hand—the hand that didn't wear the glove. 'I'm Muriel,' she said. 'I'm Arthur's sister, and Mum's second daughter.'

'But Miss Muriel,' I said to her, 'I can guess by your skin's complexion that you're not Arthur's true sister.'

'I'm his half-sister, Mr Fortune. Me and my sister Dorothy are Macphersons, Mum's proper children after she got married.'

'And your father?'

'Dad's dead. They caught him in the war.'

'I'm sorry . . .'

'Arthur, you see . . .' (she looked modest as she spoke, though I wasn't sure if it was felt or acted) '. . . Arthur was Mum's mistake before she met our Dad.'

'And Arthur: where is he?'

'In jail.'

'Ah!'

'He's always in and out of jail.'

'Oh. For what?'

'Thieving and suchlike.'

She stood and fiddled with the table-cloth frillings, then said to me: 'And didn't *your* father know about Arthur, and all the trouble Mum's had with him for more than twenty years?'

'I'm sure he didn't.'

But I began to wonder.

After a polite and careful pause, I said, 'Then Muriel, you and me are almost relatives, I'd say. We're half-half-brother and sister, or something of that kind.'

She laughed at this. 'We're not real relations, Johnny. But Arthur is a link between us, I suppose. . . .' Then she looked up at me and said, 'But do be careful what you say to Mother. She hates all coloured people now.'

'On account of my Dad and Arthur?'

'Not only that. There's Dorothy—my elder sister, Dorothy.'

'Yes?'

'She lives with a coloured boy. He's taken her away.'

'To marry?'

'No. . . . He's a Gambian.'

'Oh, those Gambians! Nigerians, of course, are friendly folks, and

Gold Coast boys respectable often, too. But Gambians! Don't judge us, please, by them. . . .'

'This one's a devil, anyway,' she told me. 'Billy Whispers is his name, and he's bad, bad, a thoroughly bad man.'

And now the old lady she came shuffling back. It was clear that she'd been thinking, and maybe refreshing herself a bit as well.

'Is your Dad rich?' she said at once.

'He's reasonably loaded.'

'In business now?'

'Export and import—he has his ups and downs.'

She stood right in front of me, nose to chest.

'Well, in return for his *greetings*, will you ask him please to make me some small return for his running away and leaving me to rear his son?'

'I could write to him, Mrs Macpherson. . . .'

'Can you imagine what it was to rear a coloured child in London twenty years ago? Can you imagine what it's like for an English girl to marry when she's got' (I saw it coming) 'a bastard nigger child?'

I made no reply whatever.

'Mother!' cried Muriel. 'That's no way to talk.'

'He'd best know what I think! I could have done better than your father, Muriel, if it hadn't been for that.'

'Mother!'

'And your sister Dorothy's going the same way.'

'Oh, Mother!'

'I was a pretty girl when I was young. . . . I could have been rich and happy. . . .'

And here—as I could see must happen—the lady broke down into her tears. I understood the way she felt, indeed I did, yet why do these women always blame the man? I'm sure Dad didn't rape her, and however young she was, she must have known a number of the facts of life. . . .

Little Muriel was easing her off into a bedroom. When she came out again, I said to her, 'Well, perhaps I should go away just now, Muriel. I'll write to my Dad much as your Mum requests. . . .'

'Stay and drink up your tea, Johnny.'

We sat there sipping on the dregs, till I said, 'What do you do for a living, Muriel?'

'I work in a tailor's, Johnny. East End, they're Jews. Cutting up shirts. . . .'

'You like that occupation?'

'No. . . . But it helps out.'

'Don't you have fun sometimes? Go dancing?'

'Not often. . . .'

And here I saw she looked down at her hand.

'You hurt yourself?' I said.

She looked up and shook her head.

'We must go out together one day, if you like to come with me,' I said to her.

She smiled.

'Next Saturday, say? Before I start out on my studies?'

She shook her head once more.

'Now listen, Muriel. *You've* got no colour prejudice, I hope. . . .'

'No, no, Johnny. Not at all. But you'd be dull with me. I don't dance, you see.'

'Don't dance? Is there *any* little girl don't dance? Well, I will teach you.'

'Yes?'

'Of course I will, Muriel. I'll teach you the basic foundations in one evening. Real bop steps, and jive, and all.'

Here she surprised me, this shy rather skinny little chick, by reaching out quite easily and giving me a full kiss on the cheek.

'Johnny,' she said. 'There's one thing you could do for me. . . . Which is to get me news of my sister Dorothy. Because she hasn't been here or written for over a month, and I don't like to go out and see her south side of the Thames in Brixton, on account of that Billy Whispers.'

'Just give me the address, and I'll go see.'

'It's a house full of coloured men and English girls.'

'Just give me the address, will you, Muriel, and I'll go out that way immediately. I want to get to know the various areas of this city, if it's going to be my own.'

5

Encounter with Billy Whispers

THIS BRIXTON HOUSE stood all by itself among ruins of what I suppose was wartime damages, much like one tooth left sticking in an old man's jaw.

Now what was curious to me was this. As I approached it, I could clearly see persons standing by the upper windows, and even hear voices and the sound of a radiogram. But when I knocked on the front door of it, no one came down however long I continued on. So I walked all round this building and looked over the very broken garden wall.

There I saw a quite surprising sight: which was a tall Spade—very tall—standing in a broken greenhouse, watering plants. Now Spades do garden—it wasn't that—but not ones dressed up like he was, fit to kill: pink slacks, tartan silk outside-hanging shirt, all freshly pressed and laundered.

'What say, man?' I called out to him. 'Do you know Billy Whispers?'

Here he spun round.

'Who you?'

'Fortune from Lagos, mister. A friend of Mr Whispers' lady's family.'

As this man came out of the greenhouse, wiping his hands, I saw by the weaving, sliding way he walked towards me that he was a boxer. Round about his neck he wore a silver chain, another on each wrist, and his face had a 'better be careful or I slap you down' expression.

I waited smiling for him.

'Mr Whispers,' he said, 'is not at home to strangers.'

'His lady is?'

'What's she mean to you?'

'I have a message for her.'

At this I vaulted, like in gymnasium, over the wall, and went leisurely across to meet him.

'Haven't I seen,' I said to him, 'your photo in the newspapers?'

Now he looked proud and pleased, and said to me, 'I'm Jimmy Cannibal.'

'I thought you was. Light-heavy champion till they stole your legitimate title just a year ago?' (But as is well known, this Jimmy Cannibal lost it on a foul.)

'That's me.'

'You growing tomatoes?' I asked him, pointing to his greenhouse.

But he looked fierce again and shook his head.

'What, then?' and I started over.

He gripped me by my shoulder and spun me round. But not before I'd seen what plant it was in flower-pots inside there.

'Keep your nose out, Mr Nigeria,' he said.

So strong was he, I saw I'd better fight him with my brains.

'It's smoking weed,' I said. 'You give me some perhaps?'

'You blow your top too much, Mr Stranger.'

We stood there on the very edge of combat. But just then I heard a window scraping and, looking up, I saw a face there staring down at us: a mask of ebony, it seemed to me from there. This face talked to Jimmy Cannibal in some Gambian tongue, and then said to me, 'You may come up.'

As we both climbed the stairs (this Cannibal behind me breathing hot upon my neck), I got the feeling of every room was occupied by hearing voices, men's and women's, and sometimes the click of dice.

On a landing Cannibal edged past me, put his head round the door, then waved me in. He didn't come inside himself, but stood out there on the landing, lurking.

This Billy Whispers was a short man with broad shoulders and longer arms than even is usual with us. Elegantly dressed but quite respectable, as if on Sundays, and with a cool, cold face that gazed at me without fear or favour.

'You come inside?' he said. 'Or do you prefer to stand there encouraging draughts?'

'I'm Fortune,' I said, 'from Lagos.'

'I know a lot of Lagos boys.'

'You're Gambian, they tell me. Bathurst?'

He nodded at me and said, 'My friend was telling me of your interest in my greenhouse.'

'I saw you grew charge out there . . .'

'You want to smoke some?'

'Well, I don't mind. I used up all I had on the trip over. . . .'

'I'll roll you a stick,' this Billy Whispers said.

I sat on the bed, feeling pleased at the chance of blowing hay once more. For much as I care for alcoholic drinks of many kinds, my greatest enjoyment, ever since when a boy, is in charging with weed. Because without it, however good I feel, I'm never really on the top of my inspiration.

Meanwhile this Billy took out two cigarette-papers, and joined them together by the tongue. He peeled and broke down a piece of the ordinary fag he held between his lips, and then, from a brown-paper pack in a jar above the fireplace (a large pack, I noticed), he sprinkled a generous dose of the weed in the papers and began rolling and licking, easing the two ends of the stick into position with a match.

'But tell me,' I said, 'if it's not enquiring. You didn't grow all that hemp you have from outside in your greenhouse?'

'No, no. Is an experiment I'm making, to grow it myself from seed.'

'Otherwise you buy it?'

He nodded.

'You can get that stuff easy here?'

'It can be got. . . . Most things can be got in London when you know your way around.'

He gave the weed a final tender lick and roll, and handed it me by the thin inhaling end.

'And the Law,' I said. 'What do they have to say about consuming weed?'

'What they say is fifteen- or twenty-pound fine if you're caught. Jail on the second occasion.'

'Man! Why, these Jumbles have no pity!'

At which I lit up, took a deep drag, well down past the throat, holding the smoke in my lungs with little sharp sniffs to stop the valuable gust escaping. When I blew out, after a heavy interval, I said to him, 'Good stuff. And what do they make you pay for a stick here?'

'Retail, in small sticks, half a crown.'

'And wholesale?'

'Wholesale? For that you have to find your own supplier and make your personal arrangement.'

I took one more deep drag.

'You know such a supplier?' I enquired.

'Of course. . . . I know of several. . . .'

'You don't deal in this stuff personal, by any possible chance?'

Here Billy Whispers joined his two hands, wearing on each one a big coloured jewel.

'Mister,' he said, 'I think these are questions that you don't ask on so early an acquaintance.'

Which was true, so I smiled at him and handed him over the weed for his turn to take his drag on it.

He did this, and after some time in silence he blew on the smouldering end of the weed and said to me, 'And what is it, Fortune, I can do for you here?'

'I'm Dorothy's half-half-brother.'

'What say?'

'Arthur, her brother, is my brother too.' And I explained.

'But Dorothy she not know you,' he said to me. 'Never she's spoken to me about you.'

Then I explained some more.

'If that old lady or her sister's worried about Dorothy,' he said at last, 'just tell them to stop worrying because she's happy here with me, and will do just what I tell her.'

'Could I speak with her, perhaps?'

'No, man. You could not.'

At this state of our interview, the door was opened and into the room came a short little fattish boy, all smiles and gesticulation, of a type that beats my time: that is, the Spade who's always acting Spadish, so as to make the Jumbles think we're more cool crazy than we are, but usually for some darker purpose to deceive them. But why play this game of his with me?

'Hullo, hullo, man,' he cried to me, grasping at both my hands. 'I ain't seen you around before. . . . Shake hands with me, my name is Mr Ronson Lighter.' And he let off his silly sambo laugh.

I said, 'What say?' unsmilingly, and freed my hands. 'What say,

Mr Ronson Lighter. Did your own mother give you that peculiar name?'

He giggled like a crazy girl.

'No, no, no, mister, is my London name, on account of my well-known strong desire to own these things.'

And out of each side coat pocket he took a lighter, and sparkled the pair of them underneath my eyes.

Still not smiling, I got up on my feet.

And as I did—smack! Up in my head I got a very powerful kick from that hot weed which I'd been smoking. A kick like you get from superior Congo stuff, that takes your brain and wraps it up and throws it all away, and yet leaves your thoughts inside it sharp and clear: that makes all your legs and arms and body seem like if jet propelled without any tiring effort whatsoever.

But I watched these two, Billy Whispers and this Mr Ronson Lighter, as they talked in their barbarian Gambian language. I didn't understand no word, but sometimes I heard the name of 'Dorothy.'

So I broke in.

'I'd like to speak to her, Billy, just a moment, if you really wouldn't mind.'

They both looked up, and this Mr Ronson Lighter came dancing across and laid his hand upon my head.

'Mister,' he said, 'that's a real Bushman hair-style that you've got. Right out of the Africa jungle.'

'You got any suggestions for improving it?' I said, not moving much.

'Why, yes. Why don't you have it beautifully cut like mine?'

His own was brushed flat and low across his forehead, sticking out far in front of his eyes as if it was a cap that he had on.

'I'll tell you of my own personal hairdresser,' he said. 'The only man in town who cuts our fine hair quite properly. He'll take off your Bushman's head-dress,' and he messed up my hair again.

'But possibly *your* hair's so elegant because you wear a wig,' I said to him. And taking two handfuls of his hair, I lifted him one foot off the floor.

He yelled, and in came Jimmy Cannibal, making a sandwich of me between the two of them.

'Mr Whispers,' I said, easing out as best I could, 'I don't like familiarity from strangers. Can you tell that, please, to these two countrymen of yours?'

Billy was smiling for the first time. He had some broad gaps between all his short teeth, I saw, and pale blue gums.

I was planning perhaps to leap out through the window when the door opened yet once more, and there stood a girl that by her body's shape and looks was quite likely to be Muriel's sister. But what a difference from the little chick! Smart clothes—or what she thought was smart—bleached hair, and a look on her face like a bar-fly seeking everywhere hard for trade.

'What's all the commotion?' she enquired.

'Get out to work, Dorothy,' said Billy Whispers.

'Oh, I'm going, Billy.'

'Then move.'

She leaned on one hip, and held out her crimson hand.

'I want a taxi fare,' she said. 'And money to buy some you-know-whats.'

Whispers threw her a folded note and said, 'Now go.'

Still she stood looking what she thought was glamorous, and it's true that, in a way, it was. And me still between these two body-guards, both of them waiting to eliminate me.

'You're a nice boy,' she said to me. 'Where you from—Gambia too?'

Billy got up, strolled over and slapped her. She screamed out louder than the blow was worth, and he slapped her again harder, so she stopped. 'Now go,' he said to her again. 'And see that your evening's profitable.'

She disappeared out with a high-heel clatter. I slipped away from among the two bad boys and took Mr Billy by the arm.

'Billy Whispers,' I said, 'do you want a scene with me too here in your bedroom?'

He looked at my eyes and through beyond them, adding up, I suppose, what damage I'd do to any life, limb or furniture, before I was myself destroyed.

'Is not necessary,' he said, 'unless you think it is.

'By nature I'm peaceable. I like my life.'

'Then shoot off, Mr Fortune, now. . . .'

The two started muttering and limbering, but he frowned at them only, and they heaved away from me.

'Goodbye, Mr Whispers,' I said. 'I dare say we'll meet soon once again, when I'll offer you some hospitality of mine at that future time.'

'Is always possible, man,' he answered, 'that you and I might cross our paths some more in this big city.'

6

Montgomery sallies forth

MY FLAT (two odd rooms and a 'kitchenette', most miscellaneously furnished) is perched on the top floor of a high, narrow house near Regent's Park with a view on the Zoological Gardens, so that lions, or seals, it may be, awake me sometimes in the dawn. Beneath me are echoing layers of floor and corridors, empty now except for Theodora Pace.

When the house used to be filled with tenants, I rarely spoke to Theodora. Such a rude, hard, determined girl, packed with ability and innocent of charm, repelled me: so clearly was she my superior in the struggle for life, so plainly did she let me see she knew it. She made it so cruelly clear she thought the world would not have been in any way a different place if I had not been born.

But circumstances threw us together.

A year ago, the property changed hands, and notices to quit were served on all the tenants. All flew to their lawyers, who thought, but weren't quite sure (they never are, until the court gives judgment), that the Rent Acts protected us. A cold war began. The new landlord refused to accept our rents, some tenants lost heart and departed, and others removed themselves, enriched by sumptuous bribes. When only Theodora and I remained, the landlords sued us for trespass. We prepared for battle but, before the case came into court, the landlords withdrew the charge, paid costs, left us like twin birds in an abandoned dovecote, and sat waiting, I suppose, in their fur-lined Mayfair offices, for our deaths—or for some gross indiscretion by which they could eject us.

Throughout this crisis, Theodora behaved with Roman resolution. Uncertain how to manœuvre against anyone so powerful as a landlord, I clung steadfastly to her chariot wheels, and she dragged me with her to victory. Small wonder that the B.B.C. should pay so talented a woman a large salary for doing I never could discover what.

Thenceforth, Theodora became my counsellor: sternly offering me advice in the manner always of one casting precious pearls before some pig. (Her advice was so useful that I overcame a strong inclination to insult her.) It was through Theodora, as a matter of fact, that I'd got the job in the Colonial Department.

So on the evening of my first encounter with Johnny Fortune, I returned to my eyrie, washed off the pretences of the Welfare Office in cool water, and went down to knock on Theodora's door. She shouted, 'Come in,' but went on typing for several minutes before raising her rimless eyes and saying, 'Well? How did it go? Are you going to hold down the job this time?'

'I don't see why not, Theodora. . . .'

'It's pretty well your last chance. If you don't make good there, you'd better emigrate.'

'Don't turn the knife in the wound. I know I was a failure at the British Council, but I did quite well there before the unfortunate happening.'

'You were never the British Council type.'

'Perhaps, after all, that's just as well.'

'And until you learn to control yourself in such matters as drink, sex and extravagance, you'll never get yourself anywhere.'

'I'm learning fast, Theodora. Be merciful.'

'Let's hope so. Would you care for a gin?'

Though she'd rebuke me for tippling, Theodora was herself a considerable boozer. But liquor only made her mind more diamond sharp.

'Cheerio. What you need, Montgomery, is a wife.'

'So you have often told me.'

'You should look around.'

'I shall.'

'Meanwhile, what is it you have to *do* in that place?'

I told her about the Welfare dossiers.

'It all sounds a lot of nonsense to me,' she said, 'though I dare say it's worth twelve pounds a week for them to keep you. The chief thing for you to remember, though, is that it's just a job like any other, so don't get involved in politics, race problems, and such inessentials.'

'No.'

'To do a job well, and get on, you must never become involved in it emotionally.'

'Theodora, do tell me! What *is* it you do yourself within the B.B.C.?'

'You wouldn't understand,' she said, 'even if I told you.'

I looked round at the bookshelves, packed to the ceiling with the kind of volume that would make this library, in thirty years' time, a vintage period piece.

'I thought,' I said, 'I might go down and investigate that hostel this evening.'

'Why? Is it your business?'

'To tell you the whole truth, I'm not sure what my business is. My predecessor hadn't the time or inclination to tell me much, and my chief's away on holiday for another week. It's an awkward time for me to take over.'

'Then leave well alone. Just do the obvious things till he gets back.'

'But I've heard such complaints about our hostel. One student in particular, called Fortune, said it's quite dreadful there.'

'It probably is. All hostels are. They're meant to be.'

She started typing again.

'I'll leave you then, Theodora.'

'Very well. And do learn to use your time and get on with a bit of work. Your biography of John Knox—how many words have you written this last month?'

'Very few. I'm beginning to dislike my hero so much he's even losing his horrid fascination.'

'Persevere.'

'I shall. May I have another gin?'

'You can take the bottle with you, if you can't resist it.'

'Thank you. And what are *you* writing, Theodora?'

'A report.'

'Might I ask on what?'

'You may, but I shan't tell you.'

'Good evening, then.'

I went upstairs sadly, and changed into my suit of Barcelona blue: a dazzling affair that makes me look like an Ealing Studio gangster, and which I'd ordered when drunk in that grim city, thereby, thank goodness, abbreviating my holiday in it by one week. As I drank heavily into Theodora's gin, the notion came to me that *I* should visit these haunts against which it was my duty to warn others: the Moorhen, the Cosmopolitan dance hall, and perhaps the Moonbeam club. But first of all, I decided, adjusting the knot of my vulgarest bow tie (for I like to mix Jermyn Street, when I can afford it, with the Mile End Road), it was a more imperative duty to inspect the Welfare hostel. So down I went by the abandoned stairs and corridors, and hailed a taxi just outside the Zoo.

It carried me across two dark green parks to that S.W.1 region of our city which, since its wartime occupation by soldiers' messes and dubious embassies, has never yet recovered its dull dignity. Outside an ill-lit peeling portico the taxi halted, and I alighted to the strains of a faint calypso:

'I can't wait eternally
For my just race equality.
If Mr England voter don't toe the line,
Then maybe I will seek some other new combine'

somebody was ungratefully singing to the twang of a guitar.

I gazed up, and saw dark forms, in white singlets, hanging comfortably out of windows: surely *not* what the architect had intended.

I walked in.

There I was met by three men of a type as yet new to me: bespectacled, their curly hair parted by an effort on one side, wearing tweed suits of a debased gentlemanly cut, and hideous university ties. (*Why* do so many universities favour purple?) They carried menacing-looking volumes.

'Can I be of assistance to you?' said one to me.

'I should like to speak to the warden.'

'Warden? There is no such person here by nights.'

'We control the hostel ourselves, sir, by committee,' said another.

'I, as a matter of fact, am the present secretary.'

And he looked it.

'Oh,' I said, 'is Mr Fortune possibly in? A Lagos gentleman.'

'You could find that for yourself, sir, also his room number, by consulting the tenancy agenda on the public information board.'

He pointed a large helpful finger at some baize in the recess of the dark hall. I gave him a cold official smile, ignored the baize board, and walked upstairs to examine the common rooms and empty cubicles.

This Colonial Department hostel smelt high, I soon decided, with the odour of good intentions. The communal rooms were like those on ships—to be drifted in and out of, then abandoned. The bedrooms (cubicles!), of which I inspected one or two, though lacking no necessary piece of furniture, yet had the 'furnished' look of a domestic interior exhibited in a shop window. And over the whole building there hung an aura of pared Welfare budgets, of tact restraining antipathies, and of a late attempt to right centuries of still unadmitted wrongs.

And all this time the nasal calypso permeated the lino-laden passages. As I approached the bright light from a distant open door, I heard:

'English politician he say, "Wait and see,"
Moscow politician he say, "Come with me."
But whichever white employer tells those little white lies,
I stop my ears and hold my nose and close my eyes.'

I peered in.

Sitting on the bed, dressed in a pair of underpants decorated with palm leaves, was a stocky youth topped by an immense gollywog fuzz of hair. He grimaced pleasantly at me, humming the air till he had completed the guitar improvisation. Whereupon he slapped the instrument (as one might a child's behind) and said, 'What say, man? You like a glass of rum?'

'I'm looking,' I told him, 'for Mr J. M. Fortune.'

'Oh, that little jungle cannibal. That bongo-banging Bushman.'

'I take it,' I said, accepting some rum in a discoloured tooth-glass, 'that you yourself are not from Africa?'

'Please be to God, no, man. I'm a civilized respectable Trinidadian.'

'The Africans, then, aren't civilized?'

'They have their own tribal customs, mister, but it was because of their primitive barbarity that our ancestors fled from that country some centuries ago.'

This was accompanied by a knowing leer.

'And the song,' I asked. 'It is of your own composition?'

'Yes, man. In my island I'm noted for my celebrated performance. It's your pleasure to meet this evening no less a one than Mr Lord Alexander in person.'

And he held out a ring-encrusted hand with an immensely long, polished, little-finger nail.

'Perhaps, though,' he went on, 'as I'm seeking to make my way in *this* country, you could help me into radio or television or into some well-loaded night-spot?'

'Alas!' I told him, 'I have no contacts in those glowing worlds.'

'Then at least please speak well of me,' he said, 'and make my reputation known among your friends.'

'Willingly. Though I have to tell you that I don't care for calypso. . . .'

'Man, that's not possible!' He stood up in his flowered pants aghast. 'Surely all educated Englishmen like our scintillating music?'

'Many, yes, but not I.'

'Now, why?'

'Your lines don't scan, you accentuate the words incorrectly, and the thoughts you express are meagre and without wit.'

'But our leg-inspiring rhythm?'

'Oh, that you have, of course. . . .'

'Mr Gentleman, you disappoint me,' he said. And taking a deep draught from the rum bottle, he strolled sadly to the window, leaned out, and sang into the opulent wastes of S.W.1:

> 'This English gentleman he say to me
> He do not appreciate calypso melody.
> But I answer that calypso has supremacy
> To the Light Programme music of the B.B.C.

I made my getaway.

Prying along an adjacent marble landing (affording a vertiginous perspective of a downward-winding statue-flanked white stair), I saw a door on which was written: 'J. Macdonald Fortune, Lagos. Enter without knocking.' I did so, turned on the light, and saw a scene of agreeable confusion. Valises up-ended disgorging the bright clothes one would so wish to wear, shirts, ties and socks predominating—*none* of them fit for an English afternoon. Bundles of coconuts.

A thick stick of bananas. Bottles, half empty. Rather surprising—a pile of biographies and novels. And pinned on the walls photographs of black grinning faces, all teeth, the eyes screwed closed to the glare of a sudden magnesium flare. A recurring group was evidently a family one: Johnny; a substantial rotund African gentleman with the same air of frank villainy as was the junior Mr Fortune's; his immense wife, swathed in striped native dress; a tall serious youth beside a motor-bicycle; and a vivacious girl with a smile like that of an amiable lynx.

On the table, I noticed an unfinished letter in a swift clerical hand. I didn't disturb it, but . . .

'Dear Peach,

'How it would be great if I could show you all the strange sights of the English capital, both comical and splendid! This morning I had my interview at the Welfare Office with—well, do you remember Reverend Simpson? Our tall English minister who used to walk as if his legs did not belong to him? And spoke to us like a telephone? Well, that was the appearance of the young Mr Pew who interviewed me, preaching and pointing his hands at me as if I was to him a menacing infant. . . .'

Ah!

'. . . I have made visits, too, this afternoon, both of which will interest Dad—tell him I'm writing more about them, but don't please tell our dearest Mum or Christmas that I give you this message. Just now I have returned here to my miserable hostel (hovel!—which soon I shall be leaving permanently) to change to fresh clothes and go out in the town when it's alight.

'And Peach! It's true about the famous escalator! It can be done, early this morning I made the two-way expedition, easily dashing up again until . . .'

Should I turn over the sheet? No, no, not that. . . .

I closed the door softly and walked down the chipped ceremonial stair. At its foot, the secretary waylaid me.

'And did you then discover Mr Fortune?' he enquired.

'No.'

'Will it be necessary for me to convey to him some message of your visit?'

'No.'

He frowned.

'As secretary of the hostel committee, may I ask of your business on our premises?'

I gave him a Palmerstonian glare, but he met it with such a look of dignified solemnity that I wilted and said, 'I am the new Assistant Welfare Officer. My name is Montgomery Pew.'

'And mine, sir, is Mr Karl Marx Bo. I am from Freetown, Sierra Leone.'

We shook hands.

'I hope, sir,' he said, 'you have not the same miserable opinion of our qualities as he who previously held down your job?'

'Oh, you mustn't think that. Come, come.'

'May I offer you a cup of canteen coffee?'

'I'd love it, but really, I'm in somewhat of a hurry. . . .'

I moved towards the massive door. Mr Bo walked beside me, radiating unaffected self-righteousness.

'Here in London, I am studying law,' he told me.

'That means, I suppose, that you'll be going into politics?'

'Inevitably. We must make the most of our learning here in London. Emancipation, sir, is our ultimate objective. I predict that in the next ten years, or less, the whole of West Africa will be a completely emancipated federation.'

'Won't the Nigerians gobble you up? Or Dr Nkrumah?'

'No, sir. Such politicians clearly understand that national differences of that nature are a pure creation of colonialism. Once we have federation, such regional distinctions will all fade rapidly away.'

'Well, jolly good luck to you.

'Oh, yes! You say so! But like all Englishmen, I conceive you view with reluctance the prospect of our freedom?'

'Oh, but we give you the education to get it.'

'Not give, sir. I pay for my university through profits my family have made in the sale of cocoa.'

'A dreadful drink, if I may say so.'

He tolerantly smiled. 'You must come, sir, if you wish, to take part in one of our discussions with us, or debates.'

'Nothing would delight me more, but alas, as an official, I am debarred from expressing any personal opinion, even had I one. And now, for the present, you really must excuse me.'

And before he could recover his potential Dominion status, I was out of the door and stepping rapidly up the moonlit road. 'To the Moorhen public house,' I told a taxi driver.

He was of that kind who believe in the London cabby's reputation for dry wit.

'Better keep your hands on your pockets, Guv,' he said, 'if I take you there.'

7

Montgomery at the Moorhen

THOUGH FOND OF BARS and boozing in hotels, I'm not a lover of that gloomiest of English institutions—the public house. There is a legend of the gaiety, the heart-warming homeliness of these 'friendly inns'—a legend unshakeable; but all a dispassionate eye can see in them is the grim spectacle of 'regulars' at their belching back-slapping beside the counter or, as is more often, sitting morosely eyeing one another, in private silence, before their half-drained gassy pints. (There is also, of course, that game called darts.)

It wasn't, then, with high eagerness that I prepared to visit the Moorhen. Nor was I more encouraged when the driver, with a knowing grimace, decanted me on a corner near the complex of North London railway termini. The pub, from outside, was of a dispirited baroque. And lurking about its doors, in groups, or half invisible in the gloom, were Negroes of equivocal appearance. One of these detached himself from a wall as I stood hesitating, and approached.

'What say, mister?' he began. 'Maybe you want somesings or others?'

'Not that I'm aware of,' I replied.

'Oh, no?'

'No. . . .'

'Not this?'

Cupped in the hollow of his hand he held a little brown-paper packet two inches long or so.

'And what might that be?'

'Come now, man,' he said with a grin of understanding and positively digging me in the ribs. 'Is weed, man.'

'*Weed?* What on earth should I want with weed? Now if you had seedlings, or even the cuttings of a rose . . .'

'I see you's a humourisk,' he said.

As a matter of fact, I wasn't quite so ignorant, for I had read my Sunday papers. But this was the first time I'd seen the stuff.

'All sames,' he went on, closing his fingers over the little packet, 'if you need some charge later in your evenings, come to me. Mr Peter Pay Paul is what's my name.'

I thanked him remotely, and pushed open the door of the Moorhen's saloon.

Within, where dark skins outnumbered white by something like twenty to one, there was a prodigious bubble and clatter of sound, and what is rare in purely English gatherings—a constant movement of person to person, and group to group, as though some great invisible spoon were perpetually stirring a hot human soup. Struggling, then propelled, towards the bar, I won myself a large whisky, and moved, with the instinct of minorities, to the only other white face I could see who was not either serving behind the bar, or a whore, of whom there were a great many there, or a person of appearance so macabre as scarcely to be believed. The man whom I addressed was one of those vanishing London characters, the elderly music-hall comical, modelled perhaps on Wilkie Bard, all nose, blear eyes, greased clothes and tufts of hair. 'Cheerio!' I said to him.

He eyed me.

'Crowded tonight.'

'Yus.' (He really said 'Yus'.) 'More's the pity.'

'Oh, you think so? You don't care for crowds?'

'Course I do—when they're rispectable. But not when they're darkies like what's here and all their rubbish.'

'Rubbish?'

He gazed all round the room like a malevolent searchlight and said, 'Jus' look for yourself. And to think a year or so ago this was the cosiest little boozer for arf a mile.'

'But if,' I said, 'you don't like it, why do you come here?'

'Ho! They won't drive me out! They drove out me pals, but they won't drive me.'

'Drove them?'

'They left. Didn't care for it as it got to be ever since the Cosmopolitan opened opposyte.'

'That's the dance hall?'

'Yus. They let those darkies overrun the dance hall, but they haven't got a licence there. So what did they do? Came trooping over the road for drinks like an invasion, and turned this place into an Indian jungle.'

'And the landlord let them?'

'He can't refuse. At least he did try to for the sake of his regulars, but when he saw all the coin they dropped on to his counters, he gave up the fight, and me pals all had to move on. But not me. This is my pub and I'm staying in it till something happens and they all get thrown out again.' And this outpost of empire stared at me with neurotic, baleful zeal.

A juke-box that had been blaring out strident threepennyworths now stopped. I edged my way over to an argumentative group around it, one of whom, a hefty, vivid-looking Negro, was shouting out what sounded rather like:

'Ooso, man. See molo keneeowo p'kolosoma nyamo Ella Fitzgerald, not that other woman. See kynyomo esoloo that is my preference.'

The speaker was wearing pink trousers, a tartan silk shirt bedecked with Parker pens, and a broad-brimmed hat ironed up fore and aft like a felt helmet. A watch of gold, and silver chains, dangled on his gesticulating wrists.

A smaller man beside him, an ally apparently, turned to the others and said, 'Is best let Mr Cannibal have his own choice of record if someone will please give him a threepence bit.'

No one offered, and I ventured to hand the giant a coin.

'Oh, this is nice,' said the smaller man. 'Here is this nice personality who gives Mr Cannibal his tune!' He took the coin from me with two delicate fingers, put it in the juke-box, then said smiling wide, 'So I offer you a cigarette? And then maybe you offer me a light in your own turn?'

I took the Pall Mall, and held out my Ronson to his own. His fingers encircled it as if to guard the flame when, hey presto! the lighter was flicked from my hand, and this person had scurried through the throng towards a farther corner.

I looked about me and saw amiable laughing faces whose eyes dropped politely when mine caught theirs. I began to make my way through them towards the robber and found that, while not exactly stopping me by standing full in my tracks, they presented hard shoulders that made progress difficult.

When at last I reached the corner, I saw an ancient hair-stuffed sofa tottering against the wall. On it were seated Mr Cannibal, the little nuisance who'd taken my lighter, and a third man who wasn't talking, only listening. He was small, tightly built into his suit, at ease, alert, alarming, and compact. He glanced up at me: our eyes locked: his glare had such depth that my own sank into his, and while for two seconds I stood riveted, this stare seemed to drain away my soul.

I blinked, hemmed in behind a wall of dark faces and drape suits. Abruptly, I shook my brain, moved a pace towards the thief, and said to him: 'Can I have my lighter?'

The gabbling conversation in jungle tones went on until the third time of asking. Then the little thief looked up and said, 'What is this stranger? You ask for some light from me, or what?'

It was a shock to see how with this race, even more than with our own, an expression of great amiability can be replaced, on the same face, within seconds, by one of cold indifference and menace.

'No,' I said, enwrapping myself with draped togas of torn Union Jacks. 'Not a *light*, but the *lighter*.'

He took it out of his pocket and tossed it up and down in his hand.

'You wish to *buy* this?' he asked.

'No. Merely to have it back.'

'You mean you say that this my lighter is *your* lighter?'

'Well, my dear chap, you know it is.'

The giant got up, and so did the lighter-lifter, but not the third man, who sat looking at eternity through his lashes.

'Then what I ask,' said the culprit, 'is if your words mean that you call me now a thief?'

The giant stood looking like the Black Peril. The third man now glanced up at me again. When his eyes fixed once more on mine, I felt myself absorbed into a promiscuity of souls closer even than that which can bind, and then dissolve, two animal bodies in each other.

'No,' I said, faltering. 'Keep it.' And as I moved off: 'I hope it brings you luck.'

Rage and disgust filled my heart. 'That idiot at the Welfare Office was right!' I cried out to myself, as I heaved back through the crowd. 'Disgusting creatures! Bring back the lash, the slave trade! Long live Dr Malan!'

Standing in the doorway was a figure different from the gaudy elegants inside—one dressed in dungarees, half shaven, with anthropoid jaws and baby ears, more startling even than alarming. He gave me a great meaningless grin, held out a detaining hand and said (this is the rough equivalent), 'You want some Mexican cigaleks?'

'No, no.'

'At sree sillins for twentik, misters. . . .'

'Oh, really? Well, yes, then.'

He slipped them to me discreetly. Lighting up, awaiting for the return of my shattered poise, I asked him, 'How do you get these, then?'

Conspiratorially, he replied: 'From him G.I.s who sells me in cartoons wisouts no legal dutiks. So you better keep him secrix.'

'They sell them to you here?'

'No, out in him streek, because of Law and his narks that put the eye insides. Anysing from G.I. stores you wants I gess you: sirts, soss, ties, jackix, nylons, overcoats, socolates or any osser foots . . .'

'You make a good profit?'

He looked bland.

'I muss have profix for my risks. That is my bisnick.'

'Do other boys here have things to sell?'

'Oh, misters! Here is him big Londons Spadiss markik place! Better than Ossford Streek hisself!' And he roared out laughing loud, doubling himself up and slapping himself all over. Then he looked coyly discreet. 'Those bad boys,' he said, 'they relieves you of somesink?'

'Yes. You saw? They stole my lighter.'

'A Ronsons?'

'Yes.'

'Of course. Was Mr Ronson Lighter who took it. That is his professins: when he sees Ronson lighter, he muss steal him.'

'And who are his friends?'

'The Billy Whispers peoples. Gambian boys, real bad. Billy hisself, and Jimmies Cannibals and Mister Ronson Lighter, this that robs you.'

'What do they do for a living?'

'Prey!'

His eyes gleamed sympathetically and, I thought, with envy. Then he went on:

'That is their seats over in him corners. This is the seats of all bad Asfrican boys where they go gather makin' deals. No Asfrican boy who is not top London hustler go near their corners, and no Wess Indians dare go by never. Mister, if you have loot, or goods, or wishes they can prey on, please keep clear of him Billy Whispers and all his surrounding mens.'

He told me this as one who reveals a precious, precarious State secret. Then he looked severe.

'Those boys they sink I stupit—"Boos-a-man" [Bushman] they call me, becos I come out from my home in him interiors, not city folks like those wikit waterfronk boys. . . .' He ruminated, flashing his eyes about. 'They sink I stupit because of no educasons. But [crescendo] my blood better than their blood! My father sieftan [chieftain]!'

'Yes?'

'Yes. I sief's son.'

Diffidence but enormous pride: as if making a huge joke that was no joke, as if calling on me to recognize a splendid truth even if incredible.

'Then why do you leave your people and come here to England?'

'I? Oh, to see these sights. To live. Also, to learn my instrumink.'

'Your . . .'

'My sassofone. I work stoke in him governmik boiler-room by nights, to get loot for lessons for my instrumink. Then, when my time come, I go home to fashinate my cousins with my tunes.'

'And how are your studies progressing?'

'Whass say?'

'Are you mastering your instrument?'

'Man, up till now is my instrumink who is most times mastering me. Ah! But lissen!'

And we heard:

'You leave your mother and your brother too,
You leave the pretty wife you're never faithful to,

You cross the sea to find those streets that's paved with
gold,
And all you find is Brixton cell that's oh! so cold.'

'Thass Lord Alissander! He always come playing here evening, hopin' for sillins and publicitix.'

He plucked at my arm and led me out to the corner of the street. Mr Lord Alexander was leaning against the pub wall, strumming and singing in the middle of a softly humming circle.

'Give us some bad song now, man!'

'Some little evil tune, Lord Alexander!'

'Oh, no! No, no, not me in this respectable country. . . .

'This little Miss Commercial Road she say to me,
"I can't spend much more time in your society.
I know you keep me warmer than my white boy can do,
But my mother fears her grandson may be black as you." '

There was laughter; but on the far side of the street, standing against the brick fence that lined the bombed-out site, were two figures in mackintoshes who were now joined by a tall police Inspector with the shape of an expectant mother. The Bushman took my arm:

'Lissen, man,' he whispered, 'I soot off now, that look to me like him Law be making his customary visicts. Come! We soot off to him Cosmikpolitan dansings, and find whass cookings there. . . .'

Looking back, we saw the three coppers sweeping on the group, which scattered; and then Lord Alexander being led off, the uniformed Inspector carrying the guitar as if it was a truncheon.

8

A raid at the Cosmopolitan

THIS COSMOPOLITAN DANCE HALL is the nearest proximity I've seen yet in London to the gaiety and happiness back home.

For the very moment I walked down the carpet stair, I could see, I could hear, I could smell the overflowing joys of all my people far below. And when I first got a spectacle of the crowded ballroom, oh, what a sight to make me glad! Everywhere us, with silly little white girls, hopping and skipping fit to die! Africans, West Indians, and coloured G.I.s all boxed up together with the cream of this London female rubbish!

A weed peddler came up to me. 'Hullo, hullo, man, you're new,' this too much smiling man said.

I gave him my frown. 'And what you want?' I said.

'Is what *you* want,' he answered, and showed me his packet. 'I'm the surest sure man in the business. You can call me Mr Peter Pay Paul.'

I took it, opened it, eyed it, sniffed it. 'If this is weed,' I said, 'I'm Sugar Ray Robinson.'

His face looked full of pain. 'Then you's dissatisfied?' and he tried to snatch the little packet back.

I held it far. 'What is your foolish game, Mr Peter Pay Paul? What is this evil stuff you peddle to poor strangers?'

He glared at me hard; then smiling again, said, 'Well, I see you's a smart fellow, not rich in ignorance. So I tell you secretly. Is asthma cure I peddle to G.I.s.'

'Tell me some more.'

'This asthma cure, you see, is much like the weed to look at, but naturally is cheaper and of no effect. But G.I.s are so ignorant and anyway so high with liquor, that they buy it from me in large quantities.'

'Well, I'm no G.I., mister, nor ignorant, you'll understand.' And I pushed past him towards the edge of the dancing floor.

And there, wearing dark glasses, and standing among the awaiting pouncers, who should I see but my dearest friend of schooldays in Lagos—Hamilton! 'Hamilton!' I cried out. 'Hamilton Ashinowo, baddest bad boy of the whole mission school!'

Round about he spun, peered, took off his dark glasses (Wow! how that man had been charging, his eyes closed up almost shut), then called out: 'No! No! Is Johnny! Johnny, since when you arrive, my little boy?' And he seized me and gabbled at me in our private tribal tongue.

Hamilton, my dear friend at the mission school, had left it by expulsion two years before I came away when he was found by the Reverend Simpson selling palm wine at profitable prices from a canvas bag he kept hidden underneath his dormitory bed. Hamilton was the love and mock of all of us at school. Mock for his tall wobbling figure, his huge teeth in his pale pink gums, his arms that hung down to his knees like a chimpanzee, and for the celebrated frenzy dance of all his body when excited, that caused him to leap and break out in sharp cries of gasping joy. But loved by us all for his everywhere good nature to everyone, even those not at all deserving of it from him.

'Villainous Hamilton!' I cried out. 'Let's have a drink to celebrate this reunion.'

'Man, in this Cosmopolitan is only coffees, ciders and Coca-Colas, but if you like we can cross the road over to the Moorhen.'

'No, no, stay here and tell me all your activities since we meet. How did you get here, and what is your full present position?'

'I came here, Johnny, on a merchant ship.'

'As passenger? As crew?'

'As stowaway. Then one month in their English jail, and I'm a free British citizen again.'

'And how do you live on what?'

'Ah, now, that . . .' He smiled and wobbled. 'Well, man, I hustle If you ain't got no loot from home, and you don't like the work in the Jumble post office, or railways, for six pounds less taxes and insurances, then, man, you must hustle.'

'And what is your particular hustling?'

'Oh, Johnny, you ask such private questions! Tell me of you, now. You been here long?'

'Some few day now.'

'And you think you like this city?'

'I think yes I do, but not my lodging. I'm in that Welfare hostel.'

'Oh, no! That underpaid paradise! You enjoy it?'

'Mister, I'm moving out before the week is ended. Are rooms in town so very hard to find?'

'They can be found, yes, though Jumbles that take Spade will rob you in their charge of rent. . . .'

'Aren't there no Spades here that have houses?'

'Oh, yes. They rob you even better, but they leave you free. I live in one such house myself.'

'And that house is where?'

'By Holloway. I live out there at times.'

'At times?'

'Man, I have *several* addresses. I keep them for various private reasons of convenience.'

'Hamilton, all this is so mysterious to me.

'I tell you more later, man, far from these overhanging ears. Meantime if you leave your hostel, will you come and live with me if you prefer? The landlord is Mr Cole, an Ibo man. I pay two pounds the week which you can share.'

'Immediately, Hamilton. I move into your house tonight.'

By this time the Cosmopolitan was getting hotted hotter up. And I was struck to notice that though the band was only Jumble imitation of our style, it was quite a hep combination, with some feel of the beat, not like those dreadful records of the English bands I'd heard back home which never can play slow, and never can play easy to the limbs. Out on the floor our boys were acting cool and crazy, letting their little girls do all the work as they twisted them around; or if any of our boys did break in a quick shuffle, the chicks were left gasping tied in hopeless knots. The English boys, of which a few were out there on the floor, all leaped around their partners like some bouncing peanuts, supposing they would show these easy Spades the genuine hot footwork of the jungle. To ask for partner, as I saw, all you must do was just walk up and grab. Though I did notice some polite student boys with spectacles who bowed and enquired, in Jumble style, for which they got refusal.

Then I saw Billy Whispers' Dorothy. She danced with a G.I., dressed up sharp, with vaseline in his hair and graceful.

'Hamilton,' I said, 'do you know a Bathurst boy called Whispers?'

'That Billy? Who doesn't know of him? Now heaven help that poor G.I. if Dorothy take him home.'

'Is that Billy Whispers' racket?'

'One that he has, with robbery and violence, assisted by Ronson Lighter and by Jimmy Cannibal.'

'Why they call that boxer that? He eat his mother?'

'I expect not yet. But he tell his Jumble victims he was fed up on boiled missionary in his village. This news impress them, see, and wins their unlucky trust.'

'Hamilton, hold my cigarette, I'm going to dance with her.'

'Look after yourself then, Johnny, and don't lose me from your view.'

Dorothy's G.I. was not a bit pleased to see me, but she cut all the ground out under his long feet by saying to me, with her English idea of the speech of a tough Brooklyn chick, 'Why, hullo, feller. Never thought I'd see *you* again so soon.'

'I'm like that bad penny, Dorothy. I always keep turning myself up.'

'Aren't you going to ask me to dance?'

'Come on, then, I'll spin you round a while.'

But soon we circled far off to the quiet corner where the partners were wedged up close.

'Does Billy know you're here?' she asked me.

'Can't say. Why? You belong to that man?'

'I don't belong to nobody, see?' (This came out in her natural Brixton language—no more Brooklyn.) 'I live with Billy Whispers, yes. But only so long as I want to. Me, I walk out just when I like.'

'That's not what I thought from how he acted to you there this afternoon. It seemed like he had you all wrapped up.'

'Oh, did it!'

'I'm glad it's not so, Dorothy. Because Muriel and your mother's getting worried about the influence of Billy on you.'

She stopped dancing.

'Oh, is she! My mother—that old cow: yes, I said "cow"! And Muriel, my good little sister! Do you know why she's so good,

Johnny? Because she's deformed! She can't do any better for herself. Didn't you see her hand?'

'I saw she had the glove on it. . . .'

'She's only got three fingers on that hand.'

'She had some accident?'

'No. She was deformed from birth.'

'Which fingers has she missing?'

'The end ones. I tell her it means she'll never get married, if she can't wear a wedding ring. . . .'

'Fingers aren't everything on a body, Dorothy.'

'No, but they come in handy, don't they?'

'She's got a pretty figure, and a happier smile than you.'

'Muriel? She's never been known to smile since she was born.'

She put her arms round my neck and hung on me.

'What about your brother Arthur, Dorothy? When is he coming out?'

'It was six months he got, so it should be any time now, with the remission. But me, I don't have anything to do with him. I don't like these half white, half Africans.'

'You might have one yourself, the way you're living.'

'Are you kidding? I'd get rid of it. Anyway, I'm going to have my ovaries removed.'

'That'll be nice and comfortable.'

We circled round a bit, and I held her off from taking any too great liberty. But she pressed up close and said to me, 'Why don't you ask me out to tea one day, Johnny?'

'Oh, I drink coffee.'

'You know what I mean.'

'Don't rush me off my feet, now, Dorothy. Why you not wait until I make the offer?'

'Oh, if that's how you feel . . .' And she walked straight out of my arms. I watched her fine figure, which certainly gave you the appetite, as she vanished from my view.

As I was strolling back to look for Hamilton, who should I see, sitting at a table, but this unusual couple: a rough-looking jungle boy, who I thought by his cheek-marks might be of the Munshi tribe, and with him who else but the Welfare Office gentleman, Mr Montgomery Pew. Oh-ho! I thought. What can this be?

His long body was wrapped all round the table legs, his hungry face held up by both his hands, and his sad eyes were shooting round the room like trying to find something they could rest on with any comfort.

'Why, Mr Pew!' I said to him. 'You visiting this wicked spot to see if I obey your wise advice to me?'

'Why, Mr Fortune!' he cried back, 'do come and have a glass of this disgusting lemonade. Here is a friend of mine—Mr Bushman, I much regret I don't know your full name.'

I said a few words to this Bushman in his own Munshi tongue, which is one of the four African languages I know fluently. I said I had business to discuss with Mr Pew, and as for him, would he please cut out and hunt some crocodiles? But he answered me in his terrible style of English.

'If you spiks to me insolting,' he said, 'be very careful or I soot you.'

'What you shoot me with, man?'

This puzzled him one moment, but he said, 'I will soot you with my amonisions.'

I laughed at the Bushman's face.

'This gentleman,' said Mr Pew, 'is a chieftain's son, and as such must be treated with respect. Besides which he's been most kind and obliging to me in all manner of ways.'

I saw Mr Pew was high—real gone.

'Blow now, you chieftain's son,' I said to him. 'Chief means no nothing now to any educated Africa man.'

'Wash out for youself,' the Bushman said to me, 'or one day I take an' soot you.' But he got up, and slowly he slide away.

Mr Pew waved after him, then turned to me and said, 'A delightful personality. To tell you the truth, I find this place quite gripping. An Elizabethan fragment come to life in our regimented world.'

No sense in that bit, so I said to him, 'Don't tell me this is *your* first visit here.'

'My dear Fortune, yes, it is. Believe it or not, I've only been attached to the Welfare Office a few days.'

'And already you give good advice to Africans! Well, well. How like an Englishman, if I may say.'

'But it's my job, my duty, Mr Fortune!'

'This "Mr Fortune"! Can't you call me Johnny like the whole world do?'

'And I'm Montgomery.' He held out his hand. 'But not, please, ever "Monty", under any circumstances.'

'If you say so, Montgomery. And now you'll be looking after colonial people's welfare?'

'In my small way, I hope so. I know nothing about you all, Johnny, but I like your people. . . .'

'We never trust a man who tells us that.'

'Oh, no? No?'

'We know in five seconds if you like us without you say so. Those who *say* they like us most usually do not.'

This Montgomery now grasped my arm in the most serious way. 'Well, even if I mustn't say I like you, I *do*,' he told me.

'Oh, that's all right, then.' And I smiled my best high-grade smile.

It was fortunate for us that Hamilton came over at this moment to warn me that some trouble was expected.

'Johnny, you must come with me, there's plain-clothes Law mustering up outside.' And then in our language: 'Who is this white?'

'Not dangerous, I think. What's cooking?'

'G.I.s have stated that their overcoats have been robbed them from the cloakroom. Naturally, our boys like those nice long blue nylon weatherproofs, and do these Americans expect their entertainment here for nothing? Always causing argument and disturbances. I not surprised those Yankee whites will string them up on trees.'

'Now, Hamilton.'

'If they keep on with their foolish agitations, this nice place will soon be closed by public opinion. Come, now. Let we buy some V.P. wine before the closing, and me I'll take you to an Indian restaurant called Fakir for rice and clean cooked chicken, not like that Jumble food, all grease.'

But just then some twenty Law appeared at the entrance steps, the band stopped, and a large cop went over to the mike and shouted: 'All stay where you are for questioning. No one moves.'

'Johnny,' said Hamilton in our speech again. 'You got weed on you? If yes, do slip it in that white man's pocket while he doesn't look.'

'No, he's my friend, I think. But I'll take care. Don't you worry, Hamilton, for me.'

'If they trouble you, say you're a G.I., and ask they hand you over to the U.S. patrol. They don't know your face, so they'll release you, I expect. Me, I have little business I must do, and I go hide.'

'We scatter then, Hamilton, and all meet at this Fakir, if you give me the address. Come please, Montgomery. We make our way slowly to the exit.'

Little packs of weed were falling like leaves upon the floor. Some boys were edging over to the back ways out, but others were mostly standing still with faces innocent and proud. Six silly high G.I.s were pointing the finger at some persons they said had taken away their coats.

As we got near the stairs, we were stopped by three Law in plain clothes that made them look even more like Law.

'Just a minute, you two. Stand on one side.'

'But, mister,' I said, 'I'm a student and must be back at my residential hostel by closing time, ten-thirty.'

'And who are you?'

'My name,' Montgomery tell them, 'is Jerusalem, Lew Jerusalem, I'm here on professional duty as editor of the *Bebop Guardian*.'

Silly.

'Stand on one side, the Inspector will talk to you,' they say to him.

'But me, mister,' I said. 'Look, here is my passport, proving I've just landed in this country, and here also are my student's papers concerning my meteorological studies.'

I spoke so humble and eager, and papers are often of much assistance with the Law. But this time they didn't make their magic.

'Stand on one side as well.'

The Law was now filtering all over the big hall, picking up here a boy, there a tough or frightened chick. I could see no sign of Hamilton, and hoped he'd melted.

Our three Law were busy now questioning others, so I decided on a dash. But at the top of the stairs two more sprang out and grabbed me, and led me to their car. And that worried me, because in my coat pocket I still had some sticks of weed that I'd not wished to lose like others did by dropping them on that floor. . . .

9

Introduction to the Law

WHEN JOHNNY RAN UP THE STAIRS I felt he'd deserted me: it was clear he didn't yet regard me as a friend; and this regret first showed me I already thought of him as one. There I was, left among a herd of suspect colonials, too dispirited to mind much when we were shepherded up the steps, and surrounded by a posse of constables who escorted us down the street with careful eyes, like a crocodile of wicked juveniles. The cool air smacked my brain, and I walked with dignity, slightly apart, in the manner of a distinguished stranger, until we reached a squat, square, windowless building, and were elbowed in.

In the hall we were kept waiting quite a while, next separated into bands and taken into smaller rooms. There, to my delight, I saw Johnny, and also, among others, Mr Peter Pay Paul.

A plain-clothes officer came up to me. 'May I have your name?' This time I gave it. 'And your address? Your age? Your occupation?' All in a little notebook. The occupation particularly interested him.

Then, fixing me with that *double* look that sits in coppers' eyes ('I say this, but I don't mean it, and you know I don't, and I know you know . . .' Or, 'Yes, I'm evil too, but, you see, my evil's licensed to discover yours'), he said, 'You won't mind if we ask you to submit to a search?'

'Of course not. But why?'

'You were found in the company of persons who are suspected of smoking hemp.'

'Is this search voluntary?'

'Oh of course.' (A tight-skinned smile.)

Johnny, from his bench across the room, said in a loud voice, 'Mr Pew, if you are searched voluntary, I suggest you ask for a non-police witness to be present also.'

'Shut your trap, you,' said the Law.

'Why, Johnny?'

'The Law, when it searches, sometimes finds things on a person that the person didn't have before the search began.'

'Keep quiet.'

'Mister. Am I arrested? If so, tell me, and for what. Then you can make your search, of course, but also you must make a charge and see it sticks. But if I am not arrested, please let me speak out my mind as a free man.'

I was in admiration at such audacity. 'You know this man?' the officer said to me.

'Certainly. He's a friend of mine.'

'So much a friend, Montgomery, that will you please give me some matches for my cigarette?'

I handed Johnny the box I'd bought to replace my lighter. As he took it, the officer grabbed it from him and opened it eagerly, scrabbling among the matches. While he did this, I saw Johnny quickly put his hand up to his mouth and swallow.

'Perhaps now you give me my friend's match-box?' he said to the vexed cops.

'We'll begin this search,' the officer replied. 'Unless anyone thinks they've any further objections.'

A uniformed man came in, dashed at me first, turned my pockets vigorously out, then poked and patted around my clothing. Curious how even innocent objects, like handkerchiefs and rings of keys, look suspect on a station table.

Johnny meanwhile had emptied his own pockets on to it. 'Would you like me to undress to naked?' he enquired.

In silence, they dashed at him as well. Evidently this bull-rush, this mock assault, was part of their technique.

Nothing.

Then Mr Peter Pay Paul. They found on him six little packets. 'Is asthma cure,' he said, grinning proudly.

'You're for the cells,' said the Law.

'But no! Why? This is not weed. Is National Health medicine, I swear it on my mother's life!'

'We'll see what the magistrate says to that,' the Law replied, and dragged him off.

'Poor foolish boy,' said Johnny softly. 'This asthma trick is one he play once too much. And surely when he appears in court, the evidence by then will be real weed and not this asthma cure.'

'You mean they'd switch that stuff for something real?'

'That is their usual way back home, where their stores of impounded stocks are used for such a purpose.'

'But this is England, Johnny. Our coppers don't do that.'

He looked at me blandly. 'Oh, is that so? Then I have much to learn of England. . . .'

The Law now returned. 'We won't keep you much longer,' it said to me, 'but perhaps you'd step into the next room a minute?'

I waited for fifteen. Then the plain-clothes man came in and offered me a cigarette.

'Of course, you'll understand, Mr Pew, why we had to search you too. We know a man in your position wouldn't probably be mixed up in anything dubious, but there it is.'

'There is what?'

'We have to take precautions. And also, of course, we don't want to be accused of discrimination, do we.' He gave me an oh, so friendly smile. 'As a matter of fact, Mr Pew, I was wondering if a man with your connections mightn't be willing to do us a good turn now and then.'

I looked blank.

'You see, between you and me, this colour problem's becoming quite a problem for us, too. Particularly in the matter of dope. Of course, these boys, it doesn't do them much harm, I don't suppose, they're used to it, even though it's not within the law. But the girls, Mr Pew, the younger girls they give it to! It's corrupting them. Yes, corrupting them and making them serve these black men's evil ends.'

His eyes shone, like some fake cleric's, with a slightly mad, holy zeal.

'What has all this to do with me, officer?'

He leaned forward at my face. 'I'll ask you. Mr Pew, if in your position you don't think it your duty to pass on any information that may come your way about the sources of this drug traffic.'

I got up.

'Officer, I have no such information. And if I had, frankly . . .'

'Yes?' (A monosyllable heavy with malice and with menace.)

'I'd not at all feel it my duty to pass it on to you.

'Oh, would you not.'

He slapped his hands on his knees, smiled most unpleasantly, and rose. 'I only mentioned it, sir, because sometimes we coppers can do a good turn in return for one that's done to us. And a friend in need can sometimes be a friend indeed.'

'Yes, I see your point.'

He opened the door. 'At any rate, remember what I say, in case you might find you'd better change your mind. Just ask for the Detective-Inspector of the C.I.D.—the Vice Inspector,' he added with taut official grin.

In the corridor outside his office, I caught a glimpse of a Negro loitering. Who was it? Yes! The boxer Cannibal who'd helped steal my lighter at the Moorhen. When he saw me, he turned hurriedly away.

Johnny was waiting in the street outside. 'What keep you so long?' he asked—suspiciously, I thought.

'That Vice Inspector tried to sign me up as a nark.'

'And you accepted the offer of this Mr Purity?'

'My dear Fortune!'

I was quite offended, and we walked two blocks in silence.

'It seems to me, Johnny,' I said at last, 'that you're very well informed about the police force and their habits.'

'I should be. I'm a policeman's son.'

'But you told me your father was in business.'

'He serve one time when a younger man in the force back home. I know the Law—I know it both sides round. In Lagos, as anyone will tell you, I was something of a bad boy in my way. What they call one of the waterfront boys . . . up to various tricks, and often encountering my own Dad's former friends. . . .' He stopped and rubbed his stomach. 'Oh, heavens, I don't like the taste of that brown paper I have to swallow down when I eat those sticks of charge I had about my person.'

'I thought that might be it. I wish I had your nerve. . . .'

Another coloured man was lurking at the next corner: haunting the city thoroughfare as if poised with a spear in the deep bush. His face to me was quite invisible, but Johnny said, 'Is Hamilton,' and they began a deep conversation in a voluble, staccato rumbling tongue.

'Hamilton,' Johnny told me with admiration, 'escaped the Law's attention by crouching on top of the lavatory doors. Then he could return, when all invaders left, to pick up the weed he find undetected on the floor.'

'Come now,' said Hamilton. 'I have some V.P. wine. We go to the Fakir for some necessary eat and drink.'

We walked through the warm night, with a wide white blaze on the city sky where the summer sun refused to set.

'Johnny,' I said. 'You talk to Hamilton in African. But to others you talk in English. Why?'

'I do not speak with Hamilton in African. I speak to him in the language of our tribe. There is no "African", but many, many tribal languages.'

'How many?'

'More than one hundred in Nigeria. Some I know, like Yoruba, Hausa, Munshi and my own. But others I do not, so I speak English.'

'So you speak five languages. Bravo!'

'I teach you some Africa words one day—words of my tribe. Say "*Madu*".'

'*Madu*. What have I said?'

'"My friend." Come, we go eat. You like this Indian food?'

'No. About Indian food, there's a great mystery: how can a race so ancient and so civilized have devised anything so repellent? It always seems predigested and regurgitated. And the handkerchiefs it ruins!'

'Oh? You like that fish-and-chip stuff better? Come, we go in.'

The Indians were, as is usual, a family, and they welcomed my friends with the aloof professional deference that scarcely veils indifference and contempt. Johnny and Hamilton chose a distant corner beside an ash-tray made of an elephant's foot, and began their surreptitious chemistry with cigarette papers and little packets. After puffs, inhalations and exchange of butts, Johnny handed me the cigarette. 'It give you appetite,' he said.

'No, thanks.'

'You never smoked this stuff?'

'As a matter of fact, once, yes. In Egypt. But from a hubble-bubble.'

'And you liked it?'

'It had no effect whatever.'

'Oh-ho! Listen to this experienced Jumble man! Then either, Montgomery, your hubble-bubble contained rubbish, or you took a very feeble drag.'

'You'll have to be careful, smoking that stuff here.'

'Oh, these Indians don't mind,' said Hamilton.

'I mean here in England. Remember Inspector Purity.'

'Man,' Johnny said, 'wherever there are Spades there will be weed.'

'You smoked a lot at home?'

'In Africa, with due discretion, you can smoke in even public places.'

'Not in the main street, naturally,' Hamilton explained, 'or underneath the copper's nose, as that is useless provocation.'

'Even as babies, we may meet it,' Johnny said. 'A mother, to soothe our cries, may ease us to comfort with a gentle loving puff. Later, as boys, we make the experiment as you do here with your tobacco.'

'And do not forget,' said Hamilton, waving his hand, 'that many of us are Mahometans and cannot indulge in liquor. Weed is to us what liquor is to you.'

'But stronger, surely.'

'Depending on the quantity you partake.'

'Liquor,' said Johnny, 'opens you outwards and gives you a foolish love of fellow men, the wish to chatter to them in a cheerful, not selective way. But weed, you see, turns you happily inward to sit silent in the greater enjoyment of your personality. Try some?' And he held out the stick again.

'But it's habit-forming.'

'No,' they both said. And Johnny added, 'Charging is different from popping as liquor is.'

'Popping?'

'With needles. White stuff—man, that's danger! But not this—just you try it.'

'No, thanks. No, not for me.'

In came great piles of the predigested food, and Hamilton uncorked the V.P. wine.

Looking past his shoulder, I saw a huge shapeless man, but one with eyes a-glint, come lumbering light-toed through the door. Customers, when they saw him, lowered their eyes and talked a little louder. He had on a thick overcoat, despite the summer, and a large felt hat which he did not remove.

'Say nothing to this person,' Hamilton told me. 'He's Johnson: Johnson the tapper.'

'What's a tapper?'

'Man, you'll see.'

The huge man drew up a chair, smiled lippily at us all and reached out fat fingers to take food. Hamilton lifted the plates out of his reach. The stranger snatched up a glass of V.P. wine and drank it. 'Cigarettes?' he said to me.

I was getting some out, but felt Johnny's hand upon my wrist.

'Then give me one pound or else ten shillings,' said the intruder.

'But why?'

He stroked my arm and looked at me sideways. 'Come now, come now, come now,' he kept on saying.

The Africans ate on, taking no notice of him whatsoever.

'Come, little white friend,' said the tapper, in a soft, gentle, stupid, persistent voice. 'Give me some sustenance.' And he began patting me on the back—gently at first, then harder.

'Go away,' I said, half rising.

'Ignore him, please,' said Johnny. 'He will shoot off in time.'

'How can I ignore him?'

But sure enough, the tapper slowly stopped his patting, sat huddled a while in silence in his chair, then shambled to another table.

'It is useless,' said Johnny, 'to instruct a tapper. If you resist, he will create some foolish disturbance. If you play cool, he will lose interest of his profit, and fade away.'

'To be a tapper is a profession,' Hamilton explained to me. 'A horrible one, of course, but these people cannot be dismissed.'

'They are unfortunate, and must not be subject to humiliation, Johnny said. 'Come: do we take some coffee? You, Montgomery?'

'All right.'

'Black?'

'Yes, black.'

'I shall drink white in compliment to you. Then Hamilton will take us to the Moonbeam club, and show us the delights of London's wicked mysteries. How about chicks to dance with, Hamilton? Are they to be found upon those premises?'

'That G.I.s' rendezvous is loaded up with chicks. Chicks of all activities and descriptions, some trading, and other voluntary companions full of hope.'

'There's a little girl in Maida Vale I'd like to ask—I wonder if she'd come?'

'You know a girl already, Johnny? Speedy!'

'A family friend, Hamilton, that I must see. I have some news for her about her sister. What say we go along and pick her up?'

'We could walk out that way, this Moonbeam's open until when the dawn . . . But first, Johnny, I more like you come over and see your future home with me.'

I had a sudden inspiration. I know,' I said, 'a very nice woman to make up the party . . . a most engaging English girl, called Theodora. I'm sure she'd like to come. Let's go to my place and ask her. We could have another drink there too, I think and hope.'

We walked out through the Indians' vague bows into the star-skied town, and hailed a cab. It was the hour at which all honest Londoners have hurried to their beds and wisdom, and when the night owls, brave spirits in this nightless city, emerge to gather in the suspect cellars that nourish the resistance movement to the day.

'Why have I done this?' I reflected, as we drove home between rotting Georgian terraces, and the ominous green of the thick trees in Regent's Park which, when night falls, are reclaimed from man by a jealous, antique Nature. 'Theodora won't be in the least bit interested, and no more will these wild Africans be in her.'

We crept stealthily up through the echoing floors of my grim house. There was a light under Theodora's door. Asking my friends to wait, I knocked, and she bade me enter in her bold, emotionless tones.

It is a curiosity of Theodora's austere and purposeful nature that she wears intimate clothes of a sensual and frivolous kind. There she was, still typing away, but dressed now in a gown and nightdress made for a suppler, more yielding body.

'You were a long time at that hostel,' she said. 'Did you enjoy yourself?'

'Theodora. Would you care to go out dancing?'

'You've been drinking again, Montgomery.'

'Of course I have. Would you like to come into a world where you've never set foot before, even though it's always existed underneath your nose?'

She flipped out the sheet she was typing, and held it on her lap. 'Go on,' she said.

'I have two delightful friends outside most keen to meet you. Would you be willing to receive them, even if in your off-duty dress?'

'Negroes?'

I nodded.

Theodora took off her spectacles (which suit her), eyed me reflecting, then said, 'Bring them in.'

The Africans stood looking at Theodora with frank curiosity, an amiable show of modesty, and complete self-assurance. I introduced them.

'A nice place you have here,' said Johnny Fortune. 'You're an eager reader of literature, too, as I can see.'

'Miss Pace,' I said, 'is a doctor of some branch of learning—economics, I believe.'

'Letters,' said Theodora. 'Montgomery, please go upstairs and fetch back my bottle of gin.'

When I returned, I was disconcerted to hear Theodora say: 'This legend of Negro virility everyone believes in. Is there anything in it, would you say?'

'Lady,' Johnny answered, 'the way to find that out is surely by personal experiment.'

'And is it true,' the rash girl continued, unabashed, 'that coloured men are attracted by white women?'

'I'd say that often is the case, Miss Pace, and likewise also in the opposite direction.'

I hastened to pour out gin. I did not like my friend Theodora treating them in this clinical manner.

'Mr Fortune,' I said, 'has come here to study the movement of the isobars.'

'With what object?' Theodora asked.

'Because back home, my studies over, I'll get a good job upon the airfield.'

'I see. And you, Mr Ashinowo, as I think it was. What do you do?'

'Lady,' said Hamilton, 'at one time I pressed suits by day and worked in the Post Office by night.'

'Doing what?'

'As switchboard relief operator. But I was sacked, you see, for gossiping, they said, with some subscribers.'

'And you did?'

'I tried to make friends that way when nice voices called me up for numbers. But this, I was told, was not my duties, and they sacked me.'

'And now?'

'I live on hope mostly, and charity from the splendid National Insurance system.'

I broke in impatiently on all this. 'The point really is, Theodora, would you care to step out with us, for time is getting on.'

But politely, though quite firmly, she replied, 'No, I don't think so, thank you, Montgomery. I'm sure you gentlemen will excuse me, but I have work to do.'

'Do change your mind,' said Johnny to her. 'Even a serious lady like yourself must at times relax herself.'

She smiled and shook her head. My two friends knocked back their gins, told me they would be calling home a moment, and gave me directions where to meet them in an hour. I saw them to the door and, like two innocent conspirators, they set off loping and prowling up the street.

Theodora was typing again when I returned. 'I think I'm in danger,' I told her, 'of becoming what Americans call a nigger-lover.'

' "Negro-worshipper" is the polite phrase, I believe. You spent the whole evening with those people?'

'Yes. And I say, thank goodness they've come into our midst.'

'Why?'

'Because they bring an element of joy and fantasy and violence into our cautious, ordered lives.'

'Indeed. Isn't there another side to the coin?'

'There must be, but I haven't found it yet. Unless it is that they live too much for the day. . . .'

Theodora got up and fiddled with her documents. 'It's always a danger,' she said, 'to fall in love with another race. It makes you dissatisfied with your own.' She tucked typed sheets away in little files. 'Most races seem marvellous,' she continued, 'when one meets them for the first time. It may surprise you, Montgomery, but once I was enamoured of the Irish. Yes, think of it!' (She shuddered.) 'I loved them for what I hadn't got. But I'm damned if I love what I found out that they had.'

'You're swearing, Theodora. It's unlike you.'

'You'd better go to bed.'

I drained the gin. 'You're not coming to this ball with me, then? Those boys will certainly put it down to colour prejudice.'

'Don't be so cunning, Montgomery. It's too transparent. Your friend Fortune wouldn't think so, anyway. He's too intelligent.' Theodora tightened the gown around her waist, smoothed meditatively her lean, albeit shapely, thighs, then turned round and said to me, 'All right, very well—I'll come.'

I gazed at her awestruck. 'Might I ask, Theodora, why you've changed your inflexible mind?'

There was a pause; then: 'It will be an opportunity to study conditions.'

'What does that mean, my dear?'

'Conditions of coloured people living in London.'

'But why? Why you?'

'The Corporation might put on a series of talks. It's a topical and unusual theme.'

I drew breath. 'Theodora! I shall not be party to such a plot! If you come out with my friends, it is to come out with them, and not to ferret raw material for impartial radio programmes.'

There was a silence.

'Very well,' she said at last. 'I accept your condition. I'll get dressed.'

10

Hamilton's sad secret

HAMILTON AND I rejected possibilities of a late tube or bus, and instead sought a taxi among the endless streets that led in the direction of his Holloway home. I cannot tell you what a joy it was to see Hamilton again, just as in youth, and to know of a sure friend in this after all very unknown city. I put my arm through his, and said to him (just near a huge, empty railway station), 'Oh, Hamilton, one day we'll return together to set alight to that dreadful mission school.'

'If ever I get home, Johnny, yes, we shall.'

'But surely, Hamilton, you will go back to Lagos in the due course of time?'

'I don't know. Many things keep me here.'

'What, Hamilton? You love this country?'

'No, no, but I have means to live here in better comfort than I could hope for back home. . . .'

'What means?'

'I tell you this in a bit later time.'

He'd looked at me with an alarmed expression, quite unlike him. 'That Jumble,' he said, 'that Mr Pew. Is he to be trusted, in your opinion?'

'Why not, until he proves us otherwise?'

'I have been here two years, and still I have no Jumble friends.'

'You do not seek for them, perhaps? Whites are all right if you are proud and strong with them.'

'Friendship between us is not possible, Johnny. Their interest is to keep us washing dishes, and in their kindest words are always hidden secret double thoughts.'

'Hamilton, you know, if our people has one bad weakness, it is our jealousy always, and suspicion.'

'Suspicion of Jumbles? Jealousy of them? Why not so?'

'Even for ourselves, our people have that bad feeling. You know it, Hamilton. If one man rises up, the others try all to pull him down —even when there is no advantage to them.'

'That may be true,' said Hamilton. 'And certainly these Jumbles are more faithful to each other than we are to our own kind. When the trouble comes, they stick: our people scatter.'

A taxi cruised by, he hailed it, and gave to the driver no fixed address, but the name of the corner of two streets. Then closing the glass panel, he said to me, 'Never let your own private addresses be known in this Jumble city, especially to such as taxi drivers who make their report on passengers they carry to the Law.'

We walked from the taxi stop round several blocks, Hamilton glancing sometimes back along the streets behind, then dived in the basement of a silent house. Hamilton opened, and turned on the lights with a great smile. 'Welcome to my place,' he said, 'which is also to be from now your home.'

It certainly was a most delightful residence: with carpets and divans, and shaded lamps and a big radiogram and comfort. He turned on the sound which gave out first Lena Horne. 'She! One of my favourites,' I told him.

'Then listen to her, man, while I go change my shirt.'

Up on his walls, Hamilton had stuck many photographs: like Billy Daniels, and Dr Nkrumah, and Joe Louis in his prime, and Sugar Ray; and also Hamilton's acquaintances, all sharply dressed and grinning—rocking high with charge, I'd say, when these snaps of them were taken.

'Hamilton,' I called out, 'who's this little girl?'

He didn't answer, so I walked through the door into the kitchen. He was standing over the sink injecting his arm with a syringe.

'Hamilton!' I cried, and tried to seize it away.

'You stand back, man, from me!'

I never saw Hamilton so ferocious. His face looked at my face I thought with hatred.

He popped, then locked his syringe into a drawer.

'Come back in the big room, Johnny. You should not have left it without my invitation.'

I was silent, and in a short while he was smiling.

'Hamilton,' I said, 'how long you been on that needle?'

'One year now, I think.'

'Hamilton!'

'I'm licensed now, Johnny—no trouble with the Law. I buy my allotment, but sell half of it. That's one of my ways to live.'

'Is that the only way possible to live, old friend?'

'Don't be too hard with me, Johnny. You're new to London, and your Dad has loot to send you, don't forget. Wait till you're skinned like I was, and then see.'

'I wish it was not this, Hamilton.'

We sat for a while with only the radiogram breaking silence: then there was a soft knock, and in came a short man wearing some Jumble clerk's striped trousers, and slippers, and braces over a grease-smeared vest, and a face to match it all—quite uninviting.

'Oh, Johnny,' said Hamilton, 'this is my landlord, Mr Cole, who we call "Nat King" in honour of his great namesake. This is Johnny Fortune, Mr Cole, who'll be staying with me here from now.'

'Very pleased,' said Mr Cole. Then handed Hamilton a little sheet of paper.

'Papers are not necessary, Mr Cole. I know I owe you all of three weeks' rent.'

'Some five it is, Hamilton Ashinowo.'

'Four by next Friday.'

'How much is it, Hamilton?' I said. 'I can advance you any sum that's necessary.'

The notes passed to Hamilton and then to Mr Cole. 'A Lagos boy?' he said to me in his horrible Ibo accent.

'Yes.'

'Newcomer to town?'

'Yes.'

'Student boy, perhaps?'

'Yes, Mr Cole. I see you soon be familiar with my personal history.'

He looked at me with no smile at all, and said, 'I have to be acquainted with the residents of my house. You a gambler?'

'I might perhaps be one.'

'We must play cards some day.'

'If you say so, sir.'

'Friends come most nights into my room upstairs. You'll understand this is no common gamble-house like you may find down in the town, but serious.' He stopped by the door. 'Do your studies include a knowledge of trigonometry?' he asked me.

'Oh, I'm not that far up.'

'I'm learning it for my hobby. I thought perhaps you'd help me with the problems. But never mind, so long as you can gamble.'

He went away with his valuable pound notes.

'A mean man,' said Hamilton, 'that "Nat King" Cole. Watch out for him.'

'Mean in what way?'

'Treacherous. Nothing is meaner, Johnny, than we are when we go sour. I tell you, man, I know the London landlords. Even a white is not so mean as our race can be to us. . . .'

Hamilton was lying back now on the divan, and I saw that his two eyes slowly began to close. 'Wake up, we're going to that club,' I cried to him; but his drug worked its effect, and when I'd removed his shoes and loosened up his clothing, and stood looking sadly at him for a while, I went out once more into the London night.

It was difficult for me to find the home of Muriel and her mother, as I had forgotten the street name and number, and had only the force of instinct to guide me there. Another thought also began to strike me: this was not Lagos, where we never slumber, but a city which after midnight seemed like the Land of Deads. Would I be welcomed by those Macphersons at so late an hour?

But though the street, when I found it, was all in blackness, I was happy to see lights blazing on the Macpherson floor. This time the front door was locked shut, so I stood underneath and called up Muriel's name; and then, when no answer came, threw little blocks of earth from the outside garden at the window-panes.

With a screech one flew open, and out on to the balcony there stepped Mrs Hancock, or Macpherson. Even I was alarmed at her wild and strange appearance. She was naked except for a short nightdress, her grey hair hung down like ghost upon her shoulders, and in her hand she carried a huge book which she held upwards, like a club.

'Who is it,' she cried, 'that disturbs the Lord's servants at their midnight prayers?'

'Good evening, Mrs Macpherson,' I called up. 'Is me, Johnny Fortune, your young friend.'

'What?' she shrieked out. And to my disgust, I saw she'd snatched away her nightgown to the thigh, which shone all blue and gristly, like a meat carcass, in the electric light.

'I too,' she cried out shrill, 'I too could be evil if I wanted to, like you wicked men.'

At that she hurled the book down on my head. I picked it up: it was a black-bound hymnal. The window shut swiftly with a clatter.

Then the door opened, and out came little Muriel. 'Mum's got hysteria,' she said. 'Arthur's come back. He's been released.'

'He's in there too?'

'No. Mum refused to let him stay, so he's gone off to the Moonbeam to find some friend he can stop with.'

'That's funny, Muriel, because I came here to ask you out with me to just that place—to dance and hear about your sister Dorothy and what I have discovered.'

'Oh, I don't want to go to the Moonbeam. . . .'

'But, Muriel, I must meet Arthur, to see if I can help him. And how will I know him without you there to point him out?'

She looked upstairs. 'Mum's so hysterical,' she kept on saying.

'Well, give her back her religious volume and leave her make her prayers and singing. Who is it she's praying for—for Arthur?'

'No. For suffering humanity.'

'Oh, come along now, Muriel. I'll look after you in any place we go.'

'All right, Johnny,' she said. 'I'll get my keys.' And taking the hymnal from me, she disappeared into the madhouse up the stairs.

11

The Moonbeam club

STRANGE GIRL, THEODORA! When I'd taken a quick bath and changed once more (sober dark grey, this time) I came downstairs to find she was resplendently got up: she looked like a lively rector's daughter's notion of a sinner.

'Theodora!'

'Well?'

'You look bewitching, but bizarre.'

'You've seen me in evening dress before.'

'But this! Where did you get it?'

Though I'd not thought she had it in her, her chiselled face now looked almost demure. 'In Italy, last holidays,' she said.

'You continually amaze me.'

'Come!' she said determinedly, and took me by the arm. I trembled, and we walked out once again into the unpredictable London night.

Soon we reached the outskirts of Soho; and being already, as I imagined, one of the freemasonry of the secret coloured underground, I did not hesitate to ask the way to the Moonbeam club from any dark face I saw. Apparently some recognized me, for they gave knowing grins and said they'd seen me earlier at the Moorhen. But I, as yet, could hardly distinguish their faces one from another, and even less whether the brown eyes were baleful or benevolent. Thereby I gave offence to the Bushman, who waylaid me quite close to our final destination.

'Yous no mo' remembers me, then, mister?' he said. 'Earlier time I sell you cigaleks.'

'Oh, but of course. How are you and your instrument, my dear chap? And can you show me to the Moonbeam?'

'You dunno that ways? Come, and your lady too.' He led us down a street where, curiously enough, I'd often visited a little Italian restaurant that wasn't. But never had I thought that the bombed site across the way contained, by night, in its entrails, the Moonbeam club.

The whole street was transformed: the horrid little restaurant was dark and shuttered, and the bombed site alive with awnings, naked lights, and throngs of coloured men. Cars were parked thick outside.

'What you does,' said the Bushman, 'is spik with Mr Bumper Woodman about how he makes you a members. But take care! All those Moonbeam owners is not Asfricans, like me, but is Wess Indians.'

I thanked him, and we crossed and joined a queue of trollops and G.I.s

Mr Bumper Woodman was a coloured giant in a belted mackintosh, somewhat run to seed. His chest protruded even farther than his belly, and his face wore an impersonal scowl. He asked my name, and who had recommended me. I said Johnny Fortune had.

'Is no such man a member here.'

On the impulse of the moment I said, 'Mr Billy Whispers, then.'

'He is inside,' said Mr Woodman. 'Please now you wait, I go see.'

We watched the G.I.s streaming in, all gracefully dressed like chorus boys in a coloured revue. They moved slowly, but persistently, as men of a race which knows that, come what may, it will go on for ever.

Billy Whispers came upstairs with Mr Woodman and a third coloured man of oriental appearance.

'I am Mr Cochrane,' this third man said, in singsong Jamaican, falsetto and lilting, so like transatlantic Welsh. 'I am the resident manager of this establishment, and will wish to know your qualifications for entering, since Mr Whispers tells me your identity is quite unknown to him.'

'Good evening, Mr Whispers,' I said. 'I expect you remember me from the Moorhen earlier on.'

The African looked at me coolly, and made no reply.

'I'm to meet Johnny Fortune here, I don't know if he's turned up yet, so I thought you'd kindly sign us in.'

'You know Johnny Fortune?'

'I should say I do.'

'He's new arrived in this country.'

'I met him only this morning, but we're already quite great friends.'

'Yes? Is it? Then I shall sign you in till Johnny come, and check with him later on about you.'

'Now just a minute,' said Mr Cochrane. 'If there's a doubt about the sponsorship of this gentleman and lady, nothing can be determined that would prejudice the issue.'

'How beautifully you speak,' said Theodora, with conviction. 'You must have gone to a university like me.'

'Though not college trained, lady, I have a pretty reasonable acquaintance with general knowledge of all descriptions.'

'You sign him in, man, like I say,' said Billy, and he turned and went downstairs.

Mr Cochrane opened a huge ledger, and charged us ten shillings each. 'Our club rules are strict about introducing liquor,' he said, 'and Mr Woodman must examine you for any portable bottles.'

Mr Woodman frisked me, and asked to see in Theodora's handbag.

'You must have been a policeman once,' I said.

'Not so, man. Me boxer. Me once fight Joe Louis, but me did not altogether defeat him.'

Then we were allowed downstairs—two long floors down (can London be so deep?), past coloured photographs of American Negro singers and white starlets, all blonde hair and breasts, till we reached a little entrance hall. Nobody was about, but there was a public call-box to the outside world, embossed with a thousand pencilled phone numbers. The sound of throbbing music came from beyond the door.

'Should I dial for ambulance or fire, Theodora?'

'They always come when they're needed,' she said, and opened the Moonbeam club's inner door.

It was a long low room like the hold of a ship, no windows and only walls. At one end, in front of a huge portrait of the rising moon, was a seven-piece orchestra, only whose eyes, teeth and shirt fronts were visible at this distance. At the other, just behind us, was a soft-drink bar, with Coca-Cola advertisements and packets of assorted nuts, where teas and coffees were also being served. Among the square columns that held up the low roof were tables, some set in sombre alcoves. And between them a small floor where couples jived gently, turning continually like water-beetles making changing patterns on a pond.

By the bar, I saw Mr Karl Marx Bo. 'You're taking time off from your studies?' I asked him.

'Man, even the greatest brains must occasionally relax.'

'Please meet my friend Theodora Pace. Theodora, Mr Karl Marx Bo.'

'Good early morning to you, lady. You like I find you a table? But the drinks is much more expensive when you sit.'

He led us, without waiting for a reply, to a little gallery I hadn't seen: up six steps, and overlooking the larger trough of the dancers and the tight-packed tables.

'Theodora,' I said, 'is, like you, a student of social phenomena.'

'Is that why you bring her to this interesting G.I. knock-shop?'

'Is that what happens here, then?'

'Everything happens here, lady. But mostly it is a spot where fine young American coloureds can destroy themselves with female white trash peddled to them by West Indians and by my fellow countrymen, who collect these women's earnings and usually the G.I.'s pocket-book as well.'

'Then why do you come here, Mr Bo?' said Theodora.

'Lady, it is a weakness, but serious individual as I am, I cannot always resist the lure of a little imitation joy.'

'You found more joy in your own homeland?'

'Oh, naturally. We Africans, you see, are not a people who deposit our days in a savings bank, like you do. Our notion is that the life is given us to be enjoyed.'

Theodora fixed him firmly with her spectacles. 'But one must build,' she said. 'To build a civilization requires effort, sacrifice. If you find the English mournful, it is because we turn the easy joys into parliaments, and penicillin.' I began to think Theodora had also been at the gin. 'You will find that out,' she continued, 'when you put on shoes and come out of the easy jungle. The new African nations will have to learn to sing less, smile less, and work.'

'Theodora, you're being priggish, tactless and a bore.'

'Is all right, Mr Pew. I have no objection to this lady's open personal statements.'

'Thank you, Karl Marx,' said Theodora. 'Well, then. If your countrymen find life so enjoyable at home, why do they flock here to England?'

'Always these white people who ask us why we come here! Do we ever ask you, lady, why your people came to our country long ago?'

'Don't be so *sensitive*, Mr Bo. I'm not saying you oughtn't to come here . . .'

'Oh, thank you, thank you.'

'. . . but only asking *why* you do.'

'I came here to study, as you know.'

'You, yes. But all the others. All the hundred thousand others, or whatever the figure is, because nobody knows.'

'Your statistics are illogical, lady, if you speak of Africans. Most of that number are West Indians, and you know very well why they come here—it is to eat. Their little islands will not hold their bursting populations, and America, where they wish much more to travel, has denied them the open door. So they come here.'

Theodora leaned forward and tapped the table four times with her finger.

'Please don't be so elusive, Mr Bo,' she said. 'Do stick to the point. West Africa is prosperous, expanding, filled with opportunity. Why come here?'

'To study: law, and nursing, and et cetera . . .'

'Yes, yes, you said so.'

'Or in show business. You like the wild illusion of our African drummers.'

'Nonsense. How many Africans are there in show business in London? Fifty at most? And anyway, you know you can't compete in that with American Negroes, or even with West Indians, because your music isn't entertainment as we understand it. In fact, it's not "show business" at all.'

'Oh, no? Not entertaining to you?'

'You know very well, Mr Bo, that African music is too real, too obsessive, too wonderfully monotonous, too religious, for Europeans ever to put up with it. We like something much less authentic.'

'I see you are a serious student of our art.'

'Of course I am. I don't speak of what I don't know about.'

'Theodora, your conceit's repulsive.'

'Be quiet, Montgomery. Go on, Mr Bo. Why do you all come here?'

Beneath her fierce onslaught, Mr Bo looked dreamy, seeming to retire within himself. 'Some boys are afraid of curses,' he said softly.

'Of spells? Of witchcraft?'

'I see you smile, Miss Pace. You should not smile. I could show to you boys here, even scientific students, who believe that family of theirs have died from spells, and fear the same themselves if they return.'

'And you: you surely don't believe such nonsense yourself?'

'Anything many people believe is not exactly nonsense, Miss Theodora. You are, of course, superior to such superstitions, but then perhaps you have no wonderful sense of magic and mystery any more.'

A shrewd thrust, I thought, and Theodora clearly didn't like it. She hitched her Italian gown, and returned to the attack. 'That might account for a few dozen who stay here,' she said, 'but not for thousands.'

Mr Bo looked at her through veiled eyes, ironically. 'Others,' he said, 'come here to flee their families' great love. A family in Africa, you see, is not like here. Our whole life and business belong to every second cousin. A family only loves you and gives you some peace when you let it eat you.' Mr Bo chuckled warmly, and flung up his hands. 'Some boys are here who wish to escape those circumstances. Here you can live out your own life, even if it is miserably.'

Theodora, in the realm of the mind, is like a huntress who's not satisfied until she's bagged her lion. 'That can't be the only reason,' she said, stabbing her coffee cup with a spoon quite viciously.

Mr Bo lit two cigarettes in his lips, and passed her one.

'You seem so obstinately inclined,' he said, 'that I shall tell you the real reason for your satisfaction. It is this.' He gazed at her, and said: 'The world has broken suddenly into my country: and we are determined to break out equally into the world.'

'Go on.'

'At home there is reasonable happiness, yes, and comfort. But when in a cinema we see the London streets shining, gleaming and beckoning, we stop and think, "Here am I, shut in my prison, cut out from where there is creation, and riches, and power in the modern world. There, in that distant place, the life is bigger, wider, more significant. That is something I must see, and show I can be master of it." So we come wandering here, like the country boys back home who dream to visit the big town.'

Theodora gazed back, visibly entranced. 'All right,' she said, 'you all come here. And what do you find?'

'Find almost always great deception. Hard times, or else, like these children you see in this club here, living prosperously for a while with little crimes. In either case, it is failure for us here.'

'Then why don't you go back?'

'Because of shame. The country boy can't go back home from the city until he makes some fortune. But opportunity for this is denied to us by you.'

'Because there's a colour bar, you mean?'

'Is there a colour bar in England, Miss Theodora?'

'You know there is.'

'If you say so, then, I say it too. Universal politeness, and universal coldness. Few love us, few hate us, but everybody wish we are not here, and shows this to us by the correct, stand-away behaviour that is your great English secret of public action.'

'And you resent it.'

'No, I do not resent it. Me, I laugh. For very soon this colour bar will die away.'

'You think so?'

'I do. When we have African prime minister, who will say: "Mr England, I have a million pounds to spend in Birmingham with you, but perhaps I go spend them in Germany, or in Tokyo, Japan." This speech by our prime minister will change more hearts of yours in half a day than nice-thinking people among you fail to do in all these years. All else is useless propaganda: I mean all statements of clergymen about brothers under the skin, all efforts you make to banish your shame at ancient conduct to us by being kind to us, and condescensious.'

'I am never condescending, and not particularly kind.'

'No, lady. Perhaps you are just civilized. But if you wish for an intelligence test of your true persuasions, answer please truthfully these two questions. You also, Mr Pew.'

He pointed a finger at her, then one at me. Theodora smiled (her nose twitching, however, slightly).

'Number one. Do you agree to total political freedom for coloured races without any restrictions whatever? Miss Theodora?'

'No.'

'Mr Pew?'

'Yes.'

'Second question. Would you yourself marry a coloured man—or woman?'

'Yes,' said Theodora; and added, 'If I loved him, of course.'

'No,' I said.

'Why not, Mr Pew?'

'For the child's sake.'

'It would be racially degenerate?'

'It would be miserable.'

'Subject to social pressures? Excluded by both races?'

'Yes.'

Mr Bo glared at us.

'That is the familiar argument. But why should such a half-caste race not serve as spearhead for enlightenment? Be necessary victims in the victorious struggle?'

'Perhaps,' I could not forbear to say, 'you should ask the half-caste child what he thinks of that.'

The band stopped, and we all sipped coffee in the silence of misunderstanding. Mr Karl Marx Bo, suddenly, looked bitter.

'Well,' he said, 'you are both nice people, I am sure, but I think you also are what we despise even more than we do those who hate us—you are full-time professional admirers of the coloured peoples, who like us as you like pet animals. Miss Theodora, do you wish to dance?'

'Alas, Mr Bo! My friend Theodora is unable to.'

'Speak for yourself, Montgomery. Karl Marx, shall we take the floor?'

And she did, and twirled with him quite creditably. Admirable Theodora!

I looked round the cavern, which had a warm coloured fug and stuffiness—sticky, promiscuous and cloying, a hot grass hut in the centre of our town. The men lounged and watched, languid and attentive, the white girls sat up chattering, playing hard to get. How sad there were no coloured girls there of equal dignity and beauty to the men.

Mr Ronson Lighter came over. He handed me my Ronson lighter. He looked very cross.

'Oh, thank you,' I said.

'Billy say I to give you that.'

'Much obliged.'

'Also that you come over to speak with him.'

'I'm here with a friend.'

'That you bring her over too. He offers you both coffee.'

Billy was sitting among his henchmen in so dark a corner as to be doubly invisible. He reached up a hand, took mine, and pulled me gently down.

'Johnny, he still not come here yet?' he said.

'No. What can have happened to him?'

'Perhaps he change his mind. He was with Hamilton Ashinowo?'

'Yes.'

'Then perhaps Hamilton will offer him some special entertainment. So he change his mind and stay back home.' Mr Whispers softly laughed.

This was mysterious. So, 'Good evening, Mr Cannibal,' I said. 'I hope you had no trouble at the police station.'

There was a loud silence.

'You were in police station tonight, Jimmy?' Billy Whispers asked him.

'No.'

Billy looked at me. So did Mr Cannibal: he seemed angry and alarmed.

I said: 'Perhaps I made a mistake.'

'I hope you do,' said Billy Whispers.

The silence continued till the coffee came. 'You get this your lighter?' Whispers said to me.

'Yes. Thank you.'

'Accidents do happen. My boy did not know you was a friend of Johnny Fortune's. He is a nice boy, Johnny. Too nice for this city, I expect. I hope he may soon go back home.' He turned to a half-caste girl upon the bench. 'This is Barbara,' he said. 'She likes to dance with you.'

'I don't dance.'

'She teach you. Barbara, go with this man on to the floor.'

We went. The girl said, 'Why did you tell him you saw Jimmy at the station?'

'Why not? Wasn't he caught up in that raid like everybody else?'

'He can't have told Billy he was there. . . . I can see Billy suspects him of something. It looks like trouble to me.'

'But Mr Cannibal's his friend.'

'Cannibal's slippery. We all know that.'

She spoke with a Cardiff accent. It came oddly out of her half-African face, the sound so ill assorted with a physical beauty that had reached her from thousands of miles away.

'You come here often?' I said.

'I'm a hostess here.'

'You work for the management?'

'No. For Billy Whispers. He controls most of the hostesses here.'

'The management let him?'

'These West Indians are frightened of the Africans. They don't interfere. Can't you dance any better than that?'

'No. You were going to teach me.'

'Just hold on to me, then. Bring your body close and don't think of your feet. You like coloured girls?'

'I think so.'

'You ever been with one?'

'No.'

Barbara glanced up at me with mild surprise. We passed Theodora and Mr Karl Marx Bo. 'Come and sit down,' I said to Barbara, 'and meet my friend Theodora.'

'That fish-face woman? Isn't she a copper?'

'Not to my knowledge.'

'Are you one, by the way?'

'Heaven forfend.'

'Eh?'

'What difference does it make what I say, Barbara? Just think what you like about us. Time alone will show.'

'Tell your friends to come to Billy's table, then. I have to get back to him.' She stepped across the floor, professionally swinging her magnificent bottom.

I said to Theodora as we followed, 'Where *did* you learn to dance so well? You're a perpetual revelation.'

Lowering her voice, she said, 'I was at one time in the Wrens, and lived a rather rackety life. It's a period I prefer to forget about, and I'll thank you not to refer to it again.'

Billy waved us into his corner with a comprehensive smile. With him now there was an enormous coloured G.I., and holding both the G.I.'s hands a lovely, harsh-faced white girl.

'Is Dorothy,' said Billy, 'and her good friend Larry.'

'Hi, man. You American or British?' Larry asked me.

'British.'

'Oh, that's all right, then.'

'Larry doesn't like Americans,' Dorothy explained.

'But isn't he one?'

'Oh, yes, but not an *American*, if you see what I mean.'

She hugged him, then let out a sudden shriek. 'Look there!' she cried. 'It's my brother Arthur!'

A tall gold-skinned boy came gangling gracefully across the floor, grinning with imbecile guile, his lower lip pendent, his eyes flashing dubious charm. He kissed Dorothy, shook hands with everyone, sat down and put his arms round several shoulders.

'I come out this morning,' he told everybody. 'An' hitch-hiked up to town. An' I called at back home and found Muriel. An' she told me about our new brother Johnny. Have you seen him, Dorothy?'

'Johnny? Yes, I seen him. He's a fresh boy, just like you.'

'Ma wouldn't take me in, I've no place I can go, and I'd like to ask my new brother Johnny to help me with some loot until I can get settled. Unless you can help me, Billy, or you, Dorothy, or someone.'

He gazed lazily around, exuding animal magnetism and anxiety.

'Larry,' said Dorothy, 'you won't mind if I have this dance with my little brother?'

But Mr Cochrane, the resident manager, who'd been standing by like a janizary, stepped up. 'I'm sorry, gentlemen, and ladies too,' he said, 'but I cannot permit your wife, Billy, to take the floor in slacks.'

Billy said nothing. Larry the G.I. took Mr Cochrane's arm.

'Listen man,' he said. 'Let me instruct you about clothing. All you West Indians go about dressed in zoot-suit styles we've thrown away ten years ago, and we don't complain about you.'

'It is not a question of styles, but of being costumed respectably for my club.'

'This girl, man, is smart as any film star. They all of them wear slacks in their off-duty hours.'

'Flim star or no flim star,' said Mr Cochrane (and he did say 'flim'), 'she must please attire herself in a proper skirt.'

'Oh, blow, man,' said Ronson Lighter. 'Twist now—you dig?'

Mr Cochrane stood his ground. 'I refuse all permission. I shall stop the orchestra.'

Mr Bumper Woodman arrived with several companions. All the men stood up. I saw Theodora reaching for her handbag.

'Why, oh why,' said Mr Karl Marx Bo to Mr Cochrane, 'do you stir up trouble with your African cousins? If you want to make some trouble, why you not go and fight with Dr Malan?'

'Me tell you insults is quite ineffectual, Mr Student,' said Mr Woodman.

'Oh-ho! Listen to this veteran Caribbean pugilist!'

'Listen to these Ras Tafaris, all long hair and dirty finger-nails.'

'These sugar-cane suckers! These calypso-singing slaves.'

'Slave? My ancestor had the wisdom to leave your jungle country.'

'You ancestor was so no good, my ancestor he go sell him to Jumble slave-ship.'

'You ras-clot man—you's wasted.'

'These bumble-clot men—these pussy-clots.'

'Come to your home in Africa, man, and we teach you some good behaviour.'

At this moment of clenched fists and hands slipping inside pockets, a very tall slim man, with a piece bitten out of one ear, approached. 'Now come,' he said. 'Come, come, come, come, come.'

'Mr Jasper!' cried Dorothy. 'Are you the boss here, or aren't you? Tell your men to see reason!'

Mr Jasper listened to several explanations, then said in a high, smooth voice, 'Miss Dorothy, I lend you a skirt from out of our cabaret costumes. I hope you will accept this solution, Mr Whispers.'

'No.'

'Yes, man.'

'No, man, no.'

'Come,' I whispered to Theodora. 'This is our cue to leave.'

12

Foo-foo in the small, late hours

WHEN I ARRIVED with Muriel outside this Moonbeam club (which every Spade we met seemed heading for, like night beasts to their water-hole), I saw at once, from very much past experience, that trouble was going on inside. People were peering down the entrance stairs and jabbering, and noise of shouts and crashings floated up. I drew Muriel far into a doorway, as I expected any moment the intrusion of the Law.

Then customers came scurrying up too. Among them I see Montgomery, and with him his Miss Theodora. I said to Muriel to wait, and went across to them.

'Oh, Mr Fortune,' Theodora cried. 'There's fighting going on downstairs.'

'Your brother Arthur,' said Montgomery, 'and Billy and his friends are battling with some wild West Indians.'

Well, I suppose our African troubles aren't his business, but all the same, has he not a pair of fists to stay and help my friends?

I'd seen there were two quite old American saloon cars with drivers that seemed Africans to me. I went over quickly and asked were they for hire? They were.

'What is a place to meet not far from here?' I asked Miss Theodora.

She said the big radio building of the B.B.C.

'Get in,' I told her, 'with Montgomery. Muriel,' I shouted, 'come over here! Go quickly where this lady says,' I told the two drivers, putting pound notes in their hands, 'and all of you wait for me there till I arrive.'

Then I plunged down the Moonbeam stairs.

At the bottom, by the entrance door, I saw Dorothy and Cannibal and various other friends all torn and tattered. The West Indians had expelled them out. I told them where to scatter at the place I'd sent the cars.

'But, Johnny!' Dorothy cried out. 'Billy's still in there, and Ronson and your brother Arthur.'

'Do as I tell you, Dorothy, I am always best alone. Cannibal, now, blow with these people to the big radio building. I bring all the others soon whether dead or else alive.'

I heaved and pushed open the club door. The band was still playing, all now up upon their feet. Chicks were standing on the chairs, laughing and screaming, and G.I.s cheering and acting with no responsibility at all. On the dance floor I saw Billy with Ronson and one other, who were murdering, and being murdered, by the West Indians.

I climbed over the bar counter, and started smashing crates of Coca-Cola by heaving them with loud crashes on the floor. The band stopped and faces began to turn round in my direction. 'Look, Mr Jasper!' a tall West Indian cried. 'Your valuable stock is being depleted.'

I picked up four bottles, and burst through to the dance floor. I grabbed up the microphone, which lay there overturned, and cried out: 'Billy, we cut out! The Law will soon be intruding! Here, Billy, catch this bottle!'

We battered our way towards the door. The customers were generally friendly, and seemed to regret the ending of this silly mess. Come on, Bumper Woodman,' they kept crying to a huge West Indian. 'Show us how you beat Joe Louis to his knees.'

But it was Ronson Lighter he was fighting now, and that crooked boy, even despite his dirty blows, looked like getting massacred by the big West Indian's bulkiness, till Billy Whispers snatched the microphone from my hands and cracked this Woodman on the skull with a cruel smack. We all beat it up the stairs.

'Come on, let's run,' said Ronson Lighter. 'I smell the coming of the Law.' And we saw two beetle cars come sweeping round the distant corner.

'Not run, no,' I said, 'is better stroll rapidly like serious gentlemen.'

'Thank you,' said Billy, 'for your interference.' He wiped blood from both his hands.

'Who is this third boy?' I asked him. 'Can this be my brother Arthur?'

For I'd seen him fighting also on the Moonbeam floor, and his certain strong resemblance to my Dad, and doing him great credit with his vigorous blows; but as I walked beside him now, and he turned smiling to me, smoothing his knuckles, I also caught his mother's crazy glance in both his eyes.

'What say?' said Arthur, as we turned two swift corners. 'Bless you, my brother—you're my boy!' He put his arm around me and said softly, 'You'll help me with some loot now, Johnny, won't you.'

'We see about this, Arthur. We talk about all those things.'

By twisting around in zigzag circles, we had now arrived outside a big white block building standing on its own. Our friends were by the cars in a cluster on the street, laughing and chattering in this silent London early dawn.

Billy introduced me round. 'Come!' I cried out. 'What's needed is to celebrate our survival from these dangers. We all of us go now to my friend Hamilton's and eat some foo-foo.'

'*Foo-foo?*' said Miss Theodora, needlessly wrinkling up her nose.

'Is a standard African dish, lady, like your English shepherd pie, but I think nicer.'

This English lady smiled and shook her head.

'Then let us drop you off, Miss Theodora,' I said, 'at your house, or any other convenient point of your selection. Billy, you take Montgomery and some of us in this one car, and Miss Theodora and we here will travel in the other.'

Of course Billy understood what I intended, and our cars shot ahead through the dark, wide thoroughfares. When Miss Theodora saw we were not going near her house at all, she turned to me and said, 'Am I being kidnapped?'

I said, 'No, lady, just forcibly invited. And you have your good friend Montgomery to take care of you as well as me.'

I felt Miss Theodora next to me relax.

At my new Holloway home, I found that Hamilton had partly returned to life, and was wandering about, holding a coffee cup, with just some slacks on, and talking to Mr Cole, who was in striped pyjamas. I told them to make themselves suitable to welcome all my guests, and I took Mr Cole upon one side.

'These are good friends,' I said, 'and perhaps you could fix some liquor at a reasonable price for their entertainment that will do honour to your house.'

'You have the loot for that now?'

I gave him more pound notes, and he looked dignified, and blew.

Billy asked for the necessary meat and semolina to make foo-foo, and Hamilton took him and Cannibal and Ronson Lighter to the kitchen. Arthur all this time was following me about, his eyes with a look of admiration, and his arm always on my shoulder. 'There you go, man!' he kept saying to me. 'There you go!'

'Take it easy, bra,' I said to him. 'I see you straight tomorrow morning.'

'Tell me about my Dad. Is he a rich man? Is he loaded?'

'He's a fine man, our Dad.'

He looked at me hideous all at once. Even I was just a little scared.

'Then why's he left me skinned in hopeless destitution?'

I took no notice of this foolishness, and put some Billy Eckstine on to Hamilton's radiogram. Soon Mr Cole appeared with armfuls of Merrydown cider and Guinness stout and V.P. wine. All the while I saw that this companion of Montgomery's, this Miss Pace, examined me as if I was a zoological exhibit. I went and sat down beside her on the collapsible settee.

'So you are in the employment of the B.B.C., Miss Theodora,' I said to her. 'That's a real serious occupation.'

'I'd thought,' she said rather rapidly, 'of putting on a series of talks in which colonial citizens would relate their experiences when they arrive here.'

She looked at me. I said nothing.

'Though I'm wondering if, to tell anything like the truth, these talks might perhaps reveal more than our listeners would stand for.'

Now I can tell as well as any when a chick has been reduced by my physical appearance, and behind this white girl's word I read a positive design to drag me between sheets before too long. But this was most unattractive to me in her case, particularly as little Muriel, who was much more to my liking and intention, was standing by.

'Oh, yes, Miss Theodora?' I said, playing cool.

'"Theodora,"' she told me, 'please, no "Miss". If I do decide to go ahead with the talks, would you consider taking part?'

I told her politely it would no doubt be a pleasure; and thinking I'd done my duties as the host, I was leaving her for Muriel when she shook my hand and said, 'Then won't you dance with me?' Someone had now swept Muriel away, so I smiled at this not so tempting girl and took her hands.

But even above the high cry of Billy Eckstine we all heard a wild scream, and there was Hamilton, still half naked in his slacks in spite of what I tell him, standing stiffly by his empty bed, pointing and gazing down at it and crying, 'This poor little boy is dead!'

'Hamilton!' I ran over and held his shaking shoulders. 'What little boy?'

'Me, Johnny! Look! There I am—dead!'

'Man, you're still high! Sit down now, and act serious. There's company present all around you.'

'I'm not dead then, Johnny?'

'Oh, Hamilton!'

He began to sob.

'Come with me in the kitchen and cool down, man. You'll find they're making foo-foo there. Eat some, it will calm you. Really, my dear friend Hamilton,' I said when I'd got him past the door, 'you must get off that needle—it will kill you dead.'

'You'll have to help me, Johnny.'

But out in the kitchen, though the pots and pans were simmering, there were no Billy, Cannibal or Mr Ronson Lighter. I sat Hamilton down, gave him a cigarette, and went and looked out through the back door to the garden.

There, in the early light, I saw Billy and Ronson Lighter beating Jimmy Cannibal. This man was a boxer, yes, but Billy, I could see, was a little killer, and Ronson grabbing at Cannibal in evil places.

I opened the door and shouted: 'What is it, Billy?'

Cannibal broke free and scrambled over the garden wall.

'What for you mix in this?' cried Billy. He raised up his hands against me, then he said, 'Oh, well . . .' smoothed down his clothes, and came to the kitchen door. There was blood on Ronson Lighter's coat, and I led him to the tap.

'That Cannibal has been making a friendship with the Law,' said Billy.

'How you know that?'

'That Jumble friend of yours saw him talking with coppers in the station.'

'Montgomery tell you that? But I was there with him too.'

'You were? All the time with him?'

'No, not all the time.... Why didn't that foolish man tell *me* about he see Cannibal?'

'Is that Jumble to be trusted?'

'I think so.'

'He'd better be.'

'Billy,' I said, 'if Cannibal was with the Law, how do you know they didn't just pull him in for something? What make you think he's blowing off his top?'

'He tell us, when we ask him, he was not in there at all. So if he was, it must be for some evil purpose. I finished with that man, and if he's said a word against me... Well, if ever the Law puts the hand on me, that boy had better leave town.

'Billy, you get so excited. And your foo-foo will all be burning.'

He came over to the stove and dished it out on the big plate. 'You can't trust even your own people in this country,' he said. 'This country turns men bad.'

'Well, Billy, you was never one big angel yourself, were you?'

He gave me a sideways smile. 'Maybe I not, but I not shop my friends like Cannibal.'

Mr Cole came through the kitchen door. 'Did I hear fighting noises? I must have no fighting on my premises.'

'Play cool, man. There'll be no more battle.'

'This Hamilton,' said Mr Cole. 'He must control his conduct.'

'Who sells him this bad stuff?' I said. 'He can't get all that bad on just his legal ration.'

I caught the glance of Billy and of Cole, who looked at each other.

'Whoever sells my friend that stuff,' I said, with a hard stare at each of them, 'is going to find himself an enemy of mine. And you, Hamilton, you'd better change your habits of life unless you wish to die when still quite young.'

We all drank some ruby wine in silence; then carried the dishes in among the dancers of the bigger room.

We passed round the water to wash, and everyone sat down upon the floor: even the Jumbles, who we showed how you crouch around the dish, and take up your wad of semolina, dip it in the red peppery gravy, and scoop up your piece of meat. They did it quite free and nicely, though burning painfully in the mouth, and with sometimes the unnecessary dribbles.

'And how is recent developments in Africa?' said Mr Cole to me.

'Oh,' I told him, 'it looks like in one or two years' time we have our freedom.'

'What you need in Africa, Africa man,' said Arthur, 'is a blow-everyone-up party, including your own crooked Africa politicians.'

'This man is talking ignorant and foolish,' said Mr Karl Marx Bo. 'What's needed is more education, and more honesty.'

'They'll never let you govern yourselves, man,' said Larry the G.I.

'They will, because we'll make them,' said Mr Bo. 'And then we Africans come across and free our poor American brothers, who all they do is sit on their seats and sing their spirituals.'

Little Barbara thought this so funny, and let out a cheap laugh.

'If we don't get this freedom soon, we take it, like the Mau Mau do,' said Mr Ronson Lighter.

'Mau Mau haven't managed to take much,' said Miss Theodora, in a sharp way, 'except a lot of African lives.'

'Oh, stop all your politics,' cried Dorothy, 'while we're eating food.'

'We shoot you like Mau Mau, man,' said Ronson Lighter, pointing a pepper-pot with an evil grin upon my friend Montgomery.

'If you was in Kenya, Mr Montgomery,' said Billy Whispers, 'what side would you be?'

'My own people's, of course,' Montgomery replied. 'When trouble comes, you must go with your own tribe.'

'Oh-ho! And if I take you prisoner, you know what I do?' said Ronson Lighter to him.

I broke in. 'If I take my friend Montgomery prisoner,' I said, 'I grab away his weapon, yes, but maybe himself, I turn him loose.'

Muriel smiled up at me, and move much closer.

Hamilton jumped up. 'This man's an African!' he cried, taking Montgomery round his neck. 'I know my brother, because I see he is an African.'

'No, no, not me.'

'Yes, man! You's an African! And I prove it to you now! I give you a present, a great gift.'

Hamilton went to his cupboard, and pulled off a hanger the dress of our dear tribe. 'Come, man, you put this on!' he cried.

'I couldn't accept,' Montgomery said.

'You are my guest,' Hamilton told him severely.

'Yes, put it on,' said his friend Theodora. 'I'm sure it'll suit you to perfection.'

Hamilton pulled it on over Montgomery, and tied the cloth round his head. He looked really quite strange in it, but he stood there quite clearly filled with flattery and pleasure. He took my friend Hamilton's hand. 'I do appreciate it,' he said. 'Thank you very, very much.'

Now Billy Whispers and Ronson Lighter were starting to roll weed, in company with Hamilton and Mr 'Nat King' Cole: which I'd rather they'd practised in private in the kitchen, instead of in this public way in front of strangers. They passed the sticks round, and Dorothy was eager, and little Barbara, and my brother Arthur, as I of course expected of him.

But Muriel wouldn't touch the stuff, and our other English visiting friends, though Billy Whispers tried to press them to it, which he shouldn't do, really, because weed is something it's best not to handle unless you have the mastery of its action from experience since an earlier age. In this refusal, they had the support of Larry the G.I. and Karl Marx Bo.

'All you get out of that,' said Mr Bo, 'is crazy antics and then ruin. That rubbish is the ruin of my people.'

'Many good men,' said Larry, 'have lived inside penitentiaries on account of that goddamned ganga.'

'Just listen to this Yank,' said Dorothy, all tough and daring. 'Man, ain't you never raved nor rocked in your career?'

'With this I forget my troubles,' Arthur said, soft and silly. 'And of troubles, I say that I have plenty.'

'It'll give you plenty more,' said Muriel. 'It'll send you right back inside where you came out of.'

'Let Arthur be,' said Dorothy. 'Is he telling *you* what you should do?'

'Why let him be?' cried Karl Marx Bo. 'She's right, this chick.

Weed kills your conscience, don't we all know it? It opens the door to what is violent inside of you, and cruel, and no good sense, and full of fear.'

'It don't make you silly like this liquor does,' said Mr Cole. 'It may slow you up, your bodily movement, but it leaves you with a better control and perfect speech.'

'Perfect speech to say some rubbish like you do,' said Larry the G.I.

Little Barbara laughed. 'Why you all so serious about it, anyway?' she said. 'Isn't life hard enough without it?'

Miss Theodora, she was listening closely. She seemed a little troubled with anxiety, and also by her unusual ignorance of this subject. Though this did not stop her now from saying her word.

'But you, Mr Bo,' she asked him. 'If you know so much about it, surely you must have smoked it once yourself?'

'Who hasn't, lady!' cried this legal student. 'But some, when they burn their fingers in the fire, can learn, and others not. What this man Cole here says is true. It leaves your mind clear, yes, but only half of it, the half that has the proud and the darker thoughts. You think that the world is you, is yours, you think it is you that make the laws of all creation. Off goes your personality, you lose control of it, and in walks the dark spirit to take over. And all the time, under that stuff you say to yourself: "How can anyone as wonderful as me be wrong?" Then you go off and rob a bank, or kill your grandmother.'

The weed-smokers laughed at this serious fellow countryman. Myself, I thought the mistake was to mix up the smokers with the others. These arguments often come up when those who smoke hemp sit down with those who don't. . . .

So I got up and put on discs, and asked Muriel to dance with me. But this was the time, I could clearly see, when the party came near its death, because the light outside the curtains grew stronger than the electricity inside, and everyone was losing pleasure in the other's company. The two boys waiting with their cars outside came knocking to ask for instructions, or else they'd shoot off, and wanted more money for waiting, anyway. So Larry the G.I. went off with Dorothy, and Billy told Ronson Lighter to see little Barbara home. And in the other car, Montgomery went with Theodora and serious Mr Karl Marx Bo. I saw them off there in the already daylight street.

Dorothy leaned out and snatched a kiss I hadn't offered. 'I'll see you again soon, my man,' she said.

At the other car I shook hands in a more steady manner.

'Keep in touch, Johnny,' said Montgomery, sitting like an emir in his native dress. 'You know my telephone number.'

'And don't forget,' said Theodora, gripping my hand, 'I rely on you for my colonial programme.'

'Yes, yes, yes, yes,' I answered, and told the drivers in the Yoruba tongue to hurry them all off.

Back in the room, I found Hamilton in a deep slumber, and Cole inviting Billy and my brother Arthur to a game of dice. 'You will come too?' he said. I wished this badly, for dice are in my blood, but first there was the question of my Muriel. So they went upstairs without me, after Arthur had borrowed from me three pounds which was all that I had left.

Muriel was sitting by the radiogram. I kissed her quite freely, and she came up easily into my arms.

'Stay with me now, Muriel,' I said.

'No, Johnny, no, not here. . . .'

'Then where? This is my home, and Hamilton will sleep soundly for six hours. . . .'

'No, Johnny, not till I know you better.'

That woman's phrase! Which means, as all men know, 'Not till *I* ask you!' And why did she not go with all the others in the cars, if her real purpose was not to stay? If I had not been fond of this little child, and tired too, to tell the truth, and longing for my sleep, she would not have escaped me by her feeble answers.

So I said, 'Very well, Muriel, get all your things, and I shall go out to find your cab.'

She got up slowly, but by the door she stopped and clung and kissed me. 'Africans' skins are soft,' she said to me.

FIRST INTERLUDE

Idyll of miscegenation on the river

A PLEASURE STEAMER put out on the river, and seated in its prow alone were Muriel Macpherson and Johnny Macdonald Fortune. His left hand clasped her right, he held both on her lap, the white and brown fingers interlocking.

'It takes us an hour to reach the palace down the stream,' she told him.

'Well, I see they have beer on board, so that don't matter.'

Beside the helmsman, on the open bridge behind, a hybrid character—nautical in peaked cap and jacket of dark blue, but landlubber from the waist down with grey slacks and sandals—had taken his stance before a microphone. Crackling through amplifiers dispersed about the ship, his voice described, in accents part Cockney, part bogus North American, part the pedantic patronizing of the lecturer, the points of interest on either shore, disturbing the peace and contemplation of the few, but delighting the docile many, who swung their heads, as if spectators at a tennis match, towards the curiosities whose histories he recounted.

Muriel said: 'Do you have rivers in your country, Johnny?'

'Of course we have rivers: that's why we're called Nigeria.'

'Did you swim in them—like those boys there? You can swim, Johnny, can't you?'

He leapt, climbed on the railings of the boat, and made as if to dive. Muriel let out a scream, and clutched his ankles. He swayed. Passengers, distracted from the amplifiers, turned, frowned and laughed.

He slipped down on the deck into her arms, and held her tight a moment. 'You're a madman, Johnny Fortune! I can't trust you a split second. I must never let you out of my sight in future.' Not to be surprised again, when they sat down this time she held him closely round the shoulder.

He said: 'You're like my sister Peach. That's what she says to me as well—ah, women!'

The loud-speaker blared: 'And opposyte the old St Paul's—turn your heads this way, please' (the heads switched south) '—is the Bankside power station, a controversial electrification project, and there—the small yellow edifice is the one I'm alluding to—the former residence of Sir Christopher himself, from whence he watched across the river the lofty pile of his cathedral rising up, and then, just adjacent, in the district known previously as the "Stews"—with its bear-gardens, and colony of Dutch and Flemish women of easy virtue, as they were called (now all cleaned up, of course)—the site of the old Globe theatre, erected by the brothers Burbage in 1598 for the smash-hits of their mate Bill Shakespeare, who acted there himself in what he termed affectionately his "wooden O" . . .'

'What is Peach like?' asked Muriel.

'Peach? She is like all our women. The more she loves you, the more she tries to grasp you and take charge of you.'

'Your women are like that, out there in Africa?'

Johnny frowned.

'You know something, now? Is a secret I'm telling you, so open up the ears and close the lips. One chief reason why our boys get settled often with your white girls here is that our own back home are such big bosses. They do everything for you, yes, much more than any white girl would, and cook so well, and work, but in exchange for this, they try to gain possession of your private person.'

Muriel mused. 'But is it true' (she paused) 'that some of your boys really prefer us more?' He didn't answer, and looked downstream ahead. 'I mean,' she went on, 'like us better just because we're white?'

He turned towards her. 'That's what they say, isn't it? That's what the white newspapers all say in their Sunday editions. That all we want is rape some innocent white lady?'

'You're not being serious, Johnny.'

'As if there was any need to rape!'

'Don't flatter yourself: you're all so conceited.'

He preened himself, and looked it.

'Now on our left,' the amplifier intoned, 'we have the Billingsgate fish market and wharves, so named after Belin, legendary monarch of the Britons in their primitive era, and best known now, of course, for the fish porters' highly coloured language, of which I will attempt an imitation. Why, Gorblimey, you . . .' (the loud-speakers emitted only deafening crackles) '. . . sorry, ladies and gents, but I've been censored. Beneath us at the moment—that is, beneath the boat and underneath the river bed—is the oldest of the numerous Thames tunnels, now disused, constructed between 1825 and 1843 by Sir Marc Isambard Brunel, the Frenchman. And now, my friends and folks, arising in historic splendour on the northern bank is the ancient Tower of London, celebrated alike for its Traitors' Gate, Crown Jewels, scaffold, dungeons, ravens, Beefeaters, Bloody Tower and instruments of torture. . . .'

Johnny and Muriel barely glanced, and gazed ahead at castellated Tower Bridge, the last gate before the river becomes the ocean that weds the city to the outer world. She pressed his shoulder down a bit, and laid her head on it. 'You didn't answer me properly, though,' she said. 'Do you really like us better?'

'Does who like who?'

'You boys like us white girls.'

'Some of us do, perhaps.'

'Only some, Johnny?'

'Oh, you cannot judge by England, Muriel. There's so few of our own girls here, it has to be a white chick or else nothing. And can you imagine us with nothing?'

They kissed discreetly, with a slight grin of complicity.

'But if you had a free choice,' Muriel persisted, 'would you choose one of us? Choose us because we're different? Or because, if you marry one of us, it's easier to fit in and make a living?'

'What is this, Muriel! You make me some proposition of matrimony? Don't be so speedy, woman—we've only met up just one month. It's the man's supposed to make that invitation, didn't you know?' (She looked demure.) 'I tell you something, though, and don't forget it. If ever one of our boys does marry one of you, there's no doubt who we think is being done the favour.'

Muriel reflected, vexed, then half understanding. 'It's true,' she said, 'your boys are often better class than girls they marry here. . . .'

'Is not class I mean. Even when class and wealth is equal, is we who do the favour!'

The boat passed underneath the bridge, and faces suddenly grew darker. Muriel watched her native city as the boat chugged on between Venetian façades of eyeless warehouses, dropping into ancient Roman mud, where barges lay scattered derelicts under lattices of insect cranes. This was her first sight of Dockland, shut off from inquisitive view on land by Brobdingnagian brick walls. Missing familiar pavements and shop windows, Muriel saw her city as a place quite unfamiliar, and wondered what it might do to her, and Johnny Fortune.

'It's queer to think,' she said, 'how close we are, we two, and yet so far.'

'We're close enough.'

'Don't choke me, Johnny. No, no, I mean sharing Arthur as a brother, and yet no one drop of the same blood in our veins. . . .'

'Our blood's the same colour, Muriel, is all that matters. Everything that comes out of all human body is the same colour—did you think of that?'

She did: 'Johnny, don't be disgusting.'

Undaunted by the absence, in these lower reaches of the river, of interesting monuments, and remembering the hat he'd pass round before the journey ended, the resourceful guide still bludgeoned the passengers' defenceless ears: '. . . Wapping Old Stairs, where the bloodthirsty Judge Jeffreys was arrested in 1688, while attempting to flee the vengeance of the populace in the disguise of a sailor, and just there the former Execution Dock, where Captain Kidd and other notorious pirates were hanged in public in 1701 . . .'

Johnny tried to light a cigarette, but the breeze was too powerful, and he stubbed it out. 'You white chicks,' he said, 'are all so maidenhood and pure. You're badly brought up, you know.'

'We're not!'

'You are. And that's why you have no manners. And why you have no manners is that you let your kids run wild.'

'Didn't you run wild once?'

'I did, yes, but I also was closely instructed in excellent manners to older people and to strangers, unlike here: to say good morning and good afternoon, and always be respectful to the other man until he gave good reason to act different.'

'But Africans deceive strangers sometimes, don't they?'

'We do. We do, but we do not rub the man's face in the dirt. We may kill and rob him, yes, but we do not make him a shame to himself, like you. Kill a man, and his spirit will forgive you, but make him ashamed, and he will never so.'

Muriel just saw what he meant. She looked round at her fellow countrymen and women, and asked herself if they would. But all were now engrossed in the guide's tales of opium dens among the non-existent Chinese population of Limehouse Reach.

'I've learned a lot,' she said, 'from Arthur and his friends about how to treat you boys.'

'You speak as if we were some cattle or baboons. Respect us, that is all.'

'Oh, yes, you must be polite to coloured boys, always very polite—good manners seem to mean so much to you. But that's not all. You have to be very patient, too.'

'Are we so slow?'

'You're quick in your minds, but you mustn't ever be hurried. I can't say "Hullo—goodbye" to one of you like I can to one of our boys, without you get offended. It seems you think time's no object. . . .'

'Time is to be used. When I meet a countryman on the path back home, I talk for five minutes at least before I pass on my way.'

'That's what I mean.'

The boat swung south, and sailed down past the Isle of Dogs.

'What matters most of all,' said Muriel, softly as if to herself, 'is that you must never be afraid of a coloured man. If he bluffs you, you must say, "All right, do what you like, I'm not afraid of you,"—and you must mean it.'

Johnny Fortune laughed at her. 'I see you make a careful study of our peculiarities.'

'I've made no study, Johnny. I think you understand a man you love, that's all.'

Even to her embarrassment, he wrapped her in his arms and gave her, in full view of the passengers, a sexy squeeze. Losing interest in the guide, the tourists had taken increasing notice of the couple in the prow. They beamed at the embrace: this was how they expected a coloured man to act.

'I tell you one thing,' said Johnny, hugging her to death. 'What little white girls like most of all is force.'

'Oh, do they!'

'They do. All the boys say so.'

'Not the nice girls, they don't.'

'Oh-ho!' Johnny glared at her like a witch-doctor, and spoke in a throaty whisper. 'If you touch them gently, they just scream. So what you do? You take them to some little room up in some empty house, far off from ears, and say to them, "Scream now, lady! Scream!"'

'I wouldn't come.'

'You would. Oh, yes, you would!'

'I mean you wouldn't have to do that with me. . . . If I love a boy, I love him. If I didn't, I'd never be alone with him.'

'So you are an African! Tell me, then, Africa woman! Truthfully, now, Muriel. Why do you love us so?'

'I don't love you all—I love you.'

'Why so?'

'Because of what you said: those lovely manners you all have. And because you're all so beautiful to look at.'

'You think our ugly faces are so beautiful?'

'Not just your faces—it's the way you move. When you walk, you walk from the top of your head right down to the very tip of your toes. . . . You step out as if you owned the world. . . .'

Fortune grew bored by this. Why praise a beauty that was evident to all?

'And then,' she went on, as he turned to gaze at the liquor bar and moistened his full lips, 'you're such fun to be with. If you say, "Let's do this, or that," to a coloured boy, his first answer isn't, "No." He's ready to fall in with any bright idea.' (Johnny was no longer listening.) 'Of course, sometimes your boys get sad and gloomy, all of a sudden for no reason. . . . And often those lovely smiles of yours don't mean a thing. . . .'

Johnny was looking at a merchant ship, sailing stern first towards them down the river to the open sea. 'Come!' he said. 'Let us get ourselves some glass of lager beer.'

The little bar amidships smelt of heat, and airlessness, and stale ale. The boy serving was an undersized lad with a Tony Curtis hair-do, who slopped the lager in the glasses with amateur abandon. He eyed Johnny Fortune with enthusiasm.

'And for you what?' Johnny asked the boy. 'Some orange juice or Coke?'

'Ta, Guv, I'll have a Pepsi. You're not a boxer, are you?'

'Me? No. I box, though.'

'Of course you do. But I thought you could maybe get me Sugar's autograph.'

'I know boys who visit at his camp. Give me your name, and I shall get you this signature of Mr Robinson.'

'I'm Norman, the captain's son. Care of the boat will find me. Good 'ealth. I drink beer for choice, but Dad won't let me on his boat, I'm under age.'

The huge ship passed, and the craft rocked in its wash. Johnny looked through the port-hole, flattening his face. 'Perhaps she sail out to Africa,' he said.

'She's British,' said Muriel, squeezing up beside him. 'What a lot of ships we have.'

'So many. So old and battered.'

'We're a rich country, Johnny.'

'You? England is quite wasted, Muriel.'

'Wasted? It's not!'

'I tell you. The lands of opportunity are America, and China, and Africa, specially Nigeria.'

'Yes? Who cares, though!' She kissed him as he was still talking. 'It's hot, Johnny. Can't we get this port-hole open?'

'Hot! You call this heat? Nigeria would melt you.' He rubbed a sweaty nose against her own.

'Wait till the cold comes. Then you'll see something you don't know about.'

'Snowballs, you mean?'

'Not snow—just *cold*. You'd better buy yourself a duffel.'

'You, Muriel, will keep me warm.'

The boy came and wiped the table needlessly. He held Johnny by the arm, delicately feeling his biceps.

'You coloured boys,' he said, 'are wonderful fighters. You're the tops.' The blue eyes in his pimply face gazed at Johnny's own with rapture.

'We also have intelligent citizens, you know. There are African students who fully understand atomic energy.'

'Oh, so long as they can fight! You're brave!'

Johnny smiled with condescension, rubbed the boy's back, and pushed him gently off.

'They all love you, Johnny,' Muriel said.

'So long as you do.'

'I do. Oh yes, I do.' She stared at him, and clutched as if she feared he'd disappear. 'I'd do anything for you,' she said.

'Anything! Big words.'

'If you want to stay with me, you can. If you wanted to get married ever, you just say. If you want a child, I'll give you one—a boy: we'll call it Johnny-number-two. I'd work for you, Johnny—any work. I'd go to jail for you—do anything.'

'Muriel! Muriel! What sad thoughts you speak of.'

'You mean getting married?'

'I mean all these things that you imagine. You are my girl—it is enough. What else is there?'

'I love you, Johnny. Once we get into each other's blood, your race and mine, we never can cut free. All that matters to me is that you're brave, and beautiful, and you've got brains, so I can be proud of you. Nothing else matters to me at all.'

The boy came back. 'We're nearing Greenwich Palace now. Do you want to have a look on deck?'

Up in the sun, beneath a pink-blue sky, they watched the stately architectural rhetoric slide into view. 'I smell the sea,' said Fortune, sniffing. When Inigo Jones's splendid white cube appeared between Sir Christopher Wren's gesticulations, Muriel cried out, 'That one's for us! That's where we'll live—the little one.' They stood hand in hand by the railings to be first off at the pier, as the boat swung round the river in a circle. No one else followed them; and when the boat headed back up the river, they saw it wasn't stopping at the palaces.

Muriel called out to the helmsman. 'Can't we get off?'

'Get off, miss? No, we don't stop.

'But it said it was an excursion to Greenwich Palace.

'This is the excursion, miss. We take you there and back, to see it, but you get off where you came from in the City.'

PART II

Johnny Fortune, and his casual days

1

Pew becomes a free-lance

AN AUTUMN DAY, some three months later, found me sitting in a coffee shop frequented by B.B.C. executives, face to face with Theodora and profoundly dejected.

'You're out?' she said.

'Sacked. My interview was a disaster.'

And it had been.

My chief was one of those who think it best to be kind to be cruel. With the air of sharing a great joke, he said to me, 'Well, Pew, the blow's falling, I dare say you expected it,' and gave me a ghastly grin.

'Sir?'

'We're not taking up our option on you, Pew. I expect you'd like some reasons. I'll give you three. The police have been making enquiries about you, and we don't like that. You've visited our hostel frequently without authority and behaved oddly, so it seems. And then, Pew, in a general way, we think you've been a little too familiar with the coloured races. Oh, don't interrupt, I know we're the Welfare Office, and we're in duty bound to help these people in their hour of need. But remote control's the best, we've found. Not matiness. Not going native, if I may so express myself.'

'May *I* make an observation, chief?' I said, when I saw the game was lost.

'You may indeed, if it will ease your feelings.'

'I'm not surprised the coloured races hate us.'

He wasn't a bit disconcerted.

'But they don't, Pew, that's where you make your second big mistake. They don't like us, certainly, but they don't hate us. They just accept us as, I suppose, a necessary evil.'

Determined to have the last word, I said: 'Nothing could be worse than to be neither loved nor hated. It puts one on a level with the Swiss.'

Theodora didn't congratulate me on this rejoinder. 'It's always best,' she said, 'in tricky interviews, to say one word for every six the other person says.'

'But did I in fact say more! And, anyway, my dear Theodora, you yourself have not always been, of recent months, a model of discretion.'

'Oh, have I not?' she said, glancing round at the coffee-swilling executives.

'This series of talks of yours on the colour question has seemed to call for an awful lot of planning.'

'All B.B.C. series must be meticulously planned for months ahead.'

'No doubt, though I can't think why. But I mean you've been bringing Johnny Fortune and his pals against their wills into your flat on far too many occasions.'

'Against their wills? They've been delighted.'

'They're so polite.'

'In any case, I've not seen Johnny now for a month.'

'Nor I. He's disappeared mysteriously from his usual haunts.'

The waitress disgustedly put down the check. I reached for it. 'No,' said Theodora. 'You must economize.'

'I have in my pocket a month's salary in lieu of notice.'

'And then?'

'Then? Only Australia remains.'

Theodora snatched the check away. 'Perhaps you could free-lance for the Corporation,' she said. 'So many mediocrities get away with it.'

'Thanks, Theodora,' I said quite bitterly, and arose. She called me back, but not until I was half-way down the stairs. Her face, from that distance, looked agonized and proud. I crossly returned, and she said in a throaty whisper, 'Find him, Montgomery!' Then swirled to some raw-boned feminine executives at the adjacent table.

I went out bemused into the chilly morning and, passing despondently by one of the many dilapidated subsidiary buildings near Portland Place that house the detritus of the B.B.C., who should I see emerging but a resplendent figure whose fortunes, it seemed, had risen as my own had fallen: none other than Mr Lord Alexander in a rose suit—yes, rose—and carrying a guitar case. I hailed him, and was mortified that at first he didn't recognize me.

'You sang for me,' I reminded him, 'at the hostel some months ago.'

'Oh yes—oh yes, indeed, man. Before my unfortunate arrest, which luckily ended only in seven days.'

'And since then, my lord, since then?'

'Well, man, I've swum into the glory. Radio programmes and cabaret work, and even a number of gramophone recordings.'

'Congratulations, my dear chap. You've written some good new songs?'

'*All* my songs is good, but specially enjoyed are those on British institutions: "Toad-in-hole and Guinness stout", and "Please, Mr Attlee, don't steal my majority", and "Why do I thirst between three and five?" . . .'

'Let us thirst no more, Lord Alexander. The pub's nearby.'

'Me, I will buy you something.'

Over two light ales, I asked him if he had news of Johnny Fortune. He lowered his voice. 'They say,' he told me, 'that little boy has turned out not too good.'

'But where is he? I've been up to Holloway, I've been round all the bars, and he's nowhere to be found.'

'The boy's moved down East End, they tell me, which is a bad, bad sign.'

'Why so?'

'There's East End Spades and West End Spades. West End are perhaps wickeder, but more prosperous and reliable.'

'Do you know where I can find him in the East End?'

'Myself I don't know, but anyone would tell you at Mahomed's café in the Immigration Road. That is a central spot for all East End activities.'

I bought Alexander a return drink, thanked him heartily, and leapt into a cab.

2

Misfortunes of Johnny Fortune

'TROUBLES,' I SAID TO HAMILTON, 'do not come singly.'

'No, Johnny.'

'Never would I think I could be so very foolish.'

'No, Johnny, no.'

'Sometimes I even think I must eat up my pride and return to my Dad in Lagos like the prodigal son.'

We were sitting in my miserable room, a former sweet-shop on the ground floor of the Immigration Road. Muriel, thank goodness, was out now at her work. But Hamilton and I had little joy in our male company, for we were both quite skinned and destitute.

'You tell me to use a needle is bad,' said Hamilton, 'but to gamble away your wealth—is that not a greater injury? Two hundred pounds fly off, Johnny, in three short happy months.'

'They rose once to nearly four hundred pounds with all my profits.'

'But tumbled again to two times zero afterwards.'

I got up and combed my hair, for there was little else to do. 'Not even a fire, Hamilton. Not even a cigarette. And do you know, my greatest sorrow is the total neglect of my meteorological studies?'

'Your greatest sorrow is not that—it is that you are boxed up with this Muriel.'

And what could I say to that? At first I had been fond of that little girl, and she had given me some excellent physical satisfactions. But when all my loot was gone, and the only serious work that I could find, in the building industry, was too poor paid and degradation, she had begun to support me with her pitiful wages from the shirt factory where she was employed.

'Johnny,' said Hamilton. 'You're quite sure this little girl of yours does work in that shirt shop?'

'Of course. Now why?'

'You're positive she's not hustling?'

'Muriel, Hamilton, is no harlot like her sister Dorothy.'

'Be sure of that. Because to live on the immoral earnings of a woman is considered a serious crime in this serious country.'

'Muriel is too honest and too simple.'

'No chick is simple.'

'That is true. . . .'

'This child of hers she says is one day to be yours. You believe her story, Johnny?'

'How can I tell? It could be so. . . .'

'You will let her have it, Johnny?'

'Hamilton! I am no infant murderer.'

Hamilton stretched his long body out.

'Perhaps not,' he said. 'But if she has it, and you refuse her marriage, as I expect you to, she can then weep before the magistrate until he grants her an affiliation order. This will oblige you to support her till the infant is sixteen years of age.'

'Man, I shall skip the country if that happens.'

I looked at my dear friend's eyes. More sunken away than when first I discovered him again, and his whole body shrivelling up with that evil drug, it seemed to me that only wicked thoughts came now into his mind.

'Hamilton,' I said. 'Let's go into the street and take the air. Sitting here leaguing all the day in idleness is just a nightmare.'

'Walking gives me only a hopeless appetite.'

'When do you draw your drug ration, Hamilton?'

'Not till tomorrow. . . .'

'Oh, but come out in the air, man!'

'No, Johnny. Let me sleep here, or I think I'll tumble down and die.'

I had no coat since it was in the pawnshop, but I took up my scarf and started for the door.

Hamilton opened up one eye. 'Those Jumbles, Johnny,' he said. 'That Pew and Pace people you used to see. Can't you raise loot from them?'

'I have some pride.'

'You also have your digestion, Johnny, to consider.'

This Immigration Road is quite the queen of squalor. And though back home we have our ruined streets, they haven't the scraped grimness of this East End thoroughfare. I half shut my eyes and headed for Mahomed's café, which, though quite miserable, has the recommendation that it's open both the night and day.

This is due to the abundant energy of Mahomed, an Indian who once worked high up in a rich West End hotel, and serves you curried chicken as if you were a rajah loaded up with diamonds. His wife is a British lady with a wild love of Spades, and a horrid habit of touching you on the shoulder because she says 'to stroke a darkie brings you luck'. But you can forgive this insolence if she supplies some credit without the knowledge of Mahomed.

The Café's frequented by human dregs, and coppers' narks, and boys who come there hustling and making deals. The first face I saw, when I went in it, was the features of Mr Peter Pay Paul.

'What say, man,' I asked him. 'You still peddling that asthma cure?'

He gave me his spewed-up grin.

'I'm legitimate now,' he said. 'I sell real stuff. You buy some?'

'Roll me a stick, and I'll smoke it at your expense.'

'That's not a good business, man.' But he started rolling.

'What sentence did you get that day?'

'Case dismissed. What do you know?'

'That C.I.D. Inspector, that Mr Purity. He didn't press the charge?'

'He not in court, man—was quite a break.'

'You small beer to him, Peter, it must be.'

'If that's true, man, it's lucky. That Mr Purity looked cold hard.'

He handed me the weed.

'Peter, where you get this stuff?' I said. 'Who is your wholesaler?'

'That is my private secret, man.'

'Suppose that you cut me in on it?'

'Well, I might do . . . if you show some generosity. . . .'

'Man, I'm skinned just at present. Make a friend of me, and you won't repent of it.'

'I'll consider your request, Johnny Fortune. Give me some drag.'

Mahomed came up and bowed as he always does: this because he likes to win the affection of violent Spades who can help him if ever trouble should arise.

'An English gentleman was here looking for you, Johnny.'

'What name?'

'He tell me to say Montgomery was asking for you.'

'Ah, him. What did he need?'

'Johnny, isn't that a copper? His name was quite unknown to me, you never tell me he was a friend of yours, so I sent him farther on east down Limehouse way.'

'I don't live there.'

'To confuse the man. I said to call at 12 Rawalpindi Street, but so far as I know there isn't any such address.'

Mahomed gave us a sly, silly smile to prove his clever cunning.

'Mahomed, you're too smart. If that man calls here again, please tell him where I live.'

'He's a friend, then?'

'Is a friend, yes.'

'Oh, I apologise. You eat something?' I shook my head. 'On me, said Mahomed, and cut out behind his counter with another little bow.

I saw an old African man was watching us. 'Who is that grey old person?' I asked Peter Pay Paul.

'That old-timer? Oh, a tapper. He's always complaining about we younger boys.'

'I no tapper,' the old gentleman said. 'But all I can tell you is you boys spoil honest business since you come. Before the wartime, before you come here in all your numbers, the white folks was nice and friendly to us here.'

'They spat in your eyes and you enjoyed it, Mr Old-timer.'

'You go spoil everything. You give me some weed.'

'Blow, man. Go ask your white friends for it.'

After Mahomed's sodden chicken, we walked down the Immigration Road, Peter Pay Paul holding his weed packets in his hands constantly inside his overcoat pockets as these weed peddlers do, ready to ditch them at the slightest warning.

'I must cut out of this weed racket soon, Johnny,' he said. 'No one lasts more than three months or so, because the Law puts the eye on you before too long goes by.'

'How will you live, man, if you give it up?'

'There's the lost-property racket, but there's not much loot in that.... You go round lost-property offices asking for brief-cases, say, or gold-topped umbrellas, and claiming the nicest object you can see.'

'They give them to you without any proof?'

'You speak some very bad English, and act ignorant and helpless to them, when they ask for explanations. They end by yielding up some article which then you can sell. . . . If only I could get a camera from them, though.'

'To take street photograph?'

Peter Pay Paul stopped and laughed.

'Man,' he said, taking me by the scarf, 'you're crazy. No. Hustling with Jumble queers. You get yourself picked up by them, taken home, then photograph them by flashlight in some dangerous condition and sell them the negative for quite a price. Or sell a print and keep the negative for future use. . . . Or else beat them up and rob them, but that's dangerous, because sometimes they turn round and fight you back. . . .' Peter walked on again. 'No, straightest of all, man, is finding sleeping accommodation and company for G.I.s, or buying cheap the goods they get from PX stores, but for this you need quite a capital. Best of all, of course, is poncing on some woman, but I haven't got the beauty enough for that. Why don't you try it, Johnny?'

'My sex life is not for sale.'

'Ah, well . . .'

We turned down a side street through an alley-way into a big empty warehouse. We climbed up some wooden steps, and Peter Pay Paul knocked on a three-locked door.

'Say who!' a voice cried inside.

'Peter, man. Let me in.'

The door opened two inches, and we saw an eye. 'And this?' said the voice behind the eye.

'My good friend Fortune, out of Lagos. Let us both in.' And he whispered to me: 'A Liberian—beware of him.'

This wholesale weed peddler was a broad-chested cripple, who dragged his legs when he moved about the room, never keeping ever still. His eyes were very brown-shot inside their purple rings.

'Good morning, Mr Ruby,' said Peter Pay Paul. 'Perhaps I could introduce you a new customer.

3

Pew and Fortune go back west

I MEANDERED ABOUT LIMEHOUSE DOCKS an hour or more before I realized that Indian had made a fool of me: there was no Rawalpindi Street. So I walked back, through the ships' masts and abandoned baroque churches of Shadwell, in the direction of the Immigration Road. On the corner of a bombed site, surviving by the special providence that loves brewers, I found a pub called the Apollo Tavern. Coloured men inside were dancing softly with morning lassitude, and behind the counter there was an amiable Jew. I asked him for a Guinness, and he said: 'One Guinness stout, right, I thank you, okey-doke, here it is, one and four, everything complete.' His wife, if she was, a grim-faced Gentile, gazed at me with the rude appraisal only women give.

I sat down. A voice said: 'So you's come movinx into this areas of London eastern populations?'

It was the Bushman. I shook his hand. 'And how is your instrument?' I asked him.

'Sold, man. Bisnick is bads juss at this mominx.'

'I, too, have been unfortunate of late. This doesn't seem to be our lucky month.'

There was a gentle tap on my shoulder, and a black hand protruded holding two double whiskies in its fingers. 'Who are these for?' I asked the Bushman.

'For you, man, and for me.'

'But who is this kind person?'

'Is my tribesmans. He offer some drinks to his sief's son and to his sief's son's friend.'

I turned and looked round. The donor was joining three others, all neatly dressed, who raised their glasses politely to the Bushman.

'But who are they, Mr Bushman?'

'I tells you: is my tribesmans. I come to this Immigrasions Roats for some tribal tributes. Here they will pay some offerinx to their sief's son.'

The Bushman caught me eyeing his soiled and greasy clothes.

'Soon they will takes me out to eat him foots,' he said, 'and make me comfortables and give me presinx. Stay, now, and you will enjoy them toos.'

'But why don't you speak to them, Mr Bushman?'

'When I reaty, I spik to them. They waits for me. Then I spik.'

The offer of liquor was repeated several times. After the third double, I gave up. 'Your father,' I said, 'must be a very powerful man.'

He grunted with satisfaction. 'And one day I. Then I invites you to my jungle home, and you stays with us for evers.'

'I look forward immensely to it.'

'Stay with us for evers, or we puts you in a pot.'

'I'm bony—only good for soup.'

'All him sames, we eats you as special favour.'

'Thank you so very much. Goodbye now, my kind friend.'

The Bushman shrieked with laughter, and, as I went out, I saw the tribesmen approach him with deferential smiles.

Possessed now by that early morning drunkard's feeling which suspends time by making all time worthless, and gives the daylight a false flavour of the dark, I sauntered up the Immigration Road. A girl's voice hailed me from a ground-floor window. It was Johnny Fortune's young friend Muriel.

'Come in,' she said, opening the door, 'I want to speak with you.'

Muriel was cooking something cabbagey. The boy Hamilton was snoring on a bed. She wiped her hands on her skirt, told me to sit down, and gave me a cup of very sweet thick tea.

'Johnny will be coming in for his dinner,' she said, 'and I know he'd like to see you.'

'Oh, I've been looking for him. He lives here now?'

'Yes, here with me. I work round the corner, and cook him all his meals.'

'And Hamilton?'

'Hamilton has no room just now, so he's staying here.'

She sat down too, and leaned across the oil-cloth. 'Can't you do something to help Johnny?'

'In what way, Muriel?'

'With money.'

'Surely he has some . . .'

'It's all been spent.'

'Oh. Can't he work?'

'Johnny won't work for less than twenty pounds a week. I tell him only clever men get those jobs, and he says he is a clever man. But he doesn't get one. . . .'

'I could lend him something. . . .'

She stirred a cup. 'If only we could get married,' she said. 'I'd help him in any job he wanted.'

'Can't you get married?'

'He doesn't want to.'

She began to cry. Women are so immodest in their grief. Even when you don't care for a woman much, to see her misery openly expressed is painful.

'These boys are all the same,' she said. 'Never anything fixed or steady, they just drift . . .'

There was a clatter at the door, and in came Johnny with Mr Peter Pay Paul.

A change had come over Johnny Fortune. His body still had its animal grace and insouciance, but his face wore at times a slanting, calculating look. And though the charm was as great as ever, he was more conscious of it than before. He greeted me with what seemed genuine affection.

'Where have you hidden yourself, Johnny?' I asked him.

'Oh, times have been difficult, man. And with you? You look sharp—real smart!' And he fingered my third-best suit.

'With me, times have been disastrous.' And I told him about my exit from the Welfare Office.

'That is one big pity,' he said gravely, 'because I thought perhaps you could help me with some new business.'

'What is it? Perhaps I can.'

'Come on one side.'

He led me over to the window, though he stood away from view of the street in the half light.

'This pack,' he said, pulling a large oblong piece of newspaper from inside his shirt, 'is wholesale weed. Five pounds' worth, which

I can sell in small packs for ten to twenty pounds if I can find five pounds now for Peter Pay Paul.'

'Here they are, Johnny. Are you going to earn your living that way?'

'Thank you, man. Well, what else can I do? I know no trade, no business . . .'

'Wouldn't your father send you money?'

'No, Montgomery, I cannot tell my Dad my loot is gone and that I'm not studying meteorology. Also, he has sent loot at my request to Muriel's mother. But my brother Arthur, so I hear, has stolen it away from her . . .'

'Perhaps the time's coming, Johnny, when you should think of going home.'

'Not till I make some fortune from this city, man. To go empty-handed home would be my shame.'

He gave the notes to Peter Pay Paul and, after removing a handful of weed, pushed the paper package up the chimney.

'And how is Miss Theodora?'

'Missing you, Johnny.'

Muriel heard this.

'She'd better keep on missing him.'

'Who spoke to you, Muriel?'

'Aren't you going to give me some of that money? How do you think we'll live?'

'Be silent, woman. Go on with your cookery.'

'I'm not an African, Johnny. You can't treat me like I'm a household slave.'

He shrugged his shoulders. 'Come, Montgomery,' he said. 'This woman troubles me with her yap, yap, chatter, chatter, chatter.'

Muriel clutched his arm. 'But don't you want your dinner, Johnny? It's all cooked.'

'I have had chicken. Hamilton, wake up! We leave this sad East End to go up west.'

But Hamilton kept snoring, and Muriel wept again into the steaming pot as we went out.

4

Coloured invasion of the Sphere

Montgomery and me left Mr Peter Paul at the Aldgate station, and started the long bus ride through the City to the west. I chose the special seat which bus constructors made for those who smoke hemp (I mean the private seat, top floor at rear, which nobody can overlook), and there, while Montgomery grew more nervous, I folded up little saleable packets of my weed. 'I must kick my heel free of this miserable life,' I told Montgomery. 'I must climb back again into prosperity.'

'You might marry a fat African lady whose father owns acres of groundnuts,' he said to me.

'Oh, I could do that, perhaps, you know. But I want to go back home well loaded from this city. . . .' I folded a little packet and said to him, 'Has Miss Theodora money?'

I saw he didn't approve of this request of information, though a natural one, I thought, among two men.

'She's only her salary, I think,' he told me. 'But you mustn't play about with Theodora's feelings.'

'Why not? She likes me—no?'

'And you her?'

'I could do, if it should prove necessary. . . .'

'I'd rather you ran a whore, like Billy, than do that. Business and no pretences. . . .'

What did my nice English friend know about that kind of life? 'I may come to do just that,' I said to him.

'I hope you don't mean it. . . .'

'This Dorothy pursues me some time now. Pestering and giving me no peace at all. She wishes to leave Billy, and for me to take possession.'

'From what I can understand,' Montgomery said, 'it's the woman who takes possession of the man. She can sell him down the river any day she likes.'

Well, that was true enough from all I know of how those bad boys live—trembling, however brave, at every knock of the front door, and so afraid of the loot their women give them that they throw it all away in gamble-houses as soon as they've snatched it from her handbag. 'Oh, yes,' I said, 'these whores are always masters of their ponces. One word to the Law, and the lucky boy's inside.'

Montgomery sat looking sad, like the Reverend Simpson. 'I don't like to think of you in that miserable world,' he said.

I smiled, and patted on his anxious back. 'No real ill luck can come to me, Montgomery,' I told him. 'Look!' And I opened my tieless shirt and showed him the wonderful little blue marks tattooed upon my skin by Mum's old aunt, who knows the proper magic, and also the mission school badge I wear around my neck upon its chain. 'These will protect me always,' I explained.

'You believe that, Johnny?'

'So long as I believe it,' I said to him, 'they will protect me.'

Though it was well after morning opening time when we reached the Moorhen public house, we were surprised to find it absent of any Spade. 'There must have been some raid,' I told Montgomery. But no. A strange old Jumble man he knew, who looked at me as if I wasn't there, said all my race had left the pub and moved to another further down the road, one called the Sphere.

'But why have they gone?' Montgomery asked him.

'Because they've shut the dance hall opposyte—and high time too.'

'The Cosmopolitan? Why did they do that?' I asked.

'Moral degeneracy,' the old man said fiercely at me. 'Didn't you read it in your Sunday paper?'

'Good heavens!' I cried out. 'Have these Jumbles no mercy on our enjoyment?'

'This place is improved out of all recognition now,' the nasty old man informed us.

Dismal, dark, dreary, almost empty, I suppose that was improvement to his eyes.

We found that this Sphere was a small pub divided into more segregated sections than is usual even in these English drinking dens. Boys flitted in and out from one box to the other, and the publican, I could see, was not used to our African habit, which is to treat such places like a club, with no dishonour to be there even if you have no loot to spend. The barman, a young boy with a face like cheese, seemed worried also; and as I held my lager beer, casting my eyes around, I spoke to him freely of his look of great mistrust.

'But those lads over by the pyano,' he said to me. 'They come in here for hours and never buy a thing.'

'Why should they not? This is their meeting-place, for exchange of gossip, information, and other necessities of life.'

'But if they come in here, then they should spend.'

'Man,' I explained, 'you will find when they spend, they *do* spend. You will make more profit from them in one evening than of your bitter-sipping English customers in a whole week.'

He seemed to doubt me. 'The guv'nor tried turfing them all out at first,' he said, 'but he's given up the struggle.' He leaned across the counter. 'Tell me something,' he went on. 'You don't mind me asking?'

'Speak, man. I listen.'

'How do you tell which is which among you people?'

'You mean we all look the same like sheep?'

'No, not exactly. I mean, which is African, and which is West Indian—all I can tell is the Yanks, and then only when they open up their mouths.'

I shook my head at such enormous ignorance. 'Do you know,' I said to him, 'my grandmother cannot tell any one Englishman from another?' I left Montgomery with his whiskies, and went round into the larger bar to look for customers.

And there I caught sight of many quite familiar faces: Ronson Lighter, playing the pin-table, and Larry the G.I., and also my brother Arthur, who I was not all that pleased to talk to because of the theft of all that loot my Dad sent his Mum, and also, lurking away in an evil corner underneath the stairways, that one-time champion boxer, Jimmy Cannibal.

'What say, man,' I said to Ronson Lighter. 'Long time no see.'

'Well, look now, who's here! Where you been hiding yourself, Mr Fortune? Somebody here's been searching out for you.'

'Called what?'

'A seaman from back home who won't tell his real name, but says just to call him Laddy Boy. He has a letter for you from your sister Peach.'

'He's in here now, this seaman?'

'I haven't noticed him around yet, but if he calls, I'll hold him for you.'

'Thank you, my man. And tell me now. I'm in business, Ronson Lighter, in this article,' (and I showed him some). 'You interested at all?'

Ronson put his body so as to hide mine from the general view. 'Be careful of that little white boy Alfy Bongo,' he advised me. 'He comes here to meet our African drummers, so he says, but I think he's a queer boy, and you cannot trust them.'

I looked at this blond and pimply creature, chatting and giggling to some West Indians, and I made a clear note of his skinny, feeble frame in my recollection.

'I'll take a stick or two,' said Ronson Lighter.

'Here, man. How's our Billy?'

'I'm worried about that man, Johnny, and so is he. He thinks the Law has got the eye on him real hard. The house is being watched, we know.'

'Why should they turn the heat on Billy after all this time?'

'Is averages, Johnny. Six months they turn you loose, then one month they turn the heat. Nobody knows why. Perhaps you're next man on their Vice Department list, that's all. Or perhaps somebody been talking. Cannibal, say.' (And Ronson Lighter looked across at him.) 'Or maybe even Dorothy.'

'Not Dorothy?'

'I don't know why, man, but I believe this Dorothy plans to cut away from Billy, and she thinks the best way is to get him put inside. Perhaps,' said Ronson, lighting up his charge, 'it is because of you, who she prefers to Mr Whispers.'

'I'm not even slightly interested in that chick.'

'Oh, I believe you man, if you say so, of course.'

Ronson was dragging now, but still hadn't paid me any money. I touched on his arm and gently held out my hand.

'Will you take one of these instead?' he asked me.

They were pawn tickets for various articles. All city Spades hold pawn tickets, and if the man's honest they're quite as good as money, often better if you can get them with the discount. I took my pick.

'And Hamilton,' said Ronson Lighter. 'How does he keep?'

'Bad. He's using all his dope allowance now, not selling any. Even buying more of that poison whenever he can.'

Ronson lowered down his voice. 'You know who put him on the needle and supplied him? It was that "Nat King" Cole.'

I said to Ronson: 'Was it only Cole who did this injury to my friend? No one else you know of who was the person?'

'Who else could it be, man? No one else.'

'I thought maybe you could tell me who.'

Ronson was silent. 'No man, not me,' he said.

By now my brother Arthur had detected me, and over he came, as happy as a smiling hyena. 'How's Muriel?' was how he greeted me.

'She's well.'

'Ma's told the Law you've taken her.'

'She's not under sixteen, is she?'

'She's a minor, brother, in need of care and protection. Ma wants her sent off to a home.' Now he approached me closer. 'Johnny,' he said, 'do something for me. Lend me loot.'

'You spent all that which you took away from Mrs Macpherson?'

He smiled at me some more: I grew to hate that smile. 'All gone,' he said. 'The gamble-house way, like you did. It sure goes so fast away in there.'

'You get no more from this side of the family, Arthur.'

'Listen, now,' he said. 'I see you's selling weed. I'd like I go partners with you. I'd get you customers.'

'Thanks, brother. I prefer I operate alone.'

'You're wasted, Johnny. No good to me at all.'

I saw the human being called Alfy Bongo standing just behind me. 'What can I do for you, mister?' I said nasty.

He answered me in a great whisper, with a lot of winks. 'They tell me you've got some stuff.'

'I don't like your face,' I said to him. 'And if you speak to me again without you're spoken to, they'll have to send you into some hospital or other.'

This didn't seem to be my lucky day for gay society, because the next person who accosted me was no one less but a well-known idiot from back home called Ibrahim Tondapo, a thoroughly gilded youth who, just because his Dad owns two small cinemas that regularly catch on fire and burn up portions of the audience, allowed himself in Lagos great airs of class distinction, earning hatred and laughter everywhere around. He looked at me up and down and shook his body in his expensive suit as if he was shivering cold water off it. So 'Hullo, chieftain,' I said to him. 'How is each one of your six mothers?' (this being a reference to his not knowing really who his mother was, because his Dad is volatile, and he quite unlike any of his brothers.)

At which this foolish man spat on the floor.

I ought not to have said what I did, of course, but nor ought he to spit—is an unhealthy habit. So I slapped him on his face, and a fight began, and I was seized on by eight people and thrown out through the doors. Stupid behaviour, with my pockets stuffed with weed, but poverty and misery cause you to act desperately, as all know.

'You and I,' I shouted back at Tondapo through the door, 'will meet each other shortly once again.'

Out in the street, the boys were charging in the light of day, a habit dangerous in this city, where now the notable sweet smell of this strong stuff is well known to curious nostrils. So I crossed the road to where some builders were erecting a new construction, and among them I was surprised to see a tall West Indian toiling, one that I'd known in gamble-houses in my prosperous days. We gazed at each other quite politely, and he came over to say his word to me.

'Just look at me,' he said. 'A member of the labouring classes.'

'If a brick falls on your head, man, you'll certainly go straight up to heaven for this honest labour.'

'Yes, man, that's authentic. But wouldn't I much rather be sitting there in the Sphere consuming Stingo beer or something of that nature.'

'You're Mr Tamberlaine,' I said to him. 'I see you round some time ago, you may remember. Introducing people one to the other was your speciality.'

'Yes, that's exactly so. Pimping about the city, as you might call it, if you wanted to.' And he gave me his harmonious smile.

'And that's all over now, that kind of business?'

'Oh, no. I'm still in the market in the evenings, but find it prudent, don't you see, to have some part-time occupation in the days to justify my movements and existence if there's any police inquiries.'

'Wise, man. You's real educated.'

'There's something,' he said, 'as might interest you at a party taking place this evening, which is an exhibition by some boys from Haiti that I know of their special voodoo practices. So if your luck's not all you've been aspiring to, you've only to come and ask them for their kind assistance to alternate your fate.'

While I said yes, that I'd accept this invitation, Ronson Lighter called to me from the public house. 'This seaman's here,' he shouted out. 'This Laddy Boy.'

He was a muscle man, this individual, his arms like legs, his legs like elephants', and with a lot of rings and gold teeth and a happy look about him that these strong men have, especially when they're loaded up with loot, as merchant seamen always seem to be. He gave me the note from Peach, which, when I opened it, said this to me:

'Macdonald, what is this we hear? Bad news has reached us, by boys returning home, that you have engaged yourself with evil company, and thrown away money that Dad gave you, and broken the sequence of your serious studies. Dad says, "He'll find his feet." But I do not believe this, nor does Mum, and she will send you the fare home (paid to care of the travel company, not in cash to you), if you agree that is what's sensible to do, which our brother Christmas also thinks it is. Be wise, Johnny, and return among your own people for all our sakes that love you as you know we do.

'I tell you, your younger sister Peach is worried. And if you do not return home before New Year, let me tell you of my intentions. They are to come out to England there, to train as nurse, which full enquiries prove can be arranged. And if I do, you know you will have me watching you each second I am not on duty, which will make you ashamed of yourself before the other men.

'But come back freely, Johnny. It would be so much better for us all.

'Dad says he thank you for what you discover of those Macpherson people. He has done what he can and will do no more at all.

'Mum adds: a cable, and you have the fare home in a fortnight.

'Your sister, and you have no other,

Peach.'

'You saw my sister?' I asked Laddy Boy.

'Your family entertained me very kindly, Johnny, at your home.'

'They're all of them well back there?'

'They're well, man, but a little worrying about you. You know why. Is not my business, countryman, but you know why. . . . You take a drink?'

'I'm barred inside that pub.'

'Not with me, you're not, man, no. You're not barred in any public house that I go into.'

He took me inside, and there was no more reference to my recent wild behaviour. While I sipped my drink, I thought quite deeply. Yes, home would be beautiful again, but surely my duty was to try to rescue myself by my own efforts before seeking family aid?

In the nearby bar, I saw Montgomery talking with Larry the G.I. This gave me a new idea of how to raise some loot quickly in a last attempt, before throwing in my sponge and going back to Lagos tail between the legs.

I went to the phone box and asked for the radio corporation of the B.B.C., and for Miss Theodora Pace. After some secretaries, her voice came clear over the line towards me.

'Miss Theodora, this is Johnny Fortune.'

'Oh. One minute, please.' I heard some mutter, and a door close. 'Yes, how are you? What can I do for you?'

'You remember those radio talks we spoke about, Miss Theodora? With me as possible performer in them?'

'Yes. . . . Why've you not contacted me again?'

'Oh, there have been things, you know, so many. But this is to say I'm willing now, though there is one stipulation I should like to ask about.'

'Yes?'

'Would your officials consider a small payment in advance? Of twenty pounds?'

I knew, of course, that this was asking Theodora for the loot, but it seemed a way of doing so that could satisfy both our dignities.

'When do you want it?'

'Today. The soonest would be the best.'

There was quite a pause here before she said: 'I dare say that could be arranged. Come to the building, and ask for me at Reception, please.'

The Sphere was now closing for the afternoon, and the Spades were scattering all over town on their various errands, from this their daily joint collecting-point. I went off myself quite quietly, without telling Montgomery of my personal intentions.

5

The southern performers at the Candy Bowl

THOUGH LARRY THE G.I. had been wonderfully entertaining (telling me of how it was back home in Cleveland, Ohio, with Pop and Mom and his six young brothers, including the one who was in love with horses), I began to miss Johnny; and explored all the Sphere's bar cubicles, until I met Ronson Lighter, and learned he'd already left. These sudden disappearances I was by now used to, so I went back to Larry and suggested we both have lunch. 'Man, here's no food,' he answered. 'So why don't we go down to the Candy Bowl?'

He said this was the club most preferred by coloured Americans, and he told me he had two swell southern friends of his he'd like to have me meet—performers in the Isabel Cornwallis ballet company, now visiting the city, and stirring up a deal of excitement in balletic and concentric circles.

How little one ever knows of one's home town! I'd been in that courtyard a dozen times, but never sensed the presence of the Candy Bowl: which, it is true, looked from outside like an amateur sawmill, but once through its doors, and past a thick filter of examining attendants, it was all peeled chromium and greasy plush, with dim pink and purple lights, and strains of drum and guitar music from the basement. G.I.s, occasionally in uniform, but mostly wearing suits of best English material and of best transatlantic cut, lounged gracefully around, draped on velours benches, or elegantly perched upon precarious stools.

Sitting at a table by the wall, writing letters, were two boys in vivid Italian sweaters. 'That's the pair of them,' said Larry, '—Norbert and Moscow. Norbert you'll find highly strung, but he's quite a guy. Moscow's more quiet, a real gentleman.' We drew near to their table. 'I want you to know my good friends Norbert Salt and Moscow Gentry,' Larry said. 'Boys, this is Montgomery Pew.'

Norbert Salt had a golden face you could only describe as radiant:

candidly delinquent, and lit with a wonderful gaiety and contentment. His friend Moscow Gentry's countenance was so deep in hue that you wondered his white eyes and teeth weren't dyed black by all the surrounding blue-dark tones: a face so obscure, it was even hard to read his changes of expression.

'Montgomery,' said Larry, 'is mightily interested in the ballay.' (Not so: I've never been able to take seriously this sad, prancing art.)

'I've not seen your show yet,' I told them, 'but I look forward immensely to doing so.'

They gazed at me with total incredulity. Clearly, anybody who'd not yet seen their show was nobody. 'If you wish it,' said Moscow Gentry, 'we'd be happy to offer you seats for the first house this evening.'

'Alternatively,' said Norbert Salt, 'we could let you and Larry view a rehearsal of our recital if you'd care to.'

'Man,' said Larry, 'that's something you certainly should not miss. If these boys don't shake you in your stomach, then I'll know you're a dead duck anyway.'

I asked them about Miss Cornwallis and her balletic art.

'Cornwallis,' said Norbert, 'isn't pleased with the British this trip so very much. Two years back when we were here, we tore the place wide open, and business, as you know, was fabulous. But this time there's empty seats occasionally, and that doesn't please Cornwallis one little bit.'

'She's having to kill chickens once again in her hotel bedroom,' said Moscow Gentry.

Even Larry didn't quite get this.

Norbert Salt explained. 'Cornwallis believes in voodoo, even though she's a graduate of some university or other in the States. So when business isn't what it might be, well, she gets her Haitian drummers to come round to her hotel and practise rituals that bring customers crowding to the box office.'

'And it works?'

'Man, yes, it seems to. At lease, it's not failed to do so yet.'

'And is Miss Cornwallis's style Haitian, then?' I asked.

'Oh, no—she choreographs a cosmopolitan style,' said Norbert. 'Being herself Brazilian by birth, and internationally educated by her studies and her travels, her art's a blend of African and Afro-

Cuban, with a bit of classical combined. It makes for a dance that's accessible to cultured persons on every civilized continent.'

'And has your art been well received in Europe?'

'In Rome-Italy and Copenhagen-Denmark,' Norbert told me, 'we found they still liked us this trip as particularly as before. But as for here, I guess with all your thoughts of war you British haven't so much time for spiritual things.'

'Our thoughts of *war*?'

'Oh, yes,' said Moscow Gentry. 'You English people are constantly crazy about war.'

'Besides which,' said his friend Norbert, 'you don't appreciate the artistry of what we do. In Rome or Copenhagen, or even Madrid-Spain, we get all the top people at our recitals. But here, it's only the degenerates who really like us.'

'Can you fill a theatre in this city with degenerates for several weeks?'

'Oh, sure,' said Norbert Salt.

'Well,' I told him, nettled, 'you should be thankful to our degenerates for not thinking about war as you say the others do.'

'We don't thank anyone, sir. We perform, that's all, and if they like us, then they pay. We don't have to thank them for patronizing an entertainment that they're willing to pay for.'

I offered them a drink: they took lemon squash and tonic water. 'And this rehearsal,' I enquired. 'It takes place soon?'

'It takes place,' said Norbert, looking at a gold watch two inches wide, 'in forty minutes from this moment. I guess we should all be going to the theatre. In the Cornwallis company, we're always dead on time.'

The two young Americans made a royal progress down the streets that lay between the Candy Bowl and the Marchioness Theatre: catching the eyes of the pedestrians as much by the extravagance of their luminous sweaters and skin-tight slacks as by the eloquence of their bodily gyrations, shrill voices and vivid gesticulations; and did anyone fail to look at them, his conquest was effected by their bending down suddenly in front of him or her to adjust an enamelled shoe, so that the recalcitrant bowler-hatted or tweed-skirted natives found themselves curiously obstructed by an exotic, questioning behind.

There was some opposition to our entry at the stage door—which was manned (as these doors are) by a person who would have been disagreeable even to Sir Henry Irving. But his rude rudeness was outmanœuvred by an abrupt and devastating display of bitchiness by our two hosts. 'These ain't no stage-door gumshoes, they're *my friends*,' hissed Norbert, after an ultimate nasty salvo. He led us past the doorman's corpse to a narrow lift of the alarming kind that receives you on one side and ejects you on the other. Norbert and Moscow preceded us along a clanging concrete corridor to their dressing-room, where they immediately stripped naked, and started painting their faces and bodies in improbable jungle hues. 'The number we're rehearsing's African,' said Moscow. 'Cornwallis wasn't pleased with our performance of last evening, and she's called this rehearsal to get us in the ripe primeval mood.'

'Come and meet the girls,' said Norbert, and, still in nothing but his paint, he stepped down the corridor, and flung open the door of a larger dressing-room in which a dozen resplendent coloured girls were gilding the lilies of their beauty. He passed rapidly from one to the other, fondling each with gestures of jovial obscenity, and capering at times to the music of a portable radio they had. 'Say hullo to Louisiana,' he called out to us from a far corner. 'Boys this is Louisiana Lamont, our *ingénue*.'

She was a succulent girl with radiant eyes that positively shone. She smiled at Larry and me as if we were the two men in the world she'd most been waiting for, and said, 'My, ain't you both quite a size.'

'Just average,' said Larry, who was gigantic.

'Louisiana is our baby,' Norbert told us. 'She's just turned seventeen and she shouldn't really be travelling outside her country yet.'

'Why, Norbert! Where I come from, we's *married* at twelve years old—that was the age my Mom had me at. Why, honey, we's *grandmothers* before we're *your* age.' She offered us some sponge fingers from a paper bag. 'I do appreciate your British confectionery,' she said to me.

'Together with marmalade, meat sauces, and some cheeses,' I answered, 'biscuits are the only thing we make that's fit to eat.'

Louisiana paused in the biting of the sponge. 'Why, Montgomery!' she cried out in amaze. 'You said that just like an Englishman.'

'But I *am* an Englishman, Miss Lamont,' I told her. 'I am one.'

'I know you are. But you said it just like they do.' She appeared entranced.

A sharp bell rang.

This was the signal for a scattering and caterwauling of coloured boys and girls, racing out of dressing-rooms, tumbling downstairs in a brown and gold cascade, their voices shrill and laughing-screaming, then suddenly, with a last cry and clatter, silent. Larry and I were left alone with their memory, their odour, and little scraps on the floor of their costumes' straw and feather. He said: 'We'd best follow them down and see.'

We reached the wings in near darkness, and saw the company sitting on the stage in an oval, staring up at a woman standing in their midst who slowly revolved, talking to one and then the other, like the axis of each one of their destinies. 'That heavy piece,' said Larry, in a whisper, 'is Isabel Cornwallis herself in person.'

Miss Cornwallis was saying to her audience:

'I want you to understand. All I want is just that you understand me. Why I bring you dancers here to Europe is for a purpose. You think it's for the money I may make: well, if you think that, will you speak to my accountant, please, or else my lawyer? They'll tell you, no. It's for my art and for my people that I bring you here. The dance is an old, old art, since the days of pre-anthropology and those things. It's not just shaking your asses round like you children seem to imagine that it is. It's uplifting, and an honour to participate. It's also a source of advancement to our people. White folk imagine all we can do is jungle numbers, and ritual dances, and such. That's why I've choreographed our African and Caribbean dances in with classical European and other sources. It shows them we're up to the highest tones of their endeavour—Norbert, will you stop scratching there in your arm-pits?'

'It's an itch, Miss Cornwallis.'

'I don't want no itches in my company. I thought you understood what I'm telling to you, Norbert. You and Moscow and Jupiter here and Huntley are some of my older performers, my stars. It seems like I'm superfluous if you scratch your arm-pits during my conversation. Which reminds me to tell you what I've often said before. Dancers are desiring in their thousands to join the Isabel Cornwallis company. So I don't have to stay with you, and you don't have to stay with me, unless each party feels we want to. We're not obligated to each other in any way. But so long as I have my company, I'm going to keep up my standards of achievement.'

On and on she went, like a playback from a tape recorder. It was clear they had heard all this a million or so times before; yet were none the less fascinated by her flow.

The boy called Jupiter, a creature of breath-taking dignity and beauty, who sat in serene repose like a work of art more than one of Nature, said, in a high, squealing, petulant voice, 'Miss Cornwallis, some of the younger performers smell so bad of their perspiring it's unbearable.'

'They should use perfume, Jupiter, like you do, and I do, and all self-regarding human beings do.'

'I wish you'd tell them, Miss Cornwallis. They just stink.'

'I am telling them, Jupiter, as you can hear.'

Now it was the turn of the boy called Huntley: a slender, graceful light-skinned youth with a Roman rather than a Negro profile.

'Some of the young performers, Miss Cornwallis,' he said, in weary, spiteful, yet mellifluous tones, 'are saying I'm impolite to them when I take class. Now am I the ballet master here, or am I not? That's what I want to know.'

'You are, Huntley, since it's there in your contract that you are, but the man who's master never need be unpolite. And that reminds me, too, Huntley. You're getting so pale in this land of sunshine you look almost like a white boy now. You must have some sun-lamp treatment, Huntley, or else use a coloration lotion on your body. This is a coloured company, remember, with all that it implies.'

Larry the G.I. nudged me. 'The crazy old bitch,' he said in dangerous *sotto voce*. 'How does she get away with it? If it was me, I'd slap her down. And do you know, man? She's getting so fat only two boys of the whole company can catch her when she flies through the air like a ton of frozen meat. The others, she knocks them flat.'

Miss Isabel Cornwallis was off again. 'Just one more thing,' she said. 'These parties you've been going to, that I've heard about. I understand the gay folk, and the rich folk that you meet, and I approve of this association—it's good for the reputation of the company you should move in high society. But you, Norbert, and you,

Moscow, have been seen in peculiar assemblies, so I hear, with people of evil reputation.'

'If you're speaking of last Saturday a somebody may have told you or, Miss Cornwallis, it was at a prominent lawyer's house, and bankers and military officers and also a chief man of police were present there.'

'Now, please don't argue with me, Norbert.'

'If a party's suitable for the police chief, what can be so wrong with it as that?'

'It's not parties I'm talking about, Norbert—it's how you spend your leisure time when you're not dancing. You should be visiting the picture museums and cultural centres of which this city's provided very freely.'

'All right, Miss Cornwallis, we'll visit picture museums and study pictures.'

'Please don't argue with me, Norbert. It's not necessary.'

My trance-like fascination was interrupted when a pair of arms clasped me gently, but firmly, round the waist. I turned and saw a short, lissom figure standing on tiptoe, gazing up as if adoringly, and, beside him, a tall slender companion, holding two tapering elongated drums.

'There are the Haitian boys, the drummers,' Larry said. 'That's Hercule La Bataille who's trying to seduce you, and Hippolyte Dieudonné is this one here.'

I greeted them, disengaging myself with difficulty from the encircling arms.

'These boys,' said Larry, 'will be doing their bit of voodoo at the party tonight.'

'I turns you into hen, and eat you,' said Hercule with an abominable smile.

Hippolyte was expressionless, but gave six sharp taps on one of his drums.

'You turn this Limey into a hen, and I slit your throat,' said Larry, suddenly producing an enormous knife from inside his clothing, and brandishing it (though sheathed) before the faces of the Caribbeans.

'Larry, do be careful,' I cried out. 'Why on earth do you carry that dreadful weapon?'

'I'm never without my knife,' said Larry. 'Not in any circumstance whatsoever.'

6

Theodora lured away from culture

THE PRICE Miss Theodora made me pay for that twenty pounds she gave me at the radio corporation building was quite heavy: it was to take me that selfsame evening to a theatre, and show me a play by a French man about nothing I could get my brain to climb around. At a coffee, in the interval (for this theatre had no liquor in its sad bar), I said, 'Miss Theodora, I know this kind of entertainment is suitable for my improvement, but don't you think we could now step out into the air?'

'I did hope you'd like it, Johnny.'

'Quite over my comprehension, Theodora. Please—can't we go?'

I could see she was sad that I didn't rise up to her educational expectancies; but to hell with that, and by some violent smiles I managed to get her up into the street away from that bad place. For compensation of her feelings, I took her by the hand and pressed and rubbed it nicely as we walked along the paving-stones. Then what should I hear, rising up from underneath my feet, but the sound of real authentic African song and drumming. A door said, 'The Beni Bronze', and I pulled Miss Theodora down the steps before she quite knew what.

Just think of my pleasure when I found it was a genuine, five-drum combination, and hardly had I parked Miss Theodora on a seat beside the bar when I stepped across the floor through all the dancers and asked the band leader (who was bald on his head as any ostrich egg) if I could sit in at the bongos for a moment, at which I am quite a product. He gave his permission with a weary smile, and I asked the young bongo player, as I wedged his sweet instrument between my thighs, what this leader's name was. 'Cuthbertson,' this boy said. 'Generally called Cranium.'

I think to their surprise my performance gave some pleasure, and as soon as we'd ended I asked this Mr Cranium to come over to the bar. Theodora, I could see, was not very glad at the use I was making of the wad of notes she'd given me, and tried some attempt to pay herself, which I soon avoided. (I do hate those women fishing in their handbags. *No* woman will ever pay a drink for me—unless I hold her money for her beforehand.)

'And how is our African style appreciated in this country?' I enquired of Mr Cuthbertson.

'Just little,' he replied with sorrow. 'Only our people like it, and some few white; but West Indians and Americans—well, they like something less artistic and dynamic.'

'So you've not done so well in England, Mr Cranium?'

'I tell you something, Mr Man. Before I leave home five years ago, I dream that one day I have a lovely wife, three lovely children and a lot of money.' Here he pulled out some snapshots from his hip. 'Well, I got the lovely wife, the beautiful children too, as you can see, but, man, that loot just fails to come my way.'

This gave me a wonderful idea.

'What you require,' I said to Cranium, 'is contacts in the highest type of Jumble high-life. Well, tonight this lady here and I are going to a most special voodoo party, and why don't you come along with us and play some numbers that will win you good engagements?'

Cuthbertson thought this was a rare idea, full of brilliant possibilities; but Theodora was not pleased to hear I planned to take her to a party without asking her approval. As I waited for the club to close, I had to surmount all her oppositions by pouring gins in heavy sequence down her throat.

The address that Tamberlaine the West Indian had given me was in the fashionable area of that Marble Arch: but there's fashion and there's fashion, and none of us quite expected such a glorious block of similar flats. The doorman examined our little group, especially Cranium's combination, carrying their instruments, and would possibly have been an obstacle if Theodora (who has just that haughty way some Jumble ladies use back home to drive our people mad with hatred) hadn't kicked him round the hallway with her tongue, and got us all into a lift built to hold only five. The boys rubbed up against her in their gratitude for her display.

'Who is our host, Johnny?' she asked me.

'Theodora, if only I knew that!'

But no need to worry. It was that kind of party that once you're there, and look glamorous or in some way particular, they welcome you with happiness and push a bottle in your hand. As soon as they'd tanked themselves up a bit, the boys led by Cranium went into action, and Tamberlaine got hold of me to introduce me to our host.

'This man's a counsel in the courts of law,' he told me, 'called Mr Wesley Vial. Observe his appearance—like an eagle. Very precarious to be his victim in the dock, man, but full of charm and generosity as a hostess.'

'A hostess, Tamberlaine?'

'Well, you understand me, man.'

Mr Vial was fat, too fat, his flesh was coloured cream, his eyes sharp green, his hands most hairy and his feet small as any child's. He wore a pleated shirt that was some shirt, and when he shook my hand he held it up and looked at it like it was some precious diamond.

'You've lovely finger-nails,' he said.

'My toe-nails also have been much admired,' I told him.

'You're a witty boy as well as handsome. Now I do like that!'

The other guests of Mr Vial's were strange and fanciful—the whites very richly dressed, whether men or women, and the coloured so splendid I guessed they'd be Americans in show business at least. And this I soon learned was so, when Larry the G.I. appeared with some of this star material from the bathroom. 'Huntley,' he said, 'is going to act a dance.' And out came a naked boy wrapped round with toilet paper, who pranced among the guests and furniture, which most seemed delighted by—not me. These Americans!

A fierce voice said into my ear, 'Now listen, Johnny! Why have you brought Theodora here?'

This was Montgomery, bursting with fire and indignation.

7

Voodoo in an unexpected setting

'MONTY,' HE SAID, 'you really must cease to act the elder brother to me. I have one already, called Mr Christmas Fortune.'

'Don't call me "Monty".'

'Then what is all this, please, Mr Montgomery?'

'You're playing on Theodora's feelings to no purpose.'

'Well, if you say so, man.'

'And sponging on her too, for all I know.'

'Man,' said Johnny sullenly, 'you beat my time. What can I say to calm your interference?'

'And please,' I went desperately on, 'don't use those awful English phrases they taught you in Lagos high school.'

'Lagos high,' he said, 'is maybe better than is Birmingham low.'

'I must warn you, Johnny, if you trifle with Theodora, I'll take steps.'

'Oh, you win, man. What is it you'll do to me—you make me one dead duck?'

And away he went, indifferent and debonair, to rejoin Theodora, who, crouched like a flamingo on a cushion, was holding a little court of coloured boys lying round her, relaxed, inquisitive and amused. She was treating them to a display of mental pyrotechnics which delighted them as an athletic performance, however little note they took of what she said. And though her questions and observations were outrageous, they took no offence because they recognized in Theodora what I had never thought her to be—a natural.

Her chief interlocutor was a bland West Indian called Tamberlaine; who said:

'Oh, calm you English are, certainly, Miss Theodora, like a corpse is, and reliable, as you say; but always reliable for what no man could desire: like making sure he pays his income tax instalments highly punctually.'

'But what you haven't got,' said Norbert Salt (reluctant to see this

West Indian steal his American thunder), 'is the social graces and spontaneous conduct we're renowned for. Also,' he said, rising to his feet and clasping Moscow Gentry by the hands, 'you've not got our glorious beauty. See now, what a beautiful race we are!'

The pair posed in an arabesque, like the bronze group above the entrance to some splendid building.

'I'd like also to rebuke you, if you'll permit me,' Tamberlaine went on, his voice rising higher to attract eyes from the arabesque, 'for the peculiar observations you English make to we people in public houses, omnibuses, and elsewhere.'

'For instance?' said Theodora, resolutely impartial, her spectacles aglint.

Tamberlaine ran to the door, and reappeared wearing a bowler hat and an umbrella. 'Now I shall show you,' he announced, 'a conversation between myself and some kind English gentleman. This gentleman, he say to me' (Tamberlaine's accent became the oddest mixture of West Indian and deep Surrey) ' "I do envy you fellows your wonderful teeth." To which I reply in my mind, if not with my voice' (Tamberlaine removed the bowler), ' "Well, sir, me don't envy you your yellow horse-fangs, and if you look clearly down my throat, you'll see most of me back ones anyway is gold." '

The performance was applauded. 'Go on,' said Theodora, seemingly unmoved.

'Or else,' Tamberlaine continued, 'he come up to me and say' (bowler on), ' "Don't you miss the hot weather over here?" '

'Oh, no, man, no, not that familiar saying!' cried several voices.

'Sometimes,' the West Indian dramatist proceeded, 'this Englishman is a more serious person, with a feeling of sorrow for past wrongs committed. In this case, he will raise his hat to me and say, "I think, sir, that conditions in the Union of South Africa are a scandal." To which I inwardly reply, "Then please go there and tell Mr Strijdom of your sentiments." Or else he will look very sad and sorrowful and tell me, "You may find, sir, that there is sometimes a certain prejudice in England, but believe me, sir, that some of us are just as worried about it as you." '

Laughter and renewed applause.

'Let me tell you,' cried Norbert, snatching the stage from Tamberlaine, 'what's the craziest thing of all they say. Is this.' He wheeled, returned with a mincing step, torso rigid, legs flaying like mad stilts, stopped dead, and said, ' "I like coloured people, myself." '

'That one,' said Moscow Gentry, 'wins top prize for pure impossibility.'

Theodora was displeased: even saddened, I thought, as if at last minding more for generosity than for justice.

'You're all very unfair,' she said. 'You must remember our people often mean well, and are only shy. Often they *do* like you, and want to help you if they can, but just don't know how to tell you.'

Tamberlaine looked slightly vicious: he no doubt felt he'd got her on the run.

'Well, lady,' he said, 'all that may be. But please remember this. We're not interested in what your kind ideas about us are, but chiefly in your personal behaviour. We even prefer the man who doesn't want to help us, but is nice and easy with us, to one who wants to lecture us for our benefit.'

There was a loud clap of a pair of hands. Mr Vial stood on an occasional table in the middle of the room, supported round the hips by willing hands of manicured white guests and long Caribbean fingers.

'Miss Isabel Cornwallis,' he announced, 'has telephoned to say she can't be with us.' There were polite, disappointed cries of 'Ah!' Mr. Vial hung his head as if dejected; then, raising it up, with a bald, beaming glare, he cried, 'But the voodoo will take place all the same!'

The lights went out.

A hand took mine. 'It's all right, hon',' the voice said. 'I'm Louisiana.'

'What's going on?'

'You'll see. Sit down here. Cornwallis never meant to come—this party's not up to her degree of expectation.'

'How does she know it's not?'

'I called her up at her hotel to say so. I'm her spy, you see, in the company. I keep her informed of what's going on.'

An Anglepoise lamp, operated by the dim, green cheeks of Mr Vial, shone on the naked torso of the dancer Jupiter, who stood immobile. Hercule La Bataille and Hippolyte Dieudonné entered, carrying what looked to be a cat in a waste-paper basket. The two

Haitians knelt on either side of the basket (which they had up-ended, cat inside), and, with Jupiter towering motionless above, began chanting. It was wonderful to look at for a while, but it went on, and on, and on, and on, and on. The white guests, and even the West Indians, became restive. A Caribbean voice said, 'When you going to slay this pussy, now, man? We want some whisky down our throats.' Unmoved, the Haitians chanted. 'It usually lasts an hour,' Louisiana whispered, 'before they kill the animal.' Really, I thought! Even for the sake of higher mysteries, I can't allow that; and was about to do something inelegant and British, when I was anticipated by Theodora, who strode briskly from the floor, seized cat and basket from between the Haitians, and stumbled off into the gloom.

The three performers looked nonplussed and shocked. The lights came on, and our host Mr Vial, his face really 'distorted with fury', as they say, cried out, 'What does that bitch think she's doing?'

'She ain't no bitch, she's my lady,' said Johnny Fortune. 'Is me who bring her here.'

'You little bastard,' said Mr Vial.

Johnny reached up and pulled the knot of Mr Vial's blue bow tie undone. 'You sure you not say, "little *black* bastard"?' he asked the lawyer mildly.

Mr Vial bulldozed his face into a smile. 'Just little bastard,' he said gently.

'Oh, well, I'm legitimate, so there must be some mistake,' said Johnny. 'I see you again some day soon, my mister.' He followed Theodora out of the room.

There was a pause in the proceedings, and a certain amount of hard looks and shuffling. 'I guess everyone,' said Larry the G.I., 'is behaving most peculiar. Why don't we put on some discs and dance?'

I found myself sitting next to the star performer Huntley, who had removed the lavatory paper he had pranced in, and attired himself, instead, in a pair of Austrian *lederhosen* he had found in his host's bedroom. 'These niggers,' he said. 'It's always the same when you have them at a party.'

'But, excuse me, you . . .'

'Oh, I work in a coloured company, sure, and half of me belongs to them, I guess, but they're just so dreadful! So hopeless, so dreadful! There's always this confusion whenever they're around. Man, they can't even *work*—and I should know, I'm their ballet master. "Work like niggers"—whoever thought up that one?' He drank a glass of neat whisky and arose. 'I just can't bear them,' he said. 'I'm going back to sleep at my hotel. I've bought me a marmoset here in this city, and it's better company to me than they are.'

The party, it seemed to me, was deteriorating. I rose to go also, but was overtaken by Norbert Salt and his friend Moscow Gentry.

'Moscow and I,' said Norbert, 'have been thinking. And what we think is, it would be cheaper for us if instead of spending money at our hotel, we moved in with you. Now, you've got an apartment, haven't you?'

'That is, if it's not too far out from the city centre,' said Moscow Gentry.

I handed them the keys. 'If I ring the bell,' I said, 'I hope you'll be kind enough to let me in.'

'Oh, sure.'

'And thanks.'

In the hall there was a white boy in a barman's jacket, reading an evening paper and sipping a glass of wine. He looked up.

'I think I've seen you earlier,' he said.

'Yes? I don't remember.'

'My name's Alfy Bongo.'

'I don't remember you.'

'I work here for Mr Vial on special evenings,' said this person, taking me with two fingers by the arm. 'He's a very much nicer man than you might think.'

'And so, I'm sure, are you,' I said to Alfy Bongo, as I opened the mortice lock of Mr Vial's front door.

8

Theodora languishes, not quite in vain

THIS MISS THEODORA! Outside the Vial man's flat, I found her with the cat, two legs in each hand, searching the late darkness for a taxi. 'Let me take it for you, please,' I said to her. 'You don't want it to scratch you on your nylon blouses.'

'They're not nylon,' she said to me, and I saw she was in tears.

I took the animal.

'We walk a bit together, you and me,' I said, 'and get the fresh air in our weary choke-up lungs.'

'You'll catch cold without a coat on.'

'Me? I'm hearty! Walking warms up the circulation.'

After a silent while, she said, 'I suppose you think I oughtn't to have done that, Johnny.'

'Is for you to judge. Each man is jury of his own actions—even women.'

'I didn't mind all that much about the cat, but I couldn't bear them all enjoying themselves so much.'

This cat was wriggling, so I shoved it inside my shirt and buttoned it. 'Ju-ju is ju-ju,' I replied. 'Surely, is best to stay away from watching it, or, if you come, not interfere.'

'But you took me there to see it.'

A remark how like a woman!

'African ju-ju, or Haitian voodoo,' I explained to her, 'is not to be despised like you do through your ignorance. Medical science is, of course, a European discovery, as we know when we buy our spectacles, or have the appendix out. But living and dying is also very much a mystery of the mind that ju-ju understands.'

With my conversation, and the night air, she was recovering her usual sharp brain. 'According to what I read,' she said, 'the latest European opinion bears you out.'

A taxi sailed by, cruising cautious, slow, and eager for custom like a prostitute would do. I hailed it, and opened up the door. 'Here is your quadruped,' I said. 'What will you call it?'

'You choose a name.'

I took the cat beneath the taxi headlamps to examine it for sex. 'Tungi,' I said, 'is a nice name for a boy.' I handed it back, but she grabbed my arm as well as Tungi when I did so. 'Come home with me, please,' she asked, 'just for a while.'

I know what 'for a while' means, once a chick's got you inside her front door . . . and I wasn't eager for any close association with this not so young, young lady. All the same, she'd given me the twenty pounds, and perhaps she might be helpful to me on some later occasion. I climbed in and took the cat again, to make sure I had a good excuse not to hold whatever else that might be offered.

'And how is Muriel?' she said, in that voice women use to hide their disapproval.

'Muriel is well. Her health is good.'

'Are you fond of her, Johnny?'

' "Fond of" is not some words I use. Either is "love" or "not love" in my language.'

"So you love Muriel, then.'

'Well, yes, I do. She makes me quite mad with all her practical remarks and weepings, but I have some love for Muriel, that's certain.'

'So you'll get married soon?'

'Who said I would? Did I say so?' The cat was wriggling once more—I slapped it. 'Any conversation about loving a woman,' I exclaimed, 'ends up always with some talk by her of marriage.'

'Excuse me, Johnny.'

'Oh, I excuse you, naturally.'

This argument gave me excellent reasons for saying my farewell to her once delivered safely at her address; but when the cab stopped, she asked me to dig some earth up from the little garden there outside the rails. 'For the cat,' she said. 'He'll need a tray upstairs. Just bring it up, will you, when you've done? I'll leave the door open.'

This woman beats my time! I gathered up two handfuls, kicked the door closed behind me, and climbed three steps up at a jump, leaving trailings and spots of dirty earth upon the landings. Inside her room, the lights were already on, the radio in operation, and she was pouring out some drink in quite a hurry.

'Where is this tray?' I cried.

'What tray?'

'For Tungi your dear cat, Miss Theodora. Or shall I lay this soil upon this sofa?'

'Oh, don't be so angry with me, Johnny. I know men don't like being asked to do a menial task.'

Didn't that make it worse? She handed me some drink. I gulped it, then said, 'Goodbye, Miss Theodora, Montgomery would not approve if I should stay.'

'Him? He's nothing to me! He'll be out drinking somewhere, anyway.'

'Nothing to you, you say. Am I then something?'

This chilly lady, all skin and eagerness and spectacles, now flung herself upon me like some jaguar, and covered me in tears and kisses. I could not speak even until I'd wrestled her away. 'It's not always Spades, then,' I shouted out, 'who try to seduce white ladies, like they say.'

At this remark of mine, which I agree was not a gentleman's, like it wasn't meant to be, she stood up, smoothed all her body down, and said, 'Accept my apologies. I'm making myself just a little cheap.'

'If you say so, lady—but I didn't.'

'Don't call me "lady"!'

She was so pale and furious. 'All right, all right, Miss Theodora.'

'Or "Miss" anything.'

'Okay, Theodora. Just play cool.'

She picked up her spectacles from the floor, where they had fallen, and propped her lean body against the fireplace.

'All right,' she said. 'You know I'm in love with you, and you're not with me, and I'm not fool enough not to know that makes me just a nuisance. All that I ask you, though, is . . . that if I promise there will be no more scenes like this one, you'll stay a friend of mine.'

'Of course. I'm everybody's friend.'

'Oh, don't be so cruel! After all, I've helped you once already, and it's possible—in fact, it's very possible—I may have to do so once again.'

I got up.

'You gave me loot, yes,' I said. 'You want it back? Well, I'll have to owe it, because I need it.' And I went towards the door.

'Oh, come back,' she said. 'Let's stop quarrelling, and have a drink.'

This seemed quite reasonable to me. We clicked both our glasses, and both sat politely down.

'Even if you don't marry Muriel . . .' she began.

'Must we still speak of that?'

'Yes, because a practical matter's involved. Even if you don't marry her, she may have children.'

'One child she certainly will have.'

'Already?'

'So she has said to me.'

She frowned like some prime minister. 'When you people get independence,' she said sharp, 'we'd better change our immigration laws. Otherwise we'll soon have a half-caste population.'

'Like in the West Indian Islands, or even in parts of Africa.'

'People here don't understand what's happening.'

'Then when they do, what splendid opportunities they will have! Always you preach in England against colour bars in other countries! Now you can practise what you preach at home.'

'They just don't realize that you're here to stay. They think you're all here just temporarily.'

'Then they must learn.'

'I suppose we must.'

She reached for a note-pad and made some note on it. 'For your radio programme?' I enquired.

She nodded. 'Why won't you marry Muriel?' she said.

'For many reasons. Is a bad family, is one.'

'You mean her sister Dorothy?'

'For example, her: I do not wish a sister-in-law who is a prostitute.'

'How did she become one in the first place?'

'How should I know? Ask Mr Whispers. These boys meet some foolish chick at a dance. They take her home and give her the good time. Then suddenly—the smiles all disappear, also the money. The chick is afraid to go home to her mother. And so she accepts to step out on the streets and be agreeable . . .'

'And what do they earn?'

'The girls? Now, Theodora! Are these informations also for your broadcast programmes?'

'No, I'm just curious. Don't tell me if you don't want to.'

'A hundred pounds a week or more, if she is sharp. . . . If less than twenty a day is brought, the man will beat her.'

'What man?'

'The ponce. Her man.'

'Does he take everything?'

'If she keeps even one shilling from him, he will beat her.'

'But in return, he protects her?'

'No—not at all. She does not do her business in the house where they both live. . . . What happens outside is not his concern at all. His only thought is to be where they live at daylight to collect his loot. . . .'

'Then what does she get out of it all?'

'She? Love, so she thinks. Also the power to hold him, through fear of the Law, even though he takes everything from her.'

'And he?'

'He gets the good time: nice suits, and drinks, and taxi fares, and money to gamble all way. They never save it.'

'And can they separate if they want to?'

'The one who first will wish to leave will be the partner who is stronger. If the chick is making a good business, she can turn her eye on a new boy. Or the man may grow up to be a fashion among those women, and all then will try to steal him from his girl. Dorothy, for example: she now wishes to leave Billy Whispers, so I hear.'

'To go to whom?'

'I have been kindly suggested by her.'

'You'd not do that. . . .'

'Me? No, thank you. I have my family to think of, and my blood.'

'What will Billy Whispers do if she should go?'

'Use the razor on Dorothy, I should say. Unless she first shops him to such police officers as Mr Inspector Purity.'

'But if she does, the case must be proved in court?'

'With the woman as witness, that is not difficult at all. But when the man comes out of his jail again, that chick should leave town by the first train she can catch.'

I finished my drink, and held out my hand to thank her. 'Telephone me, Johnny,' she said. 'You've got the number.'

'I will.'

'You promise?'

'I do.'

'Kiss me goodbye.'

While holding her, I thought of Dorothy and Billy, and whether I should not go down to Brixton and advise that little Gambian to turn his Miss Dorothy loose before the trouble started. These serious thoughts were interrupted by Miss Theodora, who was saying in my ear, 'Won't you just once, Johnny? I promise I'll never ask you ever again. . . .'

Oh dear, this female person! Where was her modesty? 'Oh well, if you feel so bad,' I said to her. 'Where is it you keep your bedroom in this flat?'

9

The Blake Street gamble-house

WHEN I LEFT Mr Vial's party, I wandered across the silent reaches of Mayfair, which, in the middle night, looked like crissed-crossed canals where the water of life had drained away. In a vast, sad, dramatic square, I paused in the lamp- and moonlight, and gazed at the blue foliage of huge, languishing trees. I took out a cigarette. 'Light, Mr Pew?' said someone. 'You don't remember me?' the voice continued. 'I thought we'd be meeting again before too long.'

'You're acting mysteriously, whoever you are. You must be a member of the secret service.'

'As a matter of fact, that's what I thought you might possible be.

I turned, and saw Detective-Inspector Purity of the C.I.D. He was wearing a tuxedo with a considerable air, had his hands in his coat pockets, and an empty pipe clenched between his teeth. 'I'm out and about around the clubs tonight,' he said. 'Routine check-up, that's all it is. As I was saying. I know it's not my concern, but I thought you were doing special work of one kind or another.'

'Did you?'

He came rather nearer and put the pipe in his breast pocket. 'It stands to reason, Mr Pew, that someone from the service must be keeping an eye on these coloured folk, and I saw at once an official like yourself wouldn't be mucking in with them like you did that night we picked you up, unless you had your cover story ready....'

'If I were what you suggest, of course I wouldn't tell you.'

'Naturally... though I could always try to check.... But it's clear as daylight someone is watching these colonials—the troublesome elements among them. First the Maltese come, then the Cypriots, and now this lot! They don't make the copper's task any the easier.'

'You find that colonials are more trouble than the natives?'

'What natives? Oh, I see what you mean. No, I don't suppose so, really... but it's a new problem. When they come unstuck, of course, they get more publicity in the Press than ours do. But I don't suppose their criminality is out of all proportion. . . . It's just that they're there, you see.'

'I'll say good night to you.'

'Yes, I thought we'd be meeting again,' Inspector Purity said, falling in alongside as I moved away. 'You've been to a party, I expect?'

'That's right.'

'Good one? Jolly? There are some very nice flats around the Marble Arch . . .' He stopped a minute. 'By the way, you didn't mind me asking you what I did?'

'About my job? I've left the Colonial Department, as it happens.'

'Yes, I heard that—word gets around.' He sounded pleased. 'And now you're just a private person.'

'That's it.'

'Doing nothing so very special at all, you'd say. Well, that's interesting to know.'

We went on some way in silence. He had the art which coppers have of inserting his personality, unwelcomed and uninvited, into your own.

'And how's young Mr Fortune?'

'Who?'

'Come on, now. You know who I'm speaking of.'

I stopped. 'Is this an official interview?'

'Not exactly. No, I wouldn't say so.'

'Then good night.'

'So you have seen something of him? I thought perhaps you had. He's a nice boy, in his way.' Mr Purity took his hands from his pockets and slapped his flanks. 'I have my duty to get on with,' he said briskly. 'We never rest.' He walked on ahead and turned the corner. When I reached it, there was no sign of him.

I crossed the neutral ground of Regent Street into the upper regions of Soho. The eighteenth-century houses looked graceful, mouldering and aloof. Beside an electric power station, that had intruded itself among them, I stopped: and wondered whether the time had not now come to 'cut out', as Johnny Fortune might have said, from the society of the Spades. They were wonderful, of course—exhilarating: the temperature of your life shot up when in their company. But if you stole some of their physical vitality, you found that the price was they began to invade your soul: or rather, they did not, but your own idea of them did—for they were sublimely indifferent to anything outside themselves! And in spite of their *joie de vivre*, in any practical sense they were so impossible! 'They're dreadful! They're just quite dreadful!' I shouted out aloud, above the slight hum of the dynamos.

I turned some corners, and under a lamp saw Africans squatting on their haunches on the pavement. I stepped out on the street to make a circuit, but was hailed by one who ran crying after me, 'Lend me two pounds, man, or even one!' It was Johnny's half-brother, Arthur.

'Hullo, Arthur. What goes on there?'

'We're throwing dice. I lose a bit . . .'

'Here in the street?'

'What's wrong with here?'

'Doesn't anyone interfere?'

'Oh, we take care. We're barred at Mr Obo-King's, you see, and can't play there.'

'Mr Obo-King?'

'He owns the Blake Street gamble-house. You'll find some people you know there, if you go.'

'What number in Blake Street is it?'

'I forget the number, man, but here on this envelope it's written.' He pulled out a crumpled one on which I saw:

> Mr Arthur,
> by the Blake Street Gamble-house,
> London, Soho.

The postmark was from Manchester.

'Somebody wrote this to you there?'

'Yes, man, a friend. He plays clarinet Moss Side.

'And this got delivered?'

'Oh, everyone knows the gamble-house. It's raided regular week-ends.'

'Don't they ever close it?'

'Why should they, so long as Mr Obo-King pays his fines, and makes his little presents to the Law? Mr Obo owns several places, and they're never closed. The Law likes to keep them open, so it knows where to look for everybody.'

I gave him ten shillings. 'Best of luck,' I said.

He snatched it, and cried: 'Never say "Good luck" to any gambler! You not know that?'

'No. Sorry.'

'You see my brother Johnny?'

'Earlier on.'

'I must get to meet him again soon. This man owes me everything. I feel real sore about him.'

He ran back to the circle without thanks.

I went on to Blake Street; and only then realized that Arthur's envelope, after all, had no number on it. I walked up and down, and could find no sign of what looked to be a club, when out of the area steps from a basement I saw a coloured man cautiously emerge and, as he walked towards me, recognized Larry the G.I.

'Man, that sure was some bum evening at Mr Vial's,' he said. 'I pulled out fast when I saw how it was shaping. They was having an orgy when I left, but me, I don't care for these pig-parties or gang-bangs whatsoever.'

'Where have you been just now, Larry?'

'In and out of the gamble-house, to get me some bit of loot.'

'Did you play in there?'

'What, me? Among all those Africans when they're throwing dice? Man, are you crazy? They'd eat me. A soldier can tell dynamite when he sees it.'

'But you went in there alone?'

'Oh, no, that Tamberlaine came with me. West Indians I can partly understand, but not these African ancestors of mine.'

'How did you get the money, then?'

'Sad—but I had to sell my knife. No other way to get myself back to base. But I'll find me another there.' He shook my hands. 'So I'll be seeing you,' he said. 'Norbert and Moscow has given me your phone number where they're moving in.'

I walked up the road, and went down the gamble-house steps. The door in the area was open, and there was no one inside to stop you going in. At the end of a dim-lit corridor was another door. I was going to open it, when from inside came shouts and clatterings, two men ran out and started fighting in the area. There was a horrid scream and whimper, and quick, noisy footsteps on the metal stair up to the street. Someone had fallen at the foot of them. I ran over. 'Can I help you? Are you hurt?' I cried out.

By the light from the inner door, I could see this man was bleeding. He tilted his face, and I saw Jimmy Cannibal. He gave me a look of intense dislike, crawled to his feet, and lurched slowly up the stair. A voice from behind me said, 'Who's you?'

I turned, and saw a very fat man in a fur-lined jerkin.

'That boy's been wounded. What should we do?'

He said nothing, and struck a match under the stair. I saw him pick up a knife. He looked at me, still holding it. 'Who's you?' he said again.

'A friend of Johnny Fortune's.'

'I think I hear about you. What did you see out here?'

'You know what I saw. A fight.'

'Is best you saw nothing.' He picked up a piece of newspaper, and wrapped the knife in it. 'Who did attack him? You saw that?'

'No. It was too quick.'

'Is best you saw nothing, then. You come inside now?'

'I don't think I will.'

'Best you come in till they scatter up there in the street. Give them the time to scatter.'

He propelled me in, and shut the outer door. We stood in the dim corridor.

'How's Johnny? That boy got some loot again just now?'

'Not much.'

'He ought to get some, then. A boy like him could make some easy, and then lose it all to me.' He let out a laugh as big as his body. 'And you, are you loaded?'

'I have some money, yes.'

'Come inside, then. I give you some good excitement before you say goodbye to it.'

'Are you Mr Obo-King?'

'That's what they call me. They should so, is my name.'

He led the way into a large room with little chairs and tables where chicken and rice and foo-foo were being served. Some boys were playing a juke-box, and Mr Obo-King called to one of them, 'Take a bucket out there, man. There's some mess to wash away.' He turned again to me. 'The gambling's through here. In this next door.'

'I'll come in later. I want to eat.'

Mr Obo-King looked at me. 'Then come later. I give you some good excitement before I skin you.'

I sat down, asked for foo-foo, and looked around. Some of the men and women were dressed like birds of paradise, so that you'd turn and look at them in the street; though down here they seemed right enough, in spite of the resolute squalor of the place, and even though other customers were in the last degrees of destitution. A few seemed to have camped there for the night, for they'd kipped down on window-shelves and tables, snoring, or dreaming, possibly, of 'back home'. A short boy with a pale blue-green pasty face and enormous eyes came up and said, 'Buy me a meal, man.' As I called for it, he suddenly lifted his sweater and showed me, on his naked stomach underneath, an enormous lump. 'Hospital can do nothing—what is the future?' he said, and carried his plate away. From time to time customers emerged, always disconsolate, from the gambling room, and started long public post-mortems on their disasters. Soon the West Indian Tamberlaine came out, and said to the company in general, 'Well, I not had much, see, so I not lose much.' He spotted me, and accepted an offer of coffee. 'So voodoo is not for you,' he said. 'Perhaps you like this place better.'

'Who comes here mostly, Mr Tamberlaine?'

'If white like yourself, they's wreckage of jazz musicians, chiefly, a lot on the needle and full of despair; if coloured, well, ponces and other hustlers like myself.'

'You're a hustler, then?'

'You might say I pimp around the town, picking the pounds up where I can. I don't often gamble, though, because the winner is the table, and like all these boys I never know when to stop if fortune does the bitch on me like she do. But coloureds like gambling, don't you see—it's part of our care-free nature.'

He gave me a sarcastic grin. 'Who gambles mostly?' I said. 'Africans or West Indians?'

'What! You recognize some difference? Ain't we all just coal-black coloured skins to you?'

'Don't be offensive, Mr Tamberlaine. Like so many West Indians I've met, you seem to have, if I may say so, a large chip sitting on your shoulder.'

'Not like your African friends? They have less chip, you say?'

'Much less. Africans seem much more self-assured, more self-sufficient. They don't seem to fear we're going to take liberties with them, or patronize them, as you people do.'

'Do we now!'

'Yes, you do. Africans don't seem to care what anyone thinks of them. So even though they're more clannish and secretive, they're easier to talk to.'

Mr Tamberlaine considered this. 'Listen to me, man,' he said. 'If we's more sensitive like you say, there's reasons for it. Our islands is colonies of great antiquity, and our mother tongue is English, like your own, and not some dialects. So naturally we expect you treat us like we're British as yourself, and when you don't, we suffer and go sour. Why should we not? But Africans—what do they care of British? For African, his passport just don't mean nothing, except for travel, but for us it's loyalty.'

I couldn't resist a dig. I'd had, after all, to take so many myself in recent months. 'I think,' I said, 'it's easier for them than it is for you. They know what they are, and you're not sure. They belong much more deeply to Africa than you do to the Caribbean.'

'My ears is pointed in your direction,' said Mr Tamberlaine, sipping his coffee, 'for some more ripe instruction.'

'Here it comes, then. They speak their own private tongues, their lives are rooted in their ancient tribes, so that even when they're lonely or miserable here they feel they're sustained by the solid tribal past at home. But you, you're wanderers, cut off by centuries from Africa where you first came from, and ready to move off again from your stepping-stones strung out across the sea.'

'Our islands is stepping-stones? Thank you now, for what you call them so.'

'Wouldn't you all move on to North or South America, if they'd let you in?'

'Well, yes, perhaps we would, the way they treat us here, and how it is back home.'

'You see, then. You're not sure what you are—African, Caribbean, or American—and so you're quite ready to be British.'

'Thank you for the compliment to our patriotism. So many of our boy who serve in R.A.F. would gladly hear your words.'

I saw the conversation wasn't a success, and apologized to Mr Tamberlaine. 'I'm just saying what I think—excuse me if it gives offence.'

Mr Tamberlaine smiled politely. 'Is no offence, man. You say what's in your mind, and that's your liberty. What's certain, anyway, is that we're different, Africans and we. We don't mix much, except when we stand shoulder to shoulder against the white.'

He got up, put on his tailored duffel coat, and said, 'Now I must get out in the cold and do me pimpin'. You're not interested in anything I have to offer, I suppose?'

'Such as what, Mr Tamberlaine?'

'A little coloured lady for you? You go with her, and add to your education of these different races.'

'All right. Is it far?'

'We go down Brixton way, man, and see there. I hope you have money for the taxi, there's no all-night bus.'

10

In Billy Whispers' domain

TAMBERLAINE WAS BORED AND SILENT on the journey, except for occasional altercations with the taxi driver, to whom he gave a succession of imprecise addresses ('take us just by that football ground, that's by that Tube station, cabby, and then I'll tell you . . .'). We reached the area of chain-store windows, parks fit for violations, and squat overhanging railway bridges, all bathed in a livid phosphorescent glare, when Tamberlaine rapped the glass and shouted, 'Here now! Here!', as if the driver should have known our final destination. Tamberlaine strolled away, leaving me to settle, while the driver exhaled his spleen. 'These darkies should go back home,' he said, 'and never have come here in the first place.'

'They tip well, don't they?'

'Either they do, or they run off without paying. But it's the way they speak to you. Calling me "cabby"!'

Tamberlaine had turned a corner, and I followed him into a tottering street of late Victorian houses, where lights, despite the lateness of the hour, were shining through many a green or crimson curtain. 'This is your London Harlem,' he said to me. 'Our Caribbean home from home. We try this one,' and he climbed some chipped steps beneath a portico, knocked loud, and rang.

A head and shoulders protruded from above. 'Is Tamberlaine,' he shouted. 'Gloria, is she there?'

'No, man. Is here, but not available.'

'Aurora, now, is she there?'

'No, man. You come too late to see her.'

We tried at several other houses, without success, till the vexation of a wounded professional pride was heard in Tamberlaine's voice. 'Is nothing more to do,' he said, 'but go back to the north of London —unless you don't fear to call upon an African, which after what you say, you shouldn't.'

'If you don't, why should I?'

'This house is one of Billy Whispers', who's the devil.

'Oh, I know him.'

'You do, now?' Tamberlaine seemed mildly impressed. 'Come, then, let we go.'

It started to snow, and my West Indian Mercury pulled the hood of his duffel up over his head, drove his hands deep in the pockets, and walked on just in front of me, like some Arctic explorer heading resolutely for the Pole. After twists and turns, of which he gave no warning, we reached a bombed lot with some wreckage of buildings on it. Tamberlaine plunged down the area steps, and beat with his fingertips on the window. A voice cried, 'Say who!', and when he did, Mr Tamberlaine walked inside, and left me standing there.

After five minutes of waiting in the area, and five more strolling round the street outside, I decided to call it a day, and started off up the street. But steps came running after me. I heard a cry of 'Hey, man!', and turned to see not Tamberlaine, but Mr Ronson Lighter. He shook hands, caught me by the sleeve, and said, 'Is all right, you can come. There is a party to celebrate one boy come out of prison, but Billy say you welcome when you come.'

We climbed two floors into a large room, festively crowded, that overlooked the street. Ronson dragged me to a buffet where, under the watchful eyes of a bodyguard of three, stood piles of bottles in disarray, and plates of uninviting sandwiches. 'Give this man drink,' said Ronson. 'Is Billy say so.' One bodyguard, aloof until these words, poured out a beer glass full of whisky.

Some of the guests I knew by sight, and others even better still: there were Johnny's former landlord, 'Nat King' Cole, and the African youth, Tondapo, with whom he'd quarrelled at the Sphere, and little Barbara, the half-caste girl of the memorable evening at the Moonbeam club; and also a contingent from Mr Vial's disrupted party, among them Mr Cranium Cuthbertson and his musicians, and the dubious Alfy Bongo. Arthur was there, strolling from group to group unwelcome, with his restless smiles; and enthroned on a divan, surrounded by fierce eager faces, his handsome, debauched half-sister Dorothy. Alone by the fire, as if a guest at his own entertainment, was Billy Whispers; and Mr Tamberlaine, like a suppliant at the levee of the paramount chief, was deep in conversation with him.

Mr Ronson Lighter led me over. 'Good evening, Mr Whispers,' I said, raising my voice above the clamour. 'It's very kind of you to ask me in.'

'My party is for this boy,' said Billy Whispers, pointing with glass in hand to a huge and handsome African, who positively dripped and oozed with mindless masculine animal magnetism and natural villainy, and who now was dancing, proud and sedate, round the room with Dorothy.

'He came out yesterday,' said Tamberlaine. 'This is his home-coming among his people, but the boy is sore. His girl was not true to him while he was away; but as you can see, he's a type of boy who soon will find another.'

Billy Whispers was looking at me closely: with those eyes which fastened on your own like grappling-hooks, and lured and absorbed your psyche into the indifferent, uncensorious depths of his own malignancy. 'Tamberlaine say to me,' he remarked, 'that earlier you see Jimmy Cannibal.'

'Yes. There was a fight at Mr Obo-King's.'

'You see who fight him?' asked Ronson Lighter, with an excess of indifference.

'No. Do you know who it was?'

'I? Why should I know?'

'You not tell nobody you see this?' said Billy Whispers.

'No, not yet.'

'Is true, I hope.'

There was a crack like a plate breaking, and a yell. Whispers went over to a group. Someone was hustled out. 'To fight at a sociable gathering,' said Mr Tamberlaine, 'is so uncivilized.'

Dorothy stood in front of me, posturing like someone in an historic German film. 'Hullo there, stranger,' she said. 'Long time no see. How is my little sister Muriel and her boy friend?' I smiled at her, and didn't answer. 'Oh, snooty,' she said. 'Sarcastic and superior,' and she stalked off in a garish blaze of glory.

During this conversation, I saw Alfy Bongo eyeing me in his equivocal way: with all the appearance of deviousness and cunning, yet openly enough to let you see he knew you realized he was up to something. He sidled over and said, 'We meet again, Mr Montgomery Pew. Two fishes in the troubled water.'

He sat down beside me. 'The rumour about me with those who

just don't know,' he went on, as if aggrieved (and I'd aggrieved him), 'is that I'm working for the coppers: a nark, like. But do you really think these boys would let me come here if they thought that lie was true?'

'How should I know?'

'The Spades trust me, see? They trust the little queer boy because we're both minorities.'

'How old are you?' I asked him.

'Seventeen.'

'You're much too old for your age.'

He sighed and smiled, and looked at me appealingly. 'I've had so hard a life—if you but knew! I was brought up by the Spades—did you know that?'

'No.'

'Yes, by them. Fact. I was an orphan, see, and brought up by Mr Obo-King.'

'Is this true, or are you making it all up?'

'Why should I lie to you—what's the advantage? Yes, by Obo-King I was brought up, till I set out on my own.' He looked sad, and wizened, and resigned. 'It's all the same,' he said, 'if you don't believe me. I do odd jobs for Mr Vial and other gentleman, that's what I do. Make contacts for them that they need among the Spades.'

'Why bother to tell me?'

He sighed again. 'You're suspicious of me—why?' he said archly. 'Anyway, I'll do you one favour, all the same. You'd better be going, because there's trouble in store tonight for someone.'

'Why?'

'Oh, you *do* want to know?' He rose, assumed a bogus American stance and speech and said, 'Stick around, man, and you'll see.'

A complete stranger, wearing a dark blue suit and spectacles, said, 'Come now, sir. She wait for you, Miss Barbara. Come now with me.'

I followed him to the next floor, where he opened a door with a polite inclination, and shut it after me. Barbara was sitting by a gas fire, reading a 'true story' magazine. 'Oh, hi,' she said, finished a paragraph, then went on, 'Tamberlaine said you want to talk with me.'

'That's right, Barbara.' I sat down too.

'Do you ever read these things?' she said, handing me the book. 'But they don't know nothing about life as it really is.'

'They say truth is stranger than fiction, don't they.'

'Eh? All I know is, if you've been a kid like me in Cardiff, and seen what I seen, there'd be more to tell than you could put in any *book*. I just haven't had the life at all. Everyone uses me, white like coloured. If you're Butetown born, down Tiger Bay, your only hope is show business, or boxing if you're a boy. But me, I can't even sing a note straight.' She got up. 'Well, shall we get on with it? I don't want to miss the party.' She began taking clothes off in an indifferent casual way. 'Yes,' she went on, 'my only hope is to marry me a G.I., and get right out of this. Or maybe a white boy if he has some *position*, that's what I want, a *position*. I'm sick of these hustlers with their easy money! And do you know—I couldn't tell you who my Dad is, even if you asked? Even my Mum don't know, or so she says, can you believe it? Can you imagine? Not even to know who it was created you? Why do you leave your socks on last? It makes you look funny.'

'The linoleum's cold.'

Billy Whispers and Ronson Lighter came, without knocking, into the room. 'Go out now, Barbara,' said Ronson. 'We talk to this man alone.'

'But I'm not dressed.'

'Dress yourself on the landing, out the door. Go, now.'

I began putting clothes on too, but Ronson Lighter snatched away the essential garments, and sat on them on the bed. 'Just wait now a minute,' he said. 'We want to talk with you.'

'You're always pinching things, Ronson Lighter. One day somebody will hit you.'

'Like you will, perhaps?'

I'd noticed a kettle on the gas fire. I edged nearer.

'We give these clothes back when you speak us what you know,' said Billy Whispers.

'Don't be so *African*, Billy. You're so bloody cunning you'll fall over yourself.'

With which I grabbed the kettle and flung it at Ronson Lighter. It missed, but drenched him splendidly in scalding steam. He yelled, and held his eyes. Billy Whispers lowered his head and butted me in the stomach, which was so horribly painful that I grabbed him in the only grip I remembered from gymnasium days, the headlock, twisted his skull violently, and fell with him on the floor. His face was uppermost, and his killer's eyes glared with a hunger for death that was beyond hatred or cruelty—a look almost pure. I hung on, he seized me in the most vulnerable parts. I howled: then suddenly he let go, when fingers were thrust into his throat and nose. I saw beyond the fingers the arms and fierce face of Johnny Fortune. Ronson, prancing with rage and agony, cried, 'You take the side of this white man? You enemy of your people?' Johnny increased the pressure. 'You stop now, Billy? You stop and tell me what is this you think you doing?'

11

Back east, chastened, in the early dawn

WHEN BILLY WAS NEAR DYING, I let him just breathe, but not till he loose his tight hold of Montgomery. I stood back and waited, ready, in case these two Gambians might start some fight again. But all three in the room—Billy and Ronson Lighter and Montgomery—was rubbing themselves silently in different places. 'Put your clothes on, Montgomery,' I said. 'Is never a good choice to fight without your garments.'

These ponces' celebration parties! Always they end up in struggles. But when I came down from Theodora's flat to visit Billy and, I thought, do him a favour by my warning, I did not expect to find this sort of battle. Perhaps soon someone would tell me the reasons of this strange argument.

'I'm glad to see you, Johnny,' said Montgomery, when he was more clothed. 'Who told you I was up here?'

'That Alfy Bongo. So of course I didn't believe him, but I came upstairs to check, and heard from little Barbara you was here. Will someone now please explain to me?' I added, giving cigarettes around, for I wished to show what friendship I could to Billy and to Ronson Lighter, and not make them think the white man could rely on me entirely, always, and for everything.

Ronson speak first. 'This Jumble shop us,' he cried out. 'He sell us to the Law, and come here spying the effects.'

'What *is* all this, Ronson Lighter?'

'I tell you. Tonight we punish Cannibal in the gamble-house. Is I who do it, with the knife I buy. This Jumble see it, and go tell the Law about me.'

'So it was you, Ronson,' said Montgomery.

'You know was I. Tamberlaine tell us what you see in there.'

'But I didn't know it was you with the knife,' Montgomery said. 'And I haven't told anyone about it.'

'A-ha! Can we believe this word?' cried Billy Whispers.

'Whether you do or not, you might have asked me before you both attacked me.'

'Is you who attack us,' cried Ronson, 'with this your kettle.' He picked it up and waved it fiercely. I took it from him.

'I do not know,' I said, 'what my friend Montgomery see. But that he tell the Law, I don't believe. If he do that to you, then why he dare come here after?'

'To spy!' said Billy. 'To put the eye on us.'

'You's foolish, Billy,' I said to him. 'If anyone tell the Law of Ronson, it will be Cannibal.'

'Cannibal not dare to. He know I end his life if he start yapping.'

'Ronson try to end his life anyway, man. That takes away his fear of speaking to the Law.'

Billy Whispers looked at me as if a knife was all I was fit for too. 'Fortune, I know you's not my friend,' he said. 'You never was my friend at any time.'

I looked hard at this Gambian, to show I did not fear him. 'Billy,' I said, 'if I am not your friend, there can only be one reason. It is the drug you give to *my* friend Hamilton Ashinowo, that kill him dead and steal his life away.'

'Who say I do that?'

'Cole. I catch him at your party here downstairs and talk to him. He put the blame on you and run away.'

'And you believe that man?'

'Is true, then?'

'And if is true? I sell that stuff to Hamilton. He buy it; he want it; I give it. I satisfy his need.'

'Then do not wonder, Billy, I am not your friend.'

'So you betray me. You put the Law on me as well.'

'Billy,' I said. 'What puts the Law on you is your life here with Dorothy. Why don't you cut out, man, go up to Manchester Moss Side, or go back home?'

Billy rubbed on his throat and said, 'This is where I stay, here in this city. I fear of nobody. The man who makes me leave town is my master.'

'All right, Billy Whispers, is your life, is not mine. Now what say we go downstairs and drink a drink and soon forget all this unfriendliness?'

The room was now empty of many of its guests, especially Tamberlaine and 'Nat King' Cole. But Cranium and one of his boys was still playing on their drums, and Barbara and Dorothy was yap-yap-yapping by the fire. And shooting dice up on the floor was my brother Arthur and Alfy Bongo, and that gilded man Tondapo with who I had not yet had my explanation of his earlier behaviour to me. 'Give us some tune, Cranium,' I said. 'Come, Billy. Forget your suspecting everyone, and pour some drink.'

'Drink for you who attack me?' Billy said to Montgomery and to me.

'Oh, come now, Billy. Don't spoil this pleasant evening, or, if you like, we have to go.'

So he poured these drinks. Dorothy she came and stood by Billy, hands on hips, looking so very foolish. 'What's all this fighting?' she cried out. 'What sort of home do you think you've given me?'

Billy gave Dorothy no drink. 'Be careful, now,' he said. 'Be careful what you say to me. Be careful what you say to anybody. The one place for your trap is shut.'

Cranium Cuthbertson beat sweetly on, trying. I could see, to give some harmony to everyone's emotion. Also, he began to sing: a chant like to himself, in his own tongue, about a boy who leave the coast beside the sea and walks all his life right up to Kano, looking for blessings of his ancestors, who came from there. The boys stopped shooting dice, and all began clapping softly to the rhythm, and singing the 'Ay-yah-ah' chorus to Cranium's good song.

But the door came open, and I saw Inspector Purity of the C.I.D. and three more of his dicks. Billy had leapt quick under the table, which had a cloth. 'Stay where you are, everybody,' this Purity man said. 'I want a word with Mr Billy Whispers. Where is he?'

No one spoke. Though did I see my brother Arthur smile at Purity and look across the room towards the table?

As feet approached it, Billy did a brave and foolish thing: he rushed and jumped right through the window, glass and everything. Dorothy screamed. Two dicks ran downstairs, one stayed beside the door, and Mr Purity stepped over to the window.

We all stood still, though Cranium beat a note or two upon his drum. Purity shone down a torch. 'Got him?' he shouted.

There was a shout up back.

'What?' Mr Purity cried out. 'Well, carry him over to the car. I'll be right down.'

Dorothy ran up to Inspector Purity and caught hold of his hair. 'What are you doing to my husband?' she screamed out. He pushed her off on to the floor. 'So he's your husband, is he?' said Purity. 'I think he's living off your immoral earnings.'

'Is that the charge? Is that the charge you make?' said Ronson Lighter.

'Resisting arrest will be one charge,' said Purity, 'and no doubt there'll be others. Well, let's take a look at you all and see who we've got. Stand up, everyone, with your hands on top of your heads. Come on!'

Everybody stood up except Dorothy, and all put their hands on their heads except Montgomery and myself. Detective Purity walked round inspecting all the party, like a general, and to some he spoke.

'So you're here, Alfy,' he began. 'One day we'll have to find a little charge for you. Any suggestions, lad? I've got one or two ideas. And you,' he said to my brother Arthur. 'You getting tired of life outside the nick? Maybe we could help you back inside again. Dice, eh? That's gambling. Hullo, Barbara. Aren't you in need of some care and protection? We'll introduce you to one of our lady coppers, she'll see you home to Cardiff. Good evening, Mr Pew, or is it good morning? You keep some strange company, don't you. And you weren't altogether frank with me earlier on about your young friend here . . . Mr Fortune. How are you, son? Do you know something? We're going to nick you for peddling weed one day soon, so don't you think you'd better get aboard a ship? No, don't bother to turn your pockets out this time, we know you've put it on the fire. And you!' He'd stopped in front of Ronson Lighter, who thought he had been missed. 'You'd better come along with us as well. There's been some malicious wounding, and perhaps you can tell us something more about it. Your friend down there seems to be unconscious, and they think he's broken some legs.'

'You bastard!' Dorothy cried out from the floor.

He didn't look down, but said to her, 'We'll be sending for you, Dorothy, when we want you. Don't leave London just at present, will you? Come on now, you!' he said to Ronson. And this boy, though if it was a fight he would fear nothing, like so many of our men when big misfortune falls upon them, was quiet and quite helpless in the copper's hand.

Inspector Purity stopped by the door. 'I needn't tell you all to watch your step,' he said. 'There's not a man or woman here we haven't got a charge for when the time comes, and we feel like paying you a visit.' Then he went out with Ronson and the other copper, who had stood there waiting and not said one word.

When the door closed, Dorothy scrambled up, opened it again and cried down the stairs, 'You bastards!' Then slammed it, turned to us all and shouted, 'Somebody's shopped Billy!'

'Would it be you, Dorothy?' I said.

'Me, Johnny Fortune! Call me a whore if you want to, but I don't shop nobody. Someone here has spoken with the Law. Somebody's shopped Billy!'

Faces all looked at faces.

'Come now, Montgomery,' I said, when looking from the window I saw the Law car drive away. 'Is time to go.'

Dorothy and Barbara were weeping on each other's shoulder. 'I have my car outside,' said Ibrahim Tondapo, like some emir. 'I offer you a lift.'

I made no reply to this vain man, but went with the others down the stairs. This Ibrahim insisted foolishly on our company, so we came up to his limousine. Place in the car was refused by me to Arthur and to Alfy Bongo, who walked away chattering in spite together. The passengers I allowed were Cranium and Montgomery in the back seat, and I by Ibrahim Tondapo's side.

'Where to?' he said.

'East End for me.'

'I'll see you home, Johnny,' said Montgomery.

'For me, please, a drop-out at the Trafalgar Square,' said Cranium Cuthbertson.

Tondapo drove elegantly but too fast, anxious to demonstrate his skill. In the central city we turned Cranium loose, and drove on across the commercial area of the city's wealth, this Ibrahim trying to make eager conversation with Montgomery and with me. But I silenced my Jumble friend, and would say nothing to this African, for whom I still planned a vengeance for his earlier action in the

Sphere. So when we came to the dockside poverty of the Immigration Road, I asked him to take two turnings and then halt.

'Thank you,' I said.

'You welcome, man. Bygone is bygone.'

'Your tyre is flat.'

'No, I not think so, man.'

'I tell you is flat: your motor rumbles.'

We all got out. Montgomery noticed my intention.

'No, no, Johnny,' he cried out. 'Not any more!'

But I had heaved this Tondapo against the wall and battered him. He fight hard and bravely, but had eaten too much throughout his comfortable life. When I had laid him low, I lifted him and put his groaning body in the back seat of his vehicle.

Montgomery was in rages with me. 'You must learn to control yourself,' he said.

'And you! Fighting with two Africans in your nakedness.'

'That was a misunderstanding.'

'Let us not argue, Montgomery. There have been arguments enough.'

We walked through the dim and silence of these evil streets: all tumbling: all sad.

'Who *did* betray Whispers?' said Montgomery.

'It was not you, then?'

'Oh, don't be absurd, Johnny. Why should I?'

'That Alfy Bongo?'

'I don't understand that hobgoblin. I don't think he's working for the Law. . . . Excuse my asking, but had Arthur anything to do with it, perhaps?'

'Perhaps so. Or more perhaps is really Dorothy who spoke.'

'She didn't act like it.'

'Dorothy is tired of Billy. Maybe she's glad to see him go inside for some other charge than laying his hands upon her earnings. If she told the Law about this wounding, and of nothing else, then she will not have to appear in court against him.'

'Isn't the simplest explanation that Jimmy Cannibal told them about the attack himself? That Ronson did it, and Billy was behind it?'

'Could be so. When the court case comes, then we shall see. By the witnesses, we shall see. But what is sure is that Billy will suspect us all—you for what you saw in the gamble-house, and Dorothy that she wants to leave him, and also me.'

'Why you?'

'Because Dorothy's foolish hope is to come and live with me. I must keep clear of that evil little chicken.'

We crossed the Immigration Road.

'Inspector Purity was asking about you earlier on,' Montgomery said, and told me of that meeting. 'Be careful, Johnny.'

'I am always careful.'

'You had no weed with you tonight?'

'None left. Though if they want to take me, they would not mind if I had weed or not.'

'If that's so, why didn't they arrest you there and then? Or any of the others except Ronson?'

'The knifing was their business this evening. One operation at a time is the Law's slow and steady way. Perhaps there were also too many witnesses for the frame-up. They have their skill and patience, Montgomery, have the Law.'

Outside my sweet-shop, I said goodbye to him. 'Do not come in, Montgomery. Muriel and Hamilton will be sleeping. I telephone you.'

'You promise? Keep in touch, now, won't you.

'I speak to you on the phone tomorrow.'

'Take care, then. And thank you, Johnny, for helping me with those two boys.'

Helping him! Had I not saved his skin entirely?

'Is nothing,' I said. 'Good night now, Montgomery. I shall see you.'

He walked away, and turned and waved, and I waited till he shrunk right out of sight. Then I went indoors to my misery.

Muriel was up, in spite of it was morning. I kissed her, but she turned her face away.

'Hamilton's gone,' she said. 'They've taken him off to hospital in the ambulance. He had delirium.'

'It was real bad, this what Hamilton have?'

'I don't think he'll live, Johnny.'

I sat down by her side.

'Let us go sleep now,' I said to her. 'A great many troubles have come my way today.'

'You're bleeding, Johnny. Let me wash you.'

'Wash me, then. But I must sleep.'

She wiped the blood off from my face and fists, and gave me a cup of warm-up tea. 'You're back so late. Always back to late,' she said, taking my clean hands.

'But I am back, Muriel. Come, we go sleep.'

'I have to go to work in a few hours.'

'Before you go to work, Muriel, you sleep with me.'

12

Splendour of flesh made into dream

For several weeks, my life in the flat had been transformed: Norbert and Moscow had made themselves at home. 'It sure is Bohemian here,' Norbert said, 'and we'll not be in your way.' They hardly were, indeed; for so much did they overflow about the place, flinging heady articles of clothing everywhere, singing naked on the stairs down to the bath, entertaining, at all hours, their wide circle of acquaintances, that I became almost the interloper in my dwelling, and feared to inconvenience them, rather than they me. Yet though so entirely heartless, and so rigorously selfish, they radiated such *bonhomie*, were perpetually so high-spirited and so amiable, laughed, danced and chattered so abandonedly, that even Theodora was won over. 'Of course, I prefer Africans,' she said, 'they're more authentic. But these young Americans certainly have charm.'

Carrying her cat Tungi, she was paying me a morning visit (such as, in earlier days, she'd never made) while my lodgers were out at their rehearsal. 'I only wish,' I said, 'they wouldn't use the telephone quite so recklessly. I caught Norbert calling up Jackson, Mississippi, yesterday, and really had to put my foot down.'

'"Put your foot down"!' Theodora irritated me by repeating with superior disdain. 'You're quite unable to say no to them about anything.'

'And you, my dear Theodora?' I could not resist asking. 'Have you not succumbed, despite your initial indifference, even hostility, to coloured people?'

'My feeling for them is selective, just as it would be with one of us. I don't admire coloured people in the mass, like you do.'

'You mean you've fallen in love with one individually, and I haven't.'

Theodora, touched on the raw, assumed her severe departmental manner. 'For some time now, Montgomery,' she told me, 'I've been wanting to say just what I think. And it's this. Your interest in these people is prompted by nothing more than a vulgar, irresponsible curiosity.'

'Thank you, Theodora.'

'You like to be the odd man out, and lord it over them.'

'I'm happy with them. It's as simple as that.'

'If you call that happiness.'

'I do.'

She shifted, woman-like, her ground.

'It's the crude animal type that attracts you most of all. It's simply another form of *nostalgie de la boue*. You've taken the easy way and are losing face, even with them. Do you see anything, for instance, of the intelligent types? The coloured intellectuals?'

I decided a dressing-down was due. 'In the first place, I'd remind you, Theodora, that I see much of Mr Karl Marx Bo. I listened to him addressing a meeting only last Sunday in Hyde Park, and we had a long and angry conversation afterwards. As for you, my dear, and *your* predilections, would you really describe Johnny Fortune as an intellectual?'

'He's most intelligent.'

'I don't deny it; but not lacking, I would say, in animal attraction.'

'He's handsome, in the way they are—yes.'

'Theodora, I don't wish to be unkind, but you're pathetic. Why not admit you love him?'

She looked at me long and hard. 'Because I'm ashamed to,' she said at last. 'Not ashamed because he's coloured, or, as you say, animal, or anything else, but because it's a feeling so strong I can't control it. I'm not used to that, and I can't cope.'

I ventured to pat her on her unyielding shoulder. 'Perhaps that's good for you,' I said. 'Perhaps one should not be able to dominate every situation. . . .'

She looked to be crying, so I considerately turned away. 'They're so appalling!' she said at last, quite softly. 'So tender and so heartless. So candid and so evil!'

It was my turn now, I felt—from the depths of what was, after all, a wider experience than her own and, so I thought, one more dearly won—to lecture her.

'I don't think you must take,' I said, 'a *moral* attitude towards these people: or rather, a moral attitude within the English terms of reference. I don't think you must suppose, if they seem to you such charming sinners, beyond good and evil (or before it, rather), that the devil has therefore marked them for his own.'

'Why not?' she said, rather sulkily.

'Use your historical sense, Theodora—one certainly far better documented than my own. Remember, for instance, that in parts of Africa not a soul had ever heard of Christianity less than a hundred years ago. . . .'

'Where hadn't they, precisely?'

'Don't be pedantic. In Uganda, for example. May I go on?'

'But Johnny doesn't come from Uganda.'

'Who said he did? Can't we move, just for a second, from the particular to the general?' I was quite exasperated.

'Go on, then.'

'I shall. You should therefore remember that if coloured men seem, to your eyes, more happily amoral than we are, they have other spiritual ties, quite unknown to us, and very different from our own, that are every bit as strong.'

'Such as?'

'Don't interrupt. They have sacred tribal loyalties, for instance, of which we feel absolutely nothing that's equivalent. If Johnny had been a Gambian like those boys who set on me that evening, and of the same tribe as they were, he certainly wouldn't have helped me, however close our friendship.'

'The more fool he.'

I restrained myself. 'There's another thing,' I went on. 'The family. We think our family ties are precious, or, at any rate, that we should feel so. But they're nothing at all to theirs. Have you noticed, when an African makes a solemn promise, what he says to you?'

'I can't say I have.'

'He says, "I swear it on my mother's life."'

'And probably breaks his word.'

'Oh, no doubt! Just as we do when we swear upon our gods, or on our sacred books. The point I'm trying to convey, though, to the frosty heights of your Everest intelligence, dearest Theodora, is that there are entirely different moral concepts among different races: a fact which leads to endless misunderstandings on the political and social planes, and makes right conduct in you, for instance, seem idiotic to Johnny Fortune, and some gesture of his which he believes necessary and honourable to seem foolish, or even wicked, in your eyes.'

'Don't bully me, Montgomery,' she said. 'You're as bad as he is.'

'I'm sorry, Theodora. Let's have some coffee in the kitchen, if I can find my way through the provocative underclothes my lodgers have hung there in festoons.'

She put Tungi down and came and helped me make it, turning thoughtfully over the gossamer vests and pants that rested on the lines.

'Have you seen Johnny lately?' I asked, as I handed her a cup.

'Yes, several times, and he telephones. But I'm worried about him, Montgomery! If only he'd work!'

'He's a lazy lad, I fear.'

'Like you. How is your free-lancing going?'

'It's not.'

'I thought it wasn't. And Johnny does absolutely nothing—only stays with that squalid woman.'

'If you knew Muriel better, you'd not call her so.'

'At all events, her sister's little friend is now in jail.'

'Billy Whispers' being sentenced has nothing to do with Muriel, Theodora. Do be consistent. And don't gloat.'

'Johnny said he got six months.'

'For being an accessory to a wounding, yes. But the evidence against him was given by a Mr Cannibal—the sentence had nothing to do with Dorothy, even less with Muriel.'

She pondered and sipped her coffee. I saw her eyes become transfixed by a peculiar garment. 'What on earth's this?' she said.

'It's what the French call a "slip" or, more accurately, a "zlip". The boys wear it when they dance. Which reminds me. There's a matinée this afternoon. Would you like to come?'

'No.'

'Don't be so ungracious, Theodora. You ought to see them. After all, my guests are courteous to you round about the house....'

'Oh, very well, then. I could do with a day off—and the Corporation owe me plenty. I'll call my secretary.'

For a matinée, the place was crowded, principally with males, and with a fair peppering of coloured admirers of the Isabel Cornwallis company. I noticed, and greeted in the foyer, Mr Lord Alexander, to whom Theodora, once she heard who he was, behaved most graciously—she had apparently become a collector of his records; and also Mr Cranium Cuthbertson, who did not please her possibly because, poking her in the ribs and bending double with amusement, he cried out in a familiar fashion, 'You's the hep-cat what stole Mr Vial's puss-cat!' Bells rang, and we went inside the auditorium to see how the Cornwallis company would achieve that most difficult of theatrical feats—the creation of illusion just one hour after the midday meal.

Although I'd seen the show so often before (almost nightly), I marvelled once again at the complete transformation of these bitter, battling egoists, with their cruel jealousies and bitchy gossip, their pitiless trampling ambition, and their dreadful fear of the day, some time so near in their late thirties, when they could dance no more—into the gracious, vigorous, sensual creatures I saw upon the stage. By Miss Cornwallis' alchemy, the sweaty physical act of dancing became an efflorescence of the spirit! True, there were tricks theatrical innumerable, but Isabel Cornwallis was wiser than she knew: because her raw material, the dancers, possessed an inner dignity and nobility, of which even she could hardly be aware, but knew, by instinct, how to use. These boys and girls seemed incapable of a vulgar gesture! And as they danced, they were clothed in what seemed the antique innocence and wisdom of humanity before the Fall—the ancient, simple splendour of the millennially distant days before thought began, and civilizations . . . before the glories of conscious creation, and the horrors of conscious debasement, came into the world! In the theatre, they were *savages* again: but the savage is no barbarian—he is an entire man of a complete, forgotten world, intense and mindless, for which we, with all our conquests, must feel a disturbing, deep nostalgia. These immensely adult children, who'd carried into a later age a precious vestige of our former life, could throw off their twentieth-century garments, and all their ruthlessness and avarice and spleen, and radiate, on the stage, an atmosphere of goodness! of happiness! of love! And I thought I saw at last what was the mystery of the deep attraction to us of the Spades—the fact that they were still a mystery to themselves.

'I can't take any more,' said Theodora at the interval. 'They're too upsetting.'

'Can't you stick it out until the end? We could meet them at the stage door and have some tea.'

'You stay: I'll go back to the office.'

We went out in the foyer. 'Be sure you say something nice to them back at the flat, Theodora,' I said to her. 'You're so parsimonious with your praise.'

'I won't know what to say.'

'Just praise them. It's all they want.'

I saw her to a taxi. Hurrying back into the theatre, amid clanging bells, I was detained by the odious Alfy Bongo.

'You again!'

'Yes, it's me. Ain't they the tops?'

'Of course. I want to see them, though, not you. Farewell.'

He plucked at my arm. 'You heard Billy Whispers and Ronson Lighter have gone inside?'

'Yes, yes.'

'They should have got a good lawyer. It's hopeless without. I told them, but they wouldn't listen.'

'Look! I want to see the show.'

He followed me into the theatre, already dark. 'They should have gone to Mr Zuss-Amor,' he whispered. 'Remember the name—it's Zuss-Amor.'

13

Inspector Purity's ingenious plan

Often I had tried for many weeks to visit Hamilton in his hospital, but they were not eager to allow me near him on account of his condition being critical. But on this present visit I was called in immediately to the Sister.

'The patient is a relative of yours?' she said.

'No, he is my friend.'

'Has he relatives in this country?'

'I know of none. Why?'

'In Africa, you know his family's address?'

'Hamilton did not tell it to you?'

'He refused to . . .'

'If he did not tell you this, I do not wish to. He has his reasons that his family should not know.'

This practical woman put on her kind face. 'Your friend is very ill,' she said. 'He's on what we call the danger list. Surely he would wish his family to know?'

'I may speak with him?'

'Yes. But not for long.'

That Hamilton would soon die was certain by his waste-away appearance, and also by his special situation convenient to the door. My friend also knew that this was to be his fate, for his first words were to tell me of his understanding. He spoke without fear of this, as you would expect of Hamilton, but very sadly. I did not deny what he foretold, nor would I agree to it, but sat by him and held his bony hands.

'Speak to me of your life, Johnny. Tell me what happens to you now.'

'I must not tire you, Hamilton.'

He smiled a very little. 'What is the difference, Johnny Fortune? Speak to me. How is Muriel?'

'Muriel is gone. I also have left our house.'

'Why?'

'Dorothy has come to live there now.'

'To stay with you?'

'No, man, no—I will explain. Muriel have sickness with her coming baby, and could not work. We owed rents to the landlord, and had no loot. Dorothy, without asking us, go see the landlord, pay over our arrears, and get the rent-book for herself. Then she say to Muriel and me that we can stay there if she stay there too.'

'And you say yes?'

'No, we say no. But where could we go to? Even I began to work, Hamilton, at labouring. But before I get my first week wage, we had no other place to go, and stayed on there with Dorothy. Even after that first week, we stay some while to make some little savings.'

'And then?'

My friend's eyes showed me he guess what happen then.

'I keep away from Dorothy, Hamilton, like you would think. But one time when Muriel was out . . . well, this thing happen between me and she. Foolish, of course, I know, but a cold evening and we left alone together. . . .'

'And Dorothy tell Muriel of this happen?'

'I think no: but Muriel she guessed. A woman can always tell it, Hamilton, when you betray her. How so, I do not know; but they can tell.'

My friend turned slowly in his bed. 'And then Muriel leave you, Johnny?'

'Yes. She go back to her horrible Mrs Macpherson mother, and will not see me. She say to me, "If is Dorothy you wish, not me, then you can take her." '

'But you do not wish for Dorothy?'

'No. She ask me, of course, to stay and live off what she earn. But I wish for nothing of that woman. Though foolishly I stay in the house some weeks more for sleeping.'

'For private sleeping, Johnny?'

'Alone. Then we have quarrel, Dorothy and I, and I leave these rooms entirely. And now I stay this place, that place, with boys I know, till I can get my room.'

Hamilton thought about my story, 'These Jumble friends of yours,' he said. 'You could not stay with them?'

'Oh, you understand me, Hamilton! When Jumbles do the favour, always they ask some price. For payment of their deeds, they wish to steal your private life in some way or another.'

'And you will not return again with Muriel at any time?'

'She say to me, Hamilton, that if I do not marry her, now that she soon has the child, she does not wish to stay with me at all. But how can I marry such a woman? What would they say back home?'

Hamilton, he understood this. 'The best thing, Johnny Fortune, is certainly for you to sail to Africa. Do not leave this too late, as I do, or you will find yourself in misery like me.'

What could I say to my old friend—but that I hope the days of both of us would soon be rather brighter? I said goodbye to him, and still Hamilton would not let me tell his home address to the people in the hospital.

So I leave that sad place behind me, and walked out in the dark winter East End afternoon: no use to go back now to my labouring job, whose foreman would not give me time off to visit Hamilton, and now would certainly dismiss me for my absence. I thought of Mahomed and his café, and how a free meal of rice would give me strength, and there, playing dominoes, I meet the former weed-peddler, Peter Pay Paul.

'Mr Ruby,' he tell me, 'ask why you come for no more business.'

'I cut out that hustle too, man. I cut right out of peddling like you say is best to, when the months go by. And you, what do you do now, Peter?'

'Good times have come to me, Johnny. I doorman now at the Tobagonian Free Occupation club, and this is a profitable business.'

'Tell me now, Peter. I have no room at present. May I sleep in your cloakroom for this evening?'

'What will you pay me, man?'

'Skinned now, Peter Pay Paul. You do this for your friend.'

'Just this one night, then, Johnny. Do not please ask me the next evening, or word will reach the ear of this Tobagonian owner and I lose my good job.'

Peter supplied me with one coffee. 'Arthur is down East End,' he said. 'He asks for you from several people.'

'I do not wish to see that relative of mine ever again.'

A great pleasure came to me now, which was the arrival in Mahomed's of the seaman Laddy Boy, he who had brought the letter from my sister Peach. His ship had been sailing to the German ports, and he told us of the friendly action of the chicks he'd met in dock-side streets of Hamburg.

'I see some Lagos boy there, Johnny,' he told me now. 'In a ship coming out of Africa. He tell me some news about your family that you should hear.'

Almost I guessed what Laddy Boy would tell me. 'Your sister Peach,' he said, 'has sailed to England now to train as nurse.'

'This news is certain of her coming? I wish it was some other time she choose.'

Laddy Boy said to me: 'Tomorrow, come meet my quartermaster, Johnny. Speak to him and see if you can sign on our ship, to have some serious occupation for when your sister reaches England.'

'I have no knowledge of a sailor—will he take me?'

'We speak to him together, man. I know some secrets of his smuggling that have helped him raise his income to his benefit.'

When the half-past-five time came at last, Laddy Boy took me for some Baby Salt at the Apollo tavern. We sit there drinking quietly, I thinking of home and Lagos, and of Peach and Christmas and my Mum and Dad.

But what spoils these thoughts is Dorothy, when she come in the saloon bar with a tall G.I. She send this man over and he say to me politely, 'Your sister-in-law ask me, man, to ask if you will speak with her a minute.'

'No, man, no. Tell her I busy with my friend.'

He went back to Dorothy, but come to me once more. 'She says is important to you, what she have to tell.'

I went with Dorothy in one corner of the bar. 'Now, Dorothy,' I said. 'Please understand I do not wish to mix my life with yours. Do not pester me, please, with your company, or I turn bad on you, and we regret it.'

She was high with her drink, I saw, but quieter and more ladylike than I know her ever before.

'Look, man,' she said. 'I know the deal I offered you means nothing to you, but can't we still be friends?'

'I do not wish to be your enemy or your friend.'

'Why are you so mean to me always, Johnny? You know how gone on you I am.'

'Keep away from me, Dorothy, is all I ask you.' I got up, but she called, 'Just one thing more I want to say to you.' She got that far, then stopped, and when I waited, said, 'Get me another drink.'

'Is that it? More drink?'

I moved finally to leave her, making from now a rule that never would I answer her again. She grabbed my arm suddenly and pulled me down towards her, and said so close my ear I smell her whisky breath, 'If I leave the game, Johnny, and get off the streets for good, will you marry me?'

I pulled my arm away. 'Your life is your life, Dorothy. Do not try to mix it in with mine is all I say.'

I left this woman, and returned to Laddy Boy. When she went out some minutes later, she stopped as she passed by and said to me, 'I'll mix in, Johnny Fortune, if I want to. I always get my own way in the end.'

The G.I. shook hands to show his dislike of her behaviour, and they both left. 'That woman should drink tea,' said Laddy Boy.

I made the arrangement with him for the meeting next day with his quartermaster, and then went to see my overnight home at the Free Occupation club. Peter had not yet come back to his duty, so I waited in the hallways, where I saw a big poster of the Cranium Cuthbertson band, which said they would play at the Stepney friendly get-together where white and coloured residents were invited to know each other rather better.

'Hullo, bra,' said some voice, and it was Arthur.

'"Bra" is for Africans, not for Jumbles,' I said to him.

'Why you always insulting me, Johnny? Would our same Dad like it, if he knew?'

'Blow, man, before I do you some violence,' I said to him.

He walked back to the door, and said out loud, 'He's here!', then scattered quick. The C.I.D. Inspector Purity came in with another officer.

'We want you, Fortune,' he said. 'We'll talk to you at the station.'

These two men grabbed me, though I made no resistance and said nothing. Each held an arm, and tugged me across the pavement to their car. Peter Pay Paul came up at just this moment, and stopped still when he saw me. 'Telephone, Peter, to the radio B.B.C.!' I cried out loud. 'Speak to Miss Pace. Pace! B.B.C. radio headquarter!'

They dragged me inside the Law car. The journey was short and fast, and they did not speak. In the police station, they took me beyond the public rooms, and then, from behind me, Mr Purity struck me on the neck and I fell on the concrete. I got up, and they pulled me into a small room.

'Finger-print him, Constable,' said Purity to the other officer.

'I have no wish to be finger-printed.'

'Shut up. Over here.'

'You cannot finger-print me. I have no conviction on my record.'

The two looked at each other, then at me. The Detective-Constable, whose face was pale and miserable, came close and said, 'You're not going to co-operate?' Then he beat me round about my head.

I know the great danger of hitting back against the Law, so sat still with my hands clenched by my side. This beating went on. 'Don't bruise him,' said Mr Purity. The Constable stopped and rubbed his hands.

'Our bruises do not show in court so well as white man's do,' I said. 'This is the reason why you hit us always harder.'

Mr Purity smiled at this funny remark I made. He asked me for details of my name, and age, and this and that, and I gave him these. Then they searched me and took away every possession. Then he began asking other questions.

'In English law,' I said, 'do you not make a charge? Do you not caution a prisoner before he speaks? This is the story that they tell us in our lessons we have back home on British justice.'

Mr Purity raised up his fist. 'Do you really want to suffer?' he said to me.

'I want to know the charge. There was no drug in my possession—nothing.'

'We're not interested in drugs at present,' said Mr Purity. 'We're charging you with something that'll send you inside for quite a bit longer, as you'll see. You're a ponce, Johnny Fortune, aren't you. You've ponced on Bill Whispers' girl.'

This words were such a big surprise to me, that at first I had no speech. Then I stand up. 'You call *me* ponce?' I shouted.

'Nigger or ponce, it's all the same,' the Detective-Constable said.

I hit him not on the face, but in the stomach where I know this blow must hurt him badly, even if they kill me after. They did not kill me, but called in friends and kicked me round the floor.

After this treatment, I was left alone and even given a kind cigarette. An old officer in uniform and grey hair then visited me, and spoke to me like some friendly uncle. 'You'd better do what you're told, son,' he said, 'and let them print you. Tomorrow they'll oppose bail in court, and the screws can print you in the nick at Brixton.... You don't want to fight the whole police force, do you? You can only lose....'

'Mister, this battle is not ended,' I said to him. 'Outside in this city, London, I have friends.'

14

Mobilisation of the defence

THE MESSAGE REACHED THEODORA, in a highly garbled version, through an agitated secretary who boldly interrupted an inter-departmental conference at Broadcasting House on a projected series of talks to be called, provisionally, 'The Misfit and the Body Corporate: a survey of contemporary un-integrated types.' Theodora, scenting mischief, had asked the D.A.C. (Programmes) if she might be excused, and had parliamented with the secretary in an airless corridor outside.

'I'm sorry if I did wrong, Miss Pace, to barge in on the meeting,' the secretary whispered, 'but it sounded urgent. This person said this person was "in big trouble"—those were his words.'

'Which person?'

'The one who phoned said it. I think he must have been a native.

'You mean the African who telephones me sometimes?'

'No: an illiterate sort, Miss Pace. I could hardly understand a word he spoke. But he did say to tell you "the Law have put the hands on she Spade friend"—those were the exact words he used.'

'Thank you, Miss Lamb,' said Theodora. 'You did quite right. Please go in and tell the D.A.C. I'm called away on urgent family business. A sudden case of sickness.'

All this Theodora told me, in calm, shrill tones, over the telephone to the flat, where I was helping Norbert Salt iron the ruffles he'd sewn on to the front of a silk shirt he planned to wear with his tuxedo at a gala.

'It sounds, Theodora, as if Johnny's been arrested.'

'Of course it does. But where? And why? How does one find out?'

'Telephone the police station.'

'Which one?'

'Well, try the East End ones first. Would you like me to do it?'

'No, I'll work from here. I'll call you back when there are developments.'

'Just a minute, Theodora. Lay your hands on some money if you can—it always come in useful. And what about a lawyer?'

'I'd thought of all that. I'll call you later.'

I waited half an hour, then telephoned the B.B.C. Theodora had gone and left no message. I wondered what to do. I opened the fourth volume of the telephone directory and looked up 'Zuss-Amor'.

Though the hour was late, a female voice replied. Yes, Mr Zuss-Amor was in, but what was it about? I started to explain, but clickings in the line suggested to me someone listening on an extension. 'Look,' I said. 'May I please speak to Mr Zuss-Amor direct? Tell him I'm a friend of Alfy Bongo's.'

Immediately a male voice said, 'What sort of case is it, Mr Pew?'

'I don't know yet, my friend's only just been arrested. We're trying to find out why. He's an African.'

'Oh. Then we know what the case will probably be, don't we. I can see you here tomorrow at half-past-five.'

'But Mr Zuss-Amor, that'll be too late. Won't the case come up in court tomorrow morning?'

'He'll be formally charged tomorrow, yes, but you can take it from me, if the case is at all serious, the police will ask for a remand. There's nothing I can do till I've heard some facts from you and from the client: that is, if I agree to take the case, of course, and he agrees to me.'

'What should I do tomorrow morning?'

'Where was your friend arrested?'

'I don't know yet. He lives down in the East End.'

'It'll be Boat Street magistrates' court, most likely. Go there, try to see him, and try to get the magistrate to grant bail. I doubt if he will, though.'

'Why?'

'The police usually oppose bail in the kind of case I think it's likely to be. See you tomorrow, then, Mr Pew, and thanks for calling.'

I had a lot more to say and ask, but Mr Zuss-Amor hung up on me. The moment I put the telephone down, the bell rang, and it was Theodora.

'I'm at Aldgate, Montgomery,' she said. 'I couldn't get any sense out of the police over the phone, so I took a taxi down here and went to the station.'

'Yes, yes. And?'

'He's been arrested, but they won't tell me where he is or what the charge is.'

'Why?'

'They wanted to know what they called my "interest in the matter". I said I was willing to go bail, but they told me that was a matter for the magistrate. Then I tried to get through to Sir Wallingford Puke-Drew——'

'Sir who?'

'He's my family solicitor: the one who advised us on the eviction trouble; but there's no one in his office.'

'I've got a solicitor, Theodora. A Mr Zuss-Amor.' And I told her of our conversation.

'But what do you know about this person, Montgomery?'

'Nothing. But he's seeing me tomorrow, isn't he? We must get things moving.'

There was a slight, agitated pause. 'Suppose they convict him tomorrow before we have time to get legal advice?'

'They can't possibly do that. He has the right to apply for legal aid.'

'But does he *know* that?'

'He's not an idiot, Theodora.'

'If only I knew what it was all about.'

'Well, stop fussing, and come back here and talk about it. There's nothing else to do now that I can see. Would you like me to come down there and fetch you?'

'No. I've kept the taxi waiting.'

She arrived back, battered and dismayed as I had never seen her before. I gave her a glass of vodka (a present to the household from Moscow Gentry), and she recovered something of her poise.

'I've been thinking, Montgomery,' she said, 'and it must be one of three things. Either some act of violence, or else having that disgusting hemp in his possession, or else . . .'

'Yes?'

'You don't think this woman Muriel was a prostitute, do you?'

'I'm certain she wasn't. She wouldn't know how.'

'Would he have lived on any other woman of that type?'

'You can never be certain, Theodora, but I really don't believe he would.'

'What can you get for having Indian hemp?'

'I believe on a first conviction it's only a fine—unless they could prove he dealt in it as well.'

Theodora poured out another glassful. 'I'll have to cook up some story for the office,' she said. Then, draining it down, 'I wish I knew more about the world!'

Next morning saw us driving down to Boat Street in a taxi—I in my best suit with an unusual white shirt, and Theodora in her severest black. She opened her bag as we drew near the East End, and made herself up rather excessively. Then she took a small yellow pill, and swallowed with difficulty. 'Dexedrine,' she said. 'Want one?'

'No thanks.'

'Good for the nerves. Tones you up in an emergency.'

'Like hemp, apparently.'

'But if you've got a kind doctor or chemist, perfectly legal.'

'White man's magic.'

'No wonder they think we're hypocrites.'

The public waiting at the court were not prepossessing: though even Venus and Adonis would have looked squalid in this antechamber of the temple of justice, built in Victorian public lavatory style. When the sitting began, we squeezed in among a considerable throng, and watched a succession of small, grim cases—on all of which two dreadful old men beside me throatily passed whispered comments, invariably derogatory to the accused. Somebody nudged me. It was Mr Laddy Boy, the seaman I'd met earlier in the Sphere. He shook hands, and pursed his lips as if to say, 'I'm here, and you're here—so there's nothing to worry about at all.'

When Johnny Fortune was brought in, he looked a little shrunken and shop-soiled, but preserved, I was glad to see, his habitual buoyancy. He immediately glanced round to where the public were, saw us, nodded slightly, and then faced the magistrate.

This was one of those old gentlemen who look so amiable, but in such a neutral, meaningless sort of way that one really can't tell very much about them. The clerk read the charge, which, as I'd feared, and all the time secretly believed it would be, was one of living on the immoral earnings of a common prostitute, to wit, Dorothea Violet Macpherson. To this odious charge, Johnny Fortune pleaded not guilty in ringing, confident tones.

'Fucking ponce,' whispered one of the disgusting old men.

'These black bastards,' said the other.

Laddy Boy trod accidentally on their feet. There was some slight scuffling, and the usher turned and frowned severely.

Through watching this, I did not at first see Inspector Purity until he stepped into the box. My heart sank. He gave evidence of arrest in a clear, manly, honest voice and immediately asked for a remand.

'For how long, Detective-Inspector?' said the magistrate, as if asking a neighbour how long he wanted to borrow the lawn-mower.

'We should be ready in a week, sir.'

'Very well. What about bail?'

'We oppose bail, your Worship. The accused showed violence when under arrest, and we fear intimidation of the prosecution's witnesses.'

'I see. Have you anything to say?' the magistrate asked Johnny.

As soon as Johnny spoke, the court stiffened slightly, and all of them—audience, Press, lawyers and innumerable coppers—glanced curiously towards the dock. This was evidently not the ordinary African.

'I wish to ask that you grant me bail, sir, in order that I take law advice, prepare my case, and see my witnesses to defend me. Two white friends of good reputation are here in the court to bail for me.' (Everyone looked towards the public box.) 'I undertake no violence to anyone, unlike what has been stated by the police evidence.'

The magistrate mused, then turned. 'What do you say, Detective-Inspector?'

'An additional reason that we have, your Worship, for opposing bail, is that the prisoner refused to have his fingerprints taken. We also know the accused consorts with coloured merchant seamen, and have reason to believe he may try to stow away and leave the country without standing trial.'

Laddy Boy muttered something in African.

'Why wouldn't you have your finger-prints taken?' the magistrate asked Johnny, as if he had thereby deprived himself of a curious and amusing experience.

'My belief, sir, is that here in this country no man is forced to have prints taken of his fingers unless he has been convicted of some crime, which in my life I never have been at any time for any reason.'

The magistrate contrived both to frown and raise his brows. 'But don't you think you ought to help the officers in their enquiries?' he said, in a mild and fatherly way. 'You know, of course, I could always make an order for you to have them done.'

'If, sir, you say I must submit to finger-prints, I will. But what is most important to me is that you give me bail, because in my cell I cannot fix to be defended as I should be. I am not a stowaway, and came to England here as proper passenger paying my own fare; and shall not wish to leave in any other way before I stand my trial.'

This speech of Johnny's seemed a little too voluble, and syntactically unsound, to please the magistrate.

'No, I don't think so,' he said finally. 'You'll have every opportunity to prepare your case and take legal advice in custody. Bail refused.'

I turned in a rage to Theodora, but found she'd gone. I went outside the court with Laddy Boy.

'They put him in Brixton for remand,' the African said. 'We go and see him there and bring him liquor.'

'In prison?'

'Port wine is allowed for only on remand, but not some spirits,' he told me. 'We also take some chicken.'

This seemed to me so irrelevant to the major problems that I wanted to clout Laddy Boy. 'The thing is to get him a good lawyer and get him out!' I said crossly.

'Oh, yes, lawyer,' said Laddy Boy. 'You fix him that.'

Theodora reappeared, red-faced and furious. 'They wouldn't let me see him,' she exclaimed. 'But I spoke to the jailer. He says we can go down to Brixton this afternoon and see him there.'

We walked out in the chilly sun, breathing great gulps of air. I stopped Theodora on the pavement.

'Doesn't one thing stick out a mile?' I said.

'What sticks out a mile is that the magistrate's a moron.'

'Forget about the magistrate, Theodora! Isn't it obvious that if we can get Muriel to go into the box, he's free?'

'Why?'

'Why? Because if he lived off her moral earnings in the shirt factory, he couldn't have been living off her sister Dorothy's immoral earnings on the streets.'

'*He* could persuade Muriel—but can we? That's why they refused him bail,' cried Theodora. 'Why isn't Muriel here, anyway? She's ratted on him.'

'You speak of Muriel?' said Laddy Boy. 'She leave Johnny some many weeks now.'

'And who's he been living with since?' asked Theodora sharply.

'Sometimes Dorothy, I think, but he leave her too.'

'My God!' cried Theodora. 'The imbecile!'

'Laddy Boy,' I said. 'You don't think he *did* this with Dorothy, do you?'

The sailor looked vaguer than ever. 'Thing is to get him free,' he said. 'What he do, not matter. What matter is get him free.'

'We'd better go and see Muriel, anyway, and find out,' I said.

'Muriel, she with her mother now, Johnny tell me,' Laddy Boy said, rather indifferently.

We had a not very agreeable lunch together at a fish-and-chip place. Laddy Boy went out shopping, and, when he came back, spent much time making mysterious little bundles of what he'd bought.

'These Africans are *hopeless*,' said Theodora in a whisper like a scream.

'What *are* you up to, Laddy Boy?' I asked.

'I tip out the port wine from the bottle, and put in whisky,' Laddy Boy said proudly. 'He like that better. And in these chicken wing, I put some weed beneath the skin of it.'

'Good heavens! Don't they examine everything?'

'Oh, yes. But I do it very clever.'

'Let's hope to God you do.'

We set off to Brixton in dejected silence, only Laddy Boy undismayed. He pointed out landmarks on the way. ('That the Oval station, there,' for example.) Outside the prison gates, the taxi driver was facetious. ('Don't stay in there too long, mate, will you?' etc.) We were kept waiting in the waiting-room inside by a jailer whose face had to be seen to be believed. Laddy Boy carefully handed over his parcels, which the warder dumped like offal in a cardboard case. At last, behind the partitioned wire-netting that ran down one half of the room, Johnny Fortune made his sad appearance.

And it was sad: the buoyancy had dropped, and for the first time since I knew him I thought he looked afraid. He wasn't much interested in Theodora and in me, and talked most of the time to Laddy Boy in African. Theodora grew increasingly enraged. 'We *must* get the information out of him, Montgomery. Do interrupt that wretched African, and *talk* to Johnny.'

'The lawyer will see him for all that, Theodora. Don't be angry—just try to cheer him up.'

Almost at once, the warder said, in tones like a funeral bell, 'Time up!' At this Laddy Boy seemed suddenly overcome with hysteria and, clutching the wire-netting, cried, in English, 'My brother! Bless you, my brother! Oh, my brother!'—and tried to kiss Johnny through the grille. The warders tore him away, and Johnny was marched off. 'Any more of that,' the jailer said, 'and you'll be coming inside to keep him company.'

Out in the street, as soon as we'd turned the corner, Laddy Boy let out a roar of laughter. 'I do it!' he cried. 'I do it.'

'Do *what*, you idiot!' Theodora shouted.

'Theodora!'

'The five-pound note, he get it! I kiss it to him through the bar!'

When the ingenious seaman's mirth abated, he told us he'd screwed the note up in a ball, put it in his mouth, and passed it through the grille into Johnny Fortune's. 'But is money all that much use when you're in jail?' I asked the sailor.

Laddy Boy stopped in his tracks, and said: 'Man, in that place, loot is *everything*. You can buy *anything* if you have loot.'

'It'll make him more cheerful, then. He didn't look too happy, did he.'

'Understand me, man,' said Laddy Boy. 'It is his family he think of. Wounding or even thieving, that is nothing; but this charge they put upon him is the top disgrace.'

Nearby Lambeth town hall, Theodora insisted on entering a phone box to call up again Sir Wallingford whoever-it-was, her family solicitor. I was not surprised when she came out and told us, 'He wasn't there, but his chief clerk says it's not the sort of case they handle.'

'Very helpful. Let's stick to Zuss-Amor.'

'You want me to come with you to see him?'

'Not unless you really want to. I think it'd be much easier if I call on him alone. But first of all I'm going to try to contact Muriel. I know where her mother lives in Maida Vale.'

'I shall come too.'

'No, Theodora, you will not. The last thing likely to encourage Muriel to help Johnny is to hear a rival pleading for him to her.'

'What else can I do, then?'

'Go to your office and write some enormous memos. I'll call you as soon as I've seen Zuss-Amor.'

'I might ask the Corporation to let me appear in court as a witness to his character.'

'Suppose he gets convicted, Theodora.'

'He won't get convicted. He's innocent.'

'Yes, but if he were convicted, and you'd appeared in court, you'd lose your job.'

'I wouldn't. No one is ever dismissed from the Corporation.'

'No doubt; but I can't believe you'd rise to any further dizzy heights there if you got mixed up publicly in this case.'

'You've no guts, Montgomery. No moral fibre.'

'Oh, SHUT UP, Theodora. You're beginning to get on my tits.'

'Easy now,' said Laddy Boy.

I seized his hand, shook it, waved to Theodora, and leapt into a taxi on the rank. Then, remembering I had no money for the lawyer, had to climb ignominiously out and borrow it from her. I set off northwards in a rage.

But I got no help from the Macpherson family. A horrible old woman who admitted to being the mother refused to let me in, and though I shouted through the door for Muriel, she wouldn't come.

'She's finished with him—finished!' Mrs Macpherson yelled, sticking her face and body out at me like the figurehead of a ship. 'I don't care if they hang him for what he's done, my daughter wouldn't lift her little finger for him!' And she banged the door.

15

Wisdom of Mr Zuss-Amor

Mr zuss-amor didn't receive me at the appointed hour: he kept me waiting in a corridor upon a kitchen chair, with nothing to regale me but yesterday's daily newspaper. The typist with ornamental spectacles who'd let me in vacated her cubby-hole from time to time, stepped indifferently over my legs, and went through a door of corrugated frosted glass inscribed in black cursive letters with the name of this man on whom we now pinned our hopes.

I was reduced to reading the opinions in the leading articles when the glass door was opened from inside and a voice said, 'I'm ready for you now. Quite ready.' When I went in, the door closed and a man stood between me and it, looking me up and down. He was wispy-bald, clad in a rumpled suit of good material, cigarette ash smothered his lapels, and his hands dangled by his sides. His face, which looked battered, sharp and confident, wore a tired and hideous smile. 'I'm your guide, philosopher and friend from now on, Mr Pew,' this person said. 'Come and tell me all about it.'

I did. He listened silently till I had nothing more to say.

'Have a fag,' he said, offering me one from a battered pack. 'I chain-smoke myself—that's why I don't like appearing in court. I prefer the work here.' He lit my cigarette. 'Right. In the first place, you should understand I can't be instructed by you. You're not the accused, fortunately. It's his instructions I have to take, you see.'

'But he asked me to come here.'

'I don't disbelieve you. But if I accept this case, I'll have to send someone down to the jail to see our friend. And whatever *he* wants me to do, I'll have to.'

'Am I wasting my time, then?'

'No—nor mine either, altogether. The more I know about the background in a case like this, the better. So. A point. What is the relationship between the accused and you? I mean the *exact* relationship?'

'I am his friend.'

'For what reason?'

'Because I like him.'

'*Like* him?'

'That's what I said.'

'You like him. Oh. What I mean is—is there anything at all I ought to know you haven't told me?'

'I don't think so.'

'I see. Another point. Why did you come here to me?'

'I told you. Mr Alfy Bongo gave your name to me.'

'Alfy. He told you I was a snide lawyer, I suppose?'

'He said you were a solicitor who wins cases.'

'Flattering! Right. Now, most important of all. Have you got any money?'

'Yes. Some.'

'Pay twenty to my secretary when you leave, will you? That'll do nicely to go on with. In notes, please—no cheques, or I can't fiddle my taxes.' He gave me a frosty grin, folded his fingers, and said, 'Very well, then. From what you've said, I can practically guarantee you something: which is that your friend will lose this case.'

'Why will he? He's innocent.'

'Oh, I don't doubt it! I don't doubt it one little bit! But these cases are always lost before they go to court. Believe the expert.'

'Then we might as well have no defence?'

'Not at all—why shouldn't you? I'm here to advise you. For example. You don't always have to fight a case, Mr Pew. You can also buy it.'

'Sorry . . .'

'Though it may be expensive. You say that two police officers were involved?'

'Yes. . . .'

'And they'll have their chief to remember. . . .'

'Do you mean . . .'

'That's just exactly what I mean.'

'But they've already brought the charge.'

'I know they have. You wouldn't be here if they hadn't. But for a consideration, they might not press it in the courts. There's evidence and evidence, you know.'

'What sort of consideration?'

'I'd have to see. But you'd better be thinking in terms of hundreds: not more than two, though, I dare say.'

'Can you arrange that?'

'It can be arranged. I haven't said by whom.'

'But if they got the money . . . wouldn't they double-cross us??'

'Why should they? It's not an important case to them. And they know if they do they'd lose good business of the same description in the future. . . .'

'I see.'

'I know what's in your mind: you think I'll take a cut.'

'Well, I suppose you would, wouldn't you?'

'How right you are, Mr Pew! Think of what's involved! Professional conduct of a disgraceful nature, and so on and so forth. I'd be quite reasonable, though. I'd not kill the goose that lays the golden egg. . . .'

Mr Zuss-Amor's dentures gave me an amiable, impatient smile. He clearly had other interviews in his diary.

'I'm not sure I can raise that much money all at once.'

'Oh. We can forget it, then.'

'And in any case, I think it's better to fight them.'

The solicitor ran his hand up and down his waistcoat buttons. 'It's not exactly you who's fighting them, but your friend,' he said. 'All the same, I think your decision's perfectly right.'

'Oh? Why do you?'

'If you take it to court, you'll almost certainly go down, as I've told you, though there's always a chance, if slight. But if you give these gentlemen a little something, they'll see to it you give them some more sooner or later. And probably sooner.'

'I don't get it, I'm sorry, Mr Zuss-Amor.'

'I've no doubt your life is blameless, Mr Pew. All the same, if they decided to scrape around and look for some dirt, they'd possibly find you'd done something or other. We all have, at one time, I expect. Even the bench of bishops have a blot on their consciences somewhere, I shouldn't be surprised.'

'But how would they know it was me the money came from?'

'Now, Mr Pew! Don't underestimate the Law! They know you're the friend of the accused, they've seen you in court this morning, they know—well, I dare say they know quite a lot of things.' He took off his spectacles and wiped them with his fingers. 'Or perhaps,' he went on, 'you think *I*'d tell them who paid up. Well, even if I did, I wouldn't have to: they'd just know.'

'So that's ruled out, then.'

'Very good. Right. So we go to court. The question arises: which court do we go to?'

'Isn't that automatic?'

'To begin with, yes, it is. Everyone appears before a magistrate initially. Even if you murdered the prime minister, that's where you'd first appear. But you needn't be tried by the magistrate if you don't want to be.'

'What else can you do'

'You can elect to go before a judge and jury.'

'And which is better?'

'There are naturally pros and cons in either case.'

'Well, tell me the pros and cons.'

Mr Zuss-Amor leaned back with his hands behind his head. 'My God!' he said, 'how often I've had to explain these simple facts! Don't laymen know *anything*?'

'Perhaps, Mr Zuss-Amor, it's to your advantage that they don't.'

'Oh, quick! Below the belt, but excellent! Right. Here we go. You elect to go before the magistrate. Advantages. It's over quicker, one way or the other. Less publicity, if that should happen to matter. The sentences aren't so high as a judge can give, if you're convicted.'

'And the cons?'

'No appeal—except to the bench of magistrates. From the judge, you can go up to the House of Lords, if all is well, but as you've not got the cash, the point's academic. Trial by jury takes much longer: it may be weeks before your young friend's face to face with my Lord and his merry men. Also, it'll cost you more. There'll be more for me, of course, and we'd have to get a barrister.'

'If we went to the magistrate, we don't need one?'

'Ah—you're catching on! Correct. Solicitors can appear before the beak. Though even in the magistrates' court, a barrister can be a help if he waves his law books at the old boy without antagonizing him unduly.'

'What does a barrister cost?'

'As you'd expect, it depends on who he is. If he's any good, it won't cost you less than fifty at the least—with refreshers, of course, that you'll have to pay if the trial lasted more than a day.'

'Is it likely to?'

'I don't suppose so, but we might come on late in the afternoon and get adjourned.' He paused. 'Well, have you made up your mind?'

'I don't know yet, Mr Zuss-Amor. You'd better tell me what you advise.'

'Advise! If I say, "Go to the judge," you'll think it's because I want more money.'

'Why should I?'

'You'd be a bloody fool if you didn't. . . . But all the same, there are certainly big advantages. Though, before I tell you what they are, I should repeat what I said just now—I think in this case you'll go down anyway.'

'Why are you so sure?'

'Because, my dear man, when the Law frames a case, they make a point of seeing it sticks. They have to.'

'I see.'

'I wish you did. You want to know why you should go to the judge and jury, then. In the first place, I don't know who the magistrate will be, but nine out of ten accept police evidence: the more so, as I need hardly tell you, when the prisoner's coloured.'

'Don't juries believe policemen, too?'

'They do, yes, even more so in a way, but there's a difference: twelve men have to be persuaded, and not one. Or twelve men and women, if we're lucky enough to have any serving. But that's not the chief consideration. What comes now is a point of legal strategy, so follow me closely, Mr Pew. You elect to go before the judge and jury. Right. That means the prosecution has to state its case, so as to get you committed. In other words, we hear all their evidence and they can't alter it afterwards much, though they can add to it if they get some nice new bright ideas. But as for you, you sit tight in the dock . . .'

'It's not me, Mr Zuss-Amor.'

'. . . All right, your friend sits in the dock and keeps his mouth shut. He says nothing.'

'But he has to speak later before the judge and jury . . .'

'Of course he has to, if he's called. But by that time we know the prosecution's case, and they don't know ours at all. And if me and the barrister, whoever it is we choose, take a good look at the transcript of the prosecution's evidence before the final trial comes on, our trained legal brains may find a hole or two that can be picked in it. Because it's not all that easy to think up a consistent story of what never happened—you'd be surprised.'

'It seems we should go to the jury, then.'

Mr Zuss-Amor gave me a sweet smile, as of one who congratulates a nitwit for seeing what was perfectly evident all the time.

'If you want to know the fruits of my experience, Mr Pew,' he said, 'I'll give you these three golden rules. Never accept trial by magistrate, unless it's a five-shilling parking offence, or something of that nature. Never plead guilty—even if the Law walks in and finds you with a gun in your hand and a corpse lying on the floor. And when you're arrested, never, never say a word, whatever they do, whatever they promise or threaten—that is, if you have the nerve to stick it out. Always remember, when they've got you alone in the cells, that they also have to prove the case in the open light of day. Say nothing, sign nothing. Most cases, believe me, are lost in the first half-hour after the arrest.'

'You mean if you make a statement to them?'

'Exactly. Tell them your name, your age, your occupation and address. Not a word more. Even then, they may swear you did say this or that, but it's harder to prove you did if you've signed nothing and kept your trap shut.' Mr Zuss-Amor arose, walked to the window, and gazed out glassily. 'It's a wicked world,' he said, 'thank goodness.' He pondered a moment. 'What about witnesses?' he asked me, turning round. 'Who can we muster?'

'I've told you this girl Muriel won't speak for him.'

'It might make quite a bit of difference if she did. And it looks rather bad, doesn't it, if she won't.'

'Why?'

'Come, now! If we say, as we're going to, that the defendant was living not with a whore, Dorothy, but with his lady-love, her sister Muriel, wouldn't the jury expect to see Miss Muriel in the box and hear her say so?'

'I'll have another shot at her. Are witnesses to character any use?'

'None whatever, unless you can produce the Pope, or someone. No, we'll have to do our best with Mr Fortune himself if we can't get Muriel. Can he talk well?'

'His only trouble is that he talks too much.'

'I'll warn our counsel. Now who will we have against us? The Detective-Inspector, of course, and his Detective-Constable, I have no doubt—and even an old hand won't be able to shake *them*.'

'But what on earth can they say?'

'Oh-ho! You wait and see! You'll be surprised what that pair saw through brick walls two feet thick! And then, of course, they may call little Dorothy.'

'They're sure to, aren't they?'

'No.... She's a common prostitute, don't forget, and juries don't seem to believe a word they say. I hope they do call her, though—I'd like to see our counsel tear her guts out in cross-examination....'

Mr Zuss-Amor rubbed his chest with relish. I got up to go.

'I don't suppose you'll believe,' I said, 'that Johnny Fortune hasn't been a ponce. But isn't it clear, from all you tell me, that these cases are sometimes framed?'

'Oh, of course they are! Who said they weren't?' Mr Zuss-Amor stood face to face with me. 'I handle a lot of cases for the defence,' he said, 'that they don't like to see me get an acquittal for. So the police don't love me all that much, as you can imagine. And believe me, whenever I get into my car at night, I look it over to see if they've planted anything there.'

'You do?'

'Well, if I don't, I ought to. And that reminds me,' he went on, leaning his lower belly against the desk. 'If you can pay for it, we'll have to get a barrister who's not afraid of coppers.'

'Some of them are, then?'

'Most of them are. But one who certainly isn't is Wesley Vial—even though he's a junior.'

'A Mr Vial who lives near Marble Arch? A fat, hairy man?'

'You know him, I dare say. He's a friend of little Alfy's.'

'I know him slightly. And so does Johnny Fortune. We went to a party at his house. I don't think he likes either of us much.'

'Oh, really? Wheels within wheels, I see.' Mr Zuss-Amor sat down again. 'I won't enquire why,' he said, 'but I don't think it'll make the slightest difference. If Vial takes on the case, he'll go all out to win it for you. Shall I ask him, anyway?'

'What is a junior, exactly?'

'He's not taken silk. Doesn't mean a thing, though. Some of the best men don't bother, because when they take silk their fees have to go up, and they lose a lot of clients. Better six cases at fifty guineas than one at two hundred, don't you agree?'

'And Vial's the best man we can get?'

'At the price you can pay, undoubtedly. Your young friend will have to see him some time, too. And before he does, there's something else you might as well explain to him.' Mr Zuss-Amor looked at the ceiling, then with his mouth open at me, then continued: 'It's a delicate matter: one laymen don't always grasp at once. In a nutshell: to beat perjured evidence, you have to meet it with perjury.'

'No, I don't understand.'

'I didn't expect you would. However. Let me give you an instance. Suppose you walk out of this building and the Law arrests you on the doorstep for being drunk and disorderly in Piccadilly Circus while you were really talking here to me. What would you do?'

'Deny it.'

'Deny what?'

'The whole thing.'

'That's the point: if they took you to court, you'd be most unwise. When they go into the box—and remember, there's always more than one of them—and swear you were where you weren't, and did what you didn't, no jury will believe you if you deny their tale entirely.'

'So what do I do?'

'You say . . . having sworn by Almighty God, of course, like they have, to tell the whole truth, etcetera . . . you say that you *were* in Piccadilly Circus, yes, and you *had* taken one light ale, yes, but that you *weren't* drunk or disorderly. In other words, you tag along with their story in its inessentials, but deny the points that can get you a conviction. If you do that, your counsel can suggest the Law had made an honest error. But if you deny everything they say, the jury will accept their word against yours.'

Mr Zuss-Amor shrugged, flung out his hands, and corrugated his brows into deep furrows.

'So Johnny mustn't deny all their story, but simply say he never took money from Dorothy, or had sex with her.

'Particularly the former, of course. Yes, being an African, I don't suppose he'll mind damning his soul to get an acquittal. A lot of Christians do it. Is he one?'

'I believe so.'

'You can help him wrestle with his conscience, then. But do it before he sees Mr Vial. Because that's what Vial will want him to say, but he won't be able to put it so plain himself. It wouldn't be etiquette, not for a barrister. Dirty work of that nature's left to us solicitors, who really win the case by preparing it properly outside the court—that is, if it's the sort of case that can be won.'

Mr Zuss-Amor bared all his teeth at me. I got up and shook his hand. 'Thank you, Mr Zuss-Amor, you've made things wonderfully clear.'

He also rose. 'They need to be,' he said. 'Trials are all a matter of tactics. I don't know what happened, or if anything did happen, between that boy and that girl, any more than I suppose you really do. But believe me, when you listen to all the evidence in the court, you'll be amazed to see how little relation what's said there bears to what really occurred, so far as one knows it. It's one pack of lies fighting another, and the thing is to think up the best ones, and have the best man there to tell them for you so that justice is done.'

He opened the frosted door and let me out.

SECOND INTERLUDE

'Let Justice be done (and be seen to be)!'

THE TRIAL OF JOHNNY MACDONALD FORTUNE took place in a building, damaged in the Hitler war, which had been redecorated in a 'contemporary' style—light salmon wood, cubistic lanterns, leather cushions of pastel shades—that pleased none of the lawyers, officials or police officers who worked there. The courts looked too much like the board-rooms of progressive companies, staterooms on liners, even 'lounges' of American-type hotels, for the severe traditional taste of these professionals; and all of them, when they appeared there, injected into their behaviour an additional awesome formality to counteract the lack of majesty of their surroundings.

On the morning of the trial, Mr Zuss-Amor had a short conference with Mr Wesley Vial. In his wig and gown, Mr Vial was transformed from the obese, balding playboy of the queer theatrical parties he loved to give at his flat near Marble Arch, into a really impressive figure; impressive, that is, by his authority, which proceeded from his formidable knowledge of the operation of the law, his nerves of wire, his adaptable, synthetic charm, his aggressive ruthlessness, and his total contempt for weakness and 'fair play'. Mr Zuss-Amor, by comparison, seemed, in this décor, a shabby figure—like a nonconformist minister calling on a cardinal.

'Who have we got against us?' said Mr Zuss-Amor.

'Archie Gillespie.'

'As Crown counsel in these cases go, by no means a fool.'

'By *no* means, Mr Zuss-Amor.'

The solicitor felt rebuked. 'What was your impression of our client, Mr Vial?'

'Nice boy. Do what I can for him, of course—but what? The trouble with coloured men in the dock, you know, is that juries just can't tell a good one from a bad.'

'Can they *ever* tell that, would you say?'

'Oh, sometimes! Don't be too hard on juries.'

'We'll be having some ladies, I believe.'

'Excellent! He must flash all his teeth at them.' Mr Vial turned over the pages of the brief. 'There was nothing you could do with this Muriel Macpherson woman?'

'Nothing. I even went out and saw her myself. She's very sore with our young client, Mr Vial. Frankly, I think if we *had* called her, we'd have found ourselves asking permission to treat her as a hostile witness.'

' "Hell hath no fury," and so on. On the other hand, Gillespie tells me he's not calling the sister Dorothy. Very wise of him. He's relying on police evidence—which, I'm sorry to say, will probably be quite sufficient for his purpose.'

'Pity you couldn't have had a go at the woman Dorothy in the box, though, Mr Vial. . . .' The solicitor's eyes gleamed.

'Oh, best to keep the females out of it, on the whole. I'll see what can be done with the two officers. I've met the Inspector in the courts before . . . always makes an excellent impression. Looks like a family man who'd like to help the prisoner if he could: deeply regrets having to do his painful duty. I don't think I know the Detective-Constable. . . .'

'A new boy in the C.I.D. Very promising in the Force, I'm told. Man of few words in the box, though. Difficult to shake him, I think you'll find.'

Mr Vial put down the brief. 'And yet, you know, it *should* be possible to shake them.'

'If anyone can do it, you can.'

'I didn't mean that. I mean this charge: it's bogus. Just look at it!' (He held up the brief.) 'It stinks to high heaven!'

'You think this boy's telling the truth—or part of it?'

'I think he's telling the whole of it. I pressed him hard at our little interview, as you saw. And what did he do? He lost his temper! I've never seen such righteous indignation! I'm always impressed by honest fury in a defendant.'

Mr Zuss-Amor nodded, frowned, and scratched his bottom. 'Why do they do it, Mr Vial?' he said.

'Why do who do what?'

'Why do the police bring these trumped-up charges?'

'Oh, well . . .' The advocate sighed with all his bulk, and hitched his robe. 'You know the familiar argument as well as I do. The accused's generally done what they say he's done, but not how they say he's done it. The charge is usually true, the evidence often false. But in this case, I think both are phoney. . . . Well, we'll have to see. . . .'

The two C.I.D. officers were having a cup of tea in the police room. 'It's your first case with us in the vice game,' said the Inspector, 'but you don't have to let that worry you. The way to win a case, in my experience, is not to mind from the beginning if you lose it.'

'But we shouldn't lose this one, should we, sir?'

'I don't see how we can, Constable. But just remember what I told you. They'll keep you outside until I've given evidence, of course, but you know what I'm going to say in its essential outlines. If they ask any questions in examination that we haven't thought of, just say as little as possible: take your time, look the lawyer in the eye, and just say you don't remember.'

'He's rough, isn't he, Inspector, this Wesley Vial?'

'That fat old poof? Don't be afraid of him, son. He's sharp, mind you, but if you don't let him rattle you, there's nothing he can do.' The Inspector lit his Dunhill pipe. 'It's obvious what he'll try,' he continued. 'He'll make out that he accepts our story, but he'll try to shake us on the details, so as to put a doubt into the jury's mind.'

The constable sipped his beverage. 'They're not likely to raise the question of that bit of rough stuff at the station, are they?'

'Vial certainly won't—he knows no jury would believe it. But the boy might allege something, even though Vial's probably told him not to. Let's hope he does do. It'd make a very bad impression on the court. Drink up now, Constable, we're on in a minute or two.'

The constable swallowed. 'I'm sure you know best about not calling that girl Dorothy, sir. But don't you think if we'd had her to pin it on him good and proper . . .'

'Mr Gillespie said no, and I think he's right. I've told her to keep out of the way and keep her trap shut till the trial's over—and she will. You never know how it will be with women in the box: she may love this boy, for all we know, and might have spoken out of turn;

and if we'd called her for the prosecution, we might have found ourselves with a hostile witness on our hands.'

In the public gallery, a little minority group of Africans was collecting: among them Laddy Boy, who'd brought an air cushion and a bag of cashew nuts; the Bushman, who'd got a front seat, leaned on the railing and immediately gone to sleep; and Mr Karl Marx Bo, who planned to send by air mail a tendentious report on the trial to the Mendi newspaper of which he was part-time correspondent, if, as he hoped it would be, the result was unfavourable to the defendant.

Theodora and Montgomery arrived much too early, and sat in great discomfort on the benches that sloped steeply like a dress circle overlooking the well of the court. They wondered if they could take their overcoats off and, if so, where they could put them.

'It doesn't look very impressive,' said Theodora. 'It's much too small.'

'It looks exactly like Act III of a murder play. Which is the dock?'

'Just underneath us, I expect.'

'So we won't see him.'

'We will when he's giving evidence,' said Theodora. 'That's the witness-box there on the right.'

'Box is the word for it. It looks like an up-ended coffin.'

Mr Wesley Vial met Mr Archie Gillespie in the lawyers' lavatory. 'I do hope, Wesley,' the Crown counsel said, 'your man's English will be comprehensible. I take it you'll be putting him in the box?'

'Time alone will show, Archie. But if you want any evidence taken in the vernacular, we can always put in for an interpreter and prolong matters to your heart's content.'

'No, thank you,' said Mr Gillespie. 'Crown counsel don't draw your huge refreshers.' He dried his hands. 'Who's the judge?'

'Old Haemorrhoids.'

'My God. It would be.'

The lawyers looked at each other resignedly. There was a distant shout, and they adjusted their wigs like actors who've heard the call-boy summon them to the stage.

Johnny Fortune had been brought up from Brixton to the court in one of those police vans where the prisoners half sit in metal boxes, hardly larger than themselves. They'd arrived more than an hour before the case began, and the court jailer, after searching him yet again, said, 'Well, we won't put you in the cells unless you really want to go there. If I leave you in the room here, will you behave yourself?'

'Of course.'

'You want some cigarettes?'

'They not let me take any of my money.'

'Oh, pay me when you're acquitted!' said the jailer with a hearty laugh, and gave Johnny Fortune a half-filled pack of Woodbines and a cup of purple tea. 'I see you've got Vial,' he went on. 'That'll cost you a bit, won't it? Or should I say'—the jailer laughed roguishly—'cost your little lady and her customers?'

Johnny stood up. 'Mister, put me in your cells. I do not wish your tea or want your Woodbine.'

'No offence, lad, don't be so touchy. I know you all have to say you're innocent—I get used to it here. Come on, keep them—you've got an hour to wait.' The jailer patted his prisoner on the shoulder, and went over to gossip with a lean, powdered female constable in civilian dress, who, as they talked, looked over the jailer's shoulder at the folds in Johnny Fortune's trousers.

Everyone stood, and the judge came in wearing a wig not of the Gilbert and Sullivan variety, but a short one, slightly askew, that made him look like Dr Johnson's younger brother. The jury was new, and the case their first, so they had to be sworn in by the usher. Two of them were women: a W.V.S. housewifely person, and the other with a beret and a tailored suit whose nature it was impossible to guess at. A male juror turned out, when he swore, to be called 'Ramsay Macdonald', on hearing which Mr Vial made a slight histrionic gesture of impressed surprise to Mr Gillespie, who ignored him.

One of the two policemen in the dock nudged Johnny, and he stood. The clerk, a quite young man with a pink, pale face, read out the charge in a voice like an Old Vic juvenile's; and when he asked Johnny how he pleaded, looked up at him, across the court, with a pleading expression on his own wan face.

'I plead not guilty.'

Mr Zuss-Amor, flanking his advocate, twitched his shoulders slightly. You never could tell with defendants: he'd even known them get the plea wrong at the outset.

Mr Archie Gillespie's opening statement of the case for the Queen against the prisoner was as methodical as one would expect from a Scottish lawyer of vast experience and entire integrity. He had the great psychological advantages of believing the facts in the brief that he'd been given, or most of them, and of being quite dispassionate in his advocacy. He had no feeling of animosity towards the prisoner whatever, and this made him all the more deadly.

He began by explaining to the jury what living on the immoral earnings of a common prostitute consisted of. It was a distasteful subject, and a painful duty for the members of the jury to have to hear about it. But they were, he did not doubt, men and women of ripe experience, to whom he could speak quite frankly. Very well, then. As everyone knew, there were, unfortunately, such women as common prostitutes—selling their bodies for gain (Mr Gillespie paused, and gazed at a female juror, who licked her lips)—in our society; women whose odious commerce was—subject to certain important restrictions—not actually illegal, however reprehensible on moral grounds. But what *was* illegal—and highly so, and he would say more, revolting and abhorrent—was the practice of certain men—if one could call them men—of battening on these wretched creatures, and living on the wages of their sin; and even, in a great many cases—though he would not necessarily say it was so in the present instance—even of forcing them out on to the streets against their wills. It was not for nothing, said Mr Gillespie, removing his spectacles a moment, that such men, in the speech of a more robust age, had been known as 'bullies'.

The judge manifested a slight impatience, and Mr Gillespie took the hint. He explained to the jury that two police officers would tell them how observation had been kept on one Dorothea Violet Macpherson, a known and convicted common prostitute, who had been seen, on several nights in succession, to accost men in Hyde Park, receive sums of money from them, entice them into the undergrowth, and there have carnal knowledge of them. These officers would further tell the members of the jury how the said Dorothea Violet Macpherson was subsequently followed to an address in Immigration Road, Whitechapel, where she lived in two rooms with the accused. (Here Mr Gillespie paused, and spoke more slowly.) These officers would then tell how, on a number of occasions when observation was kept on the accused and on the said Dorothea Violet Macpherson, she was seen to hand over to him large sums of money that had come into her possession through her immoral commerce in the purlieus of Hyde Park.

The Crown counsel now glanced at Mr Vial, who sat looking into the infinite like a Buddha. 'No doubt my learned friend here will suggest to you,' he declared, 'that the accused was not present on these occasions or, alternatively, that the sums of money in question were not passed over to him or, alternatively again, that if they were, they were not those proceeding from the act of common prostitution.' Mr Gillespie waited a second, as if inviting Mr Vial to say just that: then continued, 'It will be for you, members of the jury, to decide on whose evidence you should rely: on that of the witness, or witnesses, that may be brought forward by the defence, or on that of the two experienced police officers whom I am now going to call before you.'

The Detective-Inspector walked in with a modest, capable and self-sufficient mien. He took the oath, removed a notebook from his pocket, and turned to face his counsel.

'Members of the jury,' said Mr Gillespie. 'You will observe that the Detective-Inspector is holding a small book. Inspector, will you please tell the court what this book is?'

'It's my police notebook, sir.'

'Exactly. Officers of the Crown, when giving evidence, are permitted to refer, for matters of fact—and matters of fact only—to the notes they made of a case immediately after they have performed their duties. Very well. Now, Detective-Inspector, will you please tell my Lord and members of the jury what happened, in your own words?'

In his own words, and prompted only slightly by Mr Gillespie, the officer related the detailed minutiae of the events the counsel had already outlined. By the time of the third, fourth and fifth seeing of Dorothy taking money in the park, and seeing her giving it to Johnny in the Immigration Road, the tale began to lose some of its human fascination, even though its cumulative substance added greatly to the 'weight of evidence'.

Mr Gillespie sat down, and Mr Wesley Vial arose.

'Detective-Inspector,' he said. 'Do you know who the defendant is?'

'Who he is, sir? He's an African.'

'Yes. Quite so. An African. But can you tell us anything about him?'

'I have, sir.'

'Yes, Inspector, we know you have. But I mean who he is? His family? His background? What sort of man the court has got before it?'

'No, sir. He said he was a student.'

'He said he was a student. Did you enquire of what?'

'No, sir.'

'You didn't. Did you know this young man's father, Mr David Macdonald Fortune, wears the King's Medal for valour which was awarded to him when he was formerly a sergeant in the Nigerian police force?'

'No, sir.'

'You didn't bother to find out what sort of man you had to deal with? It didn't interest you. Is that it?'

The judge stirred himself slightly, as if from a distant dream. 'I can't quite see the relevance of that, Mr Vial,' he said, in a melancholy, croaking voice. 'It's not the accused's father who's before me.'

Mr Vial bowed. 'True, my Lord. But your Lordship will appreciate, I'm sure, how vital it is for me, in a case of this description—that is, a case where the defendant is a citizen of one of the colonies of our Commonwealth—to establish clearly his social standing and reputation. The members of the jury' (Mr Vial inclined himself courteously towards them) 'may not be as familiar as we have grown to be, my Lord, with what very different sorts of African citizen are now to be found here in England among us: some, no doubt, with a background of a kind that might render an accusation of this nature unfortunately all too credible, but others—as I hope to show you is the case at present—in whom such conduct would be as totally improbable as it would were I, my Lord, or Mr Gillespie here, to be said to indulge in it.'

There was a hush, while everyone digested this. 'Yes. Well, do proceed, please, Mr Vial,' said the judge.

The defending counsel turned once more to the Crown witness.

'You have, in fact, Inspector—apart, of course, from the present case—nothing to say against the defendant?'

'No, sir. He's got no police record.

'Exactly. He's got no police record. And has he, at any time, made any statement in writing, or any verbal statement concerning the charge, by which he admits his guilt in any particular whatever?'

'No, sir.'

'So we're left with what you and your officers have seen, Inspector.'

The Inspector didn't answer. Mr Vial looked up, and barked at him, 'I say, we're left with what you tell us that you've seen. Will you please answer me, Inspector?'

'I didn't know you were asking me a question, sir.'

'You didn't know I was asking you a question. Very well. Now, I want you to tell us about these happenings in Hyde Park. You saw this woman accost various men at various times on various evenings, take money from them, and disappear with them into the . . .' (Mr Vial looked at his notes) '. . . yes, into the undergrowth, I think it was. Now let us take the first evening: the evening you tell us that the defendant later received twenty-eight pounds from this woman. How many men accosted her?'

'Five or six, sir.'

'Five—or six? Which was it? You may consult your notebook if you wish.'

'Six, sir.'

'So each man would have paid an average of four pounds thirteen shillings and fourpence for this woman's services?'

'Not necessarily, sir. She could have had some money in her bag before she went inside the park.'

'In her what, Inspector?'

'She could have had some money in her bag before she went there.'

'What bag?'

'The bag she put the money in, sir.'

'Oh.' Mr Vial picked up a document. 'But in the magistrates' court, I see you told his Worship that this woman put the money in her raincoat pocket.'

'Yes, sir.'

'Sometimes she put it in her raincoat pocket, and sometimes she put it in her bag, is that it?'

'Yes, sir.'

'I see. And then she went with these people into the undergrowth. How dark was this undergrowth?'

'Quite light enough to keep her under observation, sir.'

'Come now, Inspector. Are you telling the court a woman of this description would take a man, in a public locality like Hyde Park, into a place that was dark enough for her purposes, but light enough to be observed by two police officers—standing at a certain distance from her, I suppose?'

'We were quite near enough, sir, to see whatever happened.'

'You were quite near enough. And she never saw you?'

'No, sir.'

'On no occasion? Not once on all these evenings when you and your colleague stood peering at her while she went into the undergrowth with all these dozens of men?'

'She gave no sign of being seen, sir.'

'Not even when you followed her home?'

'No, sir.'

'What did she travel home on? A bus? A tube?'

'She usually took a bus to Victoria station, and then a tube, sir.'

'She usually did. Aren't prostitutes in the habit of taking taxis? Isn't that notorious?'

'Not all of them, sir. Not always.' The officer consulted his notebook. 'She took a taxi one night, but it's not been referred to in my evidence.'

'So you followed her by bus, or tube, or taxi to the Immigration Road—and then what?'

'We saw her go into the house, sir.'

'Saw her how? Did you follow her inside?'

'No, sir. We kept observation from the street.

'So you must have seen her through the window. Is that it?'

'Yes, sir.'

'This window had no curtains, I suppose. Is that what you have to tell us?'

'Yes, sir, it had. But they weren't always drawn over it.'

'Not always drawn across the window in the depths of winter?'

'Not always, sir.'

Mr Vial paused for quite ten seconds. 'Officer,' he said, 'if you, or I, or anyone else in his right mind were going to hand a large sum of money over to somebody else, even for a perfectly legitimate reason, would we really do it in front of an open, uncurtained window on the ground floor of a house in a busy street of a not particularly salubrious neighbourhood?'

'That's what they did, sir.'

'And if the transaction was a highly illegal one, as it would be in the present instance, wouldn't there be all the more reason to hand the money over behind closed doors and out of sight?'

'These people are very careless, sir. They're often under the influence of alcohol, and other things.'

'They'd need to be! They'd certainly need to be, to behave so rashly!' Mr Vial gazed in amazement at the judge, at the jury, at Mr Gillespie, and back again at the Detective-Inspector. 'Now, Inspector,' he said gently. 'Please understand I'm not questioning your good faith in any respect. You're an experienced officer, as my learned friend has said, and there can therefore be no question of that at all. . . . But don't you think, from what you tell us, it's possible you were mistaken?'

'No, sir. She gave him the money like I said.'

'On half a dozen occasions, a prostitute takes money out of her handbag, or raincoat, or whatever it was, and hands it over to a man in a lighted room without the curtain drawn across in full view of the general public, and does it all so slowly that anyone standing outside could count the exact number of pound notes? Is that what you're telling us?'

'Yes, sir.'

'Thank you, Inspector.' Mr Vial sat down.

The Detective-Constable was called. Examined by Mr Gillespie, he confirmed his colleague's account in all essential particulars. Mr Wesley Vial rose again.

'How long have you been with the C.I.D., Detective-Constable?'

'Two months, sir.'

'This is your first case as a C.I.D. officer?'

'Yes, sir.'

'Before you joined the C.I.D., did your duties bring you in contact with this sort of case at all?'

'No, sir. I was in Records.'

'You were in Records. Now, Constable. Since this case was first brought in the magistrates' court, you have discussed it, naturally, with the Inspector?'

'I've talked about the case in general, sir. I haven't discussed the details of the evidence.'

'Of course not. The evidence you gave is entirely your own, isn't it? But you've relied on the guidance of your superior officers to a certain extent as to how you should put it to the court?'

The judge made a slight noise. 'I don't think you should ask the witness that, Mr Vial,' he said. 'You needn't answer, Constable.'

'As you say, my Lord. I have no further questions.'

The Detective-Constable left the box and went and sat by the Inspector, who gave him a slight, official smile. 'Call the defendant,' said the usher.

Johnny Fortune left the dock, walked firmly through the court and took the oath. The assembly regarded him with a slightly increased respect; for whatever the outcome of the case, a person in the witness-box seems a very different person from one sitting between two policemen in the dock.

Mr Vial faced his client with a look stern as Gabriel's, and said: 'John Macdonald Fortune: do you know what living off the immoral earnings of a woman means?'

'Yes. I do know.'

'Have you lived off the immoral earnings of this woman?'

'No. Never.'

'Have you ever lived off the immoral earnings of any woman?'

'Never! Never would I give my blood to such a person. Never!'

Mr Vial sat down. Mr Gillespie arose.

'You say you're a student,' he began. 'A student of what?'

'Of meteorology.'

The judge leaned forward. 'What was that word?'

'Meteorology, my Lord. I'm not quite sure what it is, but no doubt we'll discover. And how long is it since you attended your last lecture?'

'Is some months now.'

'Why? Is your college on holiday?'

'No. I give up these studies.'

'So now you're not studying anything?'

'No.'

'You've not been a student for some months, in fact?'

'No.'

'And what have you lived on?'

'I work in a labouring job.'

'How long did you work in this labouring job?'

'Some few week before I get arrested.'

'Some few weeks. And at the time you were living with this woman, were you working?'

'Listen to me, sir. I live some few week when I have no money with this woman.'

'So you *did* live with her? You admit that?'

The judge croaked again. 'There's just a point here, Mr Gillespie, I think. It's possibly the language difficulty, you know.' He looked at Johnny. 'You say you lived *with* this woman. Do you mean simply that you lived in the same house, or flat, or room, or do you mean that you lived there as man and wife?'

'She not my wife.'

'We know that,' said Mr Gillespie. 'What his Lordship means is, did you have any carnal knowledge of this woman?'

'Have what?'

'Did you have intercourse with her?'

'One time I have sex with that woman, yes. One time. But I take no money from her. Never.'

'I see. You took no money from her. Who paid the rent?'

'She pay it.'

'Who bought the food?'

'She buy some small food some time.'

'So you're telling us you lived in the same room as a common prostitute, alone with her, that you had intercourse with her, that you accepted board and lodging from her, and that you took no money from her? Is that it? Answer me, will you?'

'Listen, man. I answer you. Never I take no money from that woman. Not even pennies for my bus fare.'

'You really expect the court to believe that?'

'I swear on this book here what I say will be true. And what I say is true.'

There was suddenly a yell from the public gallery. It was the Bushman. He shouted, 'God is black!' and was hustled out by a constable. The judge closed his eyes during this episode; then opened them, and said, 'Please continue, Mr Gillespie.'

'I have no more questions, my Lord.'

'Mr Vial?'

The defending counsel bowed and shook his head. Johnny went back to the dock.

The judged blinked around the court. 'Mr Gillespie, Mr Vial. Is there anything further before you address the jury?'

The counsel shook their heads.

'Then I shall adjourn for luncheon before your final address.'

Everyone rose, the judge did so rather more slowly, and disappeared beneath the rampant lion and unicorn.

Mr Zuss-Amor stood with Montgomery outside the court, waiting for Theodora. 'Well, there it is,' said the solicitor. 'I need hardly tell you that I think he's had it.'

'What does Mr Vial say?'

'He won't commit himself. But our boy made some horrible admissions. And that interruption from the gallery didn't help at all.'

'That wasn't Johnny's fault.'

'I know it wasn't, Mr Pew: but it made a very bad impression. Was that boy drunk, or what?'

'No. Just voicing his feelings, I expect.'

'I wish he'd voiced them elsewhere.'

'I didn't think the police officers were all that brilliant, anyway.'

'Oh, they're not so clever in court as they are outside it, I admit. But they do know when to keep their mouths shut.'

'The Inspector was the more convincing . . .'

'He should be, he's been lying longer.'

'I don't like that place. Everyone acts as if the wretched prisoner's the only person there who doesn't matter.'

The solicitor didn't answer that, but said, 'I wish your friend Miss Pace would hurry powdering her nose. I could do with a gin and orange.'

Crossing the corridor, Theodora was detained by a pale youth in a drape suit whose face was vaguely familiar. 'Hullo,' he said. 'I let you in at Mr Vial's party, don't you remember? They call me Alfy Bongo.'

'Oh, yes. Excuse me, please.'

'I follow all Mr Vial's cases whenever I can.'

'Please excuse me.'

'Just a minute, miss. You know your boy's going down this afternoon?'

'What do you mean—my boy?'

'He is, isn't he? I remember you two that evening. I know how you feel about him.'

'Excuse me!' She hurried on. He sidled after her. 'There's only one thing could help him, isn't there.'

She stopped. 'What?'

'If there was some other woman to speak for him.'

'What do you mean?'

'Someone like you who might have been his girl at the time they say he was poncing on that chick.'

Theodora looked at him intently.

The Inspector and the Constable were drinking Worthingtons in the saloon bar round the corner. 'I was all right, then, sir? You're not dissatisfied?'

'All right for a beginner, Constable. Cheers!'

'We'd never have had all this fuss if we could have kept it in the magistrates' court.'

'That's out of our hands, lad, when the prisoner's got the money. I wouldn't worry about the result, though, and the sentence will be stiffer here.'

'Why didn't you just take him in for hemp, Inspector? That would have been more certain, wouldn't it?'

'Of course, but he might have got away with only a fine. Even with magistrates, you can't be sure.'

'I didn't like the defending counsel. He's murder.'

'I'll get that degenerate one day, if it's the last thing I do.'

The court jailer, who'd heard how the case was going, was not quite so nice to Johnny. 'Here's your dinner,' he said, handing him a paper bag.

'I want no dinner.'

'You'd better get into the habit of doing what you're told, you know. It might come in handy after this evening.'

'He's being awkward,' said the Brixton warder.

Theodora dragged Mr Zuss-Amor away from Montgomery into the private bar. 'At this stage,' she said, 'can we call any further witnesses?'

'We could if we had one who's of any use. . . . Why?'

'I've been Johnny Fortune's mistress.'

'Go on!'

'I saw him during the time they say he was with that woman, and gave him money, and looked after him.'

'Yes. . . ? Now look, Miss Pace, it's nice of you to think of trying to help him. But can you expect me to believe that—let alone a jury?'

'I'm pregnant by him.'

'Oh. You are? No kidding?'

'Oh, don't be so stupid and familiar! I tell you I've seen the doctor!'

'Have you!'

'I love Johnny—can't you understand? I want to marry him.'

'You do?' The solicitor shook his head dubiously. 'And you're prepared to swear all this in court—is that it?'

'Yes.'

'Well . . . I'll have to see Mr Vial and hear what he thinks.'

'Hurry up, then.'

'You'd better come with me. He'll want to question you a bit.'

When the trial resumed, Mr Vial asked the judge's permission to call another witness. 'I apologize, my Lord, to you, and to my learned friend, for any apparent discourtesy to the court. The fact is that my witness, who is, as you will see, a person of irreproachable character and reputation, has felt hitherto a quite understandable reluctance to appear in a case of this description; but since the evidence she will give——'

'Is this a woman, then?' said the judge.

'Indeed, my Lord.'

'I see. Go on.'

'Thank you, my Lord. Since, as I say, the evidence she will give, with your permission, will be of capital importance in establishing the innocence of the defendant beyond all possible doubt, she has felt it her duty—greatly, I may say, to her credit— to overcome any natural scruples and appear before the court.

'Have you anything to say, Mr Gillespie?' asked the judge.

'Not at this juncture, my Lord. I think any observations I may wish to make would best be kept until I have an opportunity of hearing this witness, and of cross-examination.'

'Very well, Mr Vial.'

Theodora entered the box and took the oath. She looked firm, tranquil, dignified and womanly, though with a slight hint of the repentant sinner.

Mr Vial quickly established that her name was Theodora Huntington Pace, her age twenty-eight, her state a spinster, and her occupation that of Assistant Supervisor of Draft Planning at the B.B.C. She had known the defendant since the previous summer, when she first met him at an interview in connection with his participation in a series of radio programmes. 'Please continue, Miss Pace,' said Mr Vial.

'I got to know Mr Fortune very well,' she said, in steady, almost semi-official tones. 'I grew to admire his qualities of character and intelligence, and soon became very fond of him.'

'And this feeling of yours, Miss Pace. It was reciprocated?'

'Yes,' said Theodora. 'I think it was.'

'Please tell the court what happened then.'

Theodora slightly lowered her voice, and looked up steadily. 'I became his mistress.'

'I see. And then?'

'I asked Mr Fortune to come and live with me, but he is very independent by nature, and preferred we should have separate establishments.'

'And during the period that we have heard about in court this morning. You saw the defendant?'

'Frequently.'

'And is it not a fact that you were able to help him financially when this was necessary?'

'I know Mr Fortune comes from a substantial business family in Nigeria, and that he would have no difficulty in calling on them for money if he needed it. He is, however, I'm sorry to say, something of a spendthrift . . .' (she paused slightly) . . . 'and on occasions when he was hard up I had no reluctance whatever in lending him whatever money he might want to tide him over.'

'So that during the period in question, he was in no need of money?'

'Why should he be? No. He had only to come to me.'

'Thank you, Miss Pace.'

Mr Gillespie got up.

'Miss Pace,' he said. 'In view of what you have told the court this afternoon, why did you not come forward this morning to speak for the accused on this very serious charge?'

Theodora glanced towards the dock, then said quietly: 'Mr Fortune forbade me to.'

'He forbade you? Why?'

'He wished to face this charge alone. Knowing his innocence, and being sure of an acquittal, he did not wish my name to be mentioned in any way.'

'I see, I see. And now he's *not* so sure of an acquittal—is that it?'

'I heard Mr Fortune giving evidence this morning. English is not his mother tongue, and an African has greater difficulty in expressing himself clearly than many of us realize. With this language handicap I didn't feel he was doing his case justice, and I therefore felt I ought to appear myself, even if against his wishes, to tell the court what I knew.'

'Did you, Miss Pace! Then please tell my Lord how you account for the fact that if the accused, as you say, had only to come to you for money, he chose to live with a prostitute in an East End slum?'

'Mr Fortune, as I have said, is a very independent man, and preferred to live his Bohemian student life in a quarter inhabited largely by his fellow countrymen. He told me, of course, of his staying for a while in the same house as this woman—which he regarded as an interesting way of catching a glimpse of the seamier side of London life.

'So this man, who has admitted he was a penniless labourer, prefers living in squalor with a prostitute when he has a rich mistress willing, and no doubt anxious, to accommodate him at any time?'

'I need hardly say that I would have preferred him to live in more conventional surroundings.'

'With you, in other words.'

'Yes.'

'But he didn't. Miss Pace: you have heard the accused admit that he had intercourse with this woman. Did you know of this?'

'No. I expect he was ashamed to tell me of this momentary lapse.'

'I expect so, indeed. How old did you say you were, Miss Pace.'

'Twenty-eight.'

'And the accused is eighteen?'

'Nineteen, now.'

'Is there not a considerable discrepancy between your ages?'

'Yes, unfortunately.'

'And you ask us seriously to believe——'

The judge leaned forward. 'I don't wish to hinder you, Mr Gillespie. But as the witness has admitted her relationship with the defendant, I really don't think you need press this point any further.'

Theodora turned towards the judge, and said softly, 'I am pregnant by him, my Lord. I hope to marry the defendant.'

The judge nodded slightly and said nothing. He turned to Mr Gillespie. 'I have no more questions, my Lord,' said the Crown counsel.

Theodora left the box, and the two lawyers addressed the jury.

'You must not attribute,' said Mr Gillespie, 'any undue weight to the testimony of Miss Theodora Pace. Remember that this woman who admits—indeed, I should say, glories in—an illicit relationship with the accused, is no doubt under the domination of her obsession. Keep firmly in your minds, rather, the contrast between the evidence you have heard from the two police officers, and that of the accused himself. If there may be, in the evidence of these officers, some slight discrepancies—of which my learned friend has naturally tried to make the most—you must surely conclude that the evidence of the accused is totally, utterly incredible. It simply cannot be believed! No, members of the jury: your duty in this matter is quite clear. Banish from your minds any thought that a verdict against the defendant might be imputed to anything in the nature of racial prejudice. In a British court, all men are equal before the law: and if you believe the defendant to be guilty, as you are bound to do, you should return a verdict in that sense with the same impartiality as you would show were he a fellow citizen of your own.'

To which Mr Vial, raising himself like Moses bringing down the tablets from the Mount, rejoined:

'My learned friend has asked you to discount the evidence of Miss Theodora Pace. But is her testimony not supremely to be believed? Here is a woman—a courageous woman, I would say, whatever you may think of her moral conduct (which is not what is on trial today)—who is prepared to risk—possibly even to sacrifice irrevocably—an honoured and established position in society, to bear witness to the truth, whatever the cost! Is this mere infatuation? Is this what my learned friend has called the consequences of an *obsession*?

'But even more to be believed—yes, even more—is the evidence of the defendant. My learned friend has told you that this evidence is "incredible." But is it? Is it incredible? I have no small experience of hearing witnesses in court, and from this I have learned one important lesson.' Mr Vial, who contrived to speak not like an advocate, but like the impartial spirit of justice itself, now looked very grave. 'Only a too fluent witness, members of the jury, is to be mistrusted! Only a story that has no flaw—one which the witness, or witnesses, have carefully manufactured, polished and rehearsed—is likely to be untrue. Did you not notice—and were you not impressed by it?—that the defendant at no time sought to deny facts that might have seemed prejudicial to his case? Did you not hear how he freely admitted to some few, small, discreditable facts because he knew, in his heart of hearts, that on the major issue—the essential issue you are called upon to decide—he was without guilt of any kind?' Mr Vial stood a second, hand raised aloft. 'The defendant was an angry witness, members of the jury! He was angry because he is honest: he is honest because he is innocent!

'Have a care how you deal with John Macdonald Fortune! This young man is a guest among us, who possibly has behaved foolishly, as young men will, but who has not behaved dishonourably. In this country he is a stranger: but a stranger who, coming from a country that is British, believes he is entitled to receive, and knows that he certainly will receive, that fair treatment and equal justice from his fellow men and women which has always been the glory of the British jury.'

Mr Vial sat down. The judge, his moment come at last, began his summing-up.

When he recapitulated the case of the prosecution, which he did in meticulous and admirably balanced detail, the case for the prosecution sounded quite unanswerable; but when he came to recapitulate the case for the defence, this case sounded quite unanswerable too. It was, in fact, impossible to tell what the judge thought, or even what he recommended; though he did, at one point in his dry, interminable, penetrating survey of the evidence, look up a minute at the jury and say this:

'I need hardly remind you, I suppose, that you should attach great importance, not only to the substance of the evidence that has been put before you, but equally to the demeanour of the witnesses, and to the force, the weight, I might say, of the actual words they used. Now the defending counsel, you will remember, asked the accused at one point' (the judge consulted his notes) 'if he had ever lived off the immoral earnings of any woman. To which the defendant answered in these words: "Never. Never would I give my blood to such a person. Never."' The judge blinked at the jury. 'You will have to decide whether these words which the defendant used convey to you the impression of veracity . . . of authenticity . . .'

When the judge finished—rather abruptly and unexpectedly—the clerk put the fatal question to the jury. After some slight muttering, they asked if they might retire.

'Will you be very long, do you think?' the judge asked the foreman.

'There seems to be some considerable disagreement, my Lord,' the foreman answered, glancing round at the eleven.

'I see. Very well, you may retire.'

In the emptying court, Mr Vial strolled across to the dock, leant on its edge and, ignoring the two policemen, said casually to Johnny, 'I thought the judge's summing-up was very fair, didn't you?'

'I thought you was wonderful,' said Johnny Fortune.

In the corridor outside, Theodora stood with Mr Zuss-Amor. 'Splendid, my dear,' said the solicitor. 'I'm sorry to say the Press were scribbling busily, though. I hope you don't lose your job.'

Smoking an agitated cigarette, Montgomery was accosted by the Detective-Inspector. 'Well,' said the policeman, 'whichever way it goes, there's no hard feelings on my part for your young friend. It's only another case to us.'

As the court reassembled, the usher in charge of the jury (who had sworn publicly, before they retired, upon the sacred book, that he would not divulge a word of their deliberations), whispered, as he passed by, to the two officers guarding Johnny in the dock, what their still secret verdict was. Johnny heard it too, and one of the officers patted him gently on the back of the knee.

The judge returned, and so did the jury. They did not, despite the nature of their impending verdict, gaze benevolently at the accused as juries are traditionally supposed to do, but sat like ancient monuments on their hard seats.

The clerk asked the foreman how they found. He said, 'Not guilty.'

Mr Vial then rose and said, with infinite deference, to the judge: 'May the prisoner please be discharged, my Lord?'

'He may.'

A week later, Johnny was re-arrested on the charge of being in possession of Indian hemp. Montgomery could borrow no more money quickly anywhere, and Theodora was in hospital with a breakdown and a miscarriage. 'I'll come over to the court for free, if you really want me to,' Mr Zuss-Amor told Montgomery, 'but why don't you tell him to plead guilty and settle before the magistrate? Believe me, if they don't get him for *something*, they'll never let him alone. And it'll only be a fine.'

It was, but no one had any money, and Johnny went to prison for a month.

PART III

Johnny Fortune leaves his city

1

Tidings from Theodora

THE WORD 'FREE-LANCE', I used to think, had a romantic ring; but sadly discovered, when I tried to be one, that its practice has little freedom, and the lance is a sorry weapon to tilt at literary windmills. I'd desperately succeeded in appearing in some serious periodicals that paid little, and were seen by few; and in printing some disreputable anonymous paragraphs, cruelly chopped by the sub-editors, in newspapers I'd hitherto despised. As for the B.B.C., since Theodora's departure from it, under a lowering cloud, it would not hear of any of my rich ideas.

How I missed Theodora in the house, and how unexpectedly! True, Johnny's company, since he'd come out of prison, was some small consolation: small, because a different Johnny had emerged—a rather bitter and less kindly person, a disillusioned adult Fortune who no longer seemed to think—as Johnny always had—that everything in the world would one fine day be possible.

I opened the bedroom door and looked at him still sleeping, rolled in an angry lump, his head underneath a pillow. I drew back the curtain, and let in a shaft of reconnoitring spring sun. 'Johnny,' I said, 'it's past eleven.' He bunched the sheets closer round him, and jerked himself in a tighter, unwelcoming ball. I put on the kettle, went back to the front room, and took up Theodora's letter.

'I'd forgotten, Montgomery, how ghastly the country is until I came here to recoup. The colours are green and grey, invariably, and in the village nothing happens: nothing. I'll be glad to get back to London, and only sorry, because of you, it won't be the old flat, but I just can't face living there any longer. You *will* see about the removal of my things to the new place as you promised, won't you. (Be *practical* about all this, Montgomery, for Heaven's sake.)

'I've heard from the Corporation, as I expected, that my appeal is disallowed. Their letter is roundabout and civil—almost deferential—but very clear as to essentials. My old job is out: that's definite; and if I can't "see my way", as they put it, to accepting being kicked upstairs (or rather, kicked downstairs, it really would be, as the office of the alternative job they offer in the Editing service is in the sub-basement of a former department store), they "have no alternative but to accept my offer of resignation". They're giving me a surprise farewell bonus, though: rather nice of them, don't you think, after everything?

'In fact, I really have to admit they've behaved very decently and (unlike me) quite sensibly. I broke the written and unwritten codes, and forfeited my claim to their paternalism. As the high-up I eventually got to see quite frankly said to me, "It's not so much what *you did*, Miss Pace, as that you did it without asking anyone's permission. The Corporation can't be expected to answer publicly for its servants' actions unless it knows what they're going to be." I imagine it was most of all those lurid pieces in the Press about the "B.B.C. woman" that really got them down.

'From what I hear from kind friends who've telephoned (not, of course, on the office lines), it was a close thing, all the same. My "case" went straight to the top, then down again to an appropriate level, then up even higher to the Board of Governors, then plummeted down once more—a massive file it must have been by then, I wish I could have seen it—to the person who actually had to wield the axe, or rather to his secretary (a bitch—I knew her in the Wrens—she probably drafted the letter for him herself).

'But I don't, as they say, "regret it". Being horribly competent, I can always get a job—all I really mind is having lost a battle. And I don't regret making a fool of myself in front of everybody in the court. All I deeply regret, Montgomery (oh, how I do!—you'll not understand, however much you think you do), is losing my child in that so squalid, absurd and dreadfully sad miscarriage (my first—I mean my first pregnancy, as it happens), because though I've never meant anything to Johnny Fortune, I would still have had that . . . it—he—she: anyway, a fragment of him.

'How is he? Better not tell me. I don't want to see him again. I do, of course, but I couldn't.

'And how are you, Montgomery? If you're behindhand with the

rent, as I imagine, and, as I also imagine, up to your grey eyes in debt, please let me know, and I'll do whatever I can.

'*Later.* Just been out to buy some gin. They looked at me as if I was indeed a "B.B.C. woman", but took the pound notes promptly enough.

'What's clear to me now, Montgomery—although I know you won't agree—is that love, or even friendship, for those people is *impossible*—I mean as we understand it. It's not either party's fault; it's just that in the nature of things we can never really understand each other because we see the whole world utterly differently. In a crisis each race will act according to its nature, each one quite separately, and each one be right, and hurt the other.

'It's when you see that *distant* look that sometimes comes into their opaque brown eyes that you realize it—that moment when they suddenly depart irrevocably within themselves far off towards some hidden, alien, secretive, quite untouchable horizon. . . .'

2

Appearance of a guardian angel

SINCE MY TROUBLE COME, I do not go often to the places where I go before—it is not that I fear the Law, or what it can do to me any more, but that I do not wish to be seen there by my countrymen. To be sent to jail for weed was not the big disgrace, for everybody know they never catch me if they treat me fairly; but to have a Jumble woman who I do not love speak up in court and say she have a child of me, and hear the boys say it was this woman's lies that set me free on that first charge—this is too big a shame for me. And since the sad death of Hamilton, I have no friend, except for Laddy Boy, who was now travelling again at sea, that I would wish to speak to in this city.

So what I do, as soon as Montgomery goes out, is visit cinemas and sit there by myself, or else go practising my judo and my boxing at the merchant seaman gymnasium. For now I hear that Billy Whispers also has come out of finishing his sentence, I know this boy will one day try to make some trouble for me, because he believes from what they tell him of my trial that when he go into jail, is I who takes his Dorothy.

So I sat in the darkness of the Tottenham Court picture palace this day, thinking; when near to me a white boy asked me for a match, to light his cigarette, he say, and other silly business of holding my hand too long when I pass the box, and when he gives it back to me, so that I know what his foolish hope is, and say to him, 'Mister, behave yourself, or else you come out with me and I push your face in.'

'All right, man, I come out with you,' this white boy whispered. I thought: oh, very well, if he wants hitting, then I hit him, this will be some big relief to all my feelings; but when I see his face outside the dark, I recognize it was this Alfy Bongo. 'Oh, you,' I said to him. 'Are you still living?'

'Why not, Johnny? The devil looks after his own. Won't you have a coffee with me?'

'So you are one of these foolish men who try to mess about with Spades in picture-houses?'

'Oh, I'm a little queer boy, Johnny, that's for certain; but I didn't know that it was you.'

'One day you meet some bad boy who do you some big damage.

'It wouldn't be the first time. Let's come and have some coffee, like I say.'

'Why should I come? I enjoy this film in here.'

'Listen, Johnny. Why are you so ungrateful? Didn't they tell you how I helped you at your trial?'

'I hear of this, yes; but is much better that you leave me to fight my trial alone. If this woman you speak to not go into the box, and make her statement, I go free all the same through my good lawyers.'

'You think you would have? Nobody else does—least of all Mr Vial, I can tell you that. And, anyway, who do you think found your lawyers for you?'

'Well, what good it do me—that acquittal? They catch me the second time.'

'I wish I'd known of that. If I'd known, I'd have done something for you. . . . Why didn't anyone let me know in time?'

I stopped in the street and looked at this cheeky person. 'What is all this, Alfy, you wish to do such nice things for me? You hope you have some pleasant treatment from me one day that never come?'

'Oh, no, Johnny, I know you're square. But I just like helping out the Spades.'

'You do! Oh, do you!'

'I wish I'd been born a Spade.'

'Do you now, man!'

'Yes, I do. I tell you I *do*. You have this coffee with me, Johnny, or not?'

'Oh, if you say so: let us go.'

He took me to a coffee-bar nearby, and there, when he order it, he said to me, 'And how was it in the nick? Did they beat you in there at all?'

'No, man, I play so cool. What I like least of all is your British sanitation in that place. Man, in that jail all you turn into is not any human person, but a lavatory machine.'

'And what do you do now, Johnny, with yourself?'

'What I do now? Would it surprise you, after how they treat me in those places, if now I start up some really serious hustle?'

'Don't think of that, man. You've got a record now. Second offence, and they've got you by the you-know-whats. What you should do is . . . Man, why don't you cut out and go back home?'

'How can I now, to face my family? They speak about my Dad in court—you know of that? They talk about his bravery, which I tell my white friends as a secret, not for them to put shame on my Dad by mixing his name up with that charge they put upon me.'

'I hear Billy's out. You know what he did with Dorothy?'

'No. Where she's gone?'

'Into hospital. He cut up her face.'

'Nice. Well, I'm not surprised. That thing come her way some quite long time.'

'Better be careful—you too, Johnny. Why don't you leave town a while? Go up to Liverpool Rialto way, or Manchester Moss Side?'

'Me? For fear of that man Billy? Listen now, Mr Bongo. If he kill me, he kill me. If I kill him, I kill him. Or else perhaps nobody kills nobody. We shall see.'

This Alfy Bongo person was one I couldn't quite make out. I looked hard behind his eyes, but could not see any real unfriendliness to me, or danger there.

He looked me back. 'Well, that's not the great news, is it?' he said. 'You know you're a father now, Johnny?'

'Yes? No, I not hear. . . .'

'A boy.'

'Is it then Muriel?'

'Yes. She's called it William.'

'Well—is nice for her. I hope this William turns out a nice man like his uncle Arthur, that shop me to the Law.'

'You're not going out to see your son?'

'Why, man? Let her keep this William for her pleasure.'

'She'll put an affiliation order on you, to support it. . . .'

'Oh, well. That will be just one more misery I have to suffer.'

This Alfy handed me a cigarette. 'You're turning sour, Johnny,' he said to me. 'It's bad in London, when a Spade turns sour.'

I got up to leave him. 'Spades will stay sour, man, let me tell you, till they're treated right.'

'Cheer up—they'll be treated better soon. That race crap's changing fast, believe me, Johnny.'

'Not fast enough for me, Mister Alfy Bongo. How long you think this rubbish will go on? This big, big problem that they think up out of nothing, and is nothing?'

'Not long now, man. In ten years' time, or so, they'll wonder what it was all about.'

I got up to leave him. 'Roll on that day,' I said to him. 'But I tell you this, man, and remember it. Let them kill every Spade that's in the world, and leave but just two, man and woman, and we'll fill up the whole globe once more and win our triumph!'

He asked me to come round and see him in his room in Kensington West one day, but I tell him my life is occupied, and left him and went out and caught my bus. To sleep now would be best, I thought, and I came home to where I am staying with Montgomery. When I turn round the corner to his house, I see standing by the door an African girl, and from this distance I know it is my sister Peach.

I stopped, and think quickly. I want to see Peach, but I do not want to see Peach, so I turned and run. But she see me, come running after, and hold on my coat like she tear it off my body, and there in the street hugged on to me so tight I cannot breathe, and she say nothing.

3

Disputed child of an uncertain future

FROM Johnny's vagueness, even rudeness, I could guess something had happened, but couldn't persuade him to tell me what. There were surreptitious telephone calls, and abrupt goings and comings, and a heightened air of inwardness, of 'African-ness' about him. One evening, when I saw him eyeing me steadily in a critical, almost hostile way, I said, 'Look, Johnny. You'd better tell me what's on your mind.'

He nodded and said, 'My sister Peach is here.'

'In London?'

'As training nurse. She live now at the hostel there beside her hospital.'

'Well, I'm delighted, Johnny. When am I going to meet her?'

'I do not wish you meet with her, Montgomery.'

'Why not? Oh, all right, then, if you prefer me not to. But why?'

'Because I fear you tell some things she should not hear.'

'Well—thank you! You're a nice trusting soul.'

'You blow your top too much, Montgomery. You know you do.'

'Oh, fine. Don't introduce me, then.'

'She wish to speak with you, all the same.'

'Well, make up your mind!'

'I tell her of this child of mine that Muriel has got. Peach wish to speak to you about it.'

'Why?'

'She tell you.'

'All right. When do we meet?'

'I ask her to come round this afternoon. While she is here, I stay downstairs in Theodora's place.'

'To keep an eye on me, is that it?'

'Yes. She is my sister.'

'Look, Johnny. I'm beginning to think it's time you and I should part company. If you like, I'll move out with friends, and you can stay on here by yourself until the landlords serve the summons.'

'You should not make argument, Montgomery.'

'Oh, no! What I should do is exactly what suits you.'

'What you should do, please, is see my sister Peach this afternoon because she wish to speak with you.'

We left it at that, and when the bell rang Johnny went down and let her in, but did not come up with her beyond Theodora's floor. I greeted Peach on the stairs, and ushered her into the flat. 'A cup of tea, Miss Fortune?' I said to her. 'Or I have coffee. . . .'

'No, thank you.'

How could a girl so beautiful wear such really appalling clothes? Peach had everything, and more, of Johnny's sumptuous good looks—as feminine a version as his was masculine, but with a greater air of gravity and depth. So that if one ignored (but how could one?) the rainbow shades of royal blue, and green, and crimson that she wore, she seemed one of the loveliest creatures in creation—the more so as she had such grace of easy gesture, and such self-confident, unaffected pride.

'You are my brother's friend,' she said. 'He tell me of you, and how you are his friend.'

Her English was not as eccentrically voluble as her brother's—she seemed to speak it with some difficulty. I insisted on tea, and bustled about with host-like charm which, to my mortification, made no impression on her whatever.

'I come to speak to you of Johnny's baby,' she said.

'Yes. . . ?'

'I tell him he must take it home to Africa.'

'Oh!'

'Here it will not be happy, or be well instructed.'

'No. . . . But Miss Fortune—or may I call you Peach?' (this gambit misfired too, for she made no reply) '—in English law, the baby belongs to the mother. Unless, that is, the parents were married, and even then . . .'

'It is an Africa child.'

'Well, not entirely, is it?'

'I have no money.'

'No. . . ?' (Money again!)

'My father, my mother, they have money, yes. But they will give some to my brother only for his boat fare home to Africa.'

'Yes . . . so he's told me. But I don't see . . .'

'If he have other money, then he can buy the baby from the woman.'

'Peach! You just *can't* do that here in England. Or rather . . . she ***might*** agree, but then there are regulations about adoption, and emigration, and so on and so forth . . . . Hasn't Johnny told you all this?'

'He tell me many things, but I wish to hear you speaking.'

'Well, I am! We could try, of course, but, honestly, I think it's unlikely the mother would . . . and in any case, what about that money?'

She looked at me.

'My dear Miss Fortune, *I* haven't got a cent.' (Didn't believe me, obviously.) 'If you explain everything to your parents, wouldn't they give Johnny something extra to try it with?'

'No. . . . My mother, no. My father, yes, but he listen to my mother.'

'Well, then, excuse me, Peach—but why do you want to get the child? Does Johnny want it?'

'No.'

'So *you* do.'

'No. But it is my brother's child, and will not be happy here, not well instructed.'

'That's very possible, I admit. . . . Is Johnny going back to Africa, then?'

'I tell him he should do this.'

'And he agrees?'

'Yes, when I speak to him.'

'Oh. Well, Peach—what can I do? I don't know. . . . I could try to see Muriel, if you like. . . . And perhaps I could try to get some money somehow if she agrees to listen, which I very much doubt. . . .' Suddenly I rebelled against this hypnotic girl. 'Why don't *you* talk to Muriel?' I asked.

'I do not wish to see this family. No.'

'Don't you? I can't altogether blame you. Well, shall I have a word with Johnny and see what might be done?' She'd already got up. 'But I don't think there's much hope. . . .' She was near the door.

'And how do you like the hospital—and nursing? How do you like it over here?' I asked desperately.

'Is good for me to learn these things in London.'

She went down the stairs. Faint sounds of a long confabulation in African drifted up them. The front door banged, and Johnny reappeared.

'You know it's impossible, what she wants?' I said to him. 'Didn't you tell her, before you inflicted all this on me?'

'My sister believes it would be possible.'

'Does she, indeed! And you: you don't really want young William in Lagos, do you, even if you could ever get him there?'

'If I have him in Africa, yes, then I would want him.'

I just stared at him. 'Johnny! Have you, and your sister, and your entire race, ever reflected that other people in the world want things besides yourselves?'

'I go out now, Montgomery.'

'You'd better!'

By force of habit, the only thing I could think of was to tell Theodora. I called up her village on the 'phone, and she didn't seem much surprised as I unfolded by incoherent story. She even said, 'If Muriel can be bought off, one might try to short-circuit the regulations and kidnap the child. An air passage would fix it—it's been done before.'

'But money, Theodora! Money, money, money, money, money!'

'Exactly. Listen. I'll come up to town tomorrow, and we'll pay a call together on Muriel.'

'Hadn't you better leave the negotiations to me?'

'When you tried that once before, Montgomery, you weren't particularly successful. And after all, it's my money that's going to be wasted.'

As I hung up, I registered, there and then, a vow that never after this, so long as I lived, never, would I interfere in anyone else's private affairs. Never! After which, I rang Mr Zuss-Amor to check on the legal aspects.

He was discouraging. 'The babe is hers until it's a major. Even if he married the woman it still would be—unless he could sue for divorce for some reason or other later on and get the custody—but is all that likely? Why does he want it, anyway?'

'You tell me. Can anyone understand Africans?'

'Well, it's a lesson to the boy, and to us all,' the solicitor said humorously. 'It makes you realize you've got to be very careful where you put it.'

I was glad to see Theodora back in London. She refused to come over to the house, and met me (neither of us could think, in a hurry, of a better place) at the pub round the corner from the law courts of evil memory. I expected that Theodora, too, would have changed, but the surprise was that it seemed a change for the better: she was less angular and spiky, rather more relaxed, and at moments she seemed almost matronly. In the taxi she took my arm and said, 'What's the sister like, Montgomery?'

'Like him. Less of a ruffian, though.'

'Women aren't ruffians.'

'No? Well, less of the female equivalent. Very attractive indeed she'll be in her nurse's uniform—I wish I could see her in it; but then, a nurse's uniform makes everyone look attractive.'

'Even Florence Nightingale? You're not going to propose to Peach, are you?'

'I don't think so, Theodora. What would be the use?'

'And how's he?'

'Moody. Melancholy. But a lot happier now he's decided to leave for home.'

'You really think he will?'

'Well, that's the plan; but like all African plans . . .'

'Don't tell me. We must go out to Africa, too, one day, Montgomery, as tourists. See all the sights together.'

'I bet as soon as we got there, we'd meet everyone we've known in all those disreputable clubs and places. We'd find Mr Karl Marx Bo prime minister, I expect.'

'That would be too much. Is this the street?'

'It is, but do let me go and spy out the land—I really think it would be best, Theodora.'

The flat was silent, and a neighbour told me the Macphersons had all left.

'It's Muriel I want.'

'Oh, she's gone off separate. I've got the address for forwarding—you're not from the landlord, are you?'

'No, no. A friend. Honest. . . .'

Muriel's new address was not far off. We walked up to the third floor, but there was nobody in there either.

'No sounds of a baby wailing,' I said. 'Shall we wait here till she comes?'

'I suppose we'd better.'

We sat on the stairs, talking. After two hours had gone, a young girl appeared with a baby. We introduced ourselves.

'I'm from the crèche,' she said. 'Isn't Mrs Macpherson back?'

'Not yet,' said Theodora. 'Shall I look after it for you till she comes?'

'Well, if you don't drop it . . .' she said after some persuasion, and handed the infant over to Theodora.

We looked together at William Macpherson Fortune. 'My God,' said Theodora. 'They say babies aren't like their parents. Just look at him!'

'I'm very nervous, Theodora. I don't think Muriel will approve at all.'

When she came, though, she almost seemed to have expected us, and asked us straight in to the single room. 'Do you mind if I feed William?' she said. 'Then I'll get you a cup of tea.'

Was there a faint triumph in her gesture, as there was certainly more than faint envy in Theodora? 'Is he good?' she asked the mother.

'He is now, but he won't be for long if he grows up like his father.'

She put the baby in its cot, and got us tea. 'I suppose you've come to tell me something about Johnny,' she said. 'What is it?'

By one of those accidents of nature, entirely unforeseeable (especially by a man, in the case of women), Theodora and Muriel, who'd only met so briefly and so long ago, seemed to take to each other, to be suddenly on familiar terms. Without too much beating about the bush, Theodora came to the point—or points, because there were quite a lot of them.

Muriel didn't seem surprised, or hurt, by the proposition Theodora unfolded to her.

'I know I behaved bad to Johnny,' she said. 'I know I should have spoken up for him in court. I should have, I dare say, but I just couldn't do it—I just *couldn't*. I was mad about him and Dorothy, and his doing *nothing* for me—*nothing*, can you believe it?—all the time.'

'Yes, I can understand.'

'And you spoke up for him instead.'

'Yes.'

Muriel looked at Theodora rather sharply, with a sudden hostile glint. Then said, 'Well, I don't blame you, if you loved him—he's a very lovable boy, isn't he, in his way. But me, I just can't make him out. . . . He's never loved *me*, that's certain. He's never loved any of us, from what I can see. . . .'

'No, I don't think he has.'

'And now he wants William: to get rid of me, and take William. Well, that's asking a bit much, isn't it? Just tell him to forget about it, will you? And that I'll send him some snaps from time to time if he'll give me his address. . . .'

'Quite apart from what he's asked us to tell you,' said Theodora, 'could I help out financially at all? I'd be very glad to.'

Muriel reflected. 'No, it's all right, thanks. I've got me job and all the allowances, and they look after William at the crèche. . . . Later on, when he grows up a bit, you could do something for him, if you felt like it.'

'Perhaps you'd let me be his godparent, Muriel.'

'And me,' I said, vexed that I hadn't thought of this.

'Oh, I don't believe in that. . . . But if you like to help William, as I say, or send him something for his birthday . . .'

We both wrote the date down carefully. Muriel saw us to the door.

'You can't hate them, can you,' she said, 'whatever they do to you. Me, I loved Johnny, I really did, like I never will anybody else, I don't suppose. And he was sweet to me in his way, and I had good times with him. But I never meant much to him, that was the trouble. I don't believe they understand love like we do, but that's their nature. . . .'

4

Back home aboard the 'Lugard'

IT WAS WHEN LADDY BOY RETURNED from sea that he tell me of this tugboat, called the *Lugard*, to be sailed empty from London Docks to Lagos, and that a deck-hand crew of five was needed to take her there. And when Laddy Boy did me the great favour to give me a forged seaman's book he buy, and tell me answers I must give to any questions, I made such a good impression on the captain by my strength and willingness (he was high, anyway—an Irishman) that he sign me on, and even though I cannot yet believe it, I am to go back home from England.

So on our sailing day, I met with my English friend Montgomery and my sister Peach at a dockside Chinese restaurant where they come to say goodbye to me. 'That is like the life,' I said to Montgomery. 'My sister Peach, who never wishes to leave Africa, is now in London till she becomes a nurse, and I who wished to live in this big city, go back home to all my family to take her place.'

'Soon I come home also,' said my sister, 'with my nurse's belt and badges. I shall not waste my time with foolishness like my brother.'

A sister's remark! 'Through Peach you will have news of me, Montgomery,' I said, 'and of all my activities at home.'

'Won't you be writing to me?' asked my English friend.

'Of course, of course—and soon you will come to Africa as well and visit Mum and Dad and Christmas and our family, and live with us in our home like I do when here with you.'

'Perhaps I'll go there when Peach has qualified,' said Montgomery. 'Perhaps we'll go out together.'

'Oh yes, oh yes,' I said (but Peach has her close instructions, and this also is her wish, that she shall not see Montgomery so often, and always, if so, in the company of the nurses' hostel).

I looked at my watch—a parting friendship present from Montgomery—and said that my time had come to go. We went in the streets, in sunshine, and I spoke first to my sister in our language, and then to Montgomery, my Jumble friend.

'Goodbye, Johnny,' he said. 'I can't think what to say, and how to thank you . . .'

'Thank me? Man, it is you who gave me so many good things that I needed.'

'Nothing it wasn't a joy to. . . . Shall we see you down to the dock gates?'

'No, no, please. We find a taxi for you take my sister back to hospital, and then I go on alone.'

I opened the taxi door, and gave my surprise gift to Montgomery: it is the mission school medal I wear on my neck on its chain since boyhood. 'For you,' I tell him. 'You keep it with you, please.' Then I tell the driver where he should go, and I waved to them as the taxi carried this two away.

I walked on quickly to the dock gates, to get a best bed on my ship before the other seamen come there. But by the river side, where our strong, dirty, little boat is by its mooring, I find that Laddy Boy is waiting for me.

He took my arm, and pulled me behind the shed. 'Listen, man,' he said. 'They sign on Whispers.'

'Sign Billy on?'

'Yes. As one of the five crew. I did not know. Shall I go see the captain and try to stop this?'

'Why, man? Why you do that?'

'Why? You know why.'

'Let him come travel home with me if he wants to. Why should I stop him go?'

'Johnny, is he stop you. This man will kill you on this voyage.'

I laughed now out loud at Laddy Boy. 'No one will kill me, countryman!' I cried. 'This is my city, look at it now! Look at it there—it has not killed me! There is my ship that takes me home to Africa: it will not kill me either! No! Nobody in the world will kill me ever until I die!'

Absolute Beginners

COLIN MACINNES

ALLISON & BUSBY
LONDON · NEW YORK

FOR ALFRED MARON

CONTENTS

IN JUNE

IT WAS with the advent of the Laurie London era that I realized the whole teenage epic was tottering to doom.

'Fourteen years old, that absolute beginner,' I said to the Wizard as we paused casually in the gramophone section to hear Little Laurie in that golden disc performance of his.

'From now on,' said Wizard, 'he's certainly Got The Whole World In His Hands.'

We listened to the wonder boy's nostrils spinning on.

'They buy us younger every year,' I cried. 'Why, Little Mr L.'s voice hasn't even dropped yet, so who will those tax-payers try to kidnap next?

'Sucklings,' said Wizard.

We climbed the white stair to the glass garden under the top roof of the department store, and came out on the glorious panorama, our favourite rendezvous.

I must explain the Wiz and I never come to this store to buy anything except, as today, a smoke-salmon sandwich and ice coffee. But in the first place, we have the opportunity to see the latest furnishings and fabrics, just like some married couple, and also to have the splendid outlook over London, the most miraculous I know in the whole city, and quite unknown to other nuisance-values of our age, in fact to everyone, it seems, except these elderly female Chelsea peasants who come up there for their elevenses.

Looking north you don't see much, it's true, and westward the view's entirely blocked up by the building you're inside. But twisting slowly on your bar stool from the east to south, like Cinerama, you can see clean new concrete cloud-kissers, rising up like felixes from the Olde Englishe squares, and then those gorgeous parks, with trees like classical French salads, and then again the port life down along the Thames, that glorious river, reminding you we're on an estuary, a salt inlet really, with crazy seagulls circling up from it and almost bashing their beaks against the circular plate glass, and then, before you know it, you're back again round a full circle in front of your iced coffee cup.

'Laurie L.,' I said, ''s a sign of decadence. This teenage thing is getting out of hand.'

The Wiz looked wise, like the middle feller of the three old monkeys.

'It's not the tax-payers,' he said, 'who are responsible. It's the kids themselves, for buying the EPs these elderly sordids bribe the teenage nightingales to wax.'

'No doubt,' I said, for I know better than ever to argue with the Wizard, or with anyone else who gets his kicks from an idea.

Mr Wiz continued, masticating his salmon sandwich for anyone to see, 'It's been a two-way twist, this teenage party. Exploitation of the kiddos by the conscripts, and exploitation of themselves by the crafty little absolute beginners. The net result? "Teenager"'s become a dirty word or, at any rate, a square one.'

I smiled at Mr W. 'Well, take it easy, son,' I said, 'because a sixteen year old sperm like you has got a lot of teenage living still to do. As for me, eighteen summers, rising nineteen, I'll very soon be out there among the oldies.'

The Wizard eyed me with his Somerset Maugham appearance. 'Me, boy,' he said, 'I tell you. As things are, I won't regret it when the teenage label's torn off the arse pockets of my drip-dry sky-blue jeans.'

What the Wiz said was at any rate partially true. This teenage ball had had a real splendour in the days when the kids discovered that, for the first time since centuries of kingdom-come, they'd money, which hitherto had always been denied to us at the best time in life to use it, namely, when you're young and strong, and also before the newspapers and telly got hold of this teenage fable and prostituted it as conscripts seem to do to everything they touch. Yes, I tell you, it had a real savage splendour in the days when we found that no one couldn't sit on our faces any more because we'd loot to spend at last, and our world was to be our world, the one we wanted and not standing on the doorstep of somebody else's waiting for honey, perhaps.

I got off my stool and went and stood by the glass of that tottering old department store, pressed up so close it was like I was out there in the air, suspended over space above the city, and I swore by Elvis and all the saints that this last teenage year of mine was going to be a real rave. Yes, man, come whatever, this last year of the teenage dream I was out for kicks and fantasy.

But my peace was shattered by the noise I heard of Wizard in an argument with the conscript behind the counter bar.

I should explain the Wiz has for all oldies just the same kind of hatred psychos have for Jews or foreigners or coloureds, that is, he hates everyone who's not a teenager, except for short-pant sperms and chicklets, whom I suppose he regards as teenagers in bud. The Wiz just doesn't like the population outside the teenage bracket, and takes every chance he gets to make the oldies conscious of their hair-root dyes, and sing out aloud the anthem of the teenage triumph.

Wiz has the art of clawing the poor tax-payers on the raw. Even from where I stood I saw the barman's face was lurid as a point steak, and as I approached I heard that sharp, flat, dry little voice the Wizard has, was needling him with, 'Oh, I suppose you're underpaid, boy, that's what's the matter with you. Don't like your work up here with these old hens.'

'You'd best settle up and 'op it,' said the conscript.

The Wizard turned to me. '"Op it," he says—just listen! This serf speaks authentic old-tyme *My Fair Lady* dialect.'

The Wizard's tactic always was to tempt the enemy to strike him which, because he's small, and seems so slender and so juvenile, arouses sympathy of other oldsters, the born aunts among them especially, who take his side and split the anti-teenage camp wide open. He often succeeds, because I can tell you he's completely fearless, a thoroughly vicious, dirty little pugilist, and only fails when sometimes they laugh at him, which makes him beside himself with rage.

The present argument, as I expected, was about the bill, which Wizard, when he's in the mood, will query even if it's for an item like a cup of tea. And often, even when he's loaded, he'll make out he's completely skint and say to them well, there you are, I've got no money, what you going to do about it? And this with the left breast pocket of his Continental casual jacket stuffed with notes and even visible, but his face so fierce and come-and-kill-me that it frightens them, and even me. It usually seems to work, because they say get to hell out, which he does in his own time, and at his own speed, as if it was an eight-course meal, he'd had and paid for, not just bounced a bill.

I paid for him, and Wiz didn't mind my paying, only laughed that little ha-ha laugh of his as we walked down the white and silver metal stair. 'Boy,' he said, 'you're a born adult number. With your conventional outlook, you just can't wait to be a family man.'

I was vexed at him, but answered, 'Don't be like that, Wizard. We all know you're loaded, so why do you play that kindergarten game?'

Which is a fact, I mean his being loaded, because the Wiz, in spite of his tender years, is, for his age, the number one hustler of the capital, his genius being in introducing A to B, or *vice versa*, that is to say, if someone has an article to sell, and someone else desires it, Wiz has a marvellous instinct for meeting them both and bringing them together. But, you might answer, that's what shops are for, which is exact. But not for exchanging the sort of article the Wizard's customers are interested in which, as you've guessed, are not so legal, and when I say 'article', I mean it may be the kind of services which might make you call the Wiz a pimp, or a procurer if you wanted to, not that it would worry him particularly.

I've wondered how the Wizard gets away with it, because, after all, he deals with male and female hustlers who must be wiser than he is, and certainly, at any rate, are stronger. But he handles them all right—in fact in a way that makes you proud to be a kid. And how he does it is, I think, that he's found out at a very early age what most kids never know, and what it took me years myself to discover—in fact it didn't dawn on me until this year, when the knowledge of it's come too late to use—namely, that youth has power, a kind of divine power straight from mother nature. All the old tax-payers know of this because, of course, for one thing, the poor old sordids recollect their own glorious teenage days, but yet they're so jealous of us, they hide this fact, and whisper it among themselves. As for the boys and girls, the dear young absolute beginners, I sometimes feel that if they only *knew* this fact, this very simple fact, namely how powerful they really are, then they could rise up overnight and enslave the old tax-payers, the whole dam lot of them—toupets and falsies and rejuvenators and all—even though they number millions and sit in the seats of strength. And I guess it was the fact that only little Wizard realized this, and not all the other two million teenagers they say exist throughout our country, that makes him so sour, like a general with lazy troops he can't lead into battle.

'He's got the whole wide world in his hands!
'He's got this crumby village drapers, in his hands!
'He's got . . .'

This was the Wizard, singing his improvisation on the Laurie London number. And as the stairway cage was probably built of breeze-blocks, there was a loud-hailer echo up and down the flights which astonished the lady peasants who were using it to carry home their purchases.

'Easy now,' I said, laying my hand upon the Wizard's arm.

He wrenched it away, and glared at me as if I was what I certainly *was* just at that moment, his deadliest enemy.

'Don't *touch* me!' he said, if you can call it 'said', because 'screeched' would be more like it.

'All right, big boy,' I told him, mentally washing my hands of the whole dam matter.

We came out of the glass doors into an absolutely fabulous June day, such as only that old whore London can throw up, though very occasionally. The Wizard stood looking up at me as if debating whether to insult me, or to call the cold war off.

'Dig this, Wiz,' I said to him. 'I'm not by nature given to interference, it's just that I think the way you're going on you'll kill yourself, which I'd regret.'

This seemed to please him, and he smiled. And when the little Wizard drops his guard it really is miraculous, because a really charming boy looks out at you from behind that razor-edge face of his, if only for an instant. But he didn't say anything to me.

'I got to go and see Suzette,' I told him. 'I hear she has a client for me.'

'You should like that,' said Wizard, 'after you've spent so much paying bills for *me*.'

'You're a horrid little creature, Wiz,' I told him. 'It's a wonder to me they don't use you for some experiment.'

'See you,' said Wizard. 'Please give my hate to little Suze.'

He'd hailed a cab, because Wizard only travels about in taxis, and will walk for miles rather than use the public transportation system, though I sometimes have known him take a late night bus. He had a long argument with the driver before he got in—it seems Wizard was trying to persuade the citizen to leave one door open, so that the summer breezes could ruffle the Wizard's true-blond Marlon Brando hair-do on his journey.

But I couldn't wait to see if he succeeded, because with Suzette you have to be dead on time for this reason, that if she sees any Spade she likes the look of, she'll get up at once and follow him, come what may, though I will say for her that she'll sit like her bottom was glued to the seat till whatever time you've dated her for, even if Harry Belafonte should walk by. Her name, by the way, Suzette, has been given to her because that's what, according to Suze herself, a Spade lover of hers called her once when, gazing hungrily at her from top to toe, especially toe, this Spade, who was a Fang boy from French Gaboon, said to her, '*Chérie*, you are my *Crêpe Suzette*, I'm going to eat you.' Which I've no doubt he did.

The fact is, that little sweet seventeen Suzette is Spade-crazy. I've often explained to her that to show you're a friend of the coloured races, and free from race prejudice and all that crap, you don't have to take every Spade you meet home and drag him between sheets. But Suzette is quite shameless about it, enjoys the life, and naturally is very popular among the boys. She doesn't make any money out of her activities, because though I think she'd like to, and certainly would, and quite a bit of it, if she happened to like whites, the Spades don't give her anything, not because they're not loaded or generous, both of which they very often are, but because every Spade believes, in spite of any evidence to the contrary (and there's a lot), that every woman in creation is thirsting for the honour of his company. So poor old Suzette, in spite of her being the belle of the Strutters' Ball, has to toil every day at a fashion house, which as a matter of fact is how she is so useful to me.

I now shall disclose my graft, which is peculiar. It's not that I haven't tried what's known as steady labour, both manual and brain, but that every job I get, even the well-paid ones (they were the manual), denied me the two things I consider absolutely necessary for gracious living, namely—take out a pencil, please, and write them down—to work in your own time and not somebody else's, number one, and number two, even if you can't make big money every day, to have a graft that lets you make it *sometime*. It's terrible, in other words, to live entirely without hope.

So what I am, is a photographer: street, holiday park, studio, artistic poses and, from time to time, when I can find a client, pornographic. I know it's revolting, but then it only harms the psychos who are my customers, and as for the kids I use for models, they'd do it all down to giggles, let alone for the fee I pay them. To have a job like mine means that I don't belong to great community of the mugs: the vast majority of squares who are exploited. It seems to me this being a mug or a non-mug is a thing that splits humanity up into two sections absolutely. It's nothing to do with age or sex or class or colour—either you're born a mug or born a non-mug, and me, I sincerely trust I'm born the latter.

So now you can see why, from time to time, I pay a call on Suze. For Suze, in the course of business at her fashion house, meets lots of kinky characters, usually among the daddies of the chicks who dress there, and acts as agent for me getting orders from them for my pornographic photos, drawing commission from me at the rate of 25 per cent. So you realize Suze is a sharp gal, and no doubt this is because she's not only English, but part Gibraltarian, partly Scotch and partly Jewish, which is perhaps why I get along with her, as I'm supposed to have a bit of Jewish blood from my mother's veins as well—at any rate, I know I'm circumcised.

I found Suze in her Belgravia coffee bar, just near her work, which was one of the weirdie varieties, called The Last Days of Pompeii, and done up to represent just that, with stone seats in dim nooks, and a ruined well as the centre-piece, and a mummified Roman let into a hole in one of the walls just for kicks, I dare say. Suze was allowing her *cappuccino* to grow cold, and nibbling at a cream cheese and gherkin sandwich, for Suze never eats middays, as she's inclined to plumpness, which I rather like, but makes up for it at evening time with huge plates of chicken and peas she cooks for her Spade visitors.

'Hi, darl,' she said.

'Hi, hon,' I answered.

That's how we heard two movie stars address each other at a film we went to ages ago that rather sent us, in the days when Suze and I were steady.

'How are the boys?' I asked her, sitting down opposite, and under that tiny table putting my knees to hers.

'The boys,' she said, 'are quite all right. Quite, quite okay.'

'Have you had your hundredth yet?' I asked her.

'Not yet a hundred,' Suze replied, 'not yet, no, I don't think so, not a hundred.'

I ordered my striped *cassata*. 'You ever think of marrying with one of them?' I asked her edgily, as usual slipping into that groove of nastiness that affects me whenever I talk to Suze of her love life.

She looked dreamy, and actually flipped her eye-lashes in the Italian starlet manner. 'If ever I marry,' she said, 'it will be exclusively for distinction. I mean to make a very *distinguished* marriage.'

'Not with a Spade, then.'

'No, I don't think so.' She blew a little brown nest in the white froth of her *cappuccino*. 'As a matter of fact,' she said, 'I've had an offer. Or what amounts to an offer.'

She stopped, and gazed at me. 'Go on,' I said.

'From Henley.'

'No!'

She nodded, and lowered her eyes.

'That horrible old poof!' I cried.

I should explain that Henley is the fashion designer Suzette works for, and old enough to be her aunt, quite apart from anything else.

Suze looked severe and sore at me. 'Henley,' she said, 'may be an invert, but he has distinction.'

'He's certainly got that!' I cried. 'Oh, he's certainly got that all right!'

She paused. 'Our marriage,' she continued, 'would of course be sexless.'

'You bet it would!' I yelled. I glared at her, seeking the killer phrase. 'And what will Miss Henley say,' I shouted, 'when the Spades come tramping in their thousands into his distinguished bridal chamber?'

She smiled with pity, and was silent. I could have smacked her down.

'I don't dig this, Suze,' I cried. 'You're a secretary in that place, you're not even a glamorous model. Why should he want *you*, of all people, as his front woman alibi?'

'I think he admires me.'

I glowered her 'You're marrying for loot,' I shouted out. 'With the Spades you were just a strumpet, now you're going to be a whore!'

She poked her determined, obstinate little face at mine. 'I'm marrying for distinction,' she replied, 'and that's a thing that you could never give me.'

'No, that I couldn't,' I said, very bitterly indeed.

I got up under pretext of spinning a record, pressed my three buttons wildly, and luckily got Ella, who would soothe even a volcano. I walked just a moment to the door, and really, the heat was beginning to saturate the air and hit you. 'This summer can't last,' said the yobbo behind the Gaggia, mopping his sweaty brow with his sweaty arm.

'Oh yes it can, daddy-o,' I answered. 'It can last till the calendar says stop.'

'No . . .' said the yobbo, gazing meanly up at the black-blue of that succulent June sky.

'It can shine on forever,' I hissed at him, leaning across and mingling with the steam out of his Gaggia. Then I turned away to go back and talk business with Suze. 'Tell me about this client,' I asked her, sitting down. 'Tell me the who, the when, and even, if you know it, the why.'

Suze was quite nice to me, now she'd planted her little arrow in my lungs. 'He's a diplomat,' she answered, 'or so he says.'

'Does he represent any special country?'

'Not exactly, no, he's over here for some conference, so she told me.'

'She who?'

'His woman, who came in with him to see Henley and buy dresses.'

I gazed at Suzette. 'Please tell me a thing I've always wanted to know. How do you go about raising the matter?'

'What matter?'

'That you're an agent for my camera studies.'

Suze smiled.

'Oh, it's quite simple, really. Sometimes, of course, they know of me, I mean recommended by other clients. Or else, if not, I just size them up and show them some from my collection.'

'Just like that?'

'Yes.'

'And Henley, does he know?'

'I never do it if he's there,' said Suze, 'but I expect he knows.'

'I see,' I said, not pleased somehow by this. 'I see. And what of this diplomat? How do I fix the deal?'

'*Do you mind?*' was all Suzette answered, the reason being that by now I had one of her knees caught between my two. I let go, and said, 'Well, how?'

She opened her square-sac, and handed me a shop-soiled card, which said:

Mickey Pondoroso
12B, Wayne Mews West,
London (England), S.W.1.

The address part was in printed copperplate, but the name was written in by hand.

'Oh,' I said, fingering this thing. 'Have you any idea what sort of snap he'll need?'

'I didn't go into any details.'

'Don't sound so scornful, Suze. You're taking my 25 per cent, aren t you?'

'Have you got it for me in advance?'

'No. Don't come the acid drop.'

'Well, then.'

I got up to leave. She came rather slowly after.

'I'll go out looking for this character,' I said. 'Shall I walk you back first to your emporium?'

'Better not,' she said. 'We're not supposed to bring our boy friends near the building.'

'But I'm not,' I said, 'your boy friend any longer.'

'No,' said Suzette. She kissed me quickly on my lips and ran. Then stopped running, and disappeared at walking pace.

I started off across Belgravia, in search of Mr Mickey P.

And I must say that, in its way, I rather dig Belgravia: not because of what the daddies who live there think of it, that is, the giddy summit of a mad sophistication, but because I see it as an Olde Englishe product like Changing the Guard, or Savile row suits, or Stilton cheese in big brown china jars, or any of those things they advertise in *Esquire* to make the Americans want to visit picturesque Great Britain. I mean, in Belgravia, the flower-boxes, and the awnings over doors, and the front walls painted different shades of cream. The gracious living in the red with huge green squares outside the window, and purring hired and diplomatic vehicles, and everything delivered at the door and on the slate, and little restaurants where camp creatures in cotton skin-tight slacks serve half an avocado pear at five bob, cover charge exclusive. All that seems missing from the scene is good King Ted himself. And I never cross this area without thinking it's a great white-and-green theatre with a cast of actors in a comedy I rather admire, however sad it may be to think of.

So there was I, in fact, crossing it in my new Roman suit, which was a pioneering exploit in Belgravia, where they still wore jackets hanging down over what the tailors call the seat. And around my neck hung my Rolleiflex, which I always keep at the ready, night and day, because you never know, a disaster might occur, like a plane crashing in Trafalgar Square, which I could sell to the fish-and-chip wrapper dailies, or else a scandal, like a personage seen with the wrong kind of man or woman, which little Mr Wiz would certainly know how to merchandise.

This brought me to Wayne Mews West which, like often in these London backwaters, was quite rural, with cobbles and flowers and silence and a sort of a sniff of horse manure around, when I saw a Vespa cycle with a CD plate on it parked nearby a recently built white mews flat, and crouching beside a wooden tub outside a chrome front door, a figure in a mauve Thai silk summer suit who was, would you believe it, watering a fig tree growing in the tub.

I snapped him.

'Hullo there,' he said, looking up and smiling at me. 'You like me to pose for you beside my Vespa?'

'Can't they allot you anything with four wheels?' I said. 'You must come from one of those very corrupt, small countries.'

Mr Mickey P. was naturally not pleased. 'I smashed it up,' he said. 'It was a Pontiac convertible.'

'This rule of the left we have,' I said, 'is so confusing.'

'I understand the rules,' said Mr P., 'but got run into, just.'

'You always do,' I said.

'Do what?'

'Keep still, please, and smile if you like that kind of snap.' I clicked a few. He stood by his motor-scooter as if it was an Arab pony. 'You always get run into,' I explained. 'Its always the other feller.'

Mr Pondoroso leant his scooter against the Wayne Mews wall. 'Well, I don't know,' he said, 'but there are a lot of very bad drivers in your country.'

I wound my spool. 'And what are they like in yours?' I asked him.

'In mine,' he said, 'it doesn't matter, because the roads are wide, and there are fewer autos.'

I looked up at him. I was curious to find where he came from, but didn't like asking direct questions, which seems to me a crude way of finding out things that, with a little patience, they'll tell you anyway. Besides, we were still at the sparring stage that always seems necessary with the seniors, whatever their race may be.

'You're a Latin American?' I asked him.

'I come from these parts, yes, but I live in the United States.'

'Oh, yes. You're representing bòth?'

He smiled his diplomatic smile. 'I'm in a UNO job,' he said, 'attached. Press officer to the delegation.'

I didn't ask which one it was. 'I wonder,' I said, 'if I could step inside out of this glare to change my spool?'

'To . . . ?'

'Re-charge my camera. As a matter of fact,' I said, eyeing him under the portico, 'I believe I have to talk about photography to you. Suzette sent me, you met her at Henley's place.'

He looked cautious and blank a moment, then turned on the diplomatic grin again and battered me on the shoulder. 'Come right in,' he cried, 'I've been expecting you.'

Inside it looked cool and costly—you know, with glass-topped white metal furniture, oatmeal-stained woodwork, Yank mags and indoor plants and siphons, but as if none of it belonged to him, as in fact I don't suppose it did. 'You have a drink?' he said.

'Thank you, no, I won't,' I told him.

'You don't drink?'

'No, sir, never.'

He stared at me, holding a bottle and a glass, and genuinely interested in me for the first time, so it seemed. 'Then how do you get by?' he asked me.

I've had to explain this so often before to elder brethren, that it's now almost a routine. 'I don't use the liquor kick,' I said, 'because I get all the kicks I need from me.'

'You don't drink at all?'

'Either you drink a lot,' I told him, 'or else, like me, you don't drink anything at all. Liquor's not made for zips, but for orgies or total abstinence. Those are the only wise weddings between man and bottle.'

He shook his head, and poured himself some deadly brew. 'So you're the photographer,' he said.

I saw I'd have to be very patient with this character. 'That's me,' I said. 'What kind of print might you be needing?' I went on, not sure yet what kinkiness I had to cater for.

He drew himself up and flexed his torso. 'Oh, I would want you to photograph me.'

'You?'

'Yes. Is that unusual?'

'Well, it is, a-bit-a-little. My clients usually want photographs of models doing this and that . . .'

I was trying to make it easier for the cat. But he said, 'Me, I want no models—only me.'

'Yes, I see. And you doing exactly what?'

'In athletic poses,' he replied.

'Just you alone?'

'Of course.' He saw I was still puzzled. 'In my gymnastic uniform,' he explained.

He put down his glass and bottle, and stepped into the next room while I flicked Yank mags and had a tonic water. Then out he came wearing—and I swear I'm not inventing this—a white-laced pair of navy-blue basket-ball shoes, black ballet rehearsal tights, a nude chest thatched like a Christmas card, and, on his head, a small, round, racing-swimmer's cap.

'You can begin,' he said.

'How many poses do you want?'

'About a hundred.'

'Seriously? It'll cost you quite a lot . . . You want to be *doing* anything particular, or just poses?'

'I leave this to your inspiration.'

'Okay. Just walk about, then. Do whatever comes naturally to you.'

As I clicked away, I worked out what the most was I could ask him: and I wondered if he was perhaps insolvent, or a lunatic, or in trouble with the law, like so many in the capital these days. This crazy Latin-American number was lumbering all over the furniture of his apartment, striking narcissistic poses, as if he was already gloating over the prints I'd give him of such a glorious big hunk of man.

After a while of this in silence, he perspiring, I chasing him round clicking like a professor with a bug-net, he grabbed a drink, collapsed into a white shining leather chair, and said, 'Perhaps you can help me.'

'Mr Pondoroso, I thought I was.'

'You call me Mickey.'

'If you say so,' I said to him, playing it cool, and rapidly reloading my apparatus.

'It's like this,' said Mr Mickey P. 'I have a study to complete for my organization on British folk ways in the middle of the century.'

'Fine,' I said, snapping him sitting down, his upper belly bulging over his ballet pants, so as to make my hundred quickly.

'Well, I've observed the British,' he said, 'but I've got very few interesting ideas about them.'

'How long have you been observing them?' I asked.

'Six weeks, I think, which I know is not very long, but even so, I just can't quite get perspectives.' Mickey P. peered at me between zips. 'Even the weather's wrong,' he said. 'It's reputed to be cold in the English summer, but just look at it.'

I saw what he meant. An old sun from the Sahara had crept up on us unawares, one we weren't at all ready for, and baked us into quite a different loaf from the usual soggy pre-sliced product.

'Try asking me,' I said.

'Well, let's take the two chief political parties,' he began, and I could see he was winding himself up for a big performance.

'No thank you,' I said quickly. 'I don't want to take any part of either.'

His face slipped a bit.

'They don't interest you, is that it?'

'How could they?'

'But your destinies,' he said, 'are being worked out by their initiatives . . .'

I clicked his unshaven face in a close-up horror picture. 'Whoever,' I said, 'is working out my destinies, you can be quite sure it's not those parliamentary numbers.'

'You mustn't despise politics,' he told me. 'Somebody's got to do the housekeeping.'

Here I let go my Rolleiflex, and chose my words with care.

'If they'd stick to their housekeeping, which is the only backyard they can move freely in to any purpose, and stopped playing Winston Churchill and the Great Armada when there's no tin soldiers left to play with any more, then no one would despise them, because no one would even notice them.'

Mr Pondoroso smiled. 'I guess,' he said, 'that fixes the politicians.'

'I do hope so,' I replied.

'Then take,' said Mr P., 'the Bomb. What are you going to do about *that*?'

Clearly, I had a zombie on my hands.

'Listen,' I said to him. 'No one in the world under twenty is interested in that bomb of yours one little bit.'

'Ah,' said this diplomatic cat, his face coming all over crafty, '*you* may not be, here in Europe I mean, but what of young peoples in the Soviet Union and the USA?'

'Young peoples in the Soviet Union and the USA,' I told him, clearly and very slowly, 'don't give a single lump of cat's shit for the bomb.'

'Easy, son. How you know that?'

'Man, it's only you adult numbers who want to destroy one another. And I must say, sincerely, speaking as what's called a minor, I'd not be sorry if you did: except that you'd probably kill a few millions of us innocent kiddos in the process.'

Mr P. grew a bit vexed.

'But you haven't been to America, have you!' he exclaimed. 'Or to Russia, and talked to these young people!'

'Why do I have to go, mister? You don't have to travel to know what it's like to be young, any time, anywhere. Believe me, Mr Pondoroso, youth is international, just like old age is. We're both very fond of life.'

I don't know if what I said was crap, or if anyone in the universe thinks it besides me, but at all events, it's what I honestly believe—from my own observations and from natters I've had with my old Dad.

Mr P. was looking disappointed with me. Then he brightened up a bit, raised his brows eagerly, and said, 'That leaves us with only one topic for an Englishman, but a very important one . . . (here the pronk half rose in his ballet tights and saluted) . . . and that is, Her Britannic Majesty the Queen!'

I sighed.

'No, please, not that one,' I said to him politely but very firmly, 'Really, that's a subject that we're very, very tired of. One which I just can't work up the interest to have any ideas about at all.'

Mr Pondoroso looked like he'd had a wasted afternoon. He stood up in his gymnastic uniform, which with his movements round the room had slipped a bit to show a fold of hairy olive tum, and he said to me, 'So you've not much to tell me of Britain and her position.'

'Only,' I said, 'that her position is that she hasn't found her position.'

He didn't wig this, so giving me a kindly smile, he stepped away to make himself respectable again. I put a disc on to his hi-fi, my choice being Billie H., who sends me even more than Ella does, but only when, as now, I'm tired, and also, what with seeing Suze again, and working hard with my Rolleiflex and then this moronic conversation, graveyard gloomy. But Lady Day has suffered so much in her life she carries it all for you, and soon I was quite a cheerful cat again.

'I wish I had this one,' I said, when Mr P. appeared.

'Take it, please,' he told me, beaming.

'Wait till you get my bill for the snaps before you make me gifts as well,' I warned him.

His only answer, which was rather nice of him, was to put the record in its sleeve and stick it underneath my arm like as if he was posting a letter.

I thanked him, and we went out in the sun. 'When you're tired of your Vespa,' I said wittily, 'you can give me that as well.'

Boy, can you credit it, it functioned! 'As soon as my automobile's repaired,' he said, slapping his hand down on the saddle, 'this toy is yours.'

I took his hand. 'Mickey,' I said, 'if you mean that, you're my boy. And the photos, need I say, are complimentary.'

'No, no,' he cried. 'That is another, separate business. For the pictures, I shall pay you cash.'

He darted in. I tried sitting on the scooter saddle for the feel of it, and when he darted out, with this time his mauve Thai silk jacket on, he handed me a folded cheque.

'Thank you,' I said, unfolding it. 'But, you know, this isn't cash.'

'Oh. You prefer cash?'

'It's not that, Mickey—it's just that you *said* cash, didn't you, see? But let's look where the branch is. Victoria station, lovely. And I see it's not one of the ugly crossed variety, good boy. I'll go there before they put up the shutters, fare you well.'

With which I blew, reflecting this, that if by any fragment of a chance he meant it, that is, about the scooter, and if I wanted to act quick and get the snaps developed, so as to keep contact with him and work on his conscience, if he'd got one, to secure the vehicle, I'd have to go home immediately to my darkroom.

So off I set, but stopping on the way to raid the bank, which was getting ready to close as I arrived, in fact the clerk had half the door shut, and he looked me up and down, my Spartan hair-do and my teenage drag and all, and said just, 'Yes?'

'Yes what?' I answered.

'You have *business* here?' he said to me.

'I have,' I told him.

'*Business?*' the poverty-stricken pen-pusher repeated.

'Business,' I said.

He still had his hands upon the door. 'We're closing now,' he told me.

'If my eyes don't fail me,' I replied, 'the clock above your desk says 2.56 p.m., so perhaps you'll be kind enough to get back behind it there and serve me.'

He said no more, and made his way round inside the counter, then raised his brows at me across it, and I handed over Mr Pondoroso's cheque.

'Are you,' he said, after examining it as if it was the sort of thing a bank had never seen before, 'the payee?'

'The which?'

'Is,' he said, speaking slowly and clearly, as if to a deaf Chinese lunatic, 'this-your-name-written-on-the-cheque?'

'*Jawohl, mein Kapitan*,' I said, 'it is.'

Now he looked diabolically crafty.

'And how,' he enquired, 'do I know this name is yours?'

I said, 'How do you know it isn't?'

He bit his lip, as the paperbacks say, and asked me, 'Have you any proof of your identity?'

'Yes,' I replied. 'Have you of yours?'

He shut his eyes, re-opened them and said, 'What proof?'

'In the arse pocket of my jeans here,' I said to him, slapping my hind-quarters briskly, 'I carry a perspex folder, with within it my Driving Licence, which is a clean one I'm surprised to say, my Blood Donor's Certificate, showing I've given two pints of gore so far this year, and tatty membership cards of more speakeasies and jazz clubs than I remember. You may look at them if you really want to, or you could get Mr Pondoroso on the blower and ask him to describe me, or, better still, you could stop playing games and give me the ten pounds your client has instructed you to pay me. that is, unless your till is short of loot.'

To which he answered, 'You have not yet endorsed the document on the back, please.'

I scribbled out my name. He twiddled the cheque, began writing on it and said, without looking up, 'I take it you're a minor?'

'Yes,' I said, 'if it's anything to do with anything, I am.' He still said nothing, and he still didn't hand me over my loot. 'But now I'm a big boy,' I continued, 'I don't wet my bed any longer, and know how to hit back if I'm attacked.'

He gave me the notes as if they were two deformed specimens the Bank happened to have it was ashamed of, then nipped round his counter and saw me out of the door, and locked it swiftly on my heels. I must admit this incident made me over-heated, it was all so unnecessary and so old-fashioned, treating a teenager like a kid, and I headed away from Victoria towards my home in quite a rage.

I must explain the only darkroom I possess of my own, without which, of course, I'd have to get my printing done commercially, is at my old folks' residence in Belgravia South, as they call it, namely, Pimlico. As I expect you'll have guessed, I don't like going there, and haven't lived in the place (except when they're off on their summer seaside orgy) in years. But they still keep what they call 'my room' there, out in the annexe at the back, which used to be the conservatory, full of potted flowers.

The family, if you can call it that, consists of three besides myself, plus numerous additions. The three are my poor old Dad, who isn't really all that old, only forty-eight, but who was wrecked and ruined by the 1930s, so he never fails to tell me, and then my Mum, who's much older than she lets on or, I will say this for her, looks certainly three or four years older than my Dad, and finally my half-brother Vern, who Mum had by a mystery man seven years before she tied up with my poppa, and who's the number-one weirdie, layabout and monster of the Westminster city area. As for the numerous additions, these are Mum's lodgers, because she keeps a boarding-house, and some of them, as you'd expect if you knew Ma, are lodged in very firmly, though there's nothing my Dad can do about it, apparently, as his spirits are squashed by a combination of my Mum and the 1930s and that's one of the several reasons for which I left the dear old ancestral home.

Mum won't let me have a key and, as a matter of fact, is even tough about giving one to her paid-up boarders, as she likes to see them come and go, even late at night, so though as a matter of fact I've had a key made of my own, in case of accidents, I go through the form of ringing the front doorbell, just out of politeness, and also to show her I regard myself strictly as a visitor and don't *live* there. As usual, although she gets mad if you go down the area steps and knock on the basement door, where she almost always is, Mum came out from there into the area and looked up to see who it was, before she'd come up the stairs inside and open the front door for me which she might have done, if she'd been civilized, in the first place.

There she stood, her face lighting up at the sight of a pair of slacks, even her own son's, with that sloppy sexy expression that always drove me mad, because, after all, tucked away behind all those mounds of highly desirable flesh, my Mum has got real brains. But she's only used them to make herself more appealing, like pepper and salt and garlic on an overdone pork chop.

'Hello, Blitz Baby,' she said.

Which is what she calls me, because she had me in one, in a tube shelter with an air raid warden acting as midwife, as she never tires of telling me or, worse still, other people in my presence.

'Hullo, Ma,' I said to her.

She still stood there, pink hands with detergent suds on them on her Toulouse-Lautrec hips, giving me that come-hither look she gave her lodgers, I suppose.

'Are you going to open up?' I asked her, 'or should I climb in through your front parlour window?'

'I'll send you down your father,' she answered me. 'I expect he'll be able to let you in.'

This is the trick my Mum has, to speak to me of Dad as if he's only *my* relation, only mine, that she never had anything whatever to do with (apart, of course, from having had sex with him and even marrying the poor old man). I suppose this is because, number one, Dad's what known as a failure, though I don't regard him as one exactly, as anyone could have seen he'd never have succeeded at anything anyway, and number two, to show that her first husband, whoever he was, the one who goosed her into producing that Category A morbid, my elder half-brother Vernon, was the *real* man in her life, not my own poor old ancestor. Well, that's her little bit of feminine psychology: you certainly learn a lot about women from your Mum.

I was kept there waiting a considerable time, so that if it wasn't for the need of my darkroom they'd have never seen me, when Dad appeared with that dead-duck look not merely on his face, but hanging on his whole poor old scruffy body, which makes me demented, because really he's got a lot of character, and though he's no mind to speak of, he's read a lot like I do—I mean, tried to make the best of what he's got in a way my Mum hasn't tried to do at all, or even thought of trying. As usual, he opened the door without a word except 'Hullo,' and started off up the stairs again towards his room in the attic portion of the building, which is just an act because he knows, of course, I'll follow him up there for a little chatter, if only for politeness' sake, and to show him I'm his son.

But today I didn't, partly because I was suddenly tired of his performance, and partly because I'd so much work to do immediately inside my darkroom. So out I went and, would you believe it, found that horrible old weirdie Vernon had built himself a cuckoo's nest there, which was something new.

'Hullo, Jules,' I said to him. 'And how's my favourite yobbo?'

'Don't call me Jules,' he said. 'I've already told you.'

Which he has—perhaps 200,000 times or so, ever since I invented the name for him, on account of Vernon=Verne=Jules of *Round the World in Eighty Days*.

'And what are you doing in my darkroom, Julie?' I asked this oafo brother of mine.

He'd got up off the camp bed in the corner—all blankets and no sheets, just like my Vernon—and came over and did an act he's done with monotonous regularity ever since I can remember, namely, to stand up over me, close to me, breathing heavily and smelling of putrid perspiration.

'What, again?' I said to him. 'Not another corny King Kong performance!'

His fist whisked past my snout in playful panto.

'Do grow *up*, Vernon,' I said to him, very patiently. 'You're a big boy now, more than a quarter of a century old.'

What would happen next would be either that he'd push me around in which case, of course, it would be just a massacre, except that he knew I'd get in at least one blow that would really cripple him, and perhaps even harm him for life—or else he'd suddenly feel the whole thing was beneath his dignity, and want to talk to me, talk to anyone, in fact, whatever, since the poor old ape was such an H-Certificate product he was really very lonely.

So he plucked at my short-arse Italian jacket with his great big cucumber fingers and said, 'What you wear this thing for?'

'Excuse me, Vernon,' I said, edging past him to unload my

camera on my table. 'I wear it,' I said, taking the jacket off and hanging it up, 'to keep warm in winter, and, in summer, to captivate the chicks by swinging my tail around.'

'Hunh!' he said, his mind racing fast, but nothing coming out except this noise like a polar bear with wind. He looked me up and down while his thoughts came into focus. 'Those clothes you wear,' he said at last, 'disgust me.'

And I hope they did! I had on precisely my full teenage drag that would enrage him—the grey pointed alligator casuals, the pink neon pair of ankle crêpe nylon-stretch, my Cambridge blue glove-fit jeans, a vertical-striped happy shirt revealing my lucky neck-charm on its chain, and the Roman-cut short-arse jacket just referred to . . . not to mention my wrist identity jewel, and my Spartan warrior hair-do, which everyone thinks costs me 17/6d. in Gerrard Street, Soho, but which I, as a matter of fact, do myself with a pair of nail-scissors and a three-sided mirror that Suzette's got, when I visit her flatlet up in Bayswater, w.2.

'And you, I suppose,' I said, deciding that attack was the best method of defence though oh! so wearisome, 'you imagine you look alluring in that horrible men's wear suiting that you've bought in a marked-down summer sale at the local casbah.'

'It's manly,' he said, 'and it's respectable.'

I gazed at the floppy dung-coloured garments he had on. 'Ha!' was about all I said.

'What's more,' he went on, 'I've not wasted money on it. It's my demobilization suit.'

My heaven, yes, it looked it—*yes*!

'When *you've* done your military service,' the poor old yokel said, his boot face breaking into a crafty grin, 'you'll be given one too, you'll find. *And* a decent hair-cut just for once.'

I gazed at the goon. 'Vernon,' I said, 'I'm sorry for you. Somehow you missed the teenage rave, and you never seem to have had a youth. To try to tell you the simplest facts of life is just a waste of valuable breath, however, do try to dig this, if your microbe mini-brain is capable. There's no honour and glory in doing military service, once it's compulsory. If it was voluntary, yes, perhaps, but not if you're just sent.'

'The war,' said Vern, 'was Britain's finest hour.'

'What war? You mean Cyprus, boy? Or Suez? Or Korea?'

'No, stupid. I mean the *real* war, you don't remember.'

'Well, Vernon,' I said, 'please believe me, I'm glad I don't. All of you oldies certainly seem to try to keep it well in mind, because every time I open a newspaper, or pick up a paperback, or go to the Odeon, I hear nothing but war, war, war. You pensioners certainly seem to love that old, old struggle.'

'You're just ignorant,' said Vern.

'Well, if I am, Vern, that's quite okay by me. Because I tell you: not being a mug, exactly, I've no intention of playing soldiers for the simple reasons, first of all, that big armies obviously are no longer necessary, what with the atomic, and secondly, no one is going to tell me to do anything I don't want to, no, or try to blackmail me with that crazy old mixture of threats and congratulations that a pronk like you falls for because you're a born form-filler, tax-payer and cannon-fodder . . . well, boy, just take a look in the mirror at yourself.'

That left him silent for a while. 'Come on, now,' I said. 'Be a good half-brother, and let me get on with my work. Why have you moved in this room, anyway?'

'You're wrong!' he cried. 'You'll have to do it!'

'That subject's exhausted. We've been into it thoroughly. Do forget it.'

'What we done, you gotta do.'

'Vernon,' I said, 'I hate to tell you this, but you really don't speak very good English.'

'You'll see!'

'All right,' I said, 'I'll see.'

I was trying, as you'll have realized, to drive him out of the room, but the boy is sensitive as the end of a truck, and just flopped back on his bed again, worn out by the mental effort of our conversation. So I put him out of my mind and worked on at my snaps in silence, till Dad knocked on the door with two cups of char; and standing there in the dark, with only the red light burning, we both ignored that moron, not bothering to wonder if he was awake and eaves-dropping, or dreaming of winning six Victoria Crosses.

Dad asked me for the news.

Now, this always embarrasses me, because whatever news I tell

Dad, he always comes back again to his two theme songs of, number one, what a much better time I have than he had in the 1930s, and, number two, why don't I come back 'home' again—which is what Dad really seems to believe this high-grade brothel that he lives in means to me.

'You've found that he's moved in,' said Dad, pointing in the direction of the bed. 'I tried to stop it, but I couldn't. The room's still yours, though, I've always insisted on that all the way along.'

I imagined poor Dad insisting to my Mum.

'What's she put him here for, anyway?' I asked.

'He's been quarrelling with the lodgers,' Dad said. 'There's one of them in particular, doesn't get on with him at all.'

I didn't like to ask him which or why. So, 'And how's the book going?' I asked my poor old ancestor. Which is a reference to a *History of Pimlico* Dad's said to be composing, but nobody's ever seen it, though it gives him the excuse for getting out of the house, and chatting to people, and visiting public libraries, and reading books.

'I've reached Chapter 23,' he said.

'When does that take us up to?' I asked him, already guessing the answer.

'The beginning of the 1930s,' he replied.

I gulped a bit of tea. 'I bet, Dad,' I said, 'you give those poor old 1930s of yours a bit of a bashing.'

I could feel Dad quivering with indignation. 'I certainly do, son!' he shouted in a whisper. 'You've simply no idea what that pre-war period was like. Poverty, unemployment, fascism and disaster and, worst of all, no chance, no opportunity, no sunlight at the end of the corridor, just a lot of hard, frightened, rich old men sitting on top of a pile of dustbin lids to keep the muck from spilling over!'

I didn't quite get all that, but concentrated.

'It was a terrible time for the young,' he went on, grabbing me. 'Nobody would listen to you if you were less than thirty, nobody gave you money whatever you'd do for it, nobody let you *live* like you kids can do today. Why, I couldn't even marry till the 1940s came and the war gave me some sort of a security . . . Just think of the terrible loss, though! If I'd married ten years earlier, when I was young, you and I would have only had twenty years between us instead of thirty, and me already an old man.'

I thought of pointing out to Dad that if he'd married so much earlier it might have been another woman than my Mum, in which case I wouldn't have existed, or not, at any rate, in my present particular form—but let it go. 'Hard cheese,' I said to him instead, hoping he'd got the subject out of his system for this visit. But no, he was off again.

'Just look around you, when you next go out!' he cried. 'Just look at any of the 1930s buildings! What they put up today may be ultra-modern, but at any rate it's full of light and life and air. But those 1930s buildings are all shut in and negative, with landlord and broker's man written all over them.'

'Just a minute, Dad,' I said, 'while I hang up this little lot of negatives.'

'Believe me, son, in the 1930s they hated life, they really did. It's better now, even with the bomb.'

I washed my hands under the hot tap that always runs cold as usual. 'You're topping it up a bit there, Dad, aren't you?' I said.

Dad dropped his voice even lower. 'And then, there's another thing,' he said, '—the venereal.'

'Yeah?' I said, though I was really quite a bit embarrassed, because no one likes much discussing that sort of topic with a Dad like mine.

'Yes,' he went on, '—the venereal. It was a scourge—a blight hanging over all young men. It cast a great shadow over love, and made it hateful.'

'It did?' I said. 'Didn't you have doctors, then?'

'Doctors!' he cried. 'In those days, the worst types were practically incurable, or only after years and years of anxiety and doubt . . .'

I stopped my work. 'No kidding?' I said. 'It was like that, then? Well, that's a thought!'

'Yes. No modern drugs and quick relief, like now . . .'

I was quite struck by that, but thought I'd better change the subject all the same.

'Then why aren't you cheerier, Dad?' I said to him. 'If you like the fifties better, as you say you do, why don't you enjoy yourself a bit?'

My poor old parent gulped. 'It's because I'm too old now, son,' he said. 'I should have had my youth in the 1950s, like you have, and not my middle-age.'

'Well, it's too late to alter that, Dad, isn't it. But hell, you're not yet fifty, you could get out into the world a bit . . . I mean, you're not really too old to get a job, are you, and travel around and see what sights there are? Others have done it, haven't they?'

My poor old Pop was silent.

'Why do you stay in this dump, for instance?' I said to him.

'You mean here with your mother?'

'Yes, Dad. Why?'

'He stays because he's afraid to go, and she keeps him because she wants the place to look respectable.'

This came from the bed and my charming half-brother Vernon, who we'd quite forgotten, and who evidently had been listening to us with both his red ears flapping.

'Ignore him, Dad,' I said. 'He's so easy to ignore.'

'He's nothing to do with *me*,' my father muttered, 'nothing whatever.' And he picked up the cups and made off out of the room, knocking things over.

'You,' I said to Vernon, 'are a real number one horror, a real unidentified thing from outer space.'

The trouble about Vernon, really, as I've said, is that he's one of the last of the generations that grew up before teenagers existed: in fact, he never seems to have been an absolute beginner at any time at all. Even today, of course, there are some like him, i.e., kids of the right age, between fifteen or so and twenty, that I wouldn't myself describe as teenagers: I mean not kiddos who dig the teenage *thing*, or are it. But in poor Vernon's era, the sad slob, there just weren't *any*: can you believe it? Not any authentic teenagers at all. In those days, it seems, you were just an over-grown boy, or an under-grown man, life didn't seem to cater for anything whatever else between.

So I said all this to him.

'Oh, yeah?' he answered (which he must have got from old Clark Gable pictures, like the ones you can see revivals of at the Classics).

'Yeah,' I said to him. 'And that's what explains your squalid downtrodden look, and your groaning and moaning and grouching against society.'

'Is zat so,' he said.

'Zat is, half-brother,' I replied.

I could see him limbering up his brain for a reply: believe me, even I could feel the floor trembling with the effort.

'I dunno about the trouble with *me*,' my oafo brother finally declared, 'but *your* trouble is, you have no social conscience.'

'No what?'

'No social conscience.'

He'd come up close, and I looked into his narrow, meanie eyes. 'That sounds to me,' I said, 'like a parrot-cry pre-packaged for you by your fellow squalids of the Ernie Bevin club.'

'Who put you where you are.'

'Which who? And put me where?'

And now this dear 50 per cent relative of mine came up and prodded my pectorals with a stubby, grubby digit.

'It was the Attlee administrations,' said my bro., in his whining, complaining, platform voice, 'who emancipated the working-man, and gave the teenagers their economic privileges.'

'So you approve of me.'

'What?'

'If it was the Ernie Bevin boys who gave us our privileges like you say, you must approve of us.'

'No, I don't, oh no.'

'No?'

'That was an unforeseen eventuality,' he said. 'I mean you kids getting all these high-paid jobs and leisure.'

'Not part of the master-plan?'

'No. And are you grateful to us? Not a bit of it.'

There I agreed with him at last. 'Why should we be?' I said. 'Your pinko pals did what they wanted to when they got power, and why should we nippers thank them for doing their bounden duty?'

This thought, such as it was, really halted him in his tracks. You could hear his brain racing and grinding behind his red, crunched face, till he cried excitedly, 'You're a traitor to the working-class!'

I took the goon's forefinger, which was still prodding me in the torso, and shook it away from me, and said:

'I am *not* a traitor to the working-class because I do *not* belong to the working-class, and therefore cannot be a traitor to it.'

'N—h'n!' he really said. 'You belong to the upper-class, I suppose.'

I sighed up.

'And you reject the working-classes that you sprung from.'

I sighed some more.

'You poor old prehistoric monster,' I exclaimed. 'I do *not* reject the working-classes, and I do *not* belong to the upper-classes, for one and the same simple reason, namely, that neither of them interest me in the slightest, never have done, never will do. Do try to understand that, clobbo! I'm just not interested in the whole class crap that seems to needle you and all the tax-payers—needle you all, whichever side of the tracks you live on, or suppose you do.'

He glared at me. I could see that, if once he believed that what I said I really meant, and thousands of the kiddos did the same as well, the bottom would fall out of his horrid little world.

'You're dissolute!' he suddenly cried out, 'Immoral! That's what I say you teenagers all are!'

I eyed the oafo, then spoke up slow. 'I'll tell you one thing about teenagers,' I said, 'compared with how I remember you ten years ago . . . which is we wash between our toes, and change our vests and pants occasionally, and don't keep empty bottles underneath our beds for the good reason we don't touch the stuff.'

Saying which, I left the creature; because really, all this was such a waste of time, a drag, all so obvious, and honestly, I don't like arguing. If they think that all cat's cock, well, let them think it, and good luck!

I must have been muttering this out aloud along the corridor, because a voice said, over the staircase balustrade, 'Counting your money, then, or talking to the devil? 'and of course it was my dear old Mum. There she stood, holding the railings, like someone in a Tennessee Williams film show. So, 'Hullo, Madame Blanche,' I said to her.

For a moment she started to look flattered, like women do if you say something sexy to them, no matter how intimate it is, so long as they think it's flattering to their egos, until she saw I was ice-cold and sarcastic, and her closed-for-business look came over her fine face again.

But I got in my body blow before she could. 'And how is the harem-in-reverse?' I said to her.

'Eh?' said my Ma.

'The gigolo lodgers, the Pal Joeys,' I went on, to make my meaning clear.

As if to prove my point, two of them kindly passed by at that moment, making it hard for poor old Mum to flatten me, as I could see by her bitter glare that she'd intended, which was now transformed into a sickly simper, prim and alluring, that she turned on like a light for the two beefo Malts who walked between us, oozing virility and no deodorant.

As soon as they'd squeezed by her up the stair, with much exchanging of the time of day, she whipped round on me and said, 'You little rat.'

'Mother should know,' I told her.

'You're too big for your boots,' she said.

'Shoes,' I told her.

In and out she breathed. 'You've too much spending money, that's your trouble!'

'That's just what's *not* my trouble, Ma.'

'All you teenagers have.'

I said, 'I'm really getting tired of hearing this. All right, we kids have got too much loot to spend! Well, please tell me what you propose to do about it.'

'All that money,' she said, looking at me as if I had pound notes falling out of my ears, and she could snatch them, 'and you're only minors! With no responsibilities to need all that spending money for.'

'Listen to me,' I said. 'Who made us minors?'

'What?'

'You made us minors with your parliamentary whatsits,' I told her patiently. 'You thought, "That'll keep the little bastards in their places, no legal rights, and so on," and you made us minors. Righty-o. That also freed us from responsibility, didn't it? Because how can you be responsible if you haven't any rights? And then came the gay-time boom and all the spending money, and suddenly you oldos found that though we minors had no rights, we'd got the money power. In other words—and *listen* to me, Ma—though it wasn't what you'd intended, admittedly, you gave us the money, and you took away our responsibility. Follow me so far? Well, okay! You majors find the laws you cooked up have given you all the duties, and none of the fun, and us the contrary, and you don't like it, do you. Well, as for us, the kids, we do like it, see? We like it fine, Ma. Let it stay that way!'

This left me quite exhausted. Why do I *explain* it to them, talking like a Method number, if they're not interested in me anyway?

Mum, who hadn't been taking this in (and I mean my ideas, though she naturally grasped the general gist), now changed her tactics, which made me wary, for she came down the stair in silence and beckoned me into her private parlour, as in the old way she used to for some trouble, and also as in the old way, I thought it best just not to follow her, and take my leave. But she must have guessed this, because she popped out of her parlour again, and caught me with the front door open, and grabbed my sleeve. 'I must speak to you, son,' she said.

'Speak to me outside, then,' I told her, trying to walk out of the door into the street, but she still clutched.

'No, in my room, it's vital,' she kept hissing.

Well, there we were, practically wrestling on the doorway, when she let go and said, '*Please* come in.'

I closed the door, but wouldn't move further than the corridor, and waited.

'Your father's dying,' Mum told me now.

Now, my first thought was, she's lying; and my second thought was, even if not, she's trying to get at me, because what does she care if he lives or dies? She's going to try to make me *responsible* in some way for something I'm not at all, i.e., the old blackmail of the parents and all oldies against the kiddos.

But I was wrong, it wasn't that, she wanted something from me. After a great deal of a lot of beating about the bush, she said to me, 'If anything should happen to your father, I'd want you to come back here.'

'You'd want me to,' I said. That's all.

'Yes. I'd want you to come back here.'

'And why?'

Because I really didn't know. But what gave me the clue was Mum dropping her eyes and looking modest and girlish and bashful, at first I thought for effect, but then I realized it was partly for true, and that for once she just couldn't help it.

'You want me back,' I said, 'because you'll want a man about the house.'

She mutely acquiesced, as the women's weeklies say.

'To keep the dear old place *respectable*, till you get married once again,' I continued on.

Still Ma was mute.

'Because old Vern, your previous product, is such a drip-dry drag that no one would ever take *him* for the male of the establishment.'

I got an eye-flash for that, but still no answer, while our thoughts sparred up there in silence in the air, unable to disconnect, because no matter how far you're cut off from a close relation, cut right off and eternally severed, there always remains a link of memory—I mean Mum *knew* a whole great deal about me, like nobody else did, and that held us.

'Dad's very much alive,' I said. 'He doesn't look like dying to me a bit. Not a bit, he doesn't.'

'Yes, but I tell you, the doctor's told me . . .'

'I'll take my instructions in that matter from Dad, and Dad alone,' I said. 'And if Dad ever dies, I'll take my instructions from myself.'

She could see that was that, and didn't give me, as you might have expected, a dirty look, but a puzzled one she couldn't control, such as she's given me about six times in my life, as though to say to me, what is this monster I've created?

With which I blew.

Down by the river, where I went to get a breather, I stood beside the big new high blocks of glass-built flats, like an X-ray of a stack of buildings with their skins peeled off, and watched the traffic floating down the Thames below them, very slow and sure (chug, chug) and oily, underneath the electric railway bridge (rattle, rattle), and past the power-station like a super-cinema with funnels stuck on it. Peace, perfect peace, though very murky, I decided. Hoot, hoot to you, big barge, *bon, bon voyage*. There was a merry scream, and I turned about and watched the juveniles, teenagers in bud as you might call them, wearing their little jeans and jumpers, playing in their kiddipark of Disneyland items erected by the borough council to help them straighten out their thwarted egos. When crash! Someone thumped me very painfully on the shoulder-blades.

I very slowly turned and saw the pasty, scabies-ridden countenance of Edward the Ted.

'Bang, bang,' I said, humouring the imbecile by pointing my thumb and finger at him like a pistol. 'Bad boy!'

Ed the Ted said nothing, just looked sinister, and stood breathing halitosis on me.

'And what,' I said, 'you doing pounding around down here?'

'I liv ear,' said Ed.

I gazed at the goon.

'My God, Ed,' I cried, 'you can actually talk!'

He came nearer, panting like a hippo, and suddenly twirled a key chain, that he'd been hiding in his fist and in his pocket, till it buzzed like a plane propeller between the two of us.

'What, Ed?' I said. 'No bike-chain? No flick knife? No iron bar?'

And, as a matter of fact, he wasn't wearing his full Teddy uniform either: no velvet-lined frock-coat, no bootlace tie, no four-inch solid corridor-creepers—only that insanitary hair-do, creamy curls falling all over his one-inch forehead, and his drainpipes that last saw the inside of a cleaner's in the Attlee era. To stop the chain twirling, he tried to grab it suddenly with the same hand he was spinning it with, hit his own great red knuckles, winced and looked hurt and offended, then fierce and defiant as he put the hand and the chain in his smelly old drainpipes once again.

'Arve moved,' he said. 'Darn ear.'

'And all the click?' I asked him. 'All the notorious Dockhead boys?'

'Not v' click,' said Ed-Ted. 'Jus me.'

I should explain (and I hope you'll believe it, even though it's true) that Edward and I were born and bred, if you can call it that, within a bottle's throw of each other off the Harrow road in Kilburn, and used to run around together in our short-pant days. Then, when the Ted-thing became all the rage, Edward signed up for the duration, and joined the Teddy-boy wolf cubs, or whatever they're called, and later graduated through the Ted high school up the Harrow road to the full-fledged Teddy-boy condition—slit eyes, and cosh, and words of one syllable, and dirty finger-nails and all—and left his broken-hearted Mum and Dad, who gave three rousing cheers, and emigrated down to Bermondsey, to join a gang. According to the tales Ed told me, when he left his jungle occasionally and crossed the frontier into the civilized sections of the city and had a coffee with me, he lived a high old life, brave, bold and splendid, smashing crockery in all-night caffs and crowning distinguished colleagues with tyre levers in *cul-de-sacs* and parking lots, and even appearing in a telly programme on the Ted question where he stared photogenically, and only grunted.

'And why, Ed,' I said, 'have you moved darn ear?'

'Cos me Mar as,' he said. 'She's bin re-owsed.'

He blinked at the effort of two syllables.

'So you still live with Momma?' I enquired.

He beetled at me. 'Course,' he said.

'Big boy like you hasn't got his own little hidey-hole?' I asked.

Ed bunched his torso. 'Lissen,' he said. 'I re-spek my Mar.'

'Cool, man,' I said. 'Now, tell me. What about the mob, the click? Have they been re-owsed as well?'

'Ner,' he said.

'Ner? What, then?'

At this point, our valiant Edward looked scared, and glancing round about him at the flat blocks, which towered all round like monsters, he said, 'The click's split up.'

I eyed the primitive.

'You mean,' I said, 'that bunch of tearaways have thrown you out?'

'Eh-y?' he cried.

'You heard, Ed. You've been expelled from the Ted college?'

'Naher! Me? Espel me? Wot? Lissen! Me, Ar lef *them*, see? You fink I'm sof, or sumfink?'

I shook my head at the poor goof and his abracadabra. 'Do me a favour, Ed,' I said. 'You're scared of the boys, why not admit it? Old-style Teds like you are, wasted, anyway: they've all moved out of London to the provinces.'

Edward the Ted did a little war-dance on the cracked concrete paving. 'Naher!' he kept crying, like a ten-year-old.

'The trouble is, Ed,' I said, 'you've tried to be a man without having been a teenager. You've tried to miss out one of the flights of stairs.'

At the mention of 'teenager', Ed came to a standstill and stood there, his body hunched like a great ingrowing toe-nail, staring at me as if his whole squashed personality was spitting.

'Teenagers!' he cried out. 'Kid's stuff. Teenagers!'

I just raised my brows at the poor slob, gave a little one-hand one-arm wave, and said bye-bye. As I was crossing the yard between the house blocks, like an ant upon a chess-board, a hunk of rock, clumsily aimed, of course, thank heaven, flew by and hit the imitation traction engine in the kiddi-park. 'Yank!' Ed yelled after me. 'Go ome, Yank!'

Sad.

Up out in Pimlico, the old, old city raised her bashed grey head again, like she was ashamed of her modern daughter down by the river, and I went up streets of dark purple and vomit green, all set at angles like ham sandwiches, until I reached the Buckingham Palace road, so called, and the place where the Air Terminal stands opposite the coach station.

And there, on the one side, were the glamour people setting off for foreign countries, mohair and linen suits, white air-liner vanity bags, dark sun-spectacles and pages of tickets packed to paradise, every nationality represented, and everyone equal in the sky-dominion of fast air-travel—and there, on the other side, were the peasant masses of the bus terminal shuffling along in their front-parlour-curtain dresses and cut-price tweeds and plastic mackintoshes, all flat feet and fair shares and you-in-your-small-corner-and-I-in-mine; and then, passing down the middle of them, a troop of toy soldiers, all of them with hangovers after nights of rapture down on the Dilly, and wearing ladies' fur muffs on their heads and sweaty red jackets that showed their vertebraes from neck to coccyx, and playing that prissy little pipe music like a bird making wind—and I thought, my God, my Lord, how horrible this country is, how dreary, how lifeless, how blind and busy over trifles!

After which, feeling maybe it perhaps was *me*, I walked into the little square behind the terminal, where there was the usual assortment of mums and prams and bubble-blowing occupants, and old men with boots and dandruff, and rolled fags with the tobacco dripping out at the ends, and I sat down on a wood bench beneath enormous planes, they must have been, with decorative beds and even a fountain, which is practically unknown in England, where they always remember to turn the taps off and economize with water, and noticed that hosing away there was a West Indian gardener, surrounded by a swarm of kids, all pulling at his hose, and he doing the benevolent adult performance I must say very well, and also the coloured man at ease among the hostile natives.

Now myself, I've nothing against kids, I realize that they have to be so that the race can continue, but I can't say that I like them, or approve of them. In fact, I mistrust them, and consider they're a menace, because they're so damned wilful and *energetic*, and, if you ask me, in spite of their charming little childish habits, they know perfectly well what they're up to, and see they get it, and one day, mark my words, we'll wake up and find the little horrors have risen in the night and captured the Bank of England and Buckingham Palace and the BBC. But this West Indian, he must have had paternal instincts, or something, or been trained as a lion-tamer, because he handled these little atom bombs without effort, either kidding them so that they all screamed with laughter (and him as well), or else cracking down on them in a fury, and getting immediate results. And all between this, and the hosing, he'd say a word or two to the mums and the old geezers, flaunting his BWI charms, for which I don't blame him, but was also attentive to the old chatterboxes of both sexes, till everyone I do declare actually beamed.

In fact, this coloured character struck me as so bloody *civilized*.

With which thought, I heaved myself up, there in that scented garden in the height of summer, feeling oh! so somehow saddened, and caught myself a bus. It took me across London to my manor in the area of W.10 and 11.

I'd like to explain this district where I live, because it's quite a curiosity, being one of the few that's got left behind by the Welfare era *and* the Property-owning whatsit, both of them, and is, in fact, nothing more than a stagnating slum. It's dying, this bit of London, and that's the most important thing to remember about what goes on there. To the north of it, there run, in parallel, the Harrow road I've mentioned, which you'd hurry through even if you were in a car, and a canal, called the Grand Union, that nothing floats on except cats and contraceptives, and the main railway track that takes you from London to the swede counties of the West of England. These three escape routes, which are all at different heights and levels, cut across one another at different points, making crazy little islands of slum habitation shut off from the world by concrete precipices, and linked by metal bridges. I need hardly mention that on this north side there's a hospital, a gas-works with enough juice for the whole population of the kingdom to commit suicide, and a very ancient cemetery with the pretty country name of Kensal Green.

On the east side, still in the W.10 bit, there's another railway, and a park with a name only Satan in all his splendour could have thought up, namely Wormwood Scrubs, which has a prison near it, and another hospital, and a sports arena, and the new telly barracks of the BBC, and with a long, lean road called Latimer road which I particularly want you to remember, because out of this road, like horrible tits dangling from a lean old sow, there hang a whole festoon of what I think must really be the sinisterest highways in our city, well, just listen to their names: Blechynden, Silchester, Walmer, Testerton and Bramley—can't you just smell them, as you hurry to get through the cats-cradle of these blocks? In this part, the houses are old Victorian lower-middle tumble-down, built I dare say for grocers and bank clerks and horse-omnibus inspectors who've died and gone and their descendants evacuated to the outer suburbs, but these houses live on like shells, and there's only one thing to do with them, absolutely one, which is to pull them down till not a one's left standing up.

On the south side of this area, down by the W.11, things are a little different, but in a way that somehow makes them worse, and that is, owing to a freak of fortune, and some smart work by the estate agents too, I shouldn't be surprised, there are one or two sections that are positively posh: not *fashionable*, mind you, but quite graded, with their big back gardens and that absolute silence which in London is the top sign of a respectable location. You walk about in these bits, adjusting your tie and looking down to see if your shoes are shining, when—wham! suddenly you're back in the slum area again—honest, it's really startling, like where the river joins on to the shore, two quite different creations of dame nature, cheek by thing.

Over towards the west, the frontiers aren't quite as definite, and the whole area merges into a drab and shady and semi-respectable part called Bayswater, which I would rather lie in my coffin, please believe me, than spend a night in, were it not for Suze, who's shacked up there. No! Give me our London Napoli I've been describing, with its railway scenery, and crescents that were meant to twist elegantly but now look as if they're lurching high, and huge houses too tall for their width cut up into twenty flatlets, and front façades that it never pays anyone to paint, and broken milk bottles *everywhere* scattering the cracked asphalt roads like snow, and cars parked in the streets looking as if they're stolen or abandoned, and a strange number of male urinals tucked away such as you find nowhere else in London, and red curtains, somehow, in all the windows, and diarrhoea-coloured street lighting—man, I tell you, you've only got to be there for a minute to know there's something radically *wrong*.

Across this whole mess there cuts, diagonally, yet another railway, that rides high above this slum property like a scenic railway at a fair. Boy, if you want to admire our wonderful old capital city, you should take a ride on this track some time! And just where this railway is slung over the big central road that cuts across the area north to south, there's a hole, a dip, a pocket, a really unhappy valley which, according to my learned Dad, was formerly at one time a great non-agricultural marsh. A place of evil, mister. I bet witches lived around it, and a lot still do.

And what about the human population? The answer is, this is the residential doss-house of our city. In plain words, you'd not live in our Napoli if you could live anywhere else. And that is why there are, to the square yard, more boys fresh from the nick, and national refugee minorities, and out-of-business whores, than anywhere else, I should expect, in London town. The kids live in the streets—I mean they have *charge* of them, you have to ask permission to get along them even in a car—the teenage lot are mostly of the Ted variety, the chicks mature so quick there's scarcely such a thing there as a *little* girl, the men don't talk, glance at you hard, keep moving, and don't stand with their backs to anyone, their women are mostly out of sight, with dishcloths I expect for yashmaks, and there are piles and piles of these dreadful, wasted, negative, shop-soiled kind of *old people* that make you feel it really is a tragedy to grow grey.

You're probably saying well, if you're so cute, kiddo, why do you live in such an area? So now, as a certain evening paper writes it, 'I will tell you.'

One reason is that it's so cheap. I mean, I have a rooted objection to paying rent at all, it should be free like air, and parks, and water. I don't think I'm mean, in fact I know I'm not, but I just can't bear paying more than a bob or two to landlords. But the real reason, as I expect you'll have already guessed, is that, however horrible the area is, you're *free* there! No one, I repeat it, no one, has ever asked me there what I am, or what I do, or where I came from, or what my social group is, or whether I'm educated or not, and if there's one thing I cannot tolerate in this world, it's nosey questions. And what is more, once the local bandits see you're making out, can earn your living and so forth, they don't swing it on you in the slightest you're a teenage creation—if you have loot, and can look after yourself, they treat you as a man, which is what you are. For instance, *nobody* in the area would ever have treated me like that bank clerk tried to in Belgravia. If you go in anywhere, they take it for granted that you know the scene. If you don't, it's true they throw you out in pieces, but if you do, they treat you just as one of them.

The room I inhabit in sunny Napoli, which overlooks *both* railways (*and* the foulest row of backyards to be found outside the municipal compost heaps), belongs to an Asian character called Omar, Pakistani, I believe, who's regular as clockwork—in fact, even more so, because clocks are known to stop—and turns up on Saturday mornings, accompanied by two countrymen who act as bodyguards, to collect the rents, and you'd better have yours ready. Because if you haven't, he simply grins his teeth and tells his *fellahin* to pile everything you possess neatly on the outside pavement, be it rain, or snow, or mulligatawny fog. And if you've locked the door, it means absolutely nothing to him to smash it down, and even if you're in bed, all injured innocence and indignation, he still comes in with his sickly don't-mean-a-thing kind of smile. So if you're going to be away, it's best to leave the money with a friend, or better still, pay him, as I do, monthly in advance. And when you do, he takes out a plastic bag on a long chain from a very inner pocket, and tucks the notes away, and says you must have a drink with him some time, but even when I've once or twice met him in a pub, he's never offered it, of course. Also, if you make any complaint *whatever*—I mean, even that the roof's falling in, and the water cut off—he smiles that same smile and does positively sweet bugger-all about it. On the other hand, you could invite every whore and cut-throat in the city in for a pail of gin, or give a corpse accommodation for the night on the spare bed, or even set the bloody place on fire, and he wouldn't turn a hair—or turn one if anybody complained to him about you. Not if you paid your rent, that is. In fact, the perfect landlord.

The tenants come and go, as you might expect, but among the regular squatters I have a few particular buddies, of whom I'd specially name the following three.

The first of them, on the floor below me (I'm on the top), is a boy called The Fabulous Hoplite. I'm hoping you'll not scoff at his name, because Hoplite would certainly not care for it if you did, as he's a most sensitive and dignified character, who was formerly a male whore's male maid, if the truth be told, but has now retired from that particular scene. According to report, the Hoplite has been in business with some of the city's top poof raves, and was even more in demand by the gentry than the costly glamorosos he'd shacked up with. How I know him, is on account of his being a friend of Wiz's who he admires (but nothing doing), and it was through them that I actually got my room. What the Hoplite does for a living now, apart from a bit of free-lancing on the side when conditions get too rough, is act as contact man for various gossip columnists, because though you might not think this credible, considering his background, Hoplite gets around on the Knightsbridge-Chelsea circuit in quite an important way, no doubt owing to his being very handsome in an elfin, adolescent sort of style, and certainly very witty, or should I say sharp-tongued, but most of all, because he's really very *friendly*: I mean, he really *does like* people, which a lot of people think they do, but which it seems, as a matter of fact, is really very rare.

Next, on the first floor, is in fact the best room, but I somehow don't think he'll last there, on account of really critical moments with Mr Omar, is a young coloured kid called Mr Cool (which I need hardly say is not his baptismal name, I don't suppose). Cool is a local product, I mean born and bred on this island of both races, and he wears a beardlet, and listens to the MJQ, and speaks very low, and blinks his big eyes and occasionally lets a sad, fleeting smile cross his kissable lips. He's certainly younger than I am, but he makes me feel about nine or so he's so very poised and paternal, though what the hell he does to keep himself in MJQ LPS I haven't an idea—I really haven't. I don't think it's anything illegal, which is what you might expect, because the kid is always so skint, he's only one suit (a striped Italian black), and no furniture to speak of except for his radiogram, so that either business, whatever it may be, is bad, or else, for reasons best known, he's covering up.

I miss out various rooms and floors, and come now to my particular pal, who lives in the basement and really is a horror, called Big Jill. Now Jill is a Les. and, what is more, you may not believe this, but a Les. ponce, that is to say, she keeps a string of idiotic chicklets on the game, and just sits back in her over-heated, over-decorated, over cooking-smelling basement and collects. She's in all day, and goes out as sun sets to an overnight club where she's behind the counter, and holds her court among her little Les.-ette fans. And then, in the wee small hours, she has a way, when she comes home, of stopping in the area before she goes in and yelling at the upper windows at the Hoplite or myself, to ask if we want to come down and have anything to eat. Which, as a matter of fact, we quite often do, not really for the food, but because old Jill is very wise, in spite of being not far in her twenties, and is my chief and only confidant about Suzette who I ask her advice about but, as I need hardly tell you, haven't produced for her inspection, for all my contacts with Suze are at her place over there in W.2.

So by now, of course, I had arrived there, and shot up the flights of no-lino stairs, which nobody keeps swept and ever lit (and the front door's always open) into my loft, which is one big room right across the whole top of the establishment, plus bathroom on the landing minus a bath (I use the municipal), but with basin and a convenient. And I've decorated it all in what I call anti-contemptuous style, i.e., ancient aunt Fanny wallpapers I got from some leftovers in a paint shop in the Portobello road. I've got a bed, too, a triple one, and the usual chair and table; but no other chairs, and instead a lot of cushions spread out on the floor and on top of what is my only luxury, a fitted carpet. My clothes I hang on ropes with polythene covers for the BR soot, the rest I keep in my metal cabin trunk. I don't have curtains because I like to look out, specially at night, and I'm too high for anyone to look in. The only other objects are my record-player, my pocket transistor radio, and stacks of discs and books that I've collected, hundreds of them, which every New Year's Day I have a pogrom of, and sling out everything except a very chosen few.

I was having a wash down, at the bathroom sink, when up came the Hoplite, nervously patting his hair which was done in a new style of hair-do like as if a large animal had licked the Hoplite's locks down flat, then licked the tip of them over his forehead vertical up, like a cockatoo with its crest on back-to-front. He was wearing a pair of skin-tight, rubber-glove thin, almost transparent cotton slacks, white nylon-stretch and black wafer-sole casuals, and a sort of maternity jacket, I can only call it, coloured blue. He looked over my shoulder into the mirror, patting his head and saying nothing, till when I said nothing too, he asked me, 'Well?'

'Smashing, Hoplite,' I said. 'It gives you a rugged, shaggy, Burt Lancaster appearance.'

'I'm not so sure,' the Hoplite said, 'it's me.'

'It's you, all right, boy. Of course, anything is, Fabulous. You're one who can wear *anything*, even a swimsuit or a tuxedo, and look nice in it.'

'I know you're one of my fans,' the Hoplite said, smiling sadly at me in the mirror, 'but don't mock.'

'No mockery, man. You've got dress sense.'

The Hoplite sat down on the lavatory seat, and sighed. 'It's not dress sense I need,' he said, 'but horse sense.'

I raised my brows and waited.

'Believe it or not, my dear,' the Hoplite continued sadly, 'but your old friend Fabulous, for the first time in his life—the *very* first in nineteen years (well, that's a lie, I'm twenty, really)—is deep, deep, deep in love.'

'Ah,' I replied.

There was a pause.

'You're not going to ask me with who?' he said, appealingly.

'I'm so sure you're going to tell me, Hop.'

'Sadist! And not *Hop*, please!'

'Not me. No, not a bit, I'm not. Well—who is it?'

'An Americano.'

'Ah.'

'What does this "Ah" mean?' the Hoplite said suspiciously.

'Several things. Tell me more. I can see it coming, though. He doesn't care.'

'Misery! That's it.'

'Doesn't care for the angle, Hoplite, or doesn't care for you personally, or just doesn't care for either?'

'The angle. Not bent at all, though I had hopes that perhaps he dabbled . . . And he's so, so understanding, which makes it so, so, so much worse.'

'You poor old bastard,' I said to the Hoplite, as he sat there on my john, and almost crying.

He plucked at a piece of sanitary tissue, and blew his nose. 'I only hope,' he said, 'it doesn't turn me anti-American.'

'Not that, Hoplite,' I said. 'Not you. It's a sure sign of total defeat to be anti-Yank.'

'But I thought,' said lovelorn Fabulous, rising from his seat and strolling across to gaze out on the railway tracks, 'you didn't approve of the American influence. I mean, I know you don't care for Elvis, and you do like Tommy.'

'Now listen, glamour puss,' I said, flicking his bottom with my towel. 'Because I want English kids to be English kids, not West Ken Yanks and bogus imitation Americans, that doesn't mean I'm anti the whole US thing. On the contrary, I'm starting up an anti-anti-American movement, because I just despise the hatred and jealousy of Yanks there is around, and think it's a sure sign of defeat and weakness.'

'Well, that's a relief,' said Fabulous, a bit sarcastically. So, really to hurt him, I made as if to use my towel again, and didn't.

'The thing is,' I said, 'to support the local product. America launched the teenage movement, there's no denying, and Frankie S., after all, was, in his way, the very first teenager. But we've got to produce our own variety, and not imitate the Americans—or the Ruskis, or anybody, for that matter.'

'Ah, the Russians,' said the Hoplite, with a dreamy look coming over his pretty countenance. 'You think they have teenagers over there as well?'

'You bet they have,' I said. 'Haven't you talked to any of the boys who've been over for the Congresses? They've got them just like us. But where the Russians fail, is sending us propaganda, and not sending us anyone in the flesh to look at, or to talk to.'

The Hoplite was getting a bit bored, as he does when it goes off the gossip kick into ideas. 'You're such a clever boy,' he said, patting me on the shoulder, 'and such a hard judge of the rest of us poor mortals . . . And deep down, I do believe, you're quite a patriot.'

'You bet I'm a patriot!' I exclaimed. 'It's because I'm a patriot, that I can't bear our country.'

The Hoplite was at the door. 'If you're interested at all,' he said, 'there's a party tonight, mine hostess being Miss Lament.'

'I'm not sure I care for that gimmicky girl,' I said. 'What sort of party—is it special?'

Dido Lament, I should explain, is a female columnist, and that actually is her name, or rather, her maiden name. Lament is known among us kids because she did a big investigation round the coffee bars in the days when the Rock thing first broke, and got taken up by all her clients in High Society—or rather, by the bus-queue masses who read about them in her column.

'Oh, the usual sw3 trash,' said Hoplite, waving his hands about disdainfully, though I know full well he just couldn't wait to go. 'Advertising people, and television people, and dressmaking people and show-business fringe people—all the parasites,' he said. 'Henley, I know, is going, and have reason to believe, is taking Suze.'

'He is?' I said, showing no sign of grief to this bit of pure camposity called Hoplite.

'And Wizard should be there,' he went on, 'up to no good, I doubt not, the dear lad . . .'

'YOU STUDS UP THERE!' came a great yell from the stairs. 'Come down and see your doll!'

This was Big Jill from her basement sector.

'Oh!' Hoplite cried. 'I do wish that female talent-spotter wouldn't shout so! Go to her if you want to, child, but me, I've got much better things to do.' And blowing me a kiss, he tripped off down the stairs, very sadly singing.

'Five minutes, Jill girl!' I yelled over the top of them.

Because, first of all, I wanted to glance at a snap of Suze that was taken of us both one day up on top of the Monument there in the City by a kid I handed my Rolleiflex to, to snap us, and which shows us she standing in front, and me standing round behind her, holding her arms, and looking over her head just after kissing her on the neck. And as I wandered round, putting on a garment here, and a garment there, I carried this photo, and propped it up somewhere when I had to use both hands, and gazed at the bloody thing and thought 'Oh Christ, it was only just one single summer ago, what's the use of being young if you're not loved? Well, all right—what *is* the use? What is it? Or is that obvious, I mean my question?'

So that was that, and down I went to see Big Jill.

But on the first floor landing, opposite Mr Cool's room, I noticed the door was left open, which was a sign I know that Cool had something he'd like to say to me, but was too dam proud to ask me to step in. If it had been anyone else, I would have just let the hint lie dropped there where it lay, but with the coloured boys you've got to be so careful, or otherwise they put it down to prejudice. So I put my head around the door, and jeepers-creepers, nearly had a fit because would you believe it, there were *two* Mr Cools, one coloured, and one white, or so it seemed.

'Oh, hi,' said Mr Cool, 'this is my brother, Wilf.'

'Hi, Wilf,' I said. 'That's crazy!'

'What is?' said this Wilf.

'You being the brother of my favourite Mr Cool. It nearly shook me rigid when I saw the pair of you.'

'Why did it?' said this white-skinned number, who struck me, I must say, as not being at all a swinging character like his brother —in fact, quite *un*-cool.

'Wilf's on his way,' said Mr Cool.

'Yem,' said this Wilf, and 'see you.' And he shook hands with his brother, and went out past me with not so much as a genuflection or a curtsy.

As soon as he'd gone, I said, 'Cool, please excuse me, but I don't quite dig the scene. I was quite polite to your brother, wasn't I? but he just didn't want to know.'

Mr Cool was standing very still, and very lean, and very all-by-himself, and said, 'My brother's come to warn me.'

'Of what? News me up, please.'

'Wilf's Mum's by another man, as you'll have guessed.'

'Well . . . Yes . . . So . . . ?

'He doesn't like me much, and my friends he likes even less, specially my white ones.'

'Charming! Why, please?'

'Let's not go into that. But anyway, he gets round the area and knows the scene, and he says there's trouble coming for the coloureds.'

I laughed out loud, but a bit nervously. 'Oh Cool, you know, they've been saying that for years, and nothing's happened. Well, haven't they? I know in this country we treat the coloureds all like you-know-what, but we English are too lazy, son, to be violent. Anyway, you're one of us, big boy, I mean home-grown, as much a native London kid as any of the millions, and much more so than hundreds of pure pink numbers from Ireland and abroad who've latched on to the Welfare thing, but don't belong here like you do.'

My speech made no impression on Mr Cool. 'I'm just telling you what Wilf says,' he answered. 'And all I know is, he likes coming here so little it must be *something* that makes him feel he ought to.'

'Perhaps your mother told him to,' I suggested, because I always like to think that *someone's* female parent has maternal instincts.

He shook his head. 'No, it was Wilf's idea,' he said, 'to come.'

I looked hard at Mr Cool.

'And if anything should happen,' I asked, 'whose side would your brother himself be on?'

Mr Cool blew out some smoke and said, 'Not mine. But he felt he had to come and tell me.'

As I stood there looking at the Cool, it struck me so hard how absolutely *lonely* the poor fucker was—standing there all on his Pat Malone, and yet so resolute, so touch-me-if-you-dare . . . And the nasty question grew up also in my mind as to what *I* might be doing if there should be trouble here in Napoli—I, the sharp kid, the pal of the whole wide world. Were those really my principles, or was it all on top? And although I *knew* it was the wrong thing to say, and knew it positively at the very moment, I found myself saying to Cool, 'Tell me, Cool, you're not short of anything, are you? I mean, I couldn't help you out with any loot?'

He just shook his head, which was quite awful, and I was really relieved that Big Jill hooted up the stairs—much louder, this time, was only two floors away—'STUD! Are you coming down to me?'

'Coming, doll,' I shouted and, with a wave to Cool, went down to Jill in her nether regions.

It needs a bit of an effort of imagination to see what the little Les. butterflies see in Jill because she is, to say the very least of it, so massive, and though I know she's blatant and masterful and all the rest of it, and wears slacks, of course, and even would do to a wedding at St. Paul's, I'm sure, she isn't beautiful in any way that I can see, or even *glamorous*. In fact, if it wasn't she's a city girl, you'd somehow imagine her handling horses—and perhaps, come to think of it, that *is* the appeal to the young chicks.

'You're late,' she said, 'you horrid little studlet.'

'What do you mean, "late", Big Jill? Did you and me have any sort of an appointment?'

She grabbed me abruptly like an ourang-outang, lifted me two feet off the floor, and banged me down again. 'If you were a chick,' she said, 'I'd eat you.'

'EASY, lady-killer,' I cried. 'You'll get me entangled in your cactuses.' Because it's true Jill is a great collector of indoor plants, in fact they sprout and dangle all over her basement rooms, and in the area as well.

She pushed a cup of coffee in my hands and said, 'Well, how's your sex life, junior, since the last time we met?'

'We met two days ago, Big Jill. It hasn't changed since then.'

'No? Nothing to report?'

Big Jill was standing looking at me, legs apart, with that sort of kindly, 'understanding' look that irritates you when the person just doesn't dig anything whatever about your inner character and pursuits.

'You don't understand as much as you think, Big Jill,' I said, voicing my thoughts to her.

'Oh!' she said huffily. 'Please pardon me for existing.'

'All that I mean, dear,' I said, to soften up the absurd old cow, 'is that your attitude to all those kicks is much too expert. You know so dam much, you know so dam little.'

Big Jill now dropped the wise old elder sister thing, and said, 'Clue me then, teenager. My big ears are flapping.'

'All I mean, Big Jill, is that you can't say, "How's your sex life?" just like you say, "How's the weather?" '

She sat down wrong way round on the chair, with her arms resting on the back of it, and her big tits resting on her arms. 'Obviously,' she said.

'The whole thing about sex,' I said to her, 'is that it's all very easy, and all very difficult indeed.'

'Ah . . .' said Big Jill, looking tolerant and amused, as if I was putting on a show for her.

'I mean, anyone can have a bash, that's obvious, there's nothing to it, but is there any pleasure?'

'Well, isn't there, big boy?' she asked me, giving a great, fat smile.

'Oh, of course there is, in that way, yes, but there isn't really, because you can't have it just like that without messing something else that matters up, and this brings you badly down.'

'Even if you like the party of the second part, it brings you down?' said Jill, getting interested, as I could see.

'If you *like* the other number, I mean like the looks of them, really dig them sexually—and I mean really—then it isn't quite so bad, because at least you're only acting like a pair of animals, which isn't a bad thing to do . . . But even then, you're still wrought badly down.

'Wrought down because you might lose them?'

'No, no, not that. Because you've not really got them, because they aren't the person.'

'What person?'

'The person you really dig, with all of yourself, your other half you'd give your life to.'

'You're not referring to marriage, are you?'

'No, no, no, no, no, Big Jill.'

'To *love*?'

'Yep. That's it. To it.'

Big J.'s eyes were pale, so that she seemed to be staring into herself, and not out into the room at me.

'You ever had that combo?' she enquired.

'No.'

'Not even with Suzette?'

'No. Me, yes, I was ready for that everything stage of it, but for Suze it was only a head, bodies and legs thing, when it happened.'

Big Jill looked wise, and said, 'So it was really you who broke it up, then.'

'I suppose you could say so, yes. I wanted more from Suze than she wanted to give me, and I just couldn't bear anything that was less.'

'Then why you still trail round after her? You hope she'll change?'

'Yes.'

Big Jill heaved herself up, and said, 'Well, boy, I can tell you something, which is she won't, Suzette. Not for ten or fifteen years she won't, anyway, I can promise you that. Later on, when you're both a big boy and girl, you might be able to wrap a big thing up...'

I'd moved away, and was looking out into her area Kew gardens. 'If I can work up the strength of will,' I said, 'I'm going to cut out seeing Suze at all.'

'Don't turn your back when you're talking, son. You mean live on your visions like a monk?'

I turned round and said, 'I mean shut my gate to all that nonsense.'

Big Jill came over too. 'You're too young for that,' she said. 'If you do, you'll only do yourself an injury. You shouldn't give up kicks till they don't mean a thing to you any more.' But she was quite a bit edgy, I could see. 'You're a romantic!' she said. 'A second feature Romeo!' and she took back my coffee cup as if I'd tried to rob her of it.

Well, there it is. That's what always happens if you try to tell the *truth*, they always want to know it, and nag you and persuade you against your better sense to tell it, and then they're always angry with you when they hear it, and dislike you for it. And, as a matter of fact, it wasn't even the truth I'd told Big Jill, in one respect: and that is, Suze and I hadn't made it, actually, though we'd sailed right up close so often. But even when the scene was set, and we both meant business, it hadn't happened, and I'm not sure if the real reason for this was her, or me.

I thought of all this, as I climbed out of Napoli into London, up towards N. Hill Gate. And straining up the Portobello road, I passed a crocodile of infants, and among them a number of little Spadelets, and I noticed, not for the first time, how, in the underground movement of the juveniles, they hadn't been educated up yet to the colour thing. Fists and wits, they were what mattered, and the only enemy was teacher. And as I walked on along the Bayswater road, just inside that two miles of gardens, so pretty and kind by day (but not by night), I went on thinking, as my Italian casuals carried me on.

Perhaps Big Jill's right, I think too much, but the sight of these school-kids reminded me of the man who really taught me to think at all, and that was my elementary schoolmaster, called Mr Barter. I know it's un-sharp to admit a schoolteacher ever taught you anything, but this Mr Barter, who was crosseyed, did. I got in his clutches when I was eleven, and the glorious 1950s had just begun. On account of schools being blitzed when I was an infant (which I can hardly remember, only a bit of the buzz-bombs at the end), I had to walk a mile up into Kilburn Park, to the place where this Mr Barter gave his performance. Now, dig this—because this was it. Old Mr Barter was the only man (or woman, too) in all the schools that I attended, before I packed that nonsense in three years ago, who actually made me realize two things, of which number one is, that what you learned had some actual value to you personally, and wasn't just dropped on you like a punishment, and number two, that everything you learned, you hadn't learned until you'd really dug it: i.e., made it part of your own experience. He'd tell us things—for example, like that Valparaiso was a big city in Chile, or that x+y equals something or other, or who all the Henrys were, or Georges, and he'd make us feel this crazy stuff really *concerned* us kids, was something to do with us, and had a value. Also, he made me kinky about books: he managed to teach me—to this day, I don't know how—that books were not just a thing like that—I mean, just *books* —but somebody else's mind opened up for me to look into, and he taught me the habit, later on, of actually *buying* them! Yes—I mean real books, like the serious paperbacks, which must have been unknown among the kids up in the Harrow road those days, who thought a book's an SF or a Western, if they thought it's anything.

Since we're on the subject, and I can't cause any more red faces than I already have, I'd also like to mention that the second great influence of my life was something even more embarrassing, and this is that, believe it or not, I actually was, for two whole years a *wolf cub*! Yes—me! Well . . . this is the fable. I got swung into that thing when, like all kids do, I was called up for the Sabbath school, and I soon told that Sunday lot it could please take a walk, but somehow got latched on to this wolf cub kick, because it started to fascinate me, for the following reasons. The first week I attended, dragged there by Dad, the old cub master, who I now realize was a terrible old poof, said that he wanted my attendance to be voluntary, not forced, and if after a full month I found they made it so attractive I'd want to come of my own free will, then would that show? I said, sure, yes it would, thinking, naturally, the month would soon pass by, and they began to teach me a lot of crap I found, even at that age, absolutely useless and ridiculous, like lighting fires with two matches when matches are about the cheapest thing there are to buy, and putting tourniquets on kids' legs for snake-bites when there aren't any snakes in London, and anyway, what if they bit kids on the head or other sensitive parts? yet gradually, all the same, to everyone's astonishment, I did actually begin to be a raver for those weekly meetings in the Baptist corrugated-iron temple, because I really felt—don't laugh—that for the first time, here was a family: at any rate, a lot, a mob, a click I could belong to. And though that dreadful old cub master with his awful shorts, and his floppy khaki hat, was queer as a coot and even queerer, he didn't interfere with any of us kids in any way, and actually succeeded in teaching us *morals*—can you believe it? Well—he did! He really did. I can honestly say the only ideas on morals I know anything of, were those that bent old cub master made me believe in, chiefly, I think, because he made us feel that he liked us, all us grubby-kneed little monsters, and cared what happened to us, and didn't *want* anything from us, except that we look after ourselves decently in the great big world hereafter. He was the first adult I'd ever met—even including Dad—who didn't come the adult at us—didn't use his strength, and won us over by persuasion.

That brings me to today, and to the third item in my education, my university, you might say, and that's the jazz clubs. Now, you can think what you like about the art of jazz—quite frankly, I don't really care *what* you think, because jazz is a thing so wonderful that if anybody doesn't rave about it, all you can feel for them is pity: not that I'm making out I really understand it *all*—I mean, certain LPS leave me speechless. But the great thing about the jazz world, and all the kids that enter into it, is that no one, not a soul, cares what your class is, or what your race is, or what your income, or if you're boy, or girl, or bent, or versatile, or what you are—so long as you dig the scene and can behave yourself, and have left all that crap behind you, too, when you come in the jazz club door. The result of all this is that, in the jazz world, you meet all kinds of cats, on absolutely equal terms, who can clue you up in all kinds of directions—in social directions, in culture directions, in sexual directions, and in racial directions . . . in fact, almost anywhere, really, you want to go to learn. So that's why, when the teenage thing began to seem to me to fall into the hands of exhibitionists and moneylenders, I cut out gradually from the kiddo water-holes, and made it for the bars, and clubs, and concerts where the older numbers of the jazz world gathered.

But this particular evening, I had to call at a teenage hut inside Soho, in order to contact two of my models, by names Dean Swift and the Misery Kid. Now, about Soho, there's this, that although so much crap's written about the area, of all London quarters, I think it's still one of the most authentic. I mean, Mayfair is just top spivs stepping into the slippers of the former gentry, and Belgravia, like I've said, is all flats in houses built as palaces, and Chelsea—well! Just take a look yourself, next time you're there. But in Soho, all the things they say happen, do: I mean, the vice of every kink, and speak-easies and spielers and friends who carve each other up, and, on the other hand, dear old Italians and sweet old Viennese who've run their honest, unbent little businesses there since the days of George six, and five, and backward far beyond. And what's more, although the pavement's thick with tearaways, provided you don't meddle it's really a much safer area than the respectable suburban fringe. It's not in Soho a sex maniac leaps out of a hedge on to your back and violates you. It's in the dormitory sections.

The coffee spot where I hoped I'd find my two duets was of the kind that's now the chic-est thing to date among the juniors—namely, the pig-sty variety, and adolescent bum's delight. I don't exaggerate, as you'll see. What you do is, rent premises that are just as dear as any other, rip up the linos and tear out the nice fittings if there happen to be any, put in thick wood floors and tables, and take special care not to wipe the cups properly, or sweep the butts and crusts and spittle off the floor. Candles are a help or, at a pinch, non-pearl 40-watt blue bulbs. And a juke-box just for decoration, as it's considered rather naïve to *use* one in these places.

This example was called Chez Nobody, and sure enough, sitting far apart from each other at distant tables, were the Dean and the Misery Kid. Though both are friends of mine, and, in a way, even friends of each other, these two don't mix in public, on account of the Dean being a sharp modern jazz creation, and the Kid just a skiffle survival, with horrible leanings to the trad. thing. That is to say, the Kid admires the groups that play what is supposed to be the authentic music of old New Orleans, i.e., combos of booking-office clerks and quantity-surveyors' assistants who've handed in their cards, and dedicated themselves to blowing what they believe to be the same note as the wonderful Creoles who invented the whole thing, when it all long ago began.

If you know the contemporary scene, you could tell them apart at once, just like you could a soldier or sailor, with their separate uniforms. Take first the Misery Kid and his trad. drag. Long, brushless hair, white stiff-starched collar (rather grubby), striped shirt, tie of all one colour (red today, but it could have been royal-blue or navy), short jacket but an old one (somebody's riding tweed, most likely), very, very, tight, tight, trousers with wide stripe, no sox, short *boots*. Now observe the Dean in the modernist number's version. College-boy smooth crop hair with burned-in parting, neat white Italian rounded-collared shirt, short Roman jacket *very* tailored (two little vents, three buttons), no-turn-up narrow trousers with 17-inch bottoms absolute maximum, pointed-toe shoes, and a white mac lying folded by his side, compared with Misery's sausage-rolled umbrella.

Compare them, and take your pick! I would add that their chicks, if present, would match them up with: trad. boy's girl—long hair, untidy with long fringes, maybe jeans and a big floppy sweater, maybe bright-coloured never-floralled, never-pretty dress... smudged-looking's the objective. Modern jazz boy's girl—short hemlines, seamless stockings, pointed-toed high-heeled stiletto shoes, crêpe nylon rattling petticoat, short blazer jacket, hair done up into the elfin style. Face pale—corpse colour with a dash of mauve, plenty of mascara.

I sat down just beside the Misery Kid, who was eating a gateau and had everything horrible about him, spotty, un-pressed, unlaundered, but with the loveliest pair of eyes you ever saw, brown and funny and appealing, I can only say, not that the Kid ever asks you for anything, as he only speaks in sentences of four words at his most voluble.

'Evening, Kid,' I said. 'There's been a small disaster.'

He just gazed like a fish: brows up, but not really curious.

'You recollect the snaps I took of you as the poet Chatterton with your bird as your Inspiration in some nylon net?'

'So?' said the Kid.

'It's all right, my client's not bounced the order, but I've developed the stuff, and your chick came out too indistinct by far.'

'She not meant so?'

'She's meant to be vague, Misery Kid, but she's meant to be visible behind that nylon net. Well? I expect she must have moved.'

'You pay us for a second take?'

'Certainly, Mr Bolden. But I can't pay for anything till I give the prints to Mr X-Y-Z.'

'Who he?'

'The client.'

The Misery Kid picked his nose and said, 'This client no deposit?'

'No. We've just got to do it all again, Mr Kid, to get our money. Can you raise your partner?'

'I dunno I know,' he said. 'Bell me tonight, I tell you.'

He got up, not showing his feelings, which was really rather heroic, because here was this trad. child, alone among the teenagers, in the days of prosperity, still living like a bum and a bohemian, skint and possibly even hungry, but still not arguing about the loot. If he'd argued, he'd have got some out of me, but to argue when the dirt dropped down on your head was contrary to his whole trad. ideology. As the Misery Kid passed by the Dean on his way out, Dean Swift looked up and hissed at him, 'Fascist!' which the Kid ignored. These modern jazz boys certainly do feel strongly about the trad. reaction.

The Dean came over and sat down with me. I should explain I haven't seen the Dean for several weeks, although he's my favourite and most successful model. The Dean's speciality's an unusual one, which is posing always fully dressed, and yet, somehow, managing to look pornographic. Don't ask me how! In the studio, exactly when he shouted out, 'Now!' I throw the switch, though he looks quite ordinary to me, and then, behold! when he's developed, there he is—indecent. Snaps of the Dean sell like hot ice-cream among vintage women with too many bosoms and time on their hands, and even my Ma, when she saw some photos of him was impressed—he looks so dam available, the Dean does. She actually asked to meet him, but Dean Swift is not interested in this, the chief reason being that he's a junkie.

If you have a friend who's a junkie, like I have the Dean, you soon discover there's no point whatever discussing his addiction. It's as senseless as discussing love, or religion, or things you only feel if you feel them, because the Dean, and I suppose all his fellow junkies, is convinced that this is 'a mystic way of life' (the Dean's own words), and you and I, who don't jab hot needles in our arms, are just going through life missing absolutely everything worth while in it. The Dean always says, life's just kicks. Well, I agree with him, so it is, but personally, it seems to me the big kick you should try to get by how you live it sober. But tell that to the Dean!

Why I'd not recently seen him, is that he'd until then been away inside. This has fairly often happened to the Dean, owing to his breaking into chemists' shops, and as he suffers a lot when he's cut off from the world and all it gives in there, he doesn't like you to refer to it when he emerges. At the same time, he *does* like you to say you're glad to see him once again, so it's all a trifle dicey.

'Hail, squire,' I said. 'Long time no see. How is you are we? Won't you say tell?'

The Dean smiled in his world-weary way. 'Doesn't this place stink?' he said to me.

'Well certainly, Dean Swift, it does, but do you mean its air, or just its atmosphere?'

'The both. The only civilized thing about it,' the Dean continued, 'is that they let you *sit* here, when you're skint.'

The Dean gazed round at the teenage products like a concentration camp exterminator. I should explain the Dean, though only just himself an ex-teenager, has sad valleys down his cheeks, and wears a pair of steel-rimmed glasses (which he takes off for our posing sessions), so that his Dean-look is habitually sour and solemn. (The Swift part of the thing comes from his rapid disappearance at the approach of any cowboys. You're talking to him and then, tick-tock! he's vanished.) I could see that now the Dean, as usual when skinned and vicious, was going to engage in his favourite theme, i.e., the horror of teenagers. 'Look at the beardless microbes!' he exclaimed, loud enough for everyone to hear. 'Look at the pram products at their plotting and their planning!'

And, as a matter of fact, you could see what he meant, because to see the kids hunched over the tables it *did* look as if some conspiracy was afoot to slay the elder brethren and majorities. And when I'd paid, and we went out in the roads, even here in this Soho, the headquarters of the adult mafia, you could everywhere see the signs of the un-silent teenage revolution. The disc shops with those lovely sleeves set in their windows, the most original thing to come out in our lifetime, and the kids inside them purchasing guitars, or spending fortunes on the songs of the Top Twenty. The shirt-stores and bra-stores with ciné-star photos in the window, selling all the exclusive teenage drag I've been describing. The hair-style saloons where they inflict the blow-wave torture on the kids for hours on end. The cosmetic shops—to make girls of seventeen, fifteen, even thirteen, look like pale rinsed-out sophisticates. Scooters and bubble-cars driven madly down the roads by kids who, a few years ago, were pushing toy ones on the pavement. And everywhere you go the narrow coffee bars and darkened cellars with the kids packed tight, just whispering, like bees inside the hive waiting for a glorious queen bee to appear.

'See what I mean,' the Dean said.

And the chicks, round the alleys, on that summer afternoon! Heavens, each year the teenage dream-girl has grown younger, and now, there they were, like children that've dressed up in their fashionable aunties' sharpest clothes—and suddenly you realize that it's not a game, and that these chicks mean business, and that it's not so much you, one of the boys, they aim their persons at, as their sheer, sweet, energetic legs walk down the pavement three by three, but no, at quite adult numbers, quite mature things, at whose eyes they shoot confident, proud looks there's no mistaking.

'Little madams,' said the Dean.

'There you go!' I answered.

Here Dean Swift stopped us in his tracks.

'I tell you,' he said, pulling his US-striped and rear-buckled cap down over his eyes, 'I tell you something. These teenagers are ceasing to be rational, thinking, human beings, and turning into mindless butterfiies. And they're turning into butterflies all of the same size and colour, that have to flutter round exactly the same flowers, on exactly the same gardens. Yes!' he exclaimed at a group of kiddos coming clicking, cracking prattling by. 'You're nothing but a bunch of butterflies!'

But the kidettes took no notice of the Dean whatever, because just at that moment . . . there! in his hand-styled car with his initials in its number, there sped by the newest of the teenage singing raves, with beside him his brother, and his composer, and his chicklet, and his Personal Manager, so that all that was missing was his Mum. And the kids waved, and the young Pied Piper waved his free hand back, and everyone for a few seconds was latched on to the glory.

'Singer!' cried the Dean out after him. 'Har, Har!'

He was standing out there in the road, gesticulating at the departing vehicle. Abruptly, though, he sheered off at an angle, and I had to catch him up across the way. He looked back over his neck, gripped my arm, and hurried on. 'Cowboys,' he explained.

I looked back too. 'They didn't seem to me like cowboys,' I told the Dean.

But to tell him this, was like telling some expert in Hatton Garden that you don't think that stone there is a diamond.

'I tell you this,' the Dean said fiercely. 'I can smell a copper in the dark, a hundred feet away, blindfolded. And anyway,' he continued pityingly, 'didn't you see those two were dressed in casual clothes, but with their *shoes mended*?'

That clinched the matter for the Dean.

'You don't like coppers, do you,' I said to him.

The Dean paused on his tracks. 'The only good thing about the bastards,' he said gently, 'is that they've all got themselves together into the same cowboy force. Just imagine what the world would be if monsters like them were out among the rest of us, without a label!'

The poor old Dean! He really hates the law although, unlike most that do, he doesn't fear it, really doesn't, though he's been given the matchbox treatment on more than one night occasion. Of course, all the jobs he's ever done have brought him into conflict with the cowboys—e.g., faith-healer, dance-hall instructor, club escort, property consultant and old-lady sitter.

We'd now reached a street down near 'the Front', as the girls on the game call the thoroughfare, and here the Dean whispered, 'I must have a fix very shortly, and I need a new whosit for my whatsit.' So we went into a chemist's shop nearby.

Behind the counter was a female case who didn't like the appearance of the Dean, and went into that routine that shopkeepers have perfected in the kingdom, that is, to get on the busy thing and bustle about with very necessary tasks, and when you cough or something, look up as if you'd broken into their private bedroom. And when they speak, they use a new kind of 'politeness' that's very common in our city, i.e., to say kind and courteous words, with a bitchy edge of nastiness, so they disarm you as they beat you down. To open the thing, of course, she asked us, 'Can I help you?'

Ah! but in the Dean she'd met her equal, because he has perfected, and almost patented, a style of being terribly polite in a way that doesn't mean a thing, and is in fact a mockery of the person he's polite to, though not easy for them to pin down, because the Dean acts so serious and earnest they couldn't quite make up their minds if it was sarcasm.

'Yes, Mad-ahm!' he answered, 'you certainly *can* help me, if you please, and if I'm not taking up too much of your time.'

And then they began their duel of politeness, their eyes blazing hatred at each other, and there you are, I thought, that's what happens when people grow to think that politeness, which is so lovely, is a form of weakness. And when the Dean had succeeded in luring the old slut to get out all sorts of products he didn't really need at all, he suddenly said, 'Thank you, Mad-ahm, so much,' and dipped his cap at her and went out in the sun saying, 'One of the fellow-sufferers at the Dubious will lend me what I need.'

The Dubious, I should explain, is of all the drinking-clubs that fester in Soho, the one that's in fashion just at present with the sharper characters, and there, sure enough, when I came in with the Dean, I saw, among others, Mr Call-me-Cobber, and his friend the ex-Deb-of-Last-Year: he being a telly personality from the outer colonies, and she one who slipped effortlessly off the pages of the weekly social glossies on to those of the monthly fashion ones. As a matter of fact, the ex-Deb's rather nice in a hunt ball way, but the same cannot be said of Call-me-Cobber, who really flogs that dinkum Aussie thing too hard, though on the telly screen it looks terrific, so sincere.

While the Dean went rambling off into dark corners, I snapped this drunken loving couple, propping my Rolleiflex upon the bar.

'Oh, hullo, reptile,' said the ex-Deb,' 'perhaps you can help my paramour with his new series.'

'It's called,' the Cobber said, '*Lorn Lovers*, and we're looking for persons deeply in love who fate has sundered.'

'You're too young for tears, I suppose,' the ex-Deb said to me, 'but maybe among your somewhat older companions . . . ?'

I nominated the Hoplite as Lorn Lover of the year.

'And who's he in love with?' Call-me-Cobber asked. 'We want to confront the frantic pair in front of the cameras, without either knowing beforehand what's going to hit them.'

'He's in love with an American,' I said.

'A good angle, though we'll have to pay the fee in dollars . . . Yes. confront the pair of them, and get them in a clinch.'

'It'll be sensational,' I said.

'*His* trouble,' said the ex-Deb, pointing a princess-size cigarette-holder at her lover, 'is his success. Ever since that fabulous series on the Angries, when the thing first broke, they expect the highest from him.'

'And they'll get it!' Call-me-Cobber cried. 'It's my aim, my mission, and my achievement to bring quality culture material to the pop culture masses.'

'He's the culture courtier of all time,' his lady said, as they both gulped the firewater down, then tried to kiss each other.

Call-me-Cobber looked around the basement room, where parties crouched on plastic covered seats with dim rose lights shining reflected up at them from the parquet floor. 'Today,' he announced, 'each woman, man and child in the United Kingdom can be made into a personality, a star. Whoever you are—and I repeat, whoever—we can put you in front of cameras and make you live for millions.

But no one seemed interested in this idea down there in the Dubious, so Call-me-Cobber slipped off his stool and went searching for the toilet. And the ex-Deb turned all her attention to myself, and started suddenly to get 'maternal'. Because a woman, if she's high and a bit frustrated, and you're young, is very apt, I've found, to want to show she 'understands'—though what, you never quite discover, and it's most embarrassing.

'Tell me about your camera,' the ex-Deb said, leaning across and fondling the thing and breathing spirits on me though, I must say, looking smashing.

'What you want to know about it?' I enquired.

'How did you learn to use it?' she said mysteriously.

'By trial and error.'

'Ah!'

I didn't get that 'Ah!'.

'When you were young?' she said. 'A boy?'

'That's it.'

She gazed at me as if I was straight out of Dr Barnardo's. 'You've had a hard life, I can see,' she said 'sympathetically'.

'No, I wouldn't say so'—and I wouldn't, really.

'Ah, but *I* can see you have!' she nattered on.

I gave up. 'Well—you win,' I told her.

'Your mother must have been a bitch,' she said.

Now, though I quite agreed with this, it made me furious! Who the hell did she think she was, this fashion model—Mrs Freud?

'I'll tell you something,' I said, 'about my mother. She may have her defects—who hasn't?—but she's got a lot of courage, and she's kept her looks, which are terrific.'

'You're loyal, kid,' said the ex-Deb, her swish-skirt nearly sliding her off the stool in her emotion.

'You bet,' I said, heaving her on to it again.

She held my arm, and said, 'Tell me a secret about you teenagers. Do you have a very active sex existence?'

They can't keep off it. 'No,' I replied, 'we don't.'

And, as a matter of fact, what I said was true, because although you often seen teenagers boxed up together in a free-and-easy, intimate sort of way, it doesn't very often reach the point of no return. But in this kingdom we reside in, the firm belief of the venerables seems to be that, if you see kids out and about enjoying themselves, then fleshy vices must be at the bottom of it all, somewhere, not just as it often is—frisking and frolicking, and having a carefree ball.

So as this wasn't the ex-Deb's business, anyway, I changed the subject round and said to her, 'Where will you take your holiday this year, Miss Sheba?'

'Who, me? Oh, I dunno . . . I always get taken some place or other where there's sand, and quarrels, and a quick flight home . . . And you, child? I hear all you brats are hitch-hiking across the Continent these days.'

'No longer,' I said, firmly.

'Why no longer?' she asked me, coming into focus.

'The hitch thing's out. We're tired of being molested, and arriving at destinations we didn't mean to. We pay our own fares now, like everybody else, in fact a lot of the new travel panders depend on teenage travellers.'

'So you've been in all those Continental places?'

Now, it's a funny thing . . . why should I be ashamed that I've never left our island yet? Why should I? because the reason is, although I've had opportunities enough (well, only last summer, the Marxists tried to ship me to a Youth thing in Bulgaria—think of that!), I've just not wanted to . . . Or rather . . . Well, as a matter of fact, I haven't even ever yet left London, except for once, of which I have the vaguest recollection, when I was trundled down to Brighton for the day, beside the sea, in connection with one of my Ma's manoeuvres, and all I remember of it is being parked here and there, upon the beach and up on bar stools with ginger beer, while she disappeared to mess about with the easy-money-boy who was her escort. As for the country, that great green thing that hangs around outside the capital, with animals, I've never seen it, because even when the bombs fell thickest in war-time, my old Ma refused to leave her manor, and refused to have Vern and me evacuated, come what may. And all I remember of that journey up and down to Brighton, is getting into trains and getting out—the rest was lying rocking on the hot and smelly seat, or vomiting.

Yet I must get away some day, and see the world. Not just that Continent they speak of—Paris and Rome, and all that crap—but the great wide one, like Brazil, say, or Japan, and that is why I *must* be sensible and save some loot, boy, hustle up some big stuff and depart in peace aboard some jet. So,

'No,' I replied, 'not all of them. I'm happiest in my manor, taking sunbathes in the Hyde, or doing swallows from the top board at the Hampstead ponds.'

She peered at me, her eyes swimming with the lush that she'd consumed. 'You're a poet, infant, in your way,' she said.

'Oh, I dunno about that,' I answered her.

While this ridiculous conversation of the ex-Deb and myself was still proceeding, some musicians there in the Dubious had begun to have a blow, because apparently a character called Two-Thumbs Tumbril, who plays bass, was holding some auditions for an out-of-city gig he thought might happen, if he could recruit a combo. There in the Dubious which, as I think I've said, is in a cellar, the instruments resounded with a thunderous effect, and as I listened to the sweet and soothing sound I once again reflected, thank the Lord I was born into the jazz age, what on earth could it have been when all they had to listen to was ballad tunes and waltzes? Because jazz music is a thing that, as few things do, makes you feel really at home in the world here, as if it's an okay notion to be born a human animal, or so.

A cat at the counter said, 'Nice, but they'll not make Bewley-Ooley.' Another answered, 'Well, who cares? That garden-party's for the ooblies and the Hooray Henries, anyway.' A third just said, 'Great,' with a soft dream in his eyes—but that may have been because he'd just been dragging on a splif inside the toilet.

From that same toilet, not quite yet fully adjusted before leaving, now reappeared the dinkum Call-me-Cobber number, who eyed the performers as if he was Mr Granz in person, like all these telly personalities do, acting the universal impresario to mankind. And after the bliss of hearing the boys blow in the proper company, the sight of the dinkum wrought me down a bit, because in the jazz thing, the audience is half the battle, even more than half.

'Nice,' he decided, 'but it falls between two stools. They're neither pop nor prestige-worthy.'

'That's two good stools,' I said, 'to fall between,' and slid off my own to leave them.

The ex-Deb-of-Last-Year grabbed me by the port pocket of my strides. 'Are you going to Miss Lament's?' she asked me.

'Yes, maybe I catch you there,' I told her, as I unhooked her vermilion claws.

'You leaving us?'

'Just for a moment, Knightsbridge girl,' I said.

Because I'd seen the Wiz come in the place, and wanted a swift word with my blood brother.

The Wiz was wearing a gladiator Lonsdale belt with studs on it, and this he unbuckled as he came into the Dubious, like a soldier that's been relieved from guard. But still he looked wary, as he always did, and no doubt in his sleep as well, as if the world was in the other corner of the ring where he did battle, and himself a lonesome hunter on the London jungle trail. 'Come over behind the music,' I said to him, and we got on the other side of the performers, so that their sound made a barrier that hedged us from the lush-swilling visitors around the counter.

'What's new?' I asked the Wiz.

A nice thing about Wizard is that he forgets a quarrel absolutely. A battle, with the Wiz, is always for a purpose, like a meal, and once it's over, he just doesn't seem to think of it any more at all. He eyed me with approval, and I could see that once again I was his old reliable, perhaps the only one he had outside eternity.

'I've news for you,' he said.

I must admit at feeling anxious, because the Wiz's bits of news are apt to sweep you out to sea until you can get adjusted to them.

'I'm thinking,' he said, 'of going into business with a chick.'

'Oh, are you. Clever boy. I'll visit you at Brixton,' I said, disgusted.

'You don't approve?'

'How can I? You're not that kind of hustler.'

'Try anything once . . .'

'Oh, sure. Oh sure, oh sure. Next thing is breaking and entering.'

I got up to fetch some drinks, and also to have time to think of this. Because I'd always imagined one day Wiz might go that way, but always decided he had brains enough to do better than that, and not get himself into some bower-bird's clutches. Because say what you like, in that set-up it's the female party who controls the situation, even if she gives the male one all her earnings, and he crunches her on Sunday evenings after the weekly visit to the Odeon. The simple reason being that her own activity, whatever you may think of it, is legal, and the boy's is not, and all she has to do if there's an argument is dial Detective-sergeant Someone round the corner.

'Health, wealth and happiness,' he said sarcastically.

'Happiness! You should talk!'

There was a silence. Then,

'Go on,' said Wiz. 'Let's have it.'

'What use, if you've decided?'

'Let's have it all the same.'

I groaned, I really did.

'It's just, Wiz, that it's not your kind of thing. Tell me one ponce you know who's got real brains.'

'I know of several.'

'I don't mean craft or cunning, I mean *brains*. Constructive brains.'

The Wiz said, 'I could introduce you to several bookies, club owners, car-hire proprietors, who've built up their business by loot they made when on the game before retirement.'

I said, 'I could introduce you to several Saturday-midnight-at-the-chemist's, and several in-and-out boys, and several corpses, who've had just the same idea.'

'Ah. Well, we disagree.'

I said to the lunatic, 'It may be all right for creatures who are young in *mind*, as well as age, but, let's face it, Wiz, you're too mature already. You *know* too much what you'd be doing.'

The Wizard smiled, if you can call it that. 'And this,' he said gently, 'comes from a kiddo known around the town for flogging pornographic photos.'

Oh well, hell!

'In the first place,' I said . . .

'And don't forget the second—and the third . . .'

'In the first place,' I continued, 'you know very well only *some* of my snaps are pornographic, and I'm on that kick for giggles as much as loot. In the second, as you say, you know I'm pulling out of that activity as soon as ever—as I've often told you. And in the third, yes, as you also say, are you really comparing poncing with what I do?'

'Not really,' the Wizard said, 'because it's more straightforward, and it's better paid.'

'Oh, if you say so, Sporting Life.'

There was another pause for refreshments between rounds.

'And who's the lucky chick?' I asked him.

'Oh, girl I know. Of course,' he said, 'you'll understand it's not wise to say *who*, specially to anyone who disapproves.'

'How right you are, young Wizard. Anyway, whoever it is, I pity her. You'll have a dozen on the game before you're nicked.'

'I'd not be surprised,' the Wizard said.

I drained my non-alcoholic beverage.

'Well, let me tell you, genius,' I said, 'two things, and do just listen. The first is, cute little number though you may be, you're really not the fixer type, the hustler type, because you're too dam delighted by the sport of it to take it seriously enough. The other, which you know full well, and should be ashamed of yourself for, is that you really have got brains, and if you'd had even a fragment of education, you'd have done big things, boy, and it's not too late. It's really not too late: why don't you study?'

'The school of life,' Wiz answered.

'Brixton class.'

'So what? Each occupation has its risks.'

'Fool.'

'Yeah? Oh, well . . .'

The Wizard looked up at the ceiling, because the combo had

stopped its operations for a moment. And me, I really felt I must say *something* to stop this thing: not because I disapproved of it (although I did), but because I knew that, if the Wizard did it, then I'd lose him.

But he got in first, now. 'I'll tell you something,' the Wizard said to me. 'I've thought it over carefully—and I'm safe as houses. Look!' And I looked at him. 'Imagine me in the dock! What mug—even a magistrate, let alone a jury—is going to believe a baby-face like me could be a ponce?'

I waited, then said, 'If you could see yourself in a mirror now, this very moment, you'd realize you don't look young at all. Not at all, Wiz, you don't—you look dam old.'

'Oh, I do?' said Wiz. 'Well, then, let me tell you something else. This is an old, old thing, this whore, and ponce, and client business. Since A. and Eve, there's always been the woman, and the visitor, and the local male.'

'Be the visitor, then.'

'Nobody likes the easy-money boy, there I agree. But the reasons he's disliked for, kiddo, are all very hypocritical. The client shifts his shame on to the ponce, see, and the ponce is willing to carry it for him—give him a clear, social, respectable alibi. Then, no man likes paying for what the ponce is paid for. And most of all, boy, the world is jealous of the ponce! Well, kid, and rightly!' And he smiled a great big aren't-I-clever smile.

'Fine, fine,' I cried. 'We'll have to get you testifying before those Wolfenden creations.'

'Oh, *them*,' said the Wizard. 'The last person they'd ever want to ask about the game is anyone who *knows* about it . . . a whore, a ponce, even a client. You know what the Wolfenden is for?' he went on, leaning across and grinning at me. 'It's so as to play down the queer thing in our country, and hide it behind the kosher game. It's so as to confuse the two, and get all the mugs muddled, so that if they call down fire and brimstone, they don't know on what.'

'Not so loud, Wiz,' I cried, because the combo had broken up, and someone hadn't yet put on the pick-up once again.

So there it was. Already, I was speaking *secretly* to the Wiz, like I had never done before, becoming a part of his squalid little plot, and, believe me, I was revolted.

'Christ!' I exclaimed. 'What's happening to me? My girl, I've lost her to the Spades and queers, and now my friend, I'm losing him to the girls.'

'Don't compare me with Spades,' said Wiz.

'Now, be intelligent, I wasn't. I was comparing Suze with you.'

'Nice! Perhaps it's you who's worrying most about all this, little latchkey-kid.'

'Oh, perhaps!'

'Well,' said the Wizard, making as if to rise, 'when the cowboys start to fill me in, I'll have you buzzed immediately for bail.'

'Don't talk to me like that, Wiz, *please*!'

'Oh, I know you'll come running . . . you adore me!'

This was evidently it, and I reached up and slapped the Wiz real hard. Real hard, I did. He didn't look all that surprised, and he didn't retaliate at all. He just rubbed his cheek and walked off over to the bar, so that I realized this was how he wanted it to be. Oh, fuck, I thought.

So I went out of the Dubious to catch the summer evening breeze. The night was glorious, out there. The air was sweet as a cool bath, the stars were peeping nosily beyond the neons, and the citizens of the Queendom, in their jeans and separates, were floating down the Shaftesbury avenue canals, like gondolas. Everyone had loot to spend, everyone a bath with verbena salts behind them, and nobody had broken hearts, because they all were all ripe for the easy summer evening. The rubberplants in the espressos had been dusted, and the smooth white lights of the new-style Chinese restaurants—not the old Mah Jongg categories, but the latest thing with broad glass fronts, and dacron curtainings, and a beige carpet over the interiors—were shining a dazzle, like some monster telly screens. Even those horrible old anglo-saxon public-houses—all potato crisps and flat, stale ale, and puddles on the counter bar, and spittle—looked quite alluring, provided you didn't push those two-ton doors that pinch your arse, and wander in. In fact, the capital was a night-horse dream. And I thought, 'My lord, one thing is certain, and that's that they'll make musicals one day about the glamour-studded 1950s.' And I thought, my heaven, one thing is certain too, I'm miserable.

And then, who should I see, wandering along the Soho thoroughfare, but the Kid-from-Outer-Space, who doesn't know that is his name, because I haven't told him so. This kid, who is extremely nice and that, and who I know from school days and even from the Baden-Powell contraption, belongs entirely to the Other World, i.e., as I've explained, the outer world that doesn't dig the scene, although, in many ways, they keep the whole scene going. This Outer-Space kid works for the municipal, doing whatever he does, and somehow I meet him every year or so, just once, by accident, like this, when sometimes he strays out of his four-square manor into mine, or I do, *vice versa*. And then we meet like travellers, and I tell him of the wonders of my section of the capital, real and fabled, and he tells me of his sports activities, and of his saving for a motor-scooter, and of which side of the books a debit item goes in at the municipal, or a credit does. He's sweet, but rather dull, though not a drag, exactly.

'What knot would you use,' I said, coming up beside him, and speaking from the corner of the mouth into his ear, 'to tie two ropes of unequal thickness, supposing you had two such ropes, and wanted to join the pair of them together?'

'Oh-ho, it's you, boy Mowgli,' said this Outer-Space creation, stopping and slapping my shoulder till I sank four inches into the Soho pavement.

'Me, me! How are the national problems shaping up? Give me the loaded gossip from the accountancy cats in the town hall.'

'The budget's balanced,' said the O.-S. kid, 'but the money it's balanced up with is worth only a third of itself, these days.'

'Dig! And how's the scooter whatsit? How many legs you broken besides your own?'

The O.-S. kid looked sad. 'I not got the scooter,' he replied, 'because my Ma preferred a telly.'

'Boy—you a traitor? You let old Ma tell you how to spend your personal earnings?'

'Well, son, she's getting on, she is.'

'Likes to sit there in her wicker rocker, with her eyes crossed on the commercials?'

'Don't be sarky, now. You sore about something or other?'

'Very so, I am. Oh, yes!'

'Don't spread it round about, then. Not on me.'

'Okay, colonel. I shall keep it private.'

'Say what you like, see, there's lots to be learned from television. I know it's for profits, but in its way it's a big universal education.'

'The population's seeing through the door at last, you think?'

'Well, isn't it? Tell me.'

'It's seeing only digests, slants and angles.'

'They kidding us then, those people? All those professors and authorities?'

'Why, sure they are! You think they tell us any secrets that's worth knowing? You think a professor who's studied twenty years can pop up in a studio and tell you something *real*?'

'It looks real, there up on the screen . . .'

'Oh, oh well . . . I tell you, Wolverine,' I explained to this simple, trusting soul, as we started walking down the boulevard, dodging prowlers, dodging gropers, dodging layabouts and tarts, 'I tell you. All these things—like telly witch-doctors, and advertising pimps, and show business pop song pirates—they despise us—dig?—they sell us cut-price sequins when we think we're getting diamonds.'

The boy stopped. 'Listen,' he said, 'you got to believe *something* in this world.'

'All right—you say so. Well, look right there!' I said, and pointed at a coffee bar that's even listed now in serious guidebooks, because the legend is, the top pop teenage rages were all 'discovered' there. 'See this establishment?' I said. 'See all the kids jam-packed in there beside the jukes, looking like they feel in at the prize-giving, the authentic big event?'

'I know the place. I been there.'

'I bet you have! It's made for mugs like you. Well, let me tell you —no teenage nightingale ever was "discovered" in that place until the telly cameras and the journalists moved in there for the massacre. The singing kids had all found out themselves, across the river, south, or anywhere, before those vultures gathered round to peck the kitty. I tell you, Tarzan, that fish-bowl over there is just as real as nothing.'

I could see what was happening: on account of my argument with the Wizard, and my earlier *cul-de-sac* with Suze, I was coming the acid drop with this young feller. So I did what I've found best on these occasions, namely, cut the umbilical, and I dashed into a club entrance with a wave and crying, 'Moment!', and picked up the telephone and dialled the operator, and said, hullo to her and asked her how I made a call to the prime minister, as I was a tourist from New Zealand and had the same name as Mr M., and wanted to ask the poor old geezer if we were possibly related. And after she'd sorted me out—quite nicely, I must say—I hung up and dashed out again, and found the Outer-Space kid still standing there, with his mouth open, and asked him about his sporting activities, because he was a boxer, though the singlet kind.

He said there were good fights billed south of the river soon, with some boys from his club, so why not go together? I said, oh, yes. Then he said meanwhile, what about we take in a film this evening? But that was no good to me, because you don't go into Soho to see films, because Soho *is* a film, and anyway, most times I go to cinemas I walk out half way through because all I see is a sheet hanging up there, and a lot of idiots staring at it, and hidden up behind all this there's just a boy operating the machinery with a fag hanging in his mouth even when he puts the record on for the 'God Save', and the cattle down there rise up on their corns, but not he, no! *Life* is the best film for sure, if you can see it as a film. So when I explained this, he said what about a bite?—a steak was what he actually suggested. And I said sorry, I was a vegetarian, which I am, not because of the poor animals or anything, but just because you belch much less, and red meat gives me the horrors.

So clearly, it wasn't going to be a big night out with the O.-S. kid, and now, as always happened, after being so pleased to see each other once again, we were just as glad to say farewell . . . isn't that like so many human relations? 'Remember me to your old Ma,' I said, 'and don't let her get ideas about a second telly.'

And all of a sudden I thought, I must get out of this fairground area, and have a bit of calm and meditation, so I hailed a cab and told the driver would he take me down by the embankment, end to end, first one way, and then the other. He didn't enjoy this much, because taxi-drivers, like everyone that has ponce activities, like to pretend they're necessary and useful as well as for hire, but he naturally agreed, because the adults love to take your money and make you feel they're doing you a favour, both combined.

Whoever thought up the Thames embankment was a genius. It

lies curled firm and gentle round the river like a boy does with a girl, after it's over, and it stretches in a great curve from the parliament thing, down there in Westminster, all the way north and east into the City. Going in that way, downstream, eastwards, it's not so splendid, but when you come back up along it—oh! If the tide's in, the river's like the ocean, and you look across the great wide bend and see the fairy advertising palaces on the south side beaming in the water, and that great white bridge that floats across it gracefully, like a string of leaves. If you're fortunate, the cab gets all the greens, and keeps up the same steady speed, and looking out from the upholstery it's like your own private Cinerama, except that in this one the show's never, never twice the same. And weather makes no difference, or season, it's always wonderful—the magic always works. And just above the diesel whining of the taxi, you hear those *river* noises that no one can describe, but you can always recognize. Each time I come here for the ride, in any mood, I get a lift, a rise, a hoist up into joy. And as I gazed out on the water like a mouth, a bed, a sister, I thought how, my God, I love this city, horrible though it may be, and never ever want to leave it, come what it may send me. Because though it seems so untidy, and so casual, and so keep-your-distance-from-me, if you can get to know this city well enough to twist it round your finger, and if you're its son, it's always on your side, supporting you—or that's what I imagined.

So when we returned again to Westminster, with the driver's neck all disapproval, I asked this coachman to turn south, across the stream, down to the Castle: because the thought had come to me it would be nice, after so many mixed emotions, to look in on Mannie Katz and his spouse Miriam.

Mannie I first met at a jellied eel stall near the Cambridge circus, when we both reached for the vinegar and said pardon. As you'll have guessed, the boy is Jewish, likewise Miriam (and their one off-spring), but I don't think it's only because I am a bit myself, as I've explained, on my Mum's side, that I admire this couple so. Here I must explain my attitude to the whole Jewish thing which in a word is, thank God (theirs and ours) they're here. I know all the arguments about them, back to front, and quite see what the Gentiles mean who are disturbed by them—but really! Add up all the defects that you can think of, please, and put them beside the great fact that the Jewish families *love life*, are on its side, are rinsed right out with it . . . and what do those debit things amount to? Just go inside a Jewish household, anywhere, I tell you, and however *dreadful* you may find them, what sticks out six miles and strikes you in your consciousness is that they're *living*. It's all a great noisy, boasting, arguing, complaining mess all right, but they're *alive*! And how they handle whatever stuff life's made of, like it was a material they were sampling, makes you realize immediately that they're an old, old, senior people who've been in the business of existence for a very long while indeed. I love London all right, as I've explained. But when the Jewish population have all made enough loot to take off for America, or Israel, then I'm leaving too. It would be turning out the light.

Mannie, as a matter of fact, has been to Israel, on a writers' congress there, and just missed that two-day battle with the Pharaohs we're all trying to forget. But being a Cockney kid, he's not as aggressive as the genuine Israelis who, when you meet them round the coffee bars, describe the orange-grove they live in as if it was a continent, and know the answers to absolutely everything before you've even asked the questions. Mannie's an authentic Cockney, by the way, not one of the suburban variety-bandbox imitations, and he's hard, and sad, and humorous, and sentimental, just like they are. Miriam's his second lady, and he must have married the first one from the cradle (she was one of ours—they came unstuck), because he's only just now hitting twenty, like we all are. There's also a young warrior of two years old called Saul who, in spite of all I've said in favour of Jewish family existence, is a bloody nuisance, and needs some of that Israeli discipline instead of being spoiled by the entire Katz clan, of every generation, and there are plenty.

This getting inside a Jewish home, if you yourself are not one, is a delicate operation, because although the place is yours once you're inside it, they take their time before they ask you round, and don't like sudden unexpected visits, as at present. But this I can do to the Katzes, because some time ago I did Emmanuel a big, big favour without meaning to, i.e., I introduced him to a kinky character I'd photographed, called Adam Stark, who turned out to be a crazy let's-make-a-big-loss publisher, and printed a bunch of Mannie's poems, which hit the literary headlines for a while. So that, for Auntie This and Grandma That down in the Borough road, I'm Fix-it Charlie, the clever boy who gave their young soothsayer a needful hoist. In this world, if you do the little kindly deed just at the right moment, the dividend's enormous: otherwise, it's soon forgotten. All the same, I took the precaution of stopping the cab, down by St. George's circus, and giving young Shakespeare fourpence worth of warning I was on my way.

The Katz lot—at least three dozen of them—live in a fine old reconditioned derelict, and Mannie himself came down there to admit me, wearing his uniform of blue-black corduroys, and brought me up into the best front room which I wish he wouldn't, because that meant, as soon as they heard a visitor was coming, the rest of the Katzes made it over to the favourite son to entertain his honoured guest, and disappeared themselves into the purlieus. And there, looking just like someone straight out of the O.T.—those illustrated copies with Rebecca, or maybe Rachel, hearing something marvellous, three thousand years ago, beside a well—was Miriam K., and there, doing his berserk performance on the parquet, was their youthful warrior product, Saul. Neither of them asked me why I'd come, or why I'd not been for an eternity, which in my book are two signs of civilized human beings—because, believe me, most hosts are bullies holding pistols at your head, but not this couple.

'And how are the Angries? I enquired.

Actually, Mannie wasn't in on the Angries kick, though he appeared in print about the same time that bunch of cottage journalists first caught the public nostril. Mannie's verse, of which I can dig the general gist, I think, is angry only about the grave, which he disapproves of, but for the life of the kiddos living round the Borough and in Bermondsey, he pens nothing but approval. His poems are songs of praise of youthful London: but his conversation doesn't approve of anything at all. In conversation, Mannie disapproves of *everything*, particularly of what you last said, whatever it may be.

'I see they gave you that Memorial Prize thing,' I said. 'I meant to send you a Greetings through the post, but I forgot.'

'They didn't *give* it to me, son. I won it,' Mannie said.

'Next, they'll be making you an O.B.E., or naming a street after you.'

'An O.B.E.! You think I'd accept that?'

'Yes,' said Miriam, who was making some false curls out of her infant's real curls.

'Well, what's high enough for you?' I asked. 'A life peer, would that do?'

'It's not a laughing matter,' Mannie told me. 'In England, they don't bribe you by money, but by trashy *honours*. People prefer them to mere money.'

'Not me, I'd settle for a bribe.'

'Flattery and respectability are sweeter than L.s.d.'

'You'd better change your mind then, and accept.'

'He will,' said Miriam, who was changing junior.

'Never. Not even the Laureateship.'

'Duke—you'd like that. Duke Katz of Newington Butts would suit you fine. I can see you in your robes and ping-pong titfer.'

'Unlike all my countrymen, I don't care for fancy dress,' said Mannie haughtily.

'Why you wear that velveteen creation, then?'

'Don't expect Mannie to be logical,' said his better half.

'So I'm not logical.'

'No.'

'You sure of that?'

'Yes.'

'And when I married you, I wasn't logical?'

'No. You were desperate.'

'Why was I desperate?'

'Because you'd messed up your first marriage, and wanted someone to put you together again.'

'So I messed it up.'

'You certainly helped.'

'Make a mess once, you can make another.'

'You mean us? I don't think so. Besides, I won't let you mess us up.'

'No? You won't let me?'

'No.'

As this little bit progressed, the loving pair got nearer and nearer to each other, till they were kneeling nose to nose, bawling each other out, and both clutching portions of the pride-and-joy.

'Miriam,' I said, 'your product's p-----g on the parquet.'

'That's not unusual,' said his loving Mum, and they busied themselves with rescue operations.

As I gazed down at this domestic scene, all bliss, I thought the corny old thought, why shouldn't all marriages be like this—a quarrel that goes on forever and ties the couple up in closer, tighter knots? And why can't all mums be like Miriam, young and beautiful and affectionate—and all girls, for that matter? Old Mannie certainly was a picker.

'You like a herring?' he said to me, looking up from behind his son's behind.

'Naturally, boy.'

'I get some. Don't pin Saul to the floor,' he told his wife, who gave him one of those 'Oh, well' glances, and started a little mum-and-son thing with the juvenile—we understand each other, don't we, man-child-born-of-woman?

I heard Mannie beckoning me from outside the door, with a whisper you could hear down as far as Southwark bridge, and out in the corridor he said—as if continuing a conversation we'd already started—'So it's a touch? You need a bit dinero? Five pounds do? Or three?'

'No, man. Not me.'

'Trouble? The bailiffs in? Got syphilis? The law? Need bail?'

'*No*, man. This is a sociable visit.'

'Girl trouble? Boy trouble? Horse trouble? Anything like that?'

'Oh, well . . . no, not exactly—but you know Suze.'

'Certainly, I do. Nice girl—a bit promiscuous, if you don't mind a frank opinion.'

'She's marrying Henley, so she says.'

'Yes? There'll be a quick divorce, I prophesy.'

'Why?'

'Because Suze will discover, in the course of time, that *she's* bringing more into the kitty than the rag merchant.'

'Of course! I wish you'd tell her so.'

'Not me! Never advise a woman—never advise anyone, for that matter.'

'And till she finds out—I suffer?'

Mannie laid his hands upon my shoulders, like a rabbi blessing a young foot-soldier before a hopeless battle.

'*She's* got to suffer, son,' he said, 'before you can get her, and stop suffering.'

'Nice lot of wasted suffering all round.'

Mannie looked at me with his great big oriental seen-it-all-ages-ago eyes. 'Sure,' he said. 'I'll get that herring for you.'

Out in the kitchen there, I could hear him singing—there's one, at least, I thought, who'll never be a teenage vocal star. And back in the big room, Miriam got out some photographs to show me of Emmanuel, in a white shirt, collecting his award.

'Splendid,' I said. 'He looks like that Shelley number, crossed with Groucho Marx.'

'He's sweet,' said Miriam, running a finger down her husband's photographic image.

'Bad snaps,' I told her. 'Why didn't you get me?'

She didn't answer that one, and said—turning suddenly upon me that way women do, to catch you unawares, and as if *all* the conversations that they've had with you hitherto were meaningless—'You think he's got talent, really? You think Mannie's got real talent?'

The answer came out before the thought, which is the only kind of true one. 'Yes,' I said, and she said nothing more.

In came the herrings, and the poet.

'The trouble about this country,' he explained to us, picking up a train of thought he'd dropped somewhere earlier on and left to ripen up a bit wherever it was he'd dropped it, 'is the total flight from reality in every sector.'

Miriam and I munched, waiting.

'For centuries,' this Southwark Shakespeare said, 'the English have been rich, and the price of riches is that you export reality to where it is you get your money from. And now that the market-places overseas are closing one by one, reality comes home again to roost, but no one notices it, although it's settled in to stay beside them.'

Short pause. Seemed that a question was demanded. And so,

'And so?' I said.

'A rude awakening is due,' Emmanuel said, smacking his lips around his herring, and gobbling it down like a performing seal.

I took up the old, old cudgels.

'A minute, Cockney boy,' I said. 'You talk of "the English"—aren't you one of us?'

'Me? Certainly. If you're born in this town, you're marked by it for life: specially by this area, you are.'

'And so what happens to *the English*, happens to you too?'

'Oh, positively. I'm booked on the same flight, whatever the direction.'

'So long as I know,' I said. 'I want you to be around when the big bills come in for payment.'

The chat had taken on suddenly an ever-so-slightly awkward edge, as chats will do, particularly when the tribal drums start beating in the distance—and I wanted Mannie to understand I *did* think him every bit a local, just as much as me and more, and needed him, and only feared he might get tired of us, and skip. But now he had grabbed prince Saul, and clutched him like that Epstein thing up by Oxford circus, and said to me,

'I write in the English language, boy. You take that away from me, and the whole world it and I come out of, and you cut off my strong right arm and other vital parts as well—let alone my livelihood and hopes of fame. Three of my own grandparents didn't speak a word of it. But me, I do, your speech is mine.'

'Grandmother Katz spoke English very well,' said Miriam.

'Never to me, she didn't.'

Here young Saul belched.

'Listen,' said Mannie solemnly. 'I tell you a secret: England is dreadful, and the English—they're barbarians. But three things of theirs I cherish most sincerely—the lovely tongue they thought up God knows how and I try hard to write in, and the nosey instinct of their engineers, and seamen, and explorers and scientists, to enquire, to find out why, and their own radicals that bounce up every century to flay and slay them, never mind the risk. So long as they have those things I'm glad to be with them, and will defend them . . . and everything else I can forget.'

Mannie said this so seriously, like he was taking an oath that might land him in a gas-chamber, but he'd keep it. Admitted, he was a bit conscious of saying it all, and of us his audience (particularly Saul)—but me, I believed him, and was impressed. 'I could do with a cup of tea,' I said, and this time Miriam went out to get it.

M. Katz arose and stretched himself and said, 'Heigh-ho—it's the human element. It's a wicked world.'

I by this time was wandering around this ghastly front abode—ghastly, I mean, in its furnishings and whatnot, which hadn't caught up with the contemporary kick, but nice and cosy-comfy and well used, as front room furnishings not always are. Over in one corner, almost hidden like a chamber pot behind a curtain, was a small selection of select volumes, including several of Mannie's two productions, one copy of each of these being bound in the hide of some rare animal, and enclosed in an outer covering of velours.

'They're not a bookish lot, your elders and betters,' I suggested.

'Not on my side,' said Mannie K., stepping over to finger his thin, beloved books. 'But come round to Miriam's father's place, and you'll see a whole public library, even stacked in the kitchen and the mod. cons., and most of them in German and in Russian.'

'Your folk are traders, Mannie?'

'Yes, but we have *four* rabbis in the family, if you include cousins,' he said with a ferocious grin, half pride, half horror.

'They didn't like it when little Emmanuel got on the writing kick?' I asked.

'There was a struggle. In Jewish families, Gentile boy, there always must be, over all major decisions, particularly about sons, a struggle. But as I went on working down the market, and in fact still do most of the week, they soon ungraciously surrendered. Especially when they first saw me on the telly.'

'And Miriam's lot?'

'They liked it even less. You see, I was supposed to be a bad match for the girl, and they thought, well, even if he's a peasant, at least he'll make the girl some money.'

'And so now?'

'Oh, they approve. Miriam's poppa's translated me into German and into Yiddish—but he's only got me published in the latter.'

'And they nice?'

Mannie gazed at the ceiling, stroking his tomes.

'I tell you one nice thing about them. The only three questions they asked Miriam when she dropped her bombshell were, "Is he healthy, is he a worker, do you love him?"—in that order. They didn't mention money till they saw *me*.'

Young Saul, feeling ignored, had joined us.

'They're pleased about this one, anyway,' I said.

'What? With twelve grandchildren already? Perhaps they'll take a bit of notice when *we* have our twelfth.'

'Not on your Nelly, we won't,' said Miriam, coming in bearing us the char.

So there it was: my visit to Mannie and Miriam had set me up, and given me the fortitude to have another bash at Crêpe Suzette. After all, even if it's undignified for a man to chase a girl, what had I got to lose in my position? So I asked the Katz pair if I could use their blower, and called up Suze's w.2 apartment where, quite surprisingly—or perhaps not, because boldness often *is* rewarded—she answered quite politely, and said to me, why didn't I come round and catch her before she left for the Lament performance down in s.w.3?

This time I took the metro, because I wanted to ruminate on what the best tactics would be to approach Suze—whether to try and force a show-down over Henley, or whether just to bank the fires, but keep them kindled till my turn came round one day. But this was a mistake, I mean the tube thing, because by the time I arrived outside her w.2 address, I saw Henley's vintage Rolls was parked there, and the lights blazing happily on Suze's floor upstairs.

Suze lives in a trio of Victorian bourgeois palaces that have been made over into flatlets for the new spiv intellectual lot, and on the old pillars underneath the porticos, instead of numbers 1, 2 and 3, or whatever it should be, they've written *Serpentine House*, this 'House' thing being the new way of describing any dump the landlords want to make a fast fiver out of. You press a bell, and a constipated voice answers down a loud-hailer thing (or sometimes doesn't), and you state your business into a grille as if you were broadcasting to the nation, and then there are quite a lot of clicks, and buzzes, and in you go to a hall where your bollocks freeze, even in summer, and climb in an upended coffin called the 'elevator', and jerk up past blank walls like a pit shaft till you stop with a late lurch at the requested number. At the lift gates—which it needs a strong man to open, but which close themselves before you're out—there, on the landing, rather to my surprise, stood Henley.

You'll dig Henley straight away if I describe him as a *cold* queer: i.e., he's not the swing-my-hips camp chatterbox variety, or a side-eyed crafty groping number, or the battle-scarred parachutist nail-biting type, but the smooth, collected, let's-talk-this-thing-over one.

'Good evening,' he said politely, trying to help me out of the elevator contraption.

'Well, and good evening to you,' I said. 'You've pinched my girl.'

Henley smiled just so slightly, and shook his head ever so slightly too, and said to me seriously, 'Naturally, when we're together, you can still come and see her.'

'*Can* I!' I said. 'You think I'd go near her in those circumstances?'

'Yes,' he said gently.

'Well, mister, then you don't know me!' I cried.

Hearing this frank exchange of greetings in the passage, Suzette herself emerged and stood there looking radiant: I mean, it is the only word to use that I can think of, she really shone, and wore a brittle Cinderella-in-the-ballroom-scene creation, one of those fragile things that girls, who really are so tough, as we all know, adore to climb into, to make us think they're sweet seventeen in person (which, in her case, in fact she was). She saw we'd got off to a dodgy start in our conversation, so she came out and grabbed us both, one hand apiece, and pulled us into her apartment, and did all those things with drinks, and fags, and radiograms that are supposed to melt a polar situation.

But I was not wearing that.

'You don't mind, Henley,' I said, crunching some pretzels and refusing the glass of Coke I hadn't asked for, 'if I speak my mind.'

The cat sat on an armchair, legs crossed, all laundry and hairdresser and dry-cleaner's, looking like a superior footman on his day off, but still horribly polite. 'Not a bit,' he said. 'That is, if Suzette doesn't mind.'

'We may as well have it,' Suzette said, flopping on to some cushions, and opening up a 2,000-page Yank mag.

'In the first place,' I said, beginning with the least obvious weapon, 'Suzette is working-class, like me.'

'And me,' said Henley.

'Eh?'

'My father, who's still living, was a butler,' the cat said.

'A *butler*,' I told him, 'is *not* working-class. No disrespect to your old Dad, but he's a flunkey.'

Suzette slammed down the mag, but Henley reached out what I think that he'd call a 'restraining arm', and said to me 'Very well, I'm not working-class. And so?'

'Those cross-class marriages don't work,' I told him.

'Nonsense. What next?'

'Suzette,' I continued, warming up, 'is young enough to be your great-great niece.'

'Please don't exaggerate. I know I'm much older, but I'm not yet forty-five.'

'Forty-five! You're ripe for Chelsea hospital!' I cried.

'Really,' said Henley, 'you *do* exaggerate. Take all the top film stars—Gable, and Grant, and Cooper. How old do you think they are?'

'They're not trying to marry Suze.'

'Very well,' he said. 'You think I'm senile. Anything else?'

'Point number three,' I said, 'I leave to your imagination.'

Henley uncrossed his legs, put neat, clean, effective fingers on either knee (I hope the creases of his pants didn't slice him), and said to me, 'Young man . . .'

'None of that "young man".'

'Oh, you're a *pest*,' cried Suzette.

'You bet I am!'

Slightly raising his voice, Henley continued, 'As I was about to say . . . do you know that a great many marriages between completely normal people are never consummated?'

'Then why wed?' I shouted.

'It's what the French call . . .'

'I don't care a fuck what the French call it,' I yelled. 'I call it just plain disgusting.'

Suzette was up, flashing fire. 'I do think you'd better go,' she said to me.

'Not yet. I haven't finished.'

'Let him go on,' said Henley.

'Let me my arse,' I said. 'What I want to ask you is, do you really suppose a set-up of that kind will make Suzette happy? I mean *happy*—do you understand that word?'

Henley had also risen. 'I only know,' he said very slowly to me, 'she'll make *me* happy.' And he went over and collected himself another drink.

I grabbed hold of Crêpe Suzette. 'Suzie,' I said. 'Do think!'

'Let go.'

I shook the girl. 'Do *think*,' I hissed at her.

She stood quite still, and rigid as a hop pole. Henley, from across the little room, said, 'Honestly, I do think Suzette's mind is made up, and I do think it best if you accepted the situation, at any rate for the time being.'

'You've bought her,' I said, letting go Suzette.

She aimed a swipe at me, but down I ducked. I moved over towards Henley.

'I suppose,' he said, 'you want to fight me.'

'I suppose I ought,' I said.

'Well, if you really want to, I'm quite agreeable, though I should warn you I'm a dirty fighter.'

'You're dirty all right,' I said.

'Well, go on,' he said to me, putting down his glass. 'Do for heaven's sake either begin, or, if you don't want to, sit down and not spoil everybody's evening.'

I noticed he had one hand inside his pocket. 'Key ring,' I thought, 'or maybe a lighter in the fist.' But I was only making excuses, because I knew I really didn't want to hit the man—it was Suzette I wanted to hit, or hit myself, bash my head against a concrete wall.

'We're not going to fight,' I said.

'Bravo,' he answered.

Suzette said very slowly to me, 'This is absolutely the last scene of this kind I want to see. One more, and I just won't see you ever at all, and please believe I mean it.'

'Thank you,' I said, 'for making yourself so clear. Good-bye for now, if I recover my temper I may see you down at the Lament's.'

'Just as you think,' Suze said.

Henley held out his hand, but this was too much, so with a sort of a wave I stumbled out of the door and had to wait several minutes in the passage there, hearing them nattering behind me, because that bloody elevator kept going up and down with Serpentine House residents packed in it, and wouldn't even stop when I managed to get the steel grille open while it was between floors, and stared down after it dropping into the abyss.

When finally I got out of that front door, aching like in a nightmare, as I dived down the streets, I heard a kind of death-rattle breathing just behind my ear, and whipped round to look, but there was nobody—was me. None of that! I cried, and broke all my regulations and went into a boozer and had a quick double something, and shot out again. I thought I'd go over the park, across the wide, open, lonely spaces, which also would be a short cut to Miss Lament.

On this north front of the Hyde, the terraces are great white monsters, like the shots you see in films of hotels at the Côte de France. There's the terraces for miles, like cliffs, then the Bayswater speedway with its glare lights and black pools, and the great dark green-purple park stretching on like a huge sea. The thing about the parks is, in day time they're all innocence and merriment, with dogs and perambulators and old geezers and couples wrapped up like judo performers on the green. But soon as the night falls, the whole scene reverses—into its exact opposite, in fact. In come the prowlers and the gropers and the cops and narks and whores and kinky exhibition numbers, and the thick air is filled with hundreds of suspicious, peering pairs of eyes. Everyone is seeking someone, but everyone is scared to meet that him or her they're looking for. If you're out of it, you want to go inside to see, and once you're in, you're very anxious to get out again. So in I went.

I tried not to think of Suze in there—and did. 'Suze, Suze, Suzette,' I said, and stopped, and I swear the thought of her was more me then than I was. I sat down on a bench, and my voice said, 'Boy, do be reasonable.'

One thing was right, I had to admit, in Suze's smelly plans. Until you know about loot—I mean really know, know how to handle the big stuff, know what the difference is between, let's say, five thousand pounds and ten (which are exactly the same to me), or what it's like to look at anything and say, 'I'll buy it,' or how the mugs will dance for you if you fling them down a shower of sixpences—then certainly you're still a mug yourself. The hard little biting brain inside Suzette was decided to understand this money kick, and my lord, she was going to do so, come what may.

I can't say I really minded about Henley in particular, and that twin-bed marriage thing that he was offering. What I minded was that it should be *anyone* but me—anyone at all. When she played me up with her Spade Casanovas, it was just as bad . . . except for this very big except, that I knew those adventures had no permanence attached to them. I still had my way in.

Mannie had said, 'Wait,' but how could I possibly be that wise? Would he have waited long for Miriam?

Perhaps Suze isn't me, I thought out suddenly. Perhaps I'm mistaken about this—she isn't really Juliet for my Romeo. But what does it matter, even if she isn't, if I feel she is?

'Fuck!' I cried out in a great bellow.

Three or so special investigators, who'd been approaching my bench cautiously from out of the dark green, stopped in their tracks at this, and some melted. I got up. 'Can I have a light?' the boldest said, as I passed by.

'Don't take a liberty,' I said, and hurried on.

I got on a stretch of curving roadway that was so dam black I kept walking off it, and getting tangled in the whatsits that they put there to say please-keep-off-the-thing. A light shaft suddenly appeared from nowhere, and by me there flashed a pair of mad enthusiasts in track-suits, puffing and groaning and looking bloody uncomfortable and virtuous. Good luck to them! 'God bless!' I shouted after.

Then unexpectedly, I came out on a delightful panorama of the Serpentine, lit up by green gas, and by headlamps from the cars whining across the bridge. I picked my way down by the water, and trod on a lot of ducks, they must have been, who scattered squawking sleepily. 'Keep in your own manor, where you belong,' I told them, chasing the little bastards down into the lake.

I was now beside the waves, and I could just make the sign out, 'Boats for Hire', and saw them moored fifteen feet away from me out there. So thinking, why not? anything to relieve the agony, I sat on the grass, and took off my nylon stretch and Itie clogs, and rolled up my Cambridge blues, and stepped into the drink like King Canute. By the time I reached the first boat, I was up to my navel like the hero in an Italian picture, and hoisted myself into the thing and, after a lot of bother untying a skein of greasy cables, I managed to put out to sea. As soon as I was in the middle, I let her just float along.

I lay there, ruddy uncomfortable, gazing at the stars, and thinking again of Suze, and of how absolutely nice it would be if she was there, she and me. 'Suzie, Suzette,' I said, 'I love you, girl.' And I washed my face off in the muddy, invisible slop.

Then I sat up inside that boat, and thought, how can I make a lot of money quickly, if that's what she wants to get? Naturally, I thought of Wiz, of his plans for his prosperity, but knew I could never make it that way—honest, not because of morals, or anything like that, but because that life, though it may be glamorous in its way, is so really *undignified*, if that's the word. I want to be rich all right, but I don't want to be *hooked*.

Wham! we slapped into the bottom of the bridge, the boat and I. I looked up and saw a geezer looking over, and I waved up to the silly sod, and shouted out, '*Bon soir, Monsieur!*' and he said nothing in reply, but started throwing pennies down on me, or maybe they were dollar bits, I couldn't see, and didn't care to, because this character's idea of having a ball struck me as most dangerous. So I rowed on to the other bank, and disembarked just at the Lido, and had to climb a fence to get out of the enclosure, and ripped myself in several painful places.

The law, as anyone who knows it will agree, has a genius for showing up not when you're *doing* something, as it should, presumably, but when you're quite innocent and *have* just done something. This cowboy flashed his lighthouse on me as I was putting on my shoes and socks, and stood there saying nothing, but not dowsing that annoying glim.

But I was determined he'd have to say the opening word, which he did by asking, after several long minutes, 'Well?'

'Having a paddle, officer,' I said.

'A paddle.'

'That's what I told you.'

'That's what you tell me.'

'In the old Serpentine.'

'Yeah.'

'Down there.'

'Down there, you say.'

This conversation seemed to me quite mental, so I got up, and said, 'Goodnight, officer,' and started off, but he said to me, moving up, 'Come here.'

So naturally, I ran.

One thing you learn about the law is that they don't like running because their helmets usually fall off. What's more, they don't like any kind of physical effort—in fact, the one thing coppers all have in common, apart from being tramps, is that they have a horror of physical labour of any kind, particularly manual. Just look at the expression on their faces when you see a photo of them in the papers, digging among the rushes for the killer weapon! So if you're fast on your feet, and there's only one of them, you can fairly easily elude them, which I did now by dodging behind that Peter Pan erection, and diving in some smutty bushes.

'Further on, mate—get further on' a voice said, as I'd inconsiderately got entangled with a bird and client, which of course wasn't my intention, so I bowed myself out, and got up on the road again and over it among the great dark trees, far darker than the dark sky up behind them, and I started walking normally, like some serious kiddo who's gone out nocturnal bird-watching, or learning poetry by heart for a dramatic evening at the borough hall. After trampling by mistake over some flower beds, for which I apologize, I came out on the south side of the Hyde, and escaped through the ornamental gate into the embassy section that starts up round about there.

If attending a teenage party, or in fact one of any other kind, I'd naturally wear my sharpest, coolest ensemble—possibly even my ivy-league outfit a GI got for me last year from his PX. But the Lament would be disappointed if, billing me to her public as a teenage product, I didn't show up in my full age-group regalia. So I wasn't embarrassed by my non-Knightsbridge clobber, but only a bit at being drenched downwards from the hips: however, I was hoping they'd accept that as just a bit of teenage fun.

So I rang the Dido bell. And, as often happens when you attend a party, another cat arrived on the doorstep at the same moment. Usually, they don't address you until properly introduced within, but this one was something of an exception, because, without even telling me his name, or anything, he smiled and said, 'You for the tigress's den as well?'

I didn't answer that, but smiled back just as politely (and with just as little meaning) as the cat—who was one of those young men with an old face, or old ones with a young one, hard to tell which: anyway, he had a very sharp top-person suit on, which must have cost his tailor quite a bit.

'You've known our remarkable hostess long?' he said.

'That's how it goes,' I answered, and we passed inside the block together.

No need for a lift this time, because Dido has a ground floor thing around a patio out the back, which is even selecter than a penthouse, in my opinion, because it's somehow more unexpected: I mean the patio, which was very large for London, and still full of gaps in spite of a fair number of hobos already milling around there. Lament's one of those persons who, when she throws a party, and you've just arrived, you don't have to hunt around for her under the cushions or in the toilet, to say hullo, because she's felt you directly you come in, and is on the scene immediately with a merry word of greeting. Up she glid, wearing a white hold-me-tight creation, like an enormous washable contraceptive, and with her ginger hair wind-tossed and tousled (I'll bet it took her all of half an hour), and with her radar-eyes gleaming on the target, and with her geiger-ears pinking big discoveries, and with her Casualty-Ward-10 hands slicing through the hospitable summer air, and with her feet, claws withdrawn inside the pads just for the present, very successfully and snakily carrying the lot.

'Oh, hul-*lo*, infant prodigy,' she said to me. 'You've already met my ex-lover Vendice? Are you hungering for something? Have you wet your pants?'

'Yes, yes, and no,' I told her. 'I've come straight up to your tenement from a bathe.'

'But of *course*,' she cried out, but in a low, rasping voice, as if someone had cut six of her vocal chords. Then she leaned her head until her carroty locks swept by my neck, and said, 'Any items for the column?'

'Lots. How's the price these days?'

She put her lips on my neck skin without kissing, actually. 'You'll tell me for love,' she said.

'Yes. All the dirt. A bit later,' I assured her. But she didn't hear me, because she'd swept on along her mossy hostess's track.

I think Dido's the most unscrupulous person I've yet met, though I don't mean especially about money. What I mean is, she believes everything in existence is a *deal*. For example, when she came pounding around the teenage ghetto, collecting material for her articles I've referred to, she gave all the kiddos the impression that she wanted to *buy* the teenage thing, like somebody booking a row of ringsides at the circus. And when she looks at you,—and she's always very pleased to see you—her eyes say she knows just how much your price will be. She's somewhere between 38 and 58, I'd say, and this flat of hers in the Knightsbridge red-light district must be worth a bit more than ever her column pays her, so there are no doubt other items in reserve. The sex angle, so the chatter goes, isn't bent in any direction, and no one in particular's in evidence around her garret, though there are said to be favourites, and sometimes the industrial daddies from the North move in a while to look around.

I gazed at the saleroom, to see what sorts of customers she'd mustered. I don't know if I can convey this idea exactly, but the general impression they all gave was of being well stoked with nourishment, well decked out in finery, but all on someone else's money. This is a curious thing—that you can usually tell who has their own loot, who not: rather as you can the really sexual numbers, boys and girls, from all the others, I mean the serious operators, by a sort of quietness, of purpose, of relaxation they possess.

Up came the Hoplite. He had on some Belafonte-style, straight-from-the-canefield (via the make-up room) kind of garments, with too many open necks, and tapering wrists, and shoes like tin-openers, all in light colours except for some splashes of mascara that gave his eyes melancholy and meaning. He plucked at my arm, and told me, with an agonizing sigh, 'Look, yon's the Nebraska boy.'

I saw, chatting away beneath the pergola, a perfectly ordinary young US product—fresh, washed and double-rinsed as they manufacture them in thousands over there. 'Cute,' I told Hoplite.

Cute! Oh, lordy me!'

'Well—dynamic, then.'

'That's a bit better.'

'You hitting it off, you two?'

'Ah, woe . . . !'

The Hoplite gripped my arm, gazing to and fro languorously from the Nebraskan one to me, and said, 'It's ghastly, you know. He's ever so friendly to me, and cheerful, and sometimes even grins and reaches out and *ruffles my hair*.'

'Painful. I feel for you.'

'Have pity! Ah me, ah me!'

'Ah you, all right. Where's the lush hidden?'

'It's not. You help yourself from the sideboard, just like that.'

I worked my way over with young Fabulous, who eased aside the multitude with his shapely tail.

'Ah-ha, you remind me,' I told Hop. 'The Call-me-Cobber number wants to sign you up for a television thing'—and I told him about the Lorn Lover programme project. The Hoplite looked very dubious indeed. 'Of course, you know I'd love to have my face and figure up there in between the commercials,' he told me, 'and naturally, I'd love to appear before the nation to tell it all about Nebraska. But do you think, really, public opinion's ripe yet for anything so bold?'

'You could say it's a deep and splendid friendship that unites you.'

'Well, in a sense it is.'

'I'll speak to C.-me-C., then.'

'And I will to Adonis.'

Standing there alone, clutching my lime-and-tonic, I was accosted by one of those numbers you always meet up with at a party, and she opened up to me with,

'Hullo, stranger.'

'Hi.'

'How are you called?'

'And you?'

'You tell me.'

'David Copperfield.'

She shrieked. 'I'm Little Nell.'

'There you go!'

'What do you do?'

'Only on Saturdays.'

'Naughty. No, I mean your job.'

'Photographic work.'

'For Dido?'

'I'm free-lance.'

'Plenty of windmills to tilt at?'

'That's how it goes.'

'Which end of town you live?'

'The end I sleep in.'

'No, seriously.'

Here they always give you the, 'But I'm *interested* in you,' look.

'Round w.10.'

'Oh, that's unusual.'

'Not to those who live in w.10.'

Here, having a little *thought* to wrestle with, her brain started pinking.

'Know everyone here?'

'Everyone except you.'

'But you *do* know me. I'm Little Nell.'

You see what I mean? Honestly, that's what parties always turn out to be. All the pleasure of a party is going there, up as far as the front door only.

Bits of the company had started dancing, but I didn't want to join in this activity, because either they were doing that one-two, one-two ballroom thing, which makes everybody look like waiters and usherettes out on their annual rave, or else, if they were jiving, they were all of them frantic and alarming, like a physical culture demonstration by a bunch of cats with colic, knocking themselves out quite unnecessarily, because the real way to jive is to swing your body, not your legs and arms. I must admit some of the birds tried to get aholt of me, on account of the prestige of the teenage performance, but I pleaded not guilty, and made it over to the pergola. There I unhitched my Rolleiflex, and took a few pictures just to keep my hand, in, and for a rainy day.

'I'd like some of those, if they're successful,' said a gent standing there beside me.

This gent, who wore a north-of-Birmingham suiting, was the one exception to the thing I said earlier on about their all, myself included, being a lot of parasites and ponces: I mean, he looked as if it was on himself that he depended—you know, substantial, and not throwing it all up at once. And this turned out to be the case, because he told me he was a business man, a manufacturer in the motor industry, and believe me, I got quite a kick out of knowing him, as I had never actually met a business man before—in fact, hardly believed that they existed, though realizing, of course, they must do, somewhere.

'Good for you, chairman!' I said to him, pumping his business-manly paw. 'If you ask me, you commercial cats are the only ones that really keep the nation sliding off its arse.'

'You think so?' the number asked me, giving the 'amused smile' the seniors turn on whenever anything intelligent is said by an absolute beginner.

'Naturally, I think it,' I told him, 'if I've just said it.'

'Not many would agree with you,' he said, beginning to latch on to my conception.

'You don't have to tell me! Turn on your telly, or your radio, and do you ever catch anything about business men? Does anyone write books about them in the paperbacks? And yet, don't we all live off what you do? Without you tycoons, there just wouldn't be the money for the rent.'

'You're very flattering,' this industrial number said.

'Oh, shit!' I cried. 'Will *no* one ever take my ideas seriously?' The balance-sheet product started to laugh soothingly, so I grabbed him by the lapel of his family-tailor hopsack, and said, 'Look! England was an empire—right? Now it isn't any longer—yes? So all it's got to live on will be brains and labour, i.e., scientists and engineers and business men and the multitudes of authentic toilers.'

The cat looked surprised and pleased.

'Mind you,' I added, just to bring him down a bit, 'I'm not saying business is *difficult*. I don't think it's difficult to coin loot, provided you're really interested in it—provided it's your number-one obsession.'

'I'll not disagree with you altogether there,' the boardroom product said.

'Most of us *think* we're interested in making money, but we're not: we're only interested in getting our hands on someone else's.'

He looked at me approvingly, as if he's sign me up immediately as chief tea-cup boy in his twelve-storey office block.

'And how is the car trade?' I continued.

'Don't tell a soul,' he said, looking around him, 'but it's prospering.'

'Crazy!' I said. 'But of course,' I went on, 'you know you automobile producers are a bunch of murderers?'

'Oh, yes? Would you say so?' he said, smiling 'tolerantly' again.

'Well, in a sense you are. You read the figures of the slaughter on the highways?'

'I try to forget them. What are we to do?' This automotive one was still looking a bit 'amused', but I could see I'd touched him on a nerve. 'After all,' he said, 'if you took the cars off the roads tomorrow, the whole economy would collapse. Have you considered that?'

'No,' I said.

'In addition, the export industry on which, as you've said, this country lives, requires a healthy home consumption to sustain it.'

'There you go!'

'So death on the roads is the price we pay for moving the goods around, and earning currency abroad.'

I looked at the cat. 'You've said all this before,' I told him, 'to the assembled shareholders.'

'Good heavens, no!' the number said. 'As a matter of fact, son, I say it chiefly to myself.'

'Well,' I told this industrial chieftain, 'you know as well as I do, if you're a driver, which I expect you are, that there's stacks of goons sitting behind steering-columns who *like* the idea they may mow some victim down.' I waited, but he didn't answer. 'An accelerator and a ton of metal,' I went on, 'bring out the Adolf Hitler in us all. They know there's no danger to themselves, sitting up there inside that tank, and if they make a kill, they know nobody's going to hang them.'

The profit-and-loss one now began to look a bit uneasy—I mean, not at my ideas, but *me*,—which always happens if you let loose an idea.

'Car driving,' I told him, twisting my knife round in the wo[illegible] 'is the licensed murder of the contemporary scene. It use[illegible] duelling and cut-throats, now it's killing by car.'

I saw I mustn't keep on rucking him, because, after all, this was a party, so I patted him on his hopsack, just like he'd done me, and struggled across to cut in on Call-me-Cobber, and have a spin round with the ex-Deb-of-Last-Year. But: 'Fair goes, now, fair goes,' the Cobber said, and he pulled the ex-Deb out of reach, and all I got for my attempt was her making apologetic faces at me over the Aussie's beefo shoulders.

'Aboriginal!' said Zesty-Boy Sift.

This Zesty, who had come up now beside me, was the only other teenage product present at the barbecue, and I hadn't spoken to him yet for two reasons: first, because I meant to borrow five pounds from him, and wanted to choose my moment, and second, because this Z.-B. Sift had come up very abruptly in the world since I first knew him, and I didn't want to show I was impressed.

But in actual fact, I was. In the far dawn of creation when the teenage thing was in its Eden epoch, young Zesty used to sing around the bars and caffs, and was notorious for being quite undoubtedly the crumbiest singer since—well, choose your own. *But* —here's the point—the songs he sung, their words as well as harmonies, were his invention, thought up by him in a garage in Peckham, where he used to toil by day and slumber in an old Bugatti. And though Zesty caught all the necessary US overtones to send the juveniles that he performed for, the words he thought up were actually *about* the London teenage kids—I mean not just 'Ah luv yew, Oh yess Ah du' that could be about anyone, but numbers like *Ugly Usherette*, and *Chickory with my Chick*, and *Jean, your Jeans!*, and *Nasty Newington Narcissus* which all referred to places and to persons which the kids could actually identify round the purlieus of the city.

So far, so bad, because nobody was interested in Zesty-Boy's creative efforts—particularly the way *he* marketed them—until one of the teenage yodellers who'd hit the big time remembered Zesty, and sold the whole idea of him (and of his songs) to his Personal Manager, and his A. & R. man, and his Publicity Consultant, and his Agency Booker, and I don't know who else, and behold! Zesty-Boy threw away his own guitar and saved his voice for gargling and normal speech,and started writing for the top pop canaries, and made piles—I mean literally piles—of coin from his sheet, and disc, and radio, and telly, and even filmic royalties. It was a real rags-to-riches fable: one moment Z.-B. Sift was picking up pennies among the dog-ends and spittle with a grateful grimace, the next he was installed in this same Knightsbridge area with a female secretary and a City accountant added to his list of adult staff.

'Those Aussies!' he said, 'have moved in for the slaughter. Did you know there's 60,000 of them in the country? And ever seen any of them on a building site?'

I didn't reply (except for a wise nod), because the matter of the five pounds was now uppermost in my mind, and about borrowing and lending, of which of both I have a wide experience, I could tell you several golden rules. The first is, come straight up smartly to the point: to lead up tactfully to the kill is fatal, because the candidate sniffs your sinister intention and has time to put up barricades. So I said, 'I want a fiver, Zesty.'

Zesty-Boy, I was glad to see, observed, on his side, the first golden rule of lending, which is to say yes or no *immediately*—if you don't, they'll hate you if you refuse, and never be grateful if you agree. He took out the note, said, 'Any time,' and changed the subject. As a matter of fact, in this case we both knew it was actually a gift, because in his Cinderella days I've often enough handed Zesty-Boy the odd cigarette-machine money, and as a shilling then was worth what a pound is to him now, this really was only a repayment. And I could add—since we're on this topic—that if you're in a position, ever, to be a *lender*, the two kinds of people you should most watch out for are not, as you might expect, the dear old boyhood pals of Paradise alley days, but any newcomer (because borrowers are attracted to fresh faces), or anyone you've just done a favour to (because borrowers think there where the corn grows, there's sugar-cane as well).

'Eh?' I said to Zesty-B. because, with these meditations, I hadn't been following attentively the trend his conversation had been taking.

'I said Dido's out for blood this evening. She's got the needle into Vendice, because he's not buying any more space in her fish-and-chip organ, and she's losing her cut on all the full-page spreads.'

'Bad,' I said, glancing over at the number he referred to, who was the one I'd met earlier outside the door, and who was under the arcade that ringed the patio, strip-lit with lamps all hidden, so that you always got only a reflection, and couldn't read a book there, supposing that you'd wanted to.

'What does he do, this Vendice?' I asked Zesty-Boy. 'And is that his baptismal name?'

Zesty said yes, it was, and that Vendice Partners' job was well up somewhere in the scaffolding of one of those advertising agencies that have taken over Mayfair, making it into a rather expensive slum.

'And why has Partners' pimpery taken their custom away from Dido's toilet-paper daily?' I asked Zesty-Boy.

'It may be that Dido's slipping, or the paper's slipping, or just that everything these days is falling in the fat laps of the jingle kings.'

'I wonder why Dido doesn't do a quick change and crash-land in the telly casbah?'

'Well—could she? I mean, can a journalist really do anything *else*?'

'I see what you mean.'

The time had now come for me to flatter the young Mozart in him a little. 'I heard one of your arias on the steam, last evening,' I told him. '*Separate Separates*, if I remember. Very nice.'

'Which of the boy slaves was it sung it? Strides Vandal? Limply Leslie? Rape Hunger?'

'No, no . . . Soft-Sox Granite, I think it was . . .'

'Oh, that one. A Dagenham kiddy. He's very new.'

'He sounded so. But I loved the lyric, and enjoyed the lilt.'

Zesty-Boy shot a pair of Peckham-trained eyes at me. 'Yeah?' he said.

'I tell you, man. I don't flatter.'

'Compliment accepted.' I could see the cat was pleased. 'You heard they gave me my first Golden?' he said cautiously.

'Boy, I was delighted. For *When I'm Dead, I'm Gone*, wasn't it? A million platters, man—just fancy that!' How could the Sift kid fail to be delighted? 'How long will it all last, do you suppose?' I said to him.

'Companion, who knows? I gave it only a year, two years ago. And still they come—performers and, what's more, cash customers.'

'Still only boys for singers? No signs of any breasted thrushes?'

'We've tried one or two of them, but the kids just don't want to know. No, for the minors, it's still males.'

'And all those boys from Dagenham and Hoxton and wherever. You have to teach them how to sing American?'

'Oh no, they seem to pick it up—get the notes well up there in their noses when they sing . . . Though when they *speak*, even in personal appearances, it's back to Dagenham again.'

'Weird spiel, isn't it.'

'Weird! Child, I'm telling you—it's eerie!'

You know the way that, when things start to go amiss at a function, everyone notices it long before they actually stop doing whatever it was they're doing—drinking, dancing, talking and etcetera—and this was what now occurred, because a battle was developing between our hostess and the Partners number. But soon, just as no one can resist listening to a bit of hot chat over the blower, we all turned ourselves into spectators at the gladiatorial show.

They started off with the mutes on, playing that English one-up game they teach you at Oxford, or is it Cambridge, anyway, one of those camp holiday camps, with Dido saying, at the point I managed to tune in, 'I didn't say barsted, I said bastard.'

'It's not your pronunciation, Dido, that I'm questioning,' the copy-writing cat was saying, 'but your definition.'

'Very well, I withdraw it,' Dido said, 'and say you're just a harlot.'

'Really, my dear, I don't think I'm a woman. Surely, I've given you proof positive of that . . .'

'Only just, Vendice, only just,' she said.

And so and so forth, guest and hostess, both very cool and, what was really rather horrible, without any emotion in it I could see—and the friends looking on and listening with that kind of grin the mob wear at a prize fight in the municipal baths. I must be a prude at heart, because this thing really shocks me—not bawling-outs and even fights, of course, but this methodical, public blood-letting. And I must be a snob, because I really do think that when an educated English voice is turning bitchy, it's a quite specially unpleasant sound, besides being fucking silly, and an utter drag. So I was much relieved, and I think one or two others were, when into the middle of all this stepped wedding-bells Henley with my Suze.

As it happened, I was adjacent to the stereo, so I slipped on some Basie, turned on the juice well up, and, with a low bow to Henley, grabbed the girl. Now if there's one thing among many Suze has learned from her Spade connections, it's how to dance like an angel, and enjoy it, and I myself, though perhaps a bit unpolished, have studied on hard floors around the clubs and palais and in all-night private sessions, and besides which, we know all each other's routines backwards—and sideways and front as well—so before long, there we were, weaving together like a pair of springs connected by invisible elastic wires, until we reached that most glorious moment of all in dancing, that doesn't come often, and usually, admittedly, only when you're whipping it up a bit to show the multitude—that is, the dance starts to do it for you, you don't bloody well know what you're up to any longer, except that you can't put a limb wrong anywhere, and your whole dam brain and sex and personality have actually become that dance, *are* it—it's heavenly!

When just a second we were in an electric clinch, I said, 'Where you dine? He take you somewhere nice?' And she said, 'Oh, *him*!' Boy! Can you believe it? She said it just like that! So when we were close again a second, and the Count playing wonderfully in our ears, and the whole Lament lot standing round us thirty miles or so away, I cried out to her, 'Is he you? Is he really you?' And Suzette said, 'No, you are! But I'm going to marry him!' And at that moment the music stopped, because I'd jabbed the sapphire down too near the middle in the earlier excitement of the moment.

So I bid everyone good-night, and do sleep well, and thanks for having me, and went out of the flat into the London dawn. It *was* dawn, as a matter of fact, already: or rather, to be exact, it was that moment when the day and night are fighting it out together, but you've no doubt whatever who will triumph. A cab was passing by, and slowed down politely for the wayfarer, but I didn't want to break into Zesty-Boy's fiver at the moment, and also wanted to remember what Suze said about 10,000 times, so I set off to foot it back across the city to my home up the north in Napoli.

IN JULY

PICTURE ME, up to the calves in mud at low tide beside the river, trying to pose the Hoplite and the ex-Deb up on a stranded barge. 'Don't *fuss* us,' the Hoplite said; and, 'Do hurry,' said the ex-Deb-of-Last-Year.

This was the spiel. Events of the last month had convinced me that the only way I could ever hope to make some swift dinero was by cracking into the top-flight photographic racket—i.e., produce some prints that would be so sensational that I'd make the big time in the papers and magazines, and even (this was my secret dream) succeed in holding a fabulous exhibition somewhere to which all my various contacts would bring their loaded friends. When you come to ponder on it, like I did for days, you'll see it's not so wild a notion as it might appear. After all, kids do make big money these days, as I've explained, and as for photography, well, it seems very fashionable just now to treat photographers like film stars, the reason being, I expect, that the culture-vultures get all the art kick they want out of snapshots, although actually they're dam easy to understand—and, need I say, so far as that goes, to manufacture.

But, as in everything here below, I had to find my gimmick, my approach, my slant, my angle. And after days of brooding on the problem, I hit on a plan that, so far as I can see, can't miss. It simply is, to weave a story round the two contemporary characters that everyone is interested in—i.e., the teenagers and the debs. You dig? The teenager, of humble origin—Prince Charming in reverse—encounters the Poor-Little-Rich-Girl debutante. Daddy and Pop both disapprove (as well as Mum and Mummy), so Teenage Tom and Diana Debutante have to meet clandestinely in selected spots about the capital (which I would choose for their crazy picturesqueness), and the whole collection, when completed, would comprise a stark, revealing portrait of the contemporary scene.

My chief difficulty was casting the two star parts, because although I know stacks of teenagers and a deb or two, I wanted persons I could rely on to keep the secret, and who would give me a lot of valuable time without immediate remuneration, and who, most of all, would look sensational when recorded for posterity by my Rolleiflex. The ex-Deb was the obvious selection for the female rôle, since her looks, though, to my taste, completely meaningless, are simply gorgeous—I mean, she's so dam glorious she isn't *real*—but the big question was, of course, would she accept? Well, thanks to Dean Swift, she did. Because the ex-Deb, though you couldn't precisely describe her as a junkie, climbs on the needle when being beautiful is just too much for her, and the Dean, when I introduced them, was able to help her in the matter of supplies. If you're going to tell me hooking her this way is unethical, I'm perfectly willing to agree to that, but please understand my situation in regard to Suze is urgent and rather desperate, as the performance at the registry totalizator can't be long delayed, although I haven't succeeded yet in discovering exactly when it is to be.

Now as for the boy, the obvious choice was Wiz—or, in fact, anyone at all within the age bracket other than the Fabulous Hoplite. But Wiz isn't my best friend, unfortunately, at the moment, so it was the Hop I picked. The reason is that, though Hoplite doesn't consider himself, correctly, to be an authentic teenager at all, or, for that matter, exactly a Prince Charming, he really is extremely handsome and delicious and photogenic, and the boy always has a load of spare time lying heavy on his hands. The deal here was rather dodgy, because I had to reject on Hoplite's part what the courts call a certain suggestion, and fixed it with him on the promise of a de-luxe album of himself in classic poses, which he could offer as a birthday gift to his Americano.

If you've ever tried to assemble two colourful characters like the Fabulous and the ex-Deb in the same place, on several occasions, for a certain length of time, you'll realize what I've been up against these last weeks. Particularly as, to get the London fairy-story atmosphere I'm aiming for, I've had to take them in a tanker down in Surrey docks, and in the reptile house at the zoological, and in both an ambulance and a hearse (that wasn't as difficult as it might seem), and also, actually inside the stables where our national toy soldiers groom their animals—which was a Day-to-Remember I believe I shall never forget.

'No, no, no, no,' I shouted from the foreshore, because the ex-Deb and the Hoplite had actually turned their backs on me.

'No—what?' cried my heroine, tossing her locks about, and turning in a practised pose that pointed all her salient features.

'You do *fuss* so,' the Hoplite said again, standing up to adjust his slacks, and looking like an are-you-weedy? be-like-me, advertisement.

I waded forward, and appealed to their better natures. 'Listen, *amateurs*!' I cried. 'It's your *fronts* that I'm paying for—the parts where you show some expression.'

'Paying us, infant!' said the female lead.

'If it's *expression* you want . . .' the Hoplite added. 'Besides, you've cut short a delightful conversation.'

I knew what that was. The Hop never tired of hearing of transactions in the debutante market, and chatted his leading lady endlessly on this subject, especially when I asked him for a heroic or a grief-ridden expression.

'Just one more try,' I pleaded, 'and do please recollect the script. The current situation is that Lord Myre is going to horsewhip his daughter's young heart-throb, and she's breaking the news to him that daddy's on the way down with his posse.'

'Delicious,' the Hoplite said.

'It's daddy who gets horsewhipped these days,' said the ex-Deb-of-Last-Year.

Picture, to re-cap, the scene. There, on the wharf, stood the ex-Deb's bubble-car and M. Pondoroso's Vespa (because yes, Mickey P. really had delivered the promised goods), and a band of on-lookers with complimentary tickets, and up on the bridge above us, the City citizens scurrying to and fro, the men looking like dutiful schoolkids with their brief-cases and brollies, the women as if they were hurrying to work in order to hurry home again, and out in the stream, the craft like Piccadilly circus-on-the-water, and there in the quagmire me, and this temperamental Old Vic duo. The fact is, it *was* rather difficult to concentrate, because the whole panorama was so splendid, with the sun hitting glass triangles off the water, and the summer with the season really in its grip, making the thought of those short, dark, cold days long ago seem just a nightmare.

So we decided to break off for *déjeuner*.

This we partook in a Thames-side caff up in a lane that, though I know the river frontage intricacies like the veins on my own two hands, I'd never discovered—but then, after all, who *does* know London? We found the caff by following some river toilers in there, and when we entered there was a mild sensation (whistles, stares, and dirty remarks made sideways), because, of course, the Hop and Deb are both exotic spectacles in any setting, and the more so, obviously, here. But both were more than equal to the situation, neither being the least put out by blinkless stares, and neither being, in spite of all their camp and blah, the least bit snobbish—socially, I mean, at any rate—which is one reason why I like them.

So the ex-Deb, between whiles of her salt beef, swedes and dumplings, chatted anyone who chatted her, and even did a tango with a hefty belted character when someone put some silver in the juke. And Fabulous, surrounded by gigantic, sweaty manual workers, did a great act of borrowing salt and pepper and miscellaneous sauces from lots of tables, giving as good as he got to the resident wittery, till some sour, quite exceptional, customer asked him, how was trade?

There was a slight hush at this, and Fabulous asked the customer just why he wanted to know.

'I thought you might fancy me,' this trouble-maker said, looking round for the applause which, actually, he didn't get.

'*You*?' said the Hoplite, gazing at the monster.

'That's what I said,' the cat rejoined.

'*Well*, now,' said Hop, in tones loud for all to hear. 'I don't really think so, no, I don't really think that you're exactly me. But if you bring your wife along, or your grandmother, or your sister, I dare say you'll find they'll prefer even me to anything they've had from you.'

'Prefer a poof?' the number said.

The Hoplite smiled round the room, rallying his supporters.

'Am I really the very first you've met?' he asked the character. 'You'd better go straight home and tell your mother you've seen one, before she changes you.'

This got a laugh, and the cat couldn't keep it up, and everybody changed the subject because, say what you like, although I know English workingmen are as crude as it's possible to be, they can be very civilized, when they feel like it, in the matter of behaviour.

A nautical cat, wearing a baseball cap and a bare chest marked,

'Pray for Me, Mother,' told the ex-Deb that his boat did weekly trips up to Scandinavia, and why didn't she come along on one—everyone on board would be delighted, he assured her. The ex-Deb said she'd certainly consider this (and I believe she meant it), and the Hop asked if he could sign on as deckhand for the trip, and the nautical numbers all said greaser would suit him better—and all this chat about the sea, and seafaring, and ships sailing out of London, made me begin to feel that hell, it really was ridiculous that here was I, nearly nineteen, and never yet left the city of my creation, so I determined there and then the very next thing I'd do, would be get myself a brand new passport.

When the place had cleared a bit, we got together to decide on the next location, which I wanted to be on the tea-terrace of an open-air swimming pool, with Hop explaining artificial respiration methods to the debutante. I could see that the Hoplite, in spite of his little victory, was a bit upset by the earlier occurrence, so I said, 'Never mind, Hop, small minds live in small worlds.'

'Don't they, though!' said Fabulous.

'Speaking personally,' said the ex-Deb, 'and I may be wrong, because I've no moral sense whatever—or so all the men I leave or don't like in the first place tell me—I think this game of putting everyone you meet in precise sexual categories, is just a bit absurd.'

'A drag, at any rate,' I suggested.

'No, just *absurd*. I mean,' said the ex-Deb, running her graceful fingers through her luscious locks, 'if everyone's entire life, every twenty-four hours, was filmed and tape-recorded, who exactly *would* seem normal any more?'

'Not me, for one,' said Hoplite, emphatically.

'Not you, darling, but not *anyone*,' the ex-Deb said. 'I mean, where does normality begin, and where does it definitely end? I could tell you a tale or two about *normal* men, if I felt inclined,' she added.

The Hoplite accepted courteously a Woodbine from an adjacent table. 'The world where they make laws and judgements,' he told us all, 'is way up above my poor bleeding baby head. But all I would ask is this, please: is there any other law in England that's broken every night by thousands of lucky individuals throughout the British

Isles, without anything being *done* about it? I mean, if the law knew that thousands of crimes of any other kind whatever were to be committed by persons of whom they know the names and addresses and etcetera, wouldn't they take *violent* action? But in our case, although they know perfectly well what's happening—who doesn't, after all? It's all so notorious, and such a bore—except for the sordid happenings in parks, and the classical choir-boy manoeuvre that every self-respecting bitch most cordially disapproves of, they ignore the law they're paid to enforce every bit as much as we do.'

'Occasionally,' I reminded Hop, 'they do select some more important victims . . .'

'Oh, yes . . . One or two files come up out of the pile, occasionally, I admit, but they always seem to pick someone who's helped in his career by the shameful publicity instead of ruined by it, as they'd fondly hoped, and even that sort of prosecution's getting rarer every day . . .'

We chewed the cud on this.

'I tell you, Hop,' I said, 'if ever the law *was* changed, nine-tenths of your queer fraternity would immediately go out of business.'

He gazed at me with his lovely, languorous eyes. 'Oh, of *course*, child,' he said. 'With the law as it is, being a poof is a full-time occupation for so many of the dear old queens. They're positively dedicated creatures. They feel so naughty, in their dreary little clubs and service flatlets. Heavens, don't I know!' Despite the summer heat, the Hoplite shuddered.

The ex-Deb reached out eight encircling arms and gave the Fabulous a big kiss, which he accepted bravely. 'Don't weaken, beautiful,' she said.

'I *won't*,' said the Hoplite, rising.

I gave him a lift west on my Vespa, but untied his arms and dropped him off where he couldn't see my own destination, because this was a very private and, in fact, rather weird occasion, namely, my annual outing with my Dad to see *H.M.S. Pinafore*, at the late afternoon performance.

In the far distant days before hi-fi and LPs, my Dad used to have, in our home-sour-home up in the Harrow road, a contrivance that he'd made himself out of old bicycle parts and clocks and jam tins, on which he would play, to anyone who'd listen, which was of course us kids, a selection of records that he'd come by, most of them with hardly any grooves left, so that you needed sharp ears, and a lot of experience, to tell what voice or instruments were playing, let alone the tunes. And among this collection, which Dad kept, like a miser's hoard, in a locked steel trunk under a table in the cellar, were a stack of G. & S. things which we all adored, and could sing every word of that we could make out from the records. And so, before Vern and I grew up to hate each other, and to learn from the other kids that all this G. & S. stuff was square and soppy, he and I used to sing duets, and sometimes old Dad would even join us in a trio, or sing the chorus parts that bored us, or were too difficult to understand. All this, I may say, took place when Ma was out, or very busy.

This *Pinafore* one was always my and Dad's special favourite, I think chiefly because it has such a really miraculous opening—friendly and sweet and gay and completely crazy—and many's the time we've sung the Captain's number with his crew together, even since I've grown to man's estate, and even when out, he and I, in some public place. So every year, when Dad's anniversary comes round, we go off to the matinee to see it, Dad of course telling nobody, and sit eating chocolates and ices in a state of rapture, surrounded by the other G. & S. cats.

These cats, unless you've already seen them, you would really not believe are real. The chief thing about them is that though, presumably, they must live somewhere in the capital, you've never seen anything like them anywhere until this G. & S. celebration brings them all out of hiding. The thing is, although they're by no means all old-timers, there's not a single one of them that looks as if, in any way, he belonged to the present day. Their clothes aren't old-fashioned, exactly, but *home-made*. And though they're lively enough, to judge by their applause, they seem so completely neuter, I can only call it. They look very good, of course, but only because no one has ever told them that there's such a thing as bad.

In fact, come to think of it, they're rather like Dad: he fits in here, among this audience. When I glanced along the row, I saw his face shining and smiling just like theirs, and his hand beating time with his programme-souvenir, and his lips forming the words just underneath his breath—and sometimes above it, too, when it came to the ninth encore, or to the rousing choruses. And when the Captain sang that wonderful ditty with his crew, I knew my old Dad's greatest dream was to be up there beside him on that quarter-deck —yes, here and now my poor old battered parent was really having a tremendous ball.

Come the intermission, I asked my Dad for news of Mum and Vern. 'Your mother,' he said, 'keeps saying she wants to see you.'

'She knows my address,' I said.

'I think she's expecting you to call around at home.'

'I bet she is. Well, you tell Ma the GPO run an excellent service, and a post card will cost her 3d.'

'Don't be too hard on your Mum, son.'

'You say that!'

'Yes, son, me. I don't like your taking a liberty where your mother's concerned.'

'Liberties! She's been taking diabolical liberties with all of us for years!'

This little argument with Dad flared up quite suddenly and unexpectedly, as these often do, particularly among relatives, and I could see, of course, that poor old Dad could never admit to me Mum was a bitch without admitting all the mistakes that he himself had made, and sacrifice his dignity. It was also that Dad's very conventional, and comes the *father* sometimes, or tries hard to, and you can hardly let him down.

So there was a pause, and we looked round at the G. & S. cats, jabbering delightedly away.

'And Vern?' I said fairly soon.

'He's got himself a job.'

'No!'

'In a bakery: night work.'

'I give up eating bread from this day forward.'

Dad smiled, and the little film of ice was melted. 'And the tenants?' I asked him next.

'There have been changes,' Dad said carefully. 'The Maltese are out. She's got some Cypriots instead.'

'Mum's certainly loyal to the Commonwealth.'

This just got by, and Dad said, very decidedly, 'The Cypriots are gentlemen.' I asked him why, and he said, 'They don't despise you like the Maltese do. You can see, how they behave, they come from a people, not a tribe.'

I wanted to lead up to the question of Dad's health, but this was tricky, because no one is more secretive than my poppa, and also, how could I do it so that he wouldn't guess that I had anything to fear about him?'

'And how you been personally, Dad?' was all I could find to say.

'How I been?'

'Yes. I mean, how you been feeling in yourself?'

Dad stared at me. 'As usual,' he said, whatever that meant.

Actually, ever since Mum's disclosure, I was hatching a bit of a plot concerning Dad. It's like this. A year ago, when I was still quite a kid, I had food poisoning. That's what I had—but that's not what the doctors told me. What they *said* I had was almost everything *except* food poisoning. Believe me, I'm not making this up. When the local expert at the surgery threw in his hand, I went into hospital on the national health, where at least three of them probed me, gave me pills and injections, and discharged me as cured, exactly as before. For days I ran temperatures, and vomited almost hourly. I nearly went home again just then, back to my Mum and Dad, because I was beginning to get really scared.

Then I had an inspiration. Everybody knows that Harley street and thereabouts is where the best doctors ply their trade, and so I thought—why shouldn't they ply it now on me? I went up there one day, and decided that I'd choose the same street number as the day of the month it happened to be, and ring on the bell, and see what happened. The trouble was there turned out to be six bells—so I rang them all. If you don't believe this fable, please recall that I was drunk with fever, and just didn't care what happened: all I wanted was to reach somebody who *knew*. Well, the six bells were all answered by the same person: i.e., a sort of nurse-secretary (I'd say nurse as far up as the bosom, and secretary above that), and I didn't have to choose which of the six medicos, because I collapsed in the marble hallway, and Dr A. R. Franklyn chose me.

This was the medical cat who cured me. When I came round, vomiting again, and got him into focus, I saw a tall, serious young-looking man who asked me to tell him all about it, which I did. He gave me an hour's examination, and then said, 'Well, I don't know what's the matter with you, but we must find out.' I can't tell you how much these words of Dr F.'s impressed me. Because all the other Emergency-Ward-10 numbers had assured me they knew *exactly* what the matter was (though they were very vague about the details of it), but Dr A. R. Franklyn of Harley street said he didn't know—and got an ambulance and whipped me inside one of those eighty-guinea-a-week clinics where they pierce your ear-lobes, or change your sex for you, for three-figure fees—all without any mention of who was eventually going to pay what.

To cut a long whatsit short, with two days of poking things into every gap I owned, he found there was an abscess, and pierced it, and down went the temperature, and that was that, except that I had to stay on another week inside the hospital, which I didn't really enjoy exactly, on account of the nurses. I know nurses are wonderful and everything, and the whole dam community would collapse without them, but they're bossy. They know every man remembers that, way back in time, when he was an infant, he was bossed about by women, and when they get you on that rubber mattress, between those sheets starched like cardboard, and never enough blankets, they work on those babyhood memories, and try to make you feel you're back again in that cosy little cot where females used to rock you, and push bottles at you, and take every kind of liberty. But I got by. And every day Dr A. R. Franklyn would call in to say, 'Hi!', and he always treated me, in front of those stacks of nurses, as if I was a cabinet minister or someone—I mean, he was so wonderfully *polite*. Considering who he was, and me, I really think he had the nicest manners I have ever seen in anyone, and I shan't forget it.

But the day they turned me loose, he didn't show up at all, and so I didn't have a chance to thank him, or to raise the tricky question of how all this medical luxury was going to be paid for. I wrote him, of course, but though he answered very nicely, he didn't refer at all to the financial aspect. So I did this. While I was in the place, I'd whiled away many a weary moment with my Rolleiflex, and some of the snaps I took of everyone were really rather intimate and funny, so I picked out the best, and made enlargements, and put them in an album, and dropped it in at Harley street, and he wrote back and said, if ever I fell into his clutches again, which he sincerely hoped I wouldn't, he'd make sure my Rolleiflex was confiscated first.

You must see by now what was in my mind: it was somehow to get Dr F. to see my Dad without Dad exactly knowing why.

By this time, of course, we were back in the auditorium, but in the second half of *H.M.S. Pinafore* the marvellous magic of the first half gets lost somehow . . . I dare say old G. & S. were in a bit of a hurry, or felt the whole thing was becoming something of a drag—anyway, the plot of the musical doesn't thicken, but evaporates. We both knew, of course, that there'd be this bit of an anti-climax, but it was a disappointment all the same, and we came out into the night air together feeling a little bit lost and cheated.

'Well, there you go,' I said.

'Have a wet with me?' said Dad.

'Excuse me, no, Dad, I have to pound around a bit tonight . . .'

'Oh. See me to my bus, then?'

'Sure.'

I took his arm, and he said, 'How's your work? You've not been using your darkroom much of late, I've noticed . . .'

I expect even Dad was beginning to guess what must have been obvious to anyone, namely, that having a darkroom at Ma's Rowton House was only an excuse to keep in touch with him . . . well, yes, and I suppose in a way her, too . . . because up in my shack at Napoli, there were dozens of places I could develop in, and as for darkrooms, the electric fused or packed in at the meters with such monotonous regularity there'd be no lack of rooms dark enough to operate in for hours.

'That trip!' I said to Dad, to take his thoughts away. 'That ship trip up the river. Don't forget, you promised we'd do it this year for my birthday—all the way up to . . . where did you say it was?'

'Reading.'

'There you go! Well, that's a date, then? You'll book the tickets?'

Dad said yes, he would, of course, and I hoisted him on his number something bus, and waved him out of sight, and stepping back on to the pavement, was nearly crunched by a Lagonda.

'Careful, teenager,' cried the driver, and he pulled up sharply at a red.

I get so tired of characters in motor vehicles behaving like duchesses, when usually the car's not even their own, but part-paid on the never-never, or borrowed from the firm without the board of management's permission, and all they really are is human animals travelling much too fast with their arses suspended six inches above the asphalt—that I stepped round smartly to give this Stirling Moss a bawling out, and saw it was the advertising monarch, Vendice Partners.

'Oh, hullo, trade wind,' I said to him. 'Where did you blow in from?'

'Come and have a drink?' the Partners person asked me, opening his noiseless, squeakless door.

I held my hand on it. 'You haven't apologized,' I said, 'for trying to take my life.'

'Jump in. We're very sorry.'

'Come along, the lights are changing,' said the cat sitting by his side.

I thought quick, oh well, my Vespa will look after itself, and perhaps this V. Partners will be of use to me over my photographic exhibition, so I climbed in the rear seat, with a fine view of their stiff white collars and Turkish-bathed necks and un-hip Jermyn street hair-does, and Vendice half turned and said. 'This is Amberley Drove.'

'Don't *turn* like that, Vendice!' I cried. 'How do you do, Mr Drove.'

'You're nervous?' the Partners number said.

'Always, when I'm not driving.'

'Then you must be nervous very often,' said my fellow passenger, in a great big booming 'friendly' voice, and treating me to a doglike grin. 'The London track,' he continued, 'is becoming a real menace.'

'Some day, it'll just seize up,' I told him. 'It'll just get stuck, and everyone will have to walk home.'

'I can see you're an optimist,' he said.

'You bet,' I told him.

As you can see, I wasn't hitting it off with this Amberley Drove creation. I could see he was marked down by fate as one of those English products such as you'd make a circuit of five miles to keep away from, not because he's dangerous at all, really, but because these hefty rugger-bugger types are so dam *boyish*, and beneath their thick heads and thin skins, such bullies, longing, I expect, for the happy days in the past when they could bash the heads of juniors at their academy, or the future ones when they hope to bash someone else's in some colony, provided they're too small and powerless to hit back.

'Amberley,' said Mr P., 'is much concerned with questions of the moment. He's a leader-writer.'

'Is that so,' I said. 'I've always wondered what they looked like. It doesn't trouble you,' I asked the Drove one, 'that no one ever reads that stuff of yours?'

'Ah, but they do.'

'Who do?'

'Members of parliament... foreign newspapers... City people...'

'But anybody *real*?'

Vendice laughed. 'You know, Amberley,' he said, 'I believe the young man's got something.'

The Drove let out a laugh that would chill your bones, and said, 'The leader columns are angled at the more intelligent portions of the population—few though they may be.'

'You mean I'm a dope,' I said.

'I mean you talk like one.'

We'd pulled up outside one of those buildings down by Pall Mall that looked like abandoned Salvation Army hostels, and Amberley Drove got out, and carried on quite a long conversation through the car door with Vendice that was evidently way up above my head, then said to me, 'I tremble to think, young man, that our country's future's in hands like yours,' didn't wait for an answer (there wasn't going to be one, anyway), and leapt up the steps, three or more at a time, and disappeared into his clubman's emporium.

I climbed over the back seat beside Vendice. 'He's too young to act like that,' I said. 'He should wait till he's a bit more senile.'

Vendice smiled, did some fancy stuff among the traffic, and said to me, 'I thought you'd like him.'

I wanted to broach this photographic topic, but the fact was, I found V. Partners rather paralysing. He was so cool, and polite, and sarcastic, and gave you the impression, so much, that he just didn't believe in a dam thing—not *any*thing—so all I could find to say to him, after a while, was, 'Tell me, Mr Partners, what is advertising *for*? I mean, what *use* is it?'

'That,' he replied immediately, 'is the one question we must never pause to answer.'

We'd now stopped outside a classified building in the Mayfair area, and he said to me, 'I've got some papers to pick up. Would you care to look inside?'

I can only describe the atmosphere of the joint by telling you it was like a very expensive tomb. Of course, all the staff had left, and the lights were dim where they ought not to be, which made it all a bit sepulchral, but it did look, as a tomb does, or a monument, like something made very big by people who want to prove something that they don't believe in, but desperately need to. Vendice's office was on the second floor, all done in white and gold and mauve. The papers were laid out on the table in coloured folders with perspex covers, and I asked him what their contents were all about.

'About Christmas,' he told me.

'I don't dig.'

He held up one of the folders. 'This about a product,' he said, 'that will be flooding the stores, we hope, at Yuletide.'

'But this is July.'

'We must plan ahead, must we not.'

I admit I shuddered. Not at the notion of his cashing in on Xmas, particularly, because everyone does that, but at the whole idea of the festive season, which comes up like an annual nightmare. The thing that's always struck me about Merry Xmas is that it's the one day of the year when you mustn't drop in on your friends, because everyone's locked tight inside his private fortress. You can smell it already when the leaves are getting golden, then those trashy cards begin arriving which everyone collects like trophies, to show how many pals they've got, and the horror of it mounts right up to that moment, round about 3 p.m. on the sacred afternoon, when the Queen addresses the obedient nation. This is the day of peace on earth and goodwill among men, when no one in the kingdom thinks of anyone outside it, let alone the cats next door, and everyone is dreaming cosily of himself, and reaching for his Alka-Seltzer. For two or three days, it's true, the English race all use the streets, where they never dare to loiter for the rest of the long year, because then streets are things that we must hurry through, not *stand* in, students sing ghastly carols in railway stations and shake collecting boxes at the peasants to prove the whole thing's charitable and authorized, not bohemian, and when it's all over, people behave as if a disaster had just overtaken the entire nation—I mean, they're dazed, and blink as if they'd been entombed for days, and are awaking up to life again.

'You look thoughtful,' the Partners number said.

'I am! I mean, the idea of planning for all that in mid-July. I'm really sorry for you.'

'Thank you,' he told me.

Then I took a swift grip of myself, and, sitting down firmly on a sprung white leather sofa, so that he couldn't throw me out before I'd ended, I told him of my plan for the exhibition, and asked what he could do about it to help. He didn't laugh, which was certainly something, and said, 'I've not seen any of your photographs, I believe.'

'Dido's got some . . .'

'Oh—those. Yes. But have you anything more exhibitable?'

I whipped out a folder from my inside breast, which I'd been carrying these days for emergencies like this, and handed it over to him. He looked at them carefully against the light, and said, 'They're not commercial.'

'Of course not!' I cried. 'That's the whole point about them.'

'They'd need presentation,' he continued. 'But they're very good.'

He put them down, looked at me with his 'amused' smile (I could have smacked him), and said, 'I'm a very busy man. Why should I do anything for you?'

I got up. 'The only possible reason,' I said, looking him as coolly in the eye as I was able, 'would be because you want to.'

'It's a very good one,' he said. 'I'll do it.'

I shook his hand. 'You're a nice cat,' I said.

'There, I'm afraid,' he told me, 'you're really very much mistaken. Shall we have a drink?'

He went slowly to a mirrored chest. 'Tonic for me,' I said, 'and thank you.'

I turned down V. Partners' offer of a meal, because I've always found that, whenever someone's done you an unexpected favour (I mean, as unexpected to them as it has been to yourself), it's best to keep right out of their way for just a moment, so that their promise can bite into their consciences a bit, otherwise they're apt just to talk the thing away to death immediately. So I said good-bye to him for now, and headed it out of the deserted Mayfair area, because I wanted to look in at a jazz club, for purposes best known.

You'll have dug, of course, that the Dubious, which I referred to earlier, is not a jazz club. It's a drinking club where some of the jazz community foregather, but a jazz club is a much bigger place where fans go to dance and listen, and not drink at all, except for softs and coffees. The one I was calling at is the Dickie Hodfodder Club, which consists of an enormous basement, a flight of concrete steps leading down thereto, a commissionaire, who does nothing, a ticket vendor who sells tickets, the aforesaid soft and coffee bars, several hundred fans of either sex and, of course, the Dickie Hodfodder ork, led by Richard H. in person, playing away merrily a sort of not very tidal mainstream and, alternating with them, on certain evenings, a group called Cuthberto Watkyns and Haitian Obeah, of which the less said (and heard) the kinder. My object in going was therefore not artistic, but because I thought I might catch a character called Ron Todd.

This Ron Todd is a Marxist, and closely connected with the ballad-and-blues movement, which seeks to prove that all folk music is an art of protest, which, fair enough, and also—or, at any rate, Ron Todd seeks to—that this art is somehow latched on to the achievements of the USSR, i.e., Mississippi jail songs are in praise of sputniks. Ron has some powerful contacts on the building sites, and what I wanted to ask him was if we could somehow arrange to hoist the ex-Deb and the Hoplite and my own good self and camera, up on top of one of those mammoth cranes along the south bank, and take some snapshots of the scene. Why I thought I might find him in the Hodfodder place was that I knew he admired the male vocalist in the Cuthberto Watkyns ensemble, who had some songs in dialect French about the resistance movement to Napoleon, I think it was, of the last King of the Zombies, which Ron wanted to have him perform at a ballad-and-blues festival he was MC-ing in the ice-rink up there on Denmark Hill.

But, as a matter of fact, when I got down into the sub-soil, the first person who accosted me wasn't Ron, but the last one I expected, which was Big Jill. She was wearing her suedette jeans and a woollen cap with a long hanging bobble, and was sitting at a table with some empty Pepsis, looking miserable. But when she called me over, her voice sounded loud and clear above the Hodfodder combo.

'Alone, Jill?' I said. 'All the young starlets too busy to keep you company a while?'

'Sit down, stud,' she said, 'and feast your eyes upon a vision.'

'Where?' I asked, thinking she could hardly mean the personnel of the R. Hodfodder band, though she was staring intently in their direction. 'In just a moment now,' she said.

So I stared too, over the hundred heads of the kids whipping it up in the small central space for dancing, or standing around, all in their sharpest garments, the boys tapping a knowledgeable toe or rocking slightly, the chicks looking a bit restless, eyes wandering, because, say what you like, the birds don't go much to the clubs to *listen*. When after a bit of nonsense on the drums, R. Hodfodder gripped the mike, and told us his vocalist, Athene Duncannon, would now be with us.

Big Jill rose four inches off her seat and gripped a Pepsi bottle.

Miss A. Duncannon was quite okay, and the kids certainly enjoyed her, but I must say I do think it's a mistake for young white English girls to try to give an exact imitation of Lady Day, since the best possible imitation that's conceivable would come about two million miles from what Billie H., at her best, can do to you, which is turn you completely over, so that you can't bear to hear any other singers, at any rate for an hour or so after. However, from Big Jill's point of view, I could quite see the situation, because this Athene D. was a highly flexible creation, who wore her dress tighter than her skin beneath it, and glared at the assembly in that imitation-woman manner that's getting to be fashionable among white US female vocalists, if you can judge from the poses on the LP sleeves.

'Oh!' cried Big Jill.

'Where have you been hiding yourself?' said a voice.

This was Ron Todd, who'd come up and stood by the table, looking scruffy and disapproving, in the correct ballad-and-blues manner, and who also was one of those people who believe that, if they haven't seen you for a while, then you must certainly have been out of town, or died, because they see *everyone*.

'Yes, long time no see,' I said to him. 'Come over here, I want to talk to you.'

But when I got him in a fairly vacant corner, and started my spiel about the mammoth crane, I could see he wasn't listening, but glaring across above the innocent and cheery faces of the Hodfodder fans at a number who was coming down the steps, wearing some very fancy schmutter: mauve, button-two tuxedo, laced shirt, varnished pumps with bows, and, on his arm, a nameless dame.

'That's Seth Samaritan!' cried Ron.

This was more or less how K. Marx himself might speak of the head of the Shell Oil company (if there is one), because S. Samaritan is the number-one villain of Ron's picture-book—and not only of Ron's—the reason being, that he was the first to see, a few years back, that jazz music, which used to be for kids and kicks, had money in it, and opened clubs and signed up bands, and brought in talent from afar, and turned it all into minks and Jags and a modest little home at Teddington. I tried to get Ron back on top of that south bank crane again, but it was heavy labour.

'I'd like to put him in!' cried Ron, waggling his briefcase because, like a lot of musical cats this summer, he had a thing of carrying one without a handle, but a zip complete with lock and key.

'Take it easy, Ronald. Put it all in a song.'

He stared at me. 'You've got an idea, there, you know,' he said. 'What rhymes with pieces of silver?'

I racked my brains, but had to admit I couldn't help him.

'This place is bad enough,' Ron said, waving his briefcase round the musical establishment, 'but just imagine it if Seth Samaritan moves in.'

'You're right,' I said.

Ron glared at me behind his Gilbert Harding lenses. 'You say so,' he cried, 'but do you mean it?'

'Well, yes, I do. I mean you're *right*.'

'I am?'

'Well, yes, you are. I mean there's *source* music, isn't there, and period music, that feeds on it, and just comes and goes.'

'That's it!'

'In England, most of what you hear is period. Not much source.'

'There you go!'

'And that applies as much to you ballad-and-blues puritans as it does to the jazz cats.'

This didn't go down quite so well. 'Our art's authentic,' Ron Todd said.

'It was,' I told him. 'But you don't think up enough songs of your own. Songs about the scene, I mean, about us and now. Most of your stuff is ancient English, or modern American, or weirdie minority songs from pokey corners. But what about *our* little fable? You're not really trying—any more than Dickie Hodfodder is.'

'What a comparison!' cried Ron, in high disgust.

But I saw I was breaking one of my golden rules, which is not to argue with Marxist kiddies, because they *know*. And not only do they know, they're not *responsible*—which is the exact opposite of what they think they are. I mean, this is their thing, if I dig it correctly. You're *in* history, yes, because you're budding here and now, but you're *outside* it, also, because you're living in the Marxist future. And so, when you look around, and see a hundred horrors, and not only musical, you're not responsible for them, because you're beyond them already, in the kingdom of K. Marx. But for me, I must say, all the horrors I see around me, especially the English ones, I feel responsible for, the lot, just as much as for the few nice things I dig.

But, as I thought this, my eyes had strayed away from Ron, a foot or two to that commissionaire I spoke of, who, not being interested, I suppose, in the performance, was reading an evening paper, I don't blame him, and I caught a headline. I just said, 'Excuse me,' and took the paper from him, and looked at a photograph of Suze and Henley, and ran up the steps into the street. Quite honestly, I don't know quite what happened then, because my next quite clear recollection was batting along a highway on my Vespa, which went on for miles and miles, I don't know where, until the petrol ran out, it stopped, and I was nowhere.

So I got off the vehicle, which I cared about no longer, and sat down on the verge, and watched the car lights flash by occasionally. I thought of an accident—yes, I did—but not for long, because I wasn't going to be rubbed out by a gin-soaked motorist returning to his bed out in the suburbs, and I thought of leaving the country, or dragging some chick or other to the registry and getting wed myself

—I thought, in fact, of anything but Suze, because that would be just too horribly painful at the moment, though it was really an agony not to do so—I mean not think of her—in fact practically impossible: because even when I *didn't* think of her, I felt the ache of that I wasn't—really a torture. And at that point, the verge I was sitting on turned out not to be a verge, but a pile of metals for the roadway, and the bloody thing collapsed and I slid down in a cascade on to the Vespa, overturning it.

A car pulled up, ten feet away, and a voice inside it said, 'Are you all right?'

'No!' I yelled back.

'You hurt?'

'Yes!' I cried out.

There was a bang and a thump and some feet came along, but I couldn't see the face above them in the glare, and the cat the feet belonged to asked me, 'You been drinking?'

'I never drink.'

'Oh.' The cat came nearer. 'Then what's the matter?'

At that, I let out a hysteric shout, and shrieked with laughter like a maniac. 'You *have* been drinking,' said the cat, disapprovingly.

'Well, so have you,' I said.

'As a matter of fact, you're right, I have.'

The cat lifted up my Vespa, shook it and said. 'You've run out of juice, that's what's your trouble. No juice left in this toy.'

'I've run out of juice all right.'

'Well then, it's simple. I'll siphon you some out.'

'You will?' I said, getting interested at last.

'I've said I will.'

He pushed my Vespa up by the car's arse, and rummaged in the boot, and fished out a tube and handed it to me. 'You'd better do it,' the cat said. 'I've swallowed enough strong liquor for this evening.'

So I sucked away, and spat out several mouthfuls, and the dam thing actually worked, exactly as advertised, and we listened to it gurgling into the Vespa.

'Something's just struck me,' said the cat.

'It has?'

'I've only got a gallon or so left myself. We don't want to have to siphon it all back again, do we.'

'No,' I said, making a swift bend in the tube.

'I guess you've got enough to take you back to civilization.'

'Thanks. Where *is* civilization?' I asked.

'You don't know where you are?'

'Not an idea.'

The cat made *tst-tst* noises. 'You really should lay off the stuff,' he said. 'Just turn about, follow the cats'-eyes half a mile, and then you're on the main road into London. I suppose you want London?'

I handed back the tube. 'I want the whole dam city,' I said, 'and everything contained there.'

'You're very welcome to it,' said this benefactor. 'I'm from Aylesbury, myself.'

So we shook hands, and patted each other's backs, and I saw him off, then got on my Vespa and turned back. I reached a garage before long, and got a proper fill, and had a cuppa at a drivers' all-night caff, and resumed my journey into the capital, like R. Whittington. And as I sped along, I said to myself, 'Well—goodbye happy youth: from now on I'm going to be a tough, tough nut, and if she thinks she can hurt me, she's bloody well mistaken, and as for the exhibition, I'll go ahead with it just the same, and make some loot and catch her when she falls, as she will, you bet, and then we'll see.'

I soon hit familiar sections, and found myself heading down to Pimlico because—I have to admit it—I wanted some miracle to happen and that squalid old Mum of mine to grasp what had happened to her second-born, and maybe suggest something, or even do something, or, at any rate, *say* something about it all. I reached the area, and went down the street in low, and sure enough, the lights were gleaming in her basement, so I parked the Vespa, and stepped carefully down, and took a glimpse through the window where, as you might have expected, I could see her drinking something or other with a lodger. Dad may have been right about the Cypriots, but it looked to be the same old beefo Malt to me, and honestly, though I wanted to chat Ma—I mean, in a way, I even felt I owed it to *her* to give her this opportunity—I just couldn't face opening the whole theme up with the Malt there in attendance, even though, no doubt, she'd have got rid of him, so I went up the area steps again, and headed home to see if Big Jill was back now by any chance.

Big Jill was not—at least, there was no light on—but someone else was there: guess who! It was Edward the Ted, none other, carrying a parcel, and coming out of the front door (which, as I've said, is always open) just at the moment I came in. He backed away at first until he saw that it was me, then said, 'I gotta see yer,' so I invited the goon to come up into the attic and have a natter.

I turned on the subdued lighting, of which I'm rather proud (because a theatrical kid I know, who scene-shifts at the Lane, created it all for me for ten pounds, plus the costs), and I poured the brave, bad Ed a glass of lager-and-lime, that I keep there for such visitors, and turned on C. Parker low, and took a look at him. He was wearing his summer uniform—i.e., slept-in jeans, four-inch prowlers, tiger vest and blue zip jacket (collar, of course, turned *up*—he must use whalebone), with lawn-mower hair-do and a built-in scowl. But something about Ed-Ted put me on my guard: he wasn't as beat about as he used to be, the snarl was a bit more real, and the shoulders hunched with a bit more power in them.

'Fuss ov all,' said Ted, 'abaht vese platters.'

'What platters?'

'Vese there.'

He pointed at the parcel. The soil in his nails must have been inlaid.

'What are they?'

'I wanter flog thm.'

'Let's have a look.'

Much to my surprise, they were an exceedingly hip collection.

'I didn't know you had such taste,' I said to Edward. 'In fact, I didn't know you had any taste at all.'

'Eh?' he said.

'They're knocked off, I suppose.'

A crafty grin cracked over the monster's countenance. 'Nachly,' he said.

'And what are you asking?'

'You name a figger.'

'I said, "What are you asking?"'

'Ten.'

'S.P. too high. I'll give you four.'

'Errrr!'

'Keep them then, sonny.'

'Ten, I sed.'

I shook my head. 'Well, that was fuss ov all,' I reminded him. 'What was second?'

Now Ed looked very sure of himself indeed, and said, 'Flikker sent me.'

'Did he. Who's Flikker?'

'You dunno?'

'That's why I asked you.'

Edward looked very contemptuous. 'If yer liv up ear,' he said, 'and don no oo Flikker is, yer don no nuffin.'

'Yeah. Who is he?'

'E eads me mob.'

'I thought you'd done with mobs. And they'd done with you. How did you work your passage back?'

'I don work.'

'How'd you join the mob?'

'They arst me.'

'On bended knee, did they? I wonder why?'

Ed stretched, then took from his zip jacket a small chopper, such as the butcher trims the cutlets with, unwrapped a bit of rag from off its blade, rubbed it, and said, 'I did a job.'

'You'll do a stretch, as well.'

'Not me. Ver push giv me cuvver.'

I got up, went over, held out my hand, and looked at Ed. He slapped the chopper down, blade sideways, quite hard, on my palm. When he saw I was taking it, he tried to snatch it back.

'I'll just put it there,' I said, laying it on the floor. 'I don't like to talk during meal times.'

Ed kept some eyes on the weapon, some on me. 'Well, vis is it,' he said. 'Flikker wonts ter see yer.'

'Tell him to call round.'

'Yer don *tell* Flikker.'

'*You* don't, I'm sure. Listen, Ed-Ted. If anyone wants to see me, I'm available. But I'm not being summoned by anyone except the magistrate.'

Edward arose, picked up his chopper, dangled it, returned it to his grease-gleaming jacket, and said to me, 'Orl rite. Okay. I'll tell im. An this stuff ear?'

'I'll give you four.'

'Ten's wot I sed.'

'And I sed four.'

As a matter of fact, I was getting anxious about this visit and also, I don't mind telling you, a bit scared. Because you can be as brave as a lion, which I don't pretend to be, but if fourteen of these hyenas set on you, at night, in an empty street (as they always do, and that's always about the number), believe me, there's absolutely nothing you can do, except book a bed in the general hospital. So best is, keep out of their way if you possibly can, which is fairly easy, provided you don't provoke them (or they pick on you), because if there *is* an incident, I can tell you from experience—I mean, I've seen it often enough—*no* one will help you, not even the law, unless they're quite a number too, which generally, in an area such as this, they aren't, except for traffic duty.

'I'll give you five,' I said, which was my big mistake.

'Ten.'

'Forget it, then.'

'I won't . . .' said Ed. 'Yer'll be earing frm me agen, an ver lads, and Flikker . . . An so wul vat feller e wonts aht ov it . . .'

'Who wants who out?'

'Flikker wants Cool aht ov ear.'

'Why?'

'E don av ter say why. E jus wonts im aht ov ear, an aht ov ver ole sexter. An *you've* got ter tell im, tell Cool, an see e blows.'

I stared at this English product. 'Ed,' I said, 'you can go and piss up your leg.'

Strangely enough, he smiled, if you can call that thing a smile. 'Orl rite,' he said, 'I'll take five.'

And now I made my second big mistake, which was to go over to the cabin trunk where I keep a few odd valuables, and unlock the thing, and get out a bit of loot I had there, and next thing Ed's hands were there inside it, and when I grabbed at them he pulled back and hit me on the neck, twice, quick, with his hand held on the side.

Now, I hate fighting. I mean, I'm not a coward—honestly, I don't think so—but I just hate that silly mess which, apart from the risk of getting hurt yourself, may mean you damage someone else you don't care a fuck about, and land up in the nick for wounding. So I avoid it, if I can. But on the other hand, if I'm in it, I believe quite firmly in fighting dirty—no Gentleman Jim for me—because the only object I can see in fighting, if you've got to, is to win as quickly as you can, then change the subject.

So though in great pain, my first act, while Ed was still jabbing at my neck, was to grab his jacket by both hands so that he couldn't get his paws back on the chopper, and my next was to struggle up, while he was still bashing at my face, and jump on his feet with all my nine-stone-something, and then kick him hard as I could on both his shins, just as I felt some teeth rattling and blood flowing in my eyes. He bent down, he had to, and I let go his jacket, and grabbed the lime bottle, and cracked it on Edward's skull as heavy as I knew how, and he wobbled and melted and fell over, where I kicked him in the stomach, just to make perfectly sure.

'You wasted mess of a treacherous bastard!' I exclaimed.

Ed lay there moaning. I got out his chopper, staggered over to the window, and flung it into the Napoli night, then turned up C. Parker, on account of the neighbours hearing what they shouldn't and wiped some of the blood off with a sheet, and the door opened, and there was Mr Cool.

'Hi,' Cool said. 'I heard some turmoil.'

I pointed at Ed-Ted. 'That's it,' I said.

Cool walked across and looked at him. 'Oh, that one,' he said. 'Excuse me not arriving earlier.'

'Better late than never,' I said. 'You can help me dispose of the body.'

Cool looked me over. 'You'd better go in the bathroom,' he said. 'I'll see him off.' And he took hold of the neck of Edward's jacket with two long, lean, very solid hands, and started dragging him across the floor, and out the door, and I could hear them bumping down the stairway like the removal men shifting the grand piano for you.

In the bathroom, I put myself together, and found all was well, except that I felt terrible, and I went back to my room, and took the top record from Ed's packet out of its sleeve, and put it on, and it was the MJQ playing *Concorde*, very smooth and comforting.

Cool re-appeared, nodded at the music, said, 'Nice,' and asked if he could wash, and I went with him in the bathroom. 'Where'd you stow Ed?' I asked.

'In the area. Next door. Behind the dustbins.'

'I do hope he's not dead, or dying.'

'I don't think so,' said Cool, drying his long hands. 'He'll die another day,' and he gave me a not very pleasant smile. As we went back in the room, I told him what Ed had been on about during his kindly visit.

'Wilf told me the same,' he said, '—my brother.'

'He's with that lot?'

'He'd like to be, but they won't have him, on account of me.'

'And this Flikker,' I asked Cool. 'You know him?'

'I know his appearance . . .'

'Tough number, is he?'

'Well, there's four hundred teenagers, they say, up here, who he can beckon.'

'*Four hundred?* Don't kid me, Cool.'

'Believe me. Four hundred or so.'

'And *teenagers*?'

'Well, Teds, semi-Teds . . . you know . . . local hooligans . . .'

I wish you could hear the spite Cool put into that last word! 'Well, what you think about all this?' I asked him.

Cool lit a fag. 'Something's happening,' he said.

'You mean now?'

'Something's cooking . . . Excuse me, but you wouldn't notice, son, not being coloured . . .'

'Well, tell me: what?' Because shit! I didn't want to believe this whole thing at all.

'For instance: they've taken to running us down with cars. And motor-bikes.'

'Accidents. Drunks. You *sure*?'

'It's happened so often. It's deliberate. You have to skip fast when you see them coming.'

'What else, Cool?'

'Well, there's this one. They stop you and ask you for cigarettes. If you offer them, they take the whole pack, and grin. If you don't, they take a smack at you, and run.'

'"They." How many "they"?'

'Little groups . . .'

'This thing has happened to you?'

'Yes. Also this. Few days ago, down by the tube station, they stopped me and said, "Which side you want your hair parted?"'

'And you said what?'

'Nothing.'

'You were alone?'

'Two of us. Eight or nine of them.'

'What then?'

'They said, "We hate you".'

'You answered?'

'No. Then they said, "Get back to your own country".'

'But this *is* your country, Cool.'

'You think so?'

'By Christ, I do! I tell you, man, yes, I bloody well do, it *is*!'

'That's what I told them.'

'So you answered?'

'When they said that, I did, yes.'

'What happened then?'

'They said I was a mongrel. So my friend said, "When your mother wants a good f--k, she doesn't bother about your father—she comes to me."'

'How'd they like that?'

'I don't know. Because when he said that, my friend also pulled his flick on them, and told them to come on.'

'And they did?'

'No, they didn't. But that time, they were only eight or nine.'

A look had come into Cool's eyes, as he stared at me, just like the look he must have given those Teds. 'Don't glare at me like that man,' I cried. 'I'm on your side.'

'You are?'

'Yes.'

'That's nice of you,' said Cool, but I saw he didn't mean it, or believe me.

I turned off the MJQ. 'So what's going to happen next?' I asked him.

'I don't know, boy. I wish I could tell you, but I can't. All I *do* know, is this. Up till now, it's been white Teds against whites, all their baby gangs. If they start on coloured, there's only a few thousand of us in this area, but I don't think you'll see there's many cowards.'

I couldn't take all this nightmare. I cried out, 'Cool, this is London, not some hick city in the provinces! This is London, man, a capital, a great big city where every kind of race has lived ever since the Romans!'

Cool said, 'Oh, yeah. I believe you.'

'They'd never allow it!' I exclaimed.

'Who wouldn't?'

'The adults! The men! The women! All the authorities! Law and order is the one great English thing!'

Here Cool made no reply. I took his shoulder. 'And Cool,' I said. 'You—you're one of us. You're not a Spade, exactly . . .'

He took off my hand. 'If it comes to any trouble,' he said, 'I am. And the reason I am is that they've never questioned me, never refused me, always accepted me—you understand? Even though I am part white? But *your* people . . . No. The part of me that belongs to you, belongs to them.'

And after he said that, he went out.

So what with all this, I spent an evil night: sometimes waking with pains and itches, and the red-purple glow hanging in the sky outside the window, sometimes dreaming those dreams you can't remember, except they're horrible, sometimes lying thinking, and not sure if it was me or someone else . . . But when I did wake, round about mid-day, I knew there were two things, anyway, that I must do: number one, call Dr A. R. Franklyn, on the pretext of tending my wounds, but actually to fix that rendezvous with Dad, and number two, to track down Wiz: because about all that Cool had told me, the only person who would really know—and who could match his danger, if he wanted to, with Flikker or anybody else—was Wizard. Also, I wanted to see the boy again.

When I went out, to rent a call-box, the sun was busy at it, and the day was calm. But whether it was what I'd heard, or just that I was weary, there did seem a *silence* in the air; together with a sort of *movement*: I mean, as if the air was shifting not by the wind, but by itself, to and fro, then pausing. On the steps, after a while to take this in and wonder, I called down to Jill a moment to ask if she knew Wiz's number, then checked in the area next door to see if Ed was there (he wasn't), and set off up the street to where the phones are. The glass of one box, which lord knows, is tough as iron, had been splintered in most squares of it, and in the other, the mouth-and-ear thing had been ripped out at the roots. So I went back in the cracked one, and dialled Harley street.

I got the secretary-nurse, who said she remembered me, and how was I, and that Dr F. was on his holidays, down there in Roma, at a congress, but back in a week, she thought, and would I call again? Meanwhile, was there anything? My head seemed just a chemist's job to me, so I said no, best regards to the doctor, and best to her, and thank you, I'd try another time. Then I got on the line to Wiz.

Now, as a matter of fact, I was a bit anxious about this call. In the first place, would Wiz like it? And in the second . . . well, I'd never exactly belled anyone in that kind of business before, and who would I get first on the line? The boy? The girl? The maid? One of the clients? So as *bzm-bzm* went the bell, I practised my possible openings. But I needn't have bothered, it was Wiz, he said Big Jill had told him I'd be calling, and when was I coming round? He gave me the address, and said to hit the bell marked 'Canine Perfectionist' up on top. So I buzzed off down there at once, and did that.

Another surprise was that, in addition to Wiz himself, there was Wiz's woman, who somehow I expected would be out of sight—I mean not receiving me so socially, like someone's auntie. She looked very young to me, and, as they say, 'respectable', in fact, if I'd seen her at the local whist drive (supposing I'd been there), I doubt if I'd have rumbled anything. The only point was, she had a way of *looking* at you as if you were a possibly valuable product—I mean a cake of soap, or leg of chicken, or something of that description. I suppose, too, I'd half expected to find all sorts of orgies going on—judges and bishops having a ball on voluptuous divans—but in fact the whole set-up was very ordinary—even a little prim and dainty or, as Ron Todd would say, boogewah.

While Wiz's woman was getting us a cuppa, and some Viennese gattos, I told him of Ed and Cool and Flikker and the whole scene up in Napoli. 'There seems to be something *wrong* up there,' I said.

'An what you want *me* to do?' Wiz said, not very nicely.

'I don't know, Wiz. Maybe come up and have a look.'

'Why, kiddo? In this profession, you mustn't get mixed in anything except you must.'

'No, I suppose not.'

'What you worrying about, anyway, boy? You're not a colour problem . . .'

I saw I wasn't getting my thing across to Wiz at all. There he sat, curled like a cheetah, dressed up in casuals that cost far more than usuals, smiling and smirking and fucking pleased with himself, I dare say.

'It's just, Wiz,' I said, trying a final bash, 'that I thought what I told you would disgust you, too.'

'Well,' he said, 'as a matter of fact, it does. It does, boy, it does—all these *mugs*' activities disgust me: hitting without warning, for example! The *games* people play!'

I apologized for that, and wanted to say he'd played a few, and still was, if it came to that, but you have to remember, with the Wizard, that the kid, somewhere there inside, is so very *young*. Really, in many ways, he's just a short-pant product.

He'd got up, to play some music that he'd captured on his tape-recorder. 'I know this Flikker kid,' he said, pressing button A, or B.

'Oh? Come on then, Wizard. Tell.'

He did. The Wiz, it turned out, and Flikker, were both old boys of an ecclesiastical baby-farm in Wandsworth, down by the common there—which was news to me about the Wizard, as well as about the Ted. According to Wiz, the infant Flikker had been noted for his meek and mild behaviour, and much scorned for such by the other young lost-property toughies, until the day came when, at the age of eleven, he'd drowned a junior in the Wandle river, by launching the nipper in an oil drum and dropping rocks in it till it submerged. Henceforth, the other kittens at the lost cats' home kept Flikker somewhat at a distance, which, according to Wiz's memory, surprised and pained young Flikker, who, it seemed, had no notion whatever he's done something out of the ordinary at all. Wiz told the tale as I've just done, for giggles, but even he didn't seem to think it all that laughable, I could see.

And then? I asked. Then, said the Wiz, the child had been sent away to all the delinquent cages that they have for the various age-groups, working his way upward year by year, until now, at the age of seventeen or so, he was as highly trained in anti-social conduct as any kiddo in the kingdom, and the law were only waiting for his next major operation to put him away for a really adult stretch. Heaven help, said, Wiz, the screws wherever they sent him to, because unless they beat him up and turned him mad, which they probably would do, the kid would certainly do one of them, the trouble being, so it seemed, that the boy wasn't so much exactly bad, as having no grasp at all of what being bad really *meant*. Meantime, his chief exploit, since his last home leave from the ministry, had been to wreck the Classic cinema in the Ladbroke basin, and, with some of his four hundred, drop the law's coach-and-four into a bomb site, while others engaged the cowboys in pitched battle with milk bottles and dustbin lids. 'In fact,' Wiz concluded, 'the boy should be put to sleep.'

'No one should,' I said. 'Not even you.'

At that point the phone bell rang, and Wiz's woman reappeared, and took over the captain's bridge from Wiz just for the moment very obviously, because this was business coming up. If you'd happened to hear her conversation, over crossed lines—I mean, only her end of it—it would have sounded completely ordinary, because of the careful way she chose her words, but if you knew the whole picture as we did, you could see how her spiel all dovetailed with the arrangements she was making with the randy cat at the far end of the blower. And you couldn't help wondering, from her answers, who this character might be—and whether he had any notion of the actual scene at the receiving end, and the matter-of-fact way his glamorous date was being organized for him, poor silly fucker.

After that, Wiz's woman looked at us politely, and didn't say anything, but after a while Wiz got up, as if that was what he'd been planning to do now for some time, and said why didn't he and I take a little stroll? and went out with me without saying anything to his woman, who didn't say anything to him.

There in the air, after a bit of silence, we turned into a private square, that Wiz seemed to have the key to—as a matter of fact, within sight of the department store where I mentioned earlier how we used to go together—and we sat down on two metal chairs, there in the late afternoon sun, and Wiz said, 'Boy, it's a drag: I tell you, it's a drag. As soon as I've made a bit of loot, I'm cutting out.'

'Will she let you?'

'*Let* me?'

'She seems to like you.'

'Oh, she *likes* me all right!' He laughed—quite horrible. 'But I'm turning her loose as soon as I've got just that much I need.'

'And what'll you do with that just that much?'

He looked at me. 'Kid, I dunno,' he said. 'Maybe travel. Or start some business. Something, anyway.'

He aimed a pebble at a pigeon.

'Unless you get knocked off first,' I couldn't help saying.

He gave me a shove. 'Not likely, boy, honest, it's not likely. Your bird on the streets—yes, it's dodgy. But call-girl business—it's really not so easy for them to prove.'

'There's a first time for everything, they say.'

'Oh, sure they do.'

He aimed another pebble, and scored a bull.

I said, 'You don't mind if I ask you a question, Wizard?'

'Shoot, man.'

'Your chick's had, let's say, x men. The day's work is over, and you come home to sleep. How do you feel about it?'

'About what?'

'The x men she's just had.'

Wiz looked at me: I swear I really wanted to *do* something for the boy that moment—give him a thousand pounds and see him off to some lovely south-sea island, where he could have a glorious, care-free ball. 'I don't feel about it,' he said.

'No?'

'No. Because I don't *think* about it. I don't let myself—see.'

Some kids were running to and fro, and the flowers and everything were blooming, and the birds strutting—even the one he'd scored on—and I couldn't bear it. 'See you, Wiz,' I said. 'Come up and visit me.' He didn't answer, but when I turned back at the gate to look at him, he waved.

By now it was the evening, and I wondered whether to keep my date with Hoplite. Frankly, I was quite exhausted, and not only that, I wasn't sure I really wanted to see Hop display himself in front of the TV cameras to the nation. The fact was, you see, that Call-me-Cobber had decided the Lorn Lover thing wasn't quite the suitable vehicle for Hoplite, but the kid was such a telly natur. that they'd have to place him somewhere, which they were going to do this evening in a magazine series called, *Junction!*, where they threw unexpected and unsuitable pairs and groups together in the studio, to see what happened.

But after a quick bite at a Nosh, and two strong black coffees, I felt up to the ordeal, and headed it out to the studios in a taxi. I got past the commissionaires and women at desks with cobra glasses by means I've always found effective: which is, walk firmly, boldly in as if anyone who *doesn't* know what your business is just doesn't know his own (this shames them), go smartly up the stairs, or take a lift and press some button, then knock at any door whatever, say you're lost, and you'll find a pretty secretary who'll put you on the right track, and even show it to you personally.

The one I fell on took me along to Call-me-Cobber's office, where the Aussie looked just a bit surprised to see me, but not much, because already he had a bunch of strange characters on his hands. There was Fabulous, of course, who ran up and hugged me, which was embarrassing, and four others who, I learned from the secretary, were all going to be separately rehearsed from five quite different characters who were hidden somewhere else inside the building, and then be put together at the actual performance, so that we'd see Hoplite with a rear-Admiral, an Asian gooroo with a Scottish steakhouse chef, an undischarged bankrupt and a cat from Carey street, a lady milliner and a male milliner (that was a cute one, I considered), and finally, to wind the thing up before the commercials came on to bring relief, a milk delivery roundsman and an actual cow.

While our little lot were having gins-and-oranges, and triangular sandwiches with grass in them, of which I partook too, the Cobber one was busy with a stack of telephones, like the captain of a jet before his instrument panel, bringing the craft in for a tricky landing. I don't know what it is that comes over so many numbers when they use the blower: it must give them a power thing, like driving some tatty beat-up motor also seems to, because they take liberties on the blower they never would to anyone face to face. If they're calling *out*, they tell their secretary to catch all sorts of cats, and keep them waiting at the far end, like fish on hooks, until they're kindly ready themselves to say their little piece of nonsense. And if called themselves, they'll never say, excuse me, won't ...er's in the room, or tell the cat who's buzzing them ...ll back a little later, even if the number sitting in their ...ice has something more important to tell them than the mug on the blower has. And when the dam thing rings, in any household, everyone flies to it, as if Winston Churchill's at the other end, or M. Monroe, or someone, instead of the grocer about the unpaid bill or, more likely, a wrong number. We're all too much set on gadgets, and let the dam things rule us, and that's why, back home at Napoli, I've always refused to have the blower in, but using Big Jill's or, if I don't want her to hear the message, then the public.

Well, all was rare confusion, with Call-me-Cobber using six green phones at once, and secretaries and junior male products explaining the forthcoming scene to the dazed performers, when in came a female telly queen in a dark blue suit with bits of clean, white, frilly linen sticking out at various neat and vital points, and a big, slightly wrinkled brow, and a too-powdered face and thin lips and lots of schoolteacher's calm, and a really dreadful smile, who evidently intended to straighten things out, and put us all at ease, and somebody said, just as you might say here was Lady Godiva, that this was Miss Cynthia Eve, C.B.E.

And while Cynthia Eve spread calm about, giving everyone nervous breakdowns, I had a natter with the Hoplite on an air sofa that let out a fart each time you sat on it, or even moved. 'You look glorious, Hop,' I said. 'You're going to kill them.'

'But an admiral! Baby, I shall *faint*!'

'You don't know your own strength, Hoplite. Just fire a few salvoes of broadsides at him.'

The Hoplite mopped his face, which was painted the colour of old orange peel.

'And the Nebraska kid,' I said. 'Will he be viewing? Or is he around here somewhere?'

The Hoplite gripped my arm. 'Oh, no!' he cried. 'Didn't I tell you, sweetie? It's all over between he and me!'

'Yes? It is? My heavens?'

'Over and done with!' cried the Fabulous with great emphasis. 'From the moment I saw him in a *hat*.'

'A hat, did you say?'

'Yes, a hat. Imagine it! Baby, he wore a *hat*. The whole thing faded instantly. I'm heartbroken.'

But now the sad lad, and his group of weirdie colleagues, were hustled out for their rehearsal, and I went along with the other stage-door gum-shoes to a viewing room, where we could observe the act when it finally came on. I thought about the dear old telly, and what an education it has been to one and all. I mean, until the TV thing got swinging, all we uncultured cats knew next to nothing about art, and fashion, and archaeology, and long-haired music, and all those sorts of thing, because steam radio never made them all seem real, and as for paper talk, well, no one in their senses ever believes that. But now, we'd seen all these things, and the experts and professors, and were digging their secrets and their complicated language, and having a sort of non-university education. The only catch—and, of course, there always is one—is that, when they *do* put on a programme about something I really know about—which I admit is little, but I mean jazz, or teenagers, or juvenile delinquency —the whole dam things seems utterly unreal. Cooked up in a hurry, and made to sound simpler than it is. Those programmes about kiddos, for example! Boy! I dare say they send the tax-payers, who think the veil's being lifted on the teenage orgies, but honestly, for anyone who knows the actual scene, they're crap. And maybe, in the things *we* don't know about, like all that art and culture, it's the same, but I can't judge.

Which makes me admit, it's all very well sneering at universities, and students with those awful scarves and flat-heeled shoes, but really and truly, it would be wonderful to have a bit of kosher education: I mean, to know what's up there in the sky: just up above you, like the blue over the umbrella, and find out whatever's phoney about our culture, and anything in it that may be glorious and real. But for that, you have to be caught young and study, and it's a hard task, believe me, to try to find the truth about it on your Pat Malone, because so many are anxious to mislead you, and you don't know exactly where to turn.

Well, excitement mounted, and now came the *Junction!* thing. First came some trains rushing at each other, then some racing cars doing likewise, and then some aircraft landing on the tarmac, and a voice bellowed 'Junction!' in an echo-chamber, and we found ourselves face to face with Call-me-Cobber. Believe me, the number was transformed! If you didn't know what an imbecile he was, you'd take him for a man of destiny, because he frowned and glared and spoke up so dam honest and convincing, just like W. Graham, and that nasal Aussie accent gave the exact tone of sincerity. He said life was a junction: the junction, he said, of composite opposites (he liked that group, and riffed it several times). From the shock of ideas, he told us, in this day and age, the light would shine! And the next thing we saw was the Hoplite with a cheery old geezer who'd obviously had four or five too many.

The Hop was terrific: boy! if they don't sign that cat up for a series, they're no talent-spotters. He hogged the camera—in fact, the dam thing had to keep chasing him about the studio—and spoke up like he was King Henry V in a Shakespearean performance. He told us that what he believed in was the flowering of the human personality, such as his own, and how could a personality flower in the boiler-room of a destroyer?

At this point, Call-me-Cobber interrupted him—though he found it darn difficult, and for a while you couldn't tell who was saying what—and he brought in the old rear-Admiral. The ideas, as you'll have dug, was that this nautical cat should sail in with guns blazing, fling all his grappling-irons on the Hoplite, explode his powder magazine, and keel-haul him before making him walk the plank. But all the time that Fabulous had been speaking, the old boy had been jerking his bald head like a bobbin, and punching himself on both his knees, and when he spoke up, it seemed he couldn't have agreed more with all that Fabulous had said. He told us the navy wasn't what it used to be, by God, no! In his day, it seemed, you ate salt fish for breakfast, and shaved in Nelson's blood. What the fleet needed badly, he told the viewers, and the Board of Admiralty too, was a depth-charge let off under all their bottoms, and he was very glad to hear Hoplite's constructive criticisms, and would welcome him aboard any ship that *he* commanded. Hop said that was okay by him, except for the uniform which was too much like an old-style musical, and couldn't the admiral do something about streamlining it a bit, and getting pink pom-poms for bell-bottomed-Jack like those French matelots have got. They had a bit of an argument over that, with the admiral quoting Trafalgar and the

Nile and something I didn't catch about Coburg harpoons, I think it was, and all this while Call-me-Cobber was trying to chip in, but when he did, they both rammed him immediately, the admiral bellowing 'Avast!', and the Hoplite saying, 'Keep out of this, *land-lubber*,' till eventually they had to fade the couple out, and move on to the Asian gooroo and the Scotch steak-house products, though you could still hear Hoplite and the old admiral having a private ball somewhere off scene in the background.

Well, after all this, the whole circus (except for the cow) gathered in a reception room without any air or windows, and there was more booze on the house, and Cynthia Eve, C.B.E., clapped her hands together, and addressed us. The effort had been fine, she said. Magnificent, she told us. The viewers were buzzing in with complaints and congratulations, and she looked forward to seeing the viewing figures, and some of us must certainly come again (and she gave old Hop an eerie, dazzling smile). It wasn't often, she went on, she used the word 'magnificent': if things just ticked over, all she said was, 'Thanks so much for coming,' but this time—well, she'd say it again—the only word that fitted was 'magnificent'.

But the ghost at the wedding was old Call-me-Cobber. Maybe the cat was just tired out, which was understandable, but he seemed to be thoroughly wrought down, and I felt sorry for him, and wished the ex-Deb-of-Last-Year was there so he could weep upon her shoulder. Well, come to think of it, it must be sad to be a Call-me-Cobber: because without that little television box, you're nobody; and with it, you're a king in our society—a television personality.

Out on the road, though, Hoplite was a bit sad, too: the boy's a born artist, I'm convinced, and this taste of the telly magic had disturbed him. There was also his emotional upset, and he said, 'By the way, although it's all over with Nebraska, he's asked me to visit him at his base, and in spite of all my pangs, I just can't resist the opportunity. Will you come too? I'd love to see the occupation army.'

'It'll be air personnel,' I said. 'The army's left.'

'Well, tailored uniforms, and gorgeous work clothes, like their films of prisons. You're not tempted?'

I told him okay, but I had to leave him just for now, because if I didn't, I'd have to bed down there and then upon the pavement. Because the fact was, I was spent.

IN AUGUST

For our trip up the river, Dad and I decided that we'd settle for the bit in between Windsor castle and a place called Marlow. We chose the shorter run because we found that was about all we could manage what with travelling to and fro from London, and also because Dad's health was certainly far from brilliant—and also because I'd discovered (but this was a secret that I kept from Dad) that Suze and Henley had a house down by the Thames at a village by the name of Cookham, and though I'd no intention of dropping in for tea and buttered scones, I certainly wanted to have a look at the place, as our pleasure boat sailed by, if that was possible.

There we were, then, up in the front seat, and passing under Windsor bridge. I don't know if you've ever been in a Tunnel of Love—I mean in one of those boats that wind along it in at the amusement parks—but if you have, you'll know the whole point is to get in that front seat, right up in the prow, because if you do, you have the sensation as you glide along, that you're just hanging there over the water: no boat, just you and the surroundings. Well, this was the same (except, of course, that it was light, not dark—in fact, a glorious August day), the water sparkling so that I had on my Polaroids, the diesel chugging, and old Dad there, with his open-neck shirt and sandals, and his mackintosh in a roll (trust Dad!), and puffing away like an engine at his briar. Up there behind us, was the enormous castle, just as you see it on the cinema screen when they play 'the Queen' and everyone hustles out, and there out in front of us were fields and trees and cows and things and sunlight, and a huge big sky filled with acres of fresh air, and I thought, my heavens! if this is the country, why haven't I shaken hands with it before—it's glorious!

In fact, the only dark cloud on the horizon, was Dad himself. It's like this. By means of nagging and prodding and persuading, I'd managed to get him inside Dr A. R. Franklyn's consulting-room in Harley street. Honest, it was like getting a hip cat into a symphony concert, but I succeeded. While I waited outside, reading eighteen magazines from cover to cover, Dr F. gave my Dad a thorough go-over. But all he would tell us was that he *must* get Dad into hospital for a proper examination, which he couldn't do there in Harley street even if he'd wanted to, but Dad turned this down point blank, and said he wouldn't go into hospital unless they'd tell him what was the matter—which, as I tried to explain to him (but it was like talking to a wall), was exactly what they wanted to find out, if only he'd only go inside there for a day or two. But Dad said once they get you in hospital, you're half dead already, and he wouldn't.

Well, there it was. I tried to forget it, on this sunny summer day, but there it was.

At this point, we went round a great U-bend, honking our horn like a truck in the Mile End road, and round in the other direction came two hundred or so little boats—I swear I don't exaggerate—each with one kiddo in them, sitting the wrong way round, and rowing like lunatics: a club, it must have been, of athletic juniors, each in white vest and pants and brown legs and arms and a red neck—it was cyclists they made me think of, weaving their way at speed through the city traffic—and we, of course, had to slow down almost to zero as they shot by both sides of us in their dozens. And I got up and cheered, and even old Dad did. Wonderful kiddos on that hot-pot cracking day, racing downstream as if only the salt sea would stop them!

And as we went on, I was really astonished at all the different kinds of boats they had on this old river! Boy! there's a great life on this Thames you'd never imagine, if you only saw it down in the city among the cargo ships and barges. Moored beside the stream there were square things like caravans, with proper chimneys and cats emptying slops over the side, and out in the fairway there were powered craft—some of them, believe me, you could have sailed in to South America—and occasionally we met a real old-timer, with a funnel and steam engine, like the Mississippi things they show you on the LP sleeves. And a big surprise was that there were so many sailing boats: I mean, how did they do their criss-cross performance, like Saturday night drunks, in a river as narrow as old father Thames is up there? And canoes, of course, and eskimo boats with one oar made of two (I hope you dig), and even the craziest number of them all—a flat one like a big cardboard box the same size each end, where the chick sits on cushions in the front part, with a brolly, and her stud heaves the thing along with a hop pole, just like gondolas. And the biggest surprise of all, when we got a bit further up the river, was one really large sailing boat lying there in a sort of parking lot, which, according to Dad, must have been brought up there in bits and re-assembled—anyway, I can't tell you how peculiar it was to see this big ocean boat sitting there right in the middle of the English countryside.

Surprises? Believe me, there were plenty. Did you know those river cats drive their boats on the wrong side of the water? I mean, no keep left nonsense at all for them? And dig this one. Did you know, when you go *up* stream—I do hope I make this plain—you go up hill, and so you have to use a kind of staircase, which is called locks? This is the spiel. You form up in a queue, just like at the Odeon, then, when it's your turn, sail in at one end, into a sort of square concrete well, and they shut two big doors behind you, as if you were going away inside the nick, and there you are, like pussy at the bottom of the drain. Then the lock-keeper product—with a peaked cap, and an Albert watch-chain, and rubber boots—throws some switches or other, and the water gushes in, and you'd hardly credit it, but you start going up yourself! I mean rising like in a commercial lift. And when you've got up there, you find to your amazement that the river on the far side is way up there too: i.e., at the same level as you're at yourself now in the well thing. And the lock-keeper opens two more doors, by pushing against great wooden arms they have with his arse—and a lot of kidlets helping him to do so, or maybe hindering—and you get your release papers, and your civvy clothes back and your fare money, and see! you're out in the stream again away to freedom, except that now you're that much *higher* up! Boy! I certainly dig those locks! And most of them had little gardens, like in St. James's, and tea chalets, and river cats and onlookers all jigging around and shouting, and having a great, noisy, lazy, watery ball!

'What about a pint?' said Dad, who the sight of all this water must have been making thirsty.

'Why not? Come on, I'll buy.'

'You flush these days?' Dad asked, as we made our way past the excursionists, and the skipper at his tiller, and the technical kiddo who helped him by sitting on the rail.

'I've just had a sub,' I answered, as we cracked our heads on the low door leading down into the saloon.

'For doing what?' he asked me, when I'd got the wallop and the Coke.

It's weird, isn't it, how your elders are always so suspicious when they hear that you've made money! They just can't credit that little junior has grown up a bit, and turned some honest coin.

'If you listen, Dad, I'll explain,' I said. But it was hard to concentrate, because through the portholes just beside our faces we were exactly at the water level, and you found yourself unable not to watch, just like the telly.

'I'm listening,' Dad said.

I told him how a character I knew called V. Partners, who's prominent in the advertising industry, had said he's sponsor an exhibition of my photos if I'd agree he take the best of them to publicize a skin lotion he was marketing, called *Tingle-tangle*, which was targeted at the teenage market, and that he'd given me an advance on it of two times twenty-five.

'That's not much,' said Dad—very greatly to my surprise.

'You don't think so?'

'It's not all you could have . . .'

'You mean I should have asked more?'

'Not that exactly, no. Did you sign anything?'

'I had to.'

'You're a bloody fool, son. Also,' Dad added, 'he is, because you're a minor.'

Well!

'Listen, Dad,' I said, quite a bit vexed, 'I've not got your experience, but one thing I'm not, please, is a fool.'

'Apologies,' said Dad.

'Apologies accepted.'

But I wasn't pleased—no, not at all—the more so as I thought Dad might probably be right. Vendice was very nice—and at any rate he'd listened to me, and not laughed—but of course he was in business for commercial purposes. I thought: I must get to know a lawyer.

'What time we get there?' Dad asked.

'Marlow? You thinking of that already? About six.'

'We might stay down there for tea.'

'If you want to, Dad, but I'd like to get back to the smoke, if you don't mind, because I want to take in a concert, second house.'

'That jazz?'

'Yeah. That jazz.'

'Oh, all right. Where we have mid-day grub?'

I thought quick. 'Well,' I said, 'we could have it here on the Queen Mary, or we could stop off at one of the little villages, and catch the next boat on.'

'Our tickets let us?'

'Oh, certainly. I've checked.'

'Well, we'll see,' he said.

'Okay.'

That brought back thoughts of Suze. And much as I love old Dad, taking him all in all, I couldn't but wish that, at that very moment, he wasn't there, but she. Glory! how fabulous it'd be to make this river trip with Crêpe Suzette! And why in creation didn't I think of it, back in the earlier days?

Wow! I really had a shock! Because a face—a human face—flashed by a porthole, just outside. But then I saw what it was, which was a bunch of bathers knocking themselves out in the surrounding drink, and Dad and I went upstairs to get a closer dekko. There they were—scores of them—diving off the bank, thrashing about in the river, and making the skipper swear at them by coming too near to his transatlantic. Yelling and splashing or, if they had any sense, roasting their torsos up there on the green, or just standing in plastic poses, watching. 'Good luck to you!' I shouted at an Olympic number who'd flogged it across the water in front of the ship's bows. 'Help! but I'd like to join them,' I told Dad.

After this we passed a quieter bit, with big houses with their front lawns on the river, and sometimes quite lonely, with only an angler or two sitting like they were statues, and swans coming out to hiss at us, just like alligators when the paddle-steamer sails up the Amazon, or the Zambesi, or wherever it is, to gnash at the explorers. As we passed tall banks of rushes, they seemed to bow to us, because they sank several feet, then rose again when we'd gone by. And sometimes hills popped up unexpectedly—and what was even more peculiar, popped up again (I mean the same hills) in some quite different location, because we'd gone round several mile-long bends. There were little bridges we could only just get under, like in corny films about baronial Scotland, and beside each of the locks, were weirs with notices saying 'Danger', and roaring noises like Niagara, or almost. In fact, the whole darn scene was as good as Cinerama in continuous performance, and much fresher.

The most famous of these locks, so Dad informed me—and he must have been right, because the skipper left his wheel to a skilful kiddo I admit I envied, and came along among the passengers to say the same—was one called Boulter's lock. It had a little bridge, like in Japanese murder pictures, and a big wooded island, and according to Dad, in the days of Queen Victoria and King Edward and all those historic monarchs, it was the top hip rendezvous for the dudes and toffs and mashers, and their birds. Personally (though naturally, I didn't say so), I found it a bit gloomy—a bit sad and deserted and un-contemporary, like so many glorious monuments your elders-and-betters point out to you proudly from the tops of buses. And when we sailed on afterwards into a section they called Cliveden reach (only you don't pronounce it that way, because it's a square thing to do with educated words), which apparently is one of the scenic glories of the nation, I admit I was considerably wrought down. It was like the canal at Regent's Park, only, of course, bigger: I mean great woods of dangling trees like parsley salad, wringing themselves out into the river, all rotting away gradually, and *old*: which, of course, England is, I mean all those ancient cities, but it seems even the nature part of it can look like that as well.

But now I was growing a bit nervous: because I knew when we'd get out of this Cliveden lily-pond, the next stop would be the place called Cookham. Now, when I'd imagined the whole scene, lying back at home upon my spring divan, I'd thought—well, I know it's foolish, but I had—I'd thought of Suze's house being a little white thing set beside the river, and the boat going slowly by, and she coming out just at that moment (without Henley, need I say), and seeing me there on the deck like the Captain in *H.M.S. Pinafore*, and throwing a kiss or two at me and pleading to me to alight, and the boat pulling in beside her garden, and me getting off into her arms.

Well, naturally, as the day grew older, I knew *that* wasn't going to happen, but I'd put off deciding exactly what I should do: e.g., get off or not, and how to find Suze's dwelling, if I did. But just after Cookham lock (which comes a bit before the place itself), while I was still hesitating about it all, and feeling kind of paralysed, and wondering if perhaps I even wanted to see Suze at all, it was Dad who came, unexpectedly, to my assistance—though in a very awkward way. Because when we'd set sail again after the lock thing, and I was already cursing myself for doing nothing, and we were just going to go underneath the metal bridge there, Dad slumped on to my shoulder, and passed out.

So I propped him up and ran and told the skipper, who wasn't pleased and said we could hop off at the next lock we came to. But I said no, that was no dam good, that Dad was a sick man, under Dr A. R. Franklyn's care of Harley street, and that I had to get him to the Cookham doctor quick, and if he didn't stop his boat immediately, I'd hold him personally responsible. And then I turned round to all the passengers, and said in a loud voice my Dad was dying and the skipper didn't care a darn about it—in fact, as you've guessed, I became a bit hysterical.

Well, I know mums and dads by now, and if there's one thing any official person hates, it's when they turn on him in a body—or, so far as that goes, if there's anything like a *fuss*. Some nosey, interfering passengers, thank goodness, took a look at Dad, and said I was quite right—*they* wanted to get rid of him too, I could soon see, because nobody likes sickness, especially on a holiday. So the skipper slowed the boat down, and pulled in near the bank there, and bellowed at an old geezer who was mending boats just beside the iron bridge (or that's what his sign said he was doing), and the geezer rowed out in a little boat, and we got Dad down into it, and pulled off, and the pleasure boat sailed on.

By the time we landed on the slipway, Dad had fortunately recovered; which I was bloody glad of, because I did feel a bit guilty about bundling him into the little boat—and in fact, about my whole hysterical performance. The old geezer helped him into the boathouse, into the shade, and yelled at his wife to get a cup of tea, and get on the blower to the local national health representative, who turned up before long, not very pleased to be interrupted from his test tubes and hypodermics, and Dad not very pleased to see him either, because he said this was a lot of fuss about nothing, and we should have stayed up there on the boat, and what the hell: so neither of them was very co-operative with the other. And this Cookham doctor said there was nothing much wrong with Dad that he could see (I'd heard *that* one before!), and what he needed was a rest, and then get on the bus and go straight back home to bed, and slumber.

So the boat-building geezer fixed Dad in a deck-chair with a hood on it and tassels, and his wife came up with further reviving cuppas, and I said a bus would be too slow, and cost what it would, I was going to get Dad back to London in a taxi. The geezer said he'd phone through to the local car-hire, but I said no, just to give me the address, and I'd go off and fix things personally, and that would give Dad time for a short nap to set him up again, and me a chance to have a swift dekko at this lovely beauty-spot. So off I went.

This Cookham is a real old village like you see on biscuit boxes: with a little square church, and cosy cottages, and roads made of mud, and agricultural numbers trudging about them doing whatever it is they do do. I asked one or two for the address I wanted of the car-hire, and they were very relaxed and friendly, and didn't talk a bit like country people do in variety spots and things, and when I followed their directions, I came round a stack of corners . . . and wham! I saw Suze's house there! Yes. I mean, it was the same house I'd imagined in my vision, near enough . . . at any rate, I didn't ask any more directions, but just walked in through the front garden, and round the side to the lawn beside the river, and there, sitting on the grass listening to the radio, I saw Suze. And only Suze.

'Hullo, Crêpe Suzette,' I said.

She looked up, but didn't *get* up, and stared at me a minute, and said, 'Hi.'

I came up a bit nearer. 'You all right?' I said.

'Yes,' said Suzette.

'Henley well?' I asked.

'Oh, yes,' she said.

'Can I say hullo?'

Suze had got up on her two knees, and her hands falling down between them. 'He's up there,' she said.

'In London?'

'Yeah.'

I got down on my knees too. 'So I'll miss him,' I said.

'Yes,' said Suzette.

And then—well, it was like we were shoved at each other from behind by two great enormous hands. And there we were, all mixed up in a bundle, me clinging on to Suze, she clinging on to me, and Suze sobbing like a child—I mean, great dreadful sobs more like groans, it was really awful.

Well, that went on for quite a while, and I'm not conventional, but I thought, hell! there's windows all over the dam place, even though this is the country, so I kept saying, 'Suze, Suze,' and bashing her on the back, and kissing her face when I could get at it, and 'Suze, take it easy, kid, do relax, girl, please take it easy.'

So after quite another while, she got herself straightened out, and sat back on the grass, and looked at me with her face red as a tomato, as if I was suddenly going to disappear (which you can bet I wasn't), and I said to her, because I just couldn't dam well resist it—you must remember what I'd been through myself, and that I loved this girl Suze with all my heart—I said, 'And so it didn't turn out all right, then.'

She just said, 'No,' and then kept on saying, 'No.'

Now, you must realize, all this time, I had Dad's health, too, in my mind, and the anxiety to get him back quite safe, though God knows how I wanted to remain there, so I got a bit brisk and businesslike, which I admit must have seemed very unfeeling to her, and said, 'Well, hon, why don't you skip?'

'I can't, darl,' she said.

'He can't stop you, Suze!'

'It's not that, I just can't!'

They won't give you a reason, will they! They won't ever give you a plain reason! 'Suzie, why not?' I cried.

Here we had another session of those dreadful sobs, which, honestly, were ghastly. 'Do *stop* that, Suzette!' I cried, banging the girl quite hard. Because honest, I couldn't take very much more of them.

'Because it's spoiled!' she cried, all mixed up with hair and bits of clothes, so as I could hardly dig what she was saying. 'I've spoiled what we used to be—it's gone!'

'Bollocks!' I cried indignantly. She'd got me in a grip like an all-in wrestler. 'It was a mess,' she kept saying. 'It was just a mess.'

I saw this was the moment for swift action. So I yanked her away from me so as I could *see* her (which most of the time had been quite impossible, because all I could see of her was her spine), and I said I had Dad there, and a car, and we'd both run her up to London —but though I said it at least half a dozen times or more, it just didn't register with Suze. She only kept on saying, 'No, no, no, no, no.'

So I got up and stood. 'Look, Suze,' I cried. 'I'm your boy—see? Your one and only. And I live up in London, and you know exactly where. And I'm waiting for you there, this evening, tomorrow, and every day until the day I die!' I grabbed both her shoulders, and joggled her. 'Have you heard what I said?' I shouted.

She said, yes.

'And have you understood me?'

Yes, she said, she had.

'Then I'm waiting!' I cried, and bent over and gave her a really fierce, everlasting kiss, then said, 'See you very soon,' and waved, and rushed off out of that garden like Dr Roger Bannister.

There in the road, I had to stop, because suddenly *I* felt faint, just like Dad, and had to sit down on the ground, which was the only thing I could find to sit on. Then I got up, and grabbed the first cat I saw, and asked him to lead me to the car-hire number—which he did, very nicely—and the cat was fortunately in (I mean the car-hire cat), and he came round to the boat-building place, and we collected Dad, and said goodbye and thanks very much indeed to the old geezer and his wife, and made it off for London, which the driver said would cost us exactly eight-pounds-ten.

Well, on the way home, Dad perked up quite a bit: in fact, he even started singing some George Formby numbers, and older songs he'd heard from his own dad, of Albert Chevalier and historic old veterans like that, and apparently the Cookham driver knew quite a few of them too, and they had several rousing choruses, and argued as to which old music-hall artiste first sang what. But me, need I say, I didn't feel a bit like that, and was car-sick as well, which I've always been prone to if somebody else is driving, and in fact I wanted to tell Dad about my troubles, but you can see how I couldn't—and anyway, even at the best of times you can't tell even your father and mother anything that really *matters* to you.

Soon we were in the outskirts, and though I'd enjoyed the country, I was so glad to be back there in the town again—it was like coming home. And before very long we were in Pimlico, and when we pulled up, Dad had to go in and get the money, as even between us we hadn't got enough, and that brought Mum and Vern out on the pavement, and out of his second-floor window, the beefo Malt.

*No*body seemed to dig how dangerous it had been to Dad: all we got was exclamations about why had I taken him away without telling anybody, and where the hell had we both been to, and why did a taxi cost us eight-pounds-ten—even Vern chipping in with helpful observations—till I was so embarrassed, in front of that Cookham driver, and the Pimlico population, that I went up to the bunch of them in a fury, and shouted, 'If you're going to kill my father, don't kill him in the streets, but let him get into his bed!'

This changed the atmosphere, we all tramped inside, and got Dad stowed away, and then Mum turned on me, and said now she wanted to know exactly what all this was about, and I said okay, I'd dam well tell her, and Vern tried to join in the party, but we turfed him out and went down into the parlour.

'Sit down,' said my mother.

I got hold of both her shoulders (just like I had with Suze) and shoved her in a chair—though she's a darn sight tougher—and said, 'Now, *you* sit down, Ma, and just you listen to me.'

Then I let her have it. I said she was the most selfish woman I knew of, that she'd made Dad's life a torture ever since I could remember, that as for a mess like Vern he was none of my responsibility, but as for me, her son by Dad, she's brought me up so that I just hated her, and was ashamed of her.

'Is that all?' she said, looking back at me as if she hated me too.

'That's about all,' I said.

'You want to go now, son?' she said to me next.

This took me aback a bit. I said nothing, but just waited there.

'Well,' said my mother. 'If you can take it, you can stay and listen to this. Your father's been no use to me at all ever since I married him.'

'He produced me,' I said, staring at her very, very hard.

'He just about managed that,' she said. 'That was about his lot.'

Now at that moment, I wanted to strike my mother: like she'd done me, a thousand times or more, when I couldn't hit back, and I wanted to hit her real hard—hard, and get it over; and I took a step in her direction. She saw very clearly what was coming, and she didn't move an inch. And I'm very glad to say that, when I saw this—though of course, all this happened in a moment—I didn't hit at her, but said, 'Whatever Dad may have been, or may not have been, you married him.'

'Yes, I married him,' she said, sarcastically and very bitterly.

'And whatever you feel about Dad,' I went on, 'if you made up your mind to have me, you were supposed to love me. Mothers are supposed to love their sons.'

'And sons their mothers,' my mother said.

'If they get a chance. There's not one that doesn't want to, is there? But they must get a bit of it back, a little bit of encouragement.'

At this old Mum just sighed, and gave me a crooked smile, and looked very *wise*, I must say, in her way, though very nasty, too.

'Now, you listen to me,' she said, 'and I don't give a b----r what you think. In the first place, I made you, here (and she banged her belly), and if you think that's easy, try it yourself some time. Without me, and what I went through, you'd not be here insulting me like you are. And in the next place, although your father means nothing to me at all, in fact just the contrary, I've stuck by him, not thrown him out, as I could have done a hundred times if I'd wanted, and made things very much easier for me by doing so. And in the third place, as for you . . .'

I interrupted. 'Just a minute, Ma,' I said. 'Why did you ask me, just two months ago, to come back here again, if anything went wrong with Dad?'

She didn't answer, and I pressed it home.

'Because you *can't* do without a man here—I mean, a *legal* man—and you know it, don't you. And you couldn't have got rid of Dad, like you say you could, because I know you, Ma, if you'd been able to, you would have, but you couldn't help yourself.'

She looked at me. 'You're getting sharp, aren't you, boy,' she said.

'I'm your son, Ma.'

'Yes. Yes, I suppose you are. But let me tell you this. Since that night you turned up in the tube shelter, eighteen years ago, which I don't suppose even you remember, I've seen you're fed and clothed and brought up, best I could, till you can take care of yourself, as you seem to think you can, and that was quite an effort, sometimes!' She put her old, fetching face on one side, and said, 'You're not very easy, you know. You've not always been very easy.'

'I dare say not, Ma,' I said.

'As for *loving* you,' my mother went on, 'well. Listen, son. You don't love or not love because you choose to—even your own son. You love if you do, and if you don't, you just don't, and there's no good at all pretending. You'll find out it's true what I say when you grow older. Or I dare say you're so clever that you've found it out already.'

I sat down too, three feet away from her.

'Okay, mother,' I said, after a while, 'let's leave it at that.'

'If you say so, son,' she said to me.

Then Ma did a thing she'd never done with me ever before, which is to get up and go to the glass cupboard with the orange lace cover on it, which I remember so well from all our other addresses in their turn, and which we were never allowed to go within a mile of, and she got out a bottle of port, and poured two glasses in green crystal goblets, and handed me one, and said, 'Cheerioh.'

'I don't drink, Ma,' I said.

'Don't be a cunt,' she said to me.

So we had a tipple.

Then Ma said, what about my father? Well, then—I hope it wasn't betraying Dad, but I did think she ought to know—I told her all about Dr A. R. Franklyn, and how he really ought to go into hospital, and she listened without interrupting (the first time she'd ever done *that* with me in her life, either), and just shook her head, and said, 'He'll never go in there voluntary. But give me this doctor's particulars, and if he's taken really bad again, we'll just have to put him in.'

So I did that.

Then, when I came to go, just by the doorway, there was a sort of pause, and what was in both our minds was, should we have a kiss or not? We looked at each other, then both laughed together suddenly, and she said, 'Oh well, son, let's skip it, you're a real nasty little bastard, aren't you,' and I gave her a big clump and said, 'Well, Ma, *you* should know about that,' and hopped it quickly.

I looked up at the clock at the Air Terminal, and saw if I made it quick, I'd catch the latter portion of the Czar Tusdie concert, with Maria Bethlehem singing with him as soloist. The venue was up in the north part, in a super-cinema with academy of dance attached, so on the rank there I grabbed a taxi (who'd been hoping for transatlantics at the terminal, and wasn't pleased so much with only me), and shot off up across the town. I certainly felt in need of a lift and soothing music, after all the excitements of the day.

And that's what jazz music gives you: a big lift up of the spirits, and a Turkish bath with massage for all your nerves. I know even nice cats (like my Dad, for example) think that jazz is just noise and rock and sound angled at your genitals, not your intelligence, but I want you to believe that isn't so at all, because it really makes you feel good in a very simple, but very basic, sort of way. I can best explain it by saying it just makes you feel *happy*. When I've been tired and miserable, which has been quite more than often, I've never known some good, pure jazz music fail to help me on.

Now, I've explained a club for jazz people, and also a jazz club, but a jazz concert is something different still. In this, several hundred cats, and even often these days thousands, gather in as large a hall as the impresario can hire, and listen to the best selection of soloists and combos, English and American, that the impresario can offer for the price—which is by no means low. Of course, in these concerts, even the greats often disappoint you, because a big hall or cinema is no more the real place for jazz than a railway station would be for a tea party. But if your luck is in, they often overcome this disadvantage, and you hear some really marvellous sounds. And then what's so nice is to hear them in company with so many hundreds of like-minded kiddos—sharp, and eager, and ready to give of their best, too, if the performance is up to standard—and although I know jazz addicts are supposed to be a lot of morons, you'd really be astonished how these fans will all sit and *listen*.

Well, Czar Tusdie's, of course, is one of the great bands of all time, and American, and coloured. And as for Maria Bethlehem, I'd say that, second to a great like Lady Day (who, to my mind's right up there on an Everest peak all of her very own), she's the world's best female jazz singer that there is. So you can imagine I was thoroughly impatient in that vehicle, and kept advising the driver of short cuts and to accelerate, which he took no notice of whatever.

He dropped me on the corner just before the picture-palace, and so I had to walk past the dance academy, and there, on the pavement, I paused a second, because I saw a notice on the wall which said,

CURRENT CLASSES

MEDALLISTS CLASS
BEGINNERS PROGRESSIVE CLASS
BEGINNERS PRACTICE
ABSOLUTE BEGINNERS

and I said out loud, 'Boy, that one's us! Although me, after my experiences, maybe I'm going to move up a category or two!'

Well, as I went in through the foyer, and gave my ticket up to the appropriate cat, I heard, from outside, that really marvellous sound, which is the strains of jazz music when it's real and true: truly a heavenly sound, it seems to me to be. And honestly, when I die—when that day comes that must come—I'd wish for no other ending of it all than to hear that Czar Tusdie band playing for me as it did just then: because their sound was so strong and gentle, just like it would carry you right up on its kind notes to paradise. And then there was a roar and whistles, and the fans all applauded like a football crowd, and I went in and got my seat just in time to catch the entrance of Maria.

Maria is big, and no longer a young woman, but she walked on the stage just like a girl: quick feet, easy gestures, and a face that's so darn friendly, though it can also be kidding you, and sometimes quite severe. She's like a girl, yes, but she's also, in a strange way, just like everybody's Mum: she welcomes you all, takes charge of you all, and from the very moment she comes on, you know that you're all there with her in safe hands. And straight away she swings into the song she's chosen, no tricks, no crafty pauses, no hesitation whatsoever, and what she does to the songs is unbelievable: I mean, she takes even quite familiar standards and turns them inside out, and throws them right back at you as though they've become nobody's but her own—Maria's. And she can be witty as hell, throwing everything away and shrugging, but then, the next moment, rising like a bird, and sweet or melancholy. But what*ever* she does—and this is the whole thing about Maria Bethlehem—her singing makes you feel it's absolutely wonderful to be alive and kicking, and that human beings are a dam fine wonderful invention after all.

They rose to her at the end—all those hundreds of English boys and girls, and their friends from Africa and the Caribbean—and they practically had to gouge us all out of that auditorium. Cats I didn't know from Adam said, hadn't it been great, and one cat in particular then said, had I heard about the happenings at St. Ann's Well, up in Nottingham, last evening? I asked him, what happenings? not taking it very much in (because I was still back there with Maria Bethlehem), when I realized he was saying there'd been rioting between whites and coloured, but what could you expect in a provincial dump out there among the sticks?

IN SEPTEMBER

I WAS up very early on that morning, as if with a private alarm clock in my brain, and it was one of the most beautiful young days I've ever seen. The dome of the heavens, when I looked out up at it over my geraniums, was pale pink glowing blue, with nothing in it but a few stray leaves of cloud, lit up gold and green by sun you couldn't see behind the houses. The air was fresh, blown right in from the sea, and there wasn't a sound except from hundreds of thousands of pairs of lungs, still slumbering there in Napoli. Peace, perfect peace, I thought, as I sucked in the warm air of my native city. And it was also, as it happened, my nineteenth birthday.

I put on some music and abluted, then made two Nescafés and carried one down for Hoplite. The cat was absent. Waste not want not, I decided, so carried them further down to Cool. Another cat out on the tiles last night. No use disturbing Big Jill that early, so I drank both cups on the front doorstep, and stood there taking in the scene.

And I saw this. Coming down the street, from the N. Hill Gate direction, were a group of yobbos, who most probably had been out at some all-night jungle-juice performance too, and who straggled across the street and pavement in that *messy* way they have, and whose bodies were all *wrong* somehow—I mean with lumps and bumps in the wrong places—and whose summer drag looked hastily pulled on. And coming up the street, from the Metropolitan Railway direction, were two coloured characters—not Spades, as it happened, but two Sikh warrior products, with a mauve and a lemon turban, and with stacks of hair. Well, when the two groups met, the Sikh characters stepped to one side, as you or I would do, but the yob lot halted, so as it was difficult to pass by, and there was a short pause: all this just outside my door.

Then one of the scruffos turned and looked at his choice companions, and grinned a sloppy grin, and suddenly approached the two Sikh characters and hit one of them right in the face: with his fist pointed so that the top knuckles got inside the skull. So long as I live, I swear, I shall never forget the look on that Asian number's face: it wasn't at all fear, it wasn't at all rage, it was just complete and utter unbelief and surprise.

Then the other Sikh one shouldered up beside his buddy, and the yobbos drew away a bit, then both the two groups separated, and the oafo lot went off laughing down the hill again, and the Sikhs started chattering and waving their arms about. They walked on a little bit, then turned and looked back, then went off chattering and waving again up hill out of sight and sound.

Now, you will be asking, what about me? Did I run out and take a poke at the chief yobbo, and bawl the bunch of little monsters out? The answer is—I did not. First of all, because I simply couldn't believe my eyes. And next, because the whole thing was just so *meaningless*, I suddenly felt weak and sick: I mean I've no objection, really, to men fighting if they want to, if they've got a *reason*. But this thing! Also—I don't like to say this much, but here it is—I myself was scared. It doesn't seem possible such sordids as this lot could frighten you, and certainly one wouldn't, or even two or three of them . . . But this little group: it seemed to have a horrid little mind, if you can call it that, all of its own, and a whole lot of unexpected force behind it.

I ran down in the area and called Big Jill. She took a while coming to the door, and shouted had I no discretion, there were chicks sleeping on the premises, but I shoved past her into her kitchen and told her what I'd just seen. She listened, asked me several questions, and said, 'The bastards!'

'But what should I have done, Big Jill?' I cried.

'Who—you? Oh, I dunno. I'll make you a cup of tea.'

As she started banging crockery about, and pulling her red slacks on over her huge hips without any by your leave, I found that I was shivering. When she handed me the cup, she said, 'You might like to take a look at this.'

It was a leading article in the Mrs Dale daily which the Amberley Drove character, who you may remember, wrote for, and it was about the happenings a week ago up there in Nottingham. It said the chief thing was that we must be realistic, and keep a proper sense of due proportion. It said that many influential journals—including, of course, this Mrs Dale production—had long been warning the government that unrestricted immigration, particularly of coloured persons, was most undesirable, even if such persons came here, as by far the bulk of them undoubtedly did, from countries under direct colonial rule, and countries benefiting by the Commonwealth connection. But Commonwealth solidarity was one thing, and unrestricted immigration was quite another.

Then it had a word to say about the coloured races. England, it said, was an old and highly civilized nation, but the countries of Africa and the Caribbean were very far from being so indeed. It was true that the West Indian islands had enjoyed the advantages of British government for many centuries, but even in these the cultural level was low, to say the least of it, and as for Africa, it should be remembered that, a mere hundred years ago, some parts of that vast continent had never even heard of Christianity. In their own setting, coloured folk were no doubt admirable citizens, according to the standards that prevailed there. But transported unexpectedly to a culture of a higher order, serious difficulties and frustrations must inevitably arise.

'Must I go on reading all this balls?' I shouted at Big Jill.

'It's up to you,' she said.

Then it went on to give you the facts about the coloured communities who'd come to settle here in the UK. Many were toilers, it did not deny, as could be seen by those courteous and efficient public transport servants, but many were layabouts who thrived on the three-pounds-ten they got from the National Assistance. This led to labour troubles, and we must remember that the nation had been passing through a slight, though of course temporary, recession. Pressure on housing was another problem. It was true that many coloured folk—for reasons that were more than understandable, and need not be detailed here—found difficulty in securing accommodation in the better sections of most towns. It was also true that many West Indians, in particular, had saved up enough from their wage-packets, over the years, to purchase houses, but unfortunately these were generally speaking little other than slum property, which further deteriorated when they moved into them, to the disadvantage of the rate-paying citizens as a whole. Moreover, it was not unknown for coloured landlords to evict white tenants—often old-age pensioners—by making their lives impossible.

Then there was the matter of different customs. By and large, said the article, English people were renowned for their decent and orderly behaviour. But not so the immigrants, it seemed, or very many of them. They liked haggling in the shops, prodding fruit before they bought it, leaving the hi-fi on all night, dressing in flashy clothes, and, worse still, because this made them more conspicuous, driving about in even flashier vehicles, which they had somehow managed to acquire.

Then there was the question of the women. (Old Amberley certainly went to town on this woman question!) To begin with, he said, mixed marriages—as responsible coloured persons would be the very first to agree themselves—were most undesirable. They led to a mongrel race, inferior physically and mentally, and rejected by both of the unadulterated communities. But frequently, of course—and this made the matter even graver—these tainted offspring were, in addition, the consequence of unions that were blessed neither by church nor state. More, said the piece. The well-known propensity and predilection of coloured males for securing intimate relations with white women—unfortunately, by now, a generally observed phenomenon in countries where the opportunities existed—led to serious friction between the immigrants and the men of the stock so coveted, whose natural—and, he would add—sound and proper instinct, was to protect their women-folk from this contamination, even if this led to violence which, in normal circumstances, all would find most regrettable.

But this was not all: it was time for plain speaking, and this had to be said. The record of the courts had shown—let alone the personal observations of any anxious and attentive observer—that living off the immoral earnings of white prostitutes, had now become all too prevalent among the immigrant community. No one would suggest—least of all this journal—that in each and every such immoral union, the guilty male was a coloured person since, of course—as figures published recently in its columns had unfortunately made it all too clear—the total estimated figure of active prostitutes in this country did not itself fall far short of the total numbers of male coloured immigrants of the appropriate age. Nevertheless, the disproportionate number of coloured 'bullies' could not be denied.

'Christ!' I said, putting the dam thing down. 'I just can't go on with this!'

'Stick it out,' Big Jill said. 'I'll make you another cuppa.'

Several conclusions, this Drove one continued, flowed inevitably—and urgently—from these grave matters and, more particularly, from the recent disturbances at Nottingham, which everyone—and especially his Mrs Dale daily—so greatly and so vehemently deplored. The first was, that immigration by coloured persons, whether having an identical citizenship status as ourselves or not, should be halted instantly. Indeed, the whole process should be reversed, and compulsory repatriation should be given urgent and serious consideration by the government. Meanwhile, it went without saying, law and order should be enforced most rigorously and impartially, however great the provocation may have been—and there may well, it must be admitted, have been provocation on both sides. But it was only a minority—chiefly persons known by the name of 'Teddy boys'—who had actually been guilty of a physical breach of the Queen's peace, and these youths should undoubtedly be restrained: though many might feel that such young people—who were far from being characteristic of the youth of the country as a whole—were psychopathic cases, in greater need of medical attention than of drastic punishment by the courts of law.

The occurrences at Nottingham, A. Drove wound up, could in no way be described as a 'race riot'. No comparison with large-scale disturbances in the southern states of America, or in the Union of South Africa, was therefore tenable. By the swift and determined action of the Nottingham authorities, we could rest assured that no more would be heard of such lamentable incidents—which were entirely alien to our way of life—provided, of course, immediate action along the lines suggested by the Mrs Dale daily was taken without fear or favour.

I put this thing down again. 'The man isn't even funny,' I said to Jill. 'And I don't believe he's even stupid—he's just wicked!'

'Take it easy, breezy,' said Big Jill.

'And there's quite a lot of things that he's left out!'

'I don't doubt you're right,' she said to me.

'And the whole point is—he's not denounced this thing! Not denounced this riot! All he's doing is looking round for alibis.'

Jill sat down and started on her nails. 'He's just ignorant,' she said, 'not wicked.'

I cried out: 'To be ignorant, and *tell* people, *is* wicked.'

She looked up from her nail polish. 'All it comes to,' she said, 'is if you've got a black face in a white or off-white neighbourhood, *everything* you do's conspicuous. You just stick out like a sore thumb.'

'Everything you do!' I said, picking up the Dale daily and rolling it into a tight sausage. 'But what *do* they do, different from all the hustlers living in this slum?'

'You tell me,' said Jill.

'Look! There's more coloured unemployed than white. Everyone knows that. And not only layabouts: you see them queueing at the Labour every day for hours.'

'Yeah,' said Big Jill.

'And you know what it's like when they try to get a room: "no children, no coloureds".'

'I suppose,' said Jill, 'if you hate the one, you also hate the other.'

'As for white illegitimates, are there none around here, would you really say?'

'I don't know many myself who aren't,' Big Jill said.

'And what about white chicks?' I cried. 'Don't they *like* it? I mean, hasn't everybody seen them hanging around the Spades?'

'I've seen more than a few,' Jill said.

'And those ponces. Are none of the bastards Maltese, Cypriots, even home-grown products, just occasionally?'

'Plenty,' Big Jill said, looking up.

'Oh, sorry, Big Jill.'

'It's okay, baby.'

'What's the matter with our men?' I said to her. 'Can't they hold their own women? Do they have to get this pronk (and I bashed the Dale daily on to the chair back) to help them and protect them?'

'I should have thought,' said Jill, beginning on her right hand, 'there should be more than enough girls to go round for everybody.'

I stuffed the rolled paper among the tea-leaves. 'The whole thing, anyway,' I cried, 'is that what really matters is being missed. And here it is. If every Spade in England was a hustler, that's still no excuse for setting on them ten to one.'

Big Jill didn't answer me this time, and I got up.

'I don't understand my own country any more,' I said to her. 'In the history books, they tell us the English race has spread itself all over the dam world: gone and settled everywhere, and that's one of the great, splendid English things. No one invited us, and we didn't ask anyone's permission, I suppose. Yet when a few hundred thousand come and settle among our fifty millions, we just can't take it.'

'Yep,' Big Jill said.

'Upstairs,' I continued, 'I've got a brand new passport. It says I'm a citizen of the UK and the Colonies. Nobody asked me to be, but there I am. Well. Most of these boys have got exactly the same passport as I have—and it was *we* who thought up the laws that gave it to them. But when they turn up in the dear old mother country, and show us the dam thing, we throw it back again in their faces!'

Big Jill got up too. 'You're getting worked up,' she said.

'You bet I am!'

She looked at me. 'People in glass houses . . .' she said.

'What does that mean?'

'Listen, darling. Personally, I live off mysteries, and that doesn't give me the right to be particular. As for you, you peddle pornographic pictures round the villages, and very nice ones they are, I don't deny. But that makes it rather hard for you, it seems to me, to preach at anybody.'

'I don't dig that,' I said, 'at all. You can hustle, and still be a man, not a beast.'

'If you say so, honey,' Big Jill answered. 'And now I must turf you out, the chicks will be screaming for their breakfast.'

'Oh, fine then, Big Jill.' I went to the door, and said to her, 'You are on my side, though, aren't you?'

'Oh, sure,' she said. 'I'm all for equality . . . If a coloured girl comes in here she's every bit as welcome as the others . . .'

'I see,' I said to her.

She came over and put her hammer-thrower's arm across my shoulder. 'Don't worry, son,' she said, 'and don't take things too much to heart that aren't your business. The Spades can look after themselves . . . they're big strong boys. A lot of them are boxers . . .'

'Oh, yes,' I said. 'But remember what I saw just now. Put Flikker and twenty Teds inside the ring tooled up with dusters in their gloves, and there's a sort of handicap.'

'Flikker's been sent away,' she said.

'Oh yes? He has?'

'He's on remand in custody.'

'This is the first time I've liked a magistrate.'

Big Jill came out into the area. 'It's not the Teds you have to worry about,' she said, 'but if the men join in it, too. The men round here are rather a tough lot.'

'I've noticed that,' I said to her, going out to take the padlocks off my Vespa.

'Where are you off to, baby?'

'I'm going to take a look around my manor.'

As soon as you passed into the area, you could sense that there was something on. The sun was well up now, and the streets were normal, with the cats and traffic—until suddenly you realized that they *weren't*. Because there in Napoli, you could feel a *hole*: as if some kind of life was draining out of it, leaving a sort of vacuum in the streets and terraces. And what made it somehow worse was that, as you looked around, you could see the people hadn't yet noticed the alteration, even though it was so startling to you.

Standing about on corners, and outside their houses, there were Teds: groups of them, not *doing* anything, but standing in circles, with their heads just a bit bent down. There were motor-bikes about, as well, and the kids had often got them out there at angles on the roadway, instead of parked against the kerb as usual, for a natter. Also, I noticed, as I cruised the streets, that quite a few of those battered little delivery vans that I've referred to—usually dark blue, and with the back doors tied on with wire, or one door off—had groups around them, also, who didn't seem to be mending them, or anything. There were occasional lots of chicks, giggling and letting out little yells, a bit too loud for that time of the morning. There were also more than the usual number of small kids about. As for the Spades, they seemed to creep a bit, and keep in bunches. And although they often did this anyway, a great number of them were hanging out of windows and speaking to each other loud across the streets. As I continued on, I came to patches once again where all was absolutely as before: quiet and ordinary. Then—turn a corner, and you were back once more in a part where the whole of Napoli seemed like it was *muttering*.

Then I saw my first 'incident' (as A. Drove wrote it)—or, as you know, my second. Here it was. Coming along, pushing a pram and wearing those really horrible clothes that Spade women do (not men)—I mean all colours of the spectrum and the wrong ones put together, and with shoes like Minnie Mouse—was a coloured mum with that self-satisfied expression that all mums have. Beside her was her husband, I imagine it was—anyway, he was talking at her all the time, and she wasn't listening. Then, coming from the opposite direction (and there always seems to *be* an opposite direction), was a white mum, also with kiddie-car and hubby, and whose clothes were just as dreadful as the Spade mum's were—except that the Spade girl's looked worse, somehow, because you could see, at any rate, that she was *trying*, and hadn't given up all hope of glamour.

Well, these two met and, as there's no law of the road on pavements, both angled their prams in the same direction, and collided. And that started it. Because neither would give way, and the two men both joined in, and before you knew where you were, about a hundred people, white and coloured, had appeared from absolutely nowhere. Quite honestly! I was watching the thing quite closely from near to, straddling my Vespa on the roadway, and one minute there were two (or three) people on each side, and next minute there were fifty.

Now, even then, if in normal times, the thing would have passed off, with the usual argument, and even then, if someone had stepped in and said, 'break it up,' or 'don't be so fucking idiotic,' all would have gone well—but no one said this, and as for coppers, well, of course there wasn't one. Then somebody threw a bottle, and that was it.

That milk that arrives mysteriously every morning, I suppose it brings us life, but if trouble comes, it's been put there—or the bottles it comes in have done—by the devil. And dustbins, that get emptied just as regularly, and take everything away—they and their lids, especially, have become much the same thing: I mean, the other natural city weapon of war. They were soon both flying, and I had to crouch behind my Vespa, then pull it over, when I got a chance, behind a vehicle.

Even then, it was still, in a way, if you'll believe me, rather *fun*: I mean, the bottles flying, and the odd window smashing, little boys and girls running round in circles shouting, and people weaving and dodging, like they were playing a sort of enjoyable, dirty game. Then there was a scream, and a white kid collapsed, and somebody shouted a Spade had pulled a knife. It's always those attacked who give the pretext—don't we know! Anyway, there was some blood for all to see.

Then, just as suddenly, the Spades all ran, as if someone had told them to on a walkie-talkie from headquarters somewhere—and they dived round corners and inside their houses, slamming doors. Honest! One minute there were white and coloured faces battling, and the next there were only white. There was a lot of shouting and discussion after that, and a few more bottles through the windows where a Spade or two was peeping out, and the white kid was carried on the pavement where I couldn't see him, and the law arrived in a radio-car and told everybody to disperse. And that was that. All over.

Then, a bit later, came incident number two—or three. Along another road I was prospecting, I saw driving along quite slow, because anyway it was pulling up, one of those 'flashy cars' A. Drove was on about, and four Spades in it—and the driver handling the thing in that way Spades often do, i.e., very expertly, but as if he didn't realize it was a *machine*, not a wonderful animal of some kind. Well, two of those delivery vans I spoke of sandwiched it like the law cars do in US crime films, and out from the back and front of them came about sixteen fellers—those from the back spilling out as if they were some peculiar kind of cargo the van had on board that day. And these were not Teds, but *men*—anyway, up in the twenties, somewhere, I should judge—and this time there was no previous argument whatever, they just rushed at that vehicle, and wrenched the doors open, and dragged out the Spades, and crunched them. Of course, they fought back—though once again, there was that same brief hesitation as I'd noticed with the Sikhs, that same moment of complete *surprise*. Two were left lying, and got kicked (those boys certainly knew all about vulnerable parts), and two made away, one weeping; and about a hundred of my own people gathered round about to watch.

And about those who watched, I saw something new to me, and which you may find quite incredible—but I swear it's the truth I'm telling you—they didn't even seem to *enjoy* themselves particularly—I mean, seeing all this—they didn't shout, or bawl, or cheer; they just stood by, out of harm's way, these English people did, and *watched.* Just like at home at evening, with their Ovaltine and slippers, at the telly. Quite decent, respectable people they seemed, too: white-collar workers and their wives, I expect, who'd probably been out to do their shopping. Well, they saw the lads get in the Spades' car, and drive it against a concrete lamp-standard, and climb back in their handy little delivery vans, and drive away. And once again, that was that. Except that a few coloured women came out and tended the men lying there, who the bystanders I spoke of had come up a bit nearer to, to examine.

Then came another incident—and soon, as you'll understand, I began to lose count a little, and, as time went on, lose count a bit of what time was, as well. This one was down by the Latimer road railway station, among those criss-cross of streets I mentioned earlier, like Lancaster, and Silchester, and Walmer, and Blechynden. In this part, by now, there was quite a muster: I mean, by now people realized what was happening—that there were kicks to be had if you came out in the thoroughfare, and besides, the pubs were emptying for the afternoon. And they all moved about like up in Middlesex street at the market there on Sunday, groups shifting and re-forming, searching. People were telling about what had happened here, or there, or in some other place, and they all seemed disappointed nothing was happening for them then and there.

Well, they weren't disappointed long. Because out of the Metropolitan Railway station—the dear old London Transport, we all think so safe and so reliable—came a bunch of passengers, and among them was a Spade. Just one. A boy of my own age, I'd say, carrying a hold-all and a brown paper parcel—a serious-looking kiddy with a pair of glasses, and one of those rather sad, drab suits that some Spades wear, particularly students, in order to show the English people that we mustn't think they're savages in grass skirts and bones stuck in their hair, but twentieth-century numbers just like we are. I think he was an African: anyway, there's no doubt that's where his ancestors all came from—millions of them, for centuries way back in time.

Now, this kiddy must have been rather dumb. Because he

evidently didn't rumble anything was at all unusual—perhaps he'd come down from Manchester or somewhere, to visit pals. Anyway, down the road he walked, stepping aside politely if people were in his way, and they all watching. All those eyes watching him, and the noise dropping. Then someone cried out, 'Get him!' and the Spade dug it quick enough then—and he started running down the Bramley road like lightning, though still clutching his hold-all and his parcel, and at least a hundred young men chasing after him, and hundreds of girls and kids and adults running after *them*, and even motor-bikes and cars. Some heathen god from home must have shouted sense into his ear just then, because he dived into a greengrocer's and slammed the door. And the old girl inside locked it from within, and she glared out at the crowd, and the crowd gathered round there, and they shouted—and I'm quoting their words exactly—'Let's get him!' and 'Bring him out!' and 'Lynch him!'

They cried that.

But they didn't get him. What they got, was the old greengrocer women instead, who came out of another door, and went for them. Picture this! This one old girl, with her grey hair all in a mess, and her old face flushed with fury, she stood there surrounded by this crowd of hundreds, and she bawled them out. She said they were a stack of cowards and gutter bastards, the whole lot of them, but they started shouting back at her, and I couldn't hear. But she didn't budge, the old girl, and her husband had got the shutters up inside, and by and by the law made its appearance with some vans as well this time, and they got through the crowd, and started milling round, and collected the young African, and moved among the mob in groups of six and told it to disperse—with truncheons out this time, just for a change.

I went off after this to be a bit alone. I rode out of the area to the big open space on Wormwood Scrubs, and I sat down on the grass to have a think. Because what I'd just seen in there made me feel weak and hopeless: most of all because, except for that old vegetable woman (who I bet will go straight up to heaven like a supersonic rocket when she dies—nothing can stop that one), no one, absolutely no one, had reacted against this thing. You looked round to find the members of the other team—even just a few of them—and there weren't any. I mean, any of us. The Spades were fighting back all right, of course, because they had to. But there were none of us.

When this thing happens to you, please believe me, it's just like as if the stones rise up from the pavement there and hit you, and the houses tumble, and the sky falls in. I mean, everything that you relied on, and all the natural things, do what you don't expect them to. Your sense of security, and of there being some plan, some idea behind it all somewhere, just disappears.

I dusted my arse, and rode down Wood Lane to the White City, where the old BBC's building that splendid modernistic palace, so as to send their telly messages to the nation. And I looked at it and thought, 'My God, if I could get in there and tell them—all the millions! Just take them across the railway tracks, not a quarter of a mile away, and show them what's happening in the capital city of our country!' And I'd say to them, 'If you don't want that, for Christ's sake come down and stop it—every one of you! But if that's what you do want, then I don't want you, and for me, it's good-bye England!' Then I turned back again inside the area, inside those railway tracks that hem it in—out of White City into Brown Town—and as I was travelling past the station there, I saw another small encouraging sight, and stopped and looked.

This was a small old geezer, with a cloth cap and a choker, who'd got hold of a young Spade so tight I thought at first he was arresting him, or going to damage him in some way. But no! Apparently this boy must have told the geezer he lived up in Napoli, and was a bit dubious about going home, and this old codger, feeling his youth again, must have grabbed him by the arm, and said, 'You're okay, son, come with me,' and set off holding the coloured boy with a look on his face as if to say, 'If you touch him, then you touch *me*, too!' And I wondered why it was the only two I'd seen who'd fought back had been old-timers?

But that gave me an idea. I rode back to the White City station, parked my Vespa, and went inside to have a look around. And sure enough, there was a young Spade standing there, and I went up to him, and gave a great big smile I didn't feel, and said, how's tricks? and would he care for a lift home on my Vespa? He seemed a bit doubtful, but I asked him where he lived and went on chatting him, because I've found if you keep on *talking* at anyone who suspects you, the mere sound of your voice usually wins them over, and he said Blenheim crescent, and I said hop on then, and I'll see you there. As we went out, a ticket number said, was I carrying my iron bar, just in case? Real witty.

So I batted along, and I tried to make conversation with the kiddo, but he just clung on and said, 'Yeh, man!' to everything I said, and as we reached the groups of bystanders we got one or two yells and whistles, and the odd brick, and a few kids ran out on the road in front of us, but I weaved or accelerated, and we got through to Blenheim crescent without trouble. I was keyed up, expecting motor-bike chases, and big mobs, but nothing happened. And that was the extraordinary thing that day in Napoli! It all popped up here, and subsided, then popped up there, then somewhere else, so that you never knew what streets were frantic, and what streets peaceful.

Well, I saw the kid to his door, where lots of dark faces were peering through the curtains, and he asked me in a moment. Well, frankly, *I* was a bit dubious now. It wasn't that I was afraid of my own people seeing, so very much, but I was a bit scared of the Spades themselves! After all, one white face is so much like another —especially on a day like this. However, I thought I really *must* stop being scared, or I just wouldn't get anywhere, and so I said sure, why not, I'd be glad to, but could I bring my Vespa in there and park it in the hall.

Well, he took me down to the basement, and there I found a sort of war cabinet of West Indians in progress. The boy made it clear, right away, that I wasn't a P. o.W. or something, and they patted me on the back, though several still looked dam suspicious, and wouldn't talk to me. They gave me a glass of rum, and one said to me, what did I think about all this? And I said I was disgusted and ashamed. Well, one of them said, at any rate, I was the first white man they'd seen that day who looked them in the eye when he spoke to them.

And then the phone rang, and a tall Spade with a bald head picked it up—and would you believe it, he was through on the blower to Kingston, Jamaica! And he had quite a natter with the folks back home, and I didn't much like a lot of what he said, and I wondered how my own people, out there in Kingston, surrounded by thousands of black faces, would be feeling when the news of it got around? And I also wondered whether, all over Napoli, there weren't other Spades calling Trinidad, and Ghana, and Nigeria, and Christ knows where, and telling *them* the story? And how all the whites in all *those* places would be treated, too? Because one big mistake a lot of locals make is to think that all Spades work on the London Transport or on building sites—whereas stacks of them are business and professional men, who know all the answers: for example, this bald-headed character turned out to run a chain of hairdressing establishments.

Then one of the Spades who was still suspicious of me said, did I think it was the English way of life to attack 6,000-odd in an area where there were 60,000 whites or more, and if us white boys wanted to show how brave we were, why didn't we choose an area like Harlem, where the whites were a minority? I could think of a lot of answers to that, but the others shut him up immediately—in fact, what amazed me the most, in the middle of all this, was how dam polite they all were to me. And then they started chatting about plans, and one said the law was no use whatever, they must set up vigilantes; and another said anyway, they'd got to organize as a community, and keep it that way in future; and another said up in Nottingham, they'd moved Spades out of certain areas 'for their own safety', but if anyone tried to move *him*, he was dam well staying where he was, because this was his house, and his wife and kids were born here, and he'd had a bash in the RAF, and he was one of the Queen's objects the same as any other. And I began to get embarrassed, as you can imagine, because of course I partly agreed with them, but also I wanted to stick up a bit for my own people somehow, if I could. And the hairdresser cat realized this, and he and the kid I'd brought there saw me to the door, and opened it cautiously, and said all was clear, and I trundled my Vespa down into the road. And the kid came out to the pavement, and said thanks for everything, and shook my hand and gave me one of those smiles that Spades can turn on when they feel like it.

Well now, I thought, I'd better look in back home, to see if anything was happening *there*, and also to find out if Cool was quite okay. So I started off, and made the corner, where eight or so crashed the bike, and slung me off, and next thing I was standing against a wall with faces six inches from me. And what I liked least of all was that the oafo nearest me was carrying something wrapped in a science-fiction magazine.

Now luckily, the happenings of the day had made me so indignant, I wasn't frightened any longer. And also, although I'm a nervy sort of number, when a crisis comes, I usually surprise myself by keeping calm—however much my ticker's pounding there inside. So I stayed still as a rock, and eyed the yobbos, waiting, with one hand in one pocket round my bunch of keys, and the third finger through the ring of it.

'We sore yer,' said an oafo.

'Darkie-luvver,' said another.

When I glimpsed the SF number un-wrapping his chopper, I whipped my keys across his face, and kicked another you-know-where. Then it was on! I was tensing for the death-blow as I thrashed about, when suddenly I realized I was not alone in this—in fact, for just a moment, I had nobody to fight with, because two other kids were fighting them, so without waiting to raise my hat and ask who the hell they were, I ran over to my fallen Vespa, grabbed the metal pump, and cracked it on some skulls, and see! the Teds were in flight, except for one lying whimpering on the pavement, and I was shaking hands with Dean Swift and the Misery Kid.

'Dr Livingstone, I presume,' said Swift.

'You bet your bloody life it is!' I cried.

'That feller *hurt* me,' said Misery, rubbing his hands and looking very pale and angry.

'My Gawd!' I cried, messing their hair-dos for them and almost kissing them. 'It had to take *this* to bring you two together!'

The Ted on the deck was trying to get up, and the Dean pushed him down and held his neck with his Italian shoe. 'We heard there'd been happenings,' he said, 'and thought we'd come up and take a dekko.'

'It's all in the evening papers,' said the Kid.

Well, was I un-displeased! And was I glad it was two kids of my own age, and two jazz addicts, even if of different tendencies, and even if one was a layabout and the other a junkie, because this seemed to me to show their admiration for coloured greats like Tusdie and Maria really *meant* something to them.

The Dean had picked up my Vespa, and he checked the motor, and then said, 'Well, how we to now? What we go where we do?'

'What about this one?' I said pointing to the Ted, who the Misery Kid was holding by his hair.

The Dean approached him. 'You're full of shit, aren't you,' he said, whizzing his fist round within a half-inch of the zombie's face.

'Wot I dun?' asked the yobbo.

And that's it! He'd scare you stiff inside his little group, but now he looked such a drip you couldn't even get vexed enough to crunch him.

'Wot you dun?' said Dean Swift. 'What you've done's get born—that was your big mistake.'

The yoblet, seeing he wasn't going to get fixed, had plucked up courage from somewhere. 'Ar,' he said, 'so a few of ver blacks git chived. Why oll ver fuss?'

The Dean swung him round, gave him a Stanley Matthews kick on his striped pink jeans, and told him to beat it fast. At the corner, the thing cried out, 'Cum back termorrer fer ver nest lot!' and cut out.

Well then, as we were discussing this, and examining the yobbos' chopper, who should come round the corner but a cowboy: one of that youthful, pasty sort, with shoulder-blades, and a helmet not too secure, and boots too big for his athletic feet—usually the least pleasant, those young ones, that is, if any are. And he looked at the Vespa, and we three, and the metal pump, and the chopper, and he said, 'What's this?'

'You're prompt on the scene, son,' said the Dean.

'I said, "What's this?" ' the law repeated, pointing at the chopper.

'This,' said the Dean, 'is what the local lads you can't control tried to do my pal with.'

'What pal?'

'Me,' I said.

'And why you holding that pump?'

'Because I used it to defend myself,' I told him.

'So you were in it too,' the cowboy said.

'That's right.'

'But you say you got attacked.'

'You're beginning to dig, mate,' said Dean Swift. 'You're speedy.'

The copper stared at the Dean. But the Dean had carried that look often enough before, and stared right back. 'You call me "officer",' the cowboy said.

'I didn't know you were one, captain. I thought you were a junior constable.'

The cowboy looked round, as if wishing for reinforcements, and said, 'You're all coming to the station.'

'Why?' asked Dean Swift.

'Because I say so. That's why.'

The Dean gave a crazy yell of laughter. And though I sympathized with his attitude, I wasn't pleased, because all I wanted was to get to hell out of here immediately.

'Look, captain,' said Dean Swift. 'Aren't you supposed to arrest the law-breakers? Well, that's the way they went—all the whole click of them.'

'If you don't shut your trap,' said the cowboy, 'I'll knock you off as well.'

'Why?' said the Dean. 'You afraid of Teds, then?'

'Take it easy, Dean,' I said.

'Boy, of course he is!' cried Swift, turning to Misery and me, as if he was explaining something perfectly well known to all. 'He's young, he's alone, he's not used to trouble of this kind—he's used to pinching parkers on the broad highway.'

This cop turned rather red, and, thanks to Swift's efforts, broke the number-one rule of the copper mystery, which is never to *argue*. Because as soon as the public hears a copper argue, and see he's a human being like any other (well, let's be generous), they know he's only a worried man in fancy-dress.

'We're not afraid of trouble,' the young cowboy said.

'Oh, no!' cried the Dean, really getting in the groove now. 'If there's sufficient of you, certainly you're not. We all remember how you cleared the streets so thoroughly when old B. and K. came here, or Colonel Tito. But if you're a few, and the trouble rises round you, and metal like this lot's flying, you can't take it, and can't stop it! Not here in this dump you can't, anyway. If it was Chelsea or Belgravia, you'd stop it soon enough, maybe . . .'

Now, all the while he was needling the cowboy, Swift, we both saw, was edging a bit away from him, and throwing a glance or two at Misery and me, who were doing likewise, and suddenly the Dean shouted to me, 'Your place!' and pushed the chopper at the copper (handle first, though), and when he backed away a second, we all scattered, and while the Dean lured the law, I managed to make it off with Misery on my Vespa.

I yelled at him as we bowled along: 'Our city's dangerous! They don't know it, but our city's getting dangerous!'

'You too!' the Kid cried, as we shot a junction.

'They've got to know it!' I shouted. 'We've got to tell them somehow!'

'Yeah,' Misery answered, as we turned into my alley.

There were no signs of anything back home, and I made it up to the first floor and broke in on Mr Cool. There he was, sure enough, but with one white eye and strips of plaster, and his half-brother Wilf, who you may remember. 'Hi!' we all said, and I asked Cool for the fable.

They'd got him, he said, down by Oxford gardens, where he's been visiting his Ma, when they threw burning rags in through the window, and Cool had gone out to make objections. And when the argument developed, his brother Wilf (much to my surprise, I must say) had shown that blood was thicker than prejudice, and sailed out and mixed in on Cool's behalf. A passing cat, who'd turned out, of all things, to be a county councillor, had given them a lift home in his jalopy, and there they both were for all to see.

'Well, what *you* think of all this, Wilf?' I couldn't resist asking the number.

'We ain't seen the end of it,' he said rather sourly, 'that's all I got ter say.'

'The law's losing its grip, if it ever had any,' said Mr Cool. 'The two lots are just going where it isn't, and having it out there.'

'Surprising!' the Misery Kid said.

The law never settled much round these parts, any time,' said Wilf.

Well, now I had to do a thing I'd already decided, which was make a few telephone calls. So I collected all the fourpennies I could, and went down to Big Jill's, where I found nobody in, but got the key from its hidey-hole in the toilet cistern, and fetched out my pocket diary, and started business on that blower. Because I was determined to call every cat that I could think of, and *tell* them about what was going on.

At the best of times, when you call twenty numbers in a row, as you can do to fix a party, you don't get more than half of them, as is well known. And I only got a quarter—as well as those where I couldn't hack my way beyond the secretary, or even the switch-board starlet. I got V. Partners, who listened patiently, and made some intelligent comments, and said it was disgraceful, and I must get some snaps of it, if I could, for the exhibition. Mannie was out, but Miriam dug at once what I was on about, and said she'd get Mannie over as soon as she'd made contact. I got through to Dido at the Mirabelle, and she said I was a naughty boy to break in on her evening meal, but certainly, she'd tell her editor all I said, and a lot of her best friends were coloured. At the Dubious and Chez Nobody they seemed more interested, and said they'd spread the tale around.

By this time I was running out of pennies, and had to have a summit conference with the operator as to whether I could have all the calls I was entitled to if I put in silver pieces. I drew blank with Call-me-Cobber, which perhaps was lucky, and Zesty-Boy's secretary said she'd see he got the message—yes she'd written it all down. I even called Dr A. R. Franklyn, who listened carefully, and asked how was my Dad, and said would I please be careful of myself. Then I knocked off Big Jill's meter money from the rubber ash-tray shaped like a bra she keeps it in, and called the Mrs Dale daily, and asked for Mr Drove. I got through, much to everyone's astonishment, and told him he might not remember me, but he was a lump of shit, and I'd do him if I ever saw his face again—whether carrying his furled umbrella, or not doing so. I felt better after this, and crash-landed, after the third try, at a session the ex-Deb was having out at Chiswick, and although she sounded raving to me over the blower, she said she'd be right along. I even, as well, thought of trying Suze and Henley at the Cookham place and in the London showrooms, but I skipped it. Of course I tried Wiz, but only got the dialling tone—not even Wiz's woman.

But even with the cats who dug it best, the great difficulty I had was in getting over what was *happening*: I mean, the scale of it, how serious, and that this was supposed to be the British Isles. Because even though most of them had heard something of it by now, there seemed to me to be a sort of conspiracy in the air to pretend what was happening in Napoli, wasn't happening: or, if it was, it somehow didn't signify at all.

I shot off after this up to my penthouse, to wash off the mud and blood, and have a lay down for a moment, and a bite. And while I was doing so, there was a little knock, and on me walked the Fabulous Hoplite. He was looking a bit diminuendo, and smiled rather nervously, and was wearing a beach-gown and his Sardinian slippers.

'My!' he said. 'What times we live in!'

'Sit down, beautiful. You can say that again.'

'You've been *bruised*, child,' he said, trying to grope my tribal scars.

'Hands off the model, Hop,' I told him. 'How have things been with you?'

The Hoplite got up, spun round so that the beach-gown did a Royal Ballet thing, and sat down again and said, 'Oh, no complaints . . . But I don't like all this.'

'Who does?'

'*Some*body must,' he said, 'or it wouldn't happen.'

'Clever boy. You been out at all?'

He let the gown fall open to reveal his pectorals. 'Once was enough,' he said. 'A glimpse, and I was in again.'

'Wise child.'

'I suppose *you've* been out fighting battles!' His eyes gleamed.

'The battles fought me.'

He folded the gown. 'I've heard some terrible tales . . .'

'Yeah?'

'Oh, yes. *Ecoutez-moi.* The whore at the sweet shop—the skinny bitch—said to me, "And when my husband got up, he was holding his back, and I saw there was a knife in it".'

'Whose knife?'

'A dark stranger's. Really, darling, I know you love them, but they're so *rough*. And somebody else I know has had thirty-seven stitches in his throat.'

'Just like a necklace.'

'Oh! Don't be so callous!'

The Hoplite once more arose. 'The innocent suffer for the guilty,' he said, with a little sigh. 'I expect all that most of the serfs who live in this sewer really long for, is just to be left alone—I mean, persons of both tints and textures.'

'Yep,' I said.

'Me, for example,' said the Hoplite. 'A pervert like me, with the fattest file, for my age, in the vice department's system, simply wants to avoid mud being stirred up needlessly.'

I got up too, and said, 'I love you, Hoplite, who doesn't, but I really must tell you some day that you're a tit.'

'You think so?' he said, quite pleased.

'Or, in plain speech, a fool.'

'Oh, I don't like *that* . . . Not at all. You see, I set very great store by your opinions: even though they're sometimes so severe. . . .'

'Well, if you do, Fabulous, may I say, I think the world's divided into those who, when they see a car crash, try to *do* something about it, and those who stand by and gape.'

'You looked like John the Baptist when you said that.'

'You never met him.'

The Hoplite smiled. 'But you, dear!' he said. 'We all heard you shrieking on the telephone, and isn't what you're doing exactly that? Bringing in a lot of gapers?'

'No,' I said.

'No?'

'No. I want witnesses. Friends who will witness this thing, and friends who'll show the Spades this two square miles isn't being written off as a ghetto.'

'And you think, sweet, that would improve matters?'

'Yes.'

'Really?'

'Yes. If they saw a few normal, healthy faces around here, it would lower the temperature they're all trying to build up. If the Spades saw a few hundred different kinds of kids who admired them, and the Teds saw a few hundred of the coloured nurses who'll have to stitch them up in hospital, it certainly would make a difference.'

'But they're not very *important* people.'

'Well, Hoplite, let's bring them in too! This is their big opportunity—the one they've been waiting for to prove their words about the kind of country this is! Let's have some of those public figures who haunt the telly studios, to advise us what to do! Let's have the thinkers of the left and right to tell us how they'd handle this one! Not from their home base, but from here! Let's have the bishops and ministers, to hold an inter-racial service in the open air! Isn't this their big chance? And let's have the Queen in all her glory, riding through the streets of Napoli, and saying: "You're *all* my subjects! Each and every one of you's my own!"'

The Hoplite shook his head in pity, gave me a little wave, and blew.

I got my bend-torch out of a drawer, because it's always best to have a weapon, if you can, whose explanation's innocent, and I got my blood-donor's card in its perspex folder (which I'd got when I started giving the pints after Dr F. had cured me), because this always seems to impress the law—not much, but just a bit—if they grab you and turn out your pockets, and I stuffed my new passport in my arse pocket as well, I dunno why, just for luck, I suppose. I took up my Rolleiflex, but put it down again, because it didn't seem useful any longer. Then I put on my buckle belt, and a zip jacket that's like a sabre if you swing it by one arm, and went down the stairs where, coming down as well, I ran into Cool.

'You taking the night air too?' I said.

'Yeah. I'll have a look around . . .'

'Be cool, Cool.'

'Oh, sure, white boy.'

I stopped the cat before the door, and took both his arms and looked at him, and said, 'I hope this isn't going to turn you sour, man.'

He smiled (quite rare with Cool). 'Oh, no . . .' he said. 'We don't turn sour—we must object. And you,' he added. 'I suppose it's not nice for you to feel your tribe is in the wrong.'

'Thanks, Cool,' I said. 'I bet you're the only Spade in Napoli who's thought of *us*.'

I slapped his arm, and we both went out into the dark, and this time I'd decided not to take my Vespa. On the pavement, without speaking about this, we shook hands and both went different ways.

There's no doubt night favours wickedness: I mean, I don't think the night's wicked, and I love it, but it opens the trap for all the monsters to come out. I went down by Westbourne Park station, and took a ride along the scenic railway to the Bush. The train was packed with sightseers from the West, who hopped out at different stations for the free display. From the height between the stops, you could see the odd fire and firemen and, at sudden glimpses as the train rocked by a street at right angles, the crowds, and law cars prowling, or standing parked with cowboys packed in them, waiting for action, like bullets in a clip. And when the train halted, at Ladbroke and by Latimer, you could hear loud-speakers blaring something harsh and meaningless, like at Battersea pleasure gardens, in the funfair there. And all along the ride there were patches of blue-black darkness, then sudden glares and flares of dazzling light.

But at the Bush, I was amazed. Because when I crossed over, beyond the Green, to that middle-class section outside our area—all was peace and quiet and calm and as-you-were-before. Believe me! Inside the two square miles of Napoli, there was blood and thunder, but just outside it—only across one single road, like some national frontier—you were back in the world of Mrs Dale, and What's my line? and England's green and pleasant land. Napoli was like a prison, or a concentration camp: inside, blue murder, outside, buses and evening papers and hurrying home to sausages and mash and tea.

I bought a late night edition by the telly theatre there. They were playing it up—big headlines, no paper can resist that—but also trying to play it down. Reactions from Africa and the Caribbean, it said, had been unfavourable, but much exaggerated. There was a bit of gloating in South Africa and the US South, which, in this difficult situation, was greatly to be deplored. The cardinal fact to remember was that neither at Nottingham—nor even at Notting Hill, so far—had there been any loss of actual life. Meanwhile a cat at Scotland Yard had issued a message to discourage sightseers. I threw the thing away. The law never wants you to see what it can't handle. Then I went back inside the area again.

I walked down an empty street that was lit, as a lot of them are round there, by lamps put up in Queen Boadicea's day, when I saw, coming along, three coloured cats, keeping together. I looked around to see if they were being chased or anything, but they weren't, so I went up and said, 'Hi, boys, what's cooking?'—when I saw that one of them had a spanner, it looked to be (anyway, something metal), and they made a rush. Boy, did I gallop! With those three sons of Africa racing after me and hissing! I made for a pool of light, and dodged round some vehicles, and batted across a road straight into Mr Wiz. 'Hold it!' he cried, and the coloured cats saw I had an ally, and melted like a falling gleam. 'Boy!' I cried, slapping the old Wiz like a carpet-beater. 'Am I glad to see your wicked face! Where the hell have you been, man, I've been seeking for you!' The Wizard took my arm, and said, 'Cool it, kiddo,' and just round two corners we found ourselves in the middle of a large assembly.

This lot were being addressed by a thing from the White Protection League, whose numbers were also distributing leaflets round the throng. The speaker on the portable platform was a man of quite ordinary appearance—i.e., the kind you'd find difficult to describe if someone asked you after—except that now he was lit up and jet-propelled by a sort of crazy, electric frenzy. He wasn't talking to any*body*—to any human cat you could imagine, even the very worst—but out into space, out into the night to some spirit there, some witch-doctor he was screaming to for help and blessing. And looking up at him, in the yellow-coloured glare, were the white faces he was protecting, all turned, by the municipal lamps above, into a kind of un-washed violet grey.

I nudged Wiz. 'He's round the bend,' I said.

Wiz didn't answer.

'I said he's flipped, boy!' I shouted, above the noise of the loudspeaker.

Then I looked at Wizard. And on my friend's face, as he stared up at this orator, I saw an expression that made me shiver. Because the little Wiz, so tight and sharp and trim and dangerous, had on a little smile, that showed his teeth a bit, and his wiry little body was all clenched, and something was staring through his eyes that came from God knows where, and he raised on his toes, and shot up his arms all rigid, and he cried out, shrill like a final cry, 'Keep England white!'

I stood there a moment, while the mob roared too. Then I grabbed Wizard's neck clothes with all the strength I have in my body, and I yanked him round about off balance, and I hit him with all my life behind it, and he stumbled. Then I looked round quick, and saw how it was, and ran.

Luckily, I knew Napoli: and I got away easier than I'd hoped and feared. Round by Cornwall crescent, I ran into an area, and stood there, panting. Then I crossed Ladbroke grove, and made it up the rise, keeping along the railings.

Under a light ahead, I saw a peculiar figure: it was an African trader well known round the area, a long, lean old number who runs a little shoplet specializing in imported products that the Spades like for their cuisine. He usually wears an antique suit and a battered Anthony Eden, but tonight he was in his full regalia—I mean, he had on his African robes, and was standing outside his house there, all alone, and waiting.

I went up and said 'Hi!' and asked him what the score was. He said this was his home, and his wife and children were inside it, and he didn't want to hurt anyone, but if anyone wanted to damage them, they'd have to have a word with him first. He'd been standing out there all day, and meant to continue standing there, he said, as long as these hooligans were around. I loved the way that old boy said that word, 'hooligan'! It came right out of his stomach, and he threw it up through his big lips like it was a nasty mess he was vomiting up. I said to him, 'Stick to it, daddy,' and I liked his robes, and as soon as I got a chance I was going to Africa to see all the cats wearing theirs like on the travelogues, and from out of somewhere there he fished a panatella for me, and I lit it, and made it up the road again.

Soon I could see lights. So I hurried on, and came on the outskirts of another crowd, and found they were gathered round the Santa Lucia club, which is a BWI clip-joint about as glamorous as an all-night urinal. There were several hundred milling there: and what added joy to the whole scene, was the presence of newsreel and TV cameras, with arc lamps and the odd flare and flashlight, as if the crowd were extras on a movie lot. And directing the whole lot, standing on a car roof with a microphone, was—yes, you've guessed it—Call-me-Cobber. That certainly was the evening of his career—the big scoop, our dauntless reporter right there in the firing line! And as for the Teds and hooligans, well, they can smell a camera, even a Press one, from a mile away, and there's nothing they like better than seeing their moronic faces next morning in the tabloids, so this was their big opportunity as well.

'Child!' shouted someone, and I looked across, and there, standing up in the back of a cream vintage Bentley, was the ex-Deb-of-Last-Year. I struggled across, and found she was with a bunch of Hooray Henries, who seemed, I will say this for them, a bit doubtful if all this was really so dam amusing. And as for the ex-Deb, she leaned out of her vehicle, and said, 'That crowd's nothing but a lot of bloody scum.'

'You're telling me,' I said.

'And what *is* that place?' she asked, waving a hand at the Santa Lucia club.

'A local nitery. You like to take a spin around in there?' I asked—a bit sarcastically, I must admit, because if the yelling crowd outside didn't do you, the Spades down in there, if there were any, most certainly would, if you attempted to get in.

'Certainly!' she cried, and she spoke up a bit loud even for my liking. 'I'd love to have a dance with someone African! They're the best dancers in the world!'

So she told me to get in, which I did thinking, 'Oh, well!' and the Henry at the wheel got the car up near the entrance, with everyone, when they saw the ex-Deb and the Henries, imagining, I suppose, that this was some item in the television programme. The ex-Deb and I got out, with a Hooray or two in tow, and shouldered down some steps into the basement area, and the ex-Deb banged with both hands on the locked door.

I admit I was petrified, but also so dam hysterical by now the whole thing struck me as quite funny, so I had an inspiration, and went in the outside can there, and got up on the pedestal, and, taking a chance, I shouted through the ventilator, 'Cool, if you're there, let us in, we're customers!' Then we waited a bit more outside the door, and the eye-shutter opened, and there was a noise of bolts and ironmongery, and the door opened eight inches, and we squeezed inside—but not the Hooray numbers, who got barred.

Well, down in the Santa Lucia club, they were certainly putting up an old troupers' show-must-go-on performance. Because they weren't cowering in corners, or putting up barricades, but hopping around to the strains of the juke-box, and sitting at tables drinking double rums: West Indians, a few GIs, and a small herd of brave hens from the local chickery. And all this while, from beyond the walls, that *other* noise that scared them, I hope, less than it did me. A GI nine feet high cut me out with the ex-Deb, and I sat down to have a breather. And then—out of the chicks' toilet, there walked Crêpe Suzette.

For just a minute, I was shaken rigid. Then I leapt up, shot over, and grabbed the girl. She was shook rigid too, but only a second, and we hugged like two Russian bears, then fell on two contemporary chairs.

'Crazy girl!' I shouted. 'Spill it quick! What the hell—'

She kissed me still, and said, 'I came up a week ago.'

'And you not told me? Bitch!'

'And when I heard this, I came right over.'

I looked at her. 'To be among the boys?'

'Yes.'

I kissed her at arm's length. 'Now, crazy, Suze!' I cried. 'Brave girl! Nice chicken! But it's mine you are now, not theirs.'

She shook her head. 'Not while all this goes on,' she said.

'Well, it won't forever, hon,' I told her.

'But while it does, darl, I'm staying here.'

'So long as it's clear I've got the option.'

We laughed like two hyenas, and I went and fetched two drinks, and the side window crashed, and a petrol bomb came in and rolled among the dancers and exploded, and the electrics all cut out, and there were shouts and screaming.

Then, there was a noise like thunder on the stairs outside, and a crashing and hammering on the door, and by the light of the bomb flare you could see the law rush in, and the fire service, not as if they were coming in to rescue anybody, but to capture an enemy position. Cats were being grabbed, and others weaving in all directions, and I'd lost Suze and the ex-Deb, so I followed a Spade in through the ladies' toilet, and we climbed out the window, and into a dark garden, and over a back wall.

There, this Spade and I, we both stood panting. And I said to him, 'Okay, *white trash*?' And he said to me, 'Okay, *darkie*,' and it was Cool. We both laughed—Ha! Ha! Ha!—then crept up to somebody's back door, opened it and tiptoed through the corridor to the front, and out down the steps where a kid was lying groaning, and I shone my torch on him, and I saw blood, and the blood belonged to Ed the Ted.

'Well!' said Mr Cool.

'Yeah,' I said too, and we just left him there, and went round in the street.

And there, there was a pitched battle. The Teds had got the law hemmed up against the railings—anyway, I suppose they must have been hemmed—and the rest of them were struggling with the Spades and one another, with razors and stakes and bike-chains and iron bars and even, at times, with knuckles. And soon I got scooped into the thing, and I heard a cry, 'Nigger's whore!', and through arms and bodies I saw Suze, and they'd got hold of her, some chicks as well as animals, and were rubbing dirt all over her face, and screaming if that's the colour she wanted to be, she'd got it. And I screamed out too, with all my lungs, and I fought like a maniac and couldn't get at her, and next thing I was slugged and staggered, and was vomiting.

Then someone heaved me up, and it was a Hooray Henry, and he said, 'Are you all right, old man?' And I said, 'No, old chap, and will you for Christ's sake try and get my girl.' Well, they had. Some more Hoorays and the ex-Deb had dragged her into the vintage vehicle, and I piled in too, and the Henry at the wheel said, 'Where to now?' and I said, 'Home!'

It was all I could do to keep them off the premises once we got there, because they were high and the ex-Deb, in particular, wanted to help Suze, but I said, thank you all very much, but would you please all fuck off, and leave us, which they did, and we staggered up, arm in arm, falling all over each other, and there, when we got up to my place, sitting holding his dreadful hat, was my half-brother Vern. 'Where you been?' he cried.

I didn't answer, and we both flopped. Vern came over, looked at us, and said, 'Your Dad's nearly gone. Ma said you got to come down there right away.'

'In a minute, Vern,' I said.

Then I kissed Suzette, vomit, and black face, and all.

'You got to come!' Vern kept saying, tugging me.

'In a *minute*, Jules,' I said. 'Do beat it now, boy, I'll come right down as soon as ever. Do get *out* of here just now,' and I pushed him through the door.

Then I came back to Suze and said, 'We'd better wash you.' She got up, looked at herself in the glass, and said, 'No, I like it this way. It suits me.'

'Hell, no,' I said, and went and got the bowl and things, and washed her all over, and I kissed her between, and there in my place at Napoli we made it at last, but honest, you couldn't say that it was sexy—it was just love.

Then I whipped up some eats, and we sat on the bed scoffing like some old married couple, and I stopped, and stared at her, and said, 'You're a mad girl, you know.'

She gave me a look.

'Yeah,' I said. 'And now it's going to be wedding bells.'

'Not for three years,' she said. 'There's got to be a divorce.'

'Oh, to hell with three years!' I cried, and grabbed her left hand, and pulled off Henley's Bond street ring, and went over to the window and threw it out there in Napoli. 'No reward for the finder!' I cried to the early dawn.

Then I turned round. 'What about Wiz?' I said. 'What is it makes you betray?'

'Some like it,' she said. 'It's a big kick to some,' then she went on eating.

'Well,' I said, 'old Wiz must sort it out with Satan when he meets him.'

'You believe in all that?' she said, getting up too.

'I certainly believe in Satan after tonight,' I told her, then came over again and said to her, 'The new Napoli Flikker. I hope the Spades sort him out.'

'Or you,' she said.

'No, not me, Suze. I'm cutting out of Napoli, and so are you.'

She looked at me again.

'We're off on our honeymoon,' I said, 'tomorrow. No, I mean it's today.'

She didn't let go, but shook her head. 'I'm not leaving here,' she said, with her pig-headed look returning, 'until it's over.'

I grabbed her hair and wiggled her head about. 'We'll talk about that,' I told her, 'a bit later. Now I must get down to Dad.'

'Now?'

'Yes. Bed down, chicken, I'll be back to bring you in the milk.'

I can't tell you what I felt, seeing Suze lying there on my bed, where I'd so often thought of her, and I ran back and kissed her till she struggled, then beat it out into the area and early morning.

But in the area, no Vespa! 'Good luck to them!' I cried, and started off on foot along the road. I guessed I'd have to make it up to the Gate to get a taxi, and I certainly wasn't going back into the bull-ring to ask any sort of motorist whatever for a lift. So I hoofed it along, and the streets were very quiet, like the silence after the crash of broken glass, and the green trees had the light on them again, and looked fresh and everlasting. Then some cat tried to run me down.

I whipped round, ready to murder this one, weak though I was, but who should it be but Mickey Pondoroso, at the wheel of his snazzy CD Pontiac. 'Mickey!' I cried. '*Buenas dias!* What the hell you doing in this asylum? You been studying some more conditions?'

Well, believe it or not, the diplomatic number had been doing exactly that: touring the area, poking his dam nose in everywhere, and he'd ended spending two hours at the section-house, because there'd been some little arguments over his car—and, would you believe it, too, on whether his dark face was Negroid or not, and this had infuriated the Latin American cat, because apparently his grandma *was* a Spade, and he was very proud of her and of her race, and he had stacks of cousins in the national football team which, I must know, had won the cup this year in 1958, and, by God! was going to win it next year too, and those hereafter.

I cut the cat short. 'Mickey P.,' I said, 'you're hired! You're driving me down to Pimlico, please, and it's very urgent.'

On the way, I asked Mickey which of the countries that he's been in had the least colour thing of any, and he said at once, Brazil. And I said, okay by me, the moment I've got the loot, I'm heading it out to Brazilia forever with my bird.

Because, in this moment, I must tell you, I'd fallen right out of love with England. And even with London, which I'd loved like my mother, in a way. As far as I was concerned, the whole dam group of islands could sink under the sea, and all I wanted was shake my feet off of them, and take off somewhere and get naturalized, and settle.

Mickey didn't seem to approve of this, although I'd thought the cat might be flattered. He said once a Roman, always a Roman, and in *every* country there were horrors as well as felicities—that was the word he used.

I said, that what had happened up in Napoli, could happen once again. That once you'd done some people, or group, or race a wicked injury, especially if they were weak, you'd come back and do it again, because that was how it was, and with people, too.

And he said, but didn't I realize these things could happen *any-where*?

I answered to this, I didn't mind so much its *happening*. But what I did mind is, that ever since Nottingham, more than a week ago, nobody had reacted strongly: so far as the government and top cats who control things were concerned, these riots might just not have happened at all, or have been in some other country.

Well, he delivered me at the door, and I said farewell, and thanks for the Vespa once again, I don't know what I'd have done without it, and he cut off like Fangio wherever he was going to.

The door opened up at once, and it was Ma, and I could see immediately that Dad was dead. 'Where is he?' I said, and she took me up the stairs. Ma didn't say anything, except just as we went inside the door, 'He kept asking for you, and I had to tell him you weren't there.'

I don't know if you've ever seen a corpse. As a matter of fact, it was my first time, and it really wasn't impressive very much, except for the whole thing about death and dying. I hope that's not disrespectful: but as I knew for sure, before I got there, Dad would be dead, I hadn't very much feeling left for what I saw there lying on the bed. All I felt, as a matter of fact, was so very much *older*. I felt that I'd moved one up nearer to something, now he was gone.

Old Ma was crying now. I had a good look at her, but it seemed perfectly genuine to me. After all, they'd been quite a while together, and I dare say time by itself makes something, even when there's no love at all. I gave the old girl a kiss, and rubbed her a bit, and got her downstairs, and said what about funeral arrangements. And she said she knew all that had to be done.

Then I said to her I was sorry, but I wasn't coming to the funeral. She didn't like this at all, and asked me why. I said, so far as I was concerned, Dad was what I remembered of him ever since I was a child, and I wasn't interested in corpses at all, and if she wanted flowers and hearses, that was up to her. She just stared at me and said she'd never understood me, and then she said a thing that shook me a bit in my determination, which was, had I considered what Dad himself would have wanted? So I said I'd think it over, and let her know, and meanwhile, good-bye, I was pulling out. She just looked at me again, said nothing, and went into her parlour and shut the door.

But as I was moving off, old Vern delayed me, and said he had to talk to me alone. I said I was very tired, but he pulled me out the back where I used to have my darkroom, and shut the door, and locked it, and said, 'You got to hear your father's secret.'

I asked him what.

He didn't say, but out of a corner he got the old metal box—the one you may remember where Dad used to keep the G. & S. gramophone records—and from it he took a large paper parcel, and he said, 'This is your Dad's book, he told me to give it to you personal if anything should happen.'

I opened it up, and there it was—hundreds of sheets all grubby and altered and corrected, except for the first one, where he'd written on a single page, '*History of Pimlico. For my one and only son.*'

Well, then I broke down. I sobbed like a boy, and Vern left me alone a bit, but I could see he hadn't ended, and he dragged the tin chest out and said, 'Look inside,' and there, on the bottom of it, were four big envelopes, and I opened them, and they contained stacks of pound notes.

'What's this?' I said.

'Your father's fortune. He saved it year by year.'

I looked at Vern. 'What did he say to do with it?'

Vernon swallowed a bit, didn't look his best, and finally said, 'Give it to you.'

'All of it?' I said.

'Yes.'

'And it hasn't been touched?' I said.

Old Vern looked really narked at this. 'You little bastard!' he said. 'You don't trust your own brother!'

I didn't answer that, but just looked at all this loot, and imagined Dad hoarding it and hiding it. 'And he managed to keep all that from Ma?' I said. 'Well, one up to old Dad!'

Vernon said, 'You know all this should go into the estate?'

'It should?' I said.

'That's the law,' Vern told me.

I picked up two of the envelopes, and handed them to Vern. He hesitated, then took them. 'Aren't you going to count it?' he said.

'You want to?'

'Oh, no.' He frowned. 'This is quite all right with you?' he said, very dubiously.

'I've given it to you.'

'And you won't tell Ma?'

I grabbed my two envelopes, and the *History of Pimlico*, and I held out my hand and said, 'Not if you don't, brother,' and he shook it, and managed to raise a smile, and then I beat it out of that house forever.

Up by Victoria, I bought a hold-all at a lost luggage, and put in the book and money, and made it to the Air Terminal. Because what with this all, my present feeling was I'd leave Dad's body to Ma, and Suze to get over loving Spades, and me, I was going away for a while, and perhaps not coming back.

At the Air Terminal, all was bustle. I went into the gents, and sorted out the loot which, so far as I could see, sitting counting it on the pedestal, was about two hundred, plus or minus. Then I had a wash, and grabbed my hold-all, and went up to the wicket and asked for a single ticket to Brazil.

Where in Brazil? the cat asked me.

I said, anywhere.

He said, could he see my passport—and I whipped it out, and he said I hadn't got a visa.

I asked him what the hell a visa was, and he said it was a thing you couldn't fly to Brazil without, and I said, okay, where *could* I fly to without a bloody visa? And the cat answered, quite politely, not to South America, but to parts of Continental Europe, I could, so I say okay, give me a ticket to one of those.

The wicket number told me this was the wrong terminal for Europe, I'd have to go up to Gloucester road, and I said, okay, and went out and got a cab, and drove there, and on the way, I'd decided I'd go to Norway, because I'd often heard from seamen Spades that they were nice to them up there.

Well, at Gloucester road, everything easy. They gave me a ticket to Oslo, and by now I was getting crafty, and said how much loot could I export there? and they said up to £250, but I'd better get a bit of local currency, so I did that at another wicket, and found I had an hour to wait, so I had a cuppa and a meat pie, and read the morning newspapers.

The Napoli thing was big stuff all right that morning. They had it all over the place, and most of last night's occurrences, and a lot of columns in the leader sections. They were still on about unrestricted immigration, and how unwise it was, just as if it wasn't they who'd allowed it in the first place, and patted themselves on the back for the old mother country's generous hospitality, so long as everything went swimmingly. They said Welfare was an urgent consideration, and what was needed was a lot more experienced welfare officers to iron out awkward misunderstandings. A bishop had said on the radio, Home Service, that 'various tensions and taboos divide us almost as strongly as those of race and creed in other countries.' There'd been some charges made at last, and the magistrate had advised people to stay indoors at night: meantime, the coloureds, it said, were having to get white friends to do their shopping for them. Ministers were going to fly in from the Caribbean, and from Africa, to scan the scene, and the High Commissioner of somewhere had protested. Best news of all—really heartening—was that the cabinet minister in charge of home security had received reports of all these happenings at his country house, and was studying them closely, and said the utmost strictness will be observed in the impartial enforcement of the law. Always 'enforcement': never condemning! As for me, I always thought laws had some idea behind them, some sort of principle, and it was this you should shout out above, not police courts.

Well, then the loudspeaker said it was all aboard for Oslo, and the strangest bundle of cats you can imagine got in a sort of bubble-coach which was half double-decker, and I sat up in the arse part and surveyed the streets of London as we sped. Good-bye, old town, I said, good luck! We passed quite near Shepherd's Bush, where everything seemed free from tensions and taboos, and we made it out to the airfield which, I must say, was a splendid spectacle.

But I hadn't all that time for spectacles, because they fed us into a sort of sausage-machine of escalators and officials, and I had to think fairly quickly, because my idea was, to try and find where the Brazil flight began and, if I could, dodge the Oslo flight, and get on the Brazil one instead. Because experience has taught me that the more highly planned a sausage system is, the easier to feed yourself through the wrong part of it, if you keep your nerves about you.

So we went through the customs, where they seemed surprised I had only a hold-all with a handwritten book in it, but I said I had an auntie out in Norway to look after me. And at the currency check, they said wasn't that a lot of money for so young a feller, and I said, wasn't it just! and got by that one. And at passports, they said was this my first passport, and I said my very first, and how did they like the photo, I'd taken it myself, and didn't I look a zombie? And after that, we all went into a great hall thing, overlooking the airfield through huge glass panels, and the loudspeaker announcing departures, and me keeping my ears skinned.

I got a Coke, and went and gazed, and it certainly was a sight! All those aircraft landing from outer space, and taking off to all the nations of the world! And I thought to myself, standing there looking out on all this fable—what an age it is I've grown up in, with everything possible to mankind at last, and every horror too, you could imagine! And what a time it's been in England, what a period of fun and hope and foolishness and sad stupidity!

Then they announced the flight to Rio. I joined the wrong queue, just like I was a regular traveller to there, and we had no check at the exit, nor when we walked across the tarmac to the aircraft, until we met a chick who stood with a board beside the staircase, asking people their names as they got on. I put myself in between a family, hoping they'd think I was cousin Frank or someone, and the chick asked my name, and I pointed at her list to a name she hadn't ticked, and she said, could she have my embarkation card, and I said what embarkation card? and she smiled politely and said one like all these, and so I gave her up mine, and she said, tut, tut, wasn't I a silly boy, that one was for the Oslo flight, and I'd better hurry back or I might miss it.

But I stayed down there, and watched the great plane taking off for Rio. And just as it became airborne—crash! down came the rain in torrents out the heavens, and I held up my arms in it, and opened my mouth and cried, 'More! More! More! That'll stop it up at Napoli! That'll do what the ruling olders can't do! That's the only thing to keep the whites and blacks and yellows and blues of Napoli indoors!'

Well then, just as I was going to get back into the sausage-machine to re-connect with Oslo, in taxied a plane, quite close to where I was standing, and up went the staircase in the downpour, and out came a score or so of Spades from Africa, holding hand luggage over their heads against the rain. Some had on robes, and some had on tropical suits, and most of them were young like me, maybe kiddos coming here to study, and they came down grinning and chattering, and they all looked so dam pleased to be in England, at the end of their long journey, that I was heartbroken at all the disappointments that were there in store for them. And I ran up to them through the water, and shouted out above the engines, 'Welcome to London! Greetings from England! Meet your first teen-ager! We're all going up to Napoli to have a ball!' And I flung my arms round the first of them, who was a stout old number with a beard and a brief-case and a little bonnet, and they all paused and stared at me in amazement, until the old boy looked me in the face and said to me, 'Greetings!' and he took me by the shoulder, and suddenly they all burst out laughing in the storm.

Mr Love and Justice

COLIN MACINNES

ALLISON & BUSBY
LONDON · NEW YORK

MR LOVE

Frankie love came from the sea, and was greatly ill at ease elsewhere. When on land he was harassed and didn't fit in at all. The orders he accepted without question, though a hundred grumbles, from almost any seaman, were hateful to him in a landsman's mouth. There was a deep injustice, somewhere, in all this. Landsmen, in England, depend entirely on the sea: yet seamen, who sustain them, don't regulate the landsmen's lives and have to submit, when landlocked themselves a moment, to all the landsman's meaningless caprices.

At the Dock Board the chief had said there was no ship for Frankie. Those were his words, but his eyes said, 'I get ten pounds from you before I put you in the pool.' But Frankie had only three-pounds-seven from the Labour. At the Labour exchange they'd asked what he could *do*. How to begin to explain to the quite nice young feller in the striped Italian jacket? On a ship he could do anything: off it, nothing, didn't want to—he was all at sea. 'But you can do a bit of labouring, can't you?' said the clerk, quite friendlily. How to tell him that a merchant seaman can be nothing else—that to do nothing else is a first condition of *being* a merchant seaman? The feller, trying to be helpful, had called over Mister someone who'd looked over the papers, said not a word to Frankie but, just in front of him (two feet from his face behind the grille), 'He's young enough for manual labour—twenty-six.' And, 'A bad discharge-book, too: adrift in Yokohama and repatriated at official expense.'

Frankie stepped back and stood there, feeling powerless and sick; and watched the next-comer, an Asian seaman with a turban. The Asian, at the wicket, smiled and smiled, and, as they questioned him, understood less and less. 'Can't you speak proper English?' somebody shouted at him. Frankie, in his days of glory, would hardly have spoken to the Asian at all: but now both of them were sea princes exiled in distress. He stepped up again and said, 'This man speaks *two* languages—ours and his. It's more than you can—think of that!' They answered nothing, said, 'Next, please,' and the Asian still stood and smiled.

Frankie walked out into Stepney, withered and disgusted. The clients round the Labour, apart from being landsmen, were mostly layabouts: professional scroungers such as you couldn't be on board a ship—your mates wouldn't wear it, let alone the officers. He found the Asian standing near, and turned to share with him his deep contempt for London. In the old days, Frankie thought, he and I would have signed on as pirates down by Wapping: and why not? Frankie became aware the Asian was inviting him to share a meal. 'I'm skint,' said Frankie, not because he was but in refusal. The Asian slightly shook his turbaned head and took Frankie gently by the arm: the gesture was sufficiently respectful, and they set off together in silence. Round two and a half corners they went into a Pakistani café with a smell of stale spices, a juke-box, a broken fruit-machine, and several English girls.

MR JUSTICE

BY Latimer road, Pc Edward Justice went into the London Transport gents: not for that purpose, nor (since he was uniformed) to trap some evil-doer, but simply to change his socks round from foot to foot. As he did so, balancing carefully on some sheets of tissue he'd laid out on the stone, he read the obscenities upon the wall. One said,

> Man, quite young, nice room, seeks friend for punishment. Please say who and when.

A space was left, and then in capitals:

> Men mean a great deal in my life.

Ted Justice took out the pencil from his black official note-book and wrote under the first part,

> Blond, 26, and brutal. NAP 1717.

(This was the number of his section-house.) Then, under the second message, he wrote:

> Mine too.

He left the establishment with a stern, penetrating glance at those inside it.

In the street and sun he stood, in official posture, before a haberdasher's. In the plate glass he examined himself from helmet tip to boot toe, and up again, adjusted the thin knot of his black tie, and patted his pockets down. All present and correct, sir. What they'd make of the man inside, in a moment, he couldn't tell: but the outward image was immaculate.

He caught the haberdasher's eyes beyond his own, didn't budge or change his expression in the slightest, then moved away, authority incarnate. The socks felt better: but tight and sticky, the serge was hot today. Would he make plain-clothes—*would* he? Think of it! In civvies yet unlike the other millions—up above the law!

'Not now, lady, I wouldn't,' he said to a girl-and-pram combination at a corner and, holding the traffic, he saw her personally across the road. An ugly one, unlike his own, but then for all women he had a quite authentic love: not just the copper's professional solicitude, but a real admiration and affection. Yes: even for women coppers, and some of *them* . . .

He reached the station dead on time, and calm, and spotless. The desk officer looked up and said, 'The Detective-sergeant's ready for you, Ted. Good luck.'

MR LOVE

OF the three girls casually eyeing Frankie and the Asian, one was a short, thick-set chunky woman past her first prime—and second—maybe hitting twenty-eight. Her dark hair was dyed blonde, her face the colour of electric light, and her body desirable in an overall way only (that is, though the immediate impression was attractive, no part of her, on inspection, seemed very beautiful). She spoke less than the others, was very contained and self-assured, yet when she did speak her voice was emphatic and decided. Her clothes accentuated the same features as nature did beneath them, but elsewhere were casual and slack.

After a while of merely glancing at Frank, when he made a sudden movement on his chair she began to watch him. Frankie was used to this and had no vanity about it (though about other things a lot). He knew he wasn't 'handsome' whatever that may mean (for nobody seems to know or to agree), but he also knew he was well set up, and confident, and strong, and potent; and that though he repelled a great many girls for various reasons, for the kind he liked best he'd only to whistle and they'd come. He now whistled by looking steadily at the girl ten seconds in that kind of way.

She got up, came over and holding out a florin, said, 'You got some pieces for the juke?' In reply he took sixpences out of the front pocket of his slacks and, without getting up, stretched over and dropped them in the juke-box. 'What you want?' he asked, still stretching far.

'You choose,' she told him.

'I can't see the names from here,' he said. 'You pick them.'

'I'll press these for you,' she answered, and without taking her finger off the button she moved the selector and jabbed eight times. Then she sat down at the far side of his table.

The juke-box made conversation quite impossible: but as it blared on they spoke to each other, perfectly clearly, with their eyes, their faces, and their limbs. This unspoken conversation established that they liked each other that way, and that way, at the moment, only; and reserved all their lives, and personalities, and friendship, and private particulars to themselves.

When the juke-box stopped neither of them wanted more music, and both looked up with faint resentment for anyone else who might consider feeding it again. The girl put her hands on the table round her bag: a battered, soiled affair, square-black, but efficient and businesslike as a safe is in an office that seems otherwise untidy and impractical. She said to Frankie, 'I'd say you look a bit tired.'

'You would?'

'Yes. Just look it, I mean. That's all.'

'Well, you'd be right. I have been.'

They both ignored the Asian as if he absolutely wasn't there, although at this stage his presence as unconscious chaperon was rather helpful.

'Bad times?' she said.

'Well, girl, you know how it is. No ship—no work—no money.'

'I thought you were one of those,' she said, waited for him to ask her what *she* was, and registered with approval that he didn't.

Now, she played a right card .... but a bit too early. 'Shall we take a walk?' she said.

He paused a fraction more than was usual in a man of quick decisions, and said, 'I'll take a rest here for a while.'

She moved her hands round the bag, didn't hide a slight vexation and said (but quite nicely), 'It was an invitation to you ... You've told me how you're fixed just now ...'

He answered (also without any malice), 'Another time. I won't forget you.'

The girl smiled, took up the bag, said nothing more, and after a few words with the other girls, went out. The Asian was in conversation with a countryman, and Frankie, catching up with this, said to him, 'No, friend, I'll pay ...'

'No, no!' cried the Asian, for the first time in their acquaintance letting drop the smile.

'Let me pay for myself, then,' Frankie Love said, getting up.

'No!' said the Asian, giving money to the Pakistani fiercely.

Frankie now gave him *his* first smile of the day—but a very reluctant, meagre one—and saying no more, shook hands with the Asian, patted his shoulder gently, and went out.

The girl, as he expected, was at the far corner, waiting. As she'd expected, he took his time, and when he came up she made no reference whatever to his change of mind. She shifted her handbag to the other arm, took his, and clicked along the pavement on her stiletto heels.

It was about half a mile. Near the end of the journey, well after she'd passed them, she said of two men standing beside a delivery van, 'Two coppers.'

'Yeah? How you know?'

'You shouldn't look back like that. The way they stared at us.'

'I expect quite a few men stare at you.'

'Not *that* way. It's not sex that interests them ...

'What does, then?'

She stopped at the door, took a bunch of keys from her bag, looked around, and opened it. 'What I do, does,' she said. 'You coming in?'

MR JUSTICE

THE Detective-sergeant said, 'At ease, constable, have a fag, come and sit down by me.' Ted Justice did so but with caution, mistrusting the affabilities of a superior: for no-one, he'd learned, is kindly without a motive—unless (and even then!) the old-timers who stayed stuck at uniformed sergeant, or below.

'Well, Ted,' the Detective-sergeant said, 'not to beat about the bush at all—you're in.'

'Thank you, sir.'

'In on probation, naturally. We all want to see how you shape up, and keep an eye on you generally.' He stared at Edward in a quite frankly treacherous way. 'So,' he resumed, 'as from tomorrow, civilian dress, please—you'll be drawing the appropriate allowances.'

'Thank you, sir.'

'Stand up, Ted.' Ted Justice did so. 'Take off your tunic and tie.' He hung them neatly on a chair-back. 'Come over in front of this,' and they walked over to the mirror.

Reflected behind him, Edward saw his new superior gazing with him at the mirror's image; and in it his own not very tall, and lean, and wiry and relaxed and sensual body. The Detective-sergeant ruffled Edward's hair, and he didn't flinch. 'Yes, it's extraordinary!' the Detective-sergeant said. 'You don't look like a copper—except, perhaps, for that lovely pair of blue eyes.' He laughed. 'Come and sit down again,' he said. And as Edward moved over, 'Get out of the way of walking like that, please. You're not on the beat any more, remember. It's the first thing that gives the untrained plain-clothes man away.'

'Now,' said the officer, sitting at his desk. 'Forget all you've learned till now. Forget any pals you've made. Here in the vice game, you've moved up a degree.' He paused. '*But*: and it's a very important but; though you've moved up above *them*, so far as *we're* concerned you're right down at the bottom once again. I'll be frank with you—you're not a fool. I'm opening a file on you today. If there's anything in that file that we don't like—then out you go, boy! And if you fall, and go back to the beat again, you'll fall even lower than you were before. Agreed?'

'Yes, sir,' said Edward.

'Agreed, then. Now: we're moving you over towards Royal Oak: new section-house, new surroundings. Round here, if you've done your work well, your face is probably a bit too familiar. That's all right? You accept?'

'Yes, sir.'

'Splendid: we want all this to be voluntary. Now, one other thing: and don't take it amiss. In the Force, we don't interfere in an officer's private life as far as is reasonable and possible. But in the CID, we have to. Why aren't you married?'

'Sir?'

'You're not a poof, are you?'

'No, sir.'

'Sure of that?'

'Quite sure, sir.'

'Well?'

Edward thought fast: but knew however fast he thought, the Detective-sergeant would observe it, so he said at once, 'May I ask you one question first, sir?'

'You may. Well?'

'Do I get any expenses?'

The officer looked at him blandly, and with pity. 'I don't like that question very much,' he said. 'To begin with, it's a foolish one. What we're offering you is—well, influence. If you've got any brains, then money's a secondary consideration: or should I say, where there's influence, there's money. Routine expenses can, of course, be recovered: but in this section, frankly, most of us don't bother. How you manage there, provided you keep your nose clean, is really up to you, you know. You understand me, do you?'

'Yes, sir.'

All this, which had entered one corner only of Edward's brain, had given him time to frame his answer. The difficulty was this. He had a girl (in fact a woman, since she was older than himself), and he loved her, and she him, and he had since adolescence loved no other woman in the world or, as it happened, known any other. *But*—and this was it. Her father had been 'in trouble'. And though he was—reluctantly—prepared to bless his daughter's marriage to a copper, the girl herself—who loved the officers now, in the measure

Ted was one—had told him she believed—and she was very lucid on this essential point—that while she would never leave him if he wanted her, to marry him would mean, with absolute certainty, that he'd never rise far in his career: if, indeed, once the Force knew of her, they allowed him to stay in it at all. So what to do? Pretend she did not exist? The uniformed lot might wear that one—but not the sharp boys of the CID: they'd soon discover; for if no one else told them, a nark or a disgruntled criminal would be certain to. Always, Edward had known this was the one chink in his newly burnished professional armour: but loving her so much, he had waited for time, somehow, to resolve the fatal contradiction. What he had *not* foreseen (and was blaming himself for severely at this moment) was that if *he* never spoke about her to the Force, the Force would raise the matter so abruptly.

'I'd like to be frank with you, sir,' he said (determined not to be).

'That's what we want, son. Come on—I'm waiting.'

'I've got a girl . . .'

'Yes . . .'

'But I'm not sure the Force would find her suitable.'

'Why?'

Edward Justice looked his superior officer right in the eyes and said, 'She's one of those persons, sir, who doesn't care for the officers of our Force.'

The Detective-sergeant smiled extremely unpleasantly. 'Doesn't she,' he said. 'She cares for you, I suppose, though.'

'Oh, yes, sir. And on this matter, she may alter. As you can imagine, sir, I've made it . . .'

The Detective-sergeant had got up. 'Shut up,' he said quite gently. 'Look, boy, it's simple. Change her ideas and marry her, or else . . . Well! That quite clear?'

'Of course, sir.'

'Okay. No hurry: but just get it fixed.' He smiled. 'An item for your file,' he added.

Detective-constable Justice put on his tie and jacket. 'Could I ask you, sir,' he said, 'what kind of work you have in mind for me?'

'I don't mind telling you,' the officer answered, taking his trilby hat off a filing cabinet. 'You interested in ponces at all?'

'I'm interested, sir, in whatever you tell me to be.'

'Good. We might try you out with them. What d'you say?'

Edward made no reply, and his senior put his hand on Detective-constable Justice's shoulder. 'Remember one thing,' he said. 'It's the only thing that matters—really.' He looked at Edward like a brother (as Cain, for example, did on Abel). 'Don't ever get in wrong with the Force: because if you do—well, a broken copper's the only person in the world we hate more than a criminal.'

MR LOVE

Frankie got up to make two cups of tea, and now for the first time he had a chance of looking round about her room. He liked it. It wasn't rich at all, no; yet as on a ship, nothing essential was missing. The sheets had been clean, and in the tins marked tea, and rice, and sugar, he saw there were actually these things, and plenty. It was, of course, a bit over-feminine, but then the girl was, after all, a woman. 'Sugar?' he said, looking round at her lying smoking on the bed. 'Eight lumps,' she answered. 'I'm not naturally sweet.'

He came and sat beside her and fondled her abstractedly. 'Thanks, girl,' he said. She smiled and said to him. 'There's not many, I can tell you, get a cup of tea as well.'

'I dare say not,' said Frankie.

'*Or* leave as rich as they came in,' she added.

Frankie frowned. 'I've *never* paid for it,' he said, 'and never would, and never will.'

'Oh, I was kidding.' She sipped a bit, and said, 'Not even those geisha girls, you wouldn't?'

'If a girl thinks she wants money from *me*, I'd rather go without.'

'Well, dear, being as you are, I don't expect you've often had to.'

Frankie smiled, then looked at her seriously. 'You like the life?' he said.

'I don't like or dislike, darling: I'm just used to it.'

'Been at it long?'

'Oh, ever since I can remember . . .'

'Yeah—I see. You don't mind if I ask: it doesn't upset you?'

She laughed. 'Upset me? Darling, you can believe me or not, but I just—don't—notice.'

'No? By the way: don't call me "darling", please. I told you my name's Frankie.'

'Yes. Frankie Love. You said so. And you've proved it.'

'But listen. Stop me if I'm curious. When you go out: not knowing who it's going to be. That doesn't disturb you?'

'No.'

'Not at all?'

'No. Only if they're vicious or anything, or try to rob me . . .'

'They try that? That's not right!'

'Sometimes they do . . . But you get to know the types—you'd be surprised.'

'I suppose so.' He took her hands, examined them, kissed them and said, 'But listen. All those men. Maybe two or three a day. Don't you find . . .'

'Two or three? Are you kidding? What you take me for—a mystery?'

'You're mysterious, all right.'

'Not *that* way, I'm not.'

'Yeah. But what I mean is—doesn't it disgust you any? One after another, dozens of them just like that?'

She sat up and fixed the pillows. 'Well, Frankie,' she said. 'First ask yourself this question, please. If you go with me after all those dozens—doesn't it disgust *you*?'

'No. No—but I think that's different.'

'Men do.'

'I suppose so.'

'Look, dear. If you're going into this business at all, it's best to have as many as you can, isn't it? Well, isn't it?'

'I dare say . . .'

'This isn't Mayfair, darling . . .'

'. . . Frankie . . .'

'. . . Sorry. Not Mayfair, but Stepney Green. Seamen and drunks. Thirty bob, a pound—even less, sometimes.'

'But it all adds up.'

'I'll say it does. Pass me that bag.'

'No.'

'Go on!'

'No, I don't want to touch it. I don't like women's bags.'

She jerked her head at him, reached over, and spilled its contents on the bed.

'What's this?' said Frankie. 'Your life's savings?'

'Don't be silly, boy. That's just last night's.'

'You kidding *me* now?'

'Why should I kid you?'

'All that loot?'

'Well, it's not so much . . . I pay a Bengali eight a week for this little gaff . . .'

'For *this*?'

'Frankie, if you're in business full-time, and your landlord's not ignorant, you don't get a gaff, even down here, for less. And if he *is* ignorant, believe me, it's even worse: he might shop you, or throw you out unexpectedly.'

Frankie gazed at the notes and silver on the blanket. Like money you pick up in the streets, it seemed quite different from the contents of a pay-packet—like valuable stuff that just belonged to *any*body.

'What else you spend it on?' he said.

She looked at him intently, then said, 'Oh, this and that—it soon goes, you know. Expenses are heavy: nylons, for instance. Look! You're not the first who's laddered the best part of a pound . . .' She rubbed her leg and said, 'But sometimes there's a bit over and to spare . . .'

Frankie reflected. 'Well, I suppose you get your due,' he said. 'It can't be easy . . .'

'It's not, Frank, believe me.'

'All the same. Excuse my saying so, but I think a man who *pays* for that's no man at all.'

She got up. 'Oh, I don't think much of them either. But I'm glad there's plenty of them around . . .'

'You going?'

'Yes, Frank, I have to. But you can stop here a bit, if you like, till I get back . . .'

'You'd trust me alone in here?'

'Yes, of course. What's there to pinch? You don't wear girl's clothes—at least I hope not—and I'm taking this...' And she flourished the square black bag.

Frankie got up too. 'No, I'll be off,' he said.

'Off to where?'

'I'm staying down the Rowton.'

'That sty? I hope it's not given you crabs.'

'Baby, I wash,' he said.

'Me too. Turn the other way, I'm going to before we leave.'

MR JUSTICE

ON his day off, Edward was sitting with his girl in the park at Little Venice, up by the Harrow road. He was proud of his girl because though few men looked at her immediately, once they did so their attention was apt to become transfixed. Their initial disdain was perhaps to be explained by the fact that she wore spectacles, was plump and rather dowdy; but their interest became riveted when they grew aware that she had the tranquillity, the assurance, and the indifference that can denote sexual operators conscious of their powers: aware of them not merely as one woman in competition with all the others (which is only a quarter way to success), but aware of them in themselves absolutely.

He was telling her of his first weeks in the vice game: and these weeks had not been without their tribulations. In the first place, Edward had suffered the humiliation of being himself reported as a suspect by a colleague unaware (or *was* he?) of his real identity as a plain-clothes man. Perhaps this mishap was due to the extraordinary difficulty he found in *loitering* successfully, unobserved. Only a child can rival the absolute right a uniformed officer has, in the public eyes, to linger wherever he wishes. But in plain-clothes... well, what would *you* do if told to watch a house for a couple of hours in a thoroughly inconspicuous fashion? All sorts of stratagems will suggest themselves... but the real art is simply to learn how to loiter as a pastime in itself: just as you are, without disguises; and get away with it. Among adults, Edward noticed, only American servicemen seemed quite naturally to possess this skill.

Then there was the difficulty of moving in the dark. Of course, when in uniform there'd been the manoeuvre of lurking in shop doorways, or in mews turnings. But the whole point in the Force of a uniform had been that people *should* see it, and think twice. Now he'd had to learn to embrace the darkness, to become part of it and use it for himself.

He told some of this in confidence to his girl, but not too much of it because he believed firmly in an ultimate loyalty to the Force so far as its own secrets were concerned; and had learned, in its hard and testing school, that a secret told to *any*one is no longer a secret in any real way at all. Also, he was feeling his way in the new job, and still doubtful and insecure.

'But you like it on the whole,' she said.

'Oh, yes. Who wouldn't.'

'Well, dearest, I *don't*. Oh, don't get me wrong! I mean, only because I seem to see much less of you.'

She moved her head slowly and kissed him, which she did quite un-furtively, warmly and decidedly yet in a private, serious, almost holy way (he thought) that no one in the little park could possibly take except to. He felt together with this short, wonderful embrace, the slight scratch of her spectacles, which enchanted him because of memories.

'I'll tell you one thing,' he said. 'I'm sorry the duties make me see you less because, honest, this new job makes me feel quite a bit lonely.'

'Well, naturally,' she said. 'Any new job does.'

'Not only that.' He hesitated how much to admit because he knew a man who betrays his weaknesses, even to the girl he loves, is giving her weapons for the tenderest blackmail. 'It's like this,' he said. 'The story is all coppers are just civilians like anyone else, living among them, not in barracks like on the Continent, but you and I know that's just a legend for mugs. We *are* cut off: we're *not* like everyone else. Some civilians fear us and play up to us, some dislike us and keep out of our way but no one—well, very few indeed—accepts us as just *ordinary* like them. In one sense, dear, we're like hostile troops occupying an enemy country. And say what you like, at times that makes us lonely.'

She squeezed his arm, said nothing.

'Now in this job the new one, even more so. Because not only the civvies all mistrust you, but—this is what I've discovered—the uniformed men do, too. They're jealous, I dare say, and a bit scared: I've had a few very distant looks from former pals in the past few weeks, I can tell you, and it's not so very pleasant.'

'But there's the satisfaction of your job,' she said, because she knew this was a man's great love by which, if she respected it, she could hold him all the more.

'Oh, yes . . . there's that, of course.'

The time was now approaching, as both knew, when they must have it out about the conflict of love and duty. After a silence made of gathering clouds, she broached the theme and said, 'Did they ask you about me at all?'

'Yes.'

'And what did you tell them?'

Edward was ready, this time, with his answer. He could not, he'd decided, tell her what he'd told the Detective-sergeant: that she was a copper-hater; for then she'd think that, maligning her to his other dearest love, the Force, he'd secretly wished to detach himself from her altogether. Women were so mistrustful! And when you want irreconcilables you have to lie at some point—there's really no other possible solution. So this double betrayal of the Force and her was the price he must pay for the higher idea of love. And he'd made up his mind that he'd say to her what he said now, and that was, 'Darling, I just told them I hadn't got a girl at all.'

She looked him full in the eyes and her own shut, a moment, behind her spectacles; then she said, 'That was probably best: probably the only thing to say.'

'I didn't like it, though.'

She pressed her shoulder closer to him. 'There's only one thing,' she said. 'If my Dad should ever die: have you thought of that?'

'No . . .'

She looked at him. 'In that case, we *could* get married: I mean, there'd be no objection any longer, would there?'

He considered. 'No, I don't think so, but . . . Well, your old Dad's hale and hearty, isn't he?'

'Oh, yes. No. All I meant was we mustn't rule out the possibility of marriage altogether.'

He put his arm round her shoulder. 'I should think not! And there's also this. When I get on in the CID, get influence and get to know the men up at the top, the whole position—about you, I mean—might be reconsidered. Specially if your Dad goes on keeping out of trouble.'

'Yes. Well, he has done, hasn't he, for quite a while . . . I've seen to that . . .'

'I do wish I could offer you marriage!' he exclaimed. 'Here and now! Right out in the open.'

'Well, Ted, we've had that out a thousand times, and you know I've said I understand and it's quite all right with me . . . It's you I want, not your name. And my money's good so we've no economic worries, and I'll just put up with it and hope. It's all thought out and decided . . . But there is just one thing: what if we had a baby?'

'We won't! You don't mean that you're . . .'

'No, no. But what if we *did*? It can happen. And honest, Ted, though you know I'd love and cherish it, I don't want to make your son and mine illegitimate.'

He laughed nervously and a bit crudely. 'Let's face that problem,' he said, 'if it arises. And let's hope it doesn't arise at all.'

She hid her feelings about this (which were multiple, and would have amazed and alarmed Edward considerably) and only said to him, 'I don't mind being your mistress, Ted, but not having a baby makes me feel just a bit like a whore.'

'Eh? Them? Don't talk daft. Anyway, some of them have babies, I can tell you.'

'On purpose? Do they mean to?'

'Some do, I suppose . . . They're women, after all . . .'

'You're seeing them, then, in your new job?'

Edward grew just a bit portentous. 'Actually, yes,' he said, 'it is concerned with those matters—but more so with their ponces.'

'Oh, yes. They've all got them, have they, these women?'

'Not all: no, not by any means all. The older more experienced type of girl does without, but not the majority, I'd say. They seem to need them.'

'And what are they like, those men?'

'Which? The ponces? Well, that darling's what I'm wising myself up on. It seems they're *all* types. I've had one or two pointed out that between you and me, if the vice boys hadn't assured me of it, I'd just have taken for—well, for anyone in this park.' He gazed at the inoffensive ramblers. 'But then, you see,' he continued, 'that's one of the very first things they teach you in the Force: that every-one—repeat, *every*one—however innocent-seeming, is a potential suspect.'

She gazed at the park population too. 'And how do you catch them? 'she asked.

He looked round, lowered his voice and said, 'Well, that's tricky, it appears: you wouldn't think so, but it's very tricky. Because you've got to prove several quite different things. Number one, that the girl's a known and habitual common prostitute. Number two, that she's earned all her money—or the bulk of it—from prostitution. Number three—that the money she earns this way she hands over to him—and that *he* hasn't got any other principal visible means of support.'

'I see,' she said.

'It's more than I do, believe me. There's one thing they always slip up on, though, so I'm told. If you can get the *woman* to testify against him—then you've got him! And as women have all sorts of reasons for losing interest in their fancy-man—well, dear, I leave it to your imagination!'

She shook her head and said, without condemnation, 'I think it's horrible.'

He paused, then answered, 'Well, as a matter of fact I think it is as well. Not, mind you, that I'm setting myself up as a judge: that's not *our* part of the little business; and one of the very first things we learn is not to condemn and simply to detect. But after all: even allowing for that, these ponces are doing something rather special that puts them in a class apart. I'd say they're making money out of love—or out of sex, at any rate. And personally, darling, I consider love is sacred: the one and only really sacred thing that's left: and if you make money out of *that*, then you're destructive and should be destroyed.'

MR LOVE

FRANKIE LOVE and the girl sat in a café (known to the local girls as 'judge's chambers') waiting for the arrival of the solicitor's clerk. 'Now, I don't know,' Frankie said, 'why you want to mix *me* up in all your bits of trouble.'

'Trouble? It's not trouble! Anyway, you're my friend, aren't you?'

'I'm your friend, yes, but until I get a ship or even a job I want to keep clear of law, and courts, and solicitors—the lot.'

She laughed. 'Oh, don't be so silly, Frankie! This isn't *trouble*! A soliciting charge? I've had dozens of them.'

'Then what you want me here for?'

She looked at him seriously. 'Well, Frank,' she said, 'this *is* a bit different as a matter of fact: it is a bit dodgy, and I felt the need of a pal around to give me courage.'

'Courage to do what?'

'Well, I'm not pleading guilty this time for once.'

'You usually do?'

'Always. In the first place I almost always *am*, in the second, what can you do with magistrates against copper's evidence? and in the third—well, if you plead not guilty it's a fiver instead of forty bob: or if the charge was hotted up to something worse, he might even send you to the Sessions.'

'Who might? What Sessions?'

'The magistrate. And if he did the law would have a barrister, and juries just don't like whores—however often some of them have had a go with one of us.'

'Why you taking a chance, then?'

'Well—just because I'm sick of it!'

'Of what?'

'I'll tell you. There's a young fellow—vice-squad copper—who's always asking me to take him home for free. Well, some of the girls do that—but I just won't: not if I don't *like* the feller, anyway. Last time he said, "Do what I say, or else." And this is the "or else": he's bringing a charge.'

'The bastard!' Frankie cried, genuinely revolted. 'That's not right!'

'I don't think so either.'

Frankie pondered. 'But he'll get you all the same, from what you say.'

The girl looked round the café and said gently, 'Perhaps not, you know—it all depends on the date of the alleged offence the charge is for.'

'How come?'

'Well, I've been having my whatsits this last week. With some of the girls that makes no difference—they just ram in some cotton wool and soldier on. But me, no, I'm particular: I stay at home those days—of which fact I've got witnesses.'

'But baby—he's not a mug. He won't bring a charge unless he saw you at it, will he?'

She stared at him, amused. 'Boy, are you crazy? He wouldn't even bother to leave his desk! He'd make the charge blind. Against a known and convicted common prostitute? It's a pushover!'

'Unless you can prove . . .'

'That's it: an alibi.'

'I see.'

'You do? Smart boy! Here comes the shark from the solicitor's.'

With a cheery wave and a cry of 'How do, girl!' there now approached a tall, mackintoshed, somewhat lumbering young man with dark greased hair and a sharp but uncritical regard. He sat at their table, said, 'How do?' to Frankie without asking who he was, and called out for a cup of tea and a cheese roll.

'Money, money,' he said cheerfully, holding out his hand. 'The old firm doesn't even move without a sub.'

From the black bag the girl handed him some notes which he counted, folded each one of them singly, and stuffed in a hip pocket, saying, 'Ta very much, dear.'

'It's we who keep your wife and kids for you,' the girl told him.

'Don't I know it! And the magistrates'! Have you ever thought of that? What wouldn't the courts cost the poor old taxpayers if it wasn't for all you girls and the thousands of forty bobs your little cases attract?'

'Let's talk business, son,' the girl said. 'We'll be on very soon.'

He shifted his glasses on his nose and said, 'Well, I know you girls *never* want to hear advice, which is all we're really useful for, however, mine is—let's get it over—please dear, plead guilty.'

'You know why I'm not.'

'Oh, I do! And I understand your feelings! But do you *really* want to take the law on single-handed? Do just think a bit of the consequences!'

The girl frowned. 'Not the law, stupid—only this one feller.'

The clerk looked at her. 'I'm surprised at you,' he said. 'Look! The law may have their internal wrangles and suspicions, and all be ready to shop one another if it means promotions. But to the outside world—and particularly, excuse me being frank, a girl like you—it's one for all and all for one, they live or hang together.'

'I think he's right,' said Frankie.

'You do? What do *you* know about it?' she cried.

Frankie got up. 'I'll be seeing you,' he said. 'It's none of my business anyway.'

She grabbed him by the seat of his slacks and yanked him down. 'Don't go,' she said. 'I'm sorry—I'm wrought up. I always am a bit just after my monthlies.'

There was a pause. Then the lawyer said, 'Look dear, there's another aspect. He might have brought this not to get his vengeance or anything like that, but just because he wanted a little birthday present.'

'You think so?'

'Well, it's possible, isn't it? Vice-squad boy? Now, if that's so . . . I shouldn't tell you this, my gov'nor wouldn't like it . . . why don't you settle with him? After all: even if you plead guilty it's forty bob, and if you don't there's us to pay as well in addition to all that might happen up at the Sessions if he brought in a brothel-keeping charge or something.'

'They take bribes?' said Frankie.

'Oh, don't be silly!' the girl answered.

The lawyer gave Frankie a rather puzzled look. 'Well, naturally,' he said. 'Imagine yourself please, for a moment, in their position. Girls sitting on a gold-mine, you've got complete powers of arrest, and the courts believe your word, not theirs. Your wages are maybe twelve or so a week. What would *you* do?'

'I wouldn't bring false charges,' Frankie said. 'I don't say I'd be all that particular about everything, but I couldn't bring false charges.'

The lawyer smiled slightly, and the girl was still silent. Then the lawyer said, 'Would you like me to see this feller for you?'

'Isn't it too late?' she asked.

'Oh, to withdraw the charge, it is. But not how it's pressed... there's evidence and evidence, you know.'

The girl, suddenly, slammed her bag on the formica table. 'You're all a bunch of sharks!' she cried. 'I'll plead guilty—give me back my money!'

'Now, don't be silly,' said the lawyer, his glasses almost falling off his nose in his surprise. 'You've got me down here, and you've asked me my advice . . .'

'You'd better give it back,' said Frankie.

The lawyer turned on Frankie Love, completely unimpressed. 'Now *please*,' he said. 'Don't *you* join it.'

The girl put her hand on Frankie's arm. 'He's right, dear,' she said. 'I was a bit vexed, that's all'—and she got up.

'So you won't be needing me in there,' the lawyer said, preparing to rise too. 'If you're going to plead guilty it's best for you there's no defence forces whatever to be seen.'

'I know,' she said. 'But stick around, will you, in case there are complications.'

The lawyer nodded, and called for another tea and roll. Frankie said to her, 'You want me to come with you?'

'Oh no, dear. But mind this for me, will you? They don't like to see that we're not destitute in there.' And she walked out leaving her bag beside Frankie on the table.

Gingerly, he put it on the seat beside him, the lawyer watching casually. Then Frankie said, 'Apologies for speaking out of turn just now.'

'Oh, quite okay! I know how you feel about all this.'

'How *I* feel?'

'Well—yes,' said the clerk, retreating slightly behind his spectacles and munching the second cheese roll. 'I hope she'll not be long,' he added. 'It all depends where her name is on the list.'

'You handle a lot of these cases?'

'Hundreds. And I mean hundreds. My gov'nor deals in vice business almost exclusively, and we're greatly in demand. And though everyone believes we're scoundrels (which of course we are

—har-har), we do have our uses because, believe me, without a lawyer you're just a dead duck in advance. With us to help you, you only lose a leg or maybe, if you're fortunate, a few tail feathers.'

'What: you work chiefly for these girls?'

'By no means! Very rarely, in fact—their cases are usually so simple. No. For the vice barons: the gaff landlords and the escort-businesses that handle call-girls and, of course . . .' the lawyer dropped his eyes '. . . the easy-money boys, the ponces.'

'Those bastards.'

The clerk looked up sharply. 'Yes, those ones,' he said.

Frankie Love had his hand resting on the girl's bag. Suddenly, the penny dropped.

'Here!' he cried. 'You think *I'm* one? *Me*?'

'Well, son—aren't you?'

Frankie raised his fist and cried, 'You dirty little lump of shit!'

The lawyer shot back his chair two feet without rising, looked quickly round the café and said, 'Well, excuse me, *aren't* you?'

Frankie was impressed by the total sincerity of the lawyer's complete surprise. He lowered his fist and said, 'Well, I'll be buggered! Do I look like one?'

The clerk carefully adjusted his seat and picked up his tea again. 'Boy!' he said, 'who *does*? Just do me a favour, will you? Just attend the courts for a week and *look* at them. Except for the odd exception, they all look exactly . . . well, like you and me or anyone at all.'

Frankie laughed. 'Well, I'll be fucked!' he said. 'Just fancy that!'

'You use a lot of bad language, son,' the lawyer said.

'Excuse me again: I didn't mean it.'

The lawyer said, 'Forgotten—excuse *me*, too.' He paused. 'What is your profession, then, if I might ask?'

'Seaman.'

'Seaman. Got a ship?'

'No.'

'Got some other job?'

'No. Not yet.'

'Pardon this question: please don't take it amiss: you ever taken money from that girl?'

There was quite a wait, and for the first time in many years, Frankie blushed. 'I *have* borrowed a few quid from her,' he said.

'*Borrowed.*'

'That's what I told you.'

'All right—all right. Don't hang me, sailor.' The clerk stirred his cup thoughtfully, then said, 'I'm going to tell you something if you want to hear it, but on two conditions. The first is you don't hit me, please. The second is you don't tell the girl because, after all, she's supposed to be my client. Do you agree?'

'Go on . . .'

'You seem a nice boy, and I think I ought to tell you. So here it is. If a vice copper saw you near the courts with a woman coming up on a soliciting charge, and waiting in a caff holding her bag while she went in, and he knew you'd had money from her, and he knew you'd got no job, he wouldn't *ask* you if you are a ponce, believe you me! He'd know you *were* one, and a bloody foolish one at that!'

Frankie Love looked at him steadily, then rose and said, 'Thanks. Would you do something for me, please? Give her this bag. And tell her if she comes near me again I'll crunch her.'

MR JUSTICE

'To show you the ropes,' the Detective-sergeant had said, 'I'll have you go around a while with our star sleuth, as we all call him. He's a young feller just about your age, a bit too big in his boots for a detective-constable, and chances his arm rather more than I think is wise even in our little line of business. But he's a good lad basically, and he certainly gets results. Don't make the mistake, though, of thinking you can get away with everything he does.'

The star sleuth fascinated Edward: he was born to his function like a thoroughbred to the turf, and although so young seemed to know intimately, by instinct, how the whole machinery of the Force could be made to function. During his military service, Edward had noticed the same thing in some young soldiers: there were recruits of only a fortnight who—except for certain gaps of experience, easily corrected—instinctively *knew* how the whole army functioned: what were the real rules behind Queen's Regulations, what duties you could ignore, what prohibited manoeuvres you could safely undertake. In appearance the star sleuth was remarkably nondescript (yet another advantage, Edward reflected!) but not, as he soon discovered, in character or skill.

On their first day out together the star sleuth said, 'Well, I've nothing on, let's just take a walk around.' The tone, scarcely disguised, suggested that he had a lot 'on', and considered Edward's company an imposition. As they walked round the streets between the Harrow road and the railway to the West, his companion said absolutely nothing: being one of those rare men who do not feel the nervous urge to talk so as to establish their identity, and who can remain silent without positively appearing to be rude.

Finding this unbearable, Edward commented on it: 'You're a man of few words,' he said, after fifteen minutes of none whatever.

The star sleuth looked sideways as he walked. 'I can talk quite a bit when necessary,' he said.

'Oh, I believe you,' Edward answered.

'I'll tell you something, boy,' the star sleuth said, stopping at the end of a short road leading to a brick precipice that overhung the railway lines below. 'I'm not here to *teach* you. As a matter of fact I'll be frank with you, I'm still learning as well and what I discover I like to keep strictly to myself. But: here's one tip: *learn* to be silent.'

'Not shoot off your mouth, you mean? Well, obviously.'

The star sleuth folded his arms upon the wall. 'More than that,' he said. 'Look! Suppose you've knocked off a suspect. What do you want to make him do? Talk, isn't it? Well—and believe me. The best way to do it—and the quickest and the *kindest* (he grimaced)—is to say not a word to him yourself. Not a bloody word. Make him wait, say nothing, just come in and *look* at him occasionally. If there's one thing most human beings just can't bear—particularly when they're sitting in the station—that thing is silence.'

'Sometimes you have to talk to them, don't you?'

'Why?'

'Well! Well—suppose it's not a suspect, but a nark or someone who's come to give you information.'

'Exactly the same!'

'Yes?'

'Yes! I'm telling you. Silence.'

'Why?'

'Oh—why? You want me to tell you *why*? Well, that's a bit hard until you've had the experience yourself. But try to get hold of this one.' The star sleuth stuttered slightly, as if wresting a secret from his breast. '*All* men and women you meet professionally are criminals.'

'*Every* one?'

'All. If you want to get anywhere you've got to treat everyone as such.'

Edward digested this as, below his eyes, the Plymouth Belle racketed by. 'That's going a bit far,' he said.

'Is it? Well, you know best. Wait and see.'

'You mean . . . Say someone comes in to report he's found a bicycle. You suspect him?'

'Of course. He's number one on my list.'

'It's a thought . . .' said Edward.

The star sleuth dusted his arms, and turned round to lean in the sun with his back against the wall.

'If you start with that principle,' he said, 'you really can't go wrong. And if you stick to it and are true to it, it will automatically stop you making a lot of other silly beginner's mistakes.'

'Such as what?' said Edward. 'I'm listening . . .'

'I hope so—because sonny, frankly, I don't want to waste all this if it's going to be wasted on *you*. Here are some golden rules, then: get out your note-book and write them down if you feel like it. (The star sleuth chortled.) First is—never go to them: make them come to you.'

'Who?'

'Anyone. It's just like football, boxing, bull-fighting—anything. Make them come to you and then you've got them.'

'And if you can't?'

'You're no damn good. Next, never let them get the impression they're doing the law a favour. Now, suppose someone walks out of that slum there—comes running over—"Officer, I've found a corpse!" —this is your big opportunity for a case . . . don't thank him, don't even *answer*, just make him feel he's done what he's *got* to do.'

'Yes, that seems sound.'

'Oh, *thank* you! Now, number three—and that'll do for today, I think—*never* answer questions: always ask them.'

'Oh, I know that one . . .'

'*Do* you? All right. I'm a dear old lady, I come up and say to you, "Constable, can you tell me the way to the Town Hall?"—what do you say?'

'Don't I tell her?'

'Oh—of course! But first you say, "Is it the sanitation department you need, madam, or the rates?" See? Put them on the defensive—always.'

'Oh. I get it.'

'No, you don't—you've forgotten something.'

'*I* have?'

'Yes. What else do you say to her?'

'Well—tell me.'

'You say, "By the way, madam, it's more usual these days to say 'officer', not 'constable'." '

'Correct, yes, I'd say that.'

'So there it is. All in a nutshell. Very simple!'

Without warning, the star sleuth started back up the road again. Edward Justice fell in by his side and said, 'I think some of what you tell me would surprise the old Detective-sergeant just a little.'

The star sleuth stopped. 'Oh *him*,' he said. 'What does *he* know? He belongs to the generation of Pc 49: crafty and tough and not a brain in his thick head.'

'Take it easy, mate.'

'I do, constable!'

They started off again. Ted Justice felt the conversation was now closed, but he had one final question. 'All you said about *every*one being criminal,' he asked. 'Does that apply to us as well?'

'Naturally.'

'To you and me and the Detective-sergeant?'

'Yes.'

'You don't even trust your colleagues in the Force, then?'

'Colleagues! I trust them for one thing, and one only. There are exceptions—but in a fight they're brave and they're reliable. Alone in a dark lane with a bunch of Teds they won't stab you in the back —no, they'll help you come what may. But otherwise . . .'

His voice and his whole posture and expression showed Edward clearly that the shutters were now down, and should not be prised open any more.

Out in the Harrow road the star sleuth stopped to gaze around the vital, squalid thoroughfare, and stood as if sniffing the breeze on a safari. Then he walked half a block, went into a tobacconist's, bought a packet of Senior Service and paused, undoing it, beside the notice-board outside.

On this were handwritten advertisements, some apparently of great antiquity, which mostly offered lodgings with innumerable restrictions. Other invited the purchase of items which no one (except, perhaps, a film studio shooting a Dickens story) would dream of buying. A third category, sometimes with crude photographs, advertised 'models'. The star sleuth scanned these, then withdrew a bit with Edward Justice.

'Whores, I suppose,' said Edward.

'The strange thing is though, boy, that quite a lot of them actually *are* models. In this fair land of ours there's loads of kinky characters who just like sitting and *gazing* at a chick's tits for a couple of quid. Please don't ask me why.'

'And that's quite legal?'

'More or less, it is.'

'But some of them *are* prostitutes?'

'Of course. Nothing illegal about that, either. Under the new act they mustn't solicit in the streets, and if there's more than one of them it's a brothel. Otherwise . . . it's just a business: and believe me, half the time we're called into protect *them.*'

'From the ponces?'

'Not usually . . . In the first place, a ponce with any sense won't live with his girl: they've two addresses, like any other business couple. And in the second—well frankly, most of the stories you hear about brutal bullies putting innocent teenagers on the streets are crap.'

'But that does happen?'

'Oh, yes. With young, or mental, or maybe masochistic girls. Most of the girls are tough and quite intelligent, though. They have to be. And girls of that type simply wouldn't wear it.'

'But the men *do* thump them . . .'

'Oh, frequently! But that's part of the kick: it's all for love!'

The star sleuth took Edward's arm and said, 'As we pass again, just take a look at the bottom left-hand corner one.'

Ted did, and he read:

BETTINA
Is a Continental girl
and very serious. All
poses by appointment.
VEN 5121.

Further along, the star sleuth said to Edward, 'Well?'

'I'd say she's one.'

'Of course! But what sort of one?'

Go on . . . Don't tease me, I'm very willing to learn . . .

'Well. "Continental" doesn't mean she *is*, but what she'll *do*. "All poses" rams the point home and "by appointment" says you can tell her what, over the blower, to see if your kinks match up. "Very serious", of course, suggests the sexual slant in this particular case. New Olympia typewriter with a clean ribbon, so she's possibly expensive.'

'In this area?'

'Why not? Where whores are concerned there *is* no fashionable section if she's good—I mean for where her gaff actually is. Anyway, kinky clients like a slum, and respectable gents prefer an area where they'll not be known.'

'The notice cost her much?'

'Pound a week, unless the tobacconist's an imbecile. For honest landladies, only 2s 6d or something similar.'

'But, tell me. Doesn't advertising like that put us on to her?'

'Why not? It's legal: and even if not, it'd take every cop in London to trace all the notices on boards . . . Besides: put yourself in the poor girl's place. The new laws make it difficult for them on the streets: so how *do* they contact their clients—tell me that, please?'

'No, you go on . . .'

'Well: best is, take a chance and go on the streets three months or so, and build up a clientele.'

'And give them the phone number.'

'Clever boy—exactly. Then, as we know, there's the notice-board technique. Another one: a good contact in the drinking-clubs or all-night garages: barman, doorman, owner, anybody.'

'These pimps take a cut?'

'Don't waste my time! Then there's the escort-businesses—know about them? No? All right: you're a wool-grower from New Zealand, shall we say. You want to meet a nice friendly young lady for a sociable evening out. You're with me?'

'That's legal too?'

'Who for, the agencies? Well, lots of the dates they make are kosher. But several of these agents *have* gone inside on procuring charges . . .'

'What about Madams?'

'Ah! Yes, there are those: and respectable clients actually like to deal with them because though it costs five times as much, she irons out all the awkward creases for them. Failing the Madams, a new mystery can also find a successful call-girl who'll sub-let clients to her at a percentage.'

Edward laughed. 'We do make it difficult in this country, don't we!' he said.

'That's probably half the charm: the mugs like it to be awkward and mysterious—but not, of course, too dangerous for them.'

'So the new laws have made the whole thing harder.'

'Not really. No, I wouldn't say so. Who they've made it harder for are stupid girls and semi-pros who've been knocked out of business because they can't use the streets any longer. The clever ones have just gone on the phone. And here's a funny thing: once they're established with their clients, it's actually *easier* for them.'

'It is?'

'Well yes, it is. Take gaffs. A crooked gaff with the landlord in the know cost forty a week at least with maybe key money in decent areas—when you could get them. That was for street girls. But once you're on the phone, you can get a straight place just like anyone else for ten a week or so. Of course, if the caretaker or some friendly neighbour rumbles you—out you go! But you'd really be surprised, if the girl's discreet and chooses her clients carefully, how *little* people notice. You see: English people are nosy, sure enough, as we all know; but they've also got a great thing about minding their own business. That's very valuable to the girls. So with the new laws I'd say this: there'll be just as much vice, just as many millions spent on it, but fewer women. Conclusion: profits per head—or tail—will rise. That's all.'

Edward was overwhelmed by this expertise: and, like an anxious angler, handled his companion with the utmost care lest an inappropriate reaction or remark might plunge him back into taciturnity. With prudence, though, there seemed little danger of this: like many silent men the star sleuth, once started, was a chatterbox, and opinionated (not without reason), and something of a fanatic: which the speed and urgency of his narrow voice conveyed vividly to Edward as they walked on along the Harrow road.

'And what,' Edward asked, 'about the ponces?'

'Those bastards,' said the officer, stopping by the canal bridge.

'Yes. How do they fit in?'

'They come out best of all,' the star sleuth said.

'With the new laws?'

'Yes.'

'Why?'

'Like this,' said the star sleuth, peering at the cats and contraceptives floating on the Grand Union canal. 'You're a ponce—right! Your girl is on the streets—yes? Well, if she is she's certainly had several convictions. But if she's a call-girl—particularly if she's started out as one without going on the streets at all—there's quite likely nothing known against her: no convictions, anyway. Very well. Try proving to a magistrate—let alone a jury—that the male companion of an innocent, unconvicted woman is living off her immoral earnings!'

'So what can you do about them?'

'We're working out techniques to meet the situation. The best is, opinion seems to be, to raid her premises with a warrant for suspected brothel-keeping and sweep him into the net, somehow, in the process. Then, once you've got him, a little chat will probably produce results. That is, if you can *find* him: because the craftier among the ponces are naturally very elusive. And if their woman's loyal to them it's going to be tricky in the extreme.' The star sleuth took out a halfpenny and dropped it in the canal. 'But not impossible,' he added.

MR LOVE

FRANKIE had paid his last visit to the Labour because he'd told the clerks there, without venom but with extreme precision and contempt, that he wasn't going through the comedy of 'signing on' any more just like a schoolboy, and that it was *their* job to get him a ship and if they couldn't, well then, fuck them. They'd said—also without malice but with all the equal contempt of the employed official for the jobless—that that was up to him, here was his week's money and if he didn't want any more then of course he needn't bother to sign on. With these few pounds Frankie went down among the seamen's homes of Stepney to try to arrange to stow away: not on a long trip, he was not so daft as that, but just to another port where the proportion of mariners to landsmen might be more favourable to his hopes and mental comfort.

On his way down by Leman Street, on the other side of the road, approaching him, he saw the girl: and walked straight ahead, ignoring her; but as they passed his eyes pulled his head round . . . and he saw it wasn't she but just another: and as soon as he knew it wasn't, wished it had been.

Like children (and most men), Frankie was attracted by what, for reasons of pride more than real inclination, he had rejected. The episode near the courts had left him speculating—naturally—on what, if he *had* been her ponce, the life would have been like: and as with so many of us, what we have speculated on at length becomes with time the thing we mean to do. A few weeks' reflection, too, had taught him that essentially the girl, by her oblique and crafty offer, hadn't really meant him any harm: her manoeuvre had in its way been flattering; and also—for Frankie was unusually free from self-delusion—had been one that, things being as they were, might as well be rationally considered.

The chief—in fact, the only real—reason against it all was that Frankie thought ponces were bums, and seamen princes. But suppose you were a prince without a throne? That it was criminal didn't worry him particularly, since Frankie's code of honour (which most certainly existed) at times coincided with, but at times departed completely from those enshrined by any established sets of laws. For example: he wouldn't hesitate a second to wound a man—or even, if it came to that, to kill him—if it was to help a friend—a rare and real one. And as for the sexual aspect, this didn't worry him at all: because for Frankie, sex *was* love; and sexual attachment the only profound relationship with a woman that he considered possible. The money, of course, would be—well, obviously—useful. Like many seamen, Frankie wasn't greedy about money and only felt the urgent need of it for explosive blow-outs when ashore in port. On board—with food and a berth and working clothes—he felt no need of it at all and even forgot at times, completely, how much back pay the company might owe him. But to be *destitute*: and on land! That was a real horror, a most shameful and miserable misfortune.

So—all things considered—hadn't he been a fool to turn her down so finally and abruptly? Quite clearly, poncing would be dangerous . . . you'd need to find out a lot more about the tackle and ropes of *that*. As obviously, a great deal would depend on how far you could trust the woman; and—more to the point—dominate her. Because in Frankie's sharp and hard experience a woman, like a ship, was reliable only if you had her under strict and complete control.

Nevertheless: the sea, certainly, came first—and far away so—if it would have him back. No woman and no fortune would hold him from that great and utterly dependable she. So, filled with the determination of a wise and right decision, he spent an energetic day among the nautical layabouts of Wapping. But though he drank a very great deal—and they—no one, apparently, could fix anything or even make a practical suggestion. And as night fell he grew not just dejected and intoxicated, but—worst of all for a man whose mind and spirit waxed and waned in power with the strength of his animal energy—he grew spiteful, tired and angry. 'Oh, well,' he said, 'anything rather than the Labour'—and he set off on foot to her address.

Repeated ringing brought no answer: till he became aware from the movement of a curtain that there was someone up there. He withdrew ostentatiously; returned and waited a whole hour in a near-by doorway (fortifying himself from a hip flask) and then, when another lodger entered, ran up and got his foot inside the door.

This man (in fact, the landlord) vigorously protested, but Frankie simply lifted him up and placed him on one side, walked up the stairs, banged on the door, heard angry shouts, heaved against it several times and broke inside. The girl was standing by the table holding a breadknife, and her companion, a short, dark man, remained sitting watchfully beside his loaded plate.

'Get out!' the girl cried.

'Not me,' said Frankie '—him.'

'You're drunk!' she shouted.

'Of course. Is he a customer? Tell him to go!'

'He's not. He's what *you* were too bloody high-and-mighty to want to be.'

And now the man made a rush. Frankie was used to the Maltese, and didn't underestimate them at all. They're fast, fearless, and mean business, he knew. He raised a whole leg quickly and braced himself against the wall: the Malt ran into it and lost his knife. Unfortunately for him his shoes were off his feet, and Frankie (recalling an episode in Williamstown, Victoria) had gone for both of them with all his eleven stone while keeping a fraction of a weather eye on the girl and, more particularly, her breadknife. But she didn't use it or move, and the Maltese was in agony. Frankie kicked him again, ripped his slacks down by a swift tear at his belt (another Victorian expedient), then closed in, heaved him to the open door and literally 'threw him down the stairs'.

The girl ran out and cried, 'Give him his coat here or he'll call the law!'

Frankie threw it down after him. 'You want me call the law?' the Bengali landlord echoed.

'No, no—I'll see you straight: a fiver!' cried the girl.

The front door slammed on the Maltese. They went back in the room. 'Well!' said the girl. 'You *are* a lively boy!' He grabbed her and got to work ferociously.

An hour or so later they sorted themselves out and resumed the meal abandoned by the Malt. She was gazing at him with frank admiration and also (but perhaps he missed this) with a triumphant, proprietory glint. Downing his VP wine, he said to her, 'Hand me that thing.'

'My bag?'

'You heard.'

She passed it over with a smile and he upended it. 'Not much,' he said.

'Others have been at it.'

'Not any more.'

'No? Hi! You're not going to be one of *those*, are you?' she cried as she saw him stuffing all the notes into his slacks pocket.

'One of what?'

'One who takes *everything*.'

'Why—is this all you've got?'

'Sure.'

'Don't kid me!'

'Darling, why should I? You'll soon find out.'

'Nothing hidden?'

'*Hidden?* Are you crazy? In this dump? My bag's the only safe place—it never leaves me.'

He put it down. 'Haven't you got any savings?' he asked her.

'*Savings?* Darling! What you take me for!'

'Well—we're going to change all that; we're going to save.'

'Are we? Well, dear, I'm all for it—but it's going to be up to you.'

'Okay. I'll see to it.'

'Nice of you. Meantime, could I have a couple of quid for pin money? Only two . . .'

'Of course.'

'*Thank* you. You *are* good to me!'

He kissed her and upset some crockery. She disentangled. 'And will you tell me,' she said, 'just *how* you're going to save this money?'

'*How?* Put it in the bank.'

'Oh, yes? The GPO? The Midland?'

'Well—why not?'

She looked at him. 'Darling,' she said, 'I love you, but honest, you worry me, you've got a *lot* to learn.'

'Well—teach me.'

'Suppose you're nicked—just on suspicion. And they find you've got a bank account. What then?'

'I see.'

'You do? Well, then. What next?'

'We'll put it in your name.'

'Oh! So you trust me! Suppose I walk out on you?'

'You won't.'

'Won't I? Dear, in this business you just *never* can tell.'

She got up, picked up her chair and came round and sat beside him. 'Listen,' she said. 'Let's get a few things straight. I love you, Frankie, but there'll be rows enough if I know you—and know me—and there's some we can skip by right from the start avoiding misunderstandings.'

He lit a fag. 'Okay,' he said. 'I'm new on board. Please clue me up.'

She was looking at him again. 'You know,' she said, 'before we think of anything like saving, we *must* get you a new suit.'

'Oh, that can wait.'

'And shirts and shoes and spare slacks and things.'

'Come on—get on with it. Lay down the cards.'

'Very well, then. And let's have first things first. I *don't* want a ponce who isn't faithful.'

'Why shouldn't I be?'

'That's what they all say! But please understand this, Frankie, very clearly. If you want to mess around with any other girl, do please just tell me and we'll wind it up. But don't try to deceive me.'

'That seems right enough to me. And what about you?'

'Me?'

'You and any other men.'

'I hope you don't mean the customers . . . because, darling, they just mean sweet fuck-all to me.'

'But what if one ever did?'

'I'd not see him again.'

'You promise?'

'I'm not the sort of girl who has to *promise*. If I say so, it is so.'

'Me, too. All right, then. What else?'

'I want to change my business completely. I want a big change in my whole life. I want to go on the phone.'

'Like call-girl?'

'Oh, Frankie! Your knowledge, boy!'

'I'm a seaman, do remember. I've got stacks of foreign phone numbers in my diary.'

'Throw it away, then.'

'Okay. So call-girl: why?'

'Because street business is getting too dangerous, because I'm reaching an age when I like to know *who* the client's going to be, and because I'm tired of thirty bobs and call-girl money's better.'

'All right. Will that Asian of yours let you put in your private phone?'

'You crazy, darling? We're moving out! I want to go up West.'

'I've no objection. Any particular area?'

'I thought of Kilburn: it's quiet and quite select.'

'Not too select to get a place, I hope.'

'Baby! This is a straight gaff I'll be looking for—not a crooked one. In fact . . . I've had what I think's quite a bright little idea: try and get a council flat.'

'They wouldn't get to know?'

'Well, if they do—we move. And that brings me to another point. Most of the girls, I don't mind telling you, prefer their boys *not* to have a job so as to make them more dependent. But me, darling, honest, for your own sake I'd rather you had one.'

'I don't mind. If I can get one . . . You know how I've tried . . .'

'Up West, it'll be different and I'll help you. It's protection for you —no need for you to account to anyone for your means of support; and it'd also mean that we could live together.'

'Aren't we going to do that anyway?'

'Oh, of course! But if you *haven't* got a job, it's much safer for you if I live and work in two different places.'

'I get it. All right—find me a job, then.'

She kissed him. He looked up and said, 'Baby, apart from that, what do I have to *do*?'

'Love me.'

'Of course! But nothing else? Don't you need protection or something?'

'Me? Apart from the odd sex maniac I can handle anyone: and even them I can usually spot a mile off. No: all you have to do is be.'

'Okay. But I must say, if you'll not think me ignorant, I don't quite see what *you*'ll get out of it: come to that, what any of you girls do out of having boys.'

She looked at him. 'I'm just wondering,' she said, 'just how much I ought to tell you.'

'It's up to you! This truth thing was your idea anyway.'

'Okey-doke. Well, here it is. Imagine you're a gigolo—right? You hire yourself out to a dozen women a day. How would you feel?'

'Exhausted.'

'No, I mean about your sex life?'

'Disgusted.'

'There you are, then. And wouldn't you feel the need for a real lover—far more than any ordinary woman does?'

Frankie reflected. 'I don't know about that,' he said.

'Well—we do. A ponce, dear, in many cases, is simply an unmarried husband. He's our little compensation for the kind of life we lead.'

'All the girls feel that way?'

'Not all—not even all those who *do* have ponces. With some of them it's just to show them off: that they've hooked some splendid great big hunk of man.'

'That's just like *any* girl.'

'A *lot* of things about whores are, dear, as you'll discover.'

'Well—what else?'

'This is the one I shouldn't tell you, but I will. A woman always likes to *own* a man.'

'So you own me?'

'Wait! All women like it. An old bag with a gigolo—doesn't she? A rich wife with a poor husband—doesn't she too? And even respectable women: don't they like to boss their husbands somehow if they can? Get the hooks on them some way? Well, with us it's a mania. And I won't hide it from you, so there'll be no tears, no reproaches. There's *no*body in the whole wide world who's hooked by a woman like a ponce is by a whore.'

'Why?'

'I'll put it to you straight: because he's a criminal and she's not.'

'And she could shop him?'

'Any minute of the day.'

There was silence.

'Yeah,' he said. 'Well, I see that. But it seems to me *he*'s not without weapons in his jacket, too.'

'You mean he can bash her?'

'Not only that. If she shops him, when he comes out—if they get him—then he can carve her up.'

'Oh, sure! And it's been done! But darling! She moves first!'

'Or even kill her.'

'Life imprisonment, dear.'

'Also,' he continued, 'just walk out on her.'

'If she doesn't want it?'

'Sure.'

She kissed his hands. 'Well, you know best,' she said, 'and with a nice girl like I am, I don't deny it's true. But if she's a bitch and he says cheerioh, she can make it very, very awkward for him if she wants to.'

Frankie withdrew his hands. 'You know,' he said, 'I'm beginning to wonder what the poor fucking ponce gets out of it at all.'

She laughed. 'Well!' she exclaimed. 'Nice times if she's any good, that others have to pay for. Easy money and a lot of it—a great, great deal. A big boost to his ego—doesn't it make you feel you're like a king? And then, excitement! They do actually love the life, so many of them.'

'Born to it, you'd say.'

'Yes—not like you: you're not the born type, that's why I love you.'

'And have there,' Frankie asked, 'been many others before me in your sweet life?'

'Frank,' she said. 'I'll make a bargain with you. I'll ask you no questions about anything you did before today: if you'll agree to do the same so far as my past life's concerned.'

'Seems reasonable. Okay.' He got to his feet. 'It's lucky for me,' he said, 'that men just can't do without it. None of them.'

She didn't answer that but got up too, and they started to clear the table and wash the dishes together.

'Just one more thing,' she said from among the suds, 'and then my little lecture's ended.' She turned and faced him. '*Do* be careful, please, about the law. Avoid them if you can and don't provoke them. The only good relations a ponce can have with coppers is just none at all.'

'I'm not a dope: I'll remember.'

'It's quite surprising,' she said, 'how much they'll leave you alone, even if they know quite a lot about you, if you keep right clear of them and don't draw their attention to you in any way at all.'

'Okay. I've got nothing against coppers.'

'I'm glad to hear it. A lot of ponces are just copper-haters: and that's so bloody foolish.'

'Hate them?' said Frankie, putting down a china plate. 'Well, me, I don't—why should I? They're part of the system just like ship's officers are—and I never hated them as long as they did their job efficiently and fairly. I didn't even mind unfairness or even a bit of rough-stuff provided they knew how to keep the old ship sailing on. As for the law—well, I've been knocked off once or twice and even bashed up a bit, but I've no real reason to complain. The law's got to be there just like the captain: and I'd say it's got to be respected, even by anyone who chooses to go against it.'

MR JUSTICE

EDWARD'S next task was to collect a nark or two: and this was no easy matter. A nark–copper relationship is, in a way, like that of lovers: a particular intimacy that cannot be simply handed over by one officer to another as part of the new officer's inheritance with the files and addresses and card-indexes. A nark must be personally wooed and won: or rather, he and the copper must *discover* each other, just as lovers do, and establish personal ties—the nark offering facts and admiration, the copper small rewards in kind and privilege.

The nark's chief asset in the deal is that really good informers—not so strange as it may seem—are rarer by far than really good coppers are The copper's asset is not, as one might imagine, the meagre advantages which, in reality, he can offer to the nark, but the power and prestige the nark imagines he derives from being attached, though indirectly and informally, to an immensely powerful organization. The nark may be motivated by the love of secrecy (of knowing things that *are* secret from others, however valueless in themselves), and also, it may be, by the almost voluptuous instinct that exists in certain human beings, to betray. There may even (if the nark be intelligent, which he rarely is or he wouldn't be one) exist the deep attraction of an awful fear: of playing with hot and very unpredictable fires. Fear, that is, of the Force and also, even, of what may happen to himself: for sharp narks can hardly fail to perceive how frequently, if they fall foul of an officer or he merely gets tired of them, they themselves are apt to disappear suddenly, unaccountably, inside the nick. But even this does not prevent the really devoted nark from re-assuming, on release, his former role. For narks in their humble way, like the majestic coppers whom they serve, are dedicated souls.

It was a female copper (plain-clothes—and very fetching ones) who gave Edward sound counsel on this point. 'Wait till they come to you,' she said. 'They will.' And sure enough, soon after his first weeks on the job during which he'd had the sensation all the time that dozens of invisible, unidentifiable eyes had been weighing him carefully up, a man approached him by the telephone boxes of Royal Oak tube station (where he was trying to catch a sex maniac whose habit it was to wait till a girl entered the box next to his own, immediately dial *her* number—which he'd previously noted—and when she raised the receiver in astonishment at the quick sound of the bell, utter an obscenity), and the following dialogue took place.

'He's not here today,' the nark said.

'Who isn't?'

'Who you're looking for.'

'Who am I looking for?'

'Madcap Mary.'

'Who's she?'

'He: the feller who makes the calls you're interested in.'

'What makes you think I'm interested in any calls?'

This exchange, to both officer and nark, had already established some essential factors. For all human conversations hold inside and beyond them other, and often larger, conversations that remain unspoken, of which the exchange is just the seventh part (if that's the figure) of the iceberg that breaks surface. Ted knew, for instance, this man knew who he was, what he was after, and something about it. The nark knew he knew all this and that Edward took a lively, but always conditional interest in himself. They'd also assessed quite a bit about each other's characters, and possible utility, and degrees of reliability and of menace. Beyond this there were whole mushroom clouds of supposition, waiting for crystallization in good time.

'I could do with a cup of tea,' the nark said, suddenly feigning a fairly evident mock humility.

Unlike most narks this creature was not small: nor shifty, nor furtive, nor triple-eyed, nor sordid in his attire. He looked like a bus conductor, say, of a suburban line and nearing retirement. They entered the caff separately, then joined up again after getting their two cups, as if casually, at the table near the window.

There was quite a pause, each waiting for the other to begin. The nark, being the older and the more experienced, held out longer, and Edward broke the silence with, 'And how did you know about me?'

'I always do.'

'Always? No one point me out to you?'

'Almost always.'

'How?'

The nark smiled sourly. 'If you could see yourself now,' he said, 'you'd know.'

Vexed, Edward asked him, 'Why?'

'You've got the *double* look.'

'The what?'

'You're wearing it now: watch your pals, you'll get to know it. And then, all coppers *stare*. Nobody else in England, except kids and coppers, *stare*.'

'Go on . . .'

'And then, they listen. Even if you're drunk or bore them stiff, coppers will *listen* to you.'

'But we have to.'

'I'm not saying you don't: only that you do.'

'All right. Anything else?'

'Yes, your shoes. I've never yet seen a cop, even got up as a down-and-out or something, who can bear to be seen around if he's down-at-heel.'

'Really!'

'Yes. And then you don't like running.'

'Come off it! You mean we never chase anyone?'

'Oh, of course you do: but you don't like it.'

'Why would you say we don't?'

'I dunno. Maybe because of those helmets. Even if you're not wearing them you're frightened they'll fall off. Or maybe you just don't like *hurrying*. Or exercise of any kind.'

Edward smiled, quite unpleasantly, too. 'Is that all?' he said.

'There's also your hands.'

'What about them?'

'You're working-men most of you, but you don't like manual labour. That's why quite a lot of you join the Force: to get out of manual labour.'

Edward drained his cup. 'So we're easy to spot,' he said. 'Stick out a mile, you'd say.'

The nark was unabashed. 'Most of you do, yes. That is, except for women coppers. Maybe it's just because they're fewer, or maybe we're all not quite used even now to the idea of them, but—well: even I quite often fail to spot them.'

'Even you.'

'Yes, that's what I said: even me.'

The nark eyed Edward with modest but assured professional pride. 'Don't take it hard,' he said, 'from me. I know you're just starting, and I'm only trying to be of assistance to you.'

'Thank you,' said Edward, meditating in the nark's near future some thoroughly uncomfortable moments.

'The fact is this,' the nark continued, lighting a fag and not offering Edward one. 'You may not approve of what I say, but you and me have one big thing in common: neither of us is mugs: both of us sees below the surface of how things seem.'

'Yeah,' Edward said.

'And I'll tell you something more,' the nark went on. 'It's even the same between you and the criminals, as you'll discover. Neither they nor you belong to the great world of the mugs: you know what I mean: the millions who pay their taxes by the pea-eh-why-ee, read their Sunday papers for the scandals, do their pools on Thursdays, watch the jingles on the telly, travel to and fro to work on tubes and buses in the rush hour, take a fortnight's annual holiday by the sea, and think the world is just like that.'

'I see what you mean,' said Edward Justice.

'Well, now,' said the nark. 'I don't want to waste your time. Are you interested in a little case?'

'I might be . . .'

'It's a small affair but I think it may lead to bigger. In fact, something makes me sure it will do. And if it does I hope you'll not forget me.'

The nark eyed Edward. 'Oh, of course not,' Edward said.

'Briefly, then, I want you to meet a pimp.'

Edward looked interrogative and said nothing.

'Here's the whole tale. This pimp, unless I'm much mistaken, is offering something much more interesting than he seems to be.'

'Go on . . .'

'He works in a saloon bar not far from here: empty glass collector—you know—splendid opportunities for contacts. Well: when the pub closes lots of them, specially Irish, still want to go on drinking.'

'Naturally.'

'Naturally. So he leads them—some of them—to a Cyprus caff where they can get it after hours.'

'Not interested. Liquor cases? What you take me for?'

'*Do* be patient, officer' (last word uttered in an urgent whisper). 'In this speakeasy, I think they also gamble.'

'Still not interested.'

'*And* make other contacts.

'Which?'

'Girls.'

'That's better. On the premises?'

'No.'

'Then where?'

'I don't know.'

'Oh, *don't* you. Then how you know they go after girls if you don't know where they go to—that is, if you really *don't* know?'

The nark looked pained. 'You and I,' he said, 'are just not going to get anywhere unless we trust each other—up to a point, at any rate.'

'All right—I trust you: so?'

'That's all I ask. Now, listen. He takes them off from the Cyprus caff, this pimp, in *groups* and on *foot*—they don't take taxis. Also, they don't come back. Now, then: what else but girls would keep drunken men from going back again to a speakeasy that's a spieler?'

'If it's just single girls they go to, I'm still not interested.'

'I don't expect you would be. But *can* it be single girls? Off in a group . . . no taxi . . . he can't distribute them one by one around the area, can he?'

'So you think it's a brothel.'

The nark nodded sagely.

'That *might* interest me,' said Edward.

'I thought so.'

'But you: why haven't you followed them to make sure?'

The nark looked bland. 'Tell me—why should I? It might be dangerous, you know. And I don't want to be observed. Anyway, it's not what I'm paid to do. That's where I think possibly *you* come in.'

MR JUSTICE (STILL)

THE Detective-sergeant had told Edward that 'if anything at all big comes up,' he was to inform him and not try to tackle it alone. 'If you prove to be any good,' his senior had added, 'something certainly *will* turn up, because a good copper always attracts crime to himself. But don't forget—it's only with arrest that the real problem of our job begins. There's the prisoner to be dealt with for his statement and so on, and beyond that the whole machinery of the courts we've got to persuade.' But Edward had vivid recollections of his disappointments when in uniformed days any discovery of his own produced, if reported, a host of seniors who did all the fancy work and took the credit. And knowing success is never blamed, he decided to chance his arm and handle the suspected brothel case alone.

Accordingly, and by appointment, he met the nark at the public-house in question: or rather the nark, as agreed, merely handed an empty glass at 10.15 pm (publican's time) to the individual he accused of being a pimp in order that Edward might be sure of his identity. That, so far as the nark was concerned, ended the proceedings: after this Edward was on his own.

The pimp, surprisingly, was little more than a teenager—twenty-one or two, Edward thought, and looking younger than his age. He was so surprised by the boy's appearance that against all professional etiquette he ventured a glance, in search of confirmation, at the nark—who very properly ignored it. The pimp, also, was a songster: for between his errands and still holding wallop-stained glasses in casual festoons, he'd pause at a microphone to nasally intone appalling Irish melodies much appreciated by the Celtic boozers who the farther they got from Erin's isle, adored it all the more.

At closing time, Edward lingered in the street carrying (a subtle touch, he thought) a quarter-filled can of paraffin whose purpose was that wherever he might be observed to loiter, the assumption would be he was visiting or coming from a neighbour to collect or supply this useful household fluid. At the back of his mind there was also the notion it might come in useful to hurl at somebody, if need be. For Edward was now learning what all young coppers do: that their job, at night, and even sometimes in the day can be very dangerous. The only security he felt was that he was alone: always the safest situation for any probing, nocturnal prowler. This wisdom confirmed the Detective-sergeant's diagnosis that he was born to the purple of the CID: who've soon understood the real reason why plain-clothes men are told to work, if possible, in pairs, is not for their own protection but that one can be the witness of an assault upon the other, and bring any vital messages home to base.

By now he was following a carolling party piloted by the pimp, the paraffin in his can playing lapping harmonies to their graceless melodies. The Cypriot café was not far off, and from its exterior Ted had no difficulty in observing they descended immediately to an invisible basement room. After a while of strolling and hesitation he entered, parked his paraffin tin, and ordered kebab and ladies' fingers. He ate these slowly and drank two Turkish coffees till he was the only surviving customer. Hints began to be dropped, even by the courteous Cypriots, that the time had come for him to be on his way. He therefore retreated to the road again, where he spent a tiresome, embarrassing hour of vigil.

But this delay served a purpose: his mounting irritation was now firmly concentrated on the drunks and gamblers in the cellar. Of course, he knew well—even recruit training had taught him that—you should always try to remain quite *impersonal* in your feelings about suspects, and not ever become too interested in them as individual human beings. On the other hand, a little spite and resentment would spice the eagerness to effect a capture. Edward was soon rewarded by the exaggeratedly cautious appearance of three Irishmen and the pimp. Observing (with recollections of the text-books) Alternative B, he 'followed' them from in front assisted, like a blind man's guide-dog (who, after all, doesn't know either *where* he's going), by the sound of their lurching feet behind. Soon the feet stopped, and he looked cautiously back to identify the brothel.

This word (brothel) conjured up scandalous, alluring visions. What it in London in most cases consists of is a dilapidated house with several girls in rooms with minimal accessories. But even in this basic, utilitarian form it still has, on account of the ancient mystique of the word and its frankly anti-social purpose (and the curiosity and venom these variously attract), a certain faded glamour. But not to Edward Justice. Edward did not condemn prostitutes because they were 'immoral': he did so because they sought to destroy in the most flagrant possible way his own deep belief in love. He therefore approached the establishment with intense interest and disapproval.

Lights shone from curtained windows, but the place was otherwise discreet. He knocked and nothing happened. Then he went away, returned and gave—a happy bow at a venture—three short knocks and one long. A light came on in the hall, the door opened hiding the person behind it, then closed on Edward who found himself confronting a forty-ish man in jeans. 'I don't think we've met,' this person said.

'No. I'd like to see one of the girls.'

'Busy, mister. What you got in that can?'

'Oh, that? It's for the wife.'

'She know you're here?'

'Not likely.'

'No. Well, there it is. You can call back, or if you like you can have a Maxwell House with me downstairs while you're waiting for a vacancy.'

Edward accepted. The basement room was scented in a savagely 'oriental' manner, and its furnishings were the Harrow road emporium's version of Ali Baba's cave. The stranger put on a kettle, then surprised Edward considerably by trying to give him an affectionate kiss. He preserved his calm, however. 'You're one of those,' he said, disengaging politely.

'One of the many,' his host cried gaily. 'We horrid creatures crop up *every*where!'

'So you don't cause jealousies among the girls.'

'Oh, I wouldn't say *that*. After all, in a certain way they're very fond of me, and I'm very necessary to them, too.'

'You own this place, then?'

'*Me?* Living in the basement? Silly! No—I'm their maid.'

'A male maid, like.'

'Check!' cried the male maid, pouring water on the Maxwell House. 'And now,' he continued, bringing the coffee over, 'a question or two to *you*, please. Who sent you here?'

'The Cypriot boys.'

'Which one?'

'Dark feller.'

'Darling! *All* Cypriots are dark! Nicky, was it? Constantine?'

'Nicky, I think.'

The male maid shook his head at Edward. 'Naughty!' he said. 'There *is* no Nicky.'

'Well, mate, I don't know his bloody name but he just sent me.'

Hand on a jeaned hip, the male maid eyed him. 'Do you know what?' he said. 'I think I've been a very, very stupid boy. I think you're quite probably a c–o–p.'

'Who—me?'

'You, darling.'

The male maid, darting like a gold-fish, had raced through the door, slamming it behind him, and as Edward jumped up he heard the sound from the backyard behind of an outside lavatory chain being vigorously pulled up and down like a ship's siren. By the time he got to the first floor there were signs of considerable movement. Edward banged on the nearest door whence a loud female voice bellowed at him to fuck off. The second door on the landing opened, and he was face to face with a squat woman of thoroughly unwelcoming demeanour who, blocking the whole doorway, said to him, 'Let's see your warrant.'

'Open that door there,' said Edward.

'Listen, young man. Show me your warrant or else hop it. If you don't, I'm on the blower to Detective-constable you-know-who.'

'*Who?*'

'Who will *not* be pleased you've come here pissing in his garden.'

'What you mean?'

'Son, I'm beginning to think you're stupid. What you suppose I pay twenty a week for to you people? Get going, now. And sort it all out with your own mates: they'll tell you.'

By now doors had opened, figures appeared, and several very truculent males had gathered at strategic points on stairways. Silence fell a moment, and everybody watched. Edward had never felt so solitary in his life.

'You'll hear more of this,' he said, and walked downstairs. There were shouts of laughter and crude cries of abuse.

By the door, the male maid handed him his paraffin tin. Bursting with rage, Edward knocked it out of his hand, grabbed him and manhandled him out into the street. 'I'm being *arrested*!' cried the male maid. 'First time in *years*. A thrill!'

As he marched his capture up the dark and empty roads, Edward recalled as best he could in his emotion all the golden rules of an arrest: for this, though far from being his first, was his first one in the expert CID. He longed to get at his black note-book, for facts noted down in this, he knew, had a magical effect on juries and even magistrates. An officer, by law, can produce his notebook when in court and consult it (for matters of *fact* alone, of course) when in the witness-box. The conception that these factual jottings may be fantasies or added long after their supposedly immediate inscription—or that the defendant, too, might be permitted to produce a similar jury-impressing book—does not seem to have occurred to legislators. Edward knew all this: but to him the black book was the reassuring symbol of his office; and he liked to enhance the tenuous reality of the confusing happenings of fact by giving them, as soon as possible, this inscribed, oracular dimension.

But how do you get at your note-book if you're frog-marching a delightedly wriggling suspect in the dark? The more Edward thought of the whole episode the less he liked it. On a sudden decision he stopped at a corner, let the male maid go and said, 'All right—I'm turning you loose. Now skip!'

'Oh, *are* you!' said the maid, rubbing his skinny arms.

'Hop it now,' said Edward.

The male maid stood his ground and cried, 'Copper, I *refuse* to be released.'

Edward had not quite expected this. 'Oh?' he said, as nastily as possible.

'Look, big boy,' the atrocious male maid answered. 'You've messed things up for us tonight, and I'm going to mess up a thing or two for you.'

As to his next move, Edward didn't hesitate. He hit the male maid very hard in the face, and turned and walked away. When he paused after several hundred yards to make some notes of the occurrence (and of others) in his book, he was dismayed to see the maid still following at a distance. He hurried on; and reaching the highway, by the expedient of showing his card to a uniformed man and of declaring the male maid had urinated in a public place, he shook him off and returned (determined to say nothing of all this) to the station.

Immediately on arrival, he was sent for by the Detective-sergeant. This officer, more in exasperation than in anger, blew him up. 'You'd like to know,' he said to Edward, 'what you've done wrong. Well, I'll tell you: everything.'

'Sir?'

'First and foremost—and even *you* should know this, constable—you don't tackle *any* case—any case at all—without prior notification and permission unless, of course, it comes up on you suddenly like a smash-and-grab or something.'

'Yes, sir.'

'This is a *Force*,' the officer said. 'Not a collection of Robin Hoods.'

'No, sir.'

'Next. If you want to enter a house without a warrant, I've no objection: these little matters can usually be ironed out and brothels, of course, don't expect you to have one anyway. But *please* don't enter any house at all without first checking if your colleagues happen to know much more about it already than you ever will. Particularly, constable, any suspect premises we've decided to let stay open for our own particular purposes.'

'I'm sorry, sir, I don't . . .'

'I expect not. Look! That gaff, as gaffs up this way go, is perfectly well conducted and a very useful place indeed to pick up *real* suspects in: the sort of criminal you *should* be interested in.'

'I see, sir.'

'You see!'

'I suppose, sir,' Edward said cautiously, 'the woman phoned you . . . or someone.'

'Oh—brilliant! Let me tell you something, son. That good woman you upset is much more useful to the Force at present by her information than *you* look like shaping up to be.'

'Yes, sir.'

'And now you've crashed in there like a cow in a china-shop, what use is she going to be to us? Eh? Answer me that! Or *ask* me before you do these things. That's what I'm here for: come and ask me!'

'But sir,' said Edward full of contrition, 'brothels *are* often raided, aren't they? Brothel-keeping cases *do* come up . . .'

'Naturally, boy! But do use your loaf! You only raid the place when any advantages it may have to the Force are *less* than the prestige of a cast-iron brothel-keeping case. If vice has got to flourish, it had better flourish underneath our eyes until we're ready to clamp down on it.'

'Yes, sir.'

The Detective-sergeant lit his pipe. 'You'll soon see how it is,' he said. 'Sometimes, of course, the order comes to us from on high, and then we close the place up anyway. Or maybe the Madam forgets her place and fails to be co-operative. Or maybe there's a change of personnel here at the station and somebody new in charge just doesn't like her face. Those vice hustlers know all that, and so do we: the whole thing's perfectly well understood. Except, of course, by idiots like you.'

'Yes, sir.'

A constable entered, saluted and said, 'There's a poof downstairs, sir, wants to bring an assault charge.'

'Against who?'

The constable looked at Edward.

'Oh, no!' the Detective-sergeant cried. Then, to the constable, 'Throw him out.

'He's very persistent, sir. He says if we won't wear it here he'll take it to another station.'

'*Does* he?' the Detective-sergeant said, an ominous glint appearing in his clouded eyes. 'Just wheel him in, constable, will you?' He then turned to Edward. 'You've broken,' he said, 'the first rule of the business: which is to make an arrest, and fail to bring a charge and make it stick.'

Edward said meekly, 'Can't we just charge him, sir, with being a queer?'

The Detective-sergeant didn't even bother to answer. The male maid appeared and the uniformed constable withdrew. The Detective-sergeant got up, punched the male maid five or six times very hard in an extremely dispassionate manner in the stomach, then threw him across a chair and said, 'I know you're a masochist and enjoy it, but don't provoke me or there might be an accident. Now, listen. What happened down at your place tonight just didn't happen. Do you understand? If I hear a squeak out of you, or anybody, I'm taking *you* in *not* on a vice charge which I know you wouldn't mind, but on a charge of robbing a client there and, believe me, everything will be present and correct: witnesses and stolen goods, your own sworn statement—the whole lot. You poofs have a high time in the nick, three in a cell, as we all well know. But this wouldn't be months I'd get you, sonny, it'd be years. And think of it, you might grow old and grey and unattractive, specially if I dropped a hint about you to the screws. So. Just apologize to my officer for all the trouble you've caused everyone, withdraw your charge as you pass the desk on your way out, and get back to bed again with your current husband.'

The male maid left in silence: though not without a yearning, reproachful glance at Edward.

Then the Detective-sergeant said: 'Now you, son. Please understand: I can't have anything more like this from you, either. You've got to improve your performance quite a bit or I'll lose my patience with you.'

'Yes, sir.'

'All right. Fuck off home.'

Edward stood at attention in salute, but hesitated before moving off. 'Well?' said the Detective-sergeant.

'Sir: it's just a question, sir, of procedure. This hitting them. I know the rule is you never do. But could you tell me please, sir, when you *can* do?'

A cracked smile appeared on the Detective-sergeant's life-battered countenance.

'Well, son,' he said, 'number one, in public, never. The citizens don't like it. Also, they don't believe we *do* it. Of course, if you're quite obviously attacked it's another matter.'

'Yes, sir. And in here?'

The Detective-sergeant rose and said, 'Well, constable, that depends. Personally, I don't happen to be a sadist and never do it unless it's clearly necessary to get certain results. Others do, I know, just for the heck of it: but not me.'

'No, sir.'

'If you *do* do it,' the officer continued, 'the first thing to remember is not to mark them: not to hit them where it shows next day in daylight. Never forget: they've got to be produced in court in twenty-four hours—or forty-eight, of course, if the day of arrest happens to be a Saturday.'

'And if you *do* happen to mark them, sir?'

'You say they went berserk and had to be restrained. Of course, you know—sometimes they do: I could show you a scar or two to prove it.'

'But, sir. If you bash them—don't they tell the magistrate?'

'Sometimes . . . It has been known . . . I've not met with one magistrate yet, though, who's believed it . . . Or even if they do, well, so long as they think the charge you've made against the prisoner 's quite authentic it doesn't seem to worry them unduly . . . As for juries, if a prisoner pleads violence or a forced confession,. in my experience all it does is tell against him in the verdict.'

'I see, sir.'

'Don't *rely* on that, though, constable. There's no point at all in using force just for the sake of it, unless it serves a purpose. Because —and you might as well remember this if you possibly can—your real battle isn't with the criminal but with the courts. It's only *there* that you can get him his conviction. You've got counsel up against you, and solicitors, and the witnesses for the defence, and juries and magistrates and judges—and the press, please don't forget *those* little parasites. They've all got to be defeated or convinced before your man gets his complimentary ticket for a seat in Brixton.'

'I'll remember, sir.'

'I do hope so. In the Force, constable, the greatest asset that a man can have, in my opinion, isn't all the ones you read so much about but purely and simply a sense of *order*: of thoroughly methodical procedure. If you train yourself to be methodical and avoid confusion like the plague, then you may end up Chief Constable—just think of that! Not, on your present showing, that it's very likely,' he added, turning out the light and opening the office door.

MR LOVE

A CHIEF difficulty in his new role, Frankie found, was what to do with the twenty-four hours of the day. At sea, this never had been a problem: even leisure, on board ship, seems to be purposeful: a relaxation from the tasks behind, a preparation for those ahead—time never seemed to *hang* upon a seaman's hands. Even to be unemployed was, in a sense, a full-time occupation: the hours it took to achieve the feat of the single minute's signing on at the Labour; the problems of where to sleep and how to eat, and even the sterile round in search of jobs.

But now his time-table except at certain immutable, vital points was vague in the extreme. He had to be home in his girl's new flat at Kilburn for the most important moment of their day—or night-and-day, for Frankie was finding the two radically divided sections were merging into one. This was the moment when, dismissing the last visitor, his girl produced the old black bag (to which in spite of growing prosperity she sentimentally clung) and shook its contents out upon the kitchen table. This was the hour of reckoning, the essential confrontation. Frankie must know *exactly* what she earned

—if she'd hid as much as a halfpenny their relationship would lose its fundamental basis. And she must know that *he* knew: what he then did with the money seemed of less importance to her, for she was quite un-grasping and, so long as she had what was necessary for essential housekeeping and personal adornment, she left the disposition of the funds entirely to him.

After this ceremony there was the continued proof, usually in the small hours, of Frankie's devotion to his girl. And then a number of minor but very important social imperatives: the Sunday evening visit, on her night off, to the Odeon; appearances at certain clubs which for professional purposes (but thoroughly indirect ones) she frequented; and occasional calls at lawyers' offices when minor difficulties arose, or were thought to be about to do so.

If Frankie had adhered to his original intention—backed by her own sage counsel—to get a cover job, a great many of these errands could no doubt have been avoided. But he had not. The reason wasn't simply that having enough money he didn't feel the need to: many rich men love work, after all. It was just that any sort of normal toil seemed quite incompatible with his position. In this he resembled the aristocrat who, appearing before the bankruptcy court, tells the judge with manifest and rather hopeless sincerity that he just couldn't find work appropriate to his status.

So there was a paradox (one of many now) in Frankie's life. On the one hand, time hung heavy on his hands and much ingenuity had to be expended in wasting it without total boredom. But on the other—this was the point—he *did* have the ever-present sensation of being *occupied*: of having if not a job, a function and even a 'function' in society. And apart from anything else, to remain constantly *available* so far as his girl was concerned, and constantly *watchful* himself in regard to the mysterious and ever-present law, did constitute a full-time activity of a kind.

As for the disposal of the money, this had its problems too. A growing acquaintance with his fellow ponces (which Frankie had tried to avoid but which, just as with fellow mariners on board ship, was really quite inevitable) had shown him that by and large they fell (as with all other human creatures) into two sharply divided categories: the spenders and the savers. The chief stratagem by which spender-ponces relieved themselves of the intolerable burden of holding on to money they had coveted so eagerly, was by gambling: but Frankie had tried this and found it unbearably meaningless and dull—even if he won as, being indifferent, he often did. Others invested in huge wardrobes or fast cars: but this, except among the pin-headed, was considered most unwise for it was a gross and needless provocation of the law. It was true, of course, that a great many of the more foolish girls loved their men to spend the money in this way, as a taste for visible riches bound the man to them all the closer; and its fruits were the manifest proof of their own success in their business.

As for the savers, whose usual intention was to 'cut out' one day with the girl (or possibly without her) to start a business of some kind, the chief disadvantage was that they were usually grudging and unattractive characters (as Frankie Love was not) and more, that to be a business *man*, even if a ponce, you need a business *head*: which Frankie knew he hadn't got at all. And his determination to save had been baulked, as the girl had foreseen, by the acute danger of opening any sort of an account and by his genuine reluctance to have all the money in her name: for the whole meaning of the symbolic emptying of the bag at night—the gesture which bound him absolutely to her—would have been lost if the money went back from the bag into an account that she controlled.

He therefore hit on an expedient that would have seemed inconceivable a few months ago. Frankie, like most proletarian Europeans, despised Asiatics to such a degree that you could hardly even call it contempt (quite unaware, like millions of his countrymen, that this feeling was reciprocated by Asians at much profounder levels). But in his predicament it suddenly occurred to him that throughout his considerable commerce with them, no Asian had ever robbed him: exasperated him, yes, but never deceived him over money. He accordingly approached, with the girl's full approval, her former Stepney landlord, the Bengali, and suggested that the Bengali should hold his money for him (*not* for her) on the understanding no interest whatever need be paid. With splendid visions of the acquisition of additional slum property which he could let out for vice, or for honest purposes to his fellow-countrymen at exorbitant rentals in a country that denies accommodation to a man of colour, the Bengali immediately agreed.

A man of some intelligence cannot fail, in any environment where fate thrusts him, to become interested in its workings however much he may dislike or disapprove of them. Thus reluctant, scholarly conscripts study regimental histories, and professional men who've fallen by the wayside write excellent studies about jails. In much the same spirit Frankie, despite himself, became interested in whores and ponces. And though not easily given to casual friendships he already had several acquaintances among the men—the women, so far as possible, he kept politely at a distance not because he was afraid of them in any way, but because this was the very basis of his bargain with his girl.

Among these pals there was a star ponce whom Frankie had got to know at a drinking-club patronized by the men of his profession. As with actresses or television personalities in the outer world, there is, in that of prostitution, a fashion at any particular moment for this or that ponce or whore: the less stable of the girls all endeavouring to hook the star ponce, and the less satisfied of the ponces trying to transfer their allegiance to the star whore of the moment. Dreadful quarrels, often accompanied by violence and sensational denunciations, accompany these struggles: but above all of them this star ponce friend of Frankie's rode serene. He *knew* he was a star—did not his glittering attire and his relaxed and glowing mien testify eloquently to the fact? But he was genuinely devoted to his girl and was—not unusual, perhaps surprisingly, among ponces—exceedingly good-natured. So he parried the manoeuvres of the eager whores with deft evasions and even managed not to arouse the jealousies of the men. 'It's a world!' he would say to Frankie (or Francis, as for some reason he always called him) when they sat together at the drinking-club in masculine communion.

The star ponce was Cornish and had been at sea, and shared with Frankie a deep disdain for all the multitudes who haven't. 'The sea,' he told Frankie, 'teaches you the scale of things: what matters and what really doesn't. The only ceremony I've ever seen that impressed me in the least is a sea burial: no priest, only the captain; no mourners, only the mates; no earth and worms or fire and ash-cans, but the huge sea and the fishes sailing gently through your eyes.'

'Or a ship's court,' said Frankie. 'Ever seen one of those? The old man a judge who really *knows;* and witnesses who nobody's been getting at; and sailors for your jury who know all about you and your case first hand.'

'Why did we leave it, Francis?'

'Ask yourself that, quartermaster,' Frankie said.

The star ponce beckoned for refills. When the girl (who'd brought the glasses voluntarily, for there was no service in the club) had been thanked and gone, he said to Frankie, 'That one's got her eye on you.'

'Yes, I noticed.'

'Not interested, Francis?'

'One at a time.'

'How right you are!' The star ponce smiled. 'Mind you, you can stick to one and still have others.'

'You can?'

'Some manage it. Even three or four at a time.'

'Sharp operators! And the girls know?'

'Usually the wires get crossed—and then they do. Not easy, as you can imagine, flitting from one address to another without running out of excuses and vital energy.'

'Those boys deserve their money. And the girls wear it?'

'Naturally, there are rows—a thing I personally hate. But sometimes if they're fond of the boy, even if they *do* know they accept it.'

'Who understands women?'

'Only they do.'

The star ponce offered panatellas. 'Ever thought of getting wed?' he said.

'To *her*?'

'Yeah.'

'Why should I?'

'Well—there could be reasons.'

'Such as what?'

'You might like to: like her, I mean.'

'That's a good one . . . Any others?'

'She might like it, too. And it makes them long-suffering, Francis, if you're a husband.'

'Not so likely to speak out of turn, you mean?'

'Not *quite* so likely: and she can't appear in court against you as your wife, though she can still chat about you to the coppers.'

'But does it impress the courts at all—your being married?'

'Oh, not in the least. The nicks are full of married ponces. No: it's just rather nice, that's all.'

'You done it?'

'No . . .'

'I see.'

They puffed away like two young rising statesmen. 'Getting used to the life?' the star ponce asked.

'Except for a few particulars.'

'Yeah?'

'Still can't get used to all that *money*.'

'Nor me: after all these years.'

'Really! When you think of the *millions* the mugs spend! We must be a race of randy, frustrated fools.'

'Speak for yourself: I'm Cornish. Anything else?'

'Yes. When people ask me what I *do*. I can't quite get used to that.'

'You say seaman?'

'Yes. But I know *I* don't believe it any longer.'

'I say turf accountant. I've found it explains my movements best.'

'Don't they try to place bets?'

'Sometimes . . . The question was awkward in the nick as well.'

'You been in there?'

'Didn't I tell you? One three, one six: next time's dangerous.'

'Let's hope there'll be none. And what did you tell them all in there?'

The star ponce looked ruminative and grave. 'Poncing and rape of minors are the two things criminals won't wear. Even poofs they will, but not we two. They're great snobs, the real professionals, about what a man's in for.'

'So what did you tell them?'

'That was it. I thought: well, I *am* a ponce—so what? I said poncing.'

'And?'

'They crunched me.'

'Nice! What did you say the next time?'

'Fraudulent conversion. That was quite all right. They were quite respectful.'

Frankie drank. 'They're hard on us, aren't they, in this world,' he said.

The star ponce said, 'Very. And yet—there are those two things. If there weren't any clients there couldn't be any ponces, let alone any whores. Have they thought of that at all?'

'I don't suppose so.'

'If no one will buy a product, no one will sell it or profit by its sale.'

'Just so.'

'And as for where the blame lies, if there is any, well, for every one of us and each one of our girls there must be several hundred clients or more.'

'It's mathematical.'

The star ponce turned his glorious eyes on Frankie. 'I'll tell you a thing,' he said. 'It's a triangle that won't stand up without any one of its three sides: client and whore and ponce. If the clients don't like us, well, it's simple: they should just stop being clients.'

'Then the triangle collapses.'

'But it won't! That's just the point, it won't, and everyone knows it. That's why all these new laws just shift the problem without altering it in any way at all. Because the girl, and her friend, and the man dropping in from somewhere, are as old as the Garden of Eden and even older.'

'There were only two of them in there,' said Frankie.

'Well, Adam must have doubled.' The star ponce stiffened slightly. 'Don't look now. But when you do you'll see we've got two coppers on the premises: one he, one she. Behind the telly set.'

'They come here often?' Frankie said, not looking up.

'Weekly or so—routine. Why they bother to dress up like that I can't imagine, but they prefer it that way.'

Frankie observed the couple. They looked like a pair of elderly teenagers: the man in Italian drape and pointeds with a Tab Hunter hair-do, the woman with puff-pastry locks, flowered separates, paper nylon petticoat and white stilettos. They were engaged in animated conversation intended to disguise the fact that no one else wished to speak to them: though no one, of course, would have refused to do so if invited.

'Poor fuckers,' said the star ponce. 'What must it feel like, earning your living spying on your fellow men?'

'How do they pay for all that clobber?' Frankie asked. 'Do they get expenses?'

'Not on that scale. Talk to the club owner here: he'll tell you.'

'Something for protection?'

'District-nurse money, he calls it. For their healing visits. Still, I prefer those fancy vice boys to the poker-faced lot in uniform. They may be crooked, but in my experience a man who's crooked is in some way or other human. Almost, anyway.'

Frankie looked at the star ponce and said, 'You afraid of them?'

'Who—me?' The star ponce reflected. 'Well—yes, of course,' he said, 'but not of *them*: I mean, I'm not scared of them individually or even several. I've been alone in the cells with them, Francis, and no holds barred, and I've found I haven't been afraid. But of the Force—yes, I am. You see, we come and go—and even they do: but the Force—it goes on forever.'

'Just like the world does.'

'Yes, on forever. There's always this, you see. If they really decide to turn the heat on anyone—not just one of us, but I mean on *any*one—well, they can always find *something*, can't they.'

'Or say they do . . . which amounts to much the same.'

The star ponce shook his luscious locks and said, 'Well, not exactly. If ever they get *you* in the cells, Francis, remember this. The trial's not there, it's in the open court. The mistake almost everyone makes, even quite clever people and no doubt because they're scared, is to fall for the copper's spiel of pretending it's *he* who conducts the trial. Well—it's not: there's always the lawyers and the judges.'

'So I'm discovering.'

'Well—remember it. Anyone can come unstuck, but you lessen the chances quite a bit if you remember . . . *never* speak to them. If six men try to carve you up—don't call a copper: grin and bear it. Then, if they knock you off, don't *talk*: Francis, don't ever talk. Name, address and age, that's all: just like the navy or the army. And never plead guilty—never. Because to them, whoever you are, if they take you you *are* guilty, so it makes no difference anyway. If they find you outside the Bank of England with a bag of gold—not guilty. In the courts, there's always a chance: if you talk to them or commit yourself to any plea, there's none.'

'I'll remember,' said Frankie, finishing his glass.

The star ponce emptied his too and rose. 'All the same,' he said, 'in this business, however careful you may be, you've *always* got to listen for the knock on the front door. Whenever you hear a knock, even if it's only the Plymouth Brethren calling to save souls, you've got to be alert and ready. And take your time before you open up: if they *really* want to see you, don't be in a hurry: they can always break the door down—and they will.'

MR JUSTICE

EDWARD longed to escape from the thraldom of the section-house. When he did his military service he didn't really dislike barrack-rooms—realized, in fact, that if you had to be a soldier they were the most practical and even comfortable places to be a soldier in. But in the section-house the men were all rather older, and, except for a few widowers and what is known as 'hardened' bachelors, all anxious, like him, not to be there any longer, since it wasn't really necessary for coppers to live in great male dormitories. Besides, the atmosphere of *randiness* in the place—you could only call it that—depressed him: you could feel it bursting from the rooms at night, and in the mess-hall the conversation (when it wasn't gossip about the Force) centred on 'sex' monotonously. For Edward, sex was a secret and yet a totally splendid thing: something he felt no need (like some copper puritans) to be uncomfortable about at all—very much the contrary—but one that lost all its glory and delight once it was severed, even in conversation, from the loved person who exchanged it with you.

But how to leave the section-house? The Force didn't care much for single men in lodgings; and marriage to his girl was for the moment, anyway, impossible. His sexual trysts with her at present took place at her father's house with his reluctant connivance (a reluctance, in respect of these particular premises, that Edward fully shared), or sometimes dangerously at the houses of several friends (for the trouble with friends is that they can betray you by their quite benevolent intentions), and even, on one or two extremely chancy occasions, in public places: a thing Edward had professionally a horror of, since so many who used the outer woods and gardens did so for reasons that were utterly perverse. It seemed to him that the only (relatively) safe procedure would be for her to take rooms at some discreet address, and for him to visit her there with maximum discretion likewise.

This plan he unfolded in the small back garden of her father's house in Kensal Green, while the older man morosely eyed them through the back window of the kitchen where he was engaged on his part-time trade of mending radio and telly sets and cameras and high-grade gadgets—a free-lance occupation Edward did not approve of since it had something imprecisely *shady* about it. (Somehow all those sets looked stolen, not left for repair, and anyway, how did the older man make all those contacts to get the jobs? And wasn't this still, in spite of all his promises, a cover story?) The back garden—yard, really—was hemmed in by walls and windows, but his girl and he were in its most secluded corner, and Edward (though even naked he'd have looked just as much a copper) had on very casual, un-professional attire. The girl poured tea and *listened* to him in that attentive, respectful way that women have when they hear of some plan to which they may or may not agree, but know it to be dear to their lover's heart and in its intentions, anyway, conducive to their own interests and a proof of his attachment.

'The chief obstacles,' Edward said, 'are these. Money first. Well—that's not really a problem with our joint earnings, and you know I'm not a spender; also—you never know—I may get some extra—expenses or something—to help out. Premises. That really shouldn't be difficult if we look carefully *and*—here's the important point—are willing to pay enough: say even five or six a week. Then . . . well, the whole set-up. If we take care I don't think we should attract attention, particularly if we get a place in a block that's big enough: I mean like some council flats, say, with stacks of tenants in them. Of course, everyone who's interested will know perfectly well why I visit you, but that doesn't really matter unless there's any trouble-makers among them who start shooting off their mouths. Naturally, I'll have to check carefully to see if there happen to be any other coppers living in the block. If not, then well and good, let's go ahead. And remember: we won't actually be doing anything *illegal*, will we. The worst I can expect, if the Force should discover, is a good ticking-off—and also, perhaps, some enquiries about you which may very well lead home to your Dad. (Edward glanced at the window and caught his potential father-in-law's baleful eye.) But that we'll have to leave to chance—we can't foresee *everything*, can we. The chief question that then remains is—when can I visit you? I'll have to check in at the section-house to sleep fairly often, and you've got your job to go out to during the day. So that leaves us week-ends, and also the evenings when I can plead duty or actually be out on it and spare a moment. They don't check on our time much, see, in the present job: they trust us to get on with it, and all they ask for is results.'

'I think I might know a place,' the girl said.

'Yeah? What area? Obviously, it can't be too far—unless I could get hold of a motor-bike, which might in a way be better.'

'In Kilburn,' she said.

'Up there? Well, it's a nice, quiet . . . well, *neutral* sort of area, isn't it. What particular place had you got in mind?'

'A girl at the workshops lives with her husband and kids there. And she told me you can jump the queue if you give something to the janitor. It's working-class, you know, but a privately owned block, not the municipal. So the rents are a bit high, too.'

'All this is going to need money,' Edward said. 'And that reminds me. Darling, whatever you do, *don't* take any from your father.'

'No, I know about that.'

'He's in the clear now, of course, but if you had even a penny from him, and a bit of it went to me even in a round-about way, it just wouldn't do.'

'No.'

Edward finished his fourth tea. 'And another thing,' he said. 'As soon as you're in, you'd better get on the phone.'

'I'd thought of that,' she said.

'A lot of our meetings will have to be at short notice, and that's the best way we can fix them discreetly without wasting time.'

The girl got up. 'All right,' she said. 'If you've got the time to spare now, Ted, we might take a walk over and have a look at the place.'

They went in through the back basement entrance and up the

inside stairs. The girl opened the kitchen door to say a word to her father, but when Edward tried to say goodbye to him he turned up a radio to a horrid blare. 'I really don't know why your Dad dislikes me so much,' Edward said to her as they walked across towards Queen's park. 'I know he's a copper-hater, but why should he detest me personally?'

'On account of his past,' said the girl, taking his hand and intimately locking up his fingers. 'He was framed, so he says, as you know, and you really must make allowances.'

'Oh, they all say that.'

'Yes, Ted: but it does happen, doesn't it.'

Edward sighed. The subject had come up before in his life, and by now he'd grown to live with it and it bored him. 'Well, it does,' he said. 'But in ninety-nine cases out of a hundred, even more I'd say, a case is never fixed unless we're absolutely sure the feller did it.'

'If you're all that sure, why can't you prove it properly?'

'Because that's often very, very difficult: you'd be surprised. There's laws of evidence, and legal quibbles if the case is defended, and sometimes even the old judge, though he may know as well as we do that the prisoner's guilty, brings up some act of Queen Victoria's reign or maybe earlier that destroys our case.'

The girl reflected. 'But if you fix a case, Edward, then don't you commit a crime yourself?'

'What crime? Oh, you mean perjury.'

'It *is* a crime, isn't it?'

'Oh, of course! But not, as I see it, for us officers. In the first place let me tell you, if we didn't use it there'd be stacks of known and previously convicted criminals who we'd never manage to put away at all. And then, there's another thing. You must remember, dear, that we're the only people who have to appear constantly in the courts in dozens of cases under oath. Now, if it's just the single defendant coming up once or twice—or even, let's say, as many as fifty times in his life—he only has to face the perjury problem—if it *is* one to him—on those individual occasions. But us, we have to face it every week almost of our lives. Could we *ever* be all that scrupulous? Then, there's this. Even suppose the case is straight and all our evidence is kosher. Suddenly, out of the blue, from the counsel who's cross-examining or even from our own feller for the Crown, you may get a question—one that's really got little or nothing to do with the case at all—which you simply cannot answer factually without prejudicing the whole issue. And then most of all, dear, there's your superior officers you've got to consider. Suppose Detective-inspector So-and-so says "Constable, this is the way we're handling this case"—what do I do? Tell him he's got it wrong?'

'Yes, I see all that,' she answered. 'But doesn't it mean if you commit perjury yourself that the defendant's bound to do it too, whether he wants to or not?'

'I don't see that—how come?'

'According to Dad, when the case was cooked up against him . . .'

'Cooked up!'

'Well, arranged . . . his solicitor advised him that if he denied everything the witnesses for the Force said, no one on earth—and certainly no one on the jury—would ever believe him. So he played along with their story part of the way, and just denied certain essentials. But even that didn't help him in the end . . .'

'Well, there it is, dear: that's how it goes.'

'And what's more, he says the fact you mentioned just now, Ted, that your officers have such a long experience of giving evidence makes any prisoner like an untrained amateur up against professionals.'

'Well—that's what we are. And really, dearest, the whole question about your old Dad is—did he do it or didn't he? That's what you've really got to decide before you pass any judgment on all of us.'

They were now out of Queen's park. He thought and said (a note of indignation in his voice), 'You know *really*, the public expect just a bit too much from us, don't they? They all want convictions and howl if we don't succeed in getting them! And all the responsibility for winning the cases by the right presentation of the evidence —which *has* a certain risk involved, even to us, let alone any question of our own feelings in the matter—well, *all* that responsibility *we* take off the public's shoulders on to our own. And then people turn round and tell us we *fix* all these cases.'

His fingers were clutching hers. She took a more gentle grip and said, 'Don't be upset, Ted: I *do* understand. And I dare say the judges and magistrates do as well.'

'But of course!' he cried. 'Some of them are quite simple in spite of all their law books, and don't really understand, maybe. But most of them realize that crime's *got* to be suppressed and provided we don't slip up over the technicalities they never enquire too closely into our actual methods. And that goes for all the top people in the business—I'm not speaking of the thousands of mugs, even the educated quite influential ones—but the people who really *know* the law and how it operates. They know what we do, and they know why we do it and they accept it. They never say so, of course. And if we slip up, they're pitiless. But they know.'

Near by Paddington cemetery she stopped beside the stones and railings and reached up and kissed him, without reservation of her person, warmly, entirely—a whole gift. He was soothed and enchanted because at such moments she gave him to himself: for not even the Force could offer him such self-realization as she did when she brought her love to him so utterly that he was unaware of her—only of himself. 'If only we could marry now,' he whispered into her hair. She held him closer, yet not *tight* as some girls do. A professional instinct made him cut short the embrace, though gently, and they entered together the respectable wastes of Kilburn.

Examining the area, Edward liked it. There is about Kilburn a sort of faded respectability, of self-righteous drabness, that appealed to him. For the true copper's dominant characteristic, if the truth be known, is neither those daring nor vicious qualities that are sometimes attributed to him by friend or enemy, but an ingrained conservatism, an almost desperate love of the conventional. It is untidiness, disorder, the unusual, that a copper disapproves of most of all: far more, even, than of crime, which is merely a professional matter. Hence his profound dislike of people loitering in streets, dressing extravagantly, speaking with exotic accents, being strange, weak, eccentric or simply any rare minority—of their doing, in short, anything that cannot be safely predicted.

So Kilburn was reassuring: but on the other hand it had something else that equally appealed to Edward which was that, although proper, it was also in an indefinable way equivocal. As you walked through its same and peeling (though un-slummy) streets, the façades of the houses hinted, somehow, that all was not as it seemed behind those faded doors and walls. This straitlaced seediness, this primped-up exterior behind which lurks something dubious and occasionally horrifying, is the chief feature of whole chunks of mid-twentieth-century London—as, indeed, of many of its inhabitants: the particular English mixture of lunacy and violence flourishing inside persons, and a décor, of impeccable lower-middle-class sedateness. This atmosphere appealed to Edward who, like all coppers, shunned clear pools (and even turbulent torrents) and preferred those whose surface, though quite still, could easily be stirred up into muddy little whirlpools. For if the copper is a worshipper of the conventional (so far as the world at large outside him is concerned), he is also in his inner person (being the arch empiricist) something of an anarch: a lover of stress and strain and conflict, wherein he himself may operate behind that outward, visible order he admires.

The flats the girl had in mind were of more recent construction—one of those countless anonymous 1950 blocks which, in spite of their proliferation, have as yet entirely failed to transform London from what it still after years of bombing and re-building essentially remains—a late-Victorian city. The block was tall and oblong-square and bleak and domestically adequate: perfect, in fact, for their intentions.

'Okay dear,' said Edward. 'You check with your friend and find out what the score is on the financial side, and I'll consult files and sources—very discreetly, of course—to find if anything's known to us about it. If both things tally, well, let's move in. I'm really getting tired, when I see you, of having to act as if I was a criminal.'

'The key money may be quite a bit,' she said. 'Something like fifty, I should imagine.'

Edward winced. 'Well, that's not the chief difficulty,' he said. 'Our chief obstacle is the place: if we find that's all right, the money will look after itself—it'll have to.'

He pressed her two arms, but only so, because the place was too public now for kissing; and each of them felt as well that the unknown tenants of the block were already curious neighbours. He ran for a bus and sat in a rear seat, eyeing his fellow travellers with the proprietory air of his profession as if they were all (and, indeed, the entire population of our islands) the potential inhabitants of some vast, imaginary jail. Passing the Metropolitan theatre of varieties he glanced out idly, and immediately left the bus. For he had noticed a person there whom an inborn and constantly developing instinct told him he should watch and follow.

This person set off along the Harrow road in the direction of the monumental metal bridges over the tangle of lines just outside Paddington railway station. The person's glances at certain passing citizens, all of a particular nature, confirmed Edward's suspicions of his hopes. At a square green metal urinal stuck on to a tall wall like a carbuncle, the person paused, gazed around (Edward was standing blandly at a bus stop), and entered. Five minutes elapsed: too long for nature and for innocence, and Edward pounced.

The design of male urinals, in England, and especially those dating from the heroic period of pre-World War I construction, has to be witnessed to be believed. For this simplest of acts, what one can only describe as temples, or shrines, have been erected. The larva-hued earthenware, the huge brass pipes, the great slate walls dividing the compartments, are all built on an Egyptian scale. Each visitor is isolated from his neighbour, though so close to him and in such physical communion, as if in a sort of lay confessional. Horrorpendous notices advising not to spit in the only place in the city where it wouldn't matter in the slightest, and warnings against fell diseases that can nowadays be cured by a few cordial jabs by a nurse in either buttock, abound, as do those reminding visitors about what their mothers taught them when, at the age of three or so, they were put into their first short pants. All this seems to bear witness to a really sensational and alarming fear and hatred of the flesh, even in its most natural functions, that inspired the municipal Pharaohs who designed these places. And from their ludicrous solemnity, and ribald inscriptions on the walls of a political, erotic, or merely autobiographical nature are an agreeable light relief.

As Edward expected, the person he had followed was up to no good at all and taking his place casually and, as it were, sympathetically in the adjacent compartment, he waited for his victim to make a fatal gesture. This, sure enough, he did. Whereupon Edward, making sure they were alone together, stepped quickly back behind the evildoer, said, 'I'm an officer of the law: I want to speak to you outside,' and hustled his prisoner out, barely giving him time to obey the injunction of an infantile nature just described.

Edward hurried his case along with a firm and dexterous grip, yet one which to a casual observer might seem that of a companion—perhaps a bit over-demonstrative, but certainly not ill-disposed. Round a corner, and over the western railway, they reached a lofty and secluded street.

Edward had said nothing yet (nor had the prisoner) and was, in fact, not quite sure what he was going to say. A charge of this kind, at the station, was always the subject of facetious comment, and on the part of a young CID man would certainly be esteemed detrimental to his prestige. In addition, as Edward well knew, there was the complication that it is very difficult to make such charges stick if the officer arrests the prisoner alone. In such a case, if the prisoner denies with resolution, it is one man's word against another's; and though the courts will probably believe the copper's, they prefer corroborative evidence and are apt to dismiss the case if they don't get it. The whole exploit was, in fact, an optimistic stab in a considerable darkness, and Edward had already decided to turn the prisoner loose after one of those lecturettes so gratifying to a young officer's ego. But at this moment the prisoner uttered plaintively the magic words, 'Officer, can't we talk this thing over?'

Any experienced copper knows instantly what this means. For unless the prisoner is an imbecile—that *does* happen, of course—he will know perfectly well there's no point whatever in talking anything over once the arrest is made, unless . . .

Edward stopped, backed the prisoner against a mews wall, still holding him firmly and discreetly, and said to him, 'Well?'

'I'm in your hands,' the prisoner said, 'and I don't want this thing to go any further. I'm a married man.'

'So?' Edward said.

There was a slight pause as they eyed each other well beyond the eyes. 'I've got a fiver in my pocket if you'll let me get at it,' the prisoner said.

'Have you?' said Edward, gazing at his victim with implacable denial. 'You know what an offer of that nature means?'

'I've got six or seven in all,' the prisoner said. 'That's all I've got: honest: you can search me.'

'Who are you?' said Edward.

'I'd rather not say my name.'

'Wouldn't you! Tell me what's your job.'

'Salesman.'

'Of what?'

'Vacuum cleaners.'

'With a suit like that? And that wrist watch?' Edward gave the man a wrench.

'All right. Car salesman. And I'll make it twenty.'

Edward, still holding him, put his face closer and said low, slow, and distinctly, 'You'll make it fifty. And you'll tell me where you work, and at exactly this time tomorrow—*exactly*, you understand me?—I'll be calling there *with* a colleague. And you, you'll have made arrangements to meet us alone in some room there—I don't care *where*—and hand me what I said, singles and not new ones *and* un-marked please, in a plain envelope, and then I'll forget about the whole matter and so will you. If you've got any ideas of seeing a lawyer or having any sort of reception committee for me, that's up to you. But don't forget my story will be—and it'll be ready for filing by tonight at the station—that I was unable to arrest you because on more important duties, but you attempted to commit an offence and attempted bribery to an officer in the due course of his duties. Is that quite clear?'

'I haven't got that money,' the prisoner said.

'Then you'll *get* it.'

'Fifty's a lot,' he cried.

'Quietly! So's a few weeks in the nick. You're certainly not a first offender . . .'

'I've never had a conviction . . .'

'We'll soon put that right for you if you don't do as I say. And one last thing. If you try to cross me over this you may get away with it, and you may not, but believe me, son, whatever embarrassment it might cause me, a lot of my colleagues in the Force won't like it at all, and once we've got the needle into a man that's shopped an officer, particularly a man like you, we'll see it goes in deep and *hurts* you.'

Edward gave the man a sharp twist and abruptly released him. 'Very well, officer,' he said. 'It'll be as you say.'

Edward looked at him, said nothing for a moment, and then after collecting some particulars briskly (as if at the prisoner's request), turned and walked away. Like a young soldier in battle who shoots and is shot at the first time, he felt pure elation: far greater than that in distant earlier days, of his first uniformed arrest. Then, as professional prudence descended on him again, he meditated on all the angles he could see so far. The rendezvous at the man's own office seemed to him the master-stroke. For what officer, suspected of corruption, would ever go to fetch a bribe in so compromising a place? Righteous indignation could greet any such suggestion! The only tricky moment would be leaving the office with the envelope. But he wouldn't: he'd bring the man out *with* the envelope, and take it from him somewhere else.

There only remained, so far as he could see, one problem: where to keep the money once he had it. Obviously, it would be imprudent to put even a relatively small lump sum like this in the Post Office savings—his only bankers. And perhaps as time passed, the sums might well get larger. And so? He must try to find out what the precedents in this matter in the Force might be, and even possibly consult his girl about it also.

MR LOVE

FRANKIE and his woman were well settled in: and hitherto, so far as they could see, had attracted no undue attention. Key money had been duly paid to the janitor of the block of flats they'd chosen —but since this was normal practice, excited no untoward remark. Frankie, though he still had no job, departed at fairly regular intervals as if to work, and was careful to remain quite soberly dressed—as much, so it happened, by inclination as by prudence. His girl put it about (but very casually, and without overdoing it at all) that her man had had an accident at sea and had retired, though so young, from active duty. Everyone knew, of course, that they weren't married; but this state of affairs was far from unusual among the tenants as a whole. As for the very essential maid to assist the girl in her profession, they'd decided to do without one both for caution's sake and for the following reason.

It was clearly necessary to have, if *asked* (no need to volunteer the information otherwise), an explanation of the visitors to Frankie's flat. Of course, in the girl's new status in her calling, the prices had gone up from those of Stepney days, so that fewer clients paid a greater total; but still some reason might be needed, not, perhaps, that there were so many visitors, but that so many of them—almost all, in fact—were men. In this dilemma, Frankie's woman had recourse to her old Mum: who being part gypsy, practised as faith-healer, in which art, over the years, she'd built up a considerable clientele especially among what one might call the contemporary *levellers*: small, nonconformist tradespeople who scorned received religions, scorned hospitals (except when, as sometimes happened, they were carried in there to die), scorned dignity and the intellect—scorned everything except the dogmatic certitude of their own infallibility.

The faith-healing Mum was reluctant to shift her practice entirely from Walthamstow, where she was a figure of some local weight, to Kilburn; nor did Frankie, who didn't care much for the old lady, wish to have her living in the flat. Accordingly she came across, often transported by a gratefully healed patient with a car-hire business, on certain evenings and afternoons; and to those who were at all curious about Frankie's woman the hint was dropped that the mother was initiating her daughter into the mysteries of her healing art.

The Mum, whose own legal record was unblemished, knew all she needed to about her girl's activities and accepted them entirely without censure. In her eyes, her daughter had not 'gone wrong' but merely gone slightly bent. Her attitude, perhaps, resembled that of an Inland Revenue collector whose daughter, unpredictably, has chosen to become an air-hostess: a tricky, odd profession, but one of evident advantage and repute. To Frankie she was far from cordial. She quite accepted the need for his existence, just as the hypothetical collector would have done the need of his daughter to be associated, professionally, with a pilot. It was just that she didn't *like* him: thought him a bit superior, ungrateful and, possible worse, untrustworthy.

The girl had furnished the flat in decorous and thoroughly petty-bourgeois style: it startlingly resembled those of countless other tenants of the building with its furnishings which, though solid, rather overstated their real degree of luxury. As the flat was quite exiguous, Frankie had caused some inconvenience by absolutely refusing to allow the bed he shared with her, to be shared by anyone else. Another, disguised as a 'divan', was therefore imported into the living-room, taking up too much space and forcing the Mum (and indeed Frankie, on the rare occasions he was present during business hours) to move into the kitchen, or his own bedroom. But as no arrangement, whatever, here below, is ever precisely as each one of the parties involved would wish it, the various give-and-takes were generally accepted. What anyone else, including the janitor, thought of the set-up—if they did think of it at all—remained unknown. But in prostitution, as in all other businesses, if reasonable precautions are taken any troubles are best not nervously foreseen, but resolutely faced if they should arise.

The routine of a call-girl had, for Frankie, one very big surprise. The life of a street whore in Stepney, from the little he'd seen of it, was certainly not lacking in incident and colour; and for street-girls in general, he supposed, excitement of some kind or other had been the order of every day. But for a girl 'on the phone' the life was colourless and business-like in the extreme. Those who telephoned, and who were never accepted unless already known or strongly recommended and never, even then, if proposing to bring strangers or manifestly drunk, arrived discreetly and departed likewise: even more anxious, it seemed, than Frankie's girl was, not to get involved in 'anything'.

There were as was inevitable occasional 'incidents', at none of which, hitherto, Frankie had himself been present—except once or twice off-stage in the capacity of number-one reserve; but on such occasions the trouble-maker had to face the formidable duo of Frankie's woman and her Mum or even—still formidable enough—Frankie's girl, operating solo. For she had the gift, common to most women and even the un-respectable, of making any man who steps out of line from the particular convention that he shares for the moment with her appear, even to himself, to be crudely and abysmally *wrong*.

Occasionally when Frankie timed things badly, rather dreary little tea-parties took place between himself, his girl, and her appalling Mum: on which occasions he was much vexed by their custom of ignoring him almost, or of treating him at best as a visitor in his own home or as a sort of bright young cousin: indispensable in his way, as all men must be admitted to be, but superfluous to so many of the vital feminine preoccupations. These trios would sometimes lead to rows and even, when Frankie and his girl were left alone, to violence: but it was difficult to quarrel with them, because they greeted his resentment with such totally unfeigned surprise. What on earth was eating up the boy? Goodness! he must be right out of his foolish mind!

'If an agent takes the money from the *girl*,' Frankie's woman was explaining in a conversation with her mother about the legal technicalities of brothel-keeping, 'that's an offence, yes, but not if he takes it from the *man*.'

They both glanced at Frankie.

'As things are here, though,' said the mother, 'the question doesn't seem to me to arise.'

'Oh, no!' said the girl, 'of course not. Not in a straight gaff with one girl, no. But if the place is crooked with a few of them, and the agent knows it and he takes money from the girl, then the law says he's a brothel-keeper even though he's not the landlord.'

'But not if he takes it from the man.'

'No, Mum.'

'Then we do have our uses,' Frankie said.

The women both smiled politely and a bit impatiently.

'All the same,' the old Mum said, 'I should say with the new laws making it difficult for the girls out on the streets, the crooked landlords are going to play an even bigger part than they used to do before.'

'Naturally. And you know, Mum, it's a funny thing. In the old days on the streets, in spite of all you read of in the Sundays, the business wasn't really organized to all that great extent. Among the foreign girls, yes, maybe, but most of our girls just did their own deals with the landlords. But now, with the question of rooms becoming so important, I shouldn't be surprised to see that kind of an estate-agent, and the hospitality bureaus and such, moving in on the thing in a very much bigger way.'

'That's the trouble about laws,' the mother said, pouring another great gurgling cup of tea. Her daughter continued,

'The people who pass them just don't know a thing first hand, and when they set out to alter things for the better as they call it, they end up by making them far worse. Now, take the game. Up till a year ago, it was broadly speaking single operators, single girls. Now it's going to be big business, and go all commercial. But there you are. Here in England they think that if a thing goes on behind closed doors, it's better. In fact though, as we're going to see, it's worse. I mean different, anyway.' The girl sipped ruminatively. 'I wonder,' she said, 'why they don't just leave us alone. Why it is they hate us so.'

'It's not you they hate,' Frankie said, 'it's us—and I'll tell you why?'

The two women turned and eyed him as do adults when a bright child who's overheard an adult conversation chips in with a remark that will be possibly idiotic, possibly cute, and just possibly the revelation of an infant wisdom.

'They hate us,' said Frankie, 'so far as I can see for three reasons —possibly more I haven't thought of.'

Mild curiosity sat in four female eyes.

'They *don't* hate us,' Frankie said, 'because we're wicked, and they're not.'

The word 'wicked' fell on the air with a slight embarrassment on account, in this setting, of its total irrelevance: as if, on a race-track, a jockey had suddenly implied that any doubt was possible about the value of steeple-chasing.

'Then why do they?' said the girl.

'In the first place,' said Frankie who by now had meditated long and deeply on this theme, 'they hate us because they put their own guilty feelings on our heads.'

'They feel *guilty*?' the Mum said, as if pronouncing an indecent word.

'Some of them do, Mum,' said her daughter. 'As a matter of fact for some of them that's just the kick.'

'In the second place,' Frankie continued, 'they resent having to pay for what we get free.'

'Frankie!' cried the Mum. 'Don't be so vulgar!'

'And in the third,' he went on, 'they're simply jealous of us: cock-jealous, I mean. They know if they did it as well as we do, they wouldn't need to pay a girl at all.'

'You're being disgusting,' said the Mum. But her daughter smiled. 'So now you've got *that* off your chest,' she said, as her Mum cleared away the unharmonious tea-things.

She reached over and put her arms round Frankie and just left them there, so that he felt their weight: the only moment when arms—those busy, utilitarian limbs—seem voluptuous as breasts or thighs. 'You love me, don't you, Frankie dear?' she said.

He kissed her hard and comfortably. 'I don't *love* you,' he said with friendly scorn, 'and you know I don't. But I certainly like you—and your body, well, it's strawberries and cream.'

She laughed and pulled free, though easily, when her Mum returned, in a way Frankie liked because it showed not deference to the mother, but that her physical life with Frankie was their own concern and no one else's, not even Mum's.

'People are funny,' the mother observed sagely, seating her huge self (she was one of those women whose very soul seems in their bottoms) and picking up, though at a tangent, some threads of the earlier conversation. 'When they get an idea they've very often no idea what their real idea behind it is. For instance,' she said, weighing her pendulous elbows on the stalwart table, 'take healing, such as I do. Well, it's not for *healing* in point of actual fact that a great many of them come to see me.' She looked at each of them, as if inviting the real explanation and defying them to utter it. 'They come,' she said, 'simply because they're lonely and want sympathetic company.'

'A lot of mine do, too,' the girl said.

'Oh, I suppose so,' said the Mum.

'That's what the law and watch committees and busybodies generally don't realize. A lot of the clients, if they didn't come to us, would be in mental homes. There's not a girl, among the nicer ones I mean, who's not had the experience of straightening out some kinky character and even maybe, who knows? saving his marriage for him, and his home.'

'That's a new angle,' Frankie said.

'Don't be sarcastic, Frank,' the mother told him.

'All I'm trying to show you, Frankie,' said his girl, 'is that they're just as wrong, often, to hate us as they are to hate men like you.'

'Live and let live,' said the mother, 'is my motto. But as a matter of fact, so far as the law's concerned I don't think they're unreasonable: I mean the older more experienced officers. They bear no malice usually. They just follow the book of rules.'

'Except for the ones that provoke you,' the girl said, 'or frame you, or try to take advantage of their position, I'd agree with you more or less.'

'Who does that leave?' said Frankie.

'Oh, quite a lot of them. I've even had clients among the Force,' the girl said demurely.

'But a lot of them are bent, just like you say,' said Frankie. 'Well, come to think of it, don't they *have* to be? I don't mean the station-sergeants, or the men on the beat who help old ladies across zebras, but the bright boys, the vice people, the CID. I just ask you this: how can they possibly catch real criminals unless they understand what goes on in their minds?'

The women gazed at him as he uttered this subversive thought.

'So far as I can see,' said Frankie, 'the coppers are simply criminals who don't happen to *commit* crimes—not usually, anyway—because their graft, their occupation, is not that but to *detect* them. But they've got the criminal mentality all right. Well, I mean: just take a look at some of their faces, specially the eyes! And those bodies! All sticking out in awkward, unexpected places—so peculiar!'

'I think you're exaggerating,' the mother said, after a pause.

'Oh, sure!' said Frankie. 'And besides, I've no experience, you may say. Why! Think of it! I haven't even been inside the nick yet, except for those nautical little episodes in foreign parts . . .'

'Now, now, dear,' his girl said gently.

'Don't get me wrong!' said Frankie, who was beginning to feel that most delicious of intoxications, the excitement of an *idea*, and like all drunkards cared less and less, as it inspired him, whether his audience was also drunk, or no. 'I'm not against coppers like some people are. I don't hate them or anything—not at all: why bother? All I say is they *are* like that, they're bound to be like that, and what's wrong with the set-up in this country is not what *they* are, but what all the mugs *think* they are: because the facts about them aren't generally understood and, anyway, most people just don't want to *know*.'

'And *why* don't they?' asked, or rather said, the Mum.

'Because they're all like you, dear. Comfortable clots.'

'Well!'

'Frankie!'

'Well?'

All three had risen. The Mum, with great 'dignity', collected up the bits-and-pieces women always have on such occasions (no sweeping, decisive female exit is possible without stage props—*and* the implication that if not expeditiously collected, the offending male will add injury to insult by purloining them), and made off, escorted to the balcony by her daughter, where one of those feminine duos could be heard in which both speak at once yet each absolutely understands the other. Frankie sat on the table, hands in his pockets, marshalling his forces for the ensuing row.

But it burst with the mutes on, all in undertones. The girl just looked at him, sighed a bit and said, 'I know you don't like her, Frankie, but after all she is my Mum and she's bloody useful to us.'

'I agree with every word you say.'

'Well, dear?'

Frankie took her in his arms. 'Are you *sure* she's your Mum?' he said. 'I can't imagine how an old cow like that gave birth to you.'

'I haven't seen *your* Ma ever, don't forget.'

'You'll meet her in paradise. Not here.'

'Oh? I didn't know. Well, dear, there it is. If you want to alter the arrangement say so, but we can't have little scenes like that too frequently.'

'No.' Frankie looked into her eyes affectionately and with profound but uncritical mistrust. 'You know what you're doing to me?' he said. 'I'll tell you: you're blackmailing me.'

'Over this?'

'Over everything. The threat's always there. Take it and like it, boy, or else.'

'You think so?'

'Naturally. In the game the woman picks the man, whatever he may think, and holds him not with money but with blackmail.'

'Not me. You're free to go, dear, and there'll be no come-backs. I don't want you to, you know that, but you're free.'

'Me? Are you kidding? Not in this set-up, baby—never. Once you're in you can't escape—not because of the loot, or even because of the law, but because if you like the girl a lot, as I do, then you're really hooked.'

'Well? And so?'

'Well, it's just frightening a bit, girl, that's all. Because so long as *you* like *me* it's all okay—but if one day you didn't! Or if you really lost *your* temper with me!'

'I never do. Not often, anyway.'

'Or we both got high, filled up with lush, and raised our voices!'

'That could happen, I suppose . . .'

'Or if I fell for someone else, or *you* did maybe, and you knew, and I didn't know! That would be most dangerous of all!'

They were still holding each other, firm but loose, smiling a little as they spoke. 'You know, dear,' she said, 'this conversation has come up between every ponce and every whore at some time or another, and in some form or other—all I wonder is that we've not got around to having it before.'

'You're a Jezebel,' he said.

'Oh, no. No, no, I'm square and solid, quite a trusty. But: dig this, Frank, and there's no escaping it. A whore can do without a ponce if it has to be that way: but a ponce can never do without a whore—not ever.'

'Dig.'

'That's just the situation, baby. So what you say?'

'What I say is, darling, that I'm going to rape you. Take all that off and come on in.'

MR LOVE (STILL)

When he left her sleeping, Frankie gathered in the dark some minimal possessions plus twenty pounds from the laundry-basket (where petty-cash was kept, loose under the week's linen, so that a pound note had once been sent, in error, to the laundry (and returned!)), and he walked out into the Kilburn dawn. He set off across the city at an angle to the west–east, north–south pattern of its thoroughfares and, as dawn broke, he arrived again at Stepney.

Frankie's real objection to his situation was not really any of those that had come up last evening in discussion with his girl. His objection was that, in a general way, the man–woman relationship was taking a wrong and insupportable form. Among seamen there still survives from earlier days of masculine domination the notion that the man, at least in appearances, wears the slacks; and that the woman is she who sighs at the mariner's departure and accepts, without too much question, the equally sighing wife-in-every-port. On land, in England, he'd found that the symbol of the husband was now that dreadful little twerp you saw on hoardings who wore a woman's apron while he did, alone, the washing-up. This conception would have been just as repellent to Frankie in a legitimate marriage as in any unmarried-husband-and-wife connection.

And yet he would miss his girl—and really her. In Frankie's life sexual exchange was a very serious business, and he was old enough to have discovered that contrarily to all the legends about the delights of promiscuity, if you were really good at it yourself and found a woman who enhanced your sexual splendour—and her own—this was a rare thing to be clung to and protected. She'd certainly, in this way, got in well under his skin; and no thought of her clients had disturbed his raptures. Partly, because that core of herself which she kept absolutely intact throughout all her commercial encounters was fired to greater heat by the very fact that she held it, in reserve, entirely for him. Partly, because the idea that other men coveted her was far from diminishing her attraction to him: an instinct which, when one comes to think of it, is also shared in many cases by the clients of prostitutes themselves, and also, it may be, by complaisant husbands of candidly unfaithful wives.

Stepney, in early morning, has a macabre, poetic beauty. It is one of those areas of London that is thoroughly confused about itself, being in transition from various ancient states of being to new ones it is still busy searching for. The City, which still preserves its Roman quality of ending very abruptly at its ancient gates, towers beyond Aldgate pump, then stops: so that gruesome Venetian financial palaces abut on to semi-slums. From the dowdy baroque of Liverpool street station, smoke and thunder fall on Spitalfields market with its vigorous dawn life and odour of veg, fruit and flowers—like blended essences of the citizens' duties, delights and fantasies. Below the windowless brick warehouses of the Port of London

Authority, the road life of Wentworth street—almost unknown elsewhere in London where roads are considered means by which you move from place to place, not places in themselves—bubbles, overspills and sways in argument and shrill persuasion, to the off-stage squawks of thousands of slaughtered chickens. Old Montague street with its doorless shops that open outward in the narrow thoroughfare, and its discreet, secretive synagogues, has still the flavour of a semi-voluntary ghetto. Further south, in Commercial road, are the nocturnal vice caffs that members of parliament and of Royal Commissions are wont to visit, invariably accompanied by a detective-inspector to ensure that their expedition will reveal nothing characteristic of the area; and which, when suppressed, pop up again immediately elsewhere or under different names with different men of straw at the identical old address. In Cable street, below, the castaways from Africa and the Caribbean perform a perpetual, melancholy, wryly humorous ballet of which they are themselves the only audience. Amid incredible slums—which, one may imagine, with the huge new blocks replacing them, are preserved there by authority to demonstrate the contrast of before-and-after—are pieces of railway architecture of grimly sombre grandeur. Then come the docks with masts and funnels strangely emerging above chimney-tops, and house-locked basins, the entry to which by narrow canals and swinging bridges seems, to the landsman, an impossibility, were it not for the cargo boats nestling snugly between the derelict tenements. Suddenly, beyond this, you come upon the river: which this far down, lined with wharves and cranes and bearing great ocean-loving steamers, is no longer the pretty, grubby, playground of the higher reaches but already, by now, the sea.

A great charm of the area is that only here, in one sense, is London really a capital city at all. For what, elsewhere in the world, distinguishes capitals from their bleak provincial brethren is that they're open for business all night, and for seven days in the week. Thanks to the markets, seamen, and Commonwealth minorities, in Stepney you can eat and drink, as well as other things, at any hour you choose to; and thanks to the alternation of the Jewish sabbath with the Gentile, the shops and markets never close. All that remains astonishing, since this is England, about this delightful state of affairs is that no one has yet managed to suppress it.

Frankie breakfasted in Stepney at one of those cafés usually conducted by Somalis which, unlike the more exclusive Maltese, Asian, or Caribbean establishments, are often neutral ground for clients of the most diverse nationalities. And so fell into conversation with a Glaswegian seaman, whose opening shot was to announce that he'd just come out of the nick. Observing the etiquette on these occasions, Frankie didn't ask for what and offered the mariner ten bob. This he accepted as by right. For the announcement of a recent release from prison, like that by children who tell you it's their birthday, is intended to provoke an instant, identical reaction, the scale of the subsidy varying with the degree of the donor's affluence and of intimacy, if any, with the uncaged bird.

'Yes,' said the Scot—speaking in those particular tones Scots use which suggest, with incredible self-esteem and unction (based, it would seem, on nothing very tangible), that each of their platitudes and banalities has a prodigious sagacity and savour—'it was all on account of a Salvation Army laddie.'

Frankie, whom the man bored already, expressed polite surprise.

'He came into a boozer,' the Scot continued, 'where I was partaking of a dram, and he shook his collecting-box underneath my nose, appealing to me and my mates that we should exercise a bit of self-denial.'

The Hebridian fixed his leery, bleary eyes on Frankie, who courteously raised his brows.

'Self-denial!' the Scot repeated. 'So I said to him this: that his coming into pubs where men went precisely to escape from hypocrites like him, and blackmailing everybody under the protection of his self-appointed uniform, was a form of spiritual pride which—as any Presbyterian can tell you—is the deadliest sin of all, and that his first task for the salvation of his own soul by blood and fire was to deny himself this hideous satisfaction.'

'Ah,' Frankie said.

'Whereupon,' the Scot continued, emphasizing each word as if it fell from his lips like newly minted coin, 'the Sassenachs in the boozer, one and all, took this man's side against me because the English, you see—excuse me, my very good friend—haven't the courage of their convictions and none of them, except for me, would dare to say the man was a damned imposter.'

'And so?' Frankie said.

'An argument—a fight—knocked off—the courts—previous convictions—two months—no remission.'

'Who pinched you?' Frankie asked.

'Plain-clothes. In a plain car. You know? One of those ordinary vehicles that are not quite what they seem.'

'Crafty.'

'Ah, well . . . not really so. Just, man, that I, on this particular occasion, being intoxicated was *not*.'

'And now what? Back to sea?'

'No: back for a wee spell to Glasgow. I've had an offer of a ship but me, after this experience, I must have a wee spell at hame in Bonnie Scotland . . .'

Into his tone and eyes had come dollops of the atrocious sentimentality that so frequently lies below the granite surface of the hard-headed Scot.

'Who's using the berth?'

'Who can tell? Why, man—you want it? Well, if you've got a tenner for the quartermaster and no one's preceded you in search of it, take this address and so forth and send me a post-card from the Argentine.'

He handed to Frankie a cigarette-wrapping inscribed with critical particulars, and Frankie thanked him and immediately took his leave. For he was certain—not being at all a fool—that if he didn't get out of England in a day or two he'd return, just as certainly, to Kilburn.

As he walked through Stepney, he passed by the all-night caffs that cater for the exhibitionist dregs of the vice trade and where, in the morning, a few survivors from the last night's market-place remained: either disappointed hustlers of both sexes who'd failed to connect and slept there, or dissatisfied clients who'd returned from various squalid set-ups whither their earlier imaginings had lured them not to complain (for this was useless: and who to complain to?), but as the beast returns from the smaller, empty water-hole to the larger. Among them was a sprinkling of the different, morning clientele: lorry-drivers, local workers and a few from the West of the city who'd visited the gamble-houses and called in for breakfast to count (mentally) their losses or more unlikely gains. It is at this hour, when someone sleepy is sweeping out among this driftwood, and not in the hopeful afternoon or the intoxicated evening, that moralists should paint their portraits of Gin Lane.

But for Frankie the change was that everything he'd seen earlier in these places now fell into focus. Just as a veteran, seeing soldiers drilling, finds no more mystery in their gyrations, so did Frankie recall this incident, or that person, which had seemed inexplicable but now no longer were. 'What you got in that bag?' a voice asked him sharply.

A copper was blocking the morning view: and worse still, disturbing Frankie's tranquil train of troubled thought. 'You want to have a look?' he said, dumping the bag down at the officer's highly polished feet.

'Open up,' said the officer.

Frankie bent casually, unzipped the zip and straightened himself remotely, leaving the bag still closed.

'I said open up.'

Frankie surveyed the copper, eyes to eyes. Unlike all but a fraction of the citizenry he did not fear coppers in the least: feared, perhaps, any damage, physical or worse, they might inflict on him, but not them as men at all. Nor was he in the least impressed by the art coppers have in a sudden crisis of calling up childhood memories, and suggesting to the accused that they are the father and the person they interrogate abruptly the child who, even if he hasn't broken something, feels he must have. So for a moment, there was an impasse: for the copper was young and not quite sure of the precedents in his predicament. Till Frankie, in a somewhat equivocal gesture of compromise, put a foot on one end of the hold-all which caused the other end to gape wide open, revealing his guiltless clothes.

'What's these?' said the officer.

Frankie made no reply. The officer inclined himself and rummaged. 'Are they yours?' he said, looking up.

Frankie nodded.

'I asked you a question,' said the officer.

'Yes. I heard you. And I gave you an answer.'

The officer, his decision made, stood up. 'I'm not satisfied with all this,' he said. 'I want you to come along to the station.'

Frankie zipped up the bag, lifted it and said, 'Are you arresting me?'

'I didn't say that. I said—'

'If you're not arresting me you know there's no charge to bring; and to take me to the station's just a bit of spite.'

The copper took Frankie's arm, text-book fashion. 'So you think you *are* arresting me,' Frankie said.

The officer applied the text-book pressure which should have resulted in Frankie's inevitable propulsion along the road—but somehow, he didn't move. 'You're coming in,' said the officer, heaving desperately, 'for resisting an officer in the execution of his duties as well as the other thing.'

Frankie laughed out loud. 'What other thing?' he cried.

'Come on!' cried the officer, giving a colossal shove.

Abruptly, Frankie started walking smartly forward so that the officer was now dragged behind his prisoner as is a dog-lover by a Great Dane. Round a corner Frankie stopped abruptly, making his custodian slightly overshoot him, and said, 'Son, do you really have to do this to a merchant seaman about his lawful business?'

'Is that what you say you are?' said the officer, panting.

'It's all I know, son, the sea. It's all I am and ever hope to be.'

'Oh, yes?' said the young copper, schooled in scepticism. 'Well, I don't think so. As a matter of fact,' he added with a penetrating professional stare, 'we know all about you . . .'

Despite a momentary throb, Frankie's good sense told him he could utterly ignore this classical copper's gambit. 'I'll tell you something, son,' he said, 'about you and your little lot. You *do* know secrets about people, yes: but the secrets you know are all secrets of no importance.'

The intrusion of this philosophical theme was greatly to the young officer's distaste. He searched in vain for a helpful colleague or even a law-abiding citizen, and realized that now his disagreeable choice lay between a fight or of letting, or appearing to let, Frankie escape: both detrimental to the junior constable's estimate of his dignity.

A voice said, 'Having a bit of trouble?' It was that of an older officer who had emerged from a scrap-metal yard where he had been passing the time of morning. 'This feller's awkward,' said the junior officer, giving Frankie an authoritative shake. Four hands—which, compared with two, are not as twofold but as twentyfold or more—now seized on Frankie and hustled him stationwards. The early hour, from the officers' point of view, could not have been more convenient: for Frankie was comfortably in time for the morning convoy to the magistrate's court. The old boy—one of the vanishing type whose sagacious sallies are still reported in the inside bottom columns of the evening papers—gave Frankie the option of forty shillings or of seven days. When asked if he had anything to say, Frankie remarked in a casual and reasoned tone: 'If the law takes a man in for nothing, he may decide he might as well get taken in for something.' The magistrate nodded, made no direct comment, and withdrew the option of a fine.

MR LOVE AND MR JUSTICE

THE attraction of wrestling is not so much the sport itself (if it be one), as in the survivals it enshrines of ancient customs. If anyone wants to know what an old Music Hall audience was like (when gallery boys hurled pease puddings and pigs' trotters over the cowering heads of the grilled-in musicians on to the performers), or going back a bit, what a bear-baiting public may have resembled, or further still, the spectators of a gladiatorial show—he may probably capture some of their atmospheres at a wrestling match. The audience, indeed, are much more arresting than the fighters: the faces of mild respectable men in business suits are twisted into vicious snarls, those of women, shrieking violent obscenities, wear masks of gloating ferocious glee. The bouts themselves seem to fall into two categories: comparatively straight matches of incomparable boredom in which huge hunks of living meat lie locked in painful and contorted postures; and then the 'villain-and-hero' bouts, sorts of popular moralities, wherein one wrestler becomes, presumably by pre-arrangement, St. George, and the other (usually the more polished performer) the odious dragon. It is a tribute to the artistry of these thespian practitioners of grunt-and-groan that though all but the dimmest-witted of the audience know the performance is a fake—or, one might say, an allegory—they accept the convention of this Jack-the-Giant-killer world entirely. So that when Jack, attacked basely from the rear by the treacherous giant who just a second ago was pleading on his quavering knees for mercy, outwits the monster and hurls him four feet high and six feet wide with a resounding crash on to the groaning mat, the audience yells the applause that may have greeted David as he returned from his encounter with Goliath.

Among the spectators of the bout between Boris the Bulgar and the Tasmanian Devil were Frank and his girl, now reconciled and firmly reunited and comfortably ensconced in ringside seats; and also among those present in ringsides likewise (complimentaries, in this case) were the newly installed tenants of their Kilburn flat, Edward and his beloved woman. Surrounding them was a cross-section of that part of the London populace which is rarely to be seen elsewhere (except at race meetings, certain East and South London pubs, and courts and jails), and whose chief characteristics are their uninhibited violence, their heartless bonhomie, and their total rejection alike of the left-ish Welfare State and the right-ish Property-owning democracy: a sort of Jacobean underground movement in the age of planned respectability from grave to cradle.

Up in the ring it was Boris the Bulgar (need one say?) who was cast for the role of villain. He was short, squat, bald and lithe, and probably hailed from Canning Town or Newington Butts. His face, if such one could call it, wore a built-in scowl when all was in his favour, a contortion of dreadful agony when his opponent secured a grip, and a look of abject ignominy when fortune momentarily failed to smile upon him. With the referee (a huge, sandy, mild-eyed man of tough but exquisite manners) he was on the worst of terms, perpetually disputing his decisions; and with the crowd even more so for he hurled back, in reply to their hoots and screams, base insults by voice and scandalous gesture. What a contrast was the Tasmanian Devil! A large, sad, slow-moving man whose whole bent, bruised body suggested a life of unjust suffering dedicated, much more in sorrow than in anger, to a resigned forgiveness of the world's worst treacheries and wrongs. How often did the Devil not break away, voluntarily, and release his victim from an impossible posture, chivalrously to show that even an animal so base must be given yet another chance! How obedient he was to the least remonstrance of the wise and patient referee! And how earnestly he looked up at the audience, apologizing with a wry smile for any faulty manoeuvre that had caused him untold agonies at the Bulgar's hands, shrugging sadly his red and massive shoulders at some outrageous piece of wickedness of his adversary, and occasionally, the fierce light of battle appearing in his brow-locked eyes, appealing to the masses as he held the atrocious Bulgar at his mercy for *their* impartial judgment (free from the prejudices that momentarily marred his own) to decide the exact nature of Boris's so richly merited fate.

This sealed, between contests and amid the patrons' recapitulative buzz, Edward's girl squeezes his hand and moved her hips even closer to his off-duty gaberdine. But Edward was staring into space. 'It ought to be suppressed,' he said.

'What ought, dear?' she said, surprised.

'All this,' said Edward, frowning. 'It's a disgrace.'

'But I thought you liked it.'

He looked round at her. 'Oh, yes, well I do: I mean the fight. But it's the audience I'm speaking of. I've seen more wanted men in here this evening than any day in the line-up. *And* flashing their money about—somebody's money, anyway.'

'They've got to go somewhere . . .' she suggested.

'I know where they all ought to go . . .'

She squeezed him again. 'Well, don't complain too much,' she said. 'You're doing a bit better yourself since you got your danger money.'

'Mustn't talk shop here, dear,' he said softly.

'Oh, I'm sorry. I liked the Tasmanian one, Edward. I think he was sexy.'

'That hunk of meat? Well, that's what the whole thing's meant for, I suppose. I notice there's nearly as many women here as men . . .'

'Oh yes, we love it! Those big men tied in knots!'

'Lovers' knots.'

'Oh, Ted! You can be so crude!'

A stir in the audience, and the incomprehensive barking from the man in a hired tuxedo at the mike, both heralded the next pair of warriors. Frankie looked round expectantly, but his girl chewed her cashew nuts in silence. 'Stay for this one, babe,' he said.

'Okay, Frankie, if you say so, but never again. It's such a drag.'

'This will be better: younger fellers, more your type.'

'No wrestler's my type. They all look like blown-up balloons. Me, I like lean men.'

'Skinny like me?'

'You're not skinny—not since you've been with me, anyway.'

'Not in here, darling. Watch what you say . . .'

' "Been with me". What's wrong with that? And Frankie, just look at the audience! All those old bitches: I bet they've not had a man in years—apart from hubby.'

'What's wrong with hubby? Look! Here they both come—young kiddies, like I said.'

'Yeah?' The girl scanned them casually. 'I'll wait till they get their gowns off,' she said, 'before I pronounce judgment.'

'It'll be a real fight,' said Frankie. 'There's nothing to beat a fight between two young men, provided they're reasonably matched.'

'You think they will be—in a place like this? Listen, Frankie. There's only one kind of fight I like, and that's with you on a six-foot divan.'

'This'll give you an appetite,' said Frankie.

By the unexacting standards of the grunt-and-groan game, the fight seemed to be a fair one. At any rate, plenty of things happened that surely no one could possibly have predetermined or predicted. When the two men bounced individually off the ropes to gain momentum, they collided and knocked each other out (apparently). At one moment a wrestler was sitting *on* the other's head, though this man was standing, and contrived to remain there for at least forty seconds. And at another, when one man staggered in dazed pain this may have been simulated, but hardly the sudden gesture of concern with which the man who'd hurt him ran up and stroked his arm. As the fight developed, two distinct personalities emerged. One fighter would attack sharply, and even when his hold seemed powerful and secure he'd break away abruptly, of his own accord, to mount a different, unexpected hostile manoeuvre. The other, in sharp comparison with the two earlier wrestlers whose expressions in combat had been perpetually bestial, wore a certain grace and freedom in the savagery of his face. When they were locked tight it was often quite impossible to tell, at moments, who was who and which limbs belonged to which: though the different coloured shorts they wore were something of an indication. The nicest thing about them both—and professionally the most convincing—was their apparent indifference to the audience around them to whom they paid little or no court, entirely intent on battle. The bout, which lasted (most unusual in wrestling) all its rounds, seemed inconclusive, although the referee did raise one tired arm: by the audience this was of course disputed, but rather languidly, as the fight had been too good for them to enjoy it.

At the interval most patrons went out in the long bars for some solid boozing. Criminal aristocrats, all wearing hats (they looked as if they wore them in their baths, beds and tombs), stood in little squares to talk so that there was no direction from which a stranger might approach the party unobserved. Women of hideous splendour —looking like actresses in a banned play who'd strayed outside the pass-door a moment—stood absolutely motionless with a gin glass, ignoring their escorts and ignored by them. The wrestlers of the earlier bout appeared in mufti, but betrayed by squashed ears and colossal shoulders, to have a quick one and talk contracts with alarming men who never blinked and spoke with a fraction of their mouths in voices inaudible from more than eighteen inches.

Frankie and Edward glanced at each other, their eyes locked, held for a second then fell away. Then each, as men do to assess a man, looked at the other's woman, and across both their faces there passed a flicker of slight disdain.

MR JUSTICE

A CHANGE in the laws does not fundamentally affect a copper's work: the only things that could do that are profound social and political changes, or (if such a thing, in mid-twentieth-century England, is conceivable) essential religious changes—not just of fashion (which happen so frequently and meaninglessly) but of basic form. Otherwise, if the moral structure of the nation does not alter, a change of its laws means merely, for the Force, a modification of its tactics, not its strategy (nor of its very self): the same crimes remain and the same criminals, but merely operate in different ways which have to be anticipated and assailed with fresh techniques.

This was the reason for a 'conference' (as he called his staff meetings) in the Detective-sergeant's office. There were present the star sleuth, Edward Justice, a plain-clothes copperess and one civilian: or rather, a hybrid creature—a former copper, now retired from the Force, who'd gone into business (quadrupling his income) as a private detective, while still (very naturally) maintaining his contacts among his former comrades who (knowing that only death could sunder one of their kind for ever from his calling) were prepared to trust—and use—him up to a certain point.

The Detective-sergeant addressed the little group. 'The problem as I see it 's this,' he said. 'We've got to crack down on the Madams. More and more of these girls are going on the phone, and it's the Madams who are picking out the best earners among them and organizing these high-grade semi-brothels. They're crafty, of course. There's no girls *living* on the premises, and they change them round so much, by calling them on the blower for a particular appointment with a client, that it's hard to log their visits if you keep watch—and play it straight, of course—to get the necessary number for a prosecution. Then there's the clients, too. The particular Madam we've chosen as our trial target seems to specialize in the bowler hat and rolled umbrella category, mostly elderly and—from the enquiries we've already made—the sort of mug you have to handle carefully, as they've got connections. So that's why,' the Detective-sergeant continued, eyeing the ex-copper detective with a friendly, mocking air, 'we've thought of enlisting the aid and assistance of our friend here.'

They all looked at the semi-civilian who smiled and said, 'Always happy to help you beginners out of your predicaments.'

'Now, here's the plan,' said the Detective-sergeant after a wry, polite, and not very pleasant smile. 'It's a three-pronged attack, as you'll see. Number one, we keep watch in the routine manner, naturally, and for that we'll be using the bread-delivery van.'

There was a muffled groan.

'Yes?' said the Detective-sergeant sharply.

'Sir,' someone said. 'If that van of ours keeps breaking down on bread rounds in every suspect street in north-west London, won't someone soon start to rumble us?'

'It's all we've got,' the Detective-sergeant said severely: as with so many strategists, 'the plan' already was, for him, a reality to which reality itself must needs conform; besides which—as he was scarcely able to divulge—the watchers outside were not really one of his 'prongs' at all, but were intended to serve as a decoy to the sharp-eyed Madam who, he hoped, would imagine them to be her only danger.

'The second attack,' said the Detective-sergeant, 'will be from this lassie here'—and he indicated with a sexy but official leer the horse-faced copperess who sat primly on her kitchen chair, showing a regulation inchage of her bony and well-exercised legs. 'Her task will be to follow the girls home, try to locate their addresses, if possible identify their ponces and—well, I wouldn't put it past so experienced an officer—get on friendly terms with them.'

There were discreet and cordial chortles, and the copperess, smiling slightly, showed her teeth in a grimace that hinted this feat was far from being beyond her professional (and womanly) competence.

'There's only one thing,' said the star sleuth, who hitherto had maintained an aloof and almost disdainful silence.

'Well?'

'I've checked on one or two,' he said, 'and this Madam's got a thing about using girls whose ponces we'd find it difficult to get at.'

'Lesbian girls?' said the ex-copper detective.

The star sleuth nodded.

'Yes, that's a difficulty,' the ex-officer said. 'You can get them for procuring if you're lucky, but with a living on immoral earnings charge, juries just wouldn't understand the situation. Even magistrates are sometimes a bit slow to grasp it.'

'Also,' the star sleuth continued, 'there's one girl, I know, who's shacked up with a teenager: and you realize how hard it is to pin a thing like that on one of them.'

'These teenagers!' said the ex-copper, sighing. 'They're a caution!'

The Detective-sergeant broke in with some vexation. 'I've considered these various angles,' he said, 'and as for you'—and he pointed a blunt index in the star sleuth's direction—'I hope your private investigations haven't buggered up the situation prematurely.'

The copperess looked at the varnished ceiling. 'Oh, pardon,' the Detective-sergeant said. 'It's still hard, after all these years, to remember we have ladies in the Force.' He gave her a cracked grin, and proceeded: 'So—attack number three: the place itself: and that's where our friend here (smile at the ex-copper) comes into the picture. Perhaps, then, you'd just tell these young officers in your own words the essential gist of our earlier private conversation.'

The ex-cop, his moment come, beamed with the bonhomie of someone who knows all the inner secrets but is freed from the servitude demanded to acquire them.

'As I see the picture,' he explained, 'I'm a randy guinea-pig.'

He paused for effect: but the laughter coming from the gallery, not the stalls or circle, he continued—suddenly very grave—'The spiel is this. I'm a client—yes? I've got her phone number, and I've got the name of a kosher client that you pinched for parking as my alleged sponsor, so my call to the premises won't seem untoward. I get in the place on several occasions, over a period of time, until I know the set-up in all its aspects and we're ready for the raid. When that comes—well, I'm the Roman legionary inside the Trojan horse.'

'We won't ask,' said the Detective-sergeant gaily, 'what, apart from your duties, you actually *do* in there.'

'Oh, I should think not! My report on *that* part of the business is strictly private for my missus.'

'Any questions?' said the Detective-sergeant.

After the traditional pause, the star sleuth said, 'So we don't touch the clients?'

'Not at all. Strictly not at all.'

'You'll excuse me, sir,' said the star sleuth very deferentially, 'but I do think there's one reason why you should consider it. It's this. They're the weak link. They're not doing anything illegal, as we know, like the girls and Madam are, but unlike them they're mugs, after all, and have their *respectability* to consider. And when a man's attached to that I've always found he'll talk with very little persuasion.'

'They're not guilty of anything,' said the ex-copper.

'I know that: I've just said so. But don't forget, sir. You can always *arouse* a sense of guilt, especially in a respectable man. Almost everyone feels guilty about *some*thing. And you can work on that.'

'All a bit over my head,' said the Detective-sergeant nastily. 'The orders are as I said. Anything else?'

Edward Justice said, 'Sir: what about the lawyers?'

'What lawyers? I don't get it, sonny.'

Edward looked round, feeling a lot of eyes on him, gulped, and said, 'These girls, sir, some of them, are earning several hundreds untaxed every week—they or their ponces are, I mean. And this Madam, sir, she must have a fabulous income and I dare say she'll try to protect them to a certain extent. Well, sir, if they're raided that means lawyers—big ones. And all I wanted to ask was, what the procedure in the event of arrest should be.'

Like so many young men new to a business, Edward had committed the solecism of asking a highly intelligent question that it was not appropriate he should ask, for several reasons. Firstly, because that wasn't what the particular briefing was about: one thing at a time in the Force as anywhere else. Next, because the whole subject of the triangle of criminal, copper and the courts is so intricate, practically and philosophically, that it can't possibly be explained in a short answer. Thirdly, there were aspects of this relationship so delicate that they have, in the Force, to be learned by experience rather than taught specifically.

The Detective-sergeant, eyeing Edward and remembering his own young days, said quite kindly, 'The procedure, constable, is as laid down: just follow that.'

'All I wanted to get at, sir,' said Edward, feeling from the slight electricity in the atmosphere he was 'on to' something and unable to resist the risk of burning his fingers on it, 'was this. When we detain them, how long do we keep them before we let them see their lawyers?'

The Detective-sergeant looked at him hard. 'As long as the book allows,' he said. 'Any further questions?'

There were none, and the little group dispersed. The ex-copper wanted to stay and chat the Detective-sergeant but this officer, exercising the privilege of an active if junior rank to a retired even if formerly senior colleague, turfed him politely out, detaining Edward. 'Sit down, son,' he said, 'I want to talk to you.'

The Detective-sergeant lit his pipe and said, 'Your question was quite all right, lad, but it wasn't quite the time and place to ask it. Now as for lawyers we have them too, you know, as well as anyone else; they're very good ones, believe me, and in the more important cases we get the services of the top brains in the land.'

'Yes, sir,' said Edward.

'I see, of course, the point you were getting at and I don't object at all to you considering it. A good man in the Force like I believe you to be—or getting to be with time—very naturally wants to secure a conviction if he can. That's what we're here for, after all; it's our duty to the profession and, if you like to put it that way, to society at large. We have also, of course, certain rules and regulations as to how you can get a man convicted—and as to how you can't—drawn up I don't know by who and don't much care because there they are, they exist, they've got to be observed.'

'Yes, sir.'

'*Observed* I said, mark you. But not necessarily, always, in every case to be *obeyed*.'

Here the Detective-sergeant stopped, removed his pipe and contemplated Edward in a fatherly way.

'But the point you've got to grasp,' he continued, 'is this one. If you knock a man off and don't follow the book and get a conviction, and no one asks any questions—then, well and good. And if you do it often enough you'll probably get quick promotion. On the other hand if you chance your arm and do something that's not in the book of rules and come unstuck in court or elsewhere, please don't expect anyone to protect you or excuse you; not me or anyone else, and I want to make that perfectly clear.'

'I understand, sir,' Edward said.

'I hope so. Now, about the particular question that you asked. Obviously, as I need hardly tell you, the longer you can keep a prisoner from his lawyer the better it's likely to be for your particular purposes. Most cases, in my experience, are lost or won in the first hour of the arrest—or at any rate in the first twenty-four of them. If you can keep the lawyers away from him in this critical period your battle's already more than half way over.'

'I see, sir. But . . . well, sir. If he *asks* to see his lawyer? What do you do then?'

'Come now, boy, that's up to you! Don't ask me to *be* your brains on top of everything else . . . It depends on the man, the case, the circumstances—everything! Remember the book—remember the case—and use your judgment. To give you a simple instance. Take formally preferring a charge or warning the person that anything he says will be taken down, etcetera. Well! How many cases couldn't I tell you of when I haven't bothered to do either! In the matter of the charge, you often don't know what it's going to be until you've talked to him quite a bit. And as for the warning . . . well frankly, in most cases I've simply forgotten it—I mean *forgotten* it—and there's no possible come-back there, because no one outside the Force believes that we *don't* warn them. They believe we do just like they believe we wear helmets in our sleep and can tell them the correct time without looking at our watches.'

'Yes, sir, I see.'

'I'd sum it up like this. If you're a good copper, I mean both as a man and an officer, more or less and allowing for human failings, and you're alone in a cell with a man who you know for certain is evil and anti-social, well, you must establish your moral right to prepare him for punishment as best you can. That, in my experience, is usually what the situation is: him and you: very simple, really. There are those who believe (and the Detective-sergeant glanced towards the door whence the others had departed) and who'll tell you a really good copper, professionally speaking I mean, has no conscience: can't afford to have one, or something. Well, there are wiser heads than mine in the Force, and admitted, I've stuck hitherto at Detective-sergeant. But all the same my personal conviction is that it's untrue. To be a good copper, in any sense of the word, you've got to have *certain* basic principles and stick to them.'

'Yes, sir.'

'Good. Now hop it, sonny, I've got work to do.'

When Edward was at the door, however, the Detective-sergeant said to him, 'That girl of yours, by the way. Any developments?'

Edward blushed, and hoped the reasons for it would be mistaken. 'I think things are working out, sir,' he said. 'I'm bringing her gradually round.'

'Ah. Just another thing: perhaps I shouldn't tell you this, but I will. One of our colleagues—I leave to your imagination who—has told me—unofficially, if such a thing exists—you've set up house already with the lady.'

Edward said nothing.

'No objection to that, of course,' the older officer said, 'provided you're just *visiting* her, like, and *not* living as man and wife, and provided I'm *not* formally informed by anyone—I mean in a report —and also provided, I'd say, that, as you tell me, the thing's only temporary and you'll soon be getting wed.'

'Thank you, sir,' Edward said.

'Just watch it, son. That's all.'

'I'd like to thank you, sir,' Edward said again.

The Detective-sergeant smiled. 'No need to: I may need you one day—who knows? That's one of the things about the Force, son, as you've no doubt probably discovered: it's hard to have friends. Mates, yes, dozens of them, and professionally good colleagues, too. But not many you can let yourself confide in.'

MR LOVE

In her warm and chintzy drawing-room the Madam was serving tea and holding court. If a person's identifiable with a locality, her appearance was Kensingtonian: neat, conservative, reliable and uncreative with a hint, perhaps, of the monied leisure of the Bournemouth pines. Her shoes were not smart but clean and dependable, her hair was not permed but well laundered and preserved. The tea-things were of silver, and the biscuits (which nobody took) from a Knightsbridge store. Her tones were quiet and authoritative like those of the chairwoman of a ward caucus; and she was also, if anyone had anything relevant to say, an excellent listener. Her guests were Frankie and his girl, a bisexual prostitute who was one of a team sustaining the sensational decline of a once (and in some senses, still) celebrated Lesbian socialite, and there was also present, like the footman behind the ducal chair, her confidential maid.

'So I think,' Frankie's girl was saying, 'you'll find, as I say, everything will be okay.'

The Madam gazed steadily at Frankie. 'I hope, Frank,' she said, 'you'll not take it amiss I asked your young lady to bring you here to see me, and didn't consider I was asking you to take an unnecessary risk. But the fact is, as I made quite clear to this young girl of yours, that if a girl of mine tells me she has a young man in her life —and I like and expect her to be perfectly frank about who she may be in business with—then before I ask her to help me in my own business here I have to see the young man, or other person in question, to get my own personal impression.'

'Yeah,' Frankie said.

'Frankie didn't very much want to come,' the girl said, smiling at him a little nervously because, about this, there'd been a really prodigious row. 'He took a bit of persuading, I can tell you.'

'That's understandable,' their hostess said.

There was a short pause.

'Look, lady,' Frankie said. 'My girl's here on the work, and it's not in my interest obviously, is it, to stand in her way if she thinks your place is right for her. So I don't object to this interview if it helps matters and provided, if I can say so without offence, it's the only one. There's no need for apologies because I'm not a man who does anything he doesn't want to, and if I agree to anything I don't need thanking for that reason.'

The Madam nodded with reserved approval. The maid looked non-committal, and the bisexual prostitute very dubious.

'This is a select place,' the Madam said, 'and I *mean* select. There are those who think an establishment of this nature has to be noisy, dirty, and generally disreputable. Well, not me or mine. A well-conducted meeting-place such as mine can be every bit as decorous and charming as a hotel is—or ought to be, should I say, because few are as well conducted, though I say so, as my premises.'

'*And* often have more strangers in the bedrooms I dare say,' said Frankie's girl.

The Madam smiled. 'Tea or coffee, with the morning and evening newspapers, are served to all our visitors prior to their departure,' she informed them. 'Is that not so?' she said, suddenly looking over her shoulder at her confidential maid.

'Oh, yes. *And* I press their suits for them, and sometimes wash and dry their socks.'

'Exactly! I set, as a matter of fact, great store by the pleasant character of these departures I've referred to. It's all that happens *after* rather than *before*, in my experience, that determines a satisfied client to return to the establishment again and recommend it to the right sort among his friends.'

'No throwing them out before the milk comes,' said Frankie's girl.

The Madam smiled again.

'And what about the law?' asked Frankie. 'You got them fixed?'

His hostess winced slightly and said, 'We take—I and my girls—all necessary measures and precautions. And one of those is to beg someone like yourself, Frank, who's concerned indirectly with my business, to exercise, at all times, a more than usual discretion. Especially, if I may say so, in the matter of conversations other than with, very naturally, your own young lady.'

'Check,' Frankie said.

'They never tap the phones?' Frankie's girl asked, impelled by professional curiosity.

'They're very welcome to,' the Madam answered. 'I, my girls, my dear maid here and, I may say, my clients have trained ourselves to say nothing over the telephone that could, even if recorded, be misinterpreted: I mean, constitute any proof before a court of law. In addition, the firm of solicitors who take my instructions have assured me that, as I expect you know, any evidence of this kind is, legally speaking, inadmissible.'

'So they'll have to fall back on the old tactics,' Frankie said.

'Who?'

'The coppers.'

To everyone but Frankie, the note in the conversation now seemed slightly vulgar.

'So far,' said the Madam with a marked tone of rebuke, 'as the officers of the law are concerned, I need hardly say that one's own common-sense would tell one to say nothing whatever to them without legal counsel. The services of my solicitors, need I tell you, are at the call of any girl whom I employ and who may encounter any difficulties, as much as they are to myself who pay them their fees. But there's no special need, I think, for us to anticipate any *special* difficulties. The officers of the law understand my position, just as I understand and respect their own. We have both, after all'—she smiled again—'been on this earth for centuries in one form or another.'

'I wouldn't say that,' said Frankie.

'No?'

'No. Your lot has, of course, as we all know, but from what they taught me at school coppers only came into being a hundred years or so ago.'

'You sure of that, Frankie?' said his girl.

'Well, isn't it right? Sir Robert Peel?'

Frankie's girl was pensive and amazed. 'A time before there were any coppers?' she said. 'I can't believe it.'

'The world,' Frankie said, 'seems to have got on very well for thousands of years without them, and some day I dare say they'll disappear as suddenly as they appeared. We live in the Age of Coppers: but I don't suppose, like anything else, that it'll last for ever.'

The Madam was displeased at such levity. 'I was of course referring,' she said, 'to law enforcement officers who've always existed, I believe, whatever they may have at the time been called. Two ancient institutions are involved: the profession of love, and the enforcement of the laws that govern it.'

'I still think we could do without them,' Frankie said.

The women all raised brows at this typical masculine irresponsibility (or irrelevant intellectual audacity).

'Anyway,' said Frankie, 'they're the only profession, the coppers, who've never had a hero—ever thought of that? They've put up statues to Nell Gwynne and Lady Godiva, but never so far as I know to a copper.'

'There may perhaps,' said the Madam, eyeing him acidly, 'be yet *another* male profession that's not been commemorated by a statue.'

Frankie laughed: so generous a laugh that it put everyone at ease again. 'Oh, I grant you that!' he said. 'Just imagine it! A public monument to Pal Joey! Still,' he continued, 'that's how I feel. They say that coppers suppress crime. My own belief is they create it: they spread a criminal atmosphere where none existed. After all—look at it from their point of view. A soldier to succeed needs wars, whatever he may say to the contrary. In just the same way as a copper, to get on, needs crime.'

The Madam, who'd by now decided Frankie was a nuisance but on the whole a comparatively harmless one since his girl seemed to have him well in hand, said in a spirit of compromise, 'I'm prepared to allow you, Frankie, that the recent changes in the laws, so far as our business is concerned, have led to situations which make corruption very much more probable.'

'Yeah. But try telling the British public that!'

'I should not,' said the Madam with a faint smile, 'dream of doing anything of the kind.'

'Maybe not. But until the day when they wake up and find what's happened, the great British public will continue to believe in coppers. And shall I tell you why?'

Nobody wanted to hear, but their collective, unspoken female wisdom considered it simpler to let him get it off his chest than to try to interrupt him.

'In the first place,' said Frankie, 'it's *not* because the public as a whole respects the law, but merely because it's law-abiding, which is a very different matter.'

A bell rang, and the confidential maid departed.

'As a matter of fact they're not even so much law-abiding, as *respectable*: take away an Englishman's respectability, and you've taken his most cherished possession.'

The bisexual whore rose silently and also took her leave.

'Now, deep down we English, let me tell you, are a cruel and violent race. Yes, you may look at me like that, but cruel and violent is what we are. But at the same time we're respectable, like I've said, and have to live jam-packed on a microscopic island. So what do we do? We check our violence and cruelty by force: by our own force of will and by employing a force of witch-doctors or high-priests called coppers, who help us to restrain ourselves and who we worship for it.'

Frankie's girl shifted a bit uneasily; but the Madam remained calmly poised upon her Louis XXII chair.

'And what is more, just like the tribe does to the witch-doctor, we unload our guilty feelings on the coppers; the law, here in England, is the licensed keeper of our own bad conscience.'

There was a silence.

'And there's another aspect. Being cruel and violent, the Englishman knows he *might* commit a crime: a big one: headline stuff! Of course—he doesn't. But being at heart something of a criminal, he worships the man that he himself's set up to punish him if he did so.'

The Madam at last rose. 'I see, dear,' she said gently to the girl, 'your Frank's a very thoughtful boy. I hope for your sake his cock is even bigger than his brain.'

MR JUSTICE

THE habit of coppers of wishing or being ordered to 'hunt in pairs' has one great disadvantage to lone-wolves and philosophers in the Force. Long hours shared in isolation with one single other man will cause all but the most resolute or bone-headed to exchange confidences (which they should or would have preferred to have kept to themselves) with their momentary companion. So does the warder chat with the condemned prisoner, the isolated soldier with his erstwhile foe, or do the husband and wife who've already signed the deeds of separation if circumstances force them to be alone together.

The star sleuth sat with Edward in the bread-delivery van: and even his resilient spirit was cracking beneath the strain. He deeply resented, in the first place, that the Detective-sergeant had given him (him!) this flatfoot job to do. And as for Edward, if the boy had been really stupid as most of them were, or really inspired as he himself was, his company would have been at any rate tolerable. But Edward's mixture of brains and of professional ignorance and ineptitude (for so the star sleuth esteemed him) were nicely calculated to irritate an expert performer who had but recently himself fathomed many of the major mysteries of the copper's art.

'Another one going in,' said Edward, making an entry in his note-book.

'You can see in the dark?' asked the star sleuth.

'I've trained myself to write without a light,' said Edward.

'Well, you're wasting your time. *I* fill up my note-book *after* the event by use of my well-trained memory, and keep my brains cool for the event itself.'

'Maybe,' said Edward, who was growing sure enough of himself to resent the star sleuth's patronage quite a bit. 'But we've got to make certain your evidence and mine are going to tally.'

'Time enough for that. Though I might tell you one thing, youngster, that you *don't* know yet. They'll tell you the evidence of *two* officers will always nail a conviction. Well, in a magistrate's court that may be so but not, believe me, with a judge and jury—of which I don't think you've yet had a very vast experience.'

'Why?' Edward asked, vexed not to know.

'Here's why. Let's say you and I are on a case—see?—and we've both cross-checked our evidence. Right. When *I* go in to give mine, *you* have to stay outside. And when *you* come in to give yours I can stay in court but I can't speak to you, or alter what I've already said.'

'And so?'

'And so this. The defending counsel if he's got any brains, and most of them have or they wouldn't earn their huge fees, will ask me a-hundred-and-one questions about circumstances we just didn't think of—like was the prisoner wearing a cap or was it a hat?—and then when you come in, ask you the same questions and very probably get a rather different set of answers. This sows quite a bit of doubt in the jury's mind. I've often seen an acquittal got that way.'

'So what do we do?'

'That's it. One prosecuting witness is often better than two, even if uncorroborated. You can't contradict yourself, see: that is, provided you remember all you said if there's a re-examination.'

Edward Justice pondered. 'The courts are very tricky,' he said. 'In fact, I'm beginning to realize what goes on in them's a much bigger battle than all that takes place before you and the prisoner get there.'

'Ah! The light's dawning on you at last! My goodness! If only one young copper in a hundred realized what you've just said!'

Edward was silent.

'I'll tell you something,' said the star sleuth. 'Our real enemy isn't the criminals: it's the courts.'

'Our enemy?'

'Yes. Here's how I see it. *We are the law.* I say this because in the whole United Kingdom we're the only people who really *know*—and I mean *know*—what actually goes on. You admit that's so?'

'And then?'

'Well—picture this. The set-up in the Force we can manipulate, once we know how. And the criminals—well, as you know, there's a thousand and one ways of controlling them. Even in the courts, so long as it's only at the lawyer level, there are pressures that can be brought to bear. For instance: suppose you're a barrister who sometimes prosecutes, sometimes defends. If you win a lot of acquittals you're not likely to get a lot of prosecuting work to do, are you?'

'I suppose not, but . . .'

'Or take solicitors. Most of those the criminals use are living on criminal money themselves and often getting more of it than they should, in ways their professional bodies mightn't like to hear about. Now, they know this, they know we know it and pressures can be brought to bear.'

'Yes, I see that. But when . . .'

'All right, I'm coming to that. *But*, as I said at the outset, in the courts there's one thing we can't get at at all—except in a way that I'll explain to you: and that's the magistrates and judges—certainly, at any rate, the judges—and also to a certain extent the juries. Except—and mark my words—for this: we can get at all three by working on their ignorance, fear and vanity.'

'We can?'

'We can. As for ignorance, remember this. Judges used to be lawyers, and in their careers there's not much they haven't learned about by seeing it passing before them when they were working in the courts.'

'And so?'

'But *seeing* a thing is *not* the same as *living* it. When you go to a theatre you see the show: in fact it's put on for you, and you're in the best seats with the actors all facing you and smiling. But you're still not an actor, are you? You can see a thousand shows, and still know nothing about show-business whatever. Well, with the judges it's the same: they don't really *know*; and if they don't know you can blind them, if only to a limited extent.'

'But fear, you said. They're not afraid of us . . .'

'No? You'd think so, wouldn't you? The justices, here in England, are the top men in the land: way up above the generals and admirals and cabinet ministers, even. But—never forget—judges in history *have* been tried themselves. In fact, over on the Continent it's happened in our lifetime—very often, too. They're way up there, but they've got very far to fall! And if ever they *do*, who do you think will call round in the small hours to collect them?'

'Us?'

'Exactly. We, boy, you see, are even more permanent than they are and they know it. They're not fools, and because of this somewhere deep down they fear us.'

'And their vanity? They're vain, you'd say?'

'Well—I ask you! What's the big, big bribe here in England? Come on—tell me! Is it money? Not a bit of it! Once you get above a certain level it's *honours*, man, and fancy-dress. You think I'm just being sarcastic? No, boy! To be dressed up in wigs and gowns and call himself lord and be surrounded by pomp and circumstance is worth *millions* to almost any Englishman. And judges—well, they love it! And if a man deep inside himself is vain, and what is worse—or better, from our point of view—*publicly* vain, then you can always play upon that weakness. "Yes, my lord. As you say, my lord." And, "As your lordship please." '

Edward reflected deeply, then said to the star sleuth, 'You don't think, then, that beyond us and beyond the courts and judges there's anything like an actual *justice* involved?'

'No.'

'It's all just personalities and procedure?'

'It's conventions: social customs, you might say. These change and alter, often radically, as anyone who's studied history a bit will know. But only one thing doesn't alter—and that's us: the men who *enforce* the laws, whatever they may be. And so I tell you: *we* are the courts, *we* are the judges, *we* are *justice!*' Edward, though highly excited by all this, was not sure by the soft, icy tone of his companion's voice whether he had a madman or a genius (or both) sitting beside him. Now the star sleuth's voice dropped to its normal mumble as he added, 'And even the stupid public and those fools in parliament, in their own way, admit this. Because according to the acts they've passed, if anyone shoots a lawyer—even a judge—and not for robbery, it isn't capital: but if a man kills one of us for any reason in the world, then—boy, he's hanged! This sets us up above the rest—above the lot of them, top men and all! Our lives are protected by the hangman's rope!'

Edward said deferentially but with considerable reserve (as one does when making a remark to anyone which one both wants him to believe and also be able to say, afterwards, one did not mean), 'So according to you, you should make a suspect feel that we, "the law", *are* the law.'

'Yes.'

Then Edward said, 'That's not how the Detective-sergeant sees it, I imagine.'

'I don't suppose so. That pensionable clot!'

'They don't serve their purpose then, according to you, his type?'

'Yes—for all sorts of things that don't really matter. Like clearing the public off the streets as they did so well when old Tito came here, or marshalling crowds when they indulge in political demonstrations, or for horseback parades in Hyde Park when we're drawn up just as if we were *soldiers*! for a royal inspection. For all that, yes. But for the real work: well—what do *you* think?'

'I quite like the old boy,' Edward said.

'I'm not talking about *liking*. Do you respect him?'

Edward didn't answer.

'You've got to make up your mind,' the star sleuth said, 'right from the outset which kind of copper you're going to be: a robot or a man with *power*.'

After a short pause Edward said, 'As a matter of fact, I've found the Detective-sergeant helpful to me.'

'Yeah? Well, I see nothing against that . . .'

'No. He's put me on guard against one or two little things he's mentioned.'

'He has? Such as what? Do you mean that I found out about your girl?'

'So it was you.'

'No secret about it, matey. I'm bound to investigate you a bit, aren't I, if you join our little lot and I'm going to have to put my own life and professional career to a certain extent into your two clumsy hands . . .'

'But did you have to tell anyone?'

'I didn't: nothing reported, I mean. I just *mentioned* it.'

'I don't see the difference.'

'You don't? There's a *lot* of difference, as you'll grow to learn.'

'Is there? Well, here's something for you to learn please, too. I resent your interfering with my private life, and I'll ask you here and now to stop it.'

'Oh! So I'm being threatened! Well! Listen to me, boy, I'm not in the habit of giving advice because it's a thing much too precious to give away and anyhow, the kind of person who *needs* advice never knows how to *use* it if you give it to him. But I will tell you this, and it's entirely for your own good because personally I just don't care a fuck. Drop that girl. Look at it any way you like, if you want to get on—in fact if you want to stay with us at all—well, boy, it's your only logical solution.'

MR JUSTICE (STILL)

LOOKING out of the institutional window (too tall for its width) of his nominal residence at the section-house, Edward was mildly alarmed to see his girl standing on the pavement opposite. Since no message had come up to him that anyone wanted to see him and it was scarcely probable that he'd happened to look out at the precise moment she'd arrived, he was even more alarmed. For she certainly didn't know as well as he did that the most conspicuous possible thing to do, in England, particulary for a woman, is to wait in a public street: even if she'd waited on the anonymous benches of the station itself she'd have attracted far less attention. He hurried down.

Out in the street he saw her some way off, which partly reassured him. And catching up with her he learned with approval but anxiety that she'd kept walking round the block until he'd appeared, and that a matter of some urgency—two, in fact—had brought her out of hiding. The first was that she was pregnant; the second, that someone—nobody yet knew who—had visited her father's house during his absence in peculiar circumstances.

Though she told him the first of these two things last, he genuinely considered it to be in every way the more important. For one reason because it clearly brought—in some way or another—his relationship with his girl to a state of crisis; but even more because this news excited and delighted Edward unexpectedly. Although in their discussions of this possibility they'd both agreed it was for the present highly undesirable, and had taken steps in a rather haphazard way to guard against the danger, Edward had always feared, in secret, that he was somehow incapable of paternity: just as he had not been sure until he'd first loved his girl in that complete and intimate way that he could actually *do* so, it needed the proof positive that she now gave to him that he could without any doubt become a father. Not that he had for the new life in her womb—or for what it might become—as yet any feeling, fatherly or otherwise. What he *did* feel was that his love for her—the total horizon of his whole emotional life—was now—in spite of the manifold complications—entire and wonderful.

'So what shall we do?' she said.

'Let's pop in here for a tea and a sit-down.'

Side by side, and Ted filled with an immense sense of *possession*, they discussed their predicament in quiet voices. 'I suppose you don't want to say it, Edward,' she said, 'but I *could* do away with it.'

'No!'

'Why? Because it's illegal?' And she smiled rather wryly.

'No: because it's too dangerous to you.'

'It's not really . . . Not all *that* dangerous . . .'

'You sure of that?'

'I think so.'

'No! We can't risk anything happening to you.'

'Very well, then. What?'

'You'll have to have it in the normal way.'

'But, Edward. As things are, it won't be exactly normal.'

'You mean us not being wed?'

'Yes.'

'Yes, I know. We must get the position straightened out. That's what I meant to tell you when I came out to you this evening.'

'Why?'

'They've found out about us.'

'Who?'

'Several: it's not officially known to the Force, but there's individuals who know.'

The girl looked at him and said, 'So you won't have to pretend any longer, Edward, that I don't exist.'

'No. They know.'

'I see. So what do we do?'

Edward stared into space, then said, 'If it's you or the Force, I choose you. I can always earn my living some other way, I'm competent, you know, believe me. But I've been thinking a lot, and there may be a way out.'

She looked at him harder.

'If your Dad emigrated.'

'Emigrated? Dad? Why should he?'

'If he sees it's to your advantage and to his own to make a new start, and if I make it worth his while.'

'But Edward: how can you?'

'I think I can. He must have a bit saved of his own, and I believe I can make up the single fare and enough over, given a bit of time.'

'But what difference will it make if Dad should go?'

'I've been looking into precedents: I mean of marriages with girls of—well, of dubious parentage—and it's been okay in several cases if the parents are dead, of course, or gone away for good.'

'You sure?'

'I think they'd wear it—but only if he's right out of the country: Canada or Australia—somewhere like that.'

'I see.'

'But there is one other aspect. Suppose he refused to go. I may have to ask you if you don't mind if I put pressure on him.'

'Pressure? How?'

'Make him believe we're going to get something on him.'

The girl said, 'Oh, Edward! And he's stayed in the clear so long!'

'So he says, I know. But what can we do?'

'And this money, Ted. It's a bit of a race against time, isn't it? I mean you've not got all that many months to get it, and get permission to marry, before I have the baby.'

'I've thought of that: and it's why I'll have to get it quick.'

'I still think you won't shift Dad. Him leave Kensal Green? And take money from you?'

'Well, as a matter of fact he already has done.'

'Dad has? Taken money?'

'Yes. Only to look after it, though. I've already made a bit, you see, and the best person I could think of to look after it for us—I mean the only *reliable* person—was your father.'

'And he agreed?'

'Oh, yes . . . So we've already discussed financial matters.'

'You didn't tell me, Ted.'

'No, dear. I thought it best not. Well: what you say?'

The girl stirred her empty cup. 'For me,' she said, 'it's like this. I want you, Ted, in the best way I can keep you, whatever that turns out to be—but there are limits. I don't mind so much what arrangements you have to make with Dad, but I want you to promise me if he refused to go, and you let me *have* my baby, then you'll marry me even if it means leaving the Force.'

'Okay,' said Edward. 'That's a promise. Though if he *does* refuse to go and I can't make him, I will ask you, all the same, to let me check up on the abortion aspects.'

'What do you mean?'

'Well, dear, I know it's a big sacrifice, but you've made me think and I'd like to have a word with the station doctor—very indirect, of course—about the actual danger. Because if I can't shake your Dad at once and it's only a question of the time it takes to persuade him, it's be a pity to leave the Force if we did manage to persuade him later on.'

'Yes, I see.'

Edward looked at her. 'You mean you don't want an abortion—not in any circumstances?'

'I haven't quite said that . . .'

'And you're not prepared to have the baby out of wedlock . . .'

'No, Ted. That I don't want: if I have him, I want to have him legitimate.'

'All right: I think I've got it. Thank you, dear, for being so reasonable about it all. Now, then. What about this man you said visited your Dad's place?'

'According to Dad, Ted, he's certain someone's been in the house, but there's no sign of breaking and entering or anything at all.'

'Yeah. I think I know who it might be. Your Dad didn't find anything *left* in the place? Nothing compromising, I mean?'

'He didn't say so . . .'

'And nothing missing?'

'He didn't say that either . . . But who do you think it might be, Ted? A thief?'

'No, a copper. Colleague of mine who doesn't like me.'

'But why should he try to harm Dad?'

'To try to harm me. I'll tell you who it is—in confidence—it's one of our vice boys I'm on a job with at the moment—very clever feller and very dangerous—who's got a down on me.'

'But why?'

'I really and truly don't know: but these things do happen in the Force. I'll speak to your Dad about that as well, and put him on his guard. Meantime, I think there's something *you* could do to help.'

'Me? How?'

Edward smiled at her. 'If I pointed out this feller to you, do you think you might consider trying to play up to him a bit?'

'How? You mean flirt with him, or so?'

'Yes. Nothing more than that . . . But it might help to find a way to get something on him, too, to keep him quiet.'

'Well, I'm not sure, Edward. If you think it's wise . . . But I'm not very glamorous, you know . . .'

'Nor's he. Anyway, we'll see. I'll keep you well in the picture, dear. Glory! What a morning! I'm glad all that's tidied up just now.'

He made to get up, but the girl detained him. 'There is just one other thing,' she said.

'No! Well, in for a penny . . .'

'Listen, Edward. You remember that couple we saw at the wrestling that night, and you commented on, who came to settle in the same block as we do . . .'

'Yeah . . . Whore and her ponce, I'd say. But not my area and not my business—we don't want trouble near the flat . . .'

'No, I know that. But the woman, Ted, the prostitute. She *knows* about us.'

'Knows? How can she know? What makes you think so? Anything she's said?'

'Nothing she's said, but the way she *looks* at me.'

'*Looks* at you! Oh, come off it, darling. What is this: feminine intuition?'

'Edward, she knows *something*: I'm convinced of it.'

'That we're not married, maybe.'

'Something more. The other day a uniformed officer passed by just as I passed *her*, and she looked at *him* and then she looked at me, and she smiled.'

'She smiled!'

'Yes.'

'I'll give her something to smile for . . . And the ponce? Any angles there?'

'No, I've scarcely seen him. He's very discreet.'

'He'd better be. Look, darling, I'll investigate that a bit as well, but now I really must get off down to the station. Thank you for all your loyalty, and thank you for being the most wonderful girl any man ever had and I know I don't deserve it.'

They kissed quietly, the girl very silent, and then went out of the café separately. At the station, the Detective-sergeant called Edward in and said to him, 'Lad, there's been a development.'

'In this Madam case, sir?'

'Yes. What d'you know? She's phoned us.'

'Well, she's got a sauce, sir. What was her reason?'

'There's been a theft—quite a big one, she says. From one of her clients, I dare say, though she didn't say so.'

'And you want me to go down, sir?'

'Yes. Find out all you can, of course, but be very careful *not* to give the impression we've got other ideas about her. She hasn't seen you, has she?'

'Not so far as I know, sir . . . But isn't she taking a chance calling us in like this?'

'Well, *she* evidently doesn't think so . . . Remember, as she sees it her set-up in that place is foolproof. No, her real danger as she probably weighs it up is that the client who's been robbed—if I'm right about that—is more of a danger just at present than we or anyone else are.'

'But sir: she must know *we* know what she's up to.'

'Oh, of course she does! There's no need to hide that fact when you see her—just give her no hint that we're planning a little party for her.'

Edward got up. 'Well, sir, all I can say is I wish I had her nerve.'

The Detective-sergeant smiled, then looked very cautious and said, 'It's just possible between you and me, constable, there may be another angle: and that's why I want you to tread very warily.'

'Sir?'

'It *is* just possible she's subbing somebody—somebody in the Force, I mean—and getting protection. I don't *know* this, mind you —I have to make a few discreet enquiries—but it is a possibility. If that were happening it would, of course, give her extra confidence and we'd have to find out exactly what the situation is—inter-departmentally, I mean—before we actually stage the raid we have in mind.'

'Yes, sir. May I make a suggestion?' The Detective-sergeant nodded. 'It might be, sir, that someone who's got no authority—I mean no real *position*—is taking something from her and making her believe she's got real protection when she hasn't.'

The officer smiled. 'Bright boy,' he said. 'Yes, that's another one that had occurred to me. Any ideas who it might be, if it is?'

'No, sir. Not yet, anyway . . .'

'Well, son, keep me posted. I may be the brains, but you're my eyes and ears, remember. So get out now and use them for me.'

Calling at the front door of the Madam's brothel was, for Edward, a strange experience resembling, perhaps, that of a love-lorn gas-inspector who, contemplating in vain from its exterior for so long the house of his adored one, suddenly finds he's ordered round there on routine business to check the meter. The confidential maid admitted him, and he was soon in the presence of the Madam.

It was instantly apparent that she possessed to handle Edward an enormous asset that neither of them, before meeting, could possibly have predicted. This was that the Madam was a 'motherly' person (in spite of being childless and of having had, ages ago, her ovaries removed) who could soothe the profound solitude that lay at the very centre of Edward's personality, and was the chief cause of his happiness in the Force and of his deep attachment to his girl. But this pit of loneliness was bottomless; and only time or even death would really fill it. Meanwhile, anyone who could restore to Edward something of his sense of self was certain of some measure of his gratitude.

This the old Madam, no mean empirical psychologist, spotted instantly as she sat Edward down on the chintz sofa, perched herself on a chair before him, and laid all her troubles eagerly and confidingly in his broad lap. She kept, she said, as he must know, residential chambers patronized by the very nicest kind of gent. (As a matter of fact she *did* have several curious, permanent tenants in the house in rooms unsuitable, for various reasons, for other purposes, and who she felt lent tone—if not legality—to the premises as a whole.) Very well, then. One of these gentlemen—she was most reluctant to divulge his name, but she could say he was a luminary in the legal profession—had very foolishly (as even luminaries sometimes are) brought a young woman to his apartment, and after this young woman's departure he'd noticed that a snuff-box—for the legal gentleman was addicted to this charming and old-world (or camp and disgusting) habit of taking the stuff—which was not only an heirloom of great sentimental value but also, according to the legal gent, insured for £350, had gone; and if it were not rapidly recovered he'd be forced to make the whole thing public as otherwise the insurance company wouldn't consider a claim. 'I know,' the Madam now concluded, 'that *your* only thought, officer, as the good detective I'm sure you are, is to catch the thief. But *my* chief preoccupation is to get back the snuff-box for my tenant and avoid, if possible, my house getting publicity and an undesirable bad name.'

Edward, both by interest in the Madam and by professional decorum, had said nothing yet. As she appeared to have finished (always let women *finish*, he'd discovered: there's nothing they like better than for you to interrupt them), he said to her, 'Who do you suspect? The girl?'

The Madam blinked her eyes and said, 'It must be her. Who else could it be?'

'This girl been here before?'

'Well, yes, as a matter of fact, yes, she has on one or two occasions. And I've always thought her—the little I've seen of her, of course, for I don't interfere with my tenant's private affairs though I do, naturally, keep an eye on things—a very attractive and well-spoken young lady. But there is one other thing about her.'

The Madam paused and Edward, eyeing her coolly, still said nothing.

'I happen to know,' the Madam said, 'she has a boy friend who I think she calls Frankie who I *don't* think is a very desirable sort of young man at all. I did see them once together, as it happens, and I wasn't favourably impressed by him. I'm not saying, mind you, that he did it or even that he egged her on. But I *do* know he's an undesirable influence and I have, of course, told my tenant that the girl is not to visit my house again under any circumstances whatever.'

'I may need,' said Edward, 'to talk to your tenant. But meanwhile you'd better give me the girl's address.'

The Madam instantly gave it. Edward looked at it, remained impassive, then looked at her. 'May I ask you, madam,' he said, 'how you happen to have this girl's address at your finger-tips?'

A shaft of venom came into the Madam's eyes as they fluttered, and she said, 'My tenant told me it.'

'How did *he* know?'

'*That*, I couldn't say.'

'I see. And when you saw her with this friend of hers, where was it?'

'I don't see . . .

'Where was it?'

'In the street.'

'Not here?'

'Certainly not!'

'And not at the address you've given me?'

'Of course not! I don't even know where it is—except, of course, that it's somewhere up in Kilburn.'

'Very well,' said Edward, rising. 'Thank you very much.'

The Madam came closer, looked up at him like a corrupt innocent in a Rossetti painting, and putting one ringed hand on his vigorous arm said, 'I *do* hope, officer, you can recover this jewel for me with the minimum of fuss.'

'I'll do my best.'

She lowered her eyes, then said, 'My tenant—confidentially, of course—would be willing to offer a quite considerable reward if it were returned to him without any publicity. I don't know how much —he hasn't said—but certainly at least half of its full value.'

'I'll remember that,' said Edward.

MR LOVE AND MR JUSTICE

FRANKIE was sitting drinking lager and lime with the star ponce, and his girl was sulking in the adjacent bedroom. She was sulking, in the first place, because she didn't approve of Frankie's friend being there at all. In earlier days he'd never have taken a silly chance like that (hadn't she always told him—business and pleasure *must* be kept quite separate?) and now, really, he was getting careless (the number one—short of impotence—defect in any ponce).

But the chief and most vital source of argument had been about her miscarriage. In spite of precautions unwanted pregnancies, in a prostitute's life, can occur as they can in anybody's (if only, she thought, the Americans or the Russians or whoever it was would hurry up and perfect those magic pills you popped into your mouth) and Frankie's girl, in the past, had always taken these mishaps in her stride, seen her favourite doctor (up in Tufnell Park), rested up afterwards and gone back to work again. This, without telling Frankie, she had recently done once more and he, when she told him, had exploded in a rage! Would the child have been his, he'd asked? Well—almost certainly: at any rate, very likely. Then didn't she realize, the stupid bitch, he wanted her to have his son if nature sent him? Why the hell hadn't she *consulted* him about it?

Now, in the first place, it'd honestly never occurred to her that he might feel like this; and in the second—well, both as a woman and as a prostitute wasn't it *her* affair? Why! the man was beginning to behave to her like a *husband*! And to make matters worse, because of her resting there was no ready money—and Frankie, if you please, 'didn't like to' touch their *savings*! Well! What in the hell are savings for? So she brooded in the bedroom, doing her nails nineteen times each and wondering if she should sink her dignity and go in and look at the telly. Masculine laughter, coming from the adjoining room, added mightily to her exasperation.

Looking up (as we do when the palaeolithic man inside us telegraphs his warning), she saw something that roused all her professional alertness and—like a ship's officer who, in a storm, may instantly forget a quarrel or postpone it—she hastened to the room next door. 'Frankie,' she cried. 'You remember that couple at the wrestling?'

'Eh? Yeah.'

'Well—*he's* coming over.'

'Who is it?' said the star ponce, whose reflexes were also racing at a calm and well-oiled tempo.

'A copper,' Frankie said, '—or I believe so. He's shacked up with a girl here—something shady, I don't know what—and he's never given us any kind of trouble . . .'

'Well, he's coming over,' said the girl.

'You want to go?' said Frankie to his friend.

'Why should I—if you don't want me to?'

'Thanks, pal. I may possibly need a witness. Baby, as for you, you'd better get back in that bedroom.'

The girl made as if to speak and then retired—but grabbing, on her way, a large pile of Yank mags. The two men took another tranquil drink, nerves tingling, waiting for that big event in the ponce's life—the *knock*.

It came.

Frankie got up, opened the front door, and closed it behind him so that he faced Edward on the balcony. He said nothing at all and looked at Edward, relaxed and not particularly hostile, in the eyes.

'I expect you know who I am,' said Edward.

'Sure. It's written all over you,' Frankie said.

Edward smiled slightly and said, 'Could I come in?'

'You're *asking* to?' said Frankie.

'Certainly. It's an enquiry . . . I haven't got a warrant or anything like that . . .'

'I didn't suppose you had or you wouldn't have asked me, and you wouldn't have been alone.'

'Well. Can I come in?'

'I don't see why not.'

Frankie opened the door, invited Edward to sit down but did not offer him a drink or, for that matter, introduce him to the star ponce —who throughout the interview did not look at Edward (or be seen to) any more than Edward did (or seemed to do) at him.

'I'll come straight to the point,' Edward said. 'It's about a theft. You may know nothing whatever about it, and I may be disturbing you for nothing, in which case, of course, I apologize. But on the other hand if you could help me at all over it, I think it might be to your advantage.'

'So far,' said Frankie, 'you haven't said a thing I understand.'

'No. Well, to make it brief. Can I be frank?'

'If any copper ever was . . .'

Edward smiled. 'Well, put it like this. The young lady you live with has been in business, I believe, up till quite recently at a certain premises. Do I make myself clear?'

'Go on . . .'

'Well, now. It's been reported to me that at these premises there's been a theft.'

'Yeah? Of what?'

'A snuff-box.'

'A what?'

'A jewelled snuff-box of a certain value which we—and the person who's lost it, naturally—are anxious to recover.'

'I suppose they would be.'

'Yes. Well—that's all I have to tell you.'

The two men looked at each other. And their looks had one thing in common (which is a very rare one among coppers and among ponces, and even among any men at all) which was that neither feared the other in the least.

Edward got up. 'I expect you know,' he said, 'where you can find me if there's anything that you can tell me soon. But it would have to be soon, please, because if I can't settle this thing one way then I'll be obliged, you see, to settle it another.'

'Yes,' Frankie said, rising too. 'I know where I can find you. You live over there, don't you, with a young woman?'

Edward nodded.

'I didn't know,' said Frankie, 'that in the Force they allowed you that particular kind of freedom.'

'Well,' Edward said beside the door, 'I dare say, whatever

profession or activity you may have, you never find that you're entirely free in it.'

He smiled slightly and Frankie let him out. Then cutting short the star ponce (who had accumulated a wealth of professional diagnosis of the situation that he was positively bursting his handsome body to impart), Frankie went into the bedroom, closed the door behind him, pulled his girl to her feet and said, 'Have you been stealing?'

'Stealing, Frankie?'

Frankie slapped her face. She slapped back. Frankie slapped her really hard and she fell down on the bed. Outside, the star ponce slightly smiled: the familiarity of the episode was reassuring.

The girl looked up at him and said, 'Frankie, that's the first time you've hit me.'

'It's not.'

'It's the first time you've hit me like *that.*'

'Well, I want an answer. Did you knock off a snuff-box at the Madam's?'

The girl looked incredulous, then furious, then laughing a bit hysterically she rummaged among her lingerie and cried, 'You mean *this*?'

'Yeah. Why you pinch it?'

'*Pinch* it? Are you crazy? The old bastard *gave* it to me.'

'You lying?'

'Oh, go and get stuffed, Frank! You're needling me too much!'

'He gave it to you, you say?'

'Of course he fucking gave it to me! He was high as a kite at the time and now I suppose he's saying I took it from him in his drunken stupor. Well—what should I have done? Got his permission in writing? He kept tucking it inside my bra and saying, "*Chérie*, this is for you," and crap like that.'

Frankie held the box, looked at her and said, 'I'm sorry, baby. But you should have told me.'

'What was there to tell? I've had presents before, often enough—dozens of them, I've had.'

'Things like this?'

'Why? Is it all that valuable?'

'That's what the copper was here about—I suppose you heard.'

'No. I tried to listen, but he spoke too low.'

Frankie considered, put the box in his pocket and said, 'Look, baby. I want you to go out and take a little walk.'

'Why?'

'Because I say so. Just for an hour or so.'

'You want to talk it over with your pal?'

'Yeah.'

'*I*'m too stupid to give an opinion, I suppose?'

'Just do as I say, baby, there's a honey.'

The girl agreed, not because she thought Frankie was right but because she knew the convention of male sagacity in crises—particularly those closely related to the law—was a powerful one in 'the game'; and come to that, it was the boys themselves who so often *were* in greater danger.

'Okey-doke,' she said. 'You win.'

When she'd gone, the two men embarked on their analysis of the angles. 'As I see it,' said the star ponce as a Queen's counsel might to a promising junior, 'it's quite clear the copper wants the box and not your girl. I'd also say he's called here on his own initiative. Reasons: he came alone and he was very nice, which coppers never do or are if they mean business.'

'He wants the box for himself, you think?'

'No: there's probably a reward attached. Well, if you can square it with your girl I'd say the simplest is to give it to him *but*, if you take my tip, you'll do it in front of two witnesses—outside the game, if possible—*and* if possible, invisible to him.'

'I'm certain,' said Frankie, 'he's up to something with that girl of his he doesn't want generally known. So I don't think he's likely to pursue the matter very far, knowing I might bring *that* up. I'd better try to find out exactly what his set-up with the woman is.'

'If he gets awkward at all,' said the star ponce, 'you might try to implicate her. Lay her, I mean.'

'Boy, have you *seen* her?'

'No. But all women are much the same from the navel down. There are, of course,' the star ponce continued, 'other aspects. You could consider, through your own woman, trying to have a go at him—I mean some compromising situation with witnesses and perhaps a camera.'

'Yeah.'

'Or,' the star ponce went on, warming to his work, 'there's possibly this other angle. I couldn't help hearing you and your girl having a bit of an argument.'

'No?'

'No. Now, I don't know . . . I don't know how you're fixed and I'm not trying at all to interfere. But if it *did* happen you wanted to cut out from the lass and latch on with another—and believe me, Frankie, there's plenty of them who'd not say no—this would certainly be the opportunity.'

'You mean,' said Frankie smiling slightly, 'I could just disappear and let the law take its course?'

'That's it! It's not you, after all, who's committed any theft . . . supposing, that is, she's wrong about what she said to you and it *was* one—and at any rate it *looks* like one to some people, doesn't it. Well, you could fix things in that way: just leave her and the copper to sort the matter out.'

Frankie got up. 'No, I don't think so, boy,' he said. 'I'm not tied to that chick—don't think that—I'm not tied to *any* woman and I never will be. But I'd certainly never shop her, and that's what your suggestion would amount to.'

'If you say so. What I was doing, Francis, was considering all the angles and the aspects.'

'Oh, I'm very grateful, man—don't misunderstand me.'

The star ponce rose too. 'So what you going to do—I mean with the box?' he said.

Frankie took it out of his pocket and threw it a foot in the air. 'Hang on to it a while and see. Perhaps I'll do a little investigation on my own account just like a copper. Perhaps there might even be a little bit of rough stuff, too, like they do from time to time.'

MR LOVE

In the next days Frankie took the following precautions.

He visited the Stepney Bengali, told him to draw three hundred pounds for him, bought a single air ticket to Monrovia and checked the validities in his passport.

He had a long conversation with the janitor at the Kilburn flat—who, he'd long discovered, had formerly seen harpooning service upon whalers—made him within the privacy of his quarters at the lodge a comradely gift (for old times' sake), and suggested it was undesirable to have among them in the block a copper in disguise who'd probably get busted anyway for living with a woman out of wedlock, and that if this copper's flat by any chance should become vacant somehow, he, Frankie, knew someone who'd be very glad to offer double—maybe more—the usual key-money that he, the janitor, expected.

He then followed Edward's girl one morning she went out shopping and, choosing his moment in an empty street came up suddenly beside her, immediately said, 'Give your copper boy friend this,' dropped a little package in her shopping-bag, and made off at a steady pace before she could reply.

To round matters off he sent this anonymous telegram, by telephone from a call-box, to the local station of the Force: WHERE DOES EDWARD JUSTICE LIVE AND WHY.

Finally, to clear the decks for any possible action he sent his girl to spend a short holiday with her faith-healing Mum at Walthamstow. She departed reluctantly under protest, and in the taxi said to him, 'Frankie, you ever thought of getting married?'

'We've discussed that. No.'

'I mean know. The way things are, and now you've saved up a bit.'

Frankie looked at her. 'Are you trying to tell me, babe,' he said, 'you'd consider giving up the game if we got wed?'

'Yeah. As a matter of fact that's it.'

'Well! That's rather sweet of you! But honest, baby, I'm not the marrying kind.'

'No, I suppose not. But think it over, will you, when this thing blows over? We could move up north somewhere, one of the ports, and open up a caff or club or something for the seamen.'

'And the girls!'

'Well, why not! For the both of them. But on the up-and-up—legitimate.'

He kissed her. 'I'll think about it, dear,' he said.

She reached forward, pulled aside the driver's window and yelled at his neck, 'Not that way—that way!' then took Frankie's arm again and said, 'I wish you'd let me handle all this for you, dear.'

'And what would you do?'

'Me? Use my fanny for you. I mean, find out why they're getting at you, and who, and offer him the best time of his life.'

'Thanks, dear—but no good. A copper wouldn't know a really good time if he had it.'

MR JUSTICE

EDWARD was closeted with his girl's disreputable father: who as Edward's affairs had grown in their complexity had become, in a sense, increasingly his own. For the older man this new relationship was possible because Edward now stood revealed in spite of his hateful uniform as a creature, like himself, of common clay. Not that the father ever forgot Edward's status: in spite of their growing intimacy Edward, for him, was still more a copper than a son-in-law-to-be.

Amid the confusion of the father's workroom with its radios and tellies and cameras and miscellaneous junk, Edward unfolded all the plots and counter-plots by which he was now surrounded. One matter, at any rate, was satisfactorily disposed of—or almost so—between them: the father was willing to go abroad. A sufferer from lumbago, he believed the heat of the Central African Federation would benefit his condition; and in a land where brains and technical skill were needed (and manual labour which was painful to him would be available in plenty), he thought that he would find his niche. But what, Edward countered, about the immigration regulations? Wouldn't they check up on his past career?

To overcome this obstacle the older man had imagined a truly Napoleonic solution which he now disclosed to Edward with a crafty smile. He'd not applied for a resident permit but for one for visitors, and had already been sent the appropriate application forms. To Question 18, which asked, candidly, 'Have you ever been in prison?' he had simply and boldly written, 'No': relying on the magic that a completed form held *in itself* to those who had devised it and who, he imagined, would be most unlikely to check up; anyway, his 'trouble' had been a long while ago, and if *they* said 'No,' well, all right, he'd try somewhere else climatically suitable. If the visa was granted he would go there, look around, establish contacts and, he was certain, make himself useful enough for them to want to keep him in the Federation on a permanent basis. It was really after all, he added, only *political* undesirables they were anxious to exclude from the Rhodesias.

Edward on his side disclosed the business of the snuff-box, and the hopeful prospects its probable recovery held out of supplementing the nest-egg of the prospective emigrant. Edward did not consider it likely that Frankie, given time to meditate, would refuse to yield it up; and if he did prove obstinate, that situation could be faced as it arose. To bring pressure on the ponce he had, after reflection, hit on this: he'd called up Frankie's girl from a public-box (on the number kindly supplied, for a consideration, by the flat janitor—a good friend of his and a special constable, as well as an ex-seaman on a whaler) and the moment the receiver had been raised, had said immediately, 'Miss, this is a well-wisher in the Force to say if Frankie does as he's asked I promise there'll be no further trouble,' hanging up instantly without waiting for a reply.

'So that leaves us,' Edward said, 'with one vital thing outstanding: this visit you had, and who I've told you I think is at the bottom of it.'

The ex-criminal reflected. 'What I don't fathom yet,' he said, 'is this. If as you say it's a pal of yours in the Force who's trying to harm you by framing me—and from what I know of you and your pals the thing, in itself, is very possible—why doesn't he try to plant something on *you* direct? And if he chooses me, why does he come here and not plant anything at all?'

'Look,' Edward answered. 'I love your girl: now, you believe that, don't you? whatever you think about me and about the Force. Well, this man he's a clever one. He knows if he can get at you and so get at *her*, he gets at me worse than any other way. Also, he knows I'm on my guard and naturally I'd recognize him if he came snooping around my place at all.'

'Then why did he just come snooping around mine here and nothing else? Not plant anything, if that's what you think he's up to?'

'Well, it's a way we have: perhaps I shouldn't tell you, but it's this: always reconnoitre, if you can, before you act. It's laid down in all the manuals.'

'Is it? Oh, I see.'

'Besides, he may not have had the right *thing* to plant on you until he saw the situation here: I mean, what sort of item might seem credible.'

Edward realized his girl's father was looking very hard at him indeed. 'So you *do* plant things, you bastards,' the father said.

Edward paused, then answered, 'Look: do we have to go into all that again?'

'Sonny boy!' the father said, 'let me tell you something. I'm so glad I'm not you: that's all. You've all got minds like mazes: trick upon trick until you tie yourself in knots. Take care you don't get lost inside your own maze, boy, some day!'

Edward waited patiently for the father's natural resentment to subside (coppers are used to this—as used as doctors are to pain), then said, 'Now the thing is, he may come again. And if he does, this time I want to catch him water-tight, report him to my Detective-sergeant and get him busted, or anyway transferred. My Detective-sergeant doesn't like him, you see, and *none* of us likes a man who shops his comrades.'

Now, the father waited silently.

'So here's what I suggest. He'll very probably come here again soon and if he does, this time he'll have something with him. So we've got to catch him in the act. You follow me?'

'Yeah. I'm listening.'

'Now, I want to ask my girl—your girl—to come back and stay here with you for a while.'

'Why? You were anxious enough to get her away from me a time ago . . .'

'I know. But I want her out of the flat up there until I get things straightened out with this ponce I mentioned and also—this is the point and hear me out carefully please, don't raise your voice or be hasty—I want her here *when* this so-called star-sleuth colleague of mine shows up on the premises.'

'Why?'

'To fix him.'

'How?'

Edward looked round the room. 'Now, you've got cameras,' he said, 'and flashes. I want you to lock all the rooms every night except where my girl will be sleeping. And I want you, if possible, to snap the pair of them together.'

'Together doing what?'

'Nothing! What you take me for?'

'Well, what you take *me* for?'

'I said—don't be hasty! As soon as he's in the house I'll tell her she's to run out to him, even if he doesn't come into her room at all: you know—dishevelled and distressed and so on: she'll do it all right for me.'

The father looked at Edward and shook his head. 'And that's who my daughter wants to marry,' he said simply. 'Well, I give up! And how do we know he's in the house at all? I didn't last time . . .'

'But you were out. And you weren't expecting him. Look! He's not a magician, he can only get in through the doors or windows . . . You've not got a skylight?'

'No.'

'Well, I want you to wire them all: the ones he can get in at, anyway. Can you do that?'

'I could do . . .'

'Something silent: a light comes on in your room—or a faint buzz—then you grab your camera and go into action.'

'I see. So I go to bed with my camera every night for weeks?'

'No: a week should be enough. Then the case that we're both working on is over—anyway, the raid we're planning will be—and he'll probably lay off me after that. It's because we're together on this job that he's so riled and jealous. Once it's over I'll just warn him off, and tell him I know what he's been up to.'

'Why don't you do that now?'

'Because I want to compromise him if I can: I mean, turn the tables on him so that he'll never try anything again! Show him who I am and who he is!'

The father looked at Edward with faint pity. 'You think the photo you speak of, if I took it, would do that? Do they believe photos at all, then, in your Force?'

'I won't even have to show it to them: only to him and say I've got the negative.'

'And you think he's all that dangerous to you?'

'He and my Detective-sergeant are the only colleagues, so far as I can tell, that know about me and my girl. I think the Detective-sergeant's okay—I think he likes me; and if I can shut the other one up, by the time we've got you away we can put in the application properly and get married.'

'When you've got rid of me.'

'Don't be like that! You know your girl loves me and I do her and this is the only way I can see to fix it!'

The father put his hand in quite a friendly way on Edward's arm. 'You know,' he mildly said, 'you really are a nasty piece of work—a proper little scheming bastard. Also, I think you're over-wrought and what you're asking me to do's a lot of nonsense. Why don't you take a holiday for a while?'

'My leave's not due yet—and I need it for the honeymoon.'

'Yes. That's the funny thing—she loves you. She really does: Eve alone knows why. Well, I'll see what I can do. But I want you to understand there's to be no funny business with my girl inside my house, and the only *promise* I'm making you is that if you raise the balance of the funds, I'll go.'

The front bell rang and both men stiffened, as if it were already the star sleuth on the doorstep. But it was the girl: manifestly upset, and bursting with fell tidings.

Getting her story wrong-way-round chronologically (though right way in point of urgency), she began by crying out. 'It's disappeared!' Calm and adroit questioning by Edward extracted the story of Frankie's alarming deposition of the snuff-box in her shopping-bag, how she'd got home, found out what it was, put it away safely until Edward should arrive, but that now it had gone from where she'd placed it.

'And where was that?'

'Among my lingerie.'

'And why did you go out again?'

'Just to the pictures.'

'For how long?'

'As long as the big film.'

'It *must* be him!' Edward concluded. 'Well! Now we know what he's going to try and plant here.'

'Must be who?' asked the girl.

But the men ignored her. 'It couldn't,' the father said, 'be that ponce himself who's changed his mind and got it back . . . ?'

'Listen! The man's not crazy!'

'But if it's your colleague wasn't it enough, if he wanted to compromise you, to find it in your flat?'

'No. No, because he knew I could say I had it there ready to turn it in. But if it's found *here*, then it looks black for me—*and* for you: don't forget that!'

'I hadn't,' the father said. 'But there's one more thing. Couldn't it be he'll just take it to the Madam and get the reward instead of you?'

'How does he know she's offered one?'

'Well—he might know.'

'No, I don't think so,' Edward said emphatically, sure of his diagnosis of the star sleuth's psychology. 'And what *I'm* going to do is this. Take a big chance, sit tight and wait for him to move: try to plant it here like I've explained. Then, if *you* two co-operate like you've promised, I get him *and* I get the box back and the reward!'

'What have I promised?' asked the girl with trust and deep anxiety in her eyes.

'More than perhaps you realize,' said her father.

Edward enfolded her with a truly loving arm. 'It's quite simple to explain,' he said, 'and if you come out with me in the garden I'll put you in the picture and fill in all the details for you. It's just one or two things that might look wrong, I admit, if it was any other girl than you who did them or anyone else who asked you to do them other than myself. But things, as you'll see, that are very necessary to us for our salvation.'

MR LOVE

A VOICE behind Frankie as the barber went to get hot towels said softly, 'Hullo, ponce!'

He didn't move an inch because it might be someone else the

voice referred to or, if it was to him, he was a good professional, and in any case a *man* doesn't let a stranger see he thinks he may have been insulted. He looked slowly up at the mirror but could see only a leg reflected. Then, after interminable business with the towels, he looked again and saw on the leg's knee a hand holding the unknown client's snuff-box.

This was too much. He got up, much to the hurt indignation of the barber who'd far from terminated his ministrations, and turned to see an extremely ordinary young man who (perhaps because his very nondescriptness made him the perfect substance for the imprint of his trade) had, quite unmistakably, COPPER written all over his body and the soul that looked through his eyes. The snuff-box had now disappeared, and this person rose, walked outside ahead of Frankie, strolled on a bit then stopped. Frank followed after. 'Recognize it?' the man said, whipping the thing out again.

'I might do.'

'Ah!' (Almost a sigh).

It was at once evident to Frankie that the danger was not immediate—for otherwise this cop would have said simply, 'Come along,'—and yet that in some deeper sense he couldn't fathom the danger was actually greater than if he'd been arrested on the spot. The two men stood silent, then the copper said, 'A junior colleague of mine has turned this in to me.'

'Oh, has he?'

'Yes. There's a reward attached to it, as I dare say you may have guessed.'

'Oh, is there?'

'But I'm not taking it myself, of course. Because this reward, you see, is unofficial: and me, I like doing things through channels according to the book. So I'm turning it in myself to my superiors.'

'Why you tell me all this?'

'I thought you might like to hear it.'

As Frankie well knew, most 'questions' are in reality inverted statements of the questioner that reveal facts he knows (or doesn't know—another kind of fact) as much as they may ask for them. So far, all of his own had been of the neutral, unloaded, noncommittal kind. But he now could not resist asking one that revealed to the star sleuth a very great deal indeed (even more than the words, the tone in which it was uttered)—in fact at this juncture, all he really wanted to know: and that was, 'Why did he turn it in to you, this colleague of yours you mention?'

The star sleuth smiled. 'Got windy, I expect. Shaky. Lost his nerve. Decided this thing was too hot for him to hold and he'd better surrender it and forget about any possible private arrangement.'

Frankie said nothing: but his face, the star sleuth was delighted to observe, wore the expressionless look which in strong men of generous temperament denotes a mounting anger.

'There may be repercussions, naturally,' the star sleuth added.

Frankie stood waiting for something more to happen, but nothing did. He turned and walked off, his loose lithe body unnaturally stiff. The star sleuth saw him hail a taxi.

Then he himself returned to the barber's shop and went to the public telephone. He dialled a Walthamstow number and said would they please pick up the woman he'd mentioned earlier and have her sent over, but if the man showed up not to bother about him at all or answer any questions. The customers in the shop (and the proprietor) made a great show of not listening to this, and after the officer's departure burst into speculative chatter.

MR JUSTICE

THE summons, for Edward, to the office of the Detective-sergeant reached him while he was reading back files in the CID records room. One of Edward's greatest delights since he had won himself this job was to retire, in spare moments, to the records section (presided over by a sour, grizzled, gnomic officer who was pensioned already in all but name) and there read over ancient 'cases'. These dead tales written in the stereotyped language of reports delighted him; and he loved to read into the enormous spaces between their amateur-typed lines, and fill in the wealth of probable, actual details that his imagination and his brief experience suggested to him. '*Sir: I have made discreet enquiries concerning the above-named . . .*' had, for him, all the childhood fascination of 'Once upon a time'.

These folders, dating back for years (and even more so—could he have but seen them!—the massive stacks of antique files assembled in steel cabinets at faraway headquarters), confirmed his belief that within the Force there is guarded and enshrined a principle which is eternal: that power is given by societies to enforce their order in a state of secrecy. Secrecy, order and might, for Edward, were almost holy things and all admirable *in themselves*. And of their dignity and virtue, the files and manuals and card-indexes were the sacred books that he revered.

Indeed, it was not enough to say of Edward—as might be of many excellent men among his colleagues—that he was well-qualified to be a copper: that he had strength, common-sense, intuition, and obedience to hallowed ritual and his superiors. These of themselves would have made him a man marked out for good and worthy things. But Edward possessed two rarer qualities that made his senior officers (as abbots might, or generals of an Order) observe him closely: a moral sense which, though strong, was entirely empirical and would draw its strength uncritically from the institution that he served; more precious still, an attitude towards the Force which could be described without mockery or a great exaggeration, as mystical. Powerful, secret orders of whatever kind attract such men: and the lay Force in this respect was no exception.

It caused, therefore, the Detective-sergeant (who'd recognized in Edward a man of the same qualities, but far greater potential gifts than he possessed himself) some pain to see so born a novice do such foolish things. And being old in the Force and not far from retirement (and so already almost beyond ambition), the Detective-sergeant had decided that if he could, he'd give this young postulant the penances and scourgings which alone at a critical time of his novitiate might save a born copper for the Cause. He looked up from his typewriter, told Edward severely to sit down, remorselessly banged on his page to its conclusion then whipped it out and said, 'Now look, son, this won't do. I've had more than one complaint about you.'

'Sir?'

'Yes, *sir*: several. The first is this: a telegram of all things. Take a look at it, please, and tell me just what it means.'

Edward did. 'It's evidently, sir,' he said, 'an ill-wisher who's hinting I've been staying at the flat in Kilburn with my girl I told you of already.'

'And you have been *staying* there? I mean as man and wife?'

'Yes, sir. But that's over now. She's back with her father, sir, until he goes away.'

'With her father? Going away?'

'Yes, sir. My girl's father's emigrating, and I wanted to consult you about that, sir, if I may.'

'One thing at a time. Now what about this?'

The Detective-sergeant had lifted the plastic cover of his typewriter to reveal, sitting on his potent but unglamorous desk, the snuff-box.

Instantly and calmly (for which the Detective-sergeant gave him points) Edward said, 'I've never seen that thing yet in my life, sir.'

'No?'

'But I shall tell you all I know about it.'

'I'm listening. I might tell *you* I've had it checked for prints . . .'

'You won't find mine, sir. But you might find my girl's.'

The Detective-sergeant covered it once more with the moulded plastic box. 'As a matter of fact,' he said, 'we didn't find anybody's: it's been wiped.'

This brief respite (for which Edward gave the Detective-sergeant no points) enabled Edward rapidly to readjust his theory. 'I'm not surprised to hear it's been wiped, sir,' he said steadily, 'if I'm right about who I think last had it and turned it in to you.'

'Go on . . .' said his superior.

'A colleague of mine, sir,' Edward said, his voice rising slightly (for after all, what harm *had* he done to the star sleuth? His indignation was entirely authentic), 'who saw fit to interfere in a case you gave me that I was handling in my own way one hundred per cent according to regulations, as I understand them.'

'Go on . . .' said the Detective-sergeant.

Edward now told his tale. Experience and native wit had taught him that the closer your story adheres to the truth the more convincing it will sound, and the more difficult it will be to demolish; and that having decided on a story, one must tell it (whatever it may be) with complete assurance and conviction.

His tale tallied with reality in most essential respects. He had visited the ponce Frankie on a tip-off from the Madam, and suggested he'd better find the box, or else. The ponce Frankie who, presumably, had recovered it from his woman, had later given it to Edward's girl, fearing, probably, to hand it to Edward personally. During his girl's absence from her flat the box had been purloined by, he suspected, the star sleuth.

'Why do you think *he* took it?' said the Detective-sergeant.

'Well, sir,' said Edward, risking a throw, '—didn't he?'

The Detective-sergeant smiled slightly. 'Yes. As a matter of fact, he did.'

'And why did he say he did, sir?'

'We'll come to that . . . Meanwhile, I'd like to go over your story once again. You got this box from the ponce, you say—or your girl did. Was it your intention to turn it in?'

'Of course, sir.'

'You hadn't any other plans for it?'

'Such as what, sir?'

'I'll do the questioning. And if you thought this ponce or else his whore, which are one and the same thing, had got the box, you didn't think of searching their place for it?'

'I hadn't a warrant, sir.'

'You don't need a warrant if there's strong suspicion of a felony. You didn't know *that*? And you didn't think of *arresting* anybody?'

'I had no evidence of theft, sir.'

'Or of consulting me or *anyone* as to procedure?' Edward was silent. 'And tell me constable, please. Why haven't I heard of all this from you before?'

'Look, sir! Put yourself in my position, please. I get the box—or my girl does. Then it disappears. I think I know *who's* taken it, and I think I know *why*. But how could I prove that to you, sir, or to anyone, until this man who stole it from me did whatever I thought he was going to do?'

'And what was that?'

'Make some use of it to harm me, sir.'

The Detective-sergeant looked at his protégé, head on one side, then said, 'If there's one thing I detest here in the Force, it's personal feuds mixed up with what's supposed to be our duties.'

Edward slightly hung his head and said, 'Yes, sir.'

'And secrets among ourselves, so that you don't know who in the Force knows what.'

Edward still bowed his head.

'Avoid it yourself, then. Now. The report I have when this thing was handed to me, is that it was confiscated from you when it was found you hadn't turned it in yourself immediately as you should have done. Now . . .' the senior officer raised (as if halting a two-ton truck) a hand ' . . . I'll be checking up on both your stories and I'd like a word, please, very early, with that girl of yours. Is she on the phone?'

'Yes, sir. At her father's place, she is.'

'Very well. Please ask her to step round. Now for you, we've got work for you: I want you to get a statement from the girl.'

'Which girl, sir?'

'The ponce's: the girl that stole this little object, as we've reason to believe.'

'I'd have to find her, sir.'

'You'll find her in the cells.'

'Sir?'

'We've brought her in.'

'Here, sir?'

'That's what I say.'

'And the man too?'

'No: I want you to pick him up when you've had a go at the woman who kept him in tobacco.'

'But, sir . . . who nicked her?'

The Detective-sergeant looked with kindly irony at his junior. 'I do wish,' he said, 'you younger constables would *not* use slang terms when you're on duty. It was your colleague that arrested her: the one you say has got a down on you.'

'And he hasn't questioned her, then, sir?'

'No.'

'Why?'

'Look, son. *You're* asking *me* a great many questions. He hasn't questioned her because he's lying on his bed.'

'Why, sir?'

'Why? Because he's gone sick, and our doctor has okayed it. Ulcers, he says, he's had them before—though I must say I thought only old men like me were entitled to convenient illnesses when there's a bit of work to finish.' The detective rose. 'However,' he continued, 'that's how it is: so get down to the cells, please, and see what the painted lady's got to say.'

Edward rose also, and hesitating (or seeming to) said, speaking suddenly rather fiercely, 'Sir, I hope when my girl comes here you'll remember that she's pregnant.'

'Oh—ho! And how can I remember that if I didn't know it? Well! You've been cutting things a bit fine, haven't you?'

'I'm hoping, sir, my application for a marriage permit will go through quite quickly.'

'It had better, sonny, hadn't it. Well, get on down.'

MR LOVE

FINDING his girl was gone and that he himself had not yet been molested, Frankie experienced the most unpleasant of anxieties—the sensation of being *conditionally* free: of knowing that sooner or later at some unexpected moment the tap might come upon his shoulder (or, to modernize the metaphor, the twist might come upon his biceps). No state is more unnerving: which is the reason why the Force sometimes lays in wait before it pounces.

There had also been a most unpleasant session with his girl's faith-healing Mum when he had called at Walthamstow and found the old girl prostrated. As his girl's Mum saw it . . . what on earth was a ponce *for* if not to get arrested—if arrest there must be—*instead* of the girl he batted on? To the ancient wrath of an *ad hoc* mother-in-law towards her daughter's companion was added an outraged sense of what was, professionally, appropriate.

In this confusion Frankie recalled a skipper's maxim about what to do if the ship was overtaken by a hurricane. However urgent the case may seem (this old mariner had said), and however thick and black the clouds may gather, before you *do* anything take a few minutes off, at least, and *think*.

This Frankie did in a back room at the Bengali's house in Stepney, for he'd already decided not to set foot again at Kilburn in any circumstances. He reflected on what he might owe to his girl—in the sense of loyalty—and decided he owed nothing: she'd used him, and would have dropped him if need be; he'd used her, and now he would do the same. That was the deal their life together had been based on, and now the deal was over. He'd miss her, yes, and those dawn sessions, but that was all part of being 'in business'. So now he would cut out, leave her, 'the game', and England too for quite a while.

Only two things troubled Frankie slightly about this analysis: that the girl had been knocked off for doing something which—essentially, if not technically—she had not done, that is, helping herself to the fucking snuff-box. Still, he'd done his best to straighten that out for her and she'd been a bloody fool ever to accept it.

The other thing was this mean-minded bastard who had shopped her. He'd done all the cop had asked—got him back the box so that he could collect... well anyway, although admittedly he'd stacked it on the girl to try to scare the pair of them away, they'd *got* the thing and him, he'd kept his mouth shut about the whole performance: whereupon this treacherous sod had turned it in and told them to knock off *his* girl. He'd like to *get* that copper, he decided: but though revenge was sweet, freedom was sweeter, and the thing to do now was get aboard a plane.

MR JUSTICE

Edward's interrogation of the ponce Frankie's girl had been brief and colourful. Yelling at him and calling him improper names (so that he'd had to summon the assistance of a copperess, a thing no male cop likes doing), she'd stuck to her story that the box had been a gift freely given, and when asked about her ponce had said she'd never used the monsters—and if they thought she'd got one why didn't they try to find him?

She further volubly made a point that seemed to Edward (as it might well do to many reasonable persons) a very good one: if they doubted her story, why didn't they go and ask the distinguished client who had given the box to her? Why did they always go for the girls and never for the men who prostituted them? Well—mark her words—they'd better: because if they brought this case against her she'd bloody well have this client subpoenaed—even if she had to use an Asian or an African lawyer who wouldn't be afraid of going for a colleague in the legal profession.

Left to himself Edward, of course, would have turned the girl loose, restored the box rewardless to the Madam, and have forgotten as rapidly as might be about the business. But now this was impossible: the star sleuth's report was in, and his own position, in relation to his girl, was poised in a delicate, precarious state of crisis. No: the only thing to do was ram home the charge quick and try to make it stick and get this bloody woman out of the way. As for the ponce, if he had any sense he'd skip, and Edward wouldn't try all that much to hinder him: although, to comply with the direct order of the Detective-sergeant, he must now go through the motions of trying to find Frankie.

To do so he knew it would be pointless, almost, to go to Frankie's Kilburn flat (at any rate initially), and he decided instead to conduct his faint-hearted pursuit through the medium of the star ponce. Although this man's name was not yet known to him, from enquiries among his colleagues, and a glance through the photographic albums, he was soon identified; and armed with sufficient damaging particulars to force the star ponce, unless he was an imbecile, to betray his friend, Edward set out for the drinking-club where the star and his colleagues were well known to foregather.

The news of the arrest of Frankie's girl had already spread by the ponce-prostitute bush telegraph to the confines of the club (rather as, in Pall Mall, a disaster to a senior civil servant would be known long before it hit an inside bottom column of the top people dailies). Edward, who (unlike several of his colleagues) was not a member of the club and thus not entitled to buy drinks there, adopted the sensible and conventionally acceptable tactic of going straight up to the bar (followed by twenty-eight or so pairs of eyes) and saying, 'I'm an officer on a routine check-up. I wonder if you'd let me have a drink?' This was instantly forthcoming (his offer of payment being accepted, with a slight smile, as the politer of the two alternatives), and holding the beer glass like a shield, Edward took a slow look round the room.

Seated with an air of bland wariness and attired in a superb Italianate confection which accented, just sufficiently, the superb formation of his limbs, the star ponce lightly held a brandy glass with a slim, solid hand on whose wrist delicately dangled a thin gold chain. Like two who have an unspoken agreement for a rendezvous, the ponce and Edward Justice now came together.

Edward explained that all he wanted from the ponce was this: to lead him to Frankie Love. The ponce, after suggesting, helpfully, the Kilburn flat and appearing surprised that Edward should think Frankie might not be there, said courteously that he was very sorry, he could be of no further assistance to the officer.

Edward half sighed, put down his glass, and bringing his face closer to the ponce's said very softly, 'Look, I'm sorry too, son, but it's this way. The heat's on at the station to find this boy, I've got to make an effort to do so, and you're the only man I know in town I've ever seen him with. So don't you see until I get hold of him, I'll just have to hold on to you. And I do mean hold, son. I've been looking up your file just recently, and I'd say you're about due for another spell inside. So it really is up to you to help me in my enquiries if you want to avoid anything of that nature—which, and I do mean this, would happen to you *immediately* if you don't.'

'Officer,' the star ponce said, 'I'm really very sorry but I don't know where this boy is and I cannot help you.'

Edward smiled, sighed again, got up and said, 'Well, come along.'

Not rising, and raising his voice slightly so that it could be heard at neighbouring tables, the star ponce said, 'Are you *arresting* me, officer?'

'That, we'll see.'

'No, I mean *now*. Because if you're not arresting me and bringing a charge against me that you think can stick, then I'm sorry, but I'm just not coming: not coming, I mean, merely to help you in your enquiries I know nothing of.'

'You're under arrest,' said Edward sadly.

'For what?'

'Suspected collusion. Assisting a wanted person in an attempt to evade arrest . . .'

One could have heard an ice-cube drop. Nobody moved, everybody watched.

'Dear!' said the star ponce to the girl behind the bar. 'Will you make a few phone calls for me, please?'

The girl nodded, the star ponce rose (looking more glorious even than when seated), and the pair departed amid a silence distilled of hatred, fear and alcohol.

Edward hailed a cab, and on the journey to the station neither man said a word—except over the paraphernalia of cigarette lighting. For the cigarette, in the twentieth century, is often the ultimate offering of deadly enemies just prior to a fatal issue.

At the station Edward parked the ponce in a small room for twenty minutes chiefly to let him 'get the atmosphere'. The star ponce shrank gradually and visibly, and his splendid clothes (like elegant mufti on a raw recruit) became increasingly inappropriate to their setting. In spirit, however, the ponce, who'd seen all this before, remained calm and buoyant.

Then Edward collected two colleagues skilled in these matters (always take two—for safety and as witnesses of each other) and removed the star ponce to a distant cell. As the door clinked to, Edward made his final, reasonable appeal. 'Feller,' he said, 'here is the spiel. You take me to this boy and that ends that. If not, you're going to leave this place just crunched a bit though unmarked in any way that will be proveable; furthermore I promise you a poncing charge, with all the trimmings, within twenty-four hours from this very moment.'

Inwardly in his turn, the star ponce sighed. It wasn't that he was a coward: not in a fight, anyway; and even unarmed and sober—unlike so many of the boys. But if they'd got the heat turned that hot on poor old Francis they'd get him even if they waited fifty years. He looked at the three officers—Edward watching him earnestly, the other two eyeing him with frank amusement—and he said, 'I'm not going to make a statement, officer. And whatever you may say I've said in court I shall deny it, please understand. All I'm prepared to do is this: give me a piece of paper and I'll write an address on it: that's all.'

'Very well,' said Edward, handing to the star essential stationery.

The two colleagues stood back a bit bored by this development, as the star ponce inscribed block capitals. Edward took back the book, looked at it carefully, said thank you and signalled his colleagues to open the door and go.

The star ponce also stood. 'I'm in the clear?' he said.

'No,' Edward said calmly. 'You'll stay here for just a little while.'

The door closed and the star ponce subsided on the wooden bench-cum-bed with the built-in lavatory pan.

MR LOVE

AWAITING the departure of his plane which left late at night, but sure somehow already that he wouldn't be on it, Frankie went out into Stepney to have a drink: both because his Mahometan host didn't keep alcohol and Frankie disapproved of Indian hemp (well, just didn't like it), and because he was determined, even at the risk of being caught, that he wasn't going to *hide* from anyone: be very careful, yes, and use his loaf, but not lose his self-respect by *lurking*.

In Stepney the licensing hours, though their existence is politely recognized, are dexterously evaded in a number of cordial speak-easies: where after the club below has closed at the well-regulated hour with much clanging of bolts and ritual cries of, 'Last orders, please!' selected guests proceed to upper rooms to eat, drink, embrace their girls or gamble. To such an establishment Frankie now repaired and was soon ensconced beside a whisky bottle in a second-floor room, and in the company of various citizens of the outlying countries of the British Commonwealth of nations.

Here his meal of chicken-and-peas was interrupted by an insistent summons, from the proprietor, to a public call-box insalubriously situated beside an appalling bi-sexual lavatory. The voice at the far end, agitated and thus more incomprehensible than usual, was that of the excellent Bengali: who told him 'one law man' had called at the house just after he'd left and made enquiries concerning him; that he, the Bengali, had revealed absolutely nothing and the law man had now departed; and that Frankie must take 'well care' not to return to the house as 'the eye' was certainly put upon it; and finally—in a torrent of the most urgent assurance—whatever happened he, Frankie, could absolutely rely on him, the Bengali, to safeguard all his property and hide it: as he had already done with his packed travelling bag by stuffing it, the very moment he'd heard the untoward soft knock, inside the communal dust-bin out the back.

Frankie expressed thanks and assured his friend of his total belief in his integrity (he meant this). He then hung up and without returning to the festive communal room went quickly downstairs to the street. At the door he tapped himself to check on the presence of his passport and his money: the luggage, such as it was, could be abandoned.

He set off through the Stepney streets but in an *easterly* direction. What they'd be expecting him to do, he calculated, was go to the West end of the city to an air terminal. Instead he'd make for London docks, try to get a ride or even stow away, and if he failed travel overland to an eastern port and reach the Continent of Europe. Ships, after all, were his affair and more reliable. Diagnosing thus he saw again, approaching on the further pavement and this time on night duty, the young officer who had arrested him, earlier on, over the absurdity of the bag.

In their feeling for persons they have succeeded in convicting, the officers of the Force fall into three chief types. There are those who feel that any convicted person is a 'client' who should return from time to time for treatment: if you do harm to a man, you should prove how right you were by harming him again. Then those who feel in an almost friendly fashion, well, he's done his lot, good luck to him, he's stale stuff now, let's look round for someone else. And then those (a very minor group) who just feel nothing in particular: it was 'a case'.

Unfortunately the officer now approaching Frankie belonged to category one; and recognizing his former victim (though regretting that on this occasion he didn't appear to be carrying a suspect bag) he crossed the road obliquely (and warily, too), his boots sounding like metal (as was indeed the case), and there he stopped a few feet from the pavement by which Frankie was advancing, in as safe-and-sound a position as seemed possible for the encounter.

But this time Frankie knew the danger; and approaching steadily as if he saw nothing untoward, he suddenly hurled all the small change in his pocket at the copper's face, turned abruptly down one of the eighteenth-century courts which in this section of Stepney intricately abound, and loped off fairly silently yet at considerable speed. A whistle blew, a torch shone, and feet came clanging.

Without much difficulty Frankie outwitted his pursuer by entering, while still some way ahead, one of the bombed buildings which, a generation after the end of World War II, still rot and crumble in the capital; and there he settled himself quickly down upon a pile of fairly comfortable rubble and abandoned furniture that lay timelessly dissolving in a distant corner.

'Fuck off!' said a voice.

Quite unaware, Frankie had stumbled on what was to the detritus of the floating population of the borough, their trysting-place; and the position he had selected within a few feet of those who in more pastoral surroundings might be described as a 'courting couple'. This couple clearly wanted to get on with their courting without uncouth interruption.

'Take it easy, mate,' said Frankie softly. 'I got to stay here a moment.'

The male—who by his tones and truculence Frankie observed to his dismay was drunk—repeated, 'I said, fuck off. You got no respect for privacy?'

Frankie risked a throw. 'You a seaman like I am?' he said.

'No!'

It *would* be a landsman. Frankie tried again. 'You like a pound-note, mate? I got to stay here a while—it's a bit urgent.'

From the rubble and his invisible (though audibly grunting) consort, the erotic landsman rose like an angry phoenix. 'Now, look!' he cried very much too loud for Frankie's liking. 'Just make away or I have to thump you.'

Frankie got up, biting his rage, said, 'Okay, mate,' and started slowly towards the light. Unwisely from every point of view the landsman tried to help him on his way with a parting shove. Consequently both men stumbled, and several hundredweight of miscellaneous London ruins and garbage collapsed with a resounding, thudding clatter.

A bit bashed on the head and dazed, Frankie staggered up knee-deep in obstacles as several lights came on in surrounding buildings, accompanied by cries and sleepy murmurs. As he struggled to the exit a torch shone blank-flash in his face—a startling experience at the best of times. Ten minutes later, filthy and rather battered, he was lodged in the adjacent headquarters of the Force where an interested sergeant was examining his passport and several envelopes crammed with currency.

MR JUSTICE

EDWARD, having done his duty—no more, no less—by tracing Frankie to his Stepney hide-out, and after taking the routine precaution of warning the local station that a wanted man was now at large among them, had returned to his own headquarters to draw up a nil report and—an even more pressing matter—discover what had passed, if anything, between his girl and the all too astute Detective-sergeant.

She was waiting for him in her eternally patient way amid the bleak décor of the junior officers' canteen. He sat down opposite her beneath a single shaft of strip-light, and with two coffees in paper cups from the automatic urn. 'Well, dear, let's hear what,' he said.

'The Detective-sergeant believes your story.'

'How? What?'

'The story you told him, Ted dear. That you were going to hand in the box and hadn't even had a chance to see it before it was stolen from me.'

'And what did he say about the man who stole it?'

'Nothing. No, we didn't mention him at all.'

'So he's satisfied I've done no wrong.'

'About that, he is . . . But, Edward. Now, dearest, *don't* be angry with me—but he got it out of me.'

'Got what?'

'He said it was for your good in your career, and mine.'

'What did you *say*? Tell me *what*.'

'About Dad: he knows Dad has a previous conviction.'

'Yes? Oh.'

'He asked me if *I* had and I said of course not, and he said he believed me though he'd check, but there's one thing he doesn't like about it.'

'That *I* didn't tell him, I suppose.'

'Yes: and that you *did* tell him I was a copper-hater and not that my father's been in jail. Did you really have to do that, Ted?'

'I'm sorry, dear. I'm very sorry—that was a big mistake. I was harassed and . . . well, I made a big mistake.'

'Yes, Ted. Another one you made, it seems, was to tell *me* you'd told him that you had no girl at all.'

'But he doesn't know I said that to you . . .'

'No, Ted, I know: it was only to me you lied.'

'Yes. Dearing, I'm sorry—do try to understand! But him. Was he very vexed when he discovered?'

'Not so much about that, Ted . . . about something else. That you made me pregnant before you got the whole thing settled.'

'Well! What business is that of his?'

'He said it was for two reasons, Edward. First, that he didn't like it because it wasn't right to me. Then . . .'

'To you! What does he care about you?'

'Well, Edward, I agree with him.'

'Oh, do you!'

'Yes—I do. I think he's right. He was like a father to me, Ted.'

'A father! If you only knew him! Well, what was the other thing?'

'Well, dear, you won't like this, but he says your application *may* go through if Dad leaves fairly soon, but it *won't* if I have a child before we marry, and he doesn't see us being able to do that before the application is approved.'

'It takes that long?'

'He says so.'

Edward looked at her. 'Well, there's only one thing,' he said, 'you'll have to have a miscarriage.'

His girl looked back. 'I don't want to now, Edward.'

'But you said you were willing to.'

'I did, yes, but I've thought of it, and it's got so much bigger here, and Ted, I'm going to have my baby.'

'Oh, you are.'

'Yes.'

He reached for her hands across the table, delved for them and held them. 'Darling,' he said, 'do think of this. If you have the child it seems I've got to choose between the Force and you.'

'I know,' she said. 'I've thought of that.'

'And what do you expect me to do?'

'You've got to decide, Ted. I suppose it all depends on how much you think you love me.'

Another shaft of the strip-light came on as an officer, entering suddenly, called out, 'It's okay, Ted—we've got him.'

MR LOVE AND MR JUSTICE

EDWARD was now faced by that most exhausting and complicated moment in a copper's life—the conduct of a full-scale interrogation of a prisoner. In this affair both parties have considerable tactical advantages, provided each knows what they are and how to use them.

First, the surroundings. The very word 'cells' has, to most ears, a sinister and forbidding ring. And these places are, to be sure, rebarbative enough . . . the nastiest thing about them being not that they have locks and bars, but that they are so utterly, fundamentally *utilitarian*. In them arrangements are made for prisoners to eat, sleep, and defecate: and for absolutely nothing else whatever. A man in prison is reduced to his physical essence.

From the copper's point of view the cells have the advantage, obviously, of making escape impossible to the prisoner and of filling his soul with lonely terror and foreboding. But they have this psychological *dis*advantage that in one very real sense, they are the prisoner's and not the copper's home: yes, home. The copper may lord it in his office, and of course does so over any visitor he may entice there. But in the cells the visitor in one sense is *he*, the copper, even though he has put the prisoner inside them. And if the prisoner be a man of intelligence, will and courage, the very presence of these four confining walls does help to sustain his spirits. It is he who is on the defensive, he who is fighting back. And he may well detect in even the most arrogant aggression of the interrogating copper, a hidden fear of the place of a very different kind from his own: the fear of something with which in the most final sense, he is unfamiliar.

When it comes to the actual interrogation the copper has, of course, the enormous advantage of seeming to personify the fact of prison itself, and the whole vast Force of which he is the representative. He will also possess, through skill and long practice, all the interrogator's essential arts in which the prisoner may be quite unversed. But: in this very unfamiliarity, there resides also a great strength. An adult questioning a child about a misdemeanour often finds himself exhausted by his own superior guile, and defeated by the instinctive simplicities of the apparently weaker party in the struggle. So it may be said to be with prisoners. And they also have —once again if men of indomitable stamp—one absolutely unbeatable trump card which is the fact that they *are*, in this circumstance, alone. If you are alone, you can never be betrayed; and in dealing with the many others who may confront him, the prisoner is the only person among the whole assembly who really knows *all* that everyone has said and done.

Frankie's opening gambit to his captor Edward, was in the finest tradition of the pugnacious victim: 'You're a nice bastard,' he said, as Edward carefully closed the cell door behind him.

Edward smiled slightly and looked interrogative.

'I gave you the way out,' Frankie continued, 'I gave your girl the box and all you had to do was to collect. And then you shop me. Why?'

'It's not quite as you think,' said Edward carefully—doubly so because he was keeping an eye on Frankie for sudden violence, and had his whistle handy.

'Oh, no?' said Frankie. 'Go on—tell me your fairytale.'

'What happened,' Edward said, 'is that a senior of mine who doesn't like me got hold of the box and turned it in, and made things very awkward for me, too, I can tell you.'

'For you! Well, listen to that! I dunno, son! You coppers really are a bunch of horrors.'

'You think so?'

'Yes, man, I do. A bunch of narks in uniform.

'Have a fag,' said Edward.

'"Have a fag! Have a fag!" Listen—skip it, *officer*. Now, tell me. What's the charge?'

'There may be several.'

'Thank you! And there may be lawyers, too! And some bloody expensive ones! I'd just like to make that clear. And there may be an affidavit about your visit to me—*with* a witness present, don't forget. No one will believe two ponces, I'm well aware of that, but it won't sound very nice up in the Sessions—because that's where we're going, let me tell you, you're not getting away with a magistrate's court and no publicity.'

'I understand how you feel,' Edward said.

'You kill me, son. Honest you do! And what about this tale of yours? Why *should* a *colleague* of yours do the dirty on you?'

'Don't you see?'

'I think I do: you've invented the whole dam thing.'

'No. No, I haven't. The reason my colleague made it difficult for me was that he hoped you'd do exactly what you're doing now—and that is attack me.'

'You're saying I've laid *hands* on you? Is that what you're concocting now?'

'This man hoped you would, once you thought I'd deceived you.'

'You ask me to believe that?'

'No, not particularly: I'm just telling you what happened.'

Frankie accepted, nevertheless, the ritual fag. 'The Force!' he said quietly. 'The Force! I really feel pity for you all. And if all that's so,' he continued, 'why did you come down chasing after me to Stepney?'

'I didn't.'

'Listen . . .'

'*You* listen, please. I didn't *chase* after you. I checked at your address because it was the very least I could do. Then I came back here and made no further enquiries. It's *you*, isn't it, who's got yourself foolishly arrested through no fault of mine.'

'You didn't send that bastard out looking for me?'

'I sent no one. It was your own carelessness that caused it, as you must know.'

'Thank you! And what happens now? You still holding my girl?'

'Yes.'

'And you're going to bring charges against us both—is that it?'

Edward now sat down on the bench-cum-lavatory and said to Frankie, 'Please do listen to me. I'm not asking you to do anything I say because that's your business, obviously. But I am asking you, please, just to listen.'

Frankie sat down too. 'Very well,' he said. 'I'm listening.'

'From my point of view,' said Edward carefully, '—and I *do* wish you'd realize this—the lighter you and your girl get off the better I'll be pleased.'

'Why? You like us?'

'Do please just *listen*. Because now that the box has been turned in, the less said about my part in trying to recover it the better.'

'Yeah. Corruption and bribery. Very nasty. My heart bleeds for you.'

'On the other hand,' Edward continued, 'if you and your girl *don't* want to help me, well, in for a penny in for a pound, I may as well help press the charge hard and get you both sent away as long as possible.'

Frankie looked sideways at Edward. 'You know,' he said, 'if you'd had any sense you'd have offered to split the price of the box with me, and just said you couldn't trace it.'

'I might have done,' said Edward, also looking sideways, 'if you'd seen me alone and not been so damned unpleasant and suspicious.'

'Yes, I see what you mean. It's a great pity. You could have bought yourself a nice new fridge, and I'd have bought myself some valuable protection.'

'Well, there it is,' said Edward. 'The thing's now as it is. Now, I'm asking you for no promises: I'm not a fool. But all I will say to you is *if* you leave out the part about my not wanting to turn it in—which no one will believe much anyway—then I'll say I believe your girl thought she had it as a present, and that you offered to co-operate with the authorities.'

'Yeah?'

'Yes. Now, I don't ask you to credit this, of course, before you see it happen. But I would point out this. I'm willing to take a chance on you that you don't have to at all on me. Prosecution evidence comes first at any trial and can't be altered afterwards. When your turn comes to speak, you can make it dependent on whatever it is you hear me say.'

Frankie threw his fag-end in the pan and pressed the automatic flush which sounded off like six Niagaras. 'Well obviously,' he said when the waters had subsided, 'I'll think that over. And that's really all I'm going to say just now.'

'I can't ask for more. Another fag?'

'Well, I don't mind. What about bail? What are the chances?'

'Oh, quite good, I'd say, for *one* of you at any rate . . .'

'What does that mean?'

'Well, we've got to bring a charge of theft: you do understand that, don't you? Unless we hear the owner—the original owner of the thing—saying to us it was a gift, then a charge must lay. But it needn't necessarily be on both of you.'

'Who will it be on?'

'The girl.'

'Why?'

'Look. *You* didn't sleep with this man, did you?'

'Take it easy, son, or I may smack you. And what about me?'

'Aiding and abetting—but *with*, of course, my favourable statement, in certain circumstances, coming later . . . and a charge against you might even not be made.'

'And no bail for my girl: is that it?'

'Well, it's up to the magistrate: but I'd say probably no.'

'I see.'

They smoked a moment in silence. Then Frankie said, 'You're shacked up with one too, aren't you?'

'Yes . . . You know I am.'

'I might have something to say to the court about *that* as well.'

'You'd be wasting your breath. She's already told everything to my superiors.'

'Why?'

'It came up as a result of all this: on account of you giving *her* the box, and not me as you should have done if you'd had any sense at all.'

'Dear, dear, dear. So I've landed *you* in the shit, too! Well, well. You like that girl?'

'I want to marry her.'

'You do? Now why? Is that a thing coppers do?'

'Because I love her.'

'You believe in that crap, son?'

'Yes.'

'Not just sex?'

'Without love there is no sex.'

'Well! And you tell *me* that!'

Edward paused then said, 'You won't mind my saying so, I hope, but I think what you do is just disgusting. *Not* because it's illegal—don't misunderstand me. But because it destroys the best thing there is in any man and woman.'

' "Not because it's illegal"! You don't believe in the law, then?'

'Of course I do. But the law isn't perfect and entire like love can be.'

Frankie arose. 'Well, are you *sure* of that?' he said. 'Because me I've found it's women and sex that are imperfect—just a game. But as for the law—if it's a *real* law, a true law like you get on board a ship, why! then it's really something! A thing you can respect and live for.'

'I don't know about ships,' said Edward, 'naturally. But here on land it's all made up of human beings struggling with one another, and that means imperfection. There are rules, of course, and they're mostly very clear: laws that have been laid down for centuries, I mean. But there's no such thing as *law*, like there is love.'

'Well, son. You may be right, of course, but I think you're wrong. There's three laws in the world here as I see it: the rules you speak of, the way you bastards alter and interpret them, and then—way on beyond and right in the centre of things—there's just . . . the *law*.'

Edward got up too. 'I don't really know,' he said, 'what you're talking about.'

'You may not,' said Frankie Love. 'Because if you did, you wouldn't be a copper.'

'Well,' Edward said, smiling a bit sourly. 'I may *not* be one before all that long, any more.'

'Oh? You retiring on your winnings?'

'No. My girl's pregnant, and the Force may not let me marry her.'

'You've not thought of an abortion?'

'She doesn't want one.'

'Good for her! She's too good for a copper—tell her so from me. And to marry her you'd have to resign?'

'It looks like that.'

'You're a fool, mate. No woman's worth a job—even yours—if your heart's in it.'

'Well, I don't know. I may stay on.'

'And if you do, and she has the kid, she loses you?'

'Yes.'

'And she cares for you, this woman?'

'Yes.'

'Well yes, she's quite a girl! She really is. I must try and get her away from you when I get out.'

'You'd better look after your own, hadn't you? It's she who'll be needing you—not mine.'

'What does that one mean?'

'If you get bail I suppose you'll try to skip, won't you?'

'*You* ask me to tell *you* that?'

'Yes, but I don't ask you for an answer . . .'

'So what should I do, according to you? Stay and try to take the rap for her? Say I forced her to pinch the thing or something lunatic like that?'

'That's what she's quite ready to do for you.'

'What d'you say?'

'When I saw her earlier on she said she was only prepared to make a statement if you weren't implicated.'

'*She* said *that*?'

'Yes.'

'Look—I don't believe you.'

'Ask her some time.'

'She really did say that?'

'I'm telling you.'

'Well, I'll be fucked! Well, I bloody well never!'

In the surprise of his emotion Frankie turned, spontaneously, to make brief use of the adjacent pan. This action transmitted (as is its wont) a similar desire to Edward, who after a casual 'You don't mind?' followed his prisoner's example.

'Well, well, well, well!' said Frankie. 'These chicks! They're packed with surprises!'

'They certainly are,' Edward said reflectively. 'They do things that impress you—even the worst of them.'

'You're not referring to my girl, I hope—I mean, when you say "worst"?'

'No . . . she's still a woman.'

'She's very much one, let me tell you.'

'I don't doubt your word . . .'

Frankie, in his dishevelled garments, looked at the neatly un-uniformed cop and said, 'I suppose you think that they and we men are a lot of anti-social parasites.'

'Yes. As a matter of fact I do.'

'Just about what we think of you. Isn't that crazy?'

'I suppose so . . .'

'Well, let me tell you one thing, copper. We may be that, but there's one thing we're not which you are, and that's hypocrites puffed up with spiritual pride.'

'I don't see you've got much to be proud of anyway.'

'I said *spiritual* pride. We're free from that, most of us easy-money boys. And I wouldn't change that freedom for your prim self-righteousness!'

Edward said nothing: as matter of fact he was (being very tired) getting a bit bored with Frankie and had decided to bring the interview—already somewhat excessively unconventional—to a close.

'Although,' Frankie continued with the passion for conversation induced by even a short stay between four closed walls, 'I dare say you *could* maintain we have one thing in common, you and I: in the upside-down world we both live in we've got a certain kind of freedom that none of the mugs outside will ever know. Neither of us conforms to the accepted pattern: so that we boys are free in spite of all our heart-beats, as I dare say you are in spite of all your discipline.'

Preparing for his departure, Edward had introduced a more formal note in his demeanour. Frankie noticed this and his tone altered. 'Just one thing, officer,' he said. 'You've not told me how you knew I was at Stepney.'

'No.'

'Well, aren't you going to?'

'No.'

'It wasn't my girl?'

'No.'

'Then the only other person I can think of who did know is the Bengali, who it can't be, or . . . yes! My fellow ponce! Is that it?'

'I'm not telling you.'

'So it *is*. Thanks, I'll remember! And one more thing.' Frankie came close to Edward and said to him, 'I promise you—if I lie, I die—I'll keep your name out of it if you do all you can to free my girl.'

Edward paused and said, 'You've changed your mind about her, then?'

'Not about *her* but about her position. I got her in this mess by making her give me the box, and I ought to get her out if I possibly can. So I want the charge to be put on me and only me. You'll do what you can?'

'I'll try,' said Edward. 'But you'll realize I can't promise.'

MR JUSTICE

EDWARD who with an instinct similar to Frankie's could no longer bear the thought of the Kilburn flat, and who'd decided after his late night up on duty to play truant from the section-house, had camped with the older man's permission at the house of his girl's Dad in Kensal Green. And when he awoke it was to the most delicious of situations—his girl bending over him holding a brimming cuppa, and looking down at him with love and a total preoccupation with their joint well-being. He reached up and hugged her and upset most of the tea.

'I love you, Ted,' she said, reaching an arm backward with the crockery and slops in search of an invisible piece of furniture.

'Me, too. Even more. Listen, dearest. I'm going to have it out with the Detective-sergeant.'

'How, Ted? How can you?'

'Reverse the process: turn the tables on him: go over to the attack. Either he helps me fix our marriage, or all right I resign and he loses a good man.'

'And you think that'll work, dear?'

'It might do. I'm sick of caution and of secrets anyway. What about your Dad? Is he all set to go?'

'Any time now. He says it's up to us to send him the balance he needs as soon as ever we can. If not—well, he says he'll come back.'

'He won't! I'll see to that.'

She'd sat down on the bed. 'I wish, Ted,' she said, 'that just at this moment I felt better.'

'You're not ill are you, dear?' said Edward, gently pressing his hand upon her body.

'A bit: you know how it is for me just now: and today I do feel queer.'

'Step up to the pre-natal clinic, darling. See what they have to say.'

'I mean to.'

He kissed her all over.

'You know, dear,' he said, 'that ponce was most impressed with you making up your mind to keep the baby.'

'He was? I thought they didn't like kids, those people.'

'Well—he's all for female children being born, I dare say. Is that what ours is going to be?'

'No, a boy. Has *his* woman ever had one, then?'

'No, I don't think so. . . . But she's certainly got guts—she stuck to him, and now he's going to stick to her.'

The girl shook her head vaguely, not in denial of what he said but to show how important matters prevented her thinking clearly of whatever he was saying. He kissed her again—neck this time, a favourite spot (women were so tough there, so everlasting yet so fragile and so downy)—then said, 'Out of it, dear, we're not hitched up yet and you know I've never liked you to see me dressing till we are.' She smiled at his prudery, took the cup and went away.

Edward decided not to check in at the section-house, and thus when he reached the station found his colleagues in that state of glee in which colleagues are when one of their number—especially one talented and fairly virtuous—has committed an offence of which he is as yet unaware. 'You're for the high jump,' someone said. 'The Detective-sergeant's been chasing after you all morning.'

When he came into the office, Edward found his superior relatively benign. He was standing by the window, which looked out on nothing, and he turned round to Edward and said, 'Well, there have been developments.'

'Sir?'

'With one man sick and the other—well, a bit involved—I've taken over this whole Madam case myself.'

'Yes, sir . . .'

'Now, from what I can make out this client, this eminent individual who the bloody box belongs to (the officer showed some dentures in a rather ghastly grin), thinking—and he's quite right—he might get involved himself in court proceedings, is going to make no charge and in fact is going further—he's going to say he *did* give the girl the snuff-box. These were only the Madam's words, and I'll check of course, but I've no doubt she's got full authority for them from her principal.'

'Well! He's caused us a lot of trouble over nothing, sir.'

'Hasn't he just! The public's *always* calling us in in a tizzy and then when we get their man for them refusing to co-operate in a prosecution.'

'So that puts the pair of them in the clear, sir?'

'I'm coming to that . . . But first of all, my lad, a word in *your* little red ear. The Madam also says you offered to get the box back for a bribe: "reward" she called it. But I prefer "bribe". Well?'

'I've nothing to say, sir.'

'That was correct?'

'Yes, sir.'

'Why you do this, son?'

'I needed money, sir: to help my girl's father emigrate like I told you.'

'You needed money! Really, lad, you *are* a bloody fool! You really *are*!' The Detective-sergeant looked at him. 'With a man like our colleague suffering with his ulcers on the same case with you, you thought you'd under-cut him? A sharp bastard like that? Really! Have you *no* brains in your head at all?'

'I think I'm learning, sir.'

'Well, I do hope so. Now, please in the future *do* be sensible and don't be greedier than your rank and length of service warrants.'

'No, sir.'

'Right. That's forgotten, then. You understand me?'

'Thank you, sir. Thank you very much indeed.'

'Okay. Now, as to the thieves who are no longer thieves. I'm turning the girl loose as I've nothing to hold her on. But I'm going to bring a charge against the man.'

'What charge, sir?'

'What do you think, son? Poncing. He's about due for his first experience and it might as well be now.'

'Excuse me, sir. Who will you get for witnesses? I don't think the girl will speak against him . . .'

'For witnesses? Well, I can think of two . . . Our friend the star sleuth, when he recovers, will be number one and number two, lad, will be you.'

'Me, sir?'

'Naturally. You've both kept observation on the flat—in fact you, you've been living on the doorstep—you've both seen clients come and go and there'll just be the little matter of saying that on several occasions you saw her hand him over considerable sums of money.'

'How, sir?'

'*How?* I dunno! However you like! You saw it through the window—in a club or pub—in the full light of the broad highway, if you prefer: I've known magistrates believe that . . . and funnily enough, in my experience it's even happened. These ponces get over-confident after a while and take unbelievable chances.'

'No, sir.'

'Eh?'

'I want to ask you take me off this case, sir.'

'Oh, *do* you.'

'Yes, sir.'

The senior officer looked very hard indeed at Edward. 'Tell me,' he said quietly. 'When you saw this ponce alone in the cells, did he make you any promises?'

'Such as what, sir?'

'Now—be very careful. I've gone with you a long way, but please don't start getting cheeky. Has he made any promises of payment later on?'

'No, sir.'

'Are you quite positive of that?'

'Yes, sir. He's offered me no money, and I've not agreed to accept any from him.'

'Oh, I see. But you did discuss the matter.'

'We spoke of money in a general way: but no arrangements were made of any kind, sir.'

'Did *you* make *him* any promises?'

Edward—enticed by the fatal mistake of *liking* the Detective-sergeant and of wishing to be entirely frank with him—said, 'I did promise, sir, if this theft charge had gone through, to try to make it lighter for the girl than him.'

'Why?'

'He wanted it that way, sir.'

'*Did* he! So this man *wants* to get inside the nick—is that it?'

'Not on a poncing charge, sir, naturally.'

The Detective-sergeant paused, looked at Edward in an absorbed, impersonal way then said, 'Constable, this is it. You're chief witness for the prosecution again this man—or else.'

Edward replied in a low voice, 'I wish to submit to you, sir, my resignation from the Force.'

'I can't accept it,' the Detective-sergeant instantly snapped back. 'You can forward it through channels, naturally, if you wish, but until it's agreed to or refused by the proper authorities you're still bound by your oath and still under my direct orders.'

Edward, without asking for permission, sat down on a chair. 'Don't force me to do this, sir,' he said.

The Detective-sergeant looked at him, then sat down slowly also at his desk. 'You know,' he said, 'I just can't make you out. This man hasn't got at you, you say. I don't believe he's offered you his woman, or you'd want her if he had. And you like your work—I mean you *enjoy* it, don't you?'

'There's nothing I like better, sir.'

'And you know personal feelings count as nothing when there's a job to be done?'

'I know that too, sir.'

'You're not *against* ponces going to jail by any chance, are you?'

'No, sir. That's where they belong. But I can't do it, sir, because of my girl I'm going to marry.'

'Oh? I thought I was helping you straighten all that out?'

'Please listen, sir,' said Edward carefully. 'She's pregnant, as you know. She also loves me a great deal. She knows how much I want to stay on in the Force, but that if she has the child I may be refused permission to marry her.'

'Well?'

'I'm afraid she might try to do away with it—an abortion, sir.'

'But look, constable! I understood you'd both decided to go ahead and take a chance on the permission coming through in time to rectify the situation.'

'Yes, sir, I know. But I'm afraid she won't believe we *will* get permission, and she'll destroy the child to safeguard my career. And if she does *that* for me, sir—then I think I'll lose her.'

'Why?'

'She'll cease to love me, sir.'

'Oh. Oh, I see.' The Detective-sergeant leant back reflecting, then said, 'You know, constable, it's *you* who's behaving a bit like a ponce now, isn't it?'

'Sir?'

'Hiding behind a woman's apron-strings? Protecting your livelihood by swinging your sex life on me?'

Edward was silent.

'And another thing,' said the Detective-sergeant. 'Why has this business of a pregnancy and all this talk of resigning only come up when I gave you your orders about this particular poncing case?' Edward still said nothing and his senior pressed the point hard home. 'Why didn't you mention resigning earlier on if you'd decided? It must have been in your mind . . .'

Edward said quietly, 'I only came to the decision then, sir.'

'Yeah?' The Detective-sergeant frowned and pondered. 'You're trying to lead me off the track,' he said. 'There's something at the bottom of all this—something to do with that fucking ponce.'

Edward was still silent.

'Look, boy,' said the Detective-sergeant who was really getting quite a bit exasperated. 'This thing has gone quite far enough. Here, as I see it, is the situation. I've given you an order and you say you don't want to obey it. Well! Resign by all means if you really think you want to. But meanwhile either you obey my order or, I'm sorry, but I'm going to suspend you.'

Edward got up, stood at attention and said, 'Then please suspend me, sir.'

The Detective-sergeant's face hardened. He also rose. 'In one minute from now, constable,' he said, 'I'm going to do just that. But before I do I want to make one thing very clear indeed. If I suspend you for disobeying a direct order, there'll be an enquiry. And if there's an enquiry there'll be a lot of things I'll find I have to say that I've been overlooking for you hitherto. Very well. Now, if this enquiry should go against you—as I think it will—it won't be resigning you'll be doing. It'll be dismissal, and perhaps even maybe worse. And a man *dismissed* from the Force, constable—well, he's the lowest of the low. He's lower than that ponce that you're so fond of.'

Edward stood rigid but at ease, still saying nothing.

'You're suspended, constable,' the Detective-sergeant said. 'Report to the Station-sergeant now accordingly.'

MR LOVE

FRANKIE, released on bail from the charge of living off immoral earnings, and waiting while his lawyers hoisted his case from the rough justice of the magistrate's court to the dangerous impartiality of a judge and jury, had met his former girl for a chat about it all at the drinking-club now fashionable in 'the game': the other having suffered an eclipse as these clubs do, rising and falling with the fickle inclinations of their clientele and the slow-grinding machinery of the law. She was as desirable as ever though perhaps a shade more *elderly*—a bit wiser to a world about which she was already far too wise. He was relaxed, resigned, and *saddened* as only those born innocent can be when by folly or misjudgment they have behaved in some way that violates this quality of their natures.

'My chances?' said Frankie, summing up the situation. 'Slender, but they exist. After all'—he pressed her hand—'I won't have the principal witness in the box against me.'

'If only your lawyers would let me speak *for* you, Frankie. Say you were a handsome, silly boy-friend who knew nothing and I never gave you anything. You sure that's no use to you at all?'

'Dear—who'd believe it? And they say the sight of a—excuse me —common prostitute speaking up for me will damn me as a ponce at once with any jury.'

'Yeah, I know. But I'm scared of that copper's evidence, honey, when you come up at the Sessions. It's always so thorough and so dam *convincing.*'

She drained her b. and s.—a drink which, now banished from stately clubs and homes where it so flourished in Edwardian times, survives in our day as a favourite of this very Edwardian profession. 'Which cops will it be, I wonder? That bastard who got the box, and I suppose the Kilburn kiddy.'

'He's bound to speak against me, honey. After all why shouldn't he? It's his graft.'

Frankie rose and leaned over to work the cigarette-machine behind her back. She reached for her bag, said, 'I've got florins,' but he smiled, bent down and clicked the bag shut, then undid the packet standing close beside her stool in the tenderly sexy posture of bar lovers: girl's face level with boy's belt. She took her fag, held it unlit, looked up at him and said, 'You really think, dear, you couldn't try to skip?'

'We've been into that. They've got my passport and they'll be watching me this time. I've thought of trying: stow away and get duff papers—it's not that difficult, I know. But it seems this thing is coming to me and I might as well take it on the chin.'

'The nick's the nick, dear, don't forget. And with a previous conviction for *that,* they can whip you in for nothing and get a judgment on you till the day you die.'

'I've thought of that.'

'*And*—can you travel, after? I mean, go anywhere? Once you've got a record, honey, you've got a record.'

'Yeah.'

'Frankie! I believe you *want* to go inside!'

'No . . . you think I'm crazy? But I don't mind telling you, baby, I *do* think it's written in my book.'

'Fuck that! And when you come out, dear. There'll be some loot?'

'Oh, sufficient. Though the lawyers are getting most of what I've had . . .'

'There'll be me, too, honey. I'll be your banker, never fear . . .'

Frankie looked at her and smiled. 'Never again,' he said. 'Baby, I've thought it over and it seems I'm really not the type.

'No? Well, darl, they all say that. They all say "never again" the first time they get nicked, and they all head straight back to the chicks when their bit of trouble's over.' Frankie was silent. 'You know, dear,' she went on, 'there's only one thing does really trouble me a bit. I believe if I'd had that kid of ours you really might have grown to love me.'

'D'you think so?'

'Yes, I do. I think you're the type of man who never loves a girl but loves a mother.'

'I don't know about mothers, babe,' he said, giving her a lipstick-avoiding kiss, 'but I do know you've been great to me—a good chick in bed, yes, but in many ways just like my flesh and blood—my sister.'

'Oh, thank you! Do you mind? Your sister! Well—what next?'

Frankie went over to replenish glasses, and glancing round the room he felt for the first time in what seemed so long a while quite *different* once again from all these people there: a non-ponce, in fact: a man whose sex life was once more his own absolute and undisputed property. Not that he judged them in the slightest, being no hypocrite, nor given by nature to imagine that to judge one's fellows has anything much to do with having a real sense of justice. But he did feel altered: and he had, for the first time in his life, an informed opinion on the easy-money boys.

Looking up, he saw one of them who entered and seeing him, withdrew. This was the star ponce whom Frankie, quickly abandoning the glasses on an indignant table, caught up with at the stairs. 'Hullo, man,' he said. 'Where you been hiding yourself? I've been looking for you.'

'Hi, Francis. And you, man! Where *you* been, feller—have you been away?'

'Not *yet*,' said Frankie. 'But it seems I'm going to just because someone who got scared felt they had to speak up out of turn.'

'Oh, yeah? That so? That really so?'

'That really so. Without that one man's coward's word I'd be in Africa or South America by now.'

'You would? Well now, Francis! Please don't *stare* at *me* like that, old-timer. Why! The way you stand there, making insinuations and just threatening a bit, anyone who didn't know might take you for a copper!'

The star ponce (in whose life this scene had occurred more than once before) knew exactly what he had to do: and that was get his blow in first. The wronged and righteous party in a quarrel often makes the capital mistake of forgetting—if it's going to come down to a set-to—that the villain, being such, is likely to be quicker off the mark because to counteract the power of towering indignation, he has only speed and swift decision. At least six seconds before Frankie got in his knock-out punch the star ponce had bent, pulled the blade from its plastic sheath inside his nylon sock, and stabbed Frankie neatly in the groin.

MR JUSTICE

PREFERRING for reasons best known to himself (no doubt financial) to travel like the emigrants of old by sea, Edward's father-in-law-to-be set sail (seen off by Edward not so much to shed a parting tear as to make sure he *went*) from the grubby and antique shores of Fenchurch street railway station. Though his departure now seemed so much less important the thing, once set in motion, could not be stopped because his girl's Dad had grown fond of the idea, and neither Edward nor she regretted it. The older man was in high spirits, haloed already with the aura of a tropical remittance-man; and only subdued, as Edward was much more so, by anxiety about his daughter's critical condition: the night before, attacked by sudden pains, she had been carried off to hospital. 'Send me a radiogram, boy,' the father said, 'as soon as ever they tell you what it is. And if it's serious, even if I have to get off the ship at the first port of call—well, rely on me, I'll face the journey back across old Biscay.'

'I hope that won't be necessary,' said Edward.

'Me, too. But note down my cabin number all the same.'

Edward reached by long habit for his little book, took it out, looked at it, and wrote the number there.

'Well,' said the expatriate, 'I won't keep you any longer: I know you've got to fly back to your headquarters. Well, lad, there it is. Cheerioh! All the very best! And thanks for all you've done for me and all you're going to do.'

Repressing with great difficulty an overpowering desire to say, 'Farewell, you old bastard, and whatever you do, don't come back,' Edward said (using the word for the first time). 'Good-bye, Dad, and good luck.'

The men shook hands, waved and separated, and Edward made off to the underground. At the foot of the escalator he dropped the black note-book, after looking at it once again, in the litter basket there provided. As he travelled west the docile public in the carriage, massed in long-suffering wedges of impatient and resigned humanity, now seemed to him as they had often done since his suspension not the *them* they used to be, but *us*: an us he still disapproved of in so many respects and still mistrusted: a great, confused, messy, indeterminate 'us' in need of regulation, guidance from above and order.

He had made in the past weeks several visits to the station on routine matters concerning his three rather contradictory appeals (to resign, to get married, and against unjustified suspension), but had no longer been admitted to the inner chambers of his erstwhile protector the Detective-sergeant. But to see him an imperative summons had now come; and so after a brief, fruitless telephone call to the hospital where his girl had just been taken, he walked up the breeze-block stairs and knocked, at exactly the appointed hour, upon the door.

Within he found the Detective-sergeant and, now restored to health, his own Iago, the star sleuth. The Detective-sergeant, most unusually for him, was in uniform which somehow made him look, though more official, less redoubtable. The star sleuth was in neat expressionless plain-clothes. 'Sit down,' said the Detective-sergeant.

He picked up a file, then putting on spectacles (giving him the appearance of a modern British general) he said to Edward, 'I don't want to see you just at present, constable, and I dare say you don't want to see me. Unfortunately, though, we've both got to. It's about this ponce. He's been involved in an affray in addition to being on bail on a much more serious matter. I don't know the rights and wrongs of it yet, but as it was a quarrel between ponces I don't suppose it very much matters either way. At all events, as he's out on bail and subject to the jurisdiction of the courts we've had him put into a hospital where we can keep an eye on him, so as to be ready for him when *he's* ready to face either of these charges.'

Edward and the star sleuth, neither looking at the other, preserved a silence of the kind that indicated all this had so far registered.

'Now, as regards the poncing charge,' said the Detective-sergeant looking at Edward, 'if that comes up first we're calling you as a prosecution witness. You can refuse to appear, of course, that's entirely up to you, but if you do I'd suggest you take counsel's opinion as to what your own legal position might then be. Is that understood?'

'Yes, sir. I'm ready to testify.'

'Oh. You are?'

'Yes, sir. I've decided it's my duty to the Force even though I have to leave it.'

'I'm not much interested in your motives, constable, any longer. What I'm interested in is facts. Now. If you and your colleague here are going to testify you'll have to get together and make sure your statements correspond. We'll be up at the Sessions, don't forget, with defending counsel and the whole bag of legal tricks. So I want some co-operation so that you both get the whole thing absolutely crystal clear within your two minds. What I *don't* want,' the Detective-sergeant added, putting down the dossier, 'is any conflict of evidence that might lead to an acquittal. I do *not* want, in short, if you can grasp this, the Force to be made a fool of. Any questions?'

'No, sir.'

'You?'

'No, sir.'

'Very well. That's it. You can carry on.'

The telephone rang and the Detective-sergeant, answering, looked up angrily. 'Constable,' he said to Edward. 'Did you tell them downstairs they were to put your private calls through to *my* office *here*?'

Edward got up. 'It's from the hospital, sir. My girl. She's very ill.'

'Oh. Oh, all right then. Take it.'

Edward picked up the apparatus, listened, hesitated, then said, 'Thank you. All right, thank you,' and put it down.

There was a short silence.

'Bad news?' said the Detective-sergeant, a faint glint of a former light appearing through the thunder on his brow.

'My girl's had a child, stillborn, sir.'

'Oh. Sorry, lad. Very sorry.'

The star sleuth said to Edward, 'I hope it's a natural miscarriage, not the other thing.'

Edward stared at him and tensed, but as he rushed the star sleuth saw him coming, and picking up a truncheon the Detective-sergeant used as a paper-weight he cracked it on Edward's skull between his eyes.

MR LOVE AND JUSTICE

THAN a prison there is only one place more impressive to the human spirit and even more a symbol of our mortal condition: a hospital. In prison there is the allegory of sin, punishment and (in theory at any rate) redemption. In a hospital, the deeper allegory of birth, death and (occasionally) resurrection.

Thus when respectable citizens pass by prisons (which they rarely do because jails are tucked away in improbable places) they avert their hearts and eyes from the reality that a prison is a particular extension of a society and not in any essential way a thing apart from it. And if one ponders upon prisons and, better still, goes inside one (other, of course, than as a visitor), one is forced to the conclusion that the prisoners are us: one fragment of those outside who save for chance and technicality might very well be inside; and that insofar as sin is universal all are criminals, even if not deemed so by the conventions of temporary self-invented laws.

But when it comes to hospitals the healthy man may avert his eyes and heart with greater trepidation: for birth, death and healing are by much more general consent our inescapable lot. And these beneficent places are, in their way, even more awe-inspiring because from the sentences they can pass there may be no release and no appeal on earth. And that is why the only place which coppers and criminals *really* fear are the white wards where those temporal imperfect figures, the screws and wardresses of the jails, become as guardians of something greater, the white-robed nurses and physicians.

As for the inmates, in either case they have a strong if momentary sense of solidarity. If you're in jail 'the others' is the world outside; if you're in hospital you belong to the fraternity of the sick—an aching body set apart from the community of the healthy beyond the disinfected walls. And it was not surprising that Frankie, convalescing from his wound on crutches, and Edward whose skull was healing likewise beneath an impressive turban of lint and bandages, should often have been thrown even closer together than their fates as healthy men had already brought them.

Their favourite rendezvous was the long sun-parlour where in this progressive establishment the walking-wounded were permitted to foregather, free from the martial disciplines of their wards, for chats, draughts, reading, at evenings telly-viewing, and for the calls by flower-laden visitors at the appointed hours. The nurses, in the brisk and bossy manner of their calling, came frequently to disturb the comfort and tranquility of the patients with thermometers and pills, and summonses to X-ray rooms and distant theatres, and charts to fill in with dots and crosses indicating such things as whether or not their charges had been, as they put it, 'good boys'. The doctors in their more remote and stately fashion made periodical forays, often, as with the colonel on his inspection, in files that indicated seniority and which trooper, in this army of good-health, held commissioned or non-commissioned status. But mostly the patients, attired in government dressing-gowns much too short for them (or else too long), were left to their own devices of boredom, pain, amity and tiffs.

Edward and Frankie had long ago put each other entirely 'in the picture' as to their respective pasts: the bonds of solitude, and ennui, and suffering, and even more the discovery that both were now outcasts from the law soon overcame any slight initial reluctance on either side. There was also the enormous interest and satisfaction of meeting 'the enemy' as equals on this neutral ground: as if they were two warriors of opposing camps interned, as a consequence of the misfortune of arms by some Swiss-like power, now pleased and eager with clear consciences to betray military secrets to each other.

When their two girls came to visit them in the evenings, the broken ice formed again ever so slightly: for these were both creatures from the outside world, living reminders of a troubled past and a most uncertain future. Not that either man was anxious or embarrassed by his own girl's behaviour to her sister: each woman had been most correct, and as the days passed even cordial; and the men learned to their astonishment, mild alarm, and then hilarity that the two girls carried on, outside the hospital, a certain degree of cautious social intercourse: phone calls, requests to convey parcels on a day either couldn't come and even joint excursions to their respective Odeons. And when both of the girls retired as the end of their visit was heralded by the clanging, by some eager authoritative nurse, of a bell that did more harm to broken nerves in a minute than the hours spent in the sun-parlour had healed, the two men gathered up the mags and fruit and fags they'd left, and laughed: though handing by mutual, unspoken agreement any *flowers* either girl had brought them to a horticulturist cleaning-woman to carry home. For each of them felt what many patients must have done—that it's a bit tactless of most kindly souls to bring flowers only when they visit hospitals, or graves.

Time after time they speculated on the days that lay ahead: chewing with joint professional gusto over every aspect of their own case and each other's. 'So Frankie, you don't think,' Edward said, 'you'll go down on either charge?'

'Honest, Ted, no, I don't. In the affray I was the victim, there were bags of witnesses and the feller's not marked at all himself, it seems. As soon as he comes up for trial I just can't see how they can bring me into it except as an absent witness with the affidavit that I gave them.'

'Yes, boy. But the other thing?'

'Well—you say you're out of the cowboy forces now. Of course, cop, I still don't believe you—not till I see you busted anyway, then I might. But even so I just can't see they've got the evidence, if, as you say, you've finally decided not to testify: and—remember this—the *longer* the thing's delayed the harder it is to prove.'

'Correct. What happened a year—even a month—ago convinces juries far less than what happened yesterday.'

'And what about you, boy? I'd say you're in the clear as well: dismissed, okay, but wedding bells and an honest job of some kind for the first time in your life.'

'Well, there's the enquiry I've still got to face, of course. But from what I gather although they think that officer acted within his rights by bashing me when I attacked him, they're not very pleased at it all happening inside a station. So they'll try to keep it very quiet. Otherwise, if they don't . . .' Edward's eyes gleamed slightly '. . . I might bring a civil action for assault.'

'You've been having a chat with your lawyers, too. I can see. And what of the future, sonny? What are you going to do?'

'I dunno: it's too early to say, really. Besides, outside my career I don't really *know* anything at all.'

'No coppers do.'

'Why should they? A job's a job. One thing I *had* thought of, though, is setting up with my wife when we get married in a dress-making business: that's her own trade, you see.'

'You'll need capital for that . . .'

'Well, we've got a little bit of that put by.'

'We won't ask from where. So—dressmaking: what does that mean? Little fitting-room upstairs? Places where the mugs who pay for the chicks' gowns can come in and admire their undies as they try them on?'

'I don't know about that.'

'While you and your missus go out and leave them alone there for a while? Boy, that's it! A little high-grade brothel's what your establishment will be.'

'Don't be foolish, Frankie.'

'I'm not! You'll see! The idea will grow on you.'

Edward drank reflectively from some repellent but no doubt curative beverage. 'And you, Frank,' he said. 'You'll be going back to sea?'

'Me? Oh, I'm not sure. As a matter of fact I've been turning the thing over and I think I might consider opening up a little investigation agency.'

'What does that mean?'

'You know—divorce and such-like. It's quite a busy trade and with hardly any overheads. I know a lot of the angles now and contacts, and it seems to me it's a possibility.'

'You'll have to be careful, sonny, that's all I have to say.'

'And so will you, son! We'll both of us have to be.'

An uneasiness in easy chairs, a creaking of un-oiled wheel-carriages, and a rapid extinction of pipes and cigarettes all signalled the evening visit of the house doctor. He was accompanied (as not in his formal, perilous visits to the wards by day when he came flanked by assistants and by students, and himself followed sometimes behind some mighty specialist) only and informally by the ward sister—a fierce and dreadfully cheery martinet whose days of maximum glory, as her huge, sexless, medalled breast bore witness, had been spent on hospital ships in time of war. The doctor himself was young, fair-haired, sharp, and amiable—a man of the new and blessedly rising school who believe that patients are best consulted, to obtain results, about themselves and no longer treated, in the style of some of the older physicians, as culpable and rather tiresome imbeciles.

'Having a natter?' the doctor said sitting down beside Frankie and Edward and, to the scandalized but respectful glare of the ward sister, offering them each a cigarette and taking one himself.

'That's about it, doc,' Frankie answered.

'It passes the time, sir,' Edward added.

'Your girls both well?' the doctor asked, a glance of friendly complicity coming into his sandy eyes.

They each said they were.

'Well, we hope to be turning you both loose among them before so very long,' the doctor continued, 'but please don't ask me *when* because, of course, only your specialists can give me the final okay for your release—*and* what's more we'll need the permission of the sister here.'

The three men smiled. The sister looked severe.

'Anyway,' said the doctor, rising, 'when you *do* get out you'll both have to take it easy for a bit: specially with the women and—this'll please you—work. You've both (his tone became suddenly professionally grave) sailed very close to the edge in your two very different ways. When you get your discharge come and see me, if you like, and I'll tell you all the gory details of just how bad you were. But not now. We want you to get fit, not turn into a pair of hypochondriacs.'

Left to themselves Frankie and Edward watched the night come on, a bit restive (as beasts are when they know the summons will soon be coming to the manger) and talking only spasmodically.

'You know,' Edward said, 'these hospitals are really terrific. All this goes on—all these people here—they treat you whoever you are —no questions asked—not even any money. Just so long as you're sick you're welcome. People should know about it,' he continued. 'People should know what goes on inside these places.'

'You might say, Ted,' said Frankie, 'they should know what goes on inside the cells and jails and station headquarters, too. Over in other countries where I've been and even in Europe on the Continent, thousands of people—and the very best among them—have had experience of the law from the inside on account of the political upheavals. But here everyone is so dam innocent: so simon-pure. They unload all their moral problems on to the law's shoulders and leave you boys to get on with doing just what you like in the public's name. Well, if they do that one day they'll wake up and find they've given you not physical authority but all their own moral authority as well.'

'Citizens,' said Edward, 'broadly speaking, just don't want to be responsible. I've always said that: they just don't want to know. They lack the sense of responsibility themselves and only the Force is left with any sense of obligation to the community.'

'That's just what I say, man! If you hear a scream in the night these days you say, "Oh, the law will take care of it". A hundred years ago or even fifty, our grandfathers would have grabbed hold of the poker and gone out and taken a look themselves. They'd have *done* something: not just dialled 999.'

'I guess that's the age we live in,' Edward said.

'Yes, but I don't like it, Ted. Because you cops—well, you'll switch to any boss: any boss whatever. Whoever's got a grip then you'll obey him however good or bad his acts and his ideas may be.'

'Well, Frankie, tell me! What else do people believe in any more but just authority! Whatever it may represent?'

'That's it: nothing at all! Not religions, anyway. As religions have got weaker coppers have got stronger—you ever noticed that? The cop is the priest of the twentieth-century world, inspiring fear and if you're obedient, giving you absolution. But there is one very, very big difference from the old religions. The god of the coppers *is* the copper: you're the priests of a religion without a god.'

In the gloaming Edward's face was indistinct and so was Frankie's and they talked in the direction of each other's voices. Edward said, 'If that is true, boy—and I really just don't know—all I can say is we coppers are exposed to very great moral stress: we have to deal more with Satan every day than the rest of you possibly ever dream of.'

The lights burst on and a high female voice cried, 'Beddy-byes! Come along, boys, or I'll have to spank your little bottoms! Back to your wards you go: last one turns off the telly—and the lights!'

Neither man moved—as much by disinclination as in rebellious assertion of their manhood. 'These nurses!' Frankie cried. 'The first thing I'm going to do when I get out is date *that* one and break her bloody heart for her!'

'I doubt if she'd be interested,' Edward said, returning from the light-switch where he'd gone to restore the soothing, healing twilight. 'I know you kill them, Frankie, but that one, I think you'd find she's wed to her sputum mugs and bedpans.'

'*All* chicks are interested,' Frankie said, 'unless they're frigid.'

'You sure of that? I think there are some who centre it all on their vocation or on just one single man.'

'Sex, boy, *is* a woman's chief vocation: and plenty of it.'

'Frankie: it ever occurred to you that your experience, really, is very limited?'

'Mine? Well! Well, if you say so, officer.'

'I mean this: you don't know about other kinds of women because you've never met them; and you've never met them because you're only interested in them if they play it your way.'

'Well—that may be. But you, Ted: you consider your experience is so varied, then?'

'No—not varied but I think it's deep.'

'*Deep*? Yeah? Excuse the question, boy. That girl of yours: she's not your one and only by any chance is she?'

'Yes.'

'I thought maybe so. You mean the only one you ever *had*?'

'Yes.'

'At your age? And you say *you*'ve got experience? And frankly, Ted: can I say this? that girl of yours: I know she's a loyal kid and worships you and all the rest of it but . . . well, she wears glasses! And she doesn't dress very sharp, now, does she? I mean, with a chick like that in spite of all her qualities I think you're bound to have a very blinkered vision.'

'If you wear blinkers, Frankie, you see straight: straight ahead and see where you're going to all on one track. I don't think it's real sex always to begin again and again with someone else: I don't think you add to it or build anything or go really deep.'

'That "deep" again: you've been in deep with that lass?'

'The longer it lasts the further we both seem to be from ever coming to the end of each other. I think real sex, Frankie, is quite simple: it's one girl.'

'But you've not tried others.'

'I still think what I say.'

'Well: real *love*, perhaps, if you like to call it that . . . but not real *sex*, feller—how can it possibly be?'

'I say real love *is* real sex: they're one and the same thing exactly; and you find them only in one and the same person. Break out of that and you destroy them both.'

'Well, Ted . . . all I can say is you may be correct but you can't really know that till you've tried.'

'Nor can you, Frankie, if what I say is so until *you*'ve tried it.'

Again the lights glared into flame. 'Naughty, naughty!' cried the nurse. 'Now, really! Into your beds at once you go the pair of you or I'll call sister and she'll have you both up on a fizzer before your specialists in the morning!'

Frankie and Edward rose in silence, and outside the swing door patted each other and shook hands. 'Don't die in the night,' said Frankie. 'Is that a promise?'

'And you, pal. No interfering with the night nurse, is that understood?'

They went their several ways along the dim-lit corridors. Peace settled on the hospital except for grunts and occasional sharp little cries, quickly suppressed.

In his office the size of a small bathroom, the house doctor had a cocoa with the ward sister.

'Disgusting stuff, sister,' he said smacking his lips. 'It's a shame to make the poor fellers drink it.'

'It's for their good, doctor,' she said. 'And a bit more of *that* and less of the other thing might do some good to *your* health, too.'

'Oh, doctors are never ill—didn't you know? Or nurses! You've learned that, sister, by now surely.'

The nurse, pursing her already purposeful lips, handed him two folders.

'Yes, those two,' he said. 'Quite astonishing recoveries the pair of them: they do us great credit—don't you think?'

'Us, yes *and* their specialist doctors,' said the loyal nurse.

'Oh—indeed: and dame nature, too. *This* one with the groin wound . . . well, do you know sister? I'll spare your blushes but to put it politely if it hadn't been for some crafty work on him by the specialist, that man would never have been able to love at all.'

'Better for him, perhaps. And the brain case?'

'Well, *him*—he's lucky, frankly, now to *have* a brain. If the specialist hadn't been on hand the night they brought him to us, this feller's judgment would have been seriously impaired for life.'

The ward sister took a decorous sip. 'And you think,' she said, 'that either of them will make good use of these two essential faculties?'

'Frankly no,' said the doctor cheerfully. 'Well, I mean obviously not! They're frail human creatures just like you and me—yes even you sister, I dare say. But at any rate we've given them back the spare parts that they need, and that's all a nurse and doctor—yes, and even a specialist—can do. The rest of it begins where healing always ends and life begins: *we* don't have to decide the use they'll make of their lives, thank God!'

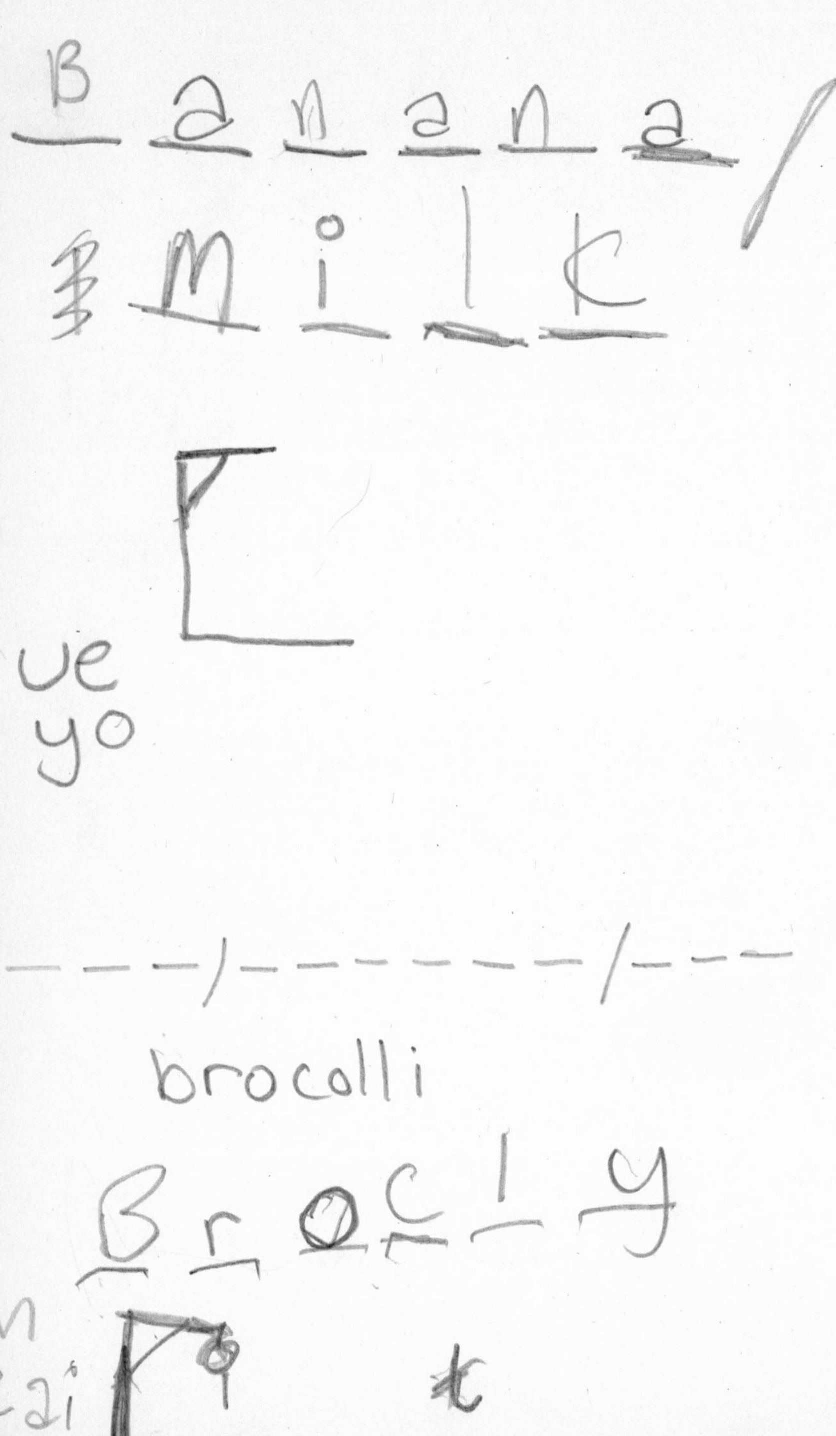

B a n a n a
m i l k
ue
yo
brocolli
B r o c l y
M
e a i
u
t